KATE CARLISLE

Ripped
from the
Pages

A Bibliophile Mystery

AN OBSIDIAN MYSTERY

OBSIDIAN
Published by the Penguin Group
Penguin Group (USA) LLC, 375 Hudson Street,
New York, New York 10014

USA | Canada | UK | Ireland | Australia | New Zealand | India | South Africa | China
penguin.com
A Penguin Random House Company

First published by Obsidian, an imprint of New American Library,
a division of Penguin Group (USA) LLC

First Printing, June 2015

LIBRARY OF CONGRESS CATALOGING-IN-PUBLICATION DATA:
    Carlisle, Kate, 1951–
    Ripped from the pages: a bibliophile mystery/Kate Carlisle.
        p. cm.— (Bibliophile mystery ; 9)
    ISBN 978-0-451-41600-1 (hardcover)
    1. Women bookbinders—Fiction. 2. Books—Conservation and restoration—Fiction.
    3. Rare books—Fiction. 4. Murder—Investigation—Fiction. I. Title.
    PS3603.A7527R57 2015
    813'.6—dc23   2015000479

Printed in the United States of America
10 9 8 7 6 5 4 3 2 1

Set in Bembo

For cheering me on like no one else can,
this one's for you, Pam.

Ripped from
the Pages

Chapter One

"Won't this be fun?" My mother squeezed me with painful enthusiasm. "Two whole months living right next door to each other. You and me. We'll be like best girlfriends."

"Or double homicide victims," my friend Robin muttered in my ear.

Naturally, my mother, who had the ultrasonic hearing ability of a fruit bat, overheard her. "Homicide? No, no. None of that talk." Leaning away from me, she whispered, "Robin, sweetie, we mustn't mock Brooklyn. She can't help finding, you know, dead people."

"Mom, I don't think Robin meant it that way."

"Of course she didn't," Mom said, and winked at Robin.

Robin grinned at me. "I love your mom."

"I do, too," I said, holding back a sigh. Mom had a point, since I did have a disturbing tendency to stumble over dead bodies. She was also right to say that I couldn't help it. It wasn't like I went out in search of them, for Pete's sake. That would be a sickness requiring immediate intervention and possibly a twelve-step program.

Hello, my name is Brooklyn, and I'm a dead-body magnet.

Robin's point was equally valid, too, though. My mother and

I could come very close to destroying each other if Mom insisted on being my BFF for the next two months.

Even though she'd raised her children in an atmosphere of peace and love and kindness, there was a limit to how much of her craziness I could take. On the other hand, Mom was an excellent cook and I could barely boil water, so I could definitely see some benefit to hanging around her house. Still, good food couldn't make up for the horror of living in close proximity to a woman whose latest idea of a good time was a therapeutic purging and bloodletting at the new panchakarma clinic over in Glen Ellen.

I focused on that as I poured myself another cup of coffee and added a generous dollop of half-and-half.

A few months ago, my hunky British ex–MI6 security agent boyfriend, Derek Stone, had purchased the loft apartment next door to mine in San Francisco. We decided to blow out the walls and turn the two lofts into one big home with a spacious office for Derek and a separate living area for visiting relatives and friends. Our reliable builder had promised it would only take two months to get through the worst of the noise and mess, so Derek and I began to plan where we would stay during the renovation. I liked the idea of spending time in Dharma, where I'd grown up, but live in my parents' house? For two months? Even though there was plenty of room for us? Never!

"It would be disastrous," I'd concluded.

Derek's look of relief had been profound. "We're in complete agreement as usual, darling."

"Am I being awful? My parents are wonderful people."

"Your parents are delightful," he assured me, "but we need our own space."

"Right. Space." I knew Derek was mainly concerned about me. He'd be spending most weeks in the city and commuting to Sonoma on the weekends. His Pacific Heights office building had two luxury guest apartments on the top floor, one of which would suit him just fine.

I could've stayed there with him, of course, but that would've meant renting studio space at the Covington Library up the hill for my work. This would entail packing up all my bookbinding equipment and supplies, including my various book presses and a few hundred other items of importance to my job. Those small studio spaces in the Covington Library basement, while cheap, were equipped with nothing but a drafting table and two chairs, plus some empty cupboards and counters.

I'm a bookbinder specializing in rare-book restoration, and I was currently working on several important projects that had to be delivered during the time we would be away from home. The original plan of staying with my parents, while less than ideal, would've allowed me access to my former mentor's fully stocked bookbinding studio just down the hill from my parents. Abraham Karastovsky had died more than a year ago, but his daughter, Annie, who lived in his house now, had kept his workshop intact. She'd also given me carte blanche to use it whenever I wanted to.

For weeks, Derek and I had tossed around various possibilities, including renting a place somewhere in the city. That seemed to be the best alternative, but at the last minute, we were given a reprieve that made everyone happy. My parents' next-door neighbors, the Quinlans, generously offered up their gorgeous French-style cottage for our use. They were off to Europe for three months, and we were welcome to live in their home while they were gone.

We offered to pay them rent, but all they required from us was that we take good care of their golden retriever, Maggie, and water their plants. When Mom offered to take care of the plants (knowing my tendency to kill them), it was too good a deal to pass up. I was hopeful that sweet old Maggie and my adorable kitten, Charlie (aka Charlemagne Cupcake Wainwright Stone, a weighty name for something so tiny and cute), would become new best friends.

So last weekend, Derek and little Charlie and I had moved out of our South of Market Street loft and turned it over to our builder, who promised to work his magic for us.

And suddenly we were living in Dharma, next door to my parents, in a lovely two-story French-style cottage that was both elegant and comfortable. The floor of the wide foyer was paved in old, smooth brick, giving the space a natural, outdoor feeling. The spacious living room was more formal, with hardwood floors covered in thick area rugs and oversized plush furniture in browns and taupes. Rustic wrought-iron chandeliers hung from the rough-hewn beams that crisscrossed the vaulted ceiling. The sage-toned kitchen was spectacular, with a twelve-foot coffered ceiling, a pizza oven, and a wide island that provided extra space for food preparation as well as seating for six. Off the kitchen was a small library with built-in bookshelves, a wood-burning fireplace, and two overstuffed leather chairs. I could already picture the two of us sitting there reading books each night by a cozy fire.

And in every room on the ground floor, dark-wood-paneled French doors opened onto an interior patio beautifully landscaped with lush plants and flowers.

Once we were unpacked and exploring the kitchen, Derek and I watched Maggie and Charlie sniff and circle each other for a few minutes. Finally, they seemed to agree that they could live in peace together. At least, I hoped so. Maggie ambled over to her bed and settled herself down on the fluffy surface. Charlie followed right behind her, clambered up and perched directly on Maggie's big paw. Maggie stared at the tiny creature for a long moment, and I prepared myself to whisk the cat away. But then Maggie let out a heavy sigh and closed her eyes. Charlie snuggled up against the big dog's soft, warm fur and was asleep several seconds later.

Derek and I exchanged smiles. I had a feeling we would all be very happy here.

And now here I was, sitting in my mother's kitchen on a bright Monday morning, drinking coffee with Robin and listening as my mother tried to brush past the fact that I did indeed have an alarming tendency to come upon dead bodies in the strangest places. Luckily, that wasn't likely to happen in Dharma anytime soon.

As I watched Mom bustle around her sunny kitchen, I wondered how I'd ever thought I could avoid seeing her every day simply because we weren't together in the same house. Not that I minded visiting with her on a regular basis. I joked about it, of course, but in truth, my mother was great, a true original and a sweet, funny woman with a good heart. All my friends loved her. She was smart and generous. But sometimes . . . well, I worried about her hobbies. She'd been heavily involved in Wicca for a while and recently had been anointed Grand Raven Mistress of her local druidic coven. Some of the spells she had cast had been alarmingly effective. She would try anything once. Lately she'd shown some interest in exorcisms. I didn't know what to expect.

I supposed I didn't have much room to criticize Mom's hobbies, given that my own seemed to revolve around crime scenes.

"Do you want some breakfast before we leave?" I asked Robin. We'd made plans to drive over to the winery this morning to watch them excavate the existing storage cave over by the cabernet vineyards. It would eventually become a large underground tasting room. Cave tastings were the hottest trend in Napa and Sonoma, and our popular Dharma winery was finally jumping on the bandwagon.

Robin pulled out a kitchen chair and sat. "I already had breakfast with Austin. He had to be on-site at seven."

"Derek left the house about that time, too. I thought he'd be driving into the city today, but he decided to hang around to watch the excavation."

"Austin was so excited, he could barely sleep last night." Robin lived with my brother Austin, with whom she had been in love since third grade. She and I had been best friends since then, too, and I loved her as much as any of my three sisters. I didn't get to see her as often as I used to when she was living in San Francisco, but I knew she was blissfully happy with Austin, who supported her sculpting work and was clearly as much in love with her as she was with him.

Austin ran the Dharma winery, and my brother Jackson managed the vineyards. My father did a great job of overseeing the entire operation, thanks to his early experience in the business world. Decades ago he'd turned his back on corporate hell and gone off to follow the Grateful Dead. Ironically, these days, Dad and four other commune members made up the winery's board of directors. He was also part of the town council, but this time around he loved all of that business stuff. It probably helped that Dad had always been remarkably laid-back and still was. I sometimes wondered if Mom had cast a mellow spell on him.

I checked the kitchen clock. It was already seven thirty. The cave excavation was scheduled to begin at eight. "I'll just fix myself a quick bowl of cereal, and then we'll go."

Robin glanced at Mom. "Becky, are you coming with us?"

"You girls go on ahead," she said, pulling a large plastic bin of homemade granola down from the cupboard. "I want to put together a basket of herbs and goodies for the cave ceremony. I'll catch up with you later."

"What cave ceremony?" I asked as I poured granola into a bowl and returned the bin to the cupboard.

She looked at me as though I'd failed my third-grade spelling test. "Sweetie, we have to bless the new space."

"Oh." I shot Robin a wary glance. "Of course we do."

Robin bumped my shoulder. "You haven't been away so long that you'd forget about the sacred cave ceremony."

"I've been busy," I mumbled. She was teasing me, but still, I should've known that my mother would want to cast a protection spell or a celebration spell to commemorate the groundbreaking of our winery's newest venture.

I could picture Mom doing a spritely interpretive dance to the wine goddess. She would chant bad haiku and sprinkle magic sparkles on the heavy tunneling machines and equipment. It would be amazing, and the heavy equipment would turn our dark storage cave into a large, magical wine-tasting space where all would be welcome.

"Oh, sweetie," Mom said, hanging a dish towel on the small rack by the sink. "While you're here, you should go to lunch at the new vegan restaurant on the Lane. They serve a turnip burger that is to die for."

I swallowed cautiously, hoping I didn't lose my breakfast. "I'll be sure to check that out, Mom."

She glanced at me and laughed. "Oh, you should see your face. Do you really think I'd be caught dead eating something so vile?"

"I . . . Okay, you got me." I shook my head and chuckled as I carried my bowl to the sink. "I was trying to remember when you turned vegan."

"I tried it once for a day and a half and vowed never again. And even then, did I ever serve my children turnips? No, never."

"You're right and I appreciate it. But I haven't seen you in a while. I was afraid maybe you'd turned into Savannah." My sister Savannah was a vegetarian now, but she'd gone through several austere phases to get there, including a few months when she would only eat fruit that had already fallen from the tree.

"No, I was just pulling your leg."

I smiled at her. "You still got it, Mom."

"I sure do." She grabbed me in another hug, and it felt good to hold on to her. "Oh, Brooklyn, I'm so happy you're here."

"So am I."

She gave me one last squeeze, then let me go. As I washed out my cereal bowl, she left the kitchen.

"Let's get going," Robin said after I put my bowl away in the cupboard. "I don't want to miss anything."

"Wait a second, girls," my mother called from her office alcove off the kitchen. She walked out, holding two tiny muslin bags tied with drawstrings, and handed one to each of us. "I want you both to carry one of these in your pocket," she said, her expression deadly serious. "It'll keep you safe."

That is the coolest, scariest piece of equipment I've ever seen," Robin said.

I had to agree. We both stared at the monstrous excavation machine that was parked at the mouth of the storage cave, waiting to roll into action. They called it a roadheader, and it was huge, weighing more than sixty tons (I'd overheard Dad gushing about its weight to Derek while they were standing around having a manly conversation about heavy equipment), and was as large as the biggest bulldozer I'd ever seen.

Extending at least fifteen feet out in front of its tanklike body was a medieval-looking articulated arm, or boom, at the tip of which was a large steel ball covered in clawlike spikes. As the machine rumbled forward, the ball rotated fast enough to tear its way through hard rock, slowly creating a tunnel. That was the theory, anyway. It hadn't started working yet. When it did, there would be dust and noise and, possibly, earthquakelike shaking. It would all be worth it when the tasting cave was completed. I could barely wait for that day.

It had always made sense to use caves for wine-barrel storage. Sonoma tended to get hot in the summer, and underground storage was the cheapest and most efficient way to maintain a constant temperature, which was vital to the health of the wine.

But over the past few years, many of the local wineries had expanded on the idea and had brought the actual wine-tasting experience into the caves. I'd done a tour of some of the tasting caves in the area, and they were beautiful, unique spaces. Some were rustic; others were elegant. One low-ceilinged, tunnel-like cave I'd visited in Napa had been excavated by hand during the days of the gold rush. You could still see the uneven spike marks on the dark stone walls made by the workers' hammers and pickaxes.

Several wineries in the area had built luxurious private dining rooms within their caves. Another offered a complete spa experience. There were waterfalls and unusual lighting and nooks and crannies to explore. One local tasting cave featured an underground library. And there was always wine.

And finally, wine-cave tasting was coming to Dharma. We already had a number of storage caves on the property, but none was big enough to use as a fully functioning tasting room. The most spacious of the storage caves was located on the opposite side of the parking lot from the current tasting room. Once the cave excavation was completed, the current tasting room would be redesigned to use for private dinners and special events.

The wide double doors at the entryway to the storage cave were made of thick wood and arched to fit the cavelike opening. With the doors opened, the passageway was broad enough to allow a truck or a forklift to drive through. The interior was dark and cool and roomy enough to hold the hundreds of oak barrels that stored the wine until it was bottled.

The barrels had been moved into the fermentation barn and to other parts of the winery to avoid possible damage from the heavy equipment that would be used to expand the cave. Geologists had already tested the hard ground above the existing cave and had approved the digging.

A crowd was beginning to gather as Robin and I planted our folding chairs on the blacktop a safe distance from the storage-cave entrance. We were drinking coffee and sharing cookies and snacks with at least fifty other commune members who were also here to watch the show.

I spied my father standing with Derek next to a massive piece of equipment. My two brothers and a couple of others were there, too, deep in conversation. They all wore hard hats and looked very manly while kibitzing with the excavation company's owner, a tall, good-looking, gray-haired man named Stan.

We had been warned that there would be a tremendous amount of dust flying and the noise would be impossible to endure without earplugs or, better yet, headphones that covered our ears completely. A while ago, Stan and his men had walked through the crowd, passing out headphones and protective goggles to anyone who wanted them.

The crowd's chatter subsided abruptly, and that was when I noticed Guru Bob walking toward the group of men. Guru Bob, otherwise known as Robson Benedict, was the avatar, the spiritual leader of the commune. My parents considered him a highly evolved conscious being, and, having known him for most of my life, I couldn't disagree. He was the reason my parents had gathered up their six small children and moved us all to Sonoma so many years ago when Guru Bob summoned them. Back in the day, he had purchased sixteen hundred acres of rich Sonoma farmland and had chosen this spot to establish his Fellowship for Spiritual Enlightenment and Higher Artistic Consciousness.

The commune members began growing grapes that first year, and, ten years later, with the winery thriving and lots of members' shops, restaurants, and B and Bs doing well, Guru Bob decided to incorporate our little community. He suggested we call the new town *Dharma*, which means "law" in Eastern philosophy.

But the word meant much more than that, according to some philosophies. When the world was first created, it was said to have emerged from chaos. As the gods stabilized the mountains and separated earth from sky, they created harmony and stability—*Dharma*. In Buddhism, the word referred to cosmic law and order. Other disciplines translated it to mean "to live in harmony with the law."

Guru Bob chose to interpret the word as the Sikhs and others had: "To follow the Path of Righteousness." That idea appealed to his followers as well, and the town of Dharma was born.

Oh, and while Guru Bob was a fun name we kids liked to use, I would never have called him that to his face. It would have been disrespectful. Funny thing, though—I'd always had the feeling he knew we called him Guru Bob and didn't mind at all.

After five minutes of serious discussion, Guru Bob waved to the rest of us and walked away, heading off toward the center of town. I knew the reason he left wasn't that he didn't have an interest in what was going on. It was more that he'd put reliable people in charge of the job and he didn't want them to think he was watching over their shoulders or micromanaging. He would show up later to see how things turned out, trusting that everything had gone according to plan.

The buzz of voices rose once again.

"I'm getting excited," Robin said.

"So am I."

She gave me a look. "You sound surprised."

"I guess I was trying to be blasé about it, but this is really fun."

"It is. And I already told you how psyched Austin is to get started."

"My dad is, too."

She laughed. "He's been talking about building this tasting cave since before I moved back up here. At least a year ago."

"I know." I sipped my coffee. "So it's about time we did it. It seems like every winery in the county has a tasting cave now."

She smirked. "And we must keep up with the trends."

I nodded, although I knew that keeping trendy wasn't the only reason the winery had finally chosen to carve out a larger space for the tasting rooms and additional barrel storage. The plain fact was that underground storage saved money. Temperatures in our existing caves didn't vary much from the recommended sixty-two degrees, which was ideal for making and storing wine. Dad had mentioned that they planned to build an interior waterfall to add to the natural humidity. Solar panels installed on the hillside above the caves would collect energy to be used for lighting the cave space and for pumping out excess moisture.

There was only one small tunnel built under the vineyards that led from one storage cave to another. More would be added, and they would be upgraded, widened, and modernized with better drainage in the floors and a thicker layer of shotcrete added to the walls for improved insulation. Shotcrete was a concretelike material applied using high-velocity hoses so that it dried quickly and covered every inch of the cave wall.

It was amazing how much cool information you could pick up from hanging around my father for a few hours. I'd learned that the winery committee had also approved plans to build a freshwater lake on the other side of Ridge Road that would eventually provide irrigation for the entire vineyard and winery. The plan was for Dharma to become self-sustaining and energy independent within five years.

A few of the men began walking toward us, away from the cave entrance where the heavy roadheader was ready to spring into action. Derek grinned as he approached, and my stomach did a little twist. There was something about a gorgeous man smiling at me that gave a boost to my day. Especially when that man was Derek Stone. The hard hat was an added treat.

"Having fun?" I asked.

"I'm having a fantastic time," he said, his British accent sounding even sexier than usual. Maybe it was the worn jeans or the heavy work boots he was wearing. Then again, he sounded sexy in a business suit, too.

I handed him my coffee mug. He took a sip and handed it back to me. "Thanks, love." Then he moved behind my chair so he wouldn't block my view, and we all waited for the show to begin.

A few seconds later, the sound of a loud, powerful engine erupted, and anyone who wasn't wearing a headset immediately fumbled to get one on. A cloud of thick dust erupted from the cave doorway and filled the air. I adjusted my goggles to watch the roadheader extend its claw arm deeper into the storage cave, where I imagined it clawing its way through the thick stone. A Dumpster-sized vessel rolled out on a track, carrying a pile of broken-down gravel that was dumped off to the side. I figured that pile would be massive by the time the job was done.

On the drive over, Robin had explained that the initial excavation would take several long weeks, possibly a few months. It all depended on the thickness and resistance of the stone.

But barely five minutes after the digging began, the earsplitting noise suddenly stopped. One of Stan's men, the one who was spotting for the driver, came running out of the storage cave.

"We've broken through some sort of wall," he explained loudly to my father and the other men. He didn't sound happy about it.

I looked up at Derek and saw him frowning. The experts had determined that most of the ground under the hillside was solid rock and heavily compressed soil. What did he mean, *We've broken through*? Was the dirt and stone beneath the vineyards less solid than the geologists had thought?

Dad, Derek, Austin, Jackson, and a few others went running toward the cave, where the roadheader had come to a complete stop. I glanced at Robin and without saying a word, we both jumped up and went running after them. No way were the boys going to have all the fun.

Eighteen narrow inches separated the massive roadheader from the sides of the storage-cave door, so we were able to slide past and enter the cool, dark space.

The dust was just clearing as Robin and I joined Derek and the others at the far end of the room where they stared at a jagged, gaping hole in what had been a solid stone wall a few minutes ago.

It looked broken, like an egg that was dropped and cracked open. Fissure lines radiated out from the large gash in the middle of the wall.

"We don't know how stable the walls are," Austin said to the small crowd, "so I'd like everyone to leave the cave for their own safety."

The commune members walked away, whispering quietly to one another. No one knew what this new development would mean to the tasting room plans, never mind the structural viability of the underground space.

I was too curious to leave. I noticed Robin wasn't going anywhere, either. But I sort of wished we'd both been given hard hats to wear. In lieu of that, I stuck my hand in my pocket to make sure my mom's little herb packet was still there. It was probably silly, but I felt better carrying it.

Derek flicked on a small flashlight and studied the open gash. About two feet wide and about four feet off the floor, it was just low enough that I could climb up and through it if I were brave enough. Was there some space back there? A tunnel, maybe? There had to be something.

Thanks to the beams from Derek's flashlight, I could see that the wall itself was at least four inches thick.

I moved closer and touched the grainy surface. "Is this concrete?"

"Looks like it," Derek said, exchanging a look with me. A wall of concrete meant that it was manmade. The excavation crew must have thought the concrete had been applied to the surface of the storage-cave walls and figured that behind the concrete were natural rock and packed earth.

"Can you see inside the hole?" I asked.

"Barely," he said, aiming the light directly into the hole in the wall. He leaned his head inside to take a look.

I held my breath. What if some wild creature was living in there? I shoved my hand back into my pocket and touched that small bag of herbs again. It gave me the oddest sense of well-being.

"Idiot," I whispered under my breath. "It's just some weeds in a bag." But I continued to rub the thin muslin packet anyway, hedging my bets while briefly considering slipping it into Derek's pocket.

Derek pulled his head back and handed the flashlight to Austin, who leaned in to take a look. "Holy Mother."

"What is it?" Robin demanded.

"You've got to see it for yourself."

"Let me see," I said, sounding like a typical younger sister. But Austin handed me the light without comment. I took another deep breath, not knowing what to expect. What in the world could survive in such a small, airless space?

I stuck my head inside to take a look for myself.

"Can you see well enough?" Derek murmured in my ear as I swung the small beam of light around.

I had to blink a few times before I could make out what I was looking at. The light beam didn't illuminate the entire space, but instead landed on small objects that were indecipherable at first. Slowly, though, things began to take shape. "What in the world?"

"What is it, Brooklyn?" Robin asked.

"It's a whole bunch of . . . stuff. Different things. Furniture. A big inlaid wood wardrobe with a beautifully beveled mirror built into its front door. There's an antique table with a fancy candelabra on it. A bookshelf with lots of things on all the shelves. Silver candlesticks. A silver teapot. At least, they look like silver from here." I leaned in farther. "There's more over in this corner. Another table with some small statuary. A couple of busts. I can't tell who they are. There are two bronze horses. Oh, the horses are bookends. And there are books." I flashed Derek a quick smile, then returned to scan the space. "A glass-fronted cabinet. It's got some more silver pieces inside. Another set of candlesticks and . . . is that another silver pitcher? On a tray of some kind. It all looks like hammered silver. It must be a set."

"And there're some gold pieces over there," Austin said, pointing. He towered over me and was able to gaze around without my blocking his view.

Robin, shorter than me by almost six inches, asked Austin to give her a boost up. I stepped aside so she could take a look.

"Here you go, baby," he said, holding her by the waist and easily lifting her up to see through the opening.

Derek handed the flashlight to Austin, and he held it steady as she took a look around. "It's an old curio cabinet."

"Can you see the silver inside?" Austin asked.

"Yes. It all looks beautiful."

"Do you see the bookends?" I asked.

"Yes. And books, too."

"I know," I said, grinning. "How cool is that?"

Robin slid back down. "It figures you'd see books before anything else."

"Books and possibly artwork," Derek said, taking the flashlight back and aiming it in another direction.

I got closer and found what he was looking at, a spot along the interior wall where several rolled canvasses stood leaning against the curio cabinet like drunken soldiers.

I moved away so Dad could take a look. After a minute, he stepped back, and Jackson took his turn.

"What is all this stuff?" I asked. "What's going on here?"

Derek shook his head. "I have no idea."

"It's a treasure trove," Dad said. "Just got to figure out where it came from."

"I wish we had a better light," I muttered.

At that moment, Stan walked up and handed me and Robin our own hard hats.

"Thanks." I put the rigid plastic hat on my head and felt safer instantly.

Then Stan pulled a long, black, industrial-strength flashlight from his tool belt and handed it to Derek. "Maybe this will help."

"Thanks, mate." Derek pushed the button on the heavy foot-long torch, and the powerful light filled the room.

"Like night and day," I said, smiling at Stan. "Thanks."

He nodded and strolled back outside. A man of few words.

Derek aimed the big flashlight's beam into the interior space.

"We need to get this wall knocked down," Dad said.

"Just what I was thinking," Jackson said, glancing toward the front of the cave. "I'll go talk to Stan."

I stretched up on my toes and poked my head farther through the opening. Derek continued holding the flashlight above my head. "Wow, over there in the other corner. It's another full-sized dresser with a mirror. There's a wooden box on top of it that looks like a jewelry box."

Derek turned the beam toward the left to allow me a better glimpse.

"It's beautiful," I said. "Looks French. Inlaid wood and lots of ormolu." I was able to recognize the finely gilded decorative detailing along the edges of the piece, thanks to Guru Bob, who had an antique desk in that style that I'd admired for years. He'd been kind enough to describe the history of the design to me.

"Pricey," Dad said.

"It's definitely worth a lot," I murmured.

"But what's a fancy dresser doing in a cave?" Robin wondered aloud. "And a curio cabinet? And silver candlesticks?"

"And books," I added.

"Good question," Austin said, his tone turning suspicious. "The sooner this wall comes down, the better."

I continued to scrutinize the dresser, too fascinated by our discovery to care how utterly bizarre it was that these amazing treasures were hidden behind a solid wall of concrete inside the winery storage cave. "That's definitley a jewelry chest on top of the dresser. It's the same inlaid pattern as the dresser. I wonder if there's anything inside."

"Jewels, of course," Robin said, grinning.

Something caught my eye on the dresser. "Oh, there's a silver tray with one of those old-fashioned silver combs and a hairbrush on it. It's pretty."

"I'm sure it's pretty," Robin said, "but it's still kind of weird."

"You're right," I said, and shivered a little. "It's like somebody lives in there."

I moved out of the way, leaving Derek alone to continue examining the odd crevice. He angled the flashlight in different directions, casting light onto every inch of the space. He scanned the low ceiling and ran the beam along the rest of the walls.

I was curious to see what other bounty we would find in there, so I peeked around Derek to take another look. Seconds later, I let out a piercing shriek.

"What is it?" Austin demanded, crowding me as I tried to push away from the wall.

Robin patted my shoulder. "Knowing Brooklyn, she probably found a dead body."

Her words barely registered as I pointed a shaky finger at what I saw on the floor close to the wall.

Derek aimed the beam where I'd indicated and muttered an expletive. He stepped back from the hole in the wall, turned off the flashlight, and wrapped his arm around my shoulders.

Robin's smile faltered. "Derek?"

"You were right, Robin," Derek said, giving me a soft squeeze of sympathy. "This cave has just turned into a crime scene."

Chapter Two

In seconds, Derek and Dad had the men rounding up pickaxes and sledgehammers in order to take down the rest of the wall.

I was shuffled out of the cave and barely had time to deal with another dead-body encounter.

Stan and his men backed the huge roadheader out of the enclosed space to give everyone more room. Stan ran and grabbed his own sledgehammer and joined the workers. Concrete dust was soon billowing out of the large storage cave. I was concerned for the men, of course, since it was getting hard to breathe, but I knew Derek wouldn't stop until he could step right into that inner room. I would've grabbed a pickax and gone to work on the wall myself, but I was certain I would just be in the way. As soon as the air cleared, though, I was going to jump in and find out who that dead person was. I had other questions, too. Where had all those beautiful treasures come from? And at what price?

One of Stan's men jogged over with a handful of cheap filter masks.

"Will those help?" Robin asked.

"It'll keep some of the larger particles from getting into their lungs," he said.

Larger particles? So the smaller ones would get through? That was not a good answer. Robin and I exchanged worried looks as the man ran into the cave to hand out the masks.

Less than two minutes later, Derek and Austin stumbled out, covered in dust. Jackson, Stan, Dad, and one other man followed a few seconds later.

I rushed over to Derek, who was ripping the mask away from his mouth. "Are you all right?"

"I'm fine," he said, slapping the dust off his shirt. "But Stan was starting to wheeze, so I thought we'd better take a break. We'll wait for the dust to settle before we go back in."

"Okay. I don't want anyone to get sick from breathing that stuff."

"Nor do I," he muttered as he bent over to shake more dust out of his hair. "I think we'll be all right."

I scuffled back a few feet to avoid being enveloped in the powdery cloud he'd just created. I was getting worried. Hadn't people died from breathing the dust inside old caves? Didn't I remember hearing something about archaeologists breathing the dust of mummies' tombs? Didn't they carry strange viruses?

I guess my mind was going a little wacky while I waited for the okay to go back inside. After another half hour, I was ready to scream. I'd always thought I was a patient person, but apparently I was wrong because I was beyond anxious to get in there and figure out who had died in the cave. Everyone else was standing around, chitchatting and hacking up particles and brushing off more dust. Didn't anyone else feel the same urge I felt? Where did all that furniture come from? The silver, the art, the books. The body. Didn't anyone want answers?

"I'm going in," I declared, and began to walk toward the cave.

"Hold on," Derek said, grabbing my hand.

"Why?" I demanded, prepared to battle against Derek's innate urge to protect and defend.

He grinned. "Because I'm going with you."

"Okay." I calmed down a smidgen. "Good. We've waited long enough. We need to check out that cave and call the police."

"In that order," he murmured, clearly resolved to survey the scene of the crime before raising the alarm. He picked up the flashlight and joined me.

Much of the dust had settled, but we stirred more up with every step we took. I coughed as some of it got into my throat, and I wondered how Derek and Dad and the others had withstood it for the thirty minutes they'd been in here breathing that stuff.

When we got to the back wall, I could see how much work the men had done earlier. The opening into the hidden room was bigger now, almost the size of a small doorway, about three feet wide by five feet high. Eighteen inches still remained along the bottom of the wall, which meant we had to step carefully over the small barrier.

"Good job," I said, beaming at Derek.

"The men were on a mission."

I smiled at his words. He made it sound like he was leading his troops off to war. I ducked my head and stepped over the stone lip. Once on the other side, I was able to stand without crouching. I had expected the enclosure to feel damp or stuffy, but the air was clean and I detected a mild floral scent. It was also slightly larger than I'd thought, maybe fifteen feet long by twelve feet across, the size of a typical bedroom.

Derek joined me inside the small enclosure, flipped on Stan's flashlight, and pointed the beam toward the floor.

That was when I saw the body again.

Although he was facedown, he was obviously a man, and he was pressed up against the wall as though he'd sought out a secure resting place. I figured that was why we hadn't seen him at first. We had been diverted by all of the treasures surrounding him.

He wore an old-fashioned brown suit and had short, dark hair.

On the ground near his right arm was a well-worn brown leather suitcase.

"I wonder if he got trapped here during the 'ninety-seven earthquake," Dad said.

I glanced up. Dad stood on the other side of the barrier, but he had poked his head in so he could watch us. Austin and Robin were crowded around him. Jackson had gone back to work in the winery, and the rest of the men must have either lost interest or needed to return to their jobs as well.

"That's almost twenty years, Jim," Derek said, touching the dead man's neck and studying the change in color. "This man's skin looks and feels as if he died a few hours ago."

"Maybe the absence of air helped preserve him," I said.

"What're you saying? You think he was mummified?" Austin's wry tone gave a clear indication of his opinion of my theory.

I was used to getting snarky comments from my big brothers, so I just shrugged. "Anything's possible."

"Yes," Derek said, "but let's see if there's a more practical explanation."

"Like maybe he actually died a few hours ago," Dad suggested. "Except I don't see how that's possible."

"Nor do I," Derek said.

"Derek, did you notice how clean the air was when you first stepped inside here?"

He looked at me from across the man's body. If he hadn't detected it before, he took notice now, breathing in deeply through his nose. "Very fresh. And there's something else."

"A light floral scent, right? I was thinking it might be coming from the dresser. The owner probably used sachets in the drawers. That's what it smells like to me, anyway."

"I can smell it, too," Robin said, and I gave her a grateful smile. So I wasn't going crazy.

Derek handed me the flashlight to hold while he continued to search the man's clothing for identification.

My attention was drawn to the small leather suitcase on the other side of the body. "Can we open that?"

"I don't suppose he'll complain if we do," Derek said, interrupting his search to move the suitcase away from the dead man.

I set the flashlight down on the ground with the beam pointing to the ceiling. It diffused the light, but we had enough to see what we were doing. The brass latches were old-fashioned as well, but Derek got them unhooked and spread the suitcase open. Inside was a neatly folded stack of men's clothes packed next to a small black toiletries bag. Laid on top of the clothing was something I had not expected to see.

"It's a book," I whispered.

"A book?" Austin laughed. "Doesn't that just figure?"

"It sure does," Dad said.

Derek's lips twisted in irony as he handed me the book. "Might as well examine it. This could provide as many answers to this puzzle as anything else in this room."

"Stranger things have happened." I aimed the flashlight's beam at the book's leather cover and read the title: *Voyage au Centre de la Terre* by Jules Verne.

Journey to the Center of the Earth.

Is it totally geeky to admit that my fingers were tingling just touching it? It was covered in three-quarter morocco leather with gilding on the spine. The boards were marbled. I opened it to the title page to see the date: 1867. It was written in French. On the same page was a fanciful illustration of a view into a prehistoric world, and I was hopeful that there would be other illustrations within.

This was not the time or place to study it more fully, but as soon as we were finished here, I was going to run straight to Abraham's studio and inspect this book from cover to cover. Meanwhile, I clutched it for dear life and reluctantly returned my gaze to the body.

"We can go through the rest of the suitcase later," Derek said, turning back to the dead man. "Right now, I'd rather find out who this poor fellow is and what he's doing here."

I stared at the man's suit jacket, which fit his body well, although it was longer than most men wore their jackets these days. The shoulders were padded, and the waist was narrow.

"I'm no fashion maven," I said, stating what everyone in my world thought was obvious, "but I think that style and the shade of brown are from the forties or fifties."

I heard Robin snicker, and I shot her a smile. She was the one who knew fashion and had always been willing to share her best ideas with me.

"You're right, love," Derek said, pondering the situation. After a moment, he said, "I'd like to photograph the body before we turn him over. Can you stand up and hold the flashlight steady?"

"Sure." I stood and set the book down on the dresser nearest the wall, then picked up the flashlight and focused the beam of light directly on the dead man. Derek pulled out his phone and began snapping photographs from every possible angle.

After at least twenty clicks, he stopped and slid the phone back into his pocket. "That should do it."

"Good." I knelt down beside him. "Does he have a wallet or ID on him?"

"Not in his back pockets. I hope to find something in his suit pockets, but we'll have to turn him over to find out."

"Let's do it."

He looked up at my brother. "Austin, can you give me a hand?"

"Sure thing." My brother stepped into the space and knelt down next to Derek. Together they carefully rolled the man over onto his back while I held the flashlight.

"How did he get in here?" Austin wondered aloud, studying the man's face. "He looks like he died just a little while ago."

"And not from natural causes," I muttered as my stomach began to churn. "That's a lot of caked blood on the side of his head."

"And there's a bullet hole in his chest," Derek said flatly, pointing out the frayed hole in the lapel.

"No earthquake did that," Dad conceded.

Derek scowled. "No, a killer did that. We'd better call the authorities."

*B*efore calling the sheriff's department to report a murder from who-knew-how-long-ago, Derek searched the man's pockets thoroughly and held up his findings: a French passport and a business-sized envelope.

I was surprised when Derek slit open the envelope and pulled out its contents. He was often a stickler for following the rules, but since he'd come from the world of clandestine law enforcement in England, I knew he preferred to find the answers on his own.

"What is it?" I asked.

"A ticket," he said, holding up a rectangular piece of paper for everyone to see. "He's booked passage from New York to Southampton on the *Queen Mary*."

"The *Queen Mary*," Robin echoed. "The ocean liner?"

"Yes. It's dated April 12, 1946."

We all needed a moment to figure that one out.

Staring down at the body, Austin scratched his head. "That's, like, seventy years ago."

"Brilliant," Robin said, patting his arm. "But we just agreed that the guy looks like he died a few hours ago."

"He does," I said, "but his clothes are more in line with the date on that ticket. Like I said, the nineteen forties or fifties."

Robin shook her head slowly. "This is weird."

"Maybe he's an actor," Dad suggested, "and died wearing a costume."

"And the ticket is a prop?" Robin said.

"Or some kind of souvenir," I said.

Austin shrugged. "That makes as much sense as anything else, I guess."

"Derek, what does the passport say?"

Derek opened the passport and read the name. " 'Jean Pierre Renaud.' And the name on the passenger ticket is the same."

"That's pretty elaborate for a theatrical prop."

"It is," Derek said. "I don't believe this man was an actor, nor do I believe the ticket is a prop."

"So you believe he died here seventy years ago?" I asked. "That's awfully hard to swallow."

"It's a mystery." Derek stood and brushed more dust off his trousers. "However, if it is a case of mummification, the body will begin to decompose rapidly at this point. The authorities need to get here as quickly as possible."

"I contacted them," Dad said. "They won't be here for another forty minutes or so." He reached into his pocket for his cell phone. "I'm going to call Robson, too."

Yes, I thought. Guru Bob would certainly want to know about this. I glanced up at Derek. "I know I mentioned it first, but seriously, how in the world could this body have been mummified? Wouldn't you need to remove the organs and coat it in resin or something?" I vaguely recalled those details, thanks to a museum presentation I'd attended during a high school field trip.

He aimed the flashlight around the space. "This wall had to have been built within hours of the man's death. Once that was done, as you were correct to suggest, a lack of air, combined with this cold, dry space, helped preserve him."

"Truly bizarre," Robin murmured.

Guru Bob walked into the cave barely ten minutes after Dad

called him. Everyone stood in silence, watching his reaction to what we'd discovered.

He was clearly upset by the presence of the body. We'd all been shaken, but Guru Bob seemed to take it more personally. A man had been murdered in Dharma. His home. His sanctuary.

The mood was so somber, it felt as though we were attending a memorial service. And in a way, we were.

Guru Bob had always been as careful as one could be to keep too much negativity from touching Dharma. I knew it firsthand because I'd once brought a visitor to Dharma who turned out to be a cold-blooded killer. Guru Bob didn't blame me, of course, but I would never forgive myself for being so clueless.

"He is French," Guru Bob murmured. It was a statement, not a question.

"Yes," Derek said. "According to the passport I found in his pocket, his name is Jean Pierre Renaud."

Guru Bob flinched at the name. It was a subtle reaction, but I saw it. Did he recognize the name? Or was he simply reacting to the fact that evil had visited Dharma once again?

But if this man had died here seventy years ago, Dharma hadn't even existed yet. The winery hadn't existed. Who owned this land back then?

"Did you know him, Robson?" I asked.

He paused for a moment, and I wondered if he would answer me. Finally he nodded. "He was a friend of my grandfather."

It was my turn to flinch. I had not been expecting that answer. I recovered quickly and gazed around the enclosure. "Are these his things?" I asked.

"I do not know, gracious." Guru Bob often used the endearment, hoping to encourage the person to show a bit of grace.

He turned to Derek. "I would like you to find out as much as you can about this man and these items. How did such a collection wind up in our caves?"

"I'll be glad to look into it."

Guru Bob nodded his appreciation. "I suggest you talk to my cousin Gertrude." He smiled. "Although, officially, she is my first cousin once removed. And you must not call her Gertrude. She goes by Trudy. I believe she could be of some assistance."

Derek gave me a curious look, and I realized he'd never met the amazing Trudy.

"I'll introduce you," I said with a smile.

After Guru Bob left, I spent a few minutes strolling alone through the vineyards, silently reflecting on everything that had happened in the last few hours. I was a little ashamed to admit that the most appalling part hadn't been the discovery of the cave itself or the wondrous treasure hidden behind those thick walls. It wasn't even the fact that a man may have been murdered there and left to rot for seventy years. No, for me the worst part was that *I* had been the one to find the body.

I hated to be so self-centered and I promised the sentiment would last for only a minute, but right then and there, it was all about me. Why me?

I felt a strong, protective arm on my shoulders, and I turned and leaned against Derek.

"Don't despair, darling," he murmured.

"Me? Despair?" I tried to smile. "How did you know?"

"It's a completely rational reaction. Especially when it happens to you with such frightening regularity."

"It's not fair." I sounded whiny. That would stop in a minute, too.

"No, it's not." He wrapped his arms around me. "I'm just relieved that this one won't be pinned on you."

"Thanks a lot."

He chuckled, and we continued walking along the rows of

thick, healthy plantings. The cabernet grapes were plump and dark, and the leaves were beginning to curl and turn orange, a sure sign that autumn was closing in on us. It was my favorite season in wine country, harvest time. I looked up at Derek and realized that this would be his second harvest since we'd been together. Wow, time had sure flown by since he first chased me up here. Back then, he'd been fairly certain I was a murdering vixen who'd killed my mentor for some horrific reason he couldn't quite come up with.

Ah, memories.

A full hour later, two detectives pulled into the parking lot. Derek and I waited to greet them and lead the way to the storage cave. They introduced themselves as Detectives Phil Gordon and Hannah Parrish from the Sonoma County Sheriff's Department, and they were so pleasant, it was almost scary. I was accustomed to the good-hearted mockery dished out by Detective Inspector Lee of the San Francisco Police Department, so it was a shock to be treated respectfully by these law enforcement officers. A shock, but one I welcomed.

It probably helped when Derek mentioned his bona fides: British Royal Navy commander, ten years in British intelligence with MI6, and now president and CEO of Stone Securities, his company that provided security to the wealthiest people and most precious artwork on the planet.

"And what do you do, Ms. Wainwright?" Detective Parrish asked politely.

"I'm a bookbinder," I said.

"That sounds fascinating."

"You have no idea," Derek murmured.

Twenty minutes later, we were joined by another detective, this one from the Coroner's Unit, and an assistant from the same department.

Once we were gathered around the hole in the wall of the cave, Derek and I explained what had happened here. It quickly became clear to the sheriff's people that this was going to be an unusual case. Yes, it was a homicide. That much was obvious. But as far as determining who the killer might be, Detective Gordon admitted that for the first time in his experience, figuring out "who" wasn't as important as first figuring out "when."

"Probably the best thing to do," Detective Parrish said, "is transport the body over to our Forensics Pathology group in Fairfield. They'll be able to determine the time of death."

"Or rather, the *year* of death," Detective Gordon amended.

"Yeah, weird," Parrish muttered as she stared at all the odd and beautiful furnishings shoved into this small space.

She reminded me of Robin, not just because she kept uttering that word, but because she was petite and pretty, with dark brown hair and a fun attitude—in spite of the circumstances.

The coroner's small staff quickly took charge of Jean Pierre Renaud's body. They completed a cursory examination inside the cave and then carried him outside and into their van in under an hour.

Derek gave them both his phone number and requested that he be kept in the loop if they found out anything. Everyone from the sheriff's department promised "Commander Stone" they would do so.

I had to admit, it was pretty great to have a big hunky commander on my side. And I knew it would make Guru Bob happy to be kept informed of the details, too.

Parrish and Gordon did a cursory search in and around the small chamber. They contacted their crime scene techs to find out how soon they could get there to dust for fingerprints and collect any trace evidence they could find.

While the detectives waited for the CSI team to arrive, they rounded up the witnesses who'd seen the inside of the room or actually been inside, namely me, Derek, Robin, Austin, Dad, and Jackson.

I told Detective Parrish everything that had happened that morning: what I'd seen, what I'd smelled, what we'd assumed or theorized about the body and the ticket and the passport. Other than that, I didn't know much.

"I didn't even know that space existed until this morning," I said, wishing I'd held on to my coffee mug from earlier. "And I have no idea how that furniture and all those expensive items got there."

"Somebody here must know," she said.

"I guess. It's possible that some original members of the commune were storing stuff in there and the cave got sealed up somehow. My dad mentioned that there was a big earthquake up here a few years ago. That might've done it. I mean, that's not what killed Mr. Renaud, but that might explain how his body was trapped there."

It still didn't make sense, but I wasn't about to say that out loud. An earthquake would've had to have occurred more than fifty years ago, and it would've buried Renaud in rubble along with damaging all the furniture and treasures.

I also wasn't about to mention Guru Bob's reaction to seeing Renaud dead on the floor. I didn't feel comfortable talking about Guru Bob to the detective, as nice as she was. That Renaud had been a friend of Guru Bob's grandfather certainly had plenty of relevance, but I quickly decided to leave it to Guru Bob to enlighten the police. Maybe that made me a bad citizen, but I refused to involve Guru Bob until I talked to him about it.

And that reminded me that I'd completely forgotten about his cousin Trudy. I wanted to talk to her as soon as possible.

Trudy's was another name I didn't intend to bring up with the cops. I liked Detective Parrish, but my loyalty remained with Guru Bob and Trudy, who were like family to me.

Detective Parrish gave me an intense look. "Bottom line, Ms. Wainwright. Do you think there's something in that chamber that precipitated Mr. Renaud's death?"

I considered her question. "I have no idea. If he was killed some seventy years ago, I'm not sure there's anyone alive who might know what happened in there."

I felt another twinge as I remembered the Jules Verne book. I'd have to add that to my list of omissions, because there was no way I would mention that I'd taken it from the room. And I had to say, I didn't feel an ounce of guilt about it.

Okay, that was a lie. If I was breathing, I was pretty much guilt-ridden. I lived with it. But that didn't mean I was going to give up the book. From my earliest days of working with rare books, I'd been instructed that if all else failed, I was to *save the book*. Earlier, I'd tucked it under a blanket in the trunk of my car for safekeeping. Now, as Detective Parrish finished her questioning, I started to wonder if the book could possibly have anything to do with the murder of Mr. Renaud. I doubted it, although I wasn't sure why. I'd dealt with plenty of rare books that had incited murderous intentions.

Not that I would mention that fact to Detective Parrish, either. Most law enforcement officials rolled their eyes whenever I was silly enough to suggest that *a simple book* might be the perfect motive for cold-blooded murder. It gave me no pleasure to count how many times I'd been right.

Chapter Three

Later that afternoon, Derek hung out with my dad and brothers, drinking wine and discussing the cave within the cave and all the stuff we'd found inside its walls. I was anxious to study the Jules Verne book, so I gave Annie a quick call just to let her know I'd be using Abraham's studio. She was glad to hear from me and said I was welcome anytime, so I fished the book out from the trunk of my car and walked down the hill to Abraham's house.

I figured that if the brown suitcase was Mr. Renaud's, and he was a friend of Guru Bob's grandfather, then Guru Bob would want this book for his library collection. And if that was the case, it would need quite a bit of cleanup work before I would feel good about handing it over to him.

Even though it was obviously a rare book—I could tell by looking at the binding, the title page, and the date of publication—it had apparently belonged to a rambunctious young boy, based on the childish scrawls I'd noticed on a few pages. I would have to examine the book more closely before I would know if I could get rid of the scrawls and still maintain the book's integrity.

As I strolled along the sidewalk of the treelined road on which my parents had lived for more than twenty years, I had to smile at the hodgepodge of home styles that made up our friendly little enclave. It was typically American for our own rambling, craftsman-inspired ranch home to live in harmony with the Quinlans' two-story French cottage next door and the Westcotts' modified Tudor across the street behind a sheltering copse of oak and pine trees.

Two doors down, the Farrell family had a cool-looking California bungalow, and next door to them, the Barclays had built their house in the prairie style because of their affection for Frank Lloyd Wright. Carl Brundidge, the commune lawyer, lived in a contemporary steel-and-glass showpiece that somehow fit perfectly nicely next door to the "midcentury modern," which was how Mr. Osborne described his home, otherwise known as a good old 1950s house complete with plastic flamingoes in the garden. Years ago, he had built a geodesic dome workshop in the backyard to keep his hippie vibe alive. Next door to the Osbornes were the Howards, who lived in a glorious three-story Victorian gem. And near the bottom of the slope was Abraham's imposing Spanish colonial mansion.

Guru Bob had always encouraged his followers to do their own thing when it came to choosing their style of house. Once the winery became successful and people started making money, neighborhoods like ours popped up all over Dharma. Visitors to the area couldn't quite wrap their brains around the fact that all these beautiful homes and shops and upscale restaurants belonged to commune members. It went against their ingrained image of what a "commune" should look like.

When I reached Abraham's house, I opened the side gate, skirted the pool and patio, and continued across the lawn to the studio he'd built for his bookbinding business.

I stared at the locked door and realized that I hadn't been back here since Abraham's death. At the time, yellow crime scene tape had crisscrossed the entrance, blocking my way. I had hesitated, but had finally torn it off to get into the room. I'd been a suspect in Abraham's murder, so ripping away the tape probably wasn't the smartest thing I could've done, but I'd come up here on a mission to find a clue to his murder. And I'd found it, even though I didn't know it at the time.

Now I let out a breath, unlocked the door, and stepped inside—and realized how completely unprepared I'd been for the over-whelming sensations that bombarded me.

I could smell Abraham in here. I could hear his voice and see his ink-stained fingers from the letterpress projects he often took on in addition to the bookbinding. The scent of leather mingled with the musty fragrance of old paper. An odd waft of peppermint almost brought me to my knees.

This room held his essence.

No wonder his daughter, Annie, had left it as it was when he died.

I managed to stay on my feet, but decided to grab a high stool and sit for a minute as a barrage of memories assaulted me. I'd grown up in this room. Abraham was a huge part of my world. He was my teacher, my friend, my confessor, my taskmaster. I'd dreamed of being a bookbinder just like him ever since I was eight years old, when I watched him bring back to life a beloved book that my horrid brothers had tried to destroy. It was nothing short of miraculous to me.

I could still see him standing by the book press, wearing his black leather apron over an old white shirt with the sleeves rolled up to his elbows. He was a big, strong, barrel-chested man who had no trouble at all tightening the huge brass book press down onto a newly rebound masterpiece.

I'd watched him do it so many times that I'd figured it was easy. What a shock it had been to find out how difficult that sucker was to use. Of course, I was only eight years old at the time. To this day, I thought of Abraham's muscular arms whenever I struggled to press a book.

I pulled the stool over to the center worktable where I set down the Jules Verne book. Then I had to go through every drawer in the cluttered room to find Abraham's standing magnifying glass. After ten minutes, I finally found it jammed in a cupboard with his punches and brushes and a myriad of other tools. He'd always been kind of a slob, although he preferred to call himself an unfettered free spirit.

Under the magnifying glass, the Jules Verne book looked even worse than I'd originally thought. I could see every little flaw along its spine and knew I would have to reconstruct it. The six raised bands had become flattened from years of handling, and all the elaborate gilding had faded away. The crown of the spine was tattered and splitting away from the front hinge. The morocco leather was in decent condition overall, but the two leather corners on the front cover had begun to fray along the edges and would need to be replaced. I anticipated using all new leather on the spine and corners rather than trying to match what little was worth saving.

Opening the front cover, I could see that the marble endpapers were in remarkably good condition with no chips or tears. The pattern was a beautiful blend of dark blue and burgundy swirls and eddies. The flyleaf—those first few blank pages of a book—was another story. On the front flyleaf, a child had signed his name across the page in bold, blue ink.

Anton Benoit.

The back flyleaf had suffered much worse abuse. Here, Anton had scrawled a long message using rust-colored ink. At the end of the message there was a date, *le 6 avril 1906*, and a place, *La Croix Saint-Just, France*. And there were two childish signatures scrawled at the bottom, *Anton Benoit* and *Jean Pierre Renaud*.

Jean Pierre: The name of the dead man. He'd been a young boy when he signed his name to this page. What had brought him all the way from France to California? And what had he been doing here that got him killed? How did he know Guru Bob's grandfather?

What the heck did it all mean?

The rust-colored ink was uneven and hard to read. Thick and blotched in some spots, scratchy and thin in others, and in a few places, it faded altogether. I stared at it through the magnifying glass for a long time, holding the book closer to the lens to figure out what it was about the ink that bothered me. Abruptly I figured it out and dropped the book in disgust.

"Blood," I said. "Ew."

Since I'd grown up with brothers, I knew it made perfect sense that two boys, probably nine or ten years old, would want to cut their skin open and draw their own blood to use as ink.

I shook my head. "Idiots."

The date and the boys' names were about the extent of my ability to translate the page of French. The scratchy handwriting didn't help, but after staring at the immature penmanship for another minute, I thought I could make out the first phrase, *Nous promettons solennellement.*

"We promise . . . solemnly?" I shrugged. "Close enough."

It sounded like the two boys were pledging an oath or something to each other.

I tried to recall my high school French, but it wasn't coming back to me. Some years ago, I'd memorized a bunch of French phrases for a trip to Paris. Unfortunately, nowhere in the boys' message did it say anything about where to find *les toilettes*, so that didn't help, either.

Reminding myself of the book's subject matter, I wondered if maybe Anton and Jean Pierre had pledged to make their own journey to the center of the earth. Since I had lived with two brothers, this sounded like something a couple of boys might vow to do after reading an enthralling adventure story.

But did they really have to destroy the value of this book by writing all over it? Yes, of course they did. Children were notoriously dangerous to the health of a fine book.

I made a mental note to ask Derek to translate the French words for me, and then moved on to study the inner pages. The paper was thick and white with some foxing throughout. The occasional instance of reddish brown spots was to be expected on a book this old. Fortunately, there were no more scrawled writings from Anton or Jean Pierre on any other pages.

I did a quick survey of the rest of the book and discovered an old piece of notepaper folded and wedged between two pages, marking the beginning of chapter forty-five. At first I thought it was a bookmark, but when I unfolded it, I found a diagram with a list of numbers and more words written in French. Again, my pitiful schoolgirl French didn't help. I would have to show this to Derek, too. Naturally, he spoke flawless French among the other hundred or so languages he seemed to know.

The big school clock on the studio wall ticked off the time. That old thing had to be thirty years old, I thought fondly, realizing I'd spent over two hours here. I had to go home and get ready for dinner with Austin and Robin, so I found a short stack of soft cloths in one of Abraham's drawers, used two of them to wrap around the book for protection, and slipped the book into my tote bag.

Walking home took longer because it was all uphill, but I made it back in time to take a quick shower and dress for dinner. Derek had a glass of wine waiting for me. "Thank you. This is nice."

"I thought we could relax for a few minutes." We sat on the comfortable couch in the Quinlans' living room. Derek had placed a plate of crackers and a small triangle of softened Brie on the heavy wood coffee table. "Did you have a chance to examine the book?"

"Yes," I said, "and I was hoping you'd look at it, too. I'm in need of your translation skills."

"I assume the book is written in French."

"It is," I said, smiling. "But you don't have to translate the book for me."

"Good, because I'm fairly certain you can pick up an English version somewhere."

I gave him a look as I swirled my wine and took a taste. "What I hope you'll translate are the notes I found inside the book."

"Notes?" he said, intrigued. "I'll be happy to look them over first thing tomorrow. Do they explain everything that happened in the cave?"

I chuckled. "If only. No, the one in the book was written by two little boys long before the cave incident. And get this, they wrote it in blood."

Derek laughed, knowing my squeamishness around blood. "You must've loved discovering that."

"It's not funny. It's gross."

"That's because you were never a little boy."

"Nice of you to notice."

"I've definitely noticed." He sat back and stretched his arm across my shoulders. "Boys like to gross things. I thought you knew."

"I do. The note made me think of Jackson and Austin as kids. They probably would've done something like that. Disgusting creatures."

"Young boys are morbidly fascinated by blood. My brothers and I tried to stab or slice one another up at every opportunity."

"Oh God. And your poor mother had to put up with five of you."

"She loved every minute of it. We were angels."

"I can't wait to hear her version of the story."

He shrugged. "She might use another term to describe us."

"The word *hooligans* comes to mind," I said, laughing.

He grinned. "I suppose that's more accurate."

I took another sip of wine. "This is awfully good."

"It's the five-year-old pinot noir we tasted today. I begged your brother for a bottle to bring home."

I rested my head on his shoulder. "My hero."

"It's the least I could do, knowing you were hard at work the entire afternoon."

I sat forward, spread some cheese on a cracker and handed it to him, and then made one for myself.

"Thanks, love."

I finished my cracker and took a sip of wine. "Have you heard anything from the detectives?"

"Not yet. The crime scene lads showed up after you left. They dusted for prints and scoured through everything. We'll have to wait and see what they turn up."

"I don't know what they can tell us. It's not like they'll arrest anyone, right? The man died seventy years ago. Nobody living here now was around back then."

He swirled his wine distractedly. "So it would seem."

"You don't sound convinced."

"I'm not." He paused, weighing his words. "Don't you find it odd that Robson's grandfather knew the dead man?"

I frowned. "I suppose. But I was mostly concerned about Guru Bob because he looked so sad."

"Yes, he did." Derek nodded thoughtfully. "According to your father, Robson—Guru Bob—moved up here only about twenty-five years ago. That was when he bought all this property and started the Fellowship. But if the dead man's passport and passenger ticket are to be believed, Jean Pierre Renaud has been lying dead in that cave for close to seventy years. So where does Guru Bob's grandfather fit into those two scenarios? Was it just a coincidence?"

Knowing Derek as well as I did, I knew he didn't believe in coincidences. "You don't actually think that Guru Bob is lying, do you?"

"I believe he's got more integrity than anyone I know, but in this case . . ." Derek shook his head. "Let's allow it to play out a bit more before jumping to any conclusions."

I thought about it for a minute. "My parents must've repeated that Guru Bob story at least a hundred times. He came up here, bought a tract of land, and then we all moved up. We lived in Airstream trailers for the first year, which was torturous, but Mom and Dad assured us that all our sacrifices would be worth it. And then we started growing grapes, and you know, the rest is history."

Derek smiled. "Yes, practically legendary."

"Maybe it's the legend that's wrong," I said slowly. "Maybe Guru Bob never said anything either way, but everyone assumed that he bought the property right then and there. But what if he didn't? What if the land was always in his family?"

Derek finished the last sip of wine and set his glass on the table. "You mentioned that you'd introduce me to Robson's cousin Trudy. Can we do that tomorrow?"

"Absolutely. You'll get a kick out of her. And she'll know plenty of their family history."

"I had no idea he had relatives living nearby," Derek said as we took our glasses and cheese plate into the kitchen.

"Trudy's the only one I know of, and she's lived here longer than we have. She doesn't mingle much with the commune folks, although she's good friends with my mom. She always helps with the harvest, and she shops in town. You might recognize her when you see her."

We finished cleaning up, refilled the animals' water dishes, and then took off to meet Robin and Austin at Arugula, my sister Savannah's restaurant on the Lane in downtown Dharma.

It was less than a mile away, and we found a parking place easily enough.

The Lane—more formally known as Shakespeare Lane—had become a destination point over the last few years with its upscale shops and fabulous restaurants as well as the Dharma winery just up the road. B and Bs were beginning to sprout up all around town, and there was a small luxury hotel and spa at the far end of the town center. My sister China had a popular yarn and weaving shop, Warped, on the Lane, and now Savannah's restaurant was here and very successful. Our family was well represented on the Lane and at the winery, where my father and brothers worked.

I could tell something was bothering Robin the minute we walked in. They had already been seated at the table but stood when they saw us. I gave her a hug, and I was pretty sure I heard her growl, sort of like a bear.

I flashed a wide-eyed look at Derek, who had also noticed her mood.

I moved around to Austin and whispered, "What's up with Robin? What did you do?"

He laughed and grabbed me in a hug. "She'll be fine."

"Men are so naive," I said, patting his shoulder. But he was still grinning, so I figured he preferred to stay clueless.

I sidled up to Robin. "What's bugging you?"

She bared her teeth. "Men."

"Ah. Okay, then. How about some wine?"

"Definitely."

We waited patiently in silence while the waiter opened the bottle. Austin took a sip and approved it, and our glasses were filled. The waiter walked away, and Austin said, "I'd like to propose a toast."

As we all raised our glasses, I noticed a blinding flash of light and set my glass down. "What is that? What're you wearing?"

"Nothing," Robin barked. "Drink your damn wine."

"Nothing?" I burst out, shoving my chair back. "There's a gigantic diamond ring on your finger. What do you mean, nothing?"

"Hello?" Austin said. "I'm in the middle of making a toast."

Robin glared at Austin, then reluctantly thrust her arm out so that I could see the ring. I grabbed her hand and stared at the most gorgeous diamond ring I'd ever seen. "That's a Tiffany setting."

Her look at me dripped with suspicion. "I'm wondering how you know that, but yeah, he went to Tiffany."

"It's spectacular," I said. "And it looks beautiful on you."

She shook her head in dismay. "Can you imagine anything less practical? Tiffany! It's two and a half freaking carats! How am I supposed to wear this thing around Dharma? We live out in the country, for God's sake."

"It's the *wine* country," Austin said, laughing. "We shop at Dean and Deluca."

She ignored him. "I'm a sculptor. I can't wear this while I'm working. What were you thinking? You should've bought me a pair of earrings or something."

"Fine," Austin grumbled, then extended his wineglass. "A toast, to the woman who has agreed to be my wife. I am the happiest man in the world." He clinked glasses with Derek and slugged down a big gulp of wine.

"Aww." I jumped from my chair, misty eyed, and rounded the table to squeeze Robin in a hug. "I'm so thrilled. So happy for you."

"I don't know why," she groused, refusing to hug me back. "I should've told him no. He's such a goofball."

"You're wearing his ring," I said softly, hugging her again. "You said yes. You love him and he loves you. I'm so proud of him and so glad he finally wised up."

"That's what you think." But her tone was lighter, and I felt her chuckling as she hugged me back.

"We'll be sisters for real," I whispered.

"Oh." She pressed her hand to her lips, and her eyes filled with tears.

And my work here was done.

Derek stood and gave Austin a hearty handshake and a slap on the back. "Congratulations, mate."

"Thanks, Derek. I'm a lucky man."

"You are indeed."

I don't know why it surprised me to hear the sincerity in Derek's voice. I knew he was crazy about my family and Robin, so that wasn't the issue. Maybe it was because we'd never discussed marriage before. And why would we? We'd only known each other . . . I did the math and felt a little dizzy. We'd been together almost two years. Time had flown by. And when he bought the loft next door to mine and was the one to suggest that we merge the two together, I knew he was committed to me. I suppose I had always assumed that he simply wasn't interested in marriage. Otherwise, surely he would have proposed to me by now. Although honestly, I'd never given it that much thought. I was perfectly happy with our relationship as it was.

Savannah came out of the kitchen with a bottle of champagne for the table, and we all celebrated the engagement in style. Less than a year ago, Robin, who had been living in San Francisco at the time, was being threatened by some guys in the Russian mafia, so she'd moved up here for a while to be safe. That was when Austin had made it clear that he wanted her to stay. She had. And they'd been living together ever since.

Despite the delicious food, wine, and celebratory atmosphere, we ended the evening early because everyone had plans for the next day.

The next morning, after a breakfast of coffee, scrambled eggs, and bagels, Derek moved to the desk in the family room and began translating the pledge and the note I'd found inside *Journey to the Center of the Earth*. I opened all the curtains to let the sun pour into the room and then pulled up a chair next to him to see how he was coming along. It took him less than ten minutes to translate what was scrawled in the rust-colored ink over the back flyleaf.

"They were blood brothers," Derek explained. *"Frères du sang."*

"Sang," I mused. "Like sanguine. Bloodred."

"Exactly." He took a sip of coffee and then read what he'd translated. "'We solemnly pledge this oath in blood to be comrades, friends, defending each other until the day we die. Together we will find the volcano that holds the portal that leads to the center of the earth, and we will share equally all the treasure we find there. So help us God. Signed, Anton Benoit and Jean Pierre Renaud.'"

I smiled. "I figured they were planning a trip to the center of the earth. That was the basis for the pledge."

"That, and friendship."

My smile faded as I remembered Guru Bob's words. "Do you think Anton killed his friend?"

"I have no idea."

"Jean Pierre's body was surrounded by treasures of another sort."

"Yes." Derek was deep in thought as he perused the page again. "I think a talk with Robson's cousin Trudy is our best first step in getting to the bottom of what happened to Monsieur Renaud."

I checked the clock. "She's probably at church right now, but we could go over there in an hour or so."

"Good."

He started to push away from the desk, but I stopped him. "I have one more thing for you to look at."

He sat down. "Another note in the book?"

I opened the book and pulled out the paper I'd found wedged between the pages.

"Ah, an actual note," he said, unfolding the piece of paper. "I thought you were referring to something else written in the book."

"No. This looks like it was written by someone else."

He stared at the squiggly diagram. A few seconds later, he turned the page on its side, and then flipped it to the other side. "It looks like a map."

"A map," I said, gazing at the odd design. "I didn't think of that. I just saw the list of numbers and words on the side and hoped you'd translate them."

"I'd be glad to." He studied it for another minute. "You're right that it was written by a different person, and I'm fairly certain that person was an adult, not a child."

"I didn't spend enough time studying it," I said, taking the paper from him. I'd taken some handwriting analysis classes to help me with authenticating signatures in books, which was an occasional part of my job.

I handed the note back to Derek. "It's definitely more mature. I wonder if it was written by one of the two boys, now grown up."

"If not, the next question is, how did it get into this book?"

"Good question," I said, frowning.

"These numbers here might indicate distance. Either in meters or footsteps. We won't know until we try to follow what it says."

"Where do we start?"

He grinned. "I haven't gotten that far in the translation. Guess I'd better get busy."

"Okay, I'll wash the breakfast dishes while you figure it out."

A few minutes later, I was putting the clean dishes away, and Derek joined me at the kitchen counter. "The starting point is at a spot he calls *l'arbre souhaitant*. Translated, it means 'wishing tree.'"

"Oh." I perked up. "The Wishing Tree. You've seen it. That beautiful old oak tree growing in the grassy circle at the entrance to the winery. The roots are so big and thick that they grow above the ground and surround the base of the tree in massive gnarly knots. Water collects in the nooks and crannies and pockets of the roots like little pools, and for as far back as I can remember, it's been a tradition to toss pennies into the pools and make wishes."

"Isn't that fascinating?" he said, and grabbed my hand. "Shall we go on a treasure hunt?"

Chapter Four

Before leaving the house, Derek ran next door to get the key to the winery storage cave from my father. Then we drove over to the winery and managed to find a parking place in the crowded lot. Even this early in the day, Sundays in wine country could be challenging with so many people driving up from the Bay Area. It was especially busy this close to harvest time.

"There's the tree," I said, pointing to the beautifully gnarled oak that some claimed had been standing in that place for more than three hundred years.

"I've seen it so many times," he said. "I had no idea I could've been making wishes all along."

"Now that you know, you won't be able to stop yourself."

The tree was immense. Its heavy limbs, twisted and dark and covered in moss, reached sixty feet in all directions. Some were so old and thick that they skimmed the ground. The knobby branches used to remind me of a wicked witch's crooked fingers, stretching out to snap up the next child who came too close. Of course I didn't believe that anymore, but it always gave me a little chill when I got close enough to make a wish.

Derek gazed up through the lush, leafy branches. "Up close, it's so much bigger than I realized."

I pressed my hand against the rough trunk. "When we were young, my three sisters and Robin and I would stand on either side of the trunk and try to join hands. It was too big for us to make it."

Derek pulled some change from his pocket. "It's fitting that we make a wish first."

"Oh, that's a nice idea." I took two pennies from him and tossed them into the small pool of water near where I was standing. My wishes always started out simple, but quickly grew complicated. I liked to squeeze in a sub-wish or two, and I wasn't sure if that disqualified my main wish or not.

This time I wished for good health for everyone in my family, but then I added names to the list, like my neighbors in San Francisco and my friend Ian and a few others. They were like family, so that counted, right? Then, as always, I tagged on a wish for world peace.

"Is it safe for the tree when its roots grow above ground?" Derek wondered aloud.

"Apparently most of its roots extend down at least forty feet, so it's not as shallow as it appears."

"That must be how it's survived for so long. In England we have oaks that have been standing since the time of King Henry the Eighth and before. They always seem so majestic, as if they have stories to tell and are only waiting for someone to listen."

I squeezed his hand, pleased that we shared the same sort of daydreams. "I know just what you mean."

"I know you do, love." He took a look at the piece of paper he'd used to write out the instructions in English. I'd asked him to copy it because I didn't want to bring the original notepaper with us. It belonged with the book.

After studying his notes, Derek glanced around, checked the

sky for the position of the sun, and pointed toward the storage cave we'd excavated yesterday. "Starting here, we take one hundred forty-seven steps in a northeast direction."

"Is that it? No jogging off this way or that?"

"No, just one straight shot, according to the instructions. Although there are landmarks noted along the way."

"Should be interesting," I said, letting go of his hand. "Okay, you lead the way and I'll follow you."

He took my hand back. "I say we ought to walk side by side so we can both count. In case I lose track."

I smiled at him, knowing he wouldn't lose track. But I appreciated that he thought I'd be helpful. "All right."

"Let's go." We headed in the northeast direction he'd indicated, until we'd crossed the parking lot. I counted steps under my breath.

Derek stopped abruptly and consulted his notes. "At thirty-seven footsteps, we should be directly in front of a hedgerow."

"A hedgerow. You mean, like a row of bushes?" I looked around and pointed. "There are some on the other side, over by the tasting rooms."

"That's the wrong direction. Perhaps there were hedgerows here all those years ago."

"Maybe. Are you sure we went in the right direction?"

"Yes. Let's keep going."

We continued in a straight line until we reached number seventy-eight. "Stop here." He gazed around. "There should be a circle of rosebushes here. Red ones, for red wine."

"All the roses were moved to the other side of the vineyard a few years ago to accommodate the flow of people taking the tour. I'm afraid the bushes were getting trampled."

He frowned and stared at the instructions.

"But I'm pretty sure they used to be right in this area," I added.

"Ah. We'll go with that, then." We started up again, and this time we made it all the way to the arched double doors of the cave. Unfortunately, the entry was masked off with yellow construction tape, blocking our way.

"I guess this was necessary," I said, "but it's going to be a turn-off for the visitors. They'll think something awful happened here." I briskly waved that statement away. "I mean, something awful *did* happen here, but you know what I mean. The bright yellow isn't exactly subtle."

"True," he said dryly, "but the construction tape was prefera-ble to the detectives' crime scene tape."

"Oh, wow. They wanted to put up crime scene tape? Okay, I'll go along with the construction tape."

"Excuse me. Is this where the body was found?"

I blinked and turned. Two women in their sixties stood a few feet away, wearing jeans, sweatshirts, and sneakers. They were staring with excitement at the cave entrance.

I gave Derek a quick glance, then said, "I, um, yes, that's what I hear."

"That's so cool!" the one woman said, and turned to her friend. "I can't wait to buy some of their wine."

"Let's get over to the tasting room," the other said, and they walked away briskly.

"So much for the news being bad for business," I murmured. "That was weird. How did the word get out so quickly?"

"I can't say, but perhaps that explains the heavy crowds today."

"I thought it was because it's so close to harvest time."

It wasn't about the harvest, though, because that same basic "Where's the body?" scenario was repeated by three more visitors before I was finally able to flag down Jenny, one of the winery workers.

"Would you mind guarding the entrance while Derek and I

take another look inside? I'll call Austin and let him know where you are."

"Okay, sure," she said easily.

I warned her that people might want to know if this was where the body was found.

She waved her hand blithely. "Oh, we've already had dozens of people asking about it. Austin said to tell them, yes, a body was found near here. But if they want more info, we should send them to see the manager."

"Sounds reasonable."

I used my cell to call my brother to tell him that Derek wanted to go back into the cave to check on something. Since it was Derek, Austin didn't have a problem with the plan. I was such a clever sister.

"Be careful," Austin added. "And tell Jenny she should stay out there until you're finished."

I relayed the message to Jenny, who was perfectly happy playing traffic cop while Derek and I tore off enough of the tape to allow us to get the door opened and slide inside.

A few steps inside the cave, we found the light switch and turned it on. In the small alcove the guys used for an office, Derek found one of the flashlights that had been left there yesterday and took it in case we needed it.

"It's so quiet in here," I said, then winced. "Oh darn. I hope you kept count of your footsteps."

"I did. We hit number one hundred two at the edge of the entrance."

"So we've got forty-five steps to go."

We both counted steps as we walked slowly through the cave in the same northeast direction. At the wall between the cave and the inner chamber, we hit one hundred thirty-three.

"I'm getting a bad feeling about this," I muttered.

"Let's carry on." Derek stepped over the barrier, and I followed. We were able to take another ten steps until we stopped directly in front of the French wardrobe with the beautiful beveled mirror I'd admired on our first visit to the cave.

"I can't believe it's a dead end," I said, smacking my palm against the side of the wardrobe. "We only needed to take four more steps. Maybe whoever made that map had smaller feet than you. We should start over and go in a slightly different direction."

"I think we wound up exactly where we should have," Derek said, his gaze focused on the wardrobe.

Trying to read his mind, I turned and stared at the well-appointed antique. It was at least seven feet tall and five feet wide with the large mirrored door in the center and two smaller doors on either side. I glanced back at Derek. "What are you thinking?"

"I think we should move this piece of furniture."

"You think there's something behind it." It wasn't a question, and I wasn't about to argue with one of Derek's hunches. The fact that the thing had to weigh hundreds of pounds was immaterial.

"Let's do it."

With Derek doing most of the actual lifting and me huffing and puffing while trying to angle the piece away from the wall, we managed to move it almost two feet.

When we stood to survey the result, it took a second or two for me to comprehend what we'd uncovered: a narrow, arched entry into a deeper cave.

"Another cave?" I whispered.

"Would you prefer to go first, or shall I?" Derek asked, switching the flashlight on.

I stared at the hole in the wall and imagined all the slimy, slinky creatures that might be crawling around back there. With a slight shiver, I stepped aside. "After you."

He slipped around the dresser and disappeared into the space beyond.

"Derek?"

"Are you coming?" His voice echoed out from the enclosed space.

"You bet I am." Creepy crawlies notwithstanding, I wasn't going to let him go in there without me. Love did weird things to people.

I could see the occasional flashlight beam bouncing off the inner walls and felt a little better about stepping into the unknown.

Derek glided the beam around the room, and I followed the light, trying to get my bearings. This space was slightly larger than the outer chamber and the ceiling just high enough for Derek, who was more than six feet tall, to stand without stooping.

"Look at this," he said, focusing the beam of light on the far wall to our left.

"Oh my God," I whispered.

"Indeed," he said.

If I'd thought the outer chamber was filled with lovely treasures, this space put that one to shame.

Leaning against the walls were paintings of various sizes, still in their beautifully gilded, rococo-style frames. Next to these, I counted sixteen canvas rolls that I thought also might be paintings.

A massive oak table held at least twenty finely bound books, as well as more silver candlesticks, goblets, and urns. There were a number of small bronze or marble statues of various objects: an angel cupping the cheek of a woman; two lovers; a horse; a naked discus thrower; a woman curled up and weeping; a matching set of cherubs mounted on marble bases and each holding a gold candelabra. I counted three large marble busts of important-looking men. Off to the side were stacks of wooden crates that held a number of cases of wine. Two large wooden wine barrels stood on the other side of the table. Derek tried to move one of them and was able to do so easily. "This one is empty."

"Where in the world did all of this come from?" I wondered aloud. "It must be worth a fortune."

"A very large fortune," Derek mused, still scanning the flashlight across the treasures we'd found.

I walked over to where the canvas rolls stood and unrolled one of them at random. It was a painting of a dancing woman in the style of Renoir, with bright, bold colors in an outdoor setting. A fun-loving group of partygoers surrounded the woman, and a buxom barmaid carried a tray of drinks in the background. The canvas was almost four feet high by at least five feet wide. It couldn't be a Renoir, could it? If not, it was an excellent forgery.

"Derek, look at this."

"I'm looking at this." He turned and showed me a small framed painting of the Madonna and Child. It was stunning, only about eighteen inches tall by thirteen or fourteen inches wide. The Virgin's face was pale and lovely with soft brown eyes and a tiny cleft in her chin. Her reddish hair curled softly as it streamed over her shoulders. The child was adorably plump, with a headful of curly brown hair, wise eyes, and a knowing smile. Their delicate golden halos seemed illuminated from within. The frame was ornately carved and gilded.

"It's as beautiful as any Botticelli I've ever seen."

Derek frowned. "Yes, isn't it?"

"You don't honestly think it was painted by—"

"I do, actually," he murmured. "Or someone equally gifted."

I was in no position to argue with Derek, who had been responsible for the security of some of the most expensive artwork on earth. I gazed from the serene Madonna to the vibrant painting in my hands. "We'd better call Guru Bob. He'll know what to do."

I confess I have no idea what to do."

It might've been the first time I'd ever heard Guru Bob

admit to being clueless. I couldn't blame him. All of these priceless objects hidden away in caves for decades? On Dharma winery land? It defied explanation.

He walked around the cavernous space, taking his time and studying each piece. He was casually dressed in soft khaki trousers and a white dress shirt with comfortable-looking loafers. For him, that was casual since I rarely saw him in anything other than a suit and tie.

I walked with him, shining the flashlight on each piece. Guru Bob took my arm and wound it through his companionably. We stopped to watch as Derek unrolled each canvas.

I couldn't say if any of the paintings were originals, but I could honestly claim that we were in the midst of great works painted in the style of Renoir, Monet, Chagall, and, perhaps, Botticelli.

"Tell me, Brooklyn," said Guru Bob. "Have you any theories that might explain where this extraordinary treasure came from?"

I hesitated for a moment, then spoke. "We found a book inside the suitcase that belonged to Mr. Renaud."

He tilted his head slightly. "A book?"

"Yes. *Journey to the Center of the Earth*, by Jules Verne. I, um, took it. I didn't want the police to have it. They don't always appreciate the fragility of a rare book."

He smiled and tightened his hold on my arm. I interpreted the action as a sign of approval.

"Anyway," I continued, "inside the book was a pledge written in French and signed by two boys. There was also a piece of note-paper left inside the book. It was written by an adult, also in French. On the note was a map, and that's how we found our way into this part of the cave."

"From a map you found in the book?" He looked frankly stunned.

"Yes." I gave Derek a quick look and noticed he was listening to every word. "Derek translated the map's instructions, and they led us from the Wishing Tree directly into this part of the cave. Well, actually, we were stopped at the fancy wardrobe in the outer chamber, but Derek had the bright idea of moving it, and, sure enough, it was covering up this small opening. And that's how we found this room."

"Astounding." Guru Bob glanced over at Derek.

"It certainly is," Derek said.

"It seems you took your own journey into the center of the earth," Guru Bob said. "How resourceful of you."

"I didn't even think of that," I said, grinning at Derek.

"Thank you both for being so tenacious." He gave my arm a light squeeze and nodded to Derek. "I will be grateful for any more information you come across that might provide an answer to this remarkable puzzle."

He turned and stared again at the items scattered around the room.

"Does anything look at all familiar?" Derek asked.

"Sadly, no," Guru Bob said. He turned back to me. "You said the pledge was written by two boys, and they signed their names."

"That's right."

"Do you remember what their names were?"

"Of course," I said. "They were Jean Pierre Renaud and Anton Benoit."

He inhaled suddenly, as though he'd received a punch in the stomach. Guru Bob rarely showed emotions unless they were positive ones, but right now he looked completely flummoxed and not happy about it.

"You knew them," Derek said softly.

Guru Bob sighed. "You may recall my telling you that Jean Pierre Renaud was a friend of my grandfather."

"Yes, of course," I said, and Derek nodded.

Guru Bob sighed. "My grandfather was Anton Benoit."

Chapter Five

"Like many families, mine had its secrets," Guru Bob admitted after we'd left the darkness of the cave for a picnic table under an oak tree near the tasting room. Derek and I sat together facing Guru Bob. I hoped he didn't feel as if we were interrogating him, but it felt like that to me.

"My father rarely spoke of his parents or their life in Sonoma. Never liked to talk about growing up working in the vineyards, except to say that it was not for him. He moved our family to San Francisco when I was barely a teenager."

"What was your grandfather like?" I asked.

"He died before I was born, so I never knew him."

"I'm sorry."

"Thank you, gracious. I do know that when my grandfather and uncles reached the United States, they changed the family name of Benoit to the English version of the name, and that is how I came to have the last name of Benedict."

He pronounced the name Benoit as *Ben-wah*.

Derek leaned forward. "And you had no idea that the hidden chamber with all that artwork and furnishings even existed?"

"No idea at all." He shook his head, looking almost ashamed.

I hoped that wasn't the case, but he was clearly unhappy about the discoveries inside the caves, especially the body of Mr. Renaud. "I feel so inadequate, unable to answer your simple questions. As I said, my father was not forthcoming when it came to discussing my grandfather, or much else for that matter. You have not talked to my cousin Trudy yet, have you?"

"Not yet."

"She is your best hope for finding the answers. She is actually my father's cousin and twenty years older than I. She moved here with the rest of the family when she was a child. I will let her know you plan to visit her."

"Do you think she knew what was inside the cave?" Derek asked.

"No," he said, shaking his head for emphasis. "Absolutely not. Trudy is wonderfully impulsive and would never have been able to keep it a secret."

He was right about that. His cousin was a generous free spirit who loved life and people. She would've wanted to share all that bounty with others.

"Who lived on this land before the commune bought up all the property?" I asked.

"It belonged to my grandfather and his brothers. As they died off, their children inherited the land. Two of them returned to France and another one died, until Trudy and my father were the only ones left. When my family moved to the city, Trudy stayed and leased the land to a few local farmers, until I came back years later and asked to take it on. She was more than happy to relinquish all that responsibility, and the commune continues to pay her a monthly dividend."

"Then we'll talk to Trudy," I said.

Derek told Guru Bob that he planned to take pictures of the objets d'art and send them to his contacts at Interpol in case they'd been reported stolen by their owners.

"If more damage was done, it is best to find out sooner than later," Guru Bob said, agreeing with Derek's plan. "There has been too much secrecy. Even Trudy has never been willing to share stories of what happened to her during the war, but I have a feeling she will open up to Derek if she knows that it is part of a bigger mystery."

"I'm sure she will," I said, confident of Derek's powers of persuasion.

Guru Bob's frown softened into a smile. "My cousin does love her mysteries. And she has always had a soft spot for the British."

"Trudy is so excited to meet you," Mom said to Derek the next day as he drove across town to meet Guru Bob's cousin— or first cousin once removed, to be precise. "And you'll love her. She's a sweetie pie."

"I'm looking forward to meeting her, too," he said.

I'd given Mom the front seat while I sat in back with a pretty pink bakery box on my lap.

Trudy lived a half mile on the opposite side of the Lane from us, on a pretty, hilly street lined with sycamore trees and California bungalows of every color and size. Hers was painted pale blue with white trim, and the wide front porch held a set of cheerful white wicker chairs, perfect for relaxing on warm fall afternoons.

Trudy was smiling as she greeted us at the door, wearing chic slim jeans and a pretty green sweatshirt over a preppy blue-collared shirt. She was as tall as I was, about five feet eight, and her hair was a beautiful shade of light reddish brown.

I introduced her to Derek, and she took his arm, pulling him into the house. "I've heard all about you. You saved our Brooklyn's life."

"She's saved my life as well, on more than one occasion."

"Isn't that sweet? I like you so much already." She turned and beckoned me and Mom to follow. "Come in, come in. Amelia, is the tea ready?"

"Yes, yes," groused Trudy's companion, Amelia, as she fluffed up the pillows on the sofa in Trudy's living room. "What do you think I've been doing?"

I had never seen Amelia in a good mood, but Trudy seemed to take her companion's curmudgeonly attitude in stride. The woman was in her forties and wore a drab blue plaid dress that hung down to her calves, with a gray cardigan buttoned all the way up. Her hair was dirty blond tinged with gray and it hung in straggly clumps to her shoulders. She was a complete contrast to Trudy's brightness, cheery attire, and attitude.

I vaguely recalled that the two of them had met in the hospital when Trudy was laid up with a broken leg—or was it a fractured hip? Amelia needed a job, and Trudy hired her to be her cook, housekeeper, and general companion. Or something like that. I would have to get the complete story from my mother later.

"Wonderful," Trudy said, clapping her hands. "We'll have tea momentarily. And, Amelia, will you look at what Brooklyn brought? Our favorite cookies from Sweet Nothings."

"Sugar cookies?" Amelia asked, entrenched frown lines digging across her forehead.

"Yes, sugar cookies," I said. "They're my favorite, too. Melt in your mouth." I handed her the box, and as she grabbed it, she almost grinned. That is, she bared her teeth at me, and I was willing to take that as a smile.

"Can I help you with anything?" I asked, following her into Trudy's charming country kitchen.

"No," Amelia said curtly, pointing toward the living room. "Go sit down, and I'll bring everything out shortly."

"Okeydokey." I could take the hint. I headed back to the front room, where Trudy was clutching Derek's arm as she led him around the frilly room and showed off some of her favorite tchotchkes.

The room was full of them: a glass hummingbird hanging off a lampshade; a Belleek porcelain bell; a tiny cloisonné pillbox in the shape of a lady's handbag; and lots of books, along with dozens of framed photographs on every surface.

Mom was seated at one end of the pale green striped brocade sofa, so I took one of the overstuffed pale rose chairs and watched Trudy charm Derek. Apparently Trudy's soft spot for the British coincided with a soft spot for handsome men. And who could blame her?

Amelia walked in and placed a large silver tray on the French provincial coffee table, then left the room. She had managed to squeeze a pot of tea, a small platter of cookies, cups, saucers, utensils, and little napkins onto the tray.

Amelia showed no signs of returning, so I scooted forward in the big chair. "Shall I pour?"

"Would you, dear?" Trudy said as Derek delivered her to her place at the opposite end of the sofa from Mom. "And I'll be happy to answer any questions your Derek wishes to ask me."

Derek sat in the other chair and flashed me a quick smile as I began to pour tea into cups. I placed a small cookie on the side of each saucer and handed them to Mom, Derek, and Trudy.

"Thanks, sweetie," Mom said.

"There are more cookies on the platter," I said, although I'd counted three missing and eyed the doorway to the kitchen, where I knew Amelia was scarfing them up. I didn't mind. I just hoped she would remember to smile at me next time.

"How long have you lived in Dharma, Trudy?" Derek asked once he'd taken his first sip of the hearty English blend.

"I moved here as a small child," Trudy said. "I was barely seven years old when we left our village in France and boarded the ocean liner for America. That was in the fall of 1944."

"That must've been a treacherous time to travel," he commented.

"Indeed it was, but being a child, I saw it as a grand adventure."

"Why did you leave?" I asked.

She stared at her cookie before taking a ladylike bite. "It was critical that we leave. We lived just over four miles from Oradour-sur-Glane. The massacre there took place in June, and we were afraid that at almost any moment, the same would be done to our village."

"Where did you live?" Derek asked.

"La Croix Saint-Just. North of Oradour, along the River Glane."

"Near Limoges?" Derek asked.

"That's the nearest large city, twenty miles southeast."

He smiled. "I know the area."

"*Très bien!* Very good." Trudy laughed. "Goodness, can you believe I still slip into French if I'm not paying attention?"

To my untrained ear, her French sounded perfect, even though she'd lived in Sonoma for close to seventy years, if my quickie calculations were correct.

"What happened in that town near you?" I asked.

Derek answered, his gaze steady on me. "The Nazis gathered all of the women and children into the Catholic church, locked the doors, and began looting the village."

"The men were rounded up and herded into several area barns," Trudy continued stoically, "and killed by machine gun. Then the Nazis gassed and bombed the church with all those people inside and set fire to the rest of the town."

"Oh my God," I whispered.

"It was said to be in retaliation for some of the villagers' collaborating with la Résistance."

Mom reached across the sofa and squeezed Trudy's hand. "I'm so sorry."

"Very few escaped," Trudy said, and then turned to Derek. "So you're aware of this ugly moment in French history?"

Derek nodded. "I attended some low-level NATO meetings near Limoges a few years ago and spent a day walking through Oradour-sur-Glane. It was heartbreaking."

"Yes, it is still. Even though I was a child, I can't remember being so frightened before or since."

There was a moment of troubled silence, and then Derek asked, "Can you tell us about your father?"

"Yes, of course." She smiled. "Luc Benoit was born in La Croix Saint-Just, but to tell his story, I must begin with his father, my grandfather, Christophe Benoit, who was born and raised in the town of St. Emilion."

My eyes grew wide. "St. Emilion?"

"Yes. It is known for its Bordeaux wines. You've heard of it?"

I almost laughed at the understatement. "Yes, I've heard of it." St. Emilion was world-renowned for its premier red Bordeaux wines. Every schoolkid in Sonoma had heard of St. Emilion.

"Grandpapa grew up working in his father's winery, but on a high school trip to Limoges, he met and fell in love with my grandmother, Belle. She was from La Croix Saint-Just and had no intention of moving to St. Emilion no matter how important Christophe's winery was."

"She was a hometown girl," Mom said in complete understanding.

"Precisely," Trudy said, smiling as she nodded. "So what else could my grandfather do but move to La Croix Saint-Just and marry her? They had four sons, one of whom was my papa, Luc. His brother Anton was Robson's grandfather. Grandpapa Christophe had only ever known winemaking, so he brought with him a satchel of old-growth vines from St. Emilion and planted them in the rich soil of La Croix Saint-Just."

"How did that work out?" I wondered aloud.

"Oh, he became very successful, possibly because he was one of the few winemakers in the area."

"He would've been very popular," Mom agreed.

Derek set his empty teacup and saucer on the coffee table. "What can you tell us about his brother Anton?"

"Uncle Anton was the oldest of the four boys and very smart," she said. "They sent him to the Université de Poitiers to study medicine."

"Anton was a doctor?" I asked.

"Yes, a medical doctor by profession." She chuckled lightly. "But he was a born academic. My grandfather used to say with much affection that Anton would rather have been teaching medicine than practicing." She took a quick sip of tea before continuing the story. "Uncle Anton worked in a small clinic a distance from town until it closed, and then he became more involved in the family winery. He turned out to be excellent at winemaking because of his ability to apply biology and chemistry to the blending of the wines."

"When did he decide to come to this country?" I asked.

"It was the war," she said, her eyes unfocused as though she were recalling those days. "The Germans marched into Paris in 1940. I was too young to remember much, but I have since heard the stories repeated by my parents and grandparents."

"It had to be a horrific time," Mom said, reaching for the teapot to pour us all more tea.

"It was. By 1942, the French winemakers were fearful of having their precious vineyards burned and their wines stolen by the Nazis. My father and Uncle Anton and their two brothers began bricking up their caves and ripping out the vines so the Nazis couldn't destroy them."

I frowned. "But if they were ripping out their own vines, weren't they destroying them anyway?"

"No, no, I misspoke," Trudy said, holding her teacup steady for Mom to refill it. "The men took the ancient vines out carefully by the roots and packed them in small burlap bags with the dirt still surrounding the root ball. They hid these inside wine barrels and sent them to all parts of the world, wherever they had friends or acquaintances in the winemaking business. This way, the vines could be replanted surrounded by the dirt that had always nurtured them. The *terroir*." She looked at me. "You are familiar with the term?"

"Yes," I said, remembering my days conducting tastings at the winery. "*Terroir* is everything that gives a certain wine its specific characteristics. The dirt, the climate, the microclimate, the geological conditions. All of these affect the taste of the wine. Even other plants growing in the area will lend flavor to the wine. *Terroir* can include the type and location of a particular oak tree used to make the barrel in which it's aged, or the yeast added during fermentation."

I realized everyone was staring at me, and I winced. "Sorry. I tend to go off on the subject."

"No, no, I find it fascinating," Trudy said. "And very true. The winemakers had a need to protect their *terroir* as well as their vines, so they collected the dirt, too. And many cases of bottled wines, of course. They distributed them to those friends around the world for safekeeping."

"But you still weren't safe," Derek prompted.

Even though I knew the outcome, I was sitting on the edge of my seat. "Your parents must've been scared to death."

"It was a dark time," she said, frowning. "When the massacre occurred at Oradour, our village fathers called a town meeting. Uncle Anton suggested that everyone gather their most treasured belongings together and hide them in one safe place."

"Did they all agree?"

"Yes. The blacksmith had a false door in the floor of his shop, and they intended to hide everything in the space underneath. But then my uncle Jacques was caught by the Nazis for being part of the Resistance. We were afraid he would be tortured. He escaped, but he and his brothers decided that our entire family had to leave immediately to avoid certain death at the hands of the enemy. The men of my family used up every connection they'd ever had to get us out of the country."

"Did they leave everything with the blacksmith?" I asked.

"No. Uncle Anton, as the oldest, was in charge, and he suggested that he and my uncles collect the most valuable belongings of everyone in the village and take them out of the country with them. When the war was over, Anton would be responsible for bringing it all back safe and sound.

"Everyone agreed that this was the best solution, so for several nights, people came by our house and left the most beautiful artwork and statues and gold coins and jewelry and silver pieces. Even some furniture. The father of one of my school friends claimed to be related to the French kings. He and the men carried several exquisite pieces of furniture into our house. I remember seeing a dresser with a mirror and a vanity table. All very fancy."

At the mention of the furniture, I exchanged a glance with Derek.

"How did you get everything out of the country?" he asked.

"By the will of God," she said. "And pure luck. The small items were placed inside the wine barrels and covered in dirt. The biggest items were shipped to a company in San Francisco that Uncle Anton knew of, and he planned to take possession of them when we arrived. Those larger crates were marked as furniture. And, of course, much of it was indeed furniture."

"That must've taken some time to arrange." I was completely enthralled by her tale.

"The clock was ticking," she said. "My mother was so nervous in those days. I didn't know why until a few years later when I was finally able to understand what we'd been through."

"So everything was packed up, and that was when you left."

"We had to sneak out of the village and travel at night. Along the way we were assisted by many kind people. I was miserable and frightened, but I didn't dare complain."

"Because you might've been discovered."

"Yes," she said flatly. "We finally made it to the coast and traveled across the channel to Southampton, England. Then by boat to New York and then by train to California. The wine barrels traveled with us. It was a harrowing journey every step of the way, because we never knew when we might be stopped and searched. My father and uncles had to carry an enormous amount of cash because they didn't know when or where they might have to pay off an official."

"How awful for them," Mom murmured. "And all of you."

"Isn't it?" Trudy said, shaking her head. "Even when we arrived at the little train station in Petaluma, safe at last, my mother refused to let a porter take her suitcase. She was afraid she wouldn't get it back."

"Your poor mother," Mom said. "She had to worry about her children, too."

"Yes," Trudy murmured. "I had a younger brother, Olivier. He returned to France after the war and died a few years ago."

"I'm sorry."

"Thank you. He was a dear old thing, and his wife was lovely. They're both gone now. I remember how Ollie and I used to practice our English together every day on the boat." She seemed lost in thought for a moment but then perked up. "When we arrived in San Francisco, we collected our shipments of furniture and everything else we'd sent ahead. My father and uncles bought three cars and a truck, and we all drove out here to Sonoma."

Derek smiled calmly, even though I could tell he was anxious to get back on track. "Once they knew you were all safe, did your parents arrange to take everything back to the villagers?"

Trudy's expression was not happy. "I don't believe so, not right away. The war was still raging back home. But to be honest, I have no idea when or how they sent the items back. My parents never spoke of it."

"They never said anything about the villagers' belongings?" I asked, not quite believing what she'd said.

"When we first arrived, they talked about it. And they told us stories. We were growing older, and I think they wanted us to know some of our history. But one day, they just stopped talking about it. All of it. The artwork. The harrowing details of the trip we'd taken. The war. Even our old village in France. My parents never spoke a word about any of it again."

"Not a word?" Mom echoed in puzzlement.

"Not as far as I knew."

"Do you have any idea why?" I asked.

"No. I was still a child and didn't think to ask. I assumed my father and uncles had taken care of everything, but they never said. I decided that they simply didn't like to dwell on the past. But I wish I knew what happened. There were so many beautiful things, I would like to know that they all made it back to their rightful owners and that our French village was peaceful again. I have so many questions."

Derek and I exchanged another glance, and he reached for Trudy's hand. "We might be able to give you some of the answers you're looking for."

She trembled visibly. "What do you mean?"

"I mean, we know where the treasures are. We can take you to see them, Trudy."

She waved him away with a tired smile. "Oh, I'm too old to travel."

"You don't understand," I said, laughing. "They're only a mile away. In the wine cave."

"It's simply too much to comprehend," Trudy said. "It all looks so familiar, and yet, it's—it's . . . Oh, there's the Greniers' family portrait. Good heavens, they're all so young." She gazed at the framed oil painting for a long moment, then turned to stare at herself in the pretty gold-leaf mirror attached to a rococo vanity table. "This belonged to my girlfriend from so many years ago, Nanette Allard."

"It's beautiful," I said.

"Isn't it? I always envied her for having so many nice . . . Oh!" She inhaled so suddenly, I thought she might faint.

"Are you all right?"

"What is it?" Derek asked. "Do you remember something else?"

Trudy let out a faint trill and flitted over to the bookshelf, where she grabbed a small white marble sculpture of a bird and clutched it tightly to her bosom. "It's my missing bookend!"

She closed her eyes and simply breathed for a moment. Then she held it out for us to see. "It's a quail. I can't believe it. I haven't seen this since I was seven years old."

"It was yours when you were young?" Derek asked.

She laughed. "The set actually belonged to my father, but he gave it to me because I loved carrying it around the house. One of the set disappeared shortly after we moved here, and I was bereft. But here it is."

"Amazing," Mom said.

"I still have its mate on my mantel at home. Well, not its mate, exactly. The one I have at home is a kitten, but it's similar in size and style to this one." She turned it this way and that. "It's charming, isn't it?"

"Beautiful," I repeated, taking the sculpture when she offered it. As Trudy said, it was a quail, and its head, half of its body, and one outstretched wing were beautifully carved while the rest of its body was still encased in the small block of marble. I handed it to Derek.

"It's so simple," he said, "and yet it manages to show so much emotion and strength. The way it's carved as though it's poised to fly free from the marble reminds me of Rodin's style."

"I think so, too." Trudy let out a happy sigh. "This was done by nobody in particular and isn't worth much money, of course. But it has lots of sentimental value."

I noticed Derek's eyebrow quirk up. Did he disagree with her? Did he believe the piece might be a more important work than Trudy thought? I'd thought of Rodin, too, when I held the little sculpture. I loved his work and had enjoyed touring his museum in Paris, but I couldn't remember whether he'd ever sculpted small animals like that. Unbidden, an old news story sprang to my mind, about the Musée Rodin in Paris discovering a number of fake sculptures in other exhibitions around the world. The article mentioned a way to tell if a Rodin sculpture was an original. Knowing Derek, I suspected he already knew how to tell.

"All these fantastic paintings," Mom said as she scanned the artwork leaning against the walls. "I can't believe they've been hiding in here all these years."

"Someone went to a lot of trouble to keep them hidden," I said.

"But why?" she asked. "Everything is so beautiful. Why not share it with the world?"

"Perhaps there was an earthquake," Trudy said. "I can't imagine my father or my uncles purposely barricading this space, but an earthquake might've made it inaccessible."

"Quite possibly," Derek said, although I knew he was only saying it to placate her. We had already decided that an earthquake would've destroyed most of the valuables hidden in these chambers. There would've been rubble and stones and earth blocking the way, not smooth cement walls.

But I played along. "Yes, anything could've happened." I didn't want Trudy to worry that her family members might've done something devious. But how else could this be explained?

I glanced at Mom, who took the hint. "It's getting late. If you don't mind, I'd better go home and start dinner."

"Oh goodness," Trudy said, checking her wristwatch. "Amelia is going to scold me for being gone so long without calling."

Amelia would scold her? Sadly, I believed it and wondered if Trudy couldn't find a more pleasant companion than that sourpuss.

I led the way out of the chamber, through the storage cave, and out to the pathway that led to the parking lot.

In the car, Trudy held her quail sculpture in her lap, and we chitchatted about the awesome discovery all the way back to her house.

Derek left the motor running while he walked Trudy to her door. Once she was safe inside, Derek returned, and we took off for our side of town. I leaned forward from the backseat and touched Mom's shoulder. "Did you know any of that stuff about Guru Bob?"

"You mean that he was French? I had no idea!"

"No, I mean did you know that his family already owned this property long before we moved up here to join the Fellowship?"

She frowned. "I suppose he did. Your father and I always thought he came here and bought the property on his own."

"So Dad didn't know, either?"

Mom's shoulders dropped fractionally. "Neither of us had any idea that Robson's family owned this property." But Dad had been known to keep secrets from Mom in the past. For her own good, he'd said at the time. Her eyes narrowed with purpose. "I'll find out exactly how much your father knows when I get home."

"Go, Mom."

"Not that it should be any big deal," she argued with herself. "Robson doesn't have to tell us every detail of his life."

"True."

Then she frowned. "In fact, I'm trying to remember exactly what he *did* tell us. Maybe we all just assumed he'd purchased the land around that same time."

"Maybe."

"I'll get back to you on that."

I caught Derek watching me in the rearview mirror and grinned. He always had too good a time watching me spar with my mother.

He pulled into Mom's driveway and came to a stop.

"I'd like to return to the caves tomorrow," Mom said as she was climbing out of the car. "The space needs a spiritual cleansing."

Normally I would've rolled my eyes and tried to discourage her, but seeing as how a murder had occurred in that small cave, and lord only knew what had happened in the larger one, I figured it might actually do some good if she went ahead and cleaned it up a little, spiritually speaking.

"I'll go with you," I said.

"I'll take you both there," Derek said. "The potential value of the treasure in those caves is phenomenal, and that much money can make people do crazy things. I think we'd be wise to follow the 'safety in numbers' adage for the time being."

"I couldn't agree more," Mom said, beaming at him. "See you kids tomorrow."

Once Mom was gone, I pounced on Derek. "Do you honestly think that sculpture might be a real Rodin?"

He glanced at me sideways before backing out of my parents' driveway and pulling into the Quinlans'. "How dare you read my mind."

"It wasn't that hard," I said, chuckling. "The expression on your face made it obvious."

"It's sad," he lamented. "I used to be so mysterious. Inscrutable."

I laughed. "You're absolutely sphinxlike most of the time, but I suppose I'm getting used to you."

"The Rodin connection makes sense, though, don't you think?" Derek said as he unlocked the side door into the kitchen. "Trudy's from a prominent French family that goes back several generations. They had a winery that was popular in the area. Who's to say they didn't commission a work by Rodin at some point?"

I was momentarily distracted as canine Maggie trundled over to greet us and feline Charlie pounced on my foot. As I washed out Maggie's bowl and filled it with fresh water, I remembered what we were talking about. "It's two works," I said. "Remember the quail's mate is on Trudy's mantel?"

He stooped to pick up Charlie and nuzzled her soft neck. "Did you happen to see it when we were there?"

"No." I smiled. "There was so much other stuff to see."

"Isn't that the truth? Her home is quite like a miniature museum in and of itself."

"I agree. I'd like to visit her again to get a look at that other sculpture she was talking about."

"Yes, let's arrange that." He took out his phone and punched in a quick note to himself.

I hung up my purse on a hook by the back door and sat down at the kitchen table with my phone. "No time like the present," I said, and Googled *Rodin sculptures*. It brought me to the site of the Musée Rodin, and I scrolled through the photographs. I saw plenty of old men with their jowls and wrinkles, and beautiful women of all shapes and sizes. There were lovers embracing and angels avenging, but no charming little animals.

I reported my findings to Derek.

"It probably wasn't sculpted by Rodin, but I'd be willing to guess that it's from the same era. It's a stunning piece."

"I think so, too. And speaking of notable Frenchmen, I never would've guessed that Guru Bob was French, would you?"

"He's so well dressed and speaks so formally, I always figured he was English."

I laughed. "If only that weren't true, I'd be able to say something rude."

Derek leaned back against the kitchen counter and folded his arms across his chest. "We British are exceedingly polite, as you well know."

"And yet"—I glanced around—"I've been home for three minutes, and I don't see my glass of wine anywhere."

He slapped his forehead in mock dismay. "Butler's night off, love. I'll get right on it."

My cell phone rang at that moment, and I glanced at the screen. I chuckled as I answered the call. "Hey, Mom. Long time no see."

"Hello, sweetie," she said, speaking quietly. "Can you and Derek come over right now? Robson is here and would like to talk to all of us together. It's important."

Chapter Six

"I have been contacted by a number of media outlets," Robson said as soon as we were all gathered in my parents' large, comfortable living room. "They are asking for details and interviews."

"They've already heard about the treasure in the cave?" I frowned, trying to figure out how the word got out. "That was fast."

"No, gracious," he said. "Not the treasure. They have only asked about the body that was found."

"Oh, that makes sense." I shot Derek a quick glance. "They probably heard the news from someone at the sheriff's department."

"Perhaps." Guru Bob stood in front of my parents' dark wood and tile-framed fireplace with his hands clasped behind his back. He was a tall, fair-haired man who never seemed to age, but for the first time I noticed streaks of silver in his hair. It only made him appear more distinguished, I decided. In his present stance, he resembled an admiral handing out difficult assignments to his closest allies.

"Brooklyn, dear," he continued, "I would appreciate it if you and Derek would agree to meet and speak with the media people

who show up seeking information. Given your firsthand knowledge of the situation, you will be the best spokespeople for the
winery and the Fellowship."

I gave Mom a quick look, and she nodded her encouragement.
I couldn't figure out why.

"I'm happy to talk with them of course," I said. It was a lie. I
hated the idea of schmoozing with the press. But I wasn't about to
turn down a personal request from Guru Bob. "But wouldn't you
rather have one of your lawyers do it?"

"To put it plainly, no," he said, smiling for the first time since
we'd arrived. "The lawyers know nothing of the circumstances.
And have you ever noticed that they have a tendency to get lost in
the weeds? If you understand my meaning of that term?"

I smiled. "I do."

"It is a colorful phrase that certainly fits in this instance." He
glanced at Derek. "Now that you have talked to Trudy and know
more of the background of my family and what brought them to
Dharma, I believe you will be prepared to handle anyone who
comes asking questions."

"I appreciate your confidence," Derek said, leaning forward to
rest his elbows on his knees. I recognized the move to mean he was
pondering something deeply. "But, Robson, even though we've
talked to Trudy and we know a lot more than we did when we first
opened up the walls of the cave, we're missing quite a bit of information. Is there anything more you'd like to share with us?"

"I wish I could tell you more," Robson said, sounding frustrated, which was alarming since he rarely showed negativity.
"Frankly, I would prefer it if you could limit your conversation
with the press to the topic of Mr. Renaud's body. How he was
found. Where you found him. Details about the excavation itself.
Those sorts of things. I believe the news media will find those
unpleasant details appealing."

"No doubt," Derek said. "But I don't believe they'll be satisfied with our bare-bones explanation. A good reporter will want to investigate exactly what happened to Mr. Renaud and how he ended up inside a walled-up cave."

Guru Bob lifted his shoulders philosophically. "I fully expect that my family history and the recently discovered artwork will become fodder for some. I don't expect you to lie about it. Trying to prevaricate will only make matters worse."

"On that we agree," Derek said. "That's why I want to be absolutely sure we have all the facts before we stumble into something we know nothing about."

Guru Bob nodded calmly. "Of course."

"I can handle the press," Derek said, "but I refuse to allow Brooklyn to be a target for some reporter's misdirected sense of truth and justice."

"I can handle it," I said, even though I shivered at the thought.

Guru Bob took a long moment to consider his words and finally said, "I will have a few more things to disclose as soon as our last guest arrives."

I glanced at Mom, who shook her head, meaning that she was as clueless as I was of the identity of our missing guest.

"Please rest assured," Guru Bob continued. "Neither of you will be hung out to dry, as they say. I am the leader of this Fellowship, first of all, and second, it is my family's story that will be exploited. If any backlash or unexpected disclosure occurs, I will step forward and deal with it."

"I don't think it'll come to that," Derek said, sitting back and sounding a lot calmer than he had a minute ago. "I'm sure we'll be able to handle it with no problem. But I appreciate your willingness to come to our rescue if necessary."

Robson nodded. "You and Brooklyn have come to my rescue on more than one occasion, so if I ever have the opportunity to return the favor, I will." He scanned the room, meeting each of our gazes one by one. "It is lowering to realize that for all these years, this dark secret was festering right here in our midst. I should have had at least an inkling, but I did not. That troubles me." He shook his head. "And the fact that it is connected to my family hurts my heart."

"You can't blame yourself," I said quickly. "It all happened before you were born."

His sudden smile was luminescent. "Your defense of me is like a balm, gracious. I appreciate everything you are doing for the Fellowship and for me." He looked at Derek. "Both of you. I am grateful."

If I didn't change the subject to something less emotional and more tangible, I would burst into tears. "Robson, how many news outlets have you heard from?"

"Close to two dozen," he said. "I have made a list of their names and contact numbers."

Two dozen? I blew out a breath. "Have you considered hiring some extra security for the caves?"

"I have indeed."

There was a knock on the front door, and Mom hurried to answer it.

Guru Bob showed a hint of a smile. "Timing is everything."

As Mom led the visitor into the living room, she wore a big broad grin. And then I saw why.

"Gabriel," I whispered.

He winked and almost took my breath away. "Hey, babe."

I dashed over to grab him in a hug. "I haven't seen you in forever. How are you?"

"I'm better now." The man was too devastatingly handsome for his own good, and his dark eyes gleamed with devilish intent. With his arm still slung over my shoulders, he scanned the room. "Greetings, everyone."

"Hello, mate." Derek strolled over and gave him a hearty handshake.

Gabriel smacked him on the back. "Good to see you, man."

I glanced from one man to the other. They were both extraordinarily hot, and I knew from experience that being in the same room with them could be hazardous to a girl's ability to speak in complete sentences. While both men exuded strength and masculine self-confidence, Derek was smoother, more sophisticated, and deliberate. Gabriel was more likely to shoot from the hip. He was—and always would be—a *bad boy*.

I beamed at Guru Bob. "Your extra security?"

He chuckled. "Who else would I call?"

Gabriel had saved my life almost two years ago when I was about to be attacked in a noodle shop on Fillmore Street in the city. At the time, I thought I'd lucked out that this tall, dark, and gorgeous stranger had walked into the shop at that precise moment, but it turned out that he'd been following me—for reasons I would discover much later.

I'd never quite figured out if he was a good guy or a thief, a gun for hire or a solid citizen. Maybe all of the above. I knew he could be deadly, but that didn't matter. He had saved my life more than once, and, like Derek, he would always be a hero to me.

He went by only one name: Gabriel. Like the archangel. I figured a guy that tall, dark, and dashing probably didn't need more than just the one name. Gabriel had a knack for finding whatever it was you needed. His business card read DISCREET PROCUREMENT.

As usual, today he was dressed all in black, from his black suede bomber jacket down to his boots. The color suited him just fine. He had made a temporary home for himself here in Dharma, and I knew he'd been working on some kind of security system for Guru Bob.

He pulled a chair in from the dining room and sat down. "So, what's all the hubbub about?"

"Hubbub?" I had to laugh. "Nothing much. Just a dead body

that's been perfectly preserved for almost seventy years in a hidden cave under the vineyards, surrounded by a treasure trove of artwork and goodies that looks like something from a museum heist."

His lips twisted into a smile. "Sounds like fun."

I sat down next to Derek. "Did you know he'd be here?"

"I had my suspicions," he said, his eyes twinkling. Besides being the two most gorgeous men I'd ever seen in real life, Derek and Gabriel had become good friends and had worked or consulted with each other on a few high-profile, top secret security cases over the past year. I didn't know many of the details, which was probably just as well.

A discreet cough from Guru Bob brought us all back to attention.

"Now that Gabriel is here," he said, "I will share more information with you. And I have an additional request. It is your choice completely whether you wish to accept it or not."

"What is it?" I asked, concerned at the way he'd phrased it.

Gesturing with his hand, he singled out Derek and Gabriel. "I would appreciate it if you two would accompany me to Frenchman's Hill tomorrow. I must talk to some people about what was found in the caves."

"Absolutely," Derek said without hesitation.

Gabriel gave him a thumbs-up. "No problem."

I had every intention of going with them, but I would mention it later.

"What do the Frenchman's Hill folks have to do with the caves?" Mom asked casually, but I could hear the edge in her voice. Was she worried about more secrets?

I'd gone to high school with a few kids from Frenchman's Hill, and they all had one thing in common: they were French, duh. Their families had traveled to Sonoma from France over the past half century, settling on farmland about five miles northwest of Dharma. The area had come to be known as Frenchman's Hill.

Coincidence that so many French families had moved to the area? I thought not. Especially after hearing Trudy's stories earlier.

"It is a long story," Guru Bob said easily, taking a seat in the lyre-back chair nearest the fireplace. "If you can spare me a few more minutes?"

"Absolutely," I said. I wasn't going to miss this.

"Wait." Dad jumped up from his chair. "Since nobody's going anywhere, I've got a bottle of wine I'd like you all to try. It's a Meritage blend I'm experimenting with."

"Good idea, Jim," Guru Bob said. "We should enjoy a glass of wine as we talk."

"Thanks, Dad," I murmured as he filled my glass. He gave me a wink and turned to pour wine into Derek's glass. Dad had always had a wonderful way of defusing tension, often by changing the subject to wine, one of his favorite topics.

I swirled my wine and stared at the streaks coating the sides of the glass and slowly dripping down. These streaks were known as *wine legs,* and some wine lovers thought that the slower the legs moved, the better the quality of wine. I'd learned that it had more to do with alcohol content and good old gravity, but it was fun to zone out while watching them slide down into the liquid.

Once Dad finished pouring the wine and was back in his chair, Guru Bob began his story.

"I have a vivid memory of an incident that happened when I was ten years old. I was helping my father in the vineyards when three men approached him. They told him they were new to the area and were looking for Anton Benoit or one of his brothers. The men had recently moved to Sonoma from the village of La Croix Saint-Just, where Anton was raised."

I nodded. We had learned that from Trudy earlier that day.

"The three were trying to track down Anton," Guru Bob said, "to retrieve their family's belongings from him. My father was furious. He wanted to know why they were accusing his fa-

ther of theft. The men quickly tried to defuse his anger, admitting
that they were still learning English and had used the wrong
phrasing."

"Did they explain themselves?"

"They did, and my father calmed down. I cannot remember
all the details of their conversation, but despite their smiles and
pleasantries, I know in my heart that they believed my grandfather
was guilty of thievery."

I wasn't about to doubt Guru Bob's emotional memory. The
man could pick up on an emotion so subtle, you wouldn't even
know you were feeling it until he mentioned it.

The three men told Guru Bob's father how, during the war,
their families had entrusted Anton with their most valuable heirlooms and he had taken them to America, promising to return
them after the war. Everyone in the village had been desperate to
keep their precious belongings out of the hands of the Nazis.

It was the same basic story we'd heard from Trudy earlier
that day.

"My father was sympathetic," Guru Bob said, "but he insisted
he had no idea what the men were talking about. They tried describing some of the artwork and furnishings, but my father could
only shake his head. He was clueless. He even invited the men into
his home, but they did not find what they were looking for."

"You told us that your grandfather died before you were
born," I said, thinking back to our conversation at the picnic table
the day before.

"That is right. I never knew him. Marie, my grandmother,
though, lived until I was well into my teens, and she was
wonderful."

"I'm glad you knew her, Robson," Mom said.

"I am, too." He smiled. "So now we are all caught up-to-date.
You know about my family, and you know about the treasures.
Soon others will find out. It remains for me to immediately seek

out those French families and explain that their belongings are safe, after all."

"Do you know if any of the three men still live here?" Gabriel asked.

"I never saw them again. My father was not interested in working the land, so shortly after that, we moved to San Francisco. The land was never sold, though, so when I grew up, I was able to reclaim all of it."

"And none of your other relatives wanted the land," I said.

"Yes. As I explained yesterday, some of them returned to France. A few have died. Trudy was the only one who stayed. She has always loved it here."

I tried to do the math. My family moved here when I was eight, so that was about twenty-five years ago. "So when you reclaimed your land and started the Fellowship, the people of Frenchman's Hill had already been here for years."

"Yes. And all this time, I have kept tabs on the families living here. Back then, they were all from La Croix Saint-Just, but more recently, others have moved here from different areas. Only two of the original families decided to return to France after a few years. The others stayed and have thrived. They grow grapes, of course, and a few years ago, they created a cooperative through which they sell their grapes to the local wineries. Recently they opened their own tasting room and continue to do quite well."

"I've been to their tasting room," Dad said. "They're doing good work."

"Do you think they all moved here to find their family treasures?" I asked. "Wouldn't they have approached you on more occasions than that one time in the vineyard?"

"They have not," Robson said. "I cannot say why. Perhaps my father's anger quelled their suspicions."

Derek frowned. "And now you're going to tell them that their suspicions were justified."

"And that their raison d'être for moving here in the first place is about to pay off," I added.

"Should be fascinating," Gabriel said, chuckling. "I assume you want us there for extra muscle?"

"I do, if you would not mind." Guru Bob looked around the room, shaking his head. "One never knows how a person will react to such shocking news."

"I'm happy to tag along," Derek said. "Although I can't imagine you'll have many complaints after you tell them they're about to get back their priceless artwork and treasures."

"I hope it will be a positive visit, but I will not be surprised if we experience a confrontational moment or two."

Did I mention that Guru Bob never used contractions in his speech? It probably sounded odd to an outsider, but I was so used to it, I rarely noticed. He had once explained that it kept him consciously aware of his speech. He was all about being conscious and aware in each moment.

I was anxious about the visit to Frenchman's Hill tomorrow and was more determined than ever to go along for the ride. If nothing else, I might get a chance to say hello to one or two of my old high school friends. And it would be interesting to see how well the French folks took the good news.

Early the next morning, Derek drove to Frenchman's Hill with one contact name from Guru Bob. He had managed to track down a Monsieur Georges Cloutier and had requested a meeting with him and others who had emigrated from La Croix Saint-Just. Derek gave no clue as to the topic of the meeting except to assure him that it would be to the group's benefit. Monsieur Cloutier knew Guru Bob by reputation and was intrigued enough to make some calls and offered his home for the meeting at one o'clock that afternoon.

Before Derek left, I'd told him that I planned to drive over to the winery. I knew he didn't want me going into the caves alone, but it was important that we start an inventory of everything in there. It was the responsible thing to do. Derek had said he would try to meet me there later. I knew it was because he thought I was afraid to go into the cave alone, but I assured him that I wasn't.

"All right, love," he said. "But just in case." And he gave me an extra tight hug and kiss before he left.

Now, in the privacy of my car, I could admit to being more than a little freaked-out about going inside the cave all by myself. It was one thing to tramp around with a big hunky guy like Derek, or one of my brothers, but all alone? In the dark? With spiders?

My shoulders jerked as chills shot across them. I was not looking forward to this, but it had to be done.

I pulled into the lot and parked, grabbed my legal pad, a fold-up stool I'd borrowed from my mom, and the heavy flashlight Derek had given me. As I walked to the storage-cave entrance, I was surprised to see Gabriel approach.

"Hey, you," I said, giving him a one-arm hug. "Are you here to start setting up the security system?"

"Something like that," he said with a sideways grin, cryptic as always.

"Have you been inside already? Seen the stuff in there? It's pretty awesome, isn't it?"

"Haven't seen anything yet, but I know it's really dark in there."

I stared at him for a long moment. "Derek asked you to meet me here."

"Why would he do that? You're a big girl. You can handle this."

"That's right. I can." I unlocked the wide double doors of the storage cave.

He shrugged. "I'm just here to make sure you don't steal anything."

I laughed all the way to the back wall.

Once we'd climbed inside the chamber, Gabriel took a long look around. "What a haul," he said after a few minutes.

"It's impressive, isn't it?"

"Yeah. Now I see why Robson wants some extra muscle when he visits Frenchman's Hill."

I frowned at him. "You think they'll be angry?"

"If any of this stuff was stolen from your family, wouldn't you be?"

"I see your point, but I hope they won't take it out on Guru Bob. That wouldn't be fair."

"Emotions get in the way of reason sometimes."

"Too true," I said. With that, I continued writing down what I found. My organizational skills were outstanding, but there was so much to figure out. I finally divided my list into sections: furniture; silver; paintings; small sculptures; larger sculptures and busts; jewelry; and miscellaneous.

After I'd been working for ten minutes, Gabriel told me some of his guys had arrived, so he'd be outside working on the security system.

"I'm fine," I assured him.

"Okay, but keep in mind I'm only a piercing scream away."

I laughed again and waved him off. For the next two hours, I sifted through jewelry boxes and unrolled canvas paintings, writing down everything I saw and describing it all in detail. I took pictures of things, thinking it would help to have some visuals when I finalized my list.

Despite my brave words, it was still a little creepy exploring the dark chambers by myself with just the big flashlight for illumination. But I survived. When I got home, I transferred what I had so far on my inventory list onto a computer document. Then I printed my photos out on glossy photo paper.

I was home by noon to meet Derek, and a few minutes before one o'clock, we pulled up in front of the home of Monsieur Cloutier. Gabriel parked right behind us, with Guru Bob in the passenger seat of his sleek black BMW. Monsieur Cloutier's wife answered the door and introduced herself as Solange. She was a petite, dark-haired woman with a ready smile, and she led us out to the terrace, where a number of men and women were standing around a long table filled with platters of food.

"Did you prepare all this?" Guru Bob asked Solange. "On such short notice?"

"*Oui, monsieur,*" she said, smiling with pride as she waved us toward the table. "*C'est pour vous. S'il vous plaît*, sit. Sit. Enjoy."

"What a lovely and generous way to welcome us to your home," he said, taking her hand in both of his. "You will be joining us?"

"*Oui*, in a moment." She gave him another smile and scurried back into the house.

As soon as the men saw Guru Bob, they all approached. It was reassuring to see them recognize him as the patriarch of Dharma and treat him with respect.

We were introduced to everyone. Besides the Cloutiers, there were four men and two women. Their ages ranged from early eighties to midtwenties.

One old man, Gerard, said, "We came to Sonoma in 1952, Felix, Simon, and I, with our families. Alas, our friend Simon died years ago, but my friend Felix is still with us."

"I am indeed," a wiry, gray-haired man said, chuckling as he took hold of the arm of a younger man, pulling him forward. "This is Henri, Simon's son. He is head of his household now."

Henri appeared to be in his midfifties. He was a big friendly bear of a man with red hair and a ruddy complexion. Felix smacked him several times on the shoulder, his pride in the younger man obvious.

The first man, Gerard, extended his arm toward one of the women helping to set the table. "And that is my wife, Beatrice." She smiled and waved at us.

"And that pretty one there is Henri's wife," Felix said, pointing to the third Frenchwoman in attendance, who was presently carrying yet another platter to the table.

The woman glanced up at Felix's words and smiled indulgently.

"That is my Sophie," Henri said proudly.

The twelve of us drifted toward the table and eventually took seats, chatting about the weather and predicting whether this would be the best grape crop in history or not.

It was a beautiful fall day, and the Cloutiers' terrace overlooked the vineyards. I felt instantly at home since my parents' home had a similar view of rolling green hills covered in rows and rows of grapevines with the occasional oak tree spreading its branches in every direction.

Dining with all of these strangers was only awkward for a moment until we began to help ourselves and pass the platters to others. Everyone was smiling as we shared the food. It all looked fantastic. Slices of rare roast beef, grilled artichokes, roasted peppers in olive oil, caprese salad with fresh tomatoes and basil, grilled sausages with sautéed onions and peppers, arugula salad sprinkled with chunks of goat cheese and orange slices, asparagus in vinaigrette, and a yummy-looking quiche.

There was wine, too, of course, and by the end of the meal, we were a jolly group. Madame Cloutier began to clear the table, and Gabriel carried platters into the house. The other two women helped, and soon I could hear giggling and chatting going on inside. Minutes later, several ladies returned carrying platters of pastries sprinkled with powdered sugar. Homemade beignets!

As soon as the rest of the women and Gabriel came back outside and sat down, Monsieur Cloutier signaled that it was time to get down to business and offered Guru Bob the floor.

He began by thanking the Cloutiers for their hospitality and hoped that all of us would always be good neighbors to one another.

"We all have something in common," he continued, looking around the table, meeting the others' serious gazes. "Either we or our forefathers traveled here from La Croix Saint-Just. Some came to escape certain death. A few were on a quest for a better life. But most of you came in search of something you thought had been stolen from your family. I am here today to right a wrong."

Several of the men exchanged glances with one another but said nothing.

Guru Bob appeared to brace himself as he announced, "My grandfather was Anton Benoit."

There were a few gasps, followed by a brief silence.

"*Felon!*" Henri shouted suddenly, and pushed his chair back from the table. He stood and scowled at Guru Bob as he spewed a stream of French insults.

Both Derek and Gabriel stood immediately.

Guru Bob's expression remained calm.

"Henri, *s'il vous plaît,*" Felix said with a world-weary wave of his hand. "Be patient. Let our guest explain himself."

Henri's jaw was clenched as he appeared to weigh his odds with Derek and Gabriel. He was bigger than both of them, but it wasn't from muscle. He had to realize his chances of defeating either one of them in a fight were close to nothing.

Not that I expected Derek or Gabriel to lay one finger on Henri. They were only here for intimidation purposes. I hoped.

"Henri," Felix chided, "it is too nice a day to quarrel."

"Coquin," the big man muttered, causing Felix to roll his eyes. Henri made a show of doing the old man a favor by sitting, but it was obvious to me that he'd done so because of Derek and Gabriel's clear intention to take him on if necessary.

Derek and Gabriel sat as well. Madame Cloutier refilled Gabriel's wineglass, and he winked at her. Despite their friendly interaction, the tension around the table was now as thick as the grilled sausages we'd just eaten.

"I never met my grandfather," Guru Bob said when he had the attention of the group again. "But I heard the stories of his escape from France and how he took all of the villagers' belongings with him for safekeeping. I assumed, wrongly, that everything was returned after the war. Recently, though, I found out how wrong I was to assume such a thing."

"Blaireau," Henri muttered.

Gabriel stood, looked at Henri, and raised an eyebrow. "Dude."

Henri gave an ill-tempered shrug. *"Désolé."*

It was a poor apology. I tried to recall some of the French words my sister had taught me while I was visiting her in Paris, but *blaireau* didn't come to mind. I had a feeling it wasn't a compliment. But why was this guy insulting Guru Bob? Didn't he get that the man was bringing him good news?

"Brooklyn, dear," Guru Bob said, leaning forward to grab my attention. "Do you have the photographs?"

"I do." I pulled them out of the bag I'd set beside my chair and handed them to him.

Gabriel, instead of sitting down again, walked a few feet away from the table and leaned his back against the outside wall. From that position he had an excellent, unobstructed view of the whole table and the still-grumbling people. He folded his arms across his chest and watched the interactions from there.

"We recently excavated one of our storage caves to expand its size," Guru Bob explained. "Behind what we thought was a solid stone wall we discovered a chamber that had been sealed off for the past seventy years. Inside we found the body of a Frenchman. Jean Pierre Renaud. Did you know of him?"

Felix laid his head in his hands. He muttered a few words in French, then glanced up, his eyes wet with tears. "He was a friend. When I arrived here and sought him out, I couldn't find him. So I thought perhaps he'd moved away and lived a good long life elsewhere."

"I am sorry for your loss," Robson said. "The sheriff's department is investigating, and I will be happy to pass along any information I receive from them."

He nodded. *"Merci."*

Guru Bob took a deep breath and let it out. I could tell this wasn't easy for him. And I had a feeling it was only going to get worse.

"We discovered a number of other items behind the stone wall. I'd like you to see them." He passed a few photographs to his left, a few to his right, and a few to the people sitting across the table. The looks on their faces ran the emotional gamut from devastation to delight.

"Gerard, look," Beatrice whispered. "It is my father's escritoire."

"The Botticelli," Solange cried. Tears formed in her eyes, and she pressed a hand to her lips.

I didn't dare look at Derek, but I knew what he was thinking. It really was a Botticelli painting! My next immediate thought was, *Gabriel needs to beef up the winery security right away.*

"These are my mother's candlesticks," Henri said, slapping the photograph with the back of his hand. "She died of a broken heart, knowing she would never see her beautiful things again."

"While my words cannot possibly ease the pain you feel, please know that I am truly sorry." Guru Bob's compassion for the other man was clear in his voice.

"That's not good enough." Henri fumed for a moment, sniffing loudly like an angry bull about to strike. But one sharp glance from Felix had him gritting his teeth. He sat back in his chair, and his breath slowed. Was he trying to chill out? I hoped so. The man was a loose cannon.

But abruptly he stood again and focused on Guru Bob. "My friends think I'm wrong to direct my anger toward you, sir. But I look at you, and I see a man whose family has been in possession of our most precious heirlooms for several generations. All that time, we had nothing. So how are we to be made whole again? Will you simply return our trinkets and that will be that? No. You owe us more. Your family owes us more. Perhaps we should pay them a visit and see what appeals to us."

Sophie grabbed hold of her husband's arm. "Henri, no!"

Felix made a guttural sound of contempt, but Henri ignored both of them and continued talking. "I may not have the money or means to take you on personally, sir, but suppose I call the newspapers and tell them my story. How much is it worth to avoid negative publicity?"

Guru Bob was able to maintain his usual Zen-like calm throughout the diatribe, but Gabriel was seething and asked, "Are you talking about blackmail, Henri?"

Alarmed, I exchanged a glance with Derek, who was quick to address the cooler heads at the table. "You're all free to seek whatever counsel you wish in this matter. However, I'll caution you that the more publicity you seek regarding these valuable objects, the greater the possibility of break-ins and thefts."

"Ah, *écoutez*, Henri," Felix chided. "*Réfléchissez avant de parler à nouveau.*"

I leaned closer to Derek. "What did he say?"

He whispered in my ear, "He told Henri to listen and think before he speaks again."

"Good. He's a hothead."

Guru Bob stood once more to address everyone at the table.

"Again, I am very sorry to have caused you pain. All I can do to mitigate your years of suffering is to return everything as quickly as possible. I would ask that you each make a list of the items your families gave to my grandfather. As quickly as I receive your lists, I will see that your belongings are delivered back to you with all speed."

"Merde," Henri said with a guttural snarl. "You can take that freaking list and shove it." He glared at his friends around the table. "How can we trust him? I say we go over there and take what belongs to us."

"You need to mellow out, friend," Gabriel said, walking up behind him. "You take one step onto Dharma winery property and you'll be looking trouble right in the eye."

Derek took my hand and nodded discreetly at Guru Bob. We stood, and Derek handed Monsieur Cloutier a business card. "Please call me if you need anything."

"Merci, Monsieur Stone," he murmured.

Guru Bob bowed his head briefly to Solange. "Thank you for your warm hospitality and wonderful food. I look forward to welcoming you into my home in the future." He pulled Monsieur Cloutier aside for a brief, private word.

I thanked Solange, then turned and smiled at the others. "It was lovely to meet all of you."

I could hear Henri grumbling still, trying to incite his friends to challenge Guru Bob. We were close to the front door when I heard footsteps pounding after us.

"You are the grandson of a thief!" Henri shouted. "Why should we take your word for anything?"

Two of the Frenchmen grabbed hold of him, giving us time to walk swiftly out of the house, slip into our cars, and drive away.

Chapter Seven

"We have to make sure Guru Bob's okay," I said, trying not to wring my hands as we raced away from Frenchman's Hill.

Derek reached over and took hold of my hand. "I've already planned to follow them home."

"You're the best."

"Yes, I am."

I laughed as he knew I would. But he could tell I was still tense, so he squeezed my hand lightly. "Things will be fine, love."

My jaw clenched. "That guy was so angry."

"Henri has all the qualities of a real troublemaker, but you must've noticed that the others weren't backing him up."

"I did, and I was grateful for that. But even if Henri doesn't incite any more discord, it was still difficult to watch him attacking Guru Bob."

"Yes, it was," Derek said with a pensive frown. "But Guru Bob handled it well."

"He did. I just hope he won't feel guilty about it."

"He won't," Derek said. "He'll take action."

I squeezed his hand. Sometimes he said the best things.

Derek pulled to a stop at the curb, right behind Gabriel's

BMW. I jumped out of the car and followed Guru Bob halfway up the walkway leading to his elegant Queen Anne Victorian home at the top of the hill. "Robson."

He paused and turned, looking surprised to see me. "Brooklyn, is something wrong, dear? You seem upset. What happened?"

"That man called you names and accused you of horrible things. I just wanted to make sure you're all right."

"I am fine." He peered at me for a long moment. "You must not suffer on my behalf, gracious."

"I'm not." I frowned at myself for lying. "Well, maybe a little. I didn't like the way Henri spoke to you."

Guru Bob sighed and touched my shoulder to console me. "Henri is in pain. I did not take his harsh words to heart, and you must not, either."

"I'll try not to."

He pressed his lips together in thought. Finally he said, "My grandfather was a complicated soul. I never met him, but I had hints of him in my own father, who was a good man but not a happy one."

"I'm sorry."

Lost in his own thoughts, he didn't acknowledge my comment. "I wonder, did Anton take the treasured items strictly to help his friends and neighbors in the village? Was his purpose always altruistic? If so, why did he betray them in the end? Or did he? If he truly had no conscience, would he not have sold off the pieces? Or brazenly displayed them in his own home? He did neither. He hid them away in a cave. What does it mean?"

"I don't know," I whispered.

"And the body in the cave." It was almost as if Guru Bob had forgotten I was there. He was talking to himself, trying to work through many thoughts. "We must be asking ourselves, did Anton Benoit kill another man?"

"No," I said. "Absolutely not. I don't believe that."

His focus returned to me, and he smiled. "You have more confidence than I, gracious. Remember, I did not know my grandfather."

"If he was yours, he was a good man."

"Someday we might know the truth."

I flailed my arms out. "Now I'm worried about you all over again."

He reached out and held my shoulders, and in an instant I felt reassured. "You are an angel and a bright light in my life. Because you and Derek are here with us in Dharma, I know that all will be well."

"We'll make sure of that," I promised. "We've got your back."

He pressed his hands together in what I called his *Namaste* pose, as though he were praying. Then he bowed slightly. "Good-bye, dear."

I lifted my hand in a wave. "Bye."

He walked a few steps, then turned and grinned. "And thank you for having my back."

I laughed softly and jogged back to the car.

*A*n hour later, Gabriel showed up at our place with a six-pack of beer. I opened a bag of pretzel sticks, and we sat down at the kitchen table to commiserate.

"Well, that went well," he said after popping open three bottles and handing them out.

"Oh, just peachy," I said. "That guy Henri is going to burst a blood vessel one of these days."

Gabriel shook his head. "Dude's got some anger-management issues to work out."

"In some ways, I can't blame him," Derek said. "But he can't go around threatening Robson. He doesn't realize who he's dealing with."

I chuckled. "I think he might've gotten a clue after seeing you guys flex your muscles a few times."

"We do what we must," Derek said with a shrug.

Gabriel just chuckled and grabbed a handful of pretzels.

I told them what Guru Bob had told me earlier when we were standing in front of his house.

"Sounds like he's not sure if his grandfather killed Jean Pierre Renaud," Gabriel said.

"That's what it sounded like to me, too," I said. "But I can't imagine anyone related to Guru Bob actually killing someone, especially his best friend from childhood."

"It's hard to picture," Gabriel agreed.

I frowned into my beer. "You know how Guru Bob can present something as though it's a riddle to be solved? That's what it sounded like when he talked about his grandfather."

"Then we'll just have to solve the riddle," Derek murmured.

"Yes, but we also have to keep him safe in the meantime."

"We will, darling." He pointed his beer bottle at Gabriel. "From what I've seen, Gabriel's got almost all of Dharma wired into his security systems."

Gabriel winked at me.

"Okay, good." I took a quick sip of my beer before getting up to pull a triangle of creamy Brie out of the refrigerator. I arranged it on a plate with some water crackers and set it on the table.

"Perfect," Derek said.

"We needed more sustenance than pretzels," I said.

"Thanks, babe," Gabriel said, and reached for a cracker.

"I have a question," I said as I sat down again. "What does *blaireau* mean? Henri called Guru Bob a *blaireau*."

Gabriel grinned. "Literally, it's French for *badger*."

"A badger?" I shook my head, baffled. "What kind of an insult is that?"

"Have you ever seen a badger? Not a pretty animal."

I chuckled. "You have a point."

Derek said, "I believe Henri was calling Robson's grandfather a *blaireau*, not Robson himself."

"Oh." I thought about it. "Yeah, maybe."

"It's like calling someone a dweeb or a moron," Gabriel explained.

"In England, we prefer the term *plonker*," Derek said. "Means the same thing. Dimwit, idiot."

"I like plonker myself," I said. I tried to recall all of Henri's insults. "He also said something like *coquin*. What does that mean?"

"Rascal," Derek said, shrugging. "Scalawag."

"For real?" I was puzzled. "As fired up as Henri was, that's an awfully weak slur."

"There were women present," Gabriel surmised. "If he'd used stronger terms, the men would've kicked his ass."

"I wanted to slap him," I said, my fists bunching up at the memory. "I mean, *rascal* isn't the worst expletive in the world, but how dare he say anything like that to Guru Bob. It's not his fault his grandfather never gave that stuff back. And hey, Guru Bob went over there to let those people know their stuff was still safe and they could have it anytime. So gee, Henri, maybe you should've said, *Thank you, Badger*, instead of calling him all those rude names."

Gabriel snorted while Derek leaned over and gave my hand a comforting stroke. "Robson deliberately put himself in that role, darling. He knew what was coming, even predicted there would be some confrontations. I'd say we got off easy if Henri was the only one attempting to stir up trouble."

"There'll be more," Gabriel warned.

"I agree," Derek said soberly. "The others might have longer fuses, but a few of them will end up taking potshots, too."

I let out a little moan at the thought of more clashes with the French families. "The sooner we get rid of all that stuff, the better."

"Agreed." Derek drained his beer. "I didn't care for Henri threatening to go to the newspapers, either."

I turned to Gabriel. "How do you plan to protect the caves from Henri and rude reporters and any other troublemakers who come along?"

"The usual way," he said nonchalantly. "Satellite technology, surveillance drones, big guys with guns."

I rolled my eyes. "Okay, you don't have to tell me. I shouldn't have asked."

Derek bit back a smile. "I think he just told you, love."

I frowned at the two of them. "Drones? Are you kidding?"

Gabriel shrugged. "They work. It's a good way to keep an eye on things. I've also installed motion sensors that'll activate closed-circuit cameras."

"You've already installed them?"

"Babe," he said, and left it at that.

"Right. Of course you have. You know what you're doing. But drones? Wow." I took a long sip of beer. Times had changed.

"Brooklyn," Derek said as he tossed his beer bottle in the plastic recycling crate, "we've got to return those calls from the media people who want information."

I winced. "With everything else going on, I forgot all about that."

"We'll split up the list. You call half and I'll call half."

"That'll help ease the pain."

He smiled. "And while I'm thinking about it, I'd like to get those photos you showed to the French folks. I want to scan them and send them to Interpol in case any of the items have been reported stolen."

I pulled the pictures from my purse and handed them to him. Gabriel was smart enough to take off then, and after he'd left, Derek and I discussed our strategy for dealing with the media. I wanted to make sure we had our stories straight in order to present a united front for the sake of the Fellowship and for Guru Bob.

"Not that he has anything to hide," I said quickly. "I mean, none of us do. We just happened to find Mr. Renaud's body. And thank goodness, the sheriff's detectives are convinced that nobody living here today could've killed him. End of story."

"We both know it's not the end of the story," he said.

"No, of course not, but we're not going to discuss anything about the artwork and furnishings we found, right?"

"That's right," he said as he cleared the table. He wrapped the remaining cheese in plastic wrap and stuck it in the fridge. "At least, not during this first round of calls. It'll come up eventually, though."

"Sooner than we think," I muttered.

"Now that the French families know, it's only a matter of time."

"And who can guess what fresh hell they'll stir up." I folded the paper with Guru Bob's notes, tore it neatly in half, and handed Derek one of the sheets. "Here are your names. I guess we should get started."

"All right. I'll make my calls in the office." He studied my face. "Something's bothering you."

He knew me too well. I held up the paper with the list of names. "I'm concerned that one of these guys on the list will try to turn the story into another Robson Benedict exposé."

"You still feel the need to protect him."

"I do," I said, unsure how to explain my feelings. "He's . . . vulnerable. It's because he has so many followers and they're all thriving up here. People can be weird about that. It's as if they don't approve of all this positivity. They don't understand it."

"I see your point. He'd be a good target for some unscrupulous reporter."

"It's happened before," I said. "Every few years, some reporter will get a bug up his butt to do an in-depth story on the Fellowship. They rehash old newspaper articles and conflate us with other so-called spiritual groups that have been in trouble with the law. They attack his character and refer to Dharma as a cult." I glared at Derek. "You must know how ridiculous that is."

"Of course I do."

I sighed. "Of course you do."

He pulled me up out of my chair and wrapped his arms around me. "We can't worry about things that might not happen. As long as we're prepared to tell the truth about what we saw, how we found the body, and then direct any other questions to the sheriff's office, we'll get through this with little or no fuss."

"No fuss, no worries."

"That is to be our mantra," he said, planting a soft kiss on my forehead. "I'm hopeful we can handle most of these phone inquiries within the next few days, but some of the reporters are going to want to come up here for interviews. Let's try to put them off until next weekend."

"They'll want to come sooner," I said, sitting back at the table.

"We have a perfectly legitimate reason to hold them off. This is a spiritual community, and the members aren't available at the spur of the moment."

"True enough. We should arrange to have them all come here at the same time and do a press conference. Say, at two o'clock next Saturday afternoon."

"It might be better to do it the following Tuesday or Wednesday instead. It's so busy here on the weekends. We don't want to draw more of a crowd than we can handle."

"Good thinking. I'd hate to draw a huge crowd of bystanders while we're talking about the caves and the body and all that."

"Exactly. Now, how do you feel about telling the reporters a small white lie? We can be vague about it, but we'll let them know that, say, a week from Wednesday, at two o'clock is the first time the commune members will be available to talk."

"That's a long time from now."

"I think we'll need the time to prepare for this."

"You're probably right. It's not like I've ever given a press conference before." I wrote down the time and date, but then stopped. "There's nothing to keep them from coming up to the winery anytime they want to."

"They're welcome to do so, but they won't get the information they need for their stories until Wednesday at two o'clock."

"Okay. And just in case, I'll have Mom spread the word that nobody should talk to reporters until the official press conference a week from Wednesday." I stared across the table at him. "Are you okay with spending more time up here than you thought you would?"

"That's the best thing about being the boss," he said, grinning. "I can do what I want most of the time. The office won't be overly busy this week, so I should be able to handle things by phone. I'll work a few hours each morning and check in every afternoon."

"I don't want you to feel obligated."

"Darling." He reached across and squeezed my hand. "This is important to me, too."

"Thank you."

"And if something comes up that I can't handle by phone, I'll simply drive into the city for a few hours."

"Okay, then I won't worry about you, either."

"Please don't," he said. "I promise I won't let myself fire me."

I smiled at that. He picked up his list of names and went off to the office while I sat back down at the table to make the calls.

Forty minutes later, I was just finishing up my last call when he came back and joined me at the table.

"How did you do?" I asked after disconnecting the call.

"I spoke with eight of the people on my list. A few of them weren't happy about waiting so long, but they'll all be here a week from Wednesday. I left messages with the other four to call me back. How about you?"

"I'm waiting on two callbacks. Everyone else was willing to go along with our time frame, especially when I suggested that they could contact the sheriff's department for more information in the meantime. It was almost too easy."

"That can't be good," he said, looking amused.

"I know. Something's bound to go wrong."

I had followed Derek's advice, explaining to each reporter that Dharma was a private spiritual community and that nobody would be available to talk to them until the agreed time. It may have been a white lie, but I didn't care. It would give us some bit of control over the proceedings.

For a number of hours over the next two days, I hid myself away inside the cave and finally managed to finish my inventory. I was indebted to Gabriel and Derek, who fashioned a light tree in each of the chambers. So my eyesight was saved, and in the end, I had a list of several hundred items. I had no idea how many families might've entrusted their precious items to Guru Bob's grandfather, but I hoped they would be happy to get them back.

Altogether I counted twenty-two pairs of silver candlesticks of various sizes and shapes; six more elaborate candelabra sets (I considered them candelabra if they held at least four candles each), two of which featured golden winged cherubs at the base; fourteen marble or bronze busts of various people, including Voltaire, Victor Hugo, two of Cardinal Richelieu, several of other unnamed French dignitaries, and four anonymous beautiful women. There was also a bust of Benjamin Franklin, who apparently was adored by the French, along with an elaborate marble bust of Louis XIV.

I knew which Louis it was only because it was engraved on a plaque below the statue.

There were seven pieces of large, expensive furniture, including three dressers with mirrors, the large wardrobe that had blocked the passageway into the deeper cave, an escritoire, and the whimsical rococo-style vanity table with tufted chair and mirror that had belonged to Trudy's childhood friend Nanette. There were also several smaller tables fancy enough that some families must have worried that they might be taken by the Nazis.

In total, there were twenty-seven pieces of fine artwork, ten smaller works still in frames, including the Botticelli *Virgin and Child*, and the rest rolled up, most notably, the Renoir-like café scene and the excellent portrait of the Grenier family that Trudy had identified on her first visit to the caves.

There were thirty-two assorted animal sculptures small enough to fit in my hand. These included horses and birds and a puppy. I counted Trudy's quail in this group. I listed ten more small sculptures of various subjects: three sets of lovers sculpted in marble; five bronze angels; and the discus thrower and weeping woman I'd noticed the first time I stepped inside the cave.

I found forty-one finely bound books, most of them written in French. I hadn't been able to study the books before, but once I was alone in the cave for those long hours, I took the opportunity to thoroughly check them out. One of the villagers must have been a devotee of the poet Rainer Maria Rilke because there were beautiful first edition copies of *Letters to a Young Poet* and the *Duino Elegies*. There was also a remarkable rare copy of *Alice's Adventures in Wonderland*, or rather, *Aventures d'Alice au pays des Merveilles*. It had a striking bright blue cloth cover with gilded images of Alice on the front cover and the Cheshire cat on the back. The book had been translated into French in 1869, and it made me smile to think of the poor translator trying to convert all of the wonderfully illogical conversations that were scattered throughout the book.

The other books included French classics by Victor Hugo, Gustave Flaubert, and several by Alexandre Dumas. All of them were in good condition and some were even excellent. I estimated the value of the collection of books at about two hundred thousand dollars, but that was just off the top of my head. And that wasn't including the fourteen family Bibles, which all had thick leather bindings and elaborate family histories written within their pages.

Among the silver pieces were four complete silver tea sets and eight silver water pitchers. There were three Sèvres urns and six Meissen figurines. Within the eight jewelry boxes I found twenty-four pieces of expensive jewelry, including six diamond rings; three simple necklaces with diamond pendants; one lovely emerald and gold necklace; three red-jeweled necklaces (these were ruby or carnelian or garnet; I couldn't say for sure), two with silver settings and one with gold; four assorted diamond bracelets; six silver bracelets; and one art-deco-style chinoiserie enamel bracelet with a gold setting.

When I arrived home, I added all of these to the growing list on my computer, then printed out two copies. And then hoped that my items matched those on the French families' lists, because if there were any discrepancies on my part, I was afraid there might be an open revolt on Frenchman's Hill.

I'd honestly thought that by controlling the time, place, and circumstances of the press conference, we'd be able to skate easily through the next week or so. But I was sadly mistaken.

By the following Tuesday, word of the treasures in the caves had spread across the world. We had no idea who had started the rumors—I suspected our friends at the sheriff's department gave the information to any reporters who happened to call, or perhaps Henri had followed through on his threat to contact the local newspaper—but Guru Bob reported that he'd received inquiries from several more Bay Area television stations, six Southern California newspapers, and another four reporters from the East Coast. Online news magazines were clamoring for photos and interviews. Two Los Angeles–based entertainment channels were sending camera crews up to film around Dharma and the winery. They agreed to be here for our Wednesday afternoon session.

I figured Derek and I could handle the press and the rumors, but when Guru Bob received the telephone call from the current mayor of La Croix Saint-Just, he insisted it was time for us to regroup and summoned us to his hilltop home for a meeting. The most recent calls from reporters had nothing to do with the body in the cave. It was all about the expensive heirlooms. Poor Mr. Renaud, forgotten for seventy years, was again being ignored in favor of the alluring treasure trove.

Robson greeted Gabriel, Derek, and me at the front door and led the way into his beautiful sitting room with the wide bay-window view of the hills and vineyards of Dharma. After serving us coffee and allowing us to get comfortable, he hit us with the news. "The mayor called to let me know that he is representing the families who still remain in the village. He warned me that a few of the citizens are discussing reparations."

"That's hostile," I muttered. "Maybe they've been contacted by Henri."

Guru Bob shrugged. "They are unhappy."

"That's not your fault! You're not the one they should be threatening."

Guru Bob reached over and patted my arm. "Your fierceness is one of my secret weapons, Brooklyn."

"Sorry, but it burns me up to hear people blaming you."

"What do they think they'll get in terms of compensation?" Gabriel wondered aloud.

"I doubt it will come to that," Robson said. "The mayor was

very accommodating, despite the veiled threat he issued at the beginning of our conversation. He will e-mail us a list of the items belonging to each of the village families. Everyone will get back what is owed to them."

"Good," I said. "The sooner everything is distributed, the better."

"The mayor might've calmed down," Derek said, "but the families may still feel affronted. Have you contacted your lawyers?"

"In an abundance of caution, I have. They are researching the matter."

"It's blackmail," I grumbled.

Derek gave a subtle nod of agreement. "The lists of lost items from the mayor and from the Frenchman's Hill families will have to be compared and contrasted with Brooklyn's inventory. There may be some unclaimed items. We should come up with a plan for all of it."

Guru Bob aimed his gaze at me. "Brooklyn's inventory?"

"Yes," I said, trying not to squirm. "I thought it was important to write down everything we found in the caves. Once we get the families' lists, we can do that comparison Derek mentioned."

"That is wonderful," Robson said. "Thank you, Brooklyn."

I smiled. "I figured I might as well put my list-making obsession to good use."

Derek exchanged a subtle glance with Robson. "She's quite organized. It extends to everything in the house, right down to the spice cupboard."

"Despite a deep-seated inability to cook," I said, and shrugged.

Guru Bob beamed at me. "All things in good time."

Derek was desperately trying to hide his smile as he quickly changed the subject. "I think we should consider hiring expert appraisers, maybe from one of the auction houses, in case there are any discrepancies to deal with. They'll be able to trace the provenance of some of these items if there are disputes."

"That's a good idea." I stood to pace since I could think better on my feet. "What if some of the families have died off? Or maybe one of them came by something illegally. I mean, there are some priceless heirlooms in that cave. I've already done a preliminary examination of the books and they alone are worth a few hundred thousand dollars, just at first glance."

Derek nodded thoughtfully. "I still wonder how these families from a small French village came into possession of some of those works of art."

"Trudy said that one of her young friends claimed that her father was descended from Louis the Fourteenth and that's how the family owned one of their dressers. A reputable auction house would be able to prove it one way or another." I frowned. "The Botticelli is a complete mystery to me."

"I share many of those same concerns," Robson said, glancing from Derek to me. He took a sip of coffee and set the cup down slowly. "So this morning I contacted an art appraiser with whom I have worked in the past. He will be here next Monday and will require access to the caves."

"I'll be happy to give him the guided tour," Derek said. "Unless you'd rather do it."

"I prefer to have you do it, if you would not mind. I think it best if I avoid entering the cave unless accompanied by some of our own people."

I bristled at the implication: that others would think Guru Bob wasn't to be trusted.

He smiled at me as if he knew what I was thinking—which he probably did. "I will arrange to have Mr. Garrity meet me at the outer door of the storage-cave entrance, where I will introduce him to you."

"Sounds good." They decided on a time, and Derek typed it into his phone calendar.

I knew that the art appraiser wouldn't be the only one demanding access to the artwork. "Have you considered moving everything out of the caves and into a more accessible space? It would have to be secured, of course."

"It is a good question." Robson turned to Gabriel. "You are the security expert. What do you think?"

Gabriel considered for a few seconds before shaking his head. "We're better off leaving everything in the caves. There's only one way in and out so it's easier to guard. I've got the entire area locked up and fortified with more security than any bank in town."

"That's true enough," I said. "Never mind my question. It was just a momentary thought."

"I appreciate hearing any momentary thoughts you may have," Robson said, making me smile.

Derek tapped his fingers on the arm of his chair, a sure sign that his brain was moving ahead at lightning speed. "What would you say to the idea of taking a number of photographs of the artwork, blowing them up to poster size, and displaying them in the town hall?"

I thought about it for a moment. "But why display photographs of the items rather than wait for folks to give us a description of their possessions? Wouldn't that give someone a chance to claim an item that wasn't theirs?"

Derek shifted in his chair, crossing one leg over the other. "One reason to do so is to prove to the Frenchmen that we're being completely transparent about the treasured items we found. Essentially, we're telling the world about the discovery we made. And by the time the exhibit begins, we will have received all of their lists of lost items, so I don't think we'll run into a problem with cheating or larceny."

"I guess you're right," I said after considering his explanation. "And since reporters will be spreading the word around the country anyway, we could have something concrete to show people who come up here hoping to get a look at the caves and the treasure."

"I can guarantee those reporters will not be allowed to set foot inside the caves," Gabriel said.

I nodded. "Good."

"It would also help us get out in front of the story," Derek said. "We could advertise the exhibit from here to the Bay Area and give it an intriguing name to draw more attention to it."

"Something like The Hidden Treasures of La Croix Saint-Just? And then a subtitle with something to do with escaping the Nazis during the Second World War."

"Excellent, darling," Derek said with a grin.

"I'm not sure why, but I'm starting to love this idea." I gazed fondly at Derek. "I had no idea you had such PR and marketing savvy."

"Hidden depths," he said with a humble shrug, making me laugh.

My smile faded. "The only problem is that it's sure to attract a lot of looky-loos to Dharma."

He flashed a wry grin. "Looky-loos earn their name because they look with no intention of buying. But that won't happen in this case. Anyone driving all the way up to Dharma to see the exhibit will wind up spending the day here. They'll tour the poster display and follow it up with a visit to the winery."

"And they'll shop and have lunch on the Lane," I added. "What do you think, Robson?"

He had been listening to us toss ideas back and forth. Now he said, "There must be a greater purpose to the exhibit."

"There is," Derek said, all seriousness now. "This is how we publicly demonstrate full disclosure. The French families think we're hiding something from them, but we're not. We'll take pictures of everything exactly as we found it, including the caves themselves."

"And it'll be educational and historical, too," I added.

"All right," Robson said after a moment of consideration. "And once we have received the families' lists of belongings, I would like them to be given a tour of the caves. It is only fair that they see things as we found them."

Derek nodded. "I'll call Monsieur Cloutier to make sure, but I'm confident we'll have their lists in hand within another day or two and can schedule a tour this weekend."

"The sooner, the better," Robson said, warming up to the idea. "It is most important that we relieve the families' apprehension. That is my biggest concern."

"All of this will help address that," Derek said with conviction.

I turned to Derek. "I thought of another issue. What if the families balk at the idea of having their personal items photographed for the exhibit?"

He pondered that one. "I considered that, too, but I don't believe it's for them to decide. We're documenting a moment in history. We found this cache on winery property and are detailing it for posterity." He turned to Robson. "Do you agree?"

"I do."

"Then all that's left to do is iron out a few more details," I said. "Would you like me to organize things, or would you rather appoint someone else to do it?"

"You are my number one choice, Brooklyn dear," Robson said with a grin.

"Lucky me," I said, smiling back at him. "Do you want us to check in with you on each aspect, or shall we just run with it?"

"I trust you to do everything to perfection."

Now I laughed out loud. "We'll see how that works out."

As we gathered our things and stood to leave, Derek said, "Can you give us a bit more information about this art appraiser?"

"His name is Noland Garrity," Robson said, walking with us down the wide hall toward the front door. "I will be sure to let him know that the books are to be appraised by Brooklyn."

"Oh," I said, touched by his words. "Thank you, Robson. I'll wait to see if any of them are left behind once the families have claimed their possessions."

"So what's this appraiser guy like?" Gabriel asked.

Robson gave a mild shrug. "A curmudgeonly sort, but he is very good and very discreet. He worked for many years at Sotheby's auction house in New York and Christie's in Beverly Hills. Now he is a freelance appraiser and author."

"Sounds legitimate," Derek said. "I presume it won't be necessary to run his name through Interpol?"

Guru Bob chuckled. "No. He is quite reputable."

I watched Derek's nonreaction as he reached for the doorknob, and I knew without a doubt that he would run Garrity's name through Interpol anyway. Because that was how he rolled.

I spent the drive home making notes as Derek and I discussed everything involved in pulling this crazy idea together.

"We can get a bunch of dramatic statements from people who've been inside the caves," I said. "We've got you and Trudy, my mom and dad, and Robin and my brothers. Oh, and Stan, from the excavation company. He can talk about it from his own point of view and make it sound like an adventure." I grew more excited as I wrote down the names.

"Are you comfortable delegating some of the tasks to others?"

"Oh yeah. I think I'll ask my mom to be in charge of gathering everyone's stories. We can write them out on cards and post them on the walls along with the photographs. Like they do in art museums."

"Good idea," Derek said as he braked for the traffic light before turning onto Shakespeare Lane. "Trudy can give a historical perspective, telling how her family escaped the Nazis and traveled here. And if any of the French folks are interested in contributing, they can each tell their own personal story."

I gazed at him. "Can we pull this all together before next Wednesday when the reporters show up?"

"Why not?"

I stared at him. "Yes. Why not?" Glancing down at my list, I wondered aloud, "Will the reporters be satisfied with photographs instead of being given a tour of the caves?"

"They'll have to be, since they won't be allowed inside the caves under any circumstances."

"Good," I said. "Because letting them go inside would be a really bad idea."

"If we entertain them well enough, they'll go away satisfied."

"Entertain them?" I stared at my list. "Do you think we need music at the town hall?"

"If you'd like," he said, "but I was referring to someone giving a guided tour of the exhibit. Someone with a lot of enthusiasm."

"A docent or two?"

"Trudy would enjoy doing that, I think."

I grinned. "She would be perfect. And so would you."

"Me?" He did a double take, looking at me as if I'd grown a second head. "Absolutely not."

"But they'll love you. It's the British accent. We Yanks are suckers for it."

He rolled his eyes. "No." The light turned green, and he proceeded slowly through the intersection.

I wrote his name down. "You'll be great."

"No."

"Oh, I just realized that Robin can take the pictures. She's a fantastic photographer."

"She does have a wonderful aesthetic style," he agreed.

"I'll contact her." I added it to my list. I was going to be busy for the next few days, but I wouldn't be alone. I planned to call every member of my family and everyone else I knew in Dharma to help me out. With barely one week to pull this together, I would need all the help I could get.

*L*ate the next morning, Trudy answered the door seconds after Mom rang the bell. "Becky and Brooklyn. What a nice surprise."

"I hope you don't mind us dropping in," Mom said. "But we were in the neighborhood, and I thought, let's see if Trudy is home."

"I love spontaneity. And to tell the truth, I'm happy to see you because you've saved me a phone call." She swung the door wide open, allowing us room to come inside. "Amelia, look who's here."

If the horrified expression on the woman's face was any indication, Amelia didn't share Trudy's love of spontaneity.

"I suppose they'll want tea or something," Amelia muttered as she stomped off to the kitchen.

"That would be lovely, thank you, Amelia," Trudy called. She turned and smiled at us. "It's as if she reads my mind."

"She must be such a joy to live with," I said, biting my tongue. It's not that I enjoyed antagonizing Amelia, but her sour reaction made our impulsive visit even sweeter.

In truth, our visit wasn't impulsive at all. I wanted to see the matching bookend that Trudy had told us about the other day in the cave. Mom had agreed to be my partner in crime—well, not crime, so much as equivocation—and we had memorized our lines well.

Two hours earlier, Derek and I had accompanied my mother into the caves to watch her perform her sacred cleansing ceremony. My ears were still ringing from her enthusiastic whoops, and I could still smell the white sage smoke in my hair. Mom had outdone herself, invoking the cave goddesses to keep the place safe. I firmly believed that the cave would last another thousand years with or without Mom's help, but it couldn't hurt to add some extra insurance. Mom was, after all, the powerful Grand Raven Mistress of the Celtic Goddess Coven of greater Sonoma County. She was not to be messed with.

After the ceremony, Derek drove off in the opposite direction to meet with Monsieur Cloutier to arrange a tour of the caves for any of his community who wanted to participate.

Now Trudy led the way into the living room, and we sat around the coffee table. There was an open storage box on the table filled with photos and letters and memorabilia.

"Did we catch you at a bad time?" Mom asked.

"Oh no," Trudy said, waving her hand breezily. "I've just been going through some of my aunt Marie's old letters and photos."

"Oh, your aunt Marie is Robson's grandmother," I said, then realized I was stating the obvious. But now I was even more interested in seeing some of those letters.

"That's right," Trudy said. "She gave this box to me years ago, mainly because so many of these letters were from my mother."

"That was thoughtful of her," Mom said.

"She was a sweet lady," she said.

"What was your mother's name?" I asked.

"Camille." She smiled fondly. "I've always loved that name."

"It's a charming name," Mom said.

"Yes." Trudy sighed. "After touring the caves the other day, I was feeling sentimental about my family, so I pulled these out to read and reminisce."

"What a good idea." Mom smiled as she glanced inside the box and lifted a short stack of letters wrapped with a faded blue ribbon. She held it close to her nose and sniffed. "Oh, Brooklyn, look at this wonderful old paper."

To an outsider, it probably looked odd to be sniffing a bunch of letters, but my mom knew and appreciated that I was addicted to anything having to do with old paper and books—the look of it, the feel of leather and paper in my hands, the smells. I took the stack of letters from my mother, ran my fingers across the surface of the paper, and felt its thickness. Then I took a deep breath, absorbing its scent. "Oh, I love it. So musty and evocative of a time long ago. And this is a beautiful, high-quality paper."

"Isn't it?" Trudy said.

"Oh gosh, I'm being presumptuous." I'd just invaded her home and helped myself to her mother's precious letters. "I'm sorry, Trudy."

But Trudy was fascinated. "Not at all. I never thought about it, but of course you would appreciate old paper. Please look at anything that strikes your fancy."

But I returned the stack of beribboned letters to their place inside the box and sat down again. "People really knew how to write letters back in the day."

"They did," Trudy said. "My mother's letters are pages and pages long. She turned every little trip on the train into an adventure filled with funny events and news and odd tidbits. I can hear her voice as I'm reading."

"That's the true gift of letter writing," Mom said.

Trudy held up a faded pink envelope. "I was just trying to read this one when you knocked on the door. It's from Aunt Marie to my mother, but it's in a language I can't figure out."

"It's not written in French?" I asked.

"No." Trudy chuckled. "I have a feeling it's some sort of hybrid language the two of them made up when they were in school. They were girlfriends from a very early age and attended a convent school near Limoges. For hundreds of years, the nuns taught the ancient languages, Latin, Medieval French, Coptic, some sort of ancient Hebrew, among others."

"That must've been challenging."

"You would think so, but according to my mother, the students used to take it in stride. My mother and aunt would use a combination of those languages in their letters to each other so nobody else could understand what they wrote."

I smiled. "Little girls like to keep their secrets."

"Most definitely." She handed the pink envelope to me. "You might find this one interesting, Brooklyn. Not the letter itself, but the paper is unlike anything else in the box."

I looked at the envelope and frowned. "There's a stamp but no address written on it."

Trudy looked mildly concerned. "Oh, I didn't realize. . . ."

"It's probably explainable," I murmured. "She might've slipped another letter inside a new envelope." I rubbed the notepaper between my thumb and forefinger. The finish felt like satin, and I wondered where it had originated. I looked more closely and could make out part of a watermark. "May I take this with me for a day or two? I would love to track down this papermaker."

"Certainly." She nodded eagerly. "You've stirred my curiosity."

"Yes. Mine, too." I slipped the letter into my purse, knowing this wasn't the time to delve into its secrets. But now I was anxious to study it and hoped I could grab some time tonight before or after dinner. My friends and family were used to my getting geeky over things like this.

"Oh," Trudy said, suddenly remembering. "I was going to call you later today."

"That's right. You said something when we first arrived."

Trudy reached for a smaller piece of paper on the side table. "I have a favor to ask you, if you don't mind."

"Not at all," I said.

She hesitated as Amelia toddled in at that moment with a tray holding a small pot of tea and several mugs. Setting it down on the coffee table, Amelia made a show of rubbing her nose and glaring at Trudy's box of letters. "So much dust," she muttered.

I glanced at the tray and noticed there were no cookies being served. This time, though, Amelia was nice enough to pour the tea into our cups and pass them around. I thanked her profusely, and she gave me a glower that was meant to make me cower. Instead, I smiled and winked at her. She huffed and puffed and stomped off to the kitchen.

What were we talking about? I had to think for a minute. "Sorry, Trudy. You had a favor to ask?"

"Yes." She waved the piece of paper she'd been holding. "I received a phone call this morning from the granddaughter of an old friend. She told me the oddest thing. She read a brief story in her local newspaper about the treasure in the caves. It reminded her that I live in the area, and she asked if I would like to have a visitor for a week. Of course I was delighted to say yes."

"That'll be fun for you," Mom said.

"Won't it? After we finished our phone call, she sent me the sweetest e-mail." She waved the piece of paper again, and I assumed it was the e-mail from the girl. "She's a darling thing, but I'm concerned that she'll be bored staying here. I'm not as spry as I used to be, and I think she might appreciate meeting some people closer to her own age."

"Why would she be bored?" I said. "You're wonderful company."

"Aren't you a dear." Trudy sighed. "But she's so much younger than me. She's closer to your age, Brooklyn, and I was hoping you'd be willing to take her to lunch one day while she's here. And if the two of you get along, perhaps some evening you and Derek can take her out and introduce her to some more friends. I would pay for your meals, of course."

"Don't be silly," I said. "I'll be happy to meet her for lunch." I didn't mention how ridiculously busy I'd been lately because I figured I still had to eat lunch, right? So why not do a favor for Trudy and by extension, Guru Bob?

"When does she arrive?" Mom asked.

"Next week, on Wednesday."

I tried to visualize my calendar. Wednesday was our big press conference with all the reporters. "I'll come by on Thursday and take her to lunch, if that works for you."

"It's perfect. I'm so grateful."

"It's no problem at all," I said.

"What's her name, Trudy?" Mom asked.

"Elizabeth Trent."

"Elizabeth is one of my favorite names," Mom said fondly. "A classical, solid name for a woman."

Her comment was interesting, considering she'd named her girls Brooklyn, Savannah, China, and London, after the cities in which we were conceived or born. But I wasn't about to bust her chops in front of Trudy. I'd save it for the drive home.

Trudy handed the e-mail to Mom to read, while I glanced around the room, trying to be nonchalant. I couldn't see the sculpture anywhere, but there were so many objects on every available surface, including several small shelves affixed to the walls that held fancy commemorative teacups and such. I turned in my chair to search again, scanning the shelves on either side of the fireplace and the mantel. And there it was! The marble piece I'd been hoping to see.

Now that Trudy had rediscovered the missing twin bookend, she had cleared a miniscule section in the middle of the mantel, slightly hidden behind a cloisonné vase, to show off the creamy white bookends. Between them they held a small collection of nicely bound books.

"Oh, I just noticed your bookends!" I said, my voice rising two octaves. Did that make me sound a little phony? Probably, but Trudy was too polite to say anything. "May I see them?"

"Of course," Trudy said. "Pick them up and hold them. They love being touched."

Chapter Eight

"Trudy's house isn't part of the Dharma security grid," Gabriel told me.

Security grid? I wasn't exactly sure what he was talking about. "So she doesn't have any kind of alarm system set up?"

"Not that I know of. Is there a problem?"

"I'm worried about her," I said. "She has some valuable things in her house, but mostly I'm nervous about her safety after hearing what that hothead Henri said the other day."

"He did threaten Robson's family," Gabriel conceded, "but at the time I thought he was just blowing off steam. Maybe not, though."

"If he's pushed to the limit and makes good on his threats, he'll come after Trudy. Robson doesn't have any other relatives around here that I know of."

"I'll talk to him. After everything that's gone down lately, he'll want Trudy's home to be secured."

"Thank you," I said, relieved.

"You got it, babe."

A moment later, we hung up and I started the car. I glanced at

Mom, sitting in the passenger seat. "I have a question. What's with Amelia?"

Mom sighed. "I know she's odd, but she's very devoted to Trudy."

"Do you know the story? How did they meet?"

"They met in the hospital when she was laid up with a broken leg."

"Okay, so Trudy needed help getting around on crutches, so she hired her. That's understandable, I guess."

"No, sweetie," Mom said. "Amelia was the one with the broken leg. Trudy offered her a place to stay until she was back on her feet."

"Really?" That was a surprise. "So Trudy was the good Samaritan, not the other way around."

"If you know Trudy, it makes sense, doesn't it?"

I nodded. "Trudy is a wonderful, generous person."

"She still volunteers at the hospital. Amelia drops her off and waits for her in the car."

I laughed in surprise. "She just sits outside? She won't go inside and volunteer, too?"

"No."

"She's a piece of work," I said, shaking my head.

"I know it might not be obvious, but Amelia has been very good for Trudy."

"I don't see how. She's just so . . . mean."

"She's fiercely protective."

"You say tomato . . ." I sighed, turning onto the highway. "Have you known Amelia a long time? I don't remember seeing her around town before she moved in with Trudy."

"Amelia was never a member of the Fellowship, if that's what you mean. But then, neither was Trudy. I don't actually know how long Amelia's lived in the area, but I can't remember a time when she wasn't around. She used to run a house-cleaning business with Harmony Byers."

"Harmony Byers? Crystal and Melody's mother?"

"Yes." She saw the look on my face and added, "Harmony's a lot more sedate than her two girls."

"Thank God for that." It was a good thing we were stopped at a light, or my shock might've caused me to run the car into a side ditch. I'd gone to school with Crystal Byers. She and her sister, Melody, were two scary little peas in a pod, to say the least. The *very* least.

"Is Amelia an Ogunite?" I asked, almost afraid to hear the answer. The Byers family belonged to the Church of the True Blood of Ogun, a local religious group whose zealous members lived a few miles away in an area known as the Hollow. Their religion taught them to honor the creative spirit of the earth, but some of their adherents took that credo to a whole new level when it came to living off the land. To put it bluntly, they were gun-toting survivalists likely to shoot first and ask questions later. They were also brazen evangelists who insisted on spreading the message of Ogun to anyone standing within earshot.

If Amelia was an Ogunite, it might explain why she was so hostile to me. I'd run afoul of some church members in the not-too-distant past.

"I think Amelia might've dabbled in church philosophy a bit," Mom said. "Or maybe she just pretended to do it for Harmony's sake. But it didn't take, and I have a feeling that was why the partnership broke up."

"Lucky for Amelia," I muttered. I waited for traffic to clear before turning onto the Lane. "I can't imagine anyone being happy to work with the Byers for any length of time."

"Who can say? It might've been her broken leg that made it impossible for her to clean houses. When Trudy met Amelia in the hospital, I understand she was a pitiful sight. Trudy brought her home, fixed her up, and gave her a job."

"Trudy is a good person," I said again, because especially in this case, it bore repeating.

"Much better than any of us." Mom and I exchanged smiles. The truth was, Mom was also one of the most caring people in the whole world.

"I'll be interested to meet Trudy's friend Elizabeth," I said, then remembered Mom's conversation with Trudy. "And speaking of Elizabeth, I hear you like that name. I believe the words you used to describe it were *classical* and *solid*."

Mom's smile was smug. "If you believed me, then so did Trudy."

I frowned as I came to the Stop sign at Vivaldi Way. "So you were just handing her a line?"

"Of course not. We were having a civilized chat. Elizabeth *is* a lovely name. It's just not to my taste. But I was determined to say whatever it took to keep the conversation going so that you could do what you had to do."

I rarely gave my mother marks for subtlety, but once in a while she surprised me. "Good work, Mom."

She flashed me a sly smile. "Just doing my job."

That night, Derek and I enjoyed a quiet dinner outside on the deck with grilled steaks, baked potatoes, and a salad, my favorite meal. Sweet Maggie lounged contentedly at our feet under the table, but we kept Charlie inside the house because I was afraid she'd be the perfect snack for the red hawks that flew over the hills.

I told Derek how Mom and I had dropped in on Trudy, and I described the kitten sculpture I'd seen. "It looks so lifelike, I expected it to start prancing around like Charlie would, frisky and adorable. And it's beautifully sculpted. It may not be a Rodin, but I imagine it's worth a lot of money."

"I'm sorry to say I didn't even notice it the first time we were there," he said. "I'd like to see it."

"I didn't see it that first time, either, probably because her house is jammed with so many baubles and goodies." I gazed at him for a second, then smacked my forehead. "I can't believe I forgot I took a picture."

He chuckled as I jumped up, grabbed my phone, and scanned the photograph. "Here it is. The lighting's not that great, but I think you can get the general idea."

He studied the photograph and slid his fingers across the screen to enlarge it several times. "I'd like to see it in person, but your photo-taking skill is not bad."

"Thank you, considering I took it while Amelia was glaring at me from her kitchen hideout."

He glanced up at me. "Why?"

"She's just weird." I set the phone aside and continued eating dinner. "By the way, I talked to Gabriel about installing a security system at Trudy's house. I'm concerned about Henri's threats."

"She doesn't have an alarm on her house?"

"No, and after looking around again today, I'll bet some of her so-called tchotchkes are more valuable than she realizes. Many of them are old family heirlooms, so she might not have any idea what they originally cost."

He chewed a mouthful of steak as he considered that. "I was thinking that very thing when we were there the other day. But I didn't know her home wasn't hooked into the Dharma grid."

I paused with my fork in midair. "What exactly is the Dharma grid?"

"Robson asked Gabriel to set up a wide-area security system to protect anyone in the commune who felt that their property might be vulnerable. It also covers Robson's home, of course, and the winery, the school, the art museum, and a number of the shops and restaurants on the Lane."

I frowned. "Is this a result of that ugly incident that happened last year?"

He hesitated, but then confessed, "Yes."

"So it's all my fault."

"No, it's not." Derek grabbed hold of my forearm and gently squeezed for reassurance. "It's the fault of those friendly neighbors who turned out to be murdering psychopaths."

"I suppose." I set my fork down. "But I'm the one who brought them into our world."

"I refuse to let you beat yourself up over this," he said firmly. "It was time to raise the level of security around here anyway. The times are changing."

"You can say that again," I muttered. "Gabriel's probably got drones flying by, watching all of us."

"Yes, he does, love." He pointed to the sky. "Be sure to smile."

"Very funny." But the joke did improve my attitude. So did a sip of the full-bodied cabernet we were drinking. After savoring it for a moment, I returned to my baked potato. But then I remembered something else. "Trudy was going through some old letters of her mother's, and I took one of them with me. I want to try to track down the papermaker, but it would be fun if you could translate the contents."

"I can try," he said between bites. "Couldn't Trudy translate it for you?"

"No. She thinks it's some hybrid of schoolgirl medieval French and Latin or something. It was a letter from her aunt to her mother, and they probably wanted to keep the contents a secret."

He smiled. "I'm intrigued. Let me give it a whirl after dinner."

Once we were finished with dinner and dessert—homemade gelato from my sister Savannah's restaurant—I washed the dishes, and Derek put them away. Then I found Trudy's letter and showed it to him.

"The paper's beautiful, isn't it?" I said.

"Yes. Unusually thick. It almost has a satin finish, which seems odd to me because it's so old."

I nodded. "Some old vellum appears satiny to the look and to the touch."

He turned it over a few times, studying it.

"As I said, I'm mainly interested in the paper, but I really hope you can read this language. It would be fun to give Trudy the translation."

He sat down at the kitchen table and pulled the letter out of the envelope. After one glance at the paper, he held it up to the light instead of reading it. "That's a curious watermark."

"I thought so, too. That's how I'm hoping to trace the source of the paper." The watermark on the letter was hard to discern at first because of the writing that covered the page. But I was able to distinguish it on the back side. It was a row of stylized turtles at various intervals, and every few inches, the word *Charente* appeared.

I had learned to make watermarks while taking classes in papermaking years ago. There were several ways to do it, but the most common was to take thin wire and bend it into the shape you wanted, affix the wire to a drum—these were called dandy rolls and looked like large rolling pins—and roll the drum over the paper. Where the wire hit the paper, it created a slight indentation. You might not be able to see it unless you held it up to the light.

The process was more complicated than that, especially when it came to mass production, but that was the easiest way to explain it.

"*Charente*," Derek murmured.

"Yes," I said. "It sounds French, doesn't it? I figured it's the name of the paper company that made the stationery. But the design is unusual and artistic enough that it could also be the name of the papermaker himself. Or herself."

Derek glanced up. "It's also the name of a river in southwestern France."

"Is it? Well, maybe that's where they made the paper."

He nodded absently as he studied the page. "Perhaps."

"I want to get a better look at that mark." I jogged back to the bedroom where I had stashed my set of portable bookbinding tools. Pulling out my magnifying glass, I returned to the kitchen and sat down to study the paper more closely.

"I don't recognize the language," Derek said. "There are a few French prefixes here and there, but they're mixed up with Hebrew symbols and it's all nonsensical. At least to me."

"I'm bummed." There were so few languages he couldn't translate at least partially. "Should I ask Gabriel?"

"Certainly, but I'm not sure he'll have any better luck with it."

I scrutinized the handwriting more closely. "I guess I could ask my bibliophile chat group."

"Good idea," he said. "And describe the watermark to them, too. They always come up with interesting theories."

"That's why I thought of them." I pushed my chair back and stood.

"There is one more thing," he said, looking up at me.

"What's that?"

"The letter wasn't written by a schoolgirl. That is an adult's handwriting."

As Derek watched the late news in the family room surrounded by Maggie and Charlie, I sat alone at the desk in the Quinlans' office with my computer logged onto my online bibliophile chat group. They were in the middle of a chat about foxing, a favorite topic of bookbinders because those pesky brown spots were a perennial problem with old books.

The chat group was full of eclectic and brilliant minds, so after first apologizing for interrupting their conversation, I described the watermark and the quality of the paper and asked if anyone was familiar with it.

"It's most likely French," I added. "And probably made in the nineteen forties or fifties."

I was immediately bombarded with comments, mostly from people thanking me for changing the subject. Nobody liked talking about the heartbreak of foxing, but we couldn't help ourselves.

A few of my online friends were intrigued and promised they'd look into it and get back to me.

To thank them, I mentioned that I'd found a beautiful French edition of *Journey to the Center of the Earth* and regaled them with the childish blood oath I'd discovered on the flyleaf. The chatter picked up, and the conversation veered off into horror stories of books damaged by children.

A while later I was about to sign off but decided to throw them one more question. It wasn't exactly related to bookbinding, I explained to the group, but it was part of the letter I was researching.

I typed out the first paragraph of the letter and then asked, "Does anyone recognize this language? Our current theory is that it's a mashup of several extinct languages, including, possibly, medieval French. I appreciate any help you can give me."

I received six comments, but only one of them was helpful. Claude, a genius of a librarian from Maryland, suggested that the letter might've been written in Chouadit, an extinct Jewish language once spoken in southern France.

"The word *Chouadit* means *Jewish* in the old Judeo-Provençal language of the area," Claude wrote. "There might be some Aramaic thrown in there, too. I won't get your hopes up, but give me a day or two to work on the translation itself, and I'll let you know what I come up with."

I thanked Claude profusely, wished everyone else a good evening, and signed out of the group. I made a quick detour over to Google the word *Charente*. It turned out to be a region near Limoges as well as the name of the river that ran through the area.

Charente was also the name of a small stationery shop in San Francisco. I stared at the screen, imagining Marie Benoit traveling into the city for the day and coming across the shop. For sentimental reasons, she would want to buy a little something in the store, and so she chose a pretty package of stationery.

My imagination could get carried away sometimes.

"You're smiling," Derek said.

"Oh, I didn't realize you were standing there." I rubbed my eyes. I'd been staring at the computer for the past hour.

"I snuck up on you."

"I'm glad. It was time to quit." I shut down the computer. "And yes, I'm happy. I think I've worked out the stationery question, and the people in my chat room are the smartest people in the world. I'm lucky they let me play with them."

"You're not exactly a lightweight yourself," Derek said with a laugh. "Are you ready for bed, love?"

I yawned. "I didn't think I was, but all of a sudden I'm exhausted."

He pulled me up from my chair, and I went willingly.

By Saturday morning, we had received a complete list of heirlooms from every family involved, including those still living in France. I had cross-checked their lists with my inventory and came across at least six discrepancies. Luckily, there were more treasures listed on my inventory than the families had claimed. I figured that some people had died before they'd informed their heirs that they'd given a valuable family keepsake to Anton for safekeeping. Each of the unclaimed items would have to be given extra attention by Noland Garrity.

There were also a few instances where I might've mislabeled something. For instance, one person had listed a set of hammered silver candelabra. I remembered seeing a set of hammered silver candlesticks that held two candles each. Would one of those be considered a candelabra? Technically, I didn't think so, but maybe that was what they'd always called it. It was a small detail, but I wanted to return to the cave to make sure I wasn't mistaken.

Once I'd worked out that inconsistency, I walked over to Mom's house to see how she was coming along with the job of tracking down everyone who'd been inside the cave and getting their personal stories recorded for the upcoming exhibit. She was compiling the stories at that very moment and would be printing them out on heavy card stock. Later, the cards would be mounted on the walls of the exhibit.

She had also lined up volunteers to work in the exhibit room and outside with crowd control. Mom had been putting together events in Dharma for years, and it was pretty obvious from whom I'd inherited my organizational gene.

After talking to Mom, I drove over to the caves to meet Robin, who had agreed to take photographs of some of the most interesting items I'd inventoried inside the cave.

I considered myself the art director and presented my ideas and concepts to Robin, and I expected her to transfer my creative vision to film.

Robin laughed a lot, mostly at me as I tried to give her advice on how to take a picture. She basically considered me a nuisance, but to my credit, I handled the lighting, a piece of cake since Derek and Gabriel had set up the light trees. I borrowed two clamp lights from Austin's garage and readjusted them strategically for each shot. It was hard work, but worth it.

As we drove to her favorite printer in Santa Rosa, I gave Robin due credit. "Your photos are going to turn out absolutely fantastic."

"Thanks. Wait till you see what a great job this printer does."

The next day, we dashed back to Santa Rosa to pick up the poster-sized prints. Robin was right about the printer. The simple

posters had been transformed into artwork. Now I was getting
excited.

W hile Mom was herding the volunteers and Robin and I were
racing back and forth from Santa Rosa, Derek led the group
from Frenchman's Hill into the caves. That night as we ate dinner,
I tried to get Derek to share some crazy stories with me, but he
insisted there was nothing to tell.

"They were on their best behavior," he said, sounding almost
disappointed. "Maybe Felix had a long talk with everyone, and
they realized that Robson is not their enemy. They were all gracious and thankful and thrilled to see everything. I felt like a tour
guide with a bunch of happy people."

"I'm shocked. Even Henri was well behaved?"

"Perfectly," he admitted after taking a sip of wine. "The most
traumatic thing that happened was that some of them broke down
in tears. I can't blame them, since there is so much family history
and pain involved in all of this."

"And it's all mixed up with the war."

"Exactly. It was quite dramatic, but all good."

"I'm especially glad Henri didn't give you any trouble."

"Not a bit," Derek said. "In fact, they've all promised to come
to the winery for the Pre-Harvest celebration next week."

I had to laugh. Basically, wine-country people would dream
up almost any excuse to get together and taste wines. The annual
Pre-Harvest celebration was Dharma's official kickoff to harvest
season, and it was always a fun-filled day of wine tasting, along
with loads of great appetizers and munchies brought in by the local
chefs, including my sister Savannah.

"That should be interesting," I said. "I wonder if Madame
Cloutier could be talked into bringing some of those amazing
beignets with her."

"Let me just make a phone call," Derek said with a determined grin.

I beamed at him. "That's my hero."

*M*onday morning, I arrived at the town hall to find a squadron of volunteers standing by to hang the posters and mount the quote cards that Mom had already designed. The day before, Robin had laid out a structure for the room itself that would give each photograph its own space and lighting. As a professional sculptor, she was used to mounting art exhibits, so within hours, she had all the posters hanging on the walls and on columns around the room.

Another volunteer with some creative ability had designed a program to hand out to visitors. A different group of commune volunteers agreed to work outside with the crowds, giving directions to visitors and handing out the programs. Mom and Robin and Trudy would act as docents, answering questions and telling their own stories of their brief adventures inside the caves.

And I tried really hard, but Derek still refused to play the docent.

I wondered a few times if we were crazy to devote this much time and energy to the town hall exhibit. But the result would show the Frenchmen that Guru Bob was being completely aboveboard, and it would give the visiting reporters something to look at instead of the actual treasures inside the cave. Those were our two main purposes, and I prayed we would be successful. But beyond that, the exhibit would be a wonderful new activity for visitors and locals to experience.

I glanced around and found Robin deeply involved with a few of the more artistic types as they put the final touches to the overall layout and positioning of the posters. I knew I wasn't needed, so I let her know I was going and then rushed off to join Derek at the storage cave, where he was scheduled to meet Guru Bob and Noland Garrity, the appraiser.

While parking the car, I noticed a handsome older man talking to Guru Bob by the rounded doors leading to the storage cave. Derek was there, too, but he was more involved with studying the security box than with the conversation going on next to him. The stranger—I assumed it was Noland Garrity—was tall, just a few inches shorter than Derek and Guru Bob, who were both more than six feet tall. As I approached, I thought it was pretty great to see three tall, handsome men gathered together in one spot.

"Here is Brooklyn," Guru Bob said, sounding relieved to see me. As soon as I was close enough, he introduced me to the appraiser. "Brooklyn Wainwright, this is Noland Garrity. I've hired him to assess the items we found in the cave."

"Hello, Mr. Garrity." The man didn't smile as I shook his hand. In his white polo shirt, khaki trousers, and highly polished brown penny loafers, he was dressed for going to the country club rather than skulking through caves.

Guru Bob added, "Noland, I trust you will benefit from Brooklyn's insight and positive energy."

With that odd statement, Guru Bob bid us good-bye. That was when I noticed Mr. Garrity surreptitiously wiping his hand on his trousers—the hand he'd just used to shake mine.

I won't take it personally, I thought, and turned to watch Guru Bob walking briskly across the parking lot. Where was he off to in such a hurry? On the other hand, it was a good sign that he trusted us with his appraiser, and I smiled at Noland Garrity. "Did Robson describe some of the treasures we found? You won't believe how amazing it is."

"Yeah, that's great. Look, I don't have all day," he said, squinting up at the bright blue sky. "And why is it so damn hot up here?"

I exchanged a puzzled look with Derek. His eyebrow shot up in response. It couldn't be more than seventy degrees outside on this gorgeous fall day. What was Garrity complaining about? Maybe he was just one of those people who always complained and were never really happy. If so, I really hoped his visit would be a short one.

And what was with his brusque attitude? Was he angry about something? Could he be angry at Guru Bob for leaving him here with us? I hoped he would mellow out once he was able to get a look at all the treasures.

Derek turned away from us to lift the cover of the security box and tap a series of numbers on the keypad. When a buzzer sounded, he used his key to unlock the dead bolt on the doors. "Right this way."

Once inside the cool storage cave, Garrity grunted in dismay. "Where are you taking me? It's filthy dirty in here."

Maybe I'd been working too hard lately, because I had little patience for this man. Guru Bob had to have told him that he was going to be inside a wine cave. And, as caves went, this one was pretty much pristine. And well ventilated. I glanced around. Yes, the cement floor was swept clean, and the wine barrels were in a perfectly straight line against the walls. The cavernous space was well lighted. What was he complaining about?

"And what's that awful smell?" he asked, sniffing and looking around.

"That's the smell of expensive red wine," I said, biting my tongue not to add, *And you'll never taste a drop of it, as God is my witness.*

"Good thing I don't drink."

Aha! There was one more reason to hate him. And it was probably the reason why he was so unlikable. After spending less than five minutes with the appraiser, I was pretty sure I knew why Guru Bob had rushed off. What I wanted to know was, why did he hire him in the first place? *Curmudgeonly* didn't begin to describe Noland Garrity.

Derek continued walking to the end of the big room where the excavated hole had been enlarged. I noticed a step stool leading up to the opening and realized that sometime during the last few days, Derek had placed it there to help the people from Frenchman's Hill climb over the eighteen-inch ledge and step down into the chamber.

At the opening, Derek stopped and turned to Garrity. "I hope you're not claustrophobic, because this space we're about to enter is small and the air is a bit stale. I assure you the air is clean, but the space has been sealed up for about seventy years."

Garrity pressed his white handkerchief to his mouth and nose. "I can barely breathe already, and you're saying it'll be worse?"

"Yes, because it's a smaller enclosure. But there's plenty of air. You won't suffocate," he added dryly.

"Is that supposed to be some kind of a joke?"

"Not really," Derek said. "On the positive side, the artwork and furnishings have been sealed up as well, so their condition hasn't deteriorated."

"I'll be the judge of that."

"Indeed," Derek said affably. I didn't know how he managed to stay so upbeat. I was ready to strangle the jerk.

"Here we go," Derek said, and easily stepped over the wall.

"Wait a minute," Garrity said, stopping at the wall. He bent over the low ledge, trying to get a look at where he was about to venture. All of a sudden he began to wobble and couldn't quite right himself. "Whoa."

"Mr. Garrity, are you all right?"

"Uhh . . ."

Was he having a heart attack? I grabbed him by his belt and yanked him back from the cave opening.

He stumbled, then righted himself. It took him a few long seconds to recover his dignity, and, once he did, he gave me a look of pure contempt. "How dare you grab me like that?"

"The way you were moaning and swaying, I thought you were going to pass out."

"Look at my shirt. It's filthy." He slapped the white polo shirt to get the dirt out, but he only made it worse.

And I thought Amelia was crabby. This guy could give her lessons. I couldn't believe I'd thought he was handsome only minutes ago. Just went to show that my mother was right again. *Handsome is as handsome does.* This guy was the poster boy for that old cliché.

On his second try, he managed to make it over the wall and into the chamber. "What in the world?" His voice echoed in the small chamber. "Are there rats? It smells moldy back here."

"No, it doesn't," I said, stepping easily into the space. "It's actually very clean, and there are no rats anywhere. My mother swept every inch of it two days ago. And if you dare say one word about my mother, I will smack you—"

"Darling, Mr. Garrity would never say anything about your mother, now would you, Mr. Garrity?" Derek said, trying to calm me down while subtly warning Garrity to shut his piehole if he didn't have anything nice to say.

Garrity ignored him. "When Robson told me there was a cave, I didn't think I'd actually have to climb into it. He lied to me."

"Robson doesn't lie," Derek said, his tone deceptively mild.

The man lifted one weary shoulder. "Whatever."

I knew Derek was generally more patient than I was, but how could he tolerate this man? My respect and admiration for Derek's tolerance were growing to biblical proportions.

Ignoring the appraiser, Derek maneuvered around the small enclosure, flipping on the set of lights he'd mounted onto the five-foot light tower at the far end of the chamber. I noticed that unlike on the day Robin and I took pictures, the extension cords were tucked safely along the bottom edges of the cave. Derek had been very busy when I wasn't looking.

With the lights illuminating everything, Garrity couldn't help but glance around. "So this is it? This is what I crawled into a cave to see?"

"There's more to see in the next chamber," Derek said. "The entry is directly behind the wardrobe."

He uttered an expletive. "You can't possibly expect me to drag myself even deeper into this pit. It's filthy. I won't do it."

"That's fine, then," Derek said, his English accent brisk and to the point. Grabbing my hand, he said, "Let's go, darling." We took turns climbing over the wall and back into the larger storage area.

"Where do you think you're going?"

Derek half turned. "We're going home. You've made it quite obvious that you aren't interested in seeing the artwork and objects inside the cave. I'm sure Robson will be happy to take back the check he wrote you."

"For God's sake, I didn't mean it literally."

"Yes, you did," Derek said amiably. "So we're leaving, and I expect you to follow because I'm not leaving you in here alone."

"You don't have to be so sensitive about it."

"I'm not sensitive at all," Derek said in an even tone. "I'm complying with your wishes."

As we walked away, Garrity shouted, "Wait, damn it. Don't be so stupid."

"Don't be so stupid?" I stopped and turned. "What is wrong with you?" My jaw was clenched so tightly, I could barely think straight. "Do you think we have nothing better to do than listen to your whining all day? Honestly, you have done nothing since you got here but complain and make insulting remarks about my friends and family. If you think we're going to put up with that for one more minute, you're as crazy as I think you are."

I stared up at Derek, and he winked at me. Okay, maybe I hadn't been as eloquent as I wanted to be, but I'd meant every word. Could Derek possibly be enjoying this jerk's antics?

"All right, all right. Don't get your panties in a twist." Garrity waved his hand, dismissing me. "If you think it's so important, I'll look at the rest of the cave."

"Hey, you're not doing us any favors. You're the one getting paid to be here."

Derek quickly clutched my arm, knowing I was furious. I'd been taking Krav Maga classes with my neighbor, and I was ready to attack. He was probably smart to hold me back.

"Does this mean you'd like to see what else is in the cave?" Derek asked with a reasonableness that astounded me.

"Fine," Garrity said. "Yes, I want to see what's in the cave. Happy now?"

"That's all you had to say," Derek said, and led the way back to the wall. With great reluctance, I followed behind them both.

Once inside the chamber, Derek said, "Look around all you want."

Garrity was already scanning the items, trying not to look impressed. He pulled out a notebook and began writing. Finally he murmured, "I suppose this is an interesting collection, but it's nothing extraordinary."

"Robson may have explained that—"

"I need complete silence while I work."

"Then why don't you shut up?" I muttered.

He turned and stared at me, affronted. "You've got a mouth on you."

Derek bared his teeth in a semblance of a grin. "She does, as well as a mean left hook. Careful you don't set her off even worse."

Garrity frowned thoughtfully and went back to studying the art objects and making notes.

We were silent for another five minutes until Mr. Garrity said, "This can't be everything."

"No," Derek said patiently. "As I explained earlier, the entry to the second chamber is behind the wardrobe."

Garrity rolled his eyes.

If only Derek had brought his gun with him, I'd shoot the damn fool in the foot. But then he wouldn't be able to walk out of here. No, I would have to shoot him in the arm because there was no way I was going to be stuck dragging this whiner all the way out of the cave.

Who was I kidding? I would never point a gun at a living creature, but this guy was sorely trying my long-held peacenik values.

"It's right this way." Derek continued speaking as if Garrity hadn't said a word. "Follow me."

He slipped easily behind the large piece of furniture and disappeared into the space beyond.

"Wait. Where'd you go?"

"This way," I said, and followed Derek into the darkness. Garrity plodded behind me.

I no longer cared how much Robson admired the man's work. I refused to be nice to this guy. I didn't give a fig how brilliant an appraiser he was. How could Derek stomach the insufferable man? I didn't care if he knew art. I wanted him to go away. But now I couldn't walk out of the cave because I refused to leave Derek alone to deal with him.

Derek had set up another light tree in this space to make it easier to see the details of the artwork and other items.

In the second chamber, Noland's expression finally registered enough awe to satisfy me. When he noticed me watching him, he yawned and shrugged as if suffering from existential ennui. But he couldn't pull it off. The artwork was simply too remarkable.

After a half hour of silent observation and note taking, he turned to Derek. "I'll need complete access to these rooms if I'm to do a competent job of appraising the work. Do I get the key from you?"

"I assure you you'll have complete access." Derek handed him his business card. "Just call my cell anytime you want to look at something and I'll arrange an escort for you."

"An escort?" Garrity let loose a scornful laugh. "No, no. That's not how I work. I'll require the security code and a key to the doors so I can come and go at my own pace."

"I'm afraid that won't be possible," Derek said, and bared his teeth in a rakish smile. "That's not how I work."

Chapter Nine

By Wednesday morning, our remarkably professional-looking exhibition of The Hidden Treasures of La Croix Saint-Just was ready to be presented to the world. The subtitle of the exhibit was How One French Village Saved Its Legacy from the Nazis. That gave it a wine-country spin with the added jolt of the Nazi connection.

Within two hours of its opening, there was a line of curious visitors winding out the door and down the steps of the town hall. Mom, Robin, and Trudy, along with their exhibit staff and crowd-control volunteers, were all doing an amazing job.

I stuck around to hear people's reactions, and they were glowing, thank goodness. Everyone was intrigued with the story of the French family shipping their fellow villagers' treasured heirlooms out of the country and escaping the dreaded Nazis in the middle of the night.

At one o'clock, Derek picked me up, and we drove to Dharma's city hall for the big press conference scheduled for two o'clock that afternoon. On the drive over, we discussed our strategy again. Derek was to give a brief introduction, and I would talk about what we'd found in the cave; then we would take their questions. He insisted it would go smoothly, but I was nervous.

We parked in the city hall parking lot and stayed in the car to finish discussing what we would say. Our strategy was simple: tell the truth. Before we took any questions, we would start with the story of how we found the body in the cave and estimate how long the man had been there—omitting the name of the victim, of course. Any questions beyond the basics, even if we knew the answers, would be referred to the sheriff's department.

Next, we would discuss how we'd inadvertently found the second cave—omitting the discovery of the map on the notepaper inside *Journey to the Center of the Earth*. I insisted on this because I didn't want anyone coming after the book. In my experience, people were more than willing to kill over a valuable book. And that reminded me that I hadn't yet gone online to appraise its worth.

Finally, we would suggest to everyone that they attend the Treasures photographic exhibit at the town hall. Because there was no way in hell any of these reporters would be allowed to step one foot inside the cave if Derek had anything to say about it.

"Are you ready for this?" Derek asked.

"Sure. Do you want to embellish anything, or just give them the straight scoop?"

"There's no way you can possibly embellish anything, so please don't try."

"Why can't I embellish things?"

"Because you're a rotten liar."

"Thanks a lot." I smacked him in the arm.

He patted his heart. "I say it with love."

"I know I get a little tongue-tied and turn beet red when I'm dancing around the truth, but this is different. I can pull this off."

"There's nothing to pull off. We simply tell the truth." He quickly added, "But not the whole truth."

I grimaced. "See, this is where I get hung up. What part do we leave out?"

He grabbed my hand and kissed it. "You're scaring me to death."

"Come on. Tell me what *not* to say."

"All right." He sighed. "They already know about the dead body in the cave, of course, but they don't know that Robson's grandfather was the man's best friend—and we're not going to tell them."

"Right."

"They don't know about the book we found, with the two boys' signatures. They don't know that you found a map in the book that led us to find even more priceless objects. They don't know about Henri threatening Robson."

I nodded. "Right. Got it. Let's do this."

It was Derek's turn to look uneasy. "You should probably wait in the car."

"No way. I'm going to be awesome. Don't worry."

Shaking his head, Derek gazed out the window toward the city hall steps where the members of the press were assembling. "I suppose we ought to get out there."

I leaned forward to get a better look. "It's a bigger crowd than I expected."

"Yes." He pointed to a car parked at the end of the aisle from us. "And someone from the sheriff's department is here, too."

"Good. I'm glad you called them."

He glanced back at me. "Are you ready?"

"As ready as I'll ever be."

He sighed. "If you insist on coming along, just feign laryngitis. I'll do the talking."

I slugged his arm again, and he was smirking as we climbed out of the car to greet the press.

"We'll take a few questions now," Derek said after we'd both presented our stories and descriptions and thoughts about the body and the things we'd seen inside the caves. I'd counted thirty reporters and camera operators while Derek was talking, and they'd been respectfully silent during our presentation. Now they began shouting and waving their arms.

"Can you tell us more about the victim in the cave? How old was he?"

"Does he have a name?"

"Exactly how did he die?"

Derek gave a quick answer to each question, and I referred them to the sheriff's department for further information on the dead man. Derek then pointed to a good-looking young guy in the front row whose arm was raised in the air. "Yes, go ahead."

"Josh Atherton, *Antiquities Magazine*," he said, and smiled brightly at us both. "Thank you, Mr. Stone, Ms. Wainwright. Wow, this has been really fascinating. I wonder, do you have any idea how long ago the cave was sealed up?"

Derek spoke. "Based on the identification found on the victim, we estimate that the cave was sealed approximately seventy years ago."

"A quick follow-up if you don't mind," Atherton rushed to say. "Specifically, what identification did you find?"

"The police found the man's passport," Derek said carefully. "Apparently there was something else found on his body that gave the investigators a more specific date to work with. You'll have to contact them for more information."

More questions were blurted out, and we answered as many of them as we could. I was surprised by how many reporters asked about the murder victim since that information was available in the sheriff's records, which were open to the public.

I was finishing up an answer when a tall woman with spiky red hair interrupted. "Why won't you allow people to go inside the cave?"

Derek stepped to the microphone. "Our excavators and geologists have suggested that until we have completed the work that was interrupted, it's safer to restrict the number of people passing through. Beyond that, the cave is private property and contains many items of great value. Don't you agree it would be foolish to allow free access to the public?"

Many in the crowd shrugged in acquiescence, but I noticed a few reporters scowling, as though they were angry at us for considering them part of the general public.

Josh Atherton raised his hand again, and I pointed to him. "Mr. Atherton."

He beamed at me when I said his name. "Thank you so much. Let me preface my question by explaining that my readers truly enjoy being drawn into another world. So I was hoping you would describe what you felt when you first walked into the cave. I assume it was dark. Were you afraid? Did you notice the smells, the sights, the sounds? Do you recall the temperature?"

"It was musty and dark," I said, recalling the first time I walked into the cave. "At first I was excited and overwhelmed. I wanted to get in there and see everything. And I wasn't alone, so I was sharing the moment with others who were equally excited. But since then, I've gone there by myself, and I must admit, it's eerie. Silent. Cold. I'm reminded that this place was sealed off from the world for decades. Why? To hide a dead body? To protect those beautiful rare objects? I almost feel as though I shouldn't be there. But it's also thrilling, a punishment and a reward. The sublime and the . . ." I chewed on my lip, suddenly aware of my blathering. "Well, it's hard to explain."

"It's a weighty question," Derek said, noting my uneasiness. "Perhaps we'll end it there. Thank you all very much."

"And while you're in Dharma," I added hastily, "do take advantage of the photographic exhibit at the town hall over on Shakespeare Lane. You'll see pictures of the beautiful artwork we're talking about, and they'll answer a lot of your questions."

The crowd broke up slowly. I made eye contact and smiled at Detective Parrish, who was surrounded by reporters. Others stood chatting with one another and comparing notes. Derek signaled to the tech guy who had set up the podium and microphones. "We're done here, Willy. Thanks a lot for your help."

"No worries, man."

Derek grabbed my hand, and we walked quickly back to the car.

"Should we rescue Detective Parrish?" I asked.

He glanced over at the crowd gathered around the woman. "If she needs to talk, she knows where to find us."

"I like her. I feel bad for throwing so many questions her way."

"I like her, too, but this is part of her job. That's why she came here today."

"I guess that's true." I took one more look at the detective. She seemed perfectly calm as she was peppered with queries.

Once seated inside the car, Derek turned to me. "Are you all right? That last question was a bit personal."

"It took me by surprise. I'm still a little dazed."

"I was surprised you answered it."

"I was, too." I buckled my seat belt. "He was so nice, and the question seemed genuine. I'm afraid my answer sounded peculiar. I hope he doesn't write about how bizarre I am."

"It wasn't bizarre; it was honest." Derek started the engine and slid the stick shift into reverse. "Are you familiar with that magazine?"

"*Antiquities*? No. But I'm going to look it up."

"That's my girl."

That night we had reservations at Umbria, our favorite Italian restaurant on the Lane. We arrived early, so Derek waited at the bar while I dashed across the street to say hello to my sister China at Warped, the yarn and weaving shop she owned.

I spotted China with six ladies gathered around the giant loom at the back of the store. She waved but didn't come over, so I figured she was in the middle of a class. I took the time to wander around admiring the beautiful yarns and threads and designs she had on display. Several sets of brightly colored place mats were stacked on a shelf, and a number of intricate wall hangings were draped along one wall. A dowel hanging from the ceiling held beautifully crocheted wool scarves. Dozens of balls of colorful yarns were tossed into baskets and placed around the shop. I was drawn to a small, fluffy woven doggy bed on a side shelf and wondered if Charlie the kitten would like to sleep in something warm and cozy like that.

My sister was so talented, I thought wistfully. She was an incredible textiles artist and a beautiful mother. But then, all of my sisters were talented in one way or another, and I included myself. Not that I could weave or cook, but when it came to making or taking apart a book, I knew what I was doing. Although I had to admit I often wished I had the talent to cook something more than a boiled egg. Heck, I even screwed that up sometimes.

But hey, I also had a talent for finding dead bodies, although that wasn't anything to stand up and cheer about. I realized I was squeezing a ball of midnight blue alpaca yarn as if it were a stress toy and quickly dropped it into a nearby basket.

"Oh, hey. Hi."

I whipped around to see Josh Atherton, the reporter, standing a few feet behind me. "Oh, hi. It's Josh, right?"

"Yeah," he said. "Wow, I'm thrilled that I ran into you."

I checked to see if China was free yet. "I just stopped by for a minute."

He glanced around, looking a little awestruck. "This is such an amazing place. I mean, wow, so many great colors and patterns. Does the owner make all these things?"

"Yes, she does."

"Wow," he said again, and I wondered if I was making him nervous. "The stores up here are so full of cool stuff. Awesome." He turned in a circle, taking it all in, but then appeared to be embarrassed by his gushing, if his pink cheeks were anything to go by. "Sorry, I get distracted sometimes."

"I don't mind at all," I said, smiling. "This is my sister's store, and I happen to think it's fabulous."

"Oh." He grinned and gazed around again. "That makes it even cooler."

I chuckled.

He scratched his head, still embarrassed. "Anyway, thank you so much for answering my question earlier. I hope it didn't make you uncomfortable. I could tell you gave a heartfelt response."

"It was honest," I admitted. "But I don't usually bare my soul in public like that."

"I live for those moments." He grinned again, and I noticed he had dimples in his cheeks. He wore a thin, navy cashmere V-neck sweater over a white button-down shirt and blue jeans. His dark blond hair was a bit scruffy, and he wore wire-rimmed glasses. He was ridiculously cute.

He shoved his hands into his pockets. "I would love to set up an appointment to talk to you further. I promise I won't take up too much of your time, but I'd like to write an in-depth story on this discovery."

"I'm not the person to talk to. I can point you toward people who are more connected to the discovery."

"But I can tell you have a real emotional connection to that cave."

I shook my head. "Not really."

He smiled again. "You're being modest, but I understand." He pulled a card from his pocket and handed it to me. "Here's my cell number if you change your mind. I'm staying in the area this week, and I would consider it an honor if you called."

I glanced down at his card, then back at him. "I'll think about it."

"I hope so. Thanks again." He shook my hand heartily and walked out of the store.

"Who was that cutie pie?" my sister whispered.

I whipped around and gave her a hug. "I didn't realize you were finished. How are you?"

"Great. I've missed you. I was wondering when you'd come in to see me."

"I'm sorry I didn't come by sooner, but we've been running around forever, dealing with the cave treasures and getting the exhibit prepared."

She smiled. "You and Derek always cause such excitement when you come to Dharma."

I laughed. "Oh yeah, excitement is one word for it. Look, Derek is waiting for me over at Umbria, but can we get together for lunch sometime this week?"

"Absolutely. I'm dying to tell you about London's latest claim to fame."

"Oh no. Is she having triplets?"

China laughed. Our youngest sister, London, was always doing something that was so much more fabulous than any of us had ever done. For instance, when China's darling baby, Hannah, was born, London used the occasion to announce that she was pregnant with twins. We loved London to death, but we also enjoyed giving her grief.

London, who had been named after London, Ontario, Canada, where my mother went into labor after a Grateful Dead show, never minded our teasing. As the youngest, she was used to it.

Rather than name their children lovely, classic, *solid* names, as my mother had described *Elizabeth's*, my parents had chosen to name us after the cities in which we were either conceived or born. Because my parents had been rabid Grateful Dead fans, most of those cities were places in which the revered band had once performed. The one exception was my sister China, who was born after a protest march at the Naval Air Weapons Station at China Lake, out in the Mojave Desert.

I promised China I would call her in a few days and grabbed her for a hug good-bye, then jogged across the street to Umbria, where I found Derek in the middle of a Primitivo wine flight. Wine flights had been popular for years and were a good way to learn more about the different types of wines. A bar or winery would offer three half glasses of either the same wine from different vintages, or three red wines of varying color or richness, or three of the exact same wine that had been stored in three different types of oak barrels. Places were always coming up with new themes for their wine flights. It was a fun way to figure out how to distinguish one wine from the next.

The last time we'd visited Dharma, my father had been raving about the Primitivo grapes he had planted. They were said to possess the exact same genetic characteristics as Zinfandel, but the wines tended to be different in color, richness, and levels of earthiness. It made sense, of course, given what we already knew about the *terroir*.

Derek stood when he saw me approaching and pulled out a bar stool for me. "Darling, you're just in time to rescue me from this diabolical bartender."

"You poor thing." I sat down and smiled at the man behind the bar. I'd known him for years. "Hi, Lance."

"Hey, Brooklyn. We just added this Primitivo wine flight to our list. Would you like to try it?"

"Not tonight, thanks. I'll just help Derek with his."

I took a sip of the lightest of the three wines in the order. It was an old-vine Zinfandel from a vineyard up in Geyserville. "I like that."

"I thought you would." Lance handed me the second glass. "This is the Primitivo. It's from Abruzzi in Southern Italy."

I held up the glass and admired the color, then took a sip. "This is spicier than the first one."

"I thought so, too."

I took another small sip and savored it. "I'm getting a hint of toasted almond."

"Very good, love. I tasted more vanilla than almond."

"That's the oak you're both tasting," Lance explained. He handed me the third glass. "Here's the Barbera."

I swirled the wine, feeling only slightly pretentious. But since this was wine country, I was hardly alone. "This color is beautiful. It's the deepest of the three."

"As it should be," Derek said.

"This is the kind of wine that stains my teeth."

"We'll only have a sip or two."

I smiled and took that sip and tasted its light, sour-cherry essence. "Strange that it's so dark in color, but light in flavor."

"That's what makes it a perfect everyday wine," Lance said. "Except for the unfortunate teeth-staining part."

After a few more sips of the three wines, our hostess arrived and Derek paid the bar bill. As soon as we were seated at our table, I started to tell Derek about running into Josh Atherton. But before I could get a full sentence out, we were interrupted by our waiter, who approached with two fresh glasses of red wine and set them in front of us.

"We didn't order these," Derek murmured to the waiter.

"From the gentleman and lady over there," he said, pointing.

We turned and saw two of the reporters from our press conference at city hall. They were easy to recognize because they both had red hair and freckles. The man was short and heavy and wore denim overalls with a Hawaiian shirt, while the woman was almost six feet tall and wore a bright yellow jumpsuit with turquoise high-top tennis shoes. She was the spiky redhead who had asked the question about access to the caves. Together they were the oddest, brightest, most interesting-looking couple I'd seen in a while. And for someone living in San Francisco, that was saying a lot.

They were watching us eagerly, and since it was too late to refuse the wine, we smiled and held up our glasses in a toast. The two grinned at each other and came to our table.

"We just wanted to say a quick thank-you," the woman said, extending her hand. "I'm Darlene Smith."

"And I'm Shawn Jones," the man said. We all shook hands.

Darlene grinned. "We have a popular Bay Area news blog called Alias Smith and Jones. Not exactly original, but we've gotten a lot of mileage out of it."

"It's clever," I said. "I've heard of it."

"It's got a pretty good following, if I do say so myself," Shawn said.

"Listen," Darlene said. "We won't take up your time, but we wanted to thank you for recommending the photo exhibit. You were right—it answered a lot of questions. So . . . thanks."

"You're welcome," I said politely. "I'm glad it helped."

"Was that your mother working there?" Shawn asked. "With the blond ponytail? You two look a lot alike. Pretty."

I gave him a questioning look. "I'm not sure . . ."

Darlene rolled her eyes and elbowed Shawn in the ribs. "Dude, you sound like a stalker." She turned back to me. "Don't listen to him. We met a lovely woman named Becky, and she told us her daughter had given a press conference at city hall. We figured it was you."

"Ah." I smiled tightly, wondering what in the world my mother had told them. They were, after all, reporters, and easy to talk to, it seemed. "Yeah, that's my mom."

"She's a kick in the pants," Shawn said, rubbing his side where Darlene's elbow had made contact. "And a real beauty, just saying. She was doing the whole tour guide thing and working in a lot of her own opinions and thoughts about the caves. I wrote it all down. Really great stuff."

"I hope so." But inside I was thinking, *Oh dear, I can't wait for the exposé.*

"We're interrupting your dinner," Darlene said suddenly, nailing her partner with another elbow to the rib cage. "Let's go, Shawn. Just wanted to thank you guys again."

"You're welcome," Derek said. "Thank you for the wine. Very kind of you."

Darlene leaned closer to me and said, "Oh, honey. That voice of his makes me want to swoon." Then she pulled Shawn away and waved over her shoulder. "Great to meet you two!"

Derek and I stared at each other for a full thirty seconds before we could speak again.

No doubt about it, we were going to need more wine.

Chapter Ten

By the time I left to meet Trudy's friend Elizabeth for lunch on Thursday, I'd heard from four people who had been approached by Josh Atherton for interviews. According to China, who called me first thing, he was so nice, she couldn't say no.

His questions were good ones, too. More penetrating and insightful than the usual, "What would you do with the treasure?" According to China, most of the reporters had been asking the same litany of questions.

"And Josh is awfully cute," she added. "I was thinking I might set him up with Annie."

Annie, Abraham's once-estranged daughter, had met her father just before he died. A month after that, her mother had passed away from a long illness. Annie had decided to move to Dharma to regroup and start over, thanks to so many of Abraham's friends welcoming her as they would a beloved family member. She moved into Abraham's beautiful home, and, months later, she opened an upscale kitchenware shop on the Lane and business was booming. Annie had made a place for herself here.

"Josh is pretty cute," I agreed. "But don't forget he's a reporter and he's looking for ways to boost his story. I wouldn't get too close to him until the story's been written and published. And frankly, I doubt he'll stick around once that happens."

"Well, he's nice and Annie's lonely, so maybe I'll drop a hint or two."

I smiled as I hung up the phone. China was a much more open, generous person than I was. Of course, I'd seen the seamier side of life and no longer had the ability to openly trust people as she did. And didn't that make me sound like an old warhorse? I hated the thought that living in the city might've made me more cynical than my sisters who'd remained in the wine country.

Talking to China reminded me that I hadn't been over to see Annie at her store yet. It would be easy to drop by after lunch and say hello. I'd already been to the house to use Abraham's workshop this week, so I really needed to make the effort to see her in person and thank her.

China's phone call also reminded me that I wanted to look up Josh's credentials. Especially if he was going to go out with Annie, whom my mother considered an adopted daughter. I went online and checked the *Antiquities* Web site. The magazine came out bimonthly and had an extensive online presence. Josh was a senior editor and wrote several articles for each issue as well as a blog column once a week for the Web site.

I clicked onto a few of his articles to get an idea of his style. His personality seemed to come through in the narrative, which was completely accessible and entertaining. I wasn't used to that in an academic journal. To compare, I checked a few of his colleagues' works and found them much drier. They were a little more educational, but not fun at all. Some were downright boring.

It was good to know that Josh was exactly who he claimed to be. But I still wouldn't rush to recommend him as a date for Annie—not that my opinion would keep China from doing so.

I pulled up in front of Trudy's and saw her standing on the front porch with an attractive woman about my age. They were waiting for me, I realized, and I wondered if they'd come outside to avoid dealing with Amelia.

Maybe I was projecting, but I was still grateful to avoid the grumpy woman.

"Hi," I said, strolling up the walkway.

"Oh, Brooklyn, you made it," Trudy said, pressing a hand to her chest. Had she been nervous that I wouldn't?

I took a quick glance at my wristwatch. I was right on time. Was she that anxious to get rid of Elizabeth? Or was Amelia making life difficult for her?

The other woman bounced down the steps and extended her arm to shake my hand. "Hi, I'm Elizabeth Trent. It's so nice to meet you."

"I'm Brooklyn Wainwright. It's good to meet you, too."

I liked her immediately because of her open smile and obvious warmth. Elizabeth Trent was just plain beautiful, with long black hair, intelligent brown eyes, and olive skin. She was my height, and she wore khaki cargo pants with a white blouse and brown flats. It was uncanny how similar our outfits were—tan jeans, white blouse, and brown flats. What were the chances?

I started to walk up to the porch, but Trudy waved me away. "You girls go on now. No need to stick around and keep me company."

"Okay," I said, "but I'll stop to visit with you on the way back."

"You're a sweet peach. Now go have a good time. And thank you again, Brooklyn. I know Elizabeth will enjoy herself with you."

We both waved and climbed into my car. Elizabeth gave me a look of sheer appreciation. "Thank you so much. Trudy is wonderful, but it's nice to get out and meet people."

Driving off toward the center of town, I asked, "And how's Amelia handling things?"

"Oh." Elizabeth paused. "She seems nice."

I burst out laughing. "She's a toad, but she's a good companion for Trudy. At least, that's what my mother keeps telling me."

Elizabeth was openly relieved to hear me say what she was probably thinking. "She's friendly enough with Trudy, but I'm definitely not one of her favorites."

"Trust me. Compared to her feelings for me, she's probably deeply in love with you."

She shook her head. "I seriously doubt it."

"Oh, Amelia has no favorites. Ever. About anything or anybody." We shared a few Amelia stories, and by the time we reached the Lane and parked, we were laughing like old friends.

As we walked down the sidewalk, I pointed out spots of interest, such as the park surrounding the town hall at the end of the Lane, the in-town tasting rooms for some of the local wineries, and a few of the better restaurants, notably, my sister's Arugula.

Elizabeth gazed into each of the store windows as we passed and finally stopped to look at the items on display in the pottery shop window. "I'm going to have to devote an entire day to shopping. These stores are calling my name."

"They do that to me, too."

"The whole town is so pretty." She pointed to the row of shops across the street, one of which was China's Warped. "I love the vines growing on the buildings and all the old stone and brick facades. It's got a real old-world charm."

"I agree. If you have time after lunch, I thought we'd go over to the town hall, and I'll show you our new exhibit."

"I'd like to see it."

We walked past another few stores and stopped at the corner. "We're going to lunch across the street. I hope you like Mexican food."

"I love it," she said. "I can't get decent Mexican food where I live."

"That's a tragedy." We crossed the street and walked into El Diablo. "Here we are."

"The Devil," she said with a laugh. "What a great name."

We walked into the cool, dark restaurant. The hostess took us to a comfortable booth where a waiter appeared with chips and salsa.

Elizabeth grabbed a chip, dragged it through the salsa, and took a bite. "This salsa is fantastic."

"Everything's good here. It may be a little early, but if you like margaritas, they serve the best in the world."

"I'd love one, but I probably shouldn't indulge at lunch." She brightened. "Maybe I'll come back for dinner."

I grinned. "Excellent plan."

She crunched down on another crispy, salty chip and sighed. "I'm in heaven."

Once we'd placed our orders, Elizabeth said, "Thank you again for playing tour guide. I really appreciate it."

"It's no problem. I'm having a good time." I took a sip of water and leaned back against the classic tuck-and-roll vinyl fabric of the booth. "So, where are you living that you can't get good Mexican food? I need to know so I don't go there."

She laughed. "I live in a small town in Michigan, in the upper peninsula. I know they have some good Mexican restaurants in that part of the world, but not in my town."

"Were you born and raised there?"

"Not really. I was a navy brat, so I grew up all over the place. Even spent two years in Sicily."

"We have a naval base in Sicily?"

"Yes, we do. It was fun living there, but being a kid, I naturally whined about going home to Michigan most of the time. And once I got home, I couldn't wait to leave again."

"No wonder I can't place your accent."

"It's because I'm a mutt," she said. "I even affected an Italian accent for years after we left Sicily. I was such an annoying child."

"I'm pretty sure we were all annoying children."

"Absolutely," she said. "It's the role of children everywhere to annoy adults."

I smiled. "We sound so cynical."

"Maybe that's why we're getting along so well."

Chuckling, I grabbed another chip, dunked it into the salsa, and popped it into my mouth. "So your grandmother and Trudy were old friends?"

"Yes, my grandparents spent their honeymoon here and returned every year for vacation. At some point, Grandma Reenie met Trudy, and they became friends. After that, they corresponded and got together every year. Grandma died last year, and I haven't been very good about contacting her old friends."

"You can't be expected to do it all right away."

"I guess not." Idly, she dragged the edge of one chip through the salsa and seemed to study the pattern it made. "I had a hard time for a while. I think I fell into a depression, although I didn't recognize it at the time. Grandma was my only living relative, and we were really close."

"I'm so sorry." I already liked Elizabeth. Knowing that she'd been alone and hurting made me feel for her. "Is Reenie your grandmother's nickname?"

"Yes, short for Irene."

"Was she Irish?"

"Can you tell?" Elizabeth laughed. "She was my mom's mother. Mom was Irish down to her toes, with beautiful strawberry blond hair and a peaches and cream complexion." She brushed her hand over her head of dark hair. "Naturally, I take after my dad."

"Your hair is gorgeous."

She laughed. "I wasn't fishing for a compliment, but thank you."

There was a short pause, and we both reached for the chips.

Elizabeth sighed. "I've been doing better lately, contacting Grandma's old friends around town. And then I heard on the news that they found that treasure here, and I recalled that Trudy lived nearby, so I gave her a call. And it was the best thing I could've done. She reminds me of my grandmother in so many ways."

"That's wonderful. I hope you two have a great visit."

"I think we will. We're going champagne tasting tomorrow."

I laughed. "How fun."

I recommended a few good champagne houses, and we settled into an easy conversation over *poblano chiles rellenos* and *tacos al carbón*.

After lunch, we walked over to the town hall in the middle of the park. On the way, I explained that we'd decided to take pictures of the artwork and items we'd found in the caves and display them for anyone interested in the story. "Not only is the discovery historically important, but there are also a lot of families with a vested interest in keeping these items safe. So we decided to keep everything locked up in the storage caves and created this exhibit for the families and the community to enjoy in the meantime."

"It's fascinating," Elizabeth said. "It sounds like you were dealing with a lot of disparate parties."

"Yes, and some of them are very unhappy." I was thinking of Henri as I said it, but a picture of Noland Garrity sprang to mind and almost ruined my afternoon.

"I should think the owners would be overjoyed at the discovery."

"Well, there's a dispute over whether the items were actually stolen or just accidentally hidden away for some seventy years."

Her eyes were focused on something in the distance. "I'll be interested to see the photographs."

"Here we are." I led the way up the wide steps of the town hall and into the exhibit space.

"Amazing," Elizabeth whispered. She gazed around at the impressive display, walked to the ends of each aisle to check what was there, and then headed straight for the group of pictures detailing the *Dancing Woman* painting, the one I thought had been painted in the style of Renoir. She stared at each one of the photos for a long time and seemed to have forgotten I was there. I was fine with that, just happy to know that someone could be so engrossed in the exhibit.

I left her alone and wandered over to the next row, where the photos of the furniture were hanging. I loved the details of the inlaid wood that Robin had managed to capture with her camera and my excellent lighting.

"It just figures you'd be here."

I turned and found Noland Garrity glaring at me. I couldn't think of anything pleasant to say, so I waited for him to speak.

"This isn't art," he said derisively. "It's a pitiful excuse. I get nothing out of it. I need access to the caves, and if I can't obtain keys from your boyfriend, I'll go directly to Robson myself."

"Robson is a busy man," I said, trying for the equanimity I'd seen Derek display. "If you need access, Derek will assist you. Just call his cell number. He made it clear, he's available whenever you are."

"I just called him, and he can't be there until three o'clock. What am I supposed to do until then?"

I checked my watch. "It's two thirty. I think you'll live till three." So much for equanimity. I couldn't help the snarky comment. What was this guy's problem? I wanted to smack him.

"You have been nothing but rude and sarcastic and—"

"Good-bye, Mr. Garrity." I said it quickly and walked away before he could insult or threaten me any further because I would have to pound him into sand if he did. For the next ten minutes I skimmed the outer edges of the room until I saw him walk out the door. I breathed more easily.

What a crank! I didn't care if he knew everything there was to know about art. He was a horrible man who didn't have a clue about how to get along with people. I just prayed that he didn't treat Guru Bob the way he treated me.

I would have to remember to ask Derek to check with Interpol soon. If nothing in the caves had been reported stolen, we wouldn't need Mr. Garrity's services anymore.

But I knew Robson wouldn't get rid of the odious man until he had done a complete and thorough appraisal of everything found in the cave. Robson had expressed concern that in the case of a family member dying and leaving no heirs, we would have to dispose of the heirloom somehow. The most equitable way to handle it, we decided, was to sell the item to a museum or reputable collector and divide the proceeds among the remaining families. For that to be done fairly, an appraiser had to establish its value.

"Hey, you."

I jolted, still nervous that Garrity might sneak up on me. But this was Robin, so I relaxed instantly.

"Hi!" It was always good to see my best friend, and now I'd have a chance to introduce Elizabeth to her as well. I gave her a big hug and shook off the residual effects of Noland Garrity. "Are you working here today?"

"Not today. I brought Austin and Jackson in to see the photos."

"That's great. I know they'll love them."

My brothers were only a step or two behind Robin, and deep in conversation, probably discussing dirt or something equally captivating.

"Hi, guys."

"Hey, Brooks," Jackson said, giving me a one-armed hug. I always got a kick out of seeing Jackson after having him gone for so long. He'd spent ten years doing some job he never talked about that kept him out of the country. Once he was back home, Guru Bob enlisted him to travel for the Fellowship and the winery for two more years. Again, the reasons for all that travel weren't mentioned, at least not to my mother and me. Apparently, Jackson was good at keeping secrets. In any case, he was home for good now, and my family was glad of it. For the past year, he'd been managing the vineyards and doing a great job.

I stared at the two men I'd grown up with and couldn't help but admire them. They were both tall and good-looking, with dark blond hair like my dad. Today Jackson wore a faded denim jacket over a black T-shirt with black jeans and boots, the original cowboy hunk. Austin was dressed a bit more in the "Sonoma style" with his chambray shirt tucked into a pair of well-worn jeans. And boots. Either way, they were both pretty hunky, if I did say so myself.

"What're you doing here, Brooks?" Austin asked.

"I'm showing a friend of Trudy's around town. We had lunch at El Diablo, and now we're checking out the exhibit. I'll introduce her to you when she's finished admiring Robin's photos."

Austin glanced around the room. "Man, this is great. The photos are fantastic." He wrapped his arm around Robin's waist. "You rock, Robbie."

"Thanks, honey." Robin beamed, and the twosome wandered off to admire more of Robin's work.

I looked around for Elizabeth but didn't see her. There were three more aisles of photographs, so there was plenty to look at. I figured I'd catch up with her in a few minutes.

I thought of something and turned to my brother. "Do you want to join Derek and me for dinner tomorrow night? I thought we'd take Elizabeth to Arugula."

Jackson gave me a sideways glance. "This isn't some kind of a setup, is it?"

I was taken aback. "No." I started to laugh. "I wouldn't do that to you."

"You'd be amazed to know how many people would."

"Uh-oh. So now that Austin's spoken for, you've moved to the top of the eligibility list?"

"Exactly," he drawled. "So don't try it."

"I didn't even think of it. She's in town for only a few days, and Trudy wants her to meet people in hopes that she'll visit more often."

"Sounds reasonable," he admitted.

"I'm going to ask China and Beau to join us, and Robin and Austin, too. I thought we could make it a party. But I understand if you'd rather not."

He frowned, probably because he realized he was misjudging my intentions. "Yeah, okay, I'll join you."

"Great. Tomorrow night at seven."

"I'll be there." Jackson walked over to the first photograph on the aisle in front of us. "Robin did a good job with these."

"I think so, too. The lighting is awesome, isn't it?"

He grinned at me. "I take it you helped with the lighting?"

"Yeah."

"Well then, the lighting is phenomenal."

I heard a sharp intake of breath and turned to see Elizabeth, staring wide-eyed across the room.

"Oh, there you are, Elizabeth," I said as I went over to her. "I wanted to introduce you to my brother."

She was trying to swallow, and I wondered if she was about to choke on something. I grabbed her arm. "Are you all right?"

But she couldn't speak. Worried, I glanced back at Jackson.

But he was gone.

"What the heck?" I scanned the room to see where he'd wandered off to, but I didn't see him anywhere.

Now, that was weird.

I turned back to Elizabeth. "Did you see where he went?"

She gulped convulsively, still unable to speak.

I grabbed her arm. "Are you going to be sick? What's wrong?"

She finally shook herself out of whatever state she'd fallen into, took a deep breath, and exhaled heavily. "I'm sorry. I thought I saw someone I knew, but I was obviously mistaken."

"You mean, my brother? Tall, good-looking, denim jacket?"

"Who?" She still looked alarmed and a little dazed. "Oh. No, sorry. It was a woman. I looked out the window and was sure I saw an old friend from . . ." She inhaled deeply again and let it out. "Um . . . but it wasn't her. Sorry."

I wasn't entirely sure I believed her because I thought she'd been reacting to Jackson. But why would she lie? And where had Jackson disappeared to? "We can check outside to make sure."

"No, I already took a second look, and I was mistaken. But wow, what a shock. Sorry." She laughed ruefully. "That was weird."

"Yeah, you looked completely flabbergasted. I hope you're okay."

"I'm fine now, thanks." She linked her arm through mine, and we walked toward another aisle of photos. "These pictures are wonderful."

Clearly she wanted to get things back on track and so did I. But I was going to be talking to Jackson about this. And Derek. Most definitely Derek. "Aren't they cool? Robin took them."

"Robin?"

"Oh. Where'd she go?" I realized I hadn't had a chance to introduce them, so I glanced around but didn't see Robin or Austin anywhere. Frowning again, I said, "People seem to be disappearing right and left today. Anyway, you'll meet her tomorrow night if you'd like to join us for dinner."

"I'd love to," she said with enthusiasm. "You're so sweet to include me. I'm having such a good time."

"I'm glad." We spent another half hour at the exhibit before we both decided we were ready to go home.

. . .

*D*inner at Arugula the following night was a blast. Elizabeth regaled us with stories of Trudy on a mission to find the best champagne-tasting venues in the region. "We drove for miles over the mountains toward Napa. There were so many treacherous hairpin turns, I didn't think we'd make it out alive."

"I hate that drive," Robin said. "I'd rather go twenty miles out of my way than go over the mountain."

"I'll never do it again," Elizabeth said. "Trudy was driving as well as could be expected, but still, it was scary. And then all of a sudden, in the middle of another turn, she slammed on the brakes and whipped into this driveway. The tires were screeching! I was clutching the dashboard for dear life. We were in the most remote area of the forest and, I swear, it looked like something out of a horror film. And then this tiny one-lane road opened, and suddenly we'd arrived at a beautiful little winery surrounded by acres of vineyards, where they served the most wonderful champagne."

"I've been to that place," Austin said, nodding. "It's really good, but you've gotta want to go there. Sometimes I think the owner makes it tough on purpose so he won't have to share his champagne."

"I don't blame him," she said, "but I'm glad we found it. Seriously, though, that road is awful. Is that how you get rid of tourists? You send them up the mountain?"

"Every chance we get," Austin said with a blasé wave of his hand, and everyone laughed.

Everyone but my brother Jackson, I thought with annoyance. He'd canceled on me at the last minute, and I was still miffed. Did he really believe I was trying to set him up with Elizabeth? Well, given her reaction to seeing him—or whomever she claimed to have seen—at the town hall yesterday, I didn't think he'd have to worry about her trying to finagle a date with him. Elizabeth had looked absolutely horrified at the sight of him. She'd insisted she was looking at someone else she'd seen walking outside, but I had a feeling she was fibbing. After all, as soon as she made that face, Jackson completely disappeared from sight. Maybe he saw her first and took off running.

Why?

I might've been imagining the whole thing. Either way, I accepted that it was none of my business. But that didn't mean I wasn't going to find some answers. And it irritated me terribly that I'd completely forgotten to mention any of it to Derek. As soon as I got the chance to have a long talk with him, I was going to get his take on the situation.

I was curious. This was my brother and my new friend. My instincts told me that there was something going on there. Did they have some history between them? Maybe it had ended badly. Was there some way I could intervene—or was I playing with fire? I wasn't ready to do anything about it just yet, but I would if the right moment presented itself.

Since Derek had spent another afternoon dealing with the insufferable Noland Garrity, he was bushed by the time we got home from dinner. In spite of that, he went for an evening walk with me and Maggie before calling it a day and going off to bed. I spent a few minutes playing with Charlie and Maggie and checking my e-mail for any messages from my online group. There was nothing yet, but Claude had said to give him a few days, so I would have to be patient.

Since I was online anyway, I stopped by a few of my favorite rare-book sites to find values for comparable versions of *Journey to the Center of the Earth*. I wanted to be able to tell Robson what the book might be worth so he could make an informed decision on its fate.

The first American version of the book published in 1872 had just sold for forty thousand dollars. The description referred to it as "beyond rare," not only because of its age and its clean and bright condition, but mainly because no other copies of that edition had ever surfaced.

I made notes and moved on, searching for a French version published in the same year as my edition. I found one going for thirty-five thousand dollars and had to sit back and take a breath. High prices like this no longer astonished me, but neither did the fact that a book this rare and expensive was sometimes worth killing for.

Rather than dwell on that unhappy thought, I considered the story that the book told. I admit I'd never read *Journey to the Center of the Earth*, but I'd seen the old movie version. It had been one of my all-time favorites when I was young. I wondered again if young Anton Benoit and Jean Pierre Renaud had dreamed of traveling all those thousands of miles to find the cave that would lead them to the magical center of the earth. I believed they had had that dream, because what child hadn't? And I was especially convinced after I'd read the blood oath they'd written inside the book.

As I closed my notebook, shut down my computer, and turned off the lights, I thought how sad and oddly coincidental it was that the men's friendship had come to an end inside a cave so far away from their home. Had Anton known that Jean Pierre was dead? Was he the one who killed him? It was awful to think that anyone related to Guru Bob was capable of murder. But if it wasn't Anton, then who killed Jean Pierre Renaud?

I made sure Maggie was comfy and cozy in her bed in the den, then cuddled Charlie all the way to the bedroom, where I set her down in her little doughnut-shaped cat bed. My tiny kitten was growing up too fast. She was a few inches taller, and her pale fur was thicker and softer. Her face was just as adorable as ever, though, with tufts of light orange across her forehead and cheeks and big, inquisitive blue eyes. I gave her some light scratches behind her ears, and she purred as I gently admonished her to stay in bed. At home, she loved sleeping in her little doughnut bed, but since we'd been in Sonoma, she rarely stayed put all night. She hadn't ventured out of the bedroom and probably wouldn't, but I had found her curled up on the comfortable chintz rocking chair on more than a few occasions.

Derek woke up as soon as I climbed into bed, but he fell asleep almost as quickly after I kissed him good night. I chuckled to myself that Derek rarely went to bed this early in the city, but I guessed all this clean country air was wearing him out. Or more likely, the horrible Noland Garrity was simply exhausting to be around.

Sometime during the night, a low-pitched ringing woke me up. I blinked a few times, disoriented.

Derek sat up and grabbed his cell phone. I checked the alarm clock, saw that it was two forty-seven a.m., and almost groaned. Nothing good ever happened this late at night.

"I'll be right there," he said, and tapped the phone, ending the call.

"Who is it? What happened?" I had to shake my head back and forth to wake myself up. "Is somebody hurt?"

"Not yet," he said flatly. He was already out of bed, grabbing a shirt and pulling on a pair of jeans. "Someone tried to break into the storage cave."

Chapter Eleven

"I'm going with you." I threw on a sweater and jeans, then slipped my feet into a pair of loafers, and we were out of the house in three minutes.

"I'll bet it was Noland Garrity," I muttered as Derek drove the three miles to the winery.

"What makes you think it's him?" he asked.

"He's so arrogant. It just figures he would try to get away with something like this. I don't trust him as far as I can throw him."

"He's arrogant, but he's not stupid," Derek murmured. "Let's wait and see."

I sat back in my seat and tapped my feet anxiously until we turned onto the winery road. "Oh, hey, maybe it's Henri. He was angry enough to pull something like this."

"Perhaps, although he was on his best behavior during the tour of the cave." Derek turned into the lot and parked as close to the storage cave as we could. It was fifty yards away, and I could see some activity with Gabriel and his men, but I couldn't make out any faces.

Gabriel met us halfway.

"Did you arrest him?" I asked.

"Him?" he said, then shrugged. "Not yet. Thought I'd wait for Derek to get here before calling the cops. He's our interrogation specialist."

I looked up at Derek. "You are?"

He threw his arm around my shoulders and didn't bother to confirm or deny, which pretty much confirmed for me what Gabriel had said. "Let's go see what we've got here."

"A couple of clowns," Gabriel muttered, which made no sense, unless he was teasing Derek and me.

But as we got closer to the storage door and saw his men holding two people captive, I realized what he was talking about.

"Ma'am, please remove your ski cap," Gabriel said.

Ma'am? I watched the woman yank the ski cap off her head to reveal her shocking red hair.

"Darlene?" My gaze switched to the short man standing next to her. "Shawn? What're you guys doing here?"

"Uh, hi, Brooklyn. Hi, Derek." Shawn's voice was meek as he scratched his head. "This isn't what it looks like."

"He was using these when we got here." With the tips of his thumb and forefinger, Gabriel held out a small plastic case filled with a set of thin tools. I recognized them because Derek had a similar set. They were used specifically for picking locks.

"I can explain," Shawn said.

Darlene elbowed him. "You don't have to explain anything." She glared at me. "We're innocent."

"Carrying a set of lock picks and actually attempting to use them seems to indicate the contrary," Derek told her.

"And then there's this," Gabriel continued blithely, pointing to one of his men, who held up a crowbar in his gloved hand.

I scowled at Darlene. "You brought burglary tools and a crowbar, and you're telling me you're innocent?" I tried to block out the image of the fun-loving pair we'd met in the restaurant the other night. I needed to see them for what they were: petty thieves. "It looks to me like you were trying to break into our winery."

"That's crazy," Darlene said, trying to laugh. It sounded more like a harsh barking. "These guys have no sense of humor. We were just looking around. We wanted to get a close-up view of the whole area, the flora, the fauna, you know what I mean? It's our way of giving our readers the complete story."

"At three o'clock in the morning?" I said.

Gabriel and the others stood behind the guilty pair, arms folded across their chests as if they were all posing for the cover of *Dangerous Men* magazine, if only that were real. Gabriel was the only one who looked somewhat amused. I didn't see the slightest thing funny in any of this. I felt used.

"Well, yeah," Shawn said, his voice a little whiny as he hitched himself to Darlene's dumb story. "Late at night's the best time to experience the true sights and sounds of a place. No crowds around, no distractions. We're wordsmiths, Brooklyn. Creative people. This is how we soak up the ambience of a place. We marinate in the total atmosphere, becoming one with the setting. Our stories are better for it."

"What a bunch of bull," I muttered, feeling foolishly disillusioned and betrayed. But why? Did I really believe they were my new best friends because they'd bought us some wine? I needed to smack myself. I shook my finger at the security box in the wall by the doors. "Don't you get it? This place is locked up so tight, it squeaks. What were you thinking?"

Darlene wore a sly grin. "Shawn's got a knack for working his way around those pesky security devices."

I stared at her for a long moment, not quite believing what I'd heard her say. It was as much of an admission of guilt as anything would ever be. "Not tonight he doesn't."

Derek nodded at Gabriel. "Call the police."

. . .

I'm so bummed." Now that it was just Derek and me in the car driving home, I was pouting. "I never expected to see those two being dragged away in handcuffs. I thought they were so friendly and quirky, you know? Turns out, they're just common criminals."

"Yes, they are." Derek kept his eyes on the road, but I could see his teeth were clenched. He was as angry as I was.

"It was creepy, wasn't it? The way she was smiling there at the end?" I sighed. "I guess I owe Noland an apology for assuming it was him."

Derek glanced over at me. "No you don't, darling."

"Good, because I couldn't stomach having to apologize to him. But I'm really bummed about Darlene and Shawn."

"I think you'd be wise to stay away from reporters from now on. You have a generous heart, and they'll take advantage of that. No matter how friendly they seem, they all have their own agendas."

"Isn't that the truth," I muttered. Really, I wasn't so much furious with the thieving twosome as I was disappointed in myself. I'd assumed the two bloggers were just as innocuous as they'd claimed to be, and I couldn't have been more wrong. What did that say about my judgment?

Derek reached for my hand and held it during the rest of the ride home. We were both exhausted, but I wasn't sure I'd be able to sleep after putting up with an hour of *The Darlene and Shawn Show.* They were grifters! I was still embarrassed that I'd fallen for their friendly act.

Honestly, with everything I'd seen in the last year or so, you would've thought my rose-colored glasses would be a little dim. Guess not. Derek was right. I planned to avoid all reporters from now on unless it was an official query related to the treasures found in the cave.

My mind wandered back to the conversation I'd had with China on Tuesday. Had she already introduced Josh to Annie? I hoped not. True, he seemed a lot more trustworthy than Darlene and Shawn, but he was only here to obtain information, and he would do it by any means necessary. And what if he turned out to be no better than Shawn and Darlene? I didn't want Annie to get hurt.

Once Derek and I got home and climbed back into bed, I found out I was wrong about sleeping, too. I drifted off within seconds of my head hitting the pillow.

I woke up hours later with a kitten sniffing around my face.

"Hello, little thing," I murmured, and she head-butted my cheek, purring softly. How could I resist such a wake-up call?

And how could I resist Derek when he had coffee and English muffins ready for me when I finally dragged myself out to the kitchen?

"My life is good," I said, setting Charlie on the floor where she immediately pounced on Maggie, who didn't seem to mind a bit. I was growing to love the sweet old dog.

Leaning against Derek's back, I wrapped my arms around him.

"And so is mine," he said, squeezing my arms affectionately.

A minute later, I sat at the kitchen table. Derek kissed the top of my head before joining me. "What are your plans today?"

"I'm going to hide away in Abraham's studio and work on a few projects. How about you?"

"I'll be toiling in the fields with the menfolk."

It was a good thing I'd chewed and swallowed my bite of muffin because I burst out laughing.

"Why are you laughing at the thought of my doing an honest day's labor?"

"Because I think what you'll really be doing is drinking a lot of wine," I said, still giggling. "Not that I have anything against that sort of toiling. But mostly I'm laughing at the way you said it, with your upper-crust British accent, so erudite and sophisticated."

"Now why does that sound like an insult?" he asked, his lips twisting into a wry smile.

"You know it's not," I said, scooting my chair closer and touching his cheek. "Your erudite sophistication is just one more reason why I love you."

"You've managed to save yourself this time," he grumbled. "Pulling the 'I love you' card."

I rested my head against his arm. "It's my favorite card."

"Mine, too."

"So what's going on in the fields today? They're not starting the harvest yet, are they?"

"Not yet. We're going to walk the fields and check the grapes. Determine which area they'll harvest first."

"There will be wine, I know."

"It's part of the job." He stood, carried his dishes to the sink, and returned to the table. Taking hold of my hands, he lifted me from the chair and planted a delicious kiss on my lips. "I've got to be off. Think of me toiling under the hot sun, won't you?"

"I will. Mm, I can already picture you with your shirt off, all tanned and hot and sweaty and—"

"You have an evil streak," he whispered, effectively cutting me off as he kissed my neck and the back of my ear. Happy chills skittered through me as his lips made contact with my skin. I barely kept from melting into a puddle on the tile floor when he let me go.

I looked up and caught his self-satisfied smile. With a friendly stroke of my hair, he chuckled and walked out the door.

I brought Charlie with me to Abraham's studio to give her an intriguing new space in which to play. She prowled and sniffed every inch of the workshop while I set myself up at the center table, spreading out my tools before studying the job before me.

My friend Ian McCullough, the head curator at the Covington Library in San Francisco, had given me a three-volume set of medical books to refurbish. The subject matter was pathological anatomy, and this set was the first English edition, published in 1772. The cloth bindings were in bad shape with tearing along the edges of the spine and joints. The front covers were rubbed down to the boards. The gilded titles on the spine had faded completely.

The set wouldn't be put on display, but because it was historically significant to researchers, it would be available in the library. For that reason, Ian had asked me to replace the old cloth binding with sturdy leather.

I'd asked him to specify exactly how sturdy he wanted the leather to be, an important consideration when price was the main factor. Cowhide, for example, was generally the cheapest and most durable leather used in bookbinding, but it wasn't as pretty as goatskin or calfskin. It was also a little more difficult to work with because it wasn't quite as supple and thin as the more expensive hides. But again, because of the historical significance of the books, Ian chose to go with the high-quality, moderately priced navy blue morocco leather I'd suggested. With gold tooling on the spines, the books would be both handsome and somber, as befitted their subject matter.

Replacing cloth with leather was going to be a relatively simple job. The tricky part would be to make sure all three books remained a matched set when I was finished with the repair. The key was finding a piece of leather big enough for three books—or having two or more pieces with all the same characteristics dyed exactly the same color. Since the leather I'd chosen had come from one hide—and therefore been tanned and dyed at the same time—it wouldn't be an issue. I'd just have to make sure the gilding and binding were perfectly matched as well. I didn't foresee any problems.

Since volume three was the least damaged of the set, I decided to repair it first.

The cloth covering the spine was in sad shape, dangling by threads along the front joint. It was an easy job to cut away the rest of it and trim off the loose bits. I measured and cut a piece of thin cardboard to use as a spine liner, about the weight of a manila folder, and attached it to the spine with PVA glue. This would provide a more solid base for my raised bands than the original threadbare spine.

I had decided to add raised bands to the spine, even though there were none on the original clothbound book. These days, raised bands were mainly decorative unless the book was hand-made, but I thought the addition would provide a bit more support to the spines of these books.

A raised band looked like a horizontal bump stretched across the spine of a book. Back in the old days, the cords used to sew the pages together were tied in knots and stretched across the spine. The leather binding was then stretched and molded around the cords. Once bookbinding became mechanized, the raised bands were no longer necessary to hide the cords, but the look was maintained because it was an attractive feature.

Once I had the spine liner in place and the glue had dried, I cut the individual bands from a long strip of leather, coated each piece with PVA glue, and attached them at evenly spaced intervals across the spine. Later, when the leather cover was completely finished, I would gild the book title, the author, and the volume number in separate spaces on the spine.

Now that the bands were in place, I began to strip away the old cloth cover. I used a razor, cutting it from the fore-edge and then pulling the cloth easily across the board.

I was happy to find that the boards were still in good condition so I wouldn't have to replace them.

"Meow."

I glanced down and saw Charlie gazing up at me, her little head cocked as though she were wondering what I was doing here since I wasn't playing with her.

"I'm sorry I haven't been playing with you, little one." I'd kept an eye on her all day, filled her water bowl, and made sure she didn't hurt herself. Mostly, she pushed her mouse around or napped in the rays of sunlight streaming through the windows along the south side of the studio.

"You've been very good all day," I said, checking my watch. "I think it's time to go home and see Derek."

"Meow."

"I'm glad you agree." Smiling, I picked her up and nuzzled her neck. She was the sweetest thing. I wondered if she would grow to ignore me someday, as cats sometimes did. I hoped not, because I was just tickled by her affection. I set her down and cleaned up my mess on the worktable, tossed the old book cloth into the trash can, gathered up my sleepy kitten, and walked up the hill.

Because of our middle-of-the-night sojourn to the caves the evening before, Derek and I had decided to spend a quiet evening at home. Thanks to Mom, we didn't have to make dinner. She'd prepared her famous taco casserole and had generously set aside a second smaller pan for us. It was an embarrassingly easy dish to make in the microwave, but I was still grateful that she'd done the work for us.

After dinner we took Maggie for another long walk along the ridge above my parents' home. We had both fallen for Maggie and talked about getting a dog when we returned to the city. If only we could find one just as sweet in one of the shelters around town. The only thing holding us back was that we lived in SoMA, a busy section south of Market Street in San Francisco. Would it be fair to keep a dog inside the apartment all day long except for the oc- casional walk down our crowded sidewalk? We did have a small park a block away, but was that enough? We decided to continue talking about it and see how we felt once we returned to our re-modeled apartment.

Monday morning, Derek and I were having our second cup of coffee and laughing at Charlie's pitched battle with her new stuffed mouse. Maggie got in on the action, bumping the mouse with her nose and swatting it a few times across the floor, causing Charlie to skitter after it. It was as if they were playing mouse hockey.

I was halfway through my bowl of granola with fresh blueberries and bananas, and Derek had just finished his. He stood and checked the time on his watch. "I've got to join a conference call shortly. What are you up to today?"

"I'm spending the morning at Abraham's, working on my medical texts. I want to finish the first book today. Afterward, I thought I might swing by and say hello to Annie. Do you want to come with me?"

"If it's much later in the afternoon, yes. I have a meeting with Gabriel and his team directly after lunch."

"Is something wrong with the security?"

"No, and we want to keep it that way."

"Good."

He took his cereal bowl to the sink and rinsed it out. The subject of security reminded me of the other night.

"Have you heard from the sheriff about Darlene and Shawn?" I asked.

"Brace yourself," Derek said, taking a last sip of coffee. "They were released on bail yesterday."

I grimaced. "I figured they couldn't keep them for long."

"No. They didn't actually break into the caves, after all." He rinsed his mug and tucked it into the dishwasher.

"I know, but still," I groused. "I just hope they were smart enough to leave the area."

"They informed the deputy who processed them that they were headed directly back to San Francisco."

"They'd better be." I was still smarting over the fact that I'd fallen for their friendly act.

Derek, aware of my feelings, gave my shoulder a soft squeeze before picking up my empty bowl and sticking it in the dishwasher.

"Thanks." My cell phone rang, and I recognized the local area code but not the number. "Hello?"

"Good morning, Brooklyn. It's Trudy."

My mood brightened instantly. "Trudy, hi. What's up?"

"I have a surprise for you." Her voice was brimming with excitement. "I hope you can stop by sometime today."

"A surprise? Can you give me a hint?"

"No, because you're too smart. You'd guess it right away."

I chuckled. "I don't know how smart I am, but that's all right. I'll just have to wait." I glanced at the kitchen clock and gauged how long I would need to work on the first leather binding that morning. "Would three o'clock be too late to come by?"

"Three o'clock is perfect, dear," she said. "See you then."

"Okay. Bye." I ended the call and looked at Derek. "Looks like I'm going to Trudy's this afternoon."

*D*espite my commitment to Ian and the Covington to finish the three medical books, my heart was set on taking some time with the Jules Verne book. I spent a half hour using my gum eraser to carefully wipe along the top edge of the book where most dust and grime settled. The soft eraser was also helpful around the edges of each page where stains were often found. I never used it near the printed lines because there was always a chance that I might wipe away a word. That was never a good thing.

As I turned each page, I could see what other areas would need repairs or deeper cleaning, and made notes as I went from page to page.

From my set of travel tools, I found the short brush with the stiff bristles I used to sweep away any minute bits of dirt and grime that had been ground into the sewn centers. It was important to get rid of as many of the tiny abrasive grains as possible because they could damage the paper.

After my half hour was up, I put the Jules Verne book aside to do the work I was paid to do. First, I cleaned off the table completely and washed my hands. Then I laid out the navy blue leather and, using the first medical book as my yardstick, I measured and cut the first piece, adding an extra inch to all four sides. After the piece was cut, the edges of the leather had to be pared, creating a beveled edge so the turndowns wouldn't be too bulky.

Paring leather wasn't quite the same as paring an apple. The first few dozen times I tried to pare leather had been complicated and scary moments for me. If I sliced away too much, I would ruin the entire piece and have to start over. I learned that the angle at which I held the knife was critical to my success—or failure. Learning what techniques and angles worked best took plenty of practice. And since I was left-handed, I couldn't always follow the person trying to train me. One great thing I'd done for myself was purchase an excellent left-handed paring knife.

I also sharpened my knife regularly using a whetstone and an old-fashioned leather strop. And I always pared my leather on a slab of marble. The harder the surface beneath the leather, the easier it was to do the job.

After I finished paring the new leather cover, I placed the piece on a large cookie sheet and added a thin layer of water to thoroughly moisten it. A few minutes later, I drained off the water and let it air-dry for a little while. I prepared my glue and applied it to the exposed side.

The moisture would make the leather more pliable and easier to stretch and mold to the boards. Since the leather would be moist, I wrapped the entire text block in wax paper, leaving only the front and back cover and spine free to work with. As every book lover in the world knew, moisture and paper did not play well together.

Once everything was ready to go, I balanced the book on its edge, spine side up. Picking up the sheet of leather, I draped it over the spine, adjusting it so that it was evenly centered, then used my hands to begin molding it to the spine and boards, stretching it as I went. I was working with high-quality morocco leather, so it had a bit of give, although it wasn't as stretchy as sheepskin. When I felt it staying, I began to trim the edges, being careful not to trim too close. It was always better to have too much leather than not enough.

Even though the glue would dry shortly, there was no need to rush the job. I just continued to smooth and press the leather evenly across all the surfaces in order to avoid air pockets. I returned to the spine every few minutes, using my thumbs and a bone folder to press and mold the leather against the raised bands.

"You're going to be beautiful," I murmured as I stretched the leather over onto the inside endpapers, creating the turndowns. I knew Ian would be happy with these books.

At the edges, I continued to stretch and press the leather until it overlapped onto the endpapers. I used scissors to trim away the excess and cut the corners, pinching them to make them fit together smoothly.

As the glue and leather dried, I could feel the leather shrinking a little, which was a good thing as long as I continued to smooth and press and tighten it around the folds. At the top and base of the spine, I used my thin, pointed bone folder to smooth and tuck the leather down into the spine so the headbands would show nicely.

I'd found that working with leather, even after hundreds of bookbinding jobs, was never an exact science. At this point in my career, the steps I took were instinctive; I knew what to do without much thought. I was incorporating years of skill and knowledge and experience—and adding a little touch of art.

And yet, every piece of leather was slightly different, so I was also applying a touch of science to each job. For instance, if a particular piece of leather got too stiff too quickly, I could moisten it with a damp sponge. I knew that wheat paste dried more slowly than PVA and absorbed more deeply, making for a more penetrating bond. But PVA was generally a faster surface adhesive, and I liked the way it worked along the edges of the turndowns. Each job brought its own new problems and solutions.

Unless I was attending a bookbinders' convention, there weren't a lot of people who cared to hear all these details, especially when it came to the intricacies of glue. I could go on for hours, but I usually stopped when I heard the snoring. My only consolation was that everyone could appreciate the beautiful finished product.

I took a break and ate the sandwich I'd brought with me. I used my phone to check messages, but there was nothing urgent. I was just waiting for the leather to dry. I walked outside and took a stroll around Abraham's pool and backyard area, then returned to the workshop to check my book.

The leather turndowns were dry enough, so I used my metal ruler and an X-Acto knife to trim them. They would ultimately be covered by new endpapers, so I wanted them to have a nice, even edge.

Finally, I cut two-inch-wide strips of wax paper and slipped them between the boards and endpapers to keep the leather from bleeding onto the paper.

After that, I slid the book into the wooden press until only the spine was showing, then tightened it enough to hold the book in place. I used my bone folder along the spine to further shape and emphasize the raised bands and the notches I'd made at the top and bottom of the joints near the headcaps.

I stretched my arms and rolled my shoulders a few times to get rid of the kinks and happened to look up at the clock.

"Oh rats!" I was going to be late to Trudy's if I didn't stop working right at that moment. With the book already in the press, my timing was perfect. I left it where it was, knowing that when I returned in the next day or so, the leather would be dried and the spine would be ready for gilding.

I cleaned up my work space, washed my glue brush, and raced home, where I took a quick shower and changed into a nicer pair of jeans and a sweater.

I'd managed to zone out while working on the medical book, but now I was curious all over again to know what Trudy's surprise could be. It had to have something to do with one of the art pieces in the cave. Unless it had to do with Elizabeth. Maybe she had decided to move here permanently. That would be a fun surprise.

"Doesn't do any good to speculate," I muttered as I locked up the house and jogged to my car.

I got lucky with traffic, and eight minutes later I was pulling to the curb in front of Trudy's place. I gazed at the pretty craftsman-style home and wondered if Amelia would be serving tea and cookies this afternoon. The thought made me snicker as I shut the car door and strolled up to the porch. Poor Amelia. Did she know how annoying she was? Probably not.

I climbed out of the car and glanced around Trudy's neighborhood. I'd been working inside for two days straight and hadn't been able to take advantage of the beautiful weather we'd been having lately. The air was clean, and the sky was a gorgeous shade of blue. I could smell hints of pine and newly mown grass in the light breeze. Someone must've lit a fire last night, I thought, because the smell of burning wood lingered in the air. It all reminded me of fall days when I was young, when school had just started and Halloween was right around the corner.

I smiled at the memory and climbed the steps up to Trudy's porch. I was about to knock, when a loud bang shattered the silence.

"What the—?"

That was a gunshot. I'd heard the sound before.

"Trudy!" I grabbed the door handle and found it unlocked, so I shoved the door open and ran inside. Trudy lay on the marble hearth in front of the fireplace. My stomach pitched at the sight of blood pooling under her head. Amelia was sprawled awkwardly facedown across the nearest chair.

"What the hell?" Rushing over to Trudy, I fumbled in my purse to grab my phone. I needed to call 911.

"Oh my God. Please, please be alive," I murmured as I knelt down and felt Trudy's neck for a pulse. Her skin was warm. I almost fainted with relief when I felt her strong pulse.

The floorboard creaked behind me, and I started to turn around to check on Amelia. But before I could get a glimpse of her, something hard and heavy slammed into the side of my head. All I saw was a quick flash of light before everything turned black.

Chapter Twelve

"There's my girl," Derek murmured, his sexy English accent drawing me back to Earth when I wanted to drift off to never-never land. He stroked my cheek and brushed my hair with his fingers. "Come on, love. Stay with me."

"Uhhh." I was seeing three of him, not that I minded. Derek did have the most gorgeous face I'd ever seen on a man. But oh, my head. I tried to reach up to find out why my skull was throbbing as though ten sledgehammers were slamming against it, but he grabbed my hand.

"No, darling," Derek whispered, giving my hand a kiss and a soft, comforting squeeze. "Let the paramedics do their job first."

"Para . . ." I closed my eyes and pictured Trudy lying in a pool of blood. What happened after that? My hands were folded across my stomach, and I wondered why they felt so damp. Were they covered in blood? I sucked in several great gulps of air to fight back the sickness that thought brought. My eyes fluttered open, and I wondered why firemen were walking inside Trudy's house.

"Trudy?" I uttered.

"Trudy will be fine."

"Firemen."

"Yes," he said. "They arrived with the EMTs."

I held up my hand and struggled to say the word. "Blood?"

"No, love. There's no blood on your hands."

I inhaled and exhaled slowly. Okay then, I thought, as memories of what I'd found on entering Trudy's house began swarming through my mind. Professionals were here, taking care of things. Even better, Derek was here. And best of all, I was still breathing and, apparently, so was Trudy. The bad news? "Head hurts."

"I know, love."

"Blood?" I guess I was a little obsessed.

Derek's dark eyes narrowed with concern. "Yes, a bit."

I gulped and tried to breathe. I could barely tolerate the sight of someone else's blood. I had even fainted a few times in the past, so I squeezed my eyes shut to concentrate on staying awake and conscious—and not thinking about blood. Mine or Trudy's.

When I opened my eyes again, Derek was watching me intently, but then looked away to scan the room. He gave someone a curt nod and turned back to me. "The tech will be over here in just a minute."

I could tell he was angry. Something was very wrong, but since Trudy was all right, his anger was probably due to my being hurt. Unless . . .

"Gunshot," I murmured, recalling the last sound I had heard before passing out.

"Yes," he said, through clenched teeth.

I tried to sit up. "Someone shot Trudy?"

He slipped his arms around me and eased me back to the floor. "Stay where you are until the techs are free."

"Someone shot . . . me?"

He touched my cheek again. "No, thank God."

I tried to think, tried to squeeze my eyes shut, but it hurt my head too much, so I watched his face. "Did Amelia shoot Trudy?"

"No, love," he said gently. "Just rest for a moment. We can talk about it later."

Amelia didn't shoot Trudy. Okay, good. But now I remembered what I'd seen when I first walked into the house. Trudy, bleeding on the floor by the fireplace. Amelia, sprawled across the chair. I met Derek's gaze directly. "Amelia?"

His jaw tightened, and he swiped his hand across his mouth in helpless fury.

"Amelia?" I was confused. Neither Trudy nor I had been shot. That left Amelia. But why would someone shoot her?

I must've gotten hit harder than I thought, because I couldn't connect any dots. So I stopped trying and slipped back into dreamland.

When I woke up, I was strapped to a gurney and Derek was gone. I could barely move my head and became anxious, but relaxed a little when I was able to spot Derek standing a few feet away, near Trudy's kitchen door, talking quietly to Gabriel and Robson.

I was glad to see Gabriel here, but Robson shouldn't be here. There was too much blood.

No, no. I was the one who got sick over blood. Not Robson. Trudy was his cousin, his only living relative. Somebody shot her, so of course Robson had to be here.

Wait. Did somebody shoot Trudy or did they shoot Amelia? I couldn't remember. Did they shoot me? My head was throbbing as if two jackhammers were trying to drill through my skull. Was it from a bullet? I couldn't remember what Derek had told me.

Damn it, I needed to get up and find out what had happened here. I tried to roll onto my side, but I was restrained by the straps. Frustrated, I yelled out, but even that small effort made my head pound and the noise sounded more like a low moan.

I raised my head and tried yelling again. Strobe lights flashed in my eyes, and now my head felt like it might explode. So maybe this wasn't such a good idea. My head fell back against the gurney, and I was happy to keep it there for as long as it continued to spin.

At one point I thought I saw Detective Parrish from the sheriff's department staring down at me, but I might've been hallucinating. Was she saying something? Her lips were moving, but I couldn't hear anything. I closed my eyes and fell asleep.

"Brooklyn, darling," Derek crooned a few seconds later—or it could've been an hour—and he leaned over to kiss my cheek.

"Home," I whispered.

"Soon."

Instead, two paramedics wheeled the gurney—with me on it—out to a waiting ambulance. Derek walked along beside me, holding my hand.

"Is this necessary?" I mumbled, and heard Derek chuckle. The sound soothed me as the tech pricked my skin with a needle and I floated into unconsciousness.

I gradually woke up out of a drug-induced sleep and found myself alone in a white room.

It took a little while to figure out that it was only a white curtain and that I was obviously somewhere inside the local urgent care center. I could hear activity on the other side of the curtain, and I desperately wanted to be a part of it. The fog was lifting from my brain. I needed to know exactly what had happened to Trudy and Amelia. Were they all right? And was the person who hurt them—and me—already in custody? Who was it?

Elizabeth!

I'd forgotten all about her. Where was she? Was she the one who got shot?

I took a few deep breaths and tried to do a little mental triage.

My head still ached, but it was a vague pain, thanks to whatever medication the techs had given me. It no longer felt as if my brain were going to spin off its axis, so that was reassuring. I checked my legs and arms, moving them slightly to make sure they were operational. Yes, they were fine. My stomach was good, too, as long as I didn't think too much about all that blood pooling under Trudy's head—and probably mine.

Nothing else hurt, so I figured I was okay to leave the room. I wanted to find Derek and get to the bottom of what had happened at Trudy's. I hated being left out of the loop.

I pushed myself up to a sitting position, and the world began to swerve. "Whoa," I whispered, clutching both edges of the narrow gurney. Maybe I would take things a little slower for the next few minutes.

"Isn't this perfect timing?" Derek said as he slipped through the curtain and into my space. "I thought you might try to make a move when I wasn't watching."

"Can we go? I'm fine, really."

"I saw your head wobbling just now," he countered.

"That'll pass." I hoped.

"Of course it will." He smiled grimly. "If you're sure you're ready, then let's go home. The doctor prescribed some pain medication to get you through the next few hours."

"I probably won't need it, but thanks." I started to slide off the table, and Derek grabbed me before my feet hit the floor. A good thing since I was pretty sure I would've kept going until my face was planted against the linoleum.

"Thanks again," I said, grateful to have him holding me up. "I'm going to be perfect any minute now."

"You're already perfect, love, just a tad unsteady." He had his arm securely fastened around my waist. "I'm not letting go of you, so as soon as you're fit to try walking, just say the word."

With the help of a wheelchair, we finally made it to Derek's car. It wasn't until I was buckled up safely inside the Bentley and we were driving home that I found out that Amelia was dead.

*D*erek carried me into the house and set me down on the couch with some extra pillows. I heard Maggie whine a little as she moved close and nosed my hand, then planted herself along the edge of the couch to guard me. Charlie jumped up onto the couch and curled up on my stomach. I wasn't sure I deserved so much wonderful treatment after the way I'd giggled and gossiped behind poor Amelia's back. And what must Trudy be going through, knowing that her companion had been killed inside her own home?

And where was Elizabeth?

After handing me a glass of water and one of the pills the doctors had sent home with me, Derek sat down at the foot of the couch and we talked about what had happened. I told him everything I could remember from the time I got out of my car in front of Trudy's until the moment when I lost consciousness.

"Do you know what else happened?" I asked. "Did you talk to Trudy?"

"We're piecing it together," he said. I reached out to rest my hand on his knee and felt calmer. "Trudy is still unconscious, but when she wakes up, we hope she'll be able to tell us exactly what occurred." He frowned and stood up, grabbed another pillow from one of the chairs, and shoved it behind my back so I could sit up a little straighter. He pulled my blanket up to my waist and tucked it under me. Charlie waited patiently until Derek was finished, then gingerly climbed on top of my stomach again.

"Is she too heavy for you?" Derek asked.

"No, she's perfect."

Derek adjusted the pillows again. He was nervous, I realized, fiddling with things while he figured out the best way to give me the bad news.

"Please, Derek. Just tell me what happened."

He sat on the heavy mission-style coffee table inches away from me and leaned forward, his elbows resting on his knees. "The best we can guess is that someone else was in the house with Trudy. They pulled a gun out and shot her, or tried to. We don't know why. Amelia ran over and pushed Trudy aside. The bullet grazed Trudy's shoulder and entered Amelia's chest, piercing her heart."

"Oh God." I pressed my hand to my own heart, appreciating its reassuring beat. It was painful to hear his words.

"When Trudy was pushed," he continued, "she hit her head against the tile fireplace and lost consciousness. Since you were close enough to hear the gunshot, I'm assuming the assailant was nearby as you ran inside. The minute you knelt down to help Trudy, he or she hit you with a vase filled with flowers that Trudy kept on the table by the front door."

"Are you kidding?" Now I realized why my hands and shirt had been so damp earlier. From the water in the vase. I hoped it wasn't something like a Ming vase. Of course, it would just figure that Trudy would own a Ming vase. But I was going off on another tangent and had to drag my brain back to the subject. "Poor Amelia. Poor Trudy. What did Robson say?"

"He's devastated." Derek shook his head. "It's too close to home for him. Nothing like this has ever happened here."

I nodded and felt the same disappointment and sorrow Robson must be feeling. It was as if Dharma had been living a charmed life since its beginning and now some of that innocence had been stripped away and would never come back. "That's true. Even the discovery of the body in the cave wasn't as shocking as this. Nobody knew Mr. Renaud, and he's been gone for seventy years. But

Amelia . . . I just saw her the other day. She was scowling at me."
I swallowed around the sudden lump in my throat. "Heck, when
wasn't she scowling at me?"

Derek moved to the couch, picked up Charlie and set her
down on my other side, and put his arms around me. Neither of
us spoke for a while. It was enough for me to feel his solid warmth
and the steady beat of his heart beneath my cheek.

A minute later, I suddenly sat up straight. "Wait. Where's
Elizabeth? Is she okay?"

"We don't know," he said, his jaw tightening again. "She
wasn't in the house when the police arrived, and we haven't heard
from her."

"Oh my God. Do you think the killer took her?"

"We don't know, love. There was no sign of another struggle. As
soon as Trudy wakes up, we hope she might know something."

I frowned. "Maybe she was out shopping. I hope she's okay."

"I do, too." He took my hand in his. "Can you tell me what
happened when you arrived?"

"Oh yeah." I closed my eyes to organize my thoughts, then
looked at him. "I was on the front porch when I heard the gunshot. I didn't even think twice, just pushed the door open and
went inside. I saw Trudy in front of the fireplace, and Amelia
passed out on the chair. I thought she was asleep or drunk or
something. It never occurred to me that . . ."

"Why would it?" Derek said quietly. "Why would anyone
expect this sort of violence to occur inside Trudy's home?"

"I feel so bad, though, because I sort of ignored Amelia and
went straight to Trudy. I knelt down to check her pulse and
grabbed my cell phone to call nine-one-one, and that was when I
got hit from behind."

"Did you see or hear anything?" he asked. "Smell anything?"

I put myself back in the scene. "I did, but it won't help anything. All I heard was the floorboard creaking behind me. I thought maybe it was Amelia. Maybe she woke up. Stupid." I rubbed my eyes and inched down on the couch, exhausted from the recital.

"Sleep, love," Derek whispered, and pulled the blanket up to my chin.

Two hours later, I woke up to find Gabriel and Robson seated at the dining room table with Derek. It was an oddly sweet picture to see these three powerful men sitting in the charming, old-world-style room. Lace café curtains framed the casement windows, and, outside, geraniums grew in profusion in window boxes. I loved the view from that room, but my head was still too achy to get up off the couch to join them. I did manage to overhear their conversation, though, despite its unhappy subject matter.

Guru Bob insisted on paying for Amelia's funeral.

"Does she have relatives in the area?" Derek asked.

"Trudy will know," Robson said. "As soon as she is able to speak, we will obtain the information and begin the preparations."

He sounded tired, but it was probably because he was so sad.

"I will attempt to persuade Trudy to move into my home," he continued. "There is plenty of room."

"You know she won't go for that," Gabriel said. "She's still feisty enough to fight you on it."

Guru Bob smiled, despite the lines of worry across his forehead. "Yes, I know. And I admire her lively spirit. But I am beside myself with worry, and I simply cannot bear the idea of her remaining in a home where such violence occurred. But if she insists, I would appreciate it if you would increase the security levels at her house."

"No problem."

"She knows her assailant," Derek said, not mincing words. "She saw the person aim the gun and kill Amelia. The killer knows this, so Trudy is in danger. However, I don't think moving her from her home would be the best thing for her. Especially not to your house, Robson. We don't want to endanger you, too."

He thought about that. "Then what can we do?"

"I'll move into her house," Gabriel said easily. "She's got an extra bedroom or two, and it'll only be for a few days, until she's well enough to tell us what happened."

I sat up on the couch and said, "I could move in with her. I could protect her."

Derek whipped around. "No."

Just *no*. What the heck? But the other men shook their heads in agreement with him.

"Sorry, babe," Gabriel said. "You're already on the injured list."

"I'll be fine by tomorrow."

Robson smiled. "I am grateful for your generous offer, Brooklyn, but I must agree with Derek. I will not jeopardize your health and safety any more than it already has been. And forgive me, but I have Trudy's safety to consider as well."

"I guess you're right. I wouldn't be much help in my current condition." But I glowered at Derek anyway.

Derek glared back until I raised my hands in surrender. "Okay, okay. You win."

Maybe he was right, but did he have to give me such a dirty look? I wanted to help. I knew I'd totally blown it when I arrived a few seconds too late to help Trudy or Amelia. Hell, I didn't even get a look at the killer. It was infuriating.

The front door swung open, and my mother and father charged into the room. Mom was carrying a heavy case.

Maggie jumped up and barked with delight. She ambled over and allowed Dad to pet her vigorously.

"Where is she?" Mom demanded as she whirled around, scanning the rooms. "Brooklyn? Oh, there you are. Thank Buddha."

Dad left Maggie and came to the couch, where he leaned over and gave me a light kiss on the good side of my head.

"Hi, Dad."

He sat down and held my hand as Mom set the briefcase she'd been carrying on the coffee table. She immediately pressed the back of her hand against my forehead.

"What're you doing, Mom?"

"Just checking that you don't have a fever."

"The killer didn't sneeze on me," I grumbled as I settled back against the pillows.

"Very funny." She pressed her hands to her stomach and breathed in and out. "You took ten years off my life, missy."

"Mine, too, kiddo," Dad said, sniffling a little.

They were obviously distraught, so I grabbed both of their hands and gave them a squeeze. "I'm sorry. But really, I'll be fine. I just got a little bump on the head."

Since my head was wrapped in yards of gauze and bandages, I didn't blame Mom for rolling her eyes at me.

"It looks worse than it is," I mumbled.

"Just stop talking," she advised, and opened her case to reveal a veritable pharmacopoeia of vials and potions and tinctures and God knew what else. Probably a tube of fairy dust and some eye of newt.

Heaven help me, the Grand Raven Mistress of the Celtic Goddess Coven was on a mission. And her mission was *me*.

Once upon a time, my mother would've dissolved into tears at the sight of my head bashed in. Now, though, Dad was the one tearing up while Mom was all business as she pulled out the ingredients to work one of her world-class healing and protection spells. As far as she was concerned, white magic would cure whatever ailed me.

Seriously. She believed it. The funny thing was, once in a while her crazy magic spells actually worked. But you wouldn't catch me saying that out loud.

I cast a pleading look at Derek, silently beseeching him to rescue me from Glinda the Good Witch. But Derek's eyes sparkled with laughter, and I knew I would get no support from him.

Robson gazed fondly at my mother as she prepared to terrorize me. So no help from him, either.

And forget Gabriel. Grinning shamelessly, he got up from the dining table, walked into the living room, and sat down to watch the show.

Mom pressed her fingers against the middle of my forehead—my third eye—and intoned, *"Om shanti . . . shanti . . . shanti."*

Peace.

I couldn't help but close my eyes and breathe. Repeated three times, the simple Sanskrit chant was meant to protect me from the three disturbances brought on by nature, the modern world, and one's own negativity.

I hoped it worked.

"I know you're in pain, so I'll keep it simple," Mom said, pressing two black tourmaline crystals into my hand. "Hold these. Visualize their power."

Black tourmaline. I'd seen Mom work with it before. According to her, the ancients had employed the stone as potent protection from demons and negative forces.

All black stones were protective by nature, but black tourmaline's power was further enhanced by its unique shape, a three-sided prism with vertical striations that acted as a strong deflector of negative energy.

Mom stood and closed her eyes. She reached out and touched my head with both of her hands, and began to chant:

"Goddess of Earth, Wind, Water, and Fire,

Grant me one wish I desire,

Protect my loved one from evil's spell,

Be ever watchful and guard her well.

Focus her power, make her strong,

Banish all that do her wrong.

My thanks and praise I offer thee

And as I mote, so shall it be."

A circle of white light surrounded me like mist in a forest. The black stones seemed to vibrate in my hands, sending waves of calming strength up my arms, across my shoulders, and down my spine. Glinda really did know her stuff. Within seconds, I fell sound asleep.

I woke up a while later, unsure how long I'd slept. It was evening, and the living room drapes had been pulled closed. There were no lights on, and the room was dark. Too dark. Almost depressing. I struggled to sit up, wondering where Derek was.

"Hello, gracious."

"Oh!" I jolted, and the sudden movement caused my head to ache. But I had to admit the pain wasn't as pronounced as it had been before my mother's visit, so go figure. "Hi, Robson."

He was still seated at the dining table a few yards away from me. "I apologize for frightening you."

"That's okay. I wasn't sure anyone was home."

"Derek drove to the pharmacy to obtain some instant ice packs and a heating pad for you."

"Oh, that sounds wonderful."

"Is there anything I can get you?" he asked.

It felt odd to be asking him for favors, but I plunged ahead. "Would you mind turning on some lights for me?"

"Of course not." He carried his chair over and set it down closer to the couch. After switching on several table lamps around the room, he sat and observed me. I figured I must've looked pretty bad to have him so concerned.

Maggie the dog shuffled over and settled at Guru Bob's feet while Charlie pounced against his shoe until he lifted her onto his lap. Ordinarily, Charlie would've been tucked up against me, but I had a feeling her instinctive kitty perception told her that Guru Bob was in more dire need of some affection.

"They love you," I said.

He smiled at Charlie as he stroked the kitten's back. "If only we humans could show one another as much pure love as animals do."

"If only," I murmured.

He returned his gaze to me. "I told Derek I would stay until he returned, in case there was anything you needed."

"That wasn't necessary, but thank you." I rearranged the pillows so I could sit upright and face him. "How is Trudy?"

"She is still unconscious, although the doctor indicated that she is recuperating nicely. She will stay in the hospital until she wakes up and is fully recovered. It could be a day or two." Even though his words were encouraging, he wore a worried frown.

I didn't want to sound like an alarmist and add to his worries, but I was suddenly nervous. "I hope they have someone watching her room. She's the only one who can identify Amelia's killer."

Guru Bob didn't respond right away. He was an expert at keeping his emotions in check, but the subject of Amelia and Trudy's assailant was testing his resolve. Finally he said, "It is such a blessing to have you and Derek staying in Dharma. Rest assured that he has already contacted his office to arrange a security detail and his people were quick to install a guard outside her hospital room."

"That's good." I gritted my teeth and confessed what I'd been considering for the last few hours. "I should probably move back to the city."

"Because you feel you have brought death to Dharma."

It was weird to be reminded that Guru Bob always seemed to know exactly what was going on in my head. Could he read my thoughts? Probably not, but he seemed to possess an uncanny empathic ability that most people lacked. Whatever his strengths, he blew my mind on a regular basis.

"We've talked about it before," I said, referring to my disconcerting habit of finding dead people. "But this time it's hitting too close to home. I don't want anyone else to be hurt. I feel awful about Amelia."

"And you blame yourself," he concluded.

"Well, yes." Did I? It sounded dumb to say it out loud. "Okay, I don't actually blame myself, but what the heck? I show up and somebody dies! It's creepy. If I were you or someone else, I would think twice about inviting *me* to dinner, if you know what I mean."

His smile broadened, lightening my mood despite my worries. "I used to get more sympathy from you," I grumbled.

He laughed, a deep melodic sound that was like music. "You know I have complete sympathy and concern for your feelings in this matter. I also am aware of your role in Amelia's life."

I sighed. "I didn't mean to be so antagonistic toward her, if that's what you mean. But she always seemed so annoyed to see me. I guess I let it get to me."

He sobered. "I misspoke. Let me rephrase my statement. I am aware of your role in Amelia's *death*."

"What?" It took me a few long moments to figure out what he was talking about, and I was afraid my face fell when I finally did. "Are you talking about that whole *Nemesis* thing?"

Nemesis was the name of an Agatha Christie novel in which Miss Marple received a letter from a man who'd recently died, in which he beseeched her to investigate the death of his son's fiancée. Guru Bob thought that, like Miss Marple, my destiny might somehow be wrapped up in seeking vengeance and justice for the dead who could no longer speak for themselves.

It was a little crazy, but how else could I explain my proclivity for finding dead bodies with such alarming regularity?

"Yes, gracious. I know that in your heart, you realize this, but let me make it extra clear: you are not to blame for Amelia's death.

That blame goes directly to the person who killed her in cold blood."

"I know, but come on." I flailed my arms for emphasis. "Don't you think it's a little weird that I show up in Dharma and within days, there's a dead body? And then another one? What am I doing here? How will it end?"

"I cannot say how it will end," he admitted. "But I repeat, those deaths have nothing to do with your being here."

"But—"

"Whether you were here or not, we would have opened the cave and found the body. I think that Amelia was killed because of that discovery. In other words, it would have happened anyway." He held up his hand to stop me from interrupting again. "Your reason for being here is clear. You are not the harbinger of doom, gracious. You are the bringer of justice. You will find that justice for Amelia. You will solve the puzzle of Monsieur Renaud's death. And you will do all of this because you simply cannot help yourself."

"I can't help myself." I thought about it and shook my head. "That makes me sound pitiful. And even a little ruthless."

"Not one bit," Guru Bob said with a tenacity I appreciated but didn't quite believe. "The last time we spoke of such things, you told me that each time you have been confronted with violent death, you've focused your mind on the loved ones left behind. Their pain. Their ruined lives. That is your motivation; that is your purpose in delving so deeply into the mysteries of why such a thing happened and who caused it. And that is neither ruthless nor pitiable. It is a most admirable trait."

Admirable? Sometimes I wondered, but I had to admit it felt good to know Robson's thoughts on all of this. "But the police . . ."

"You have never hindered a police investigation."

"I've tried not to," I said, grinning sheepishly. "But the police might disagree."

His smile was serene. "They are wrong."

Who was I to argue with a highly evolved conscious being? Especially one who was trying his best to cajole me out of my one-woman pity party? "Thank you."

"You are welcome." He bowed his head slightly. "Perhaps you will grant me a favor or two?"

I sat up a little straighter on the couch. "Of course, Robson. Anything."

His eyes narrowed. "Stay in Dharma. Recuperate from this attack. Then work with Derek to track down the assailant who has brought this terrible evil to our community."

"Derek wouldn't want to hear you saying that."

"He wishes to protect you from yourself."

"Yes. Even though he's perfectly happy putting himself in danger to find the answers."

"In truth, he does this best when you are by his side."

I had to smile. Returning to the city right now had never really been an option anyway, I told myself. And to tell the truth, I wouldn't have wanted to leave until Dharma was once again its peaceful, normal self. But having Robson call it a personal favor pretty much sealed my decision.

"I'll stay," I said. "But I'm afraid you might have to answer to Derek if anything happens."

He pursed his lips thoughtfully. "Perhaps we ought to keep this between ourselves for now."

"Good idea," I said with a laugh.

Chapter Thirteen

Despite my gauze-enshrouded head, I felt well enough the next morning to shower carefully and dress for the day. Over orange juice, a soft-boiled egg, and toast, Derek broke the news that Trudy remained in a coma. "But the doctors are hopeful she'll emerge within the next twenty-four hours."

"I pray they're right." I needed to ask a totally dumb question that had kept me awake for at least an hour in the middle of the night. "Did the vase break when the killer hit my head?"

Derek smiled in sympathy. "No. Whoever swung it wasn't able to do permanent damage to either your head or the vase itself."

"Small favors," I whispered. I would take them wherever I could find them. "I imagined I'd broken a Ming vase with my head."

"If it had been a Ming, you probably would've broken it. But sadly, it was harder than your delicate little head."

I chuckled. I finished my egg and toast, but lingered over my juice. "I feel like I've been out of it for a week. Is there any news? Was someone arrested? Have you seen Elizabeth? How's Trudy doing? Is Amelia being autopsied?"

"It all happened yesterday, so you haven't missed much." Derek smiled but turned somber as he began to answer my questions. "Amelia's autopsy is being performed today. I don't expect any grand revelations. And no one's been arrested. The detectives are questioning everyone they can find."

"Do they want to talk to me?"

"I called Detective Parrish to relate everything you told me yesterday, but they'll want to hear it from you eventually. I assured her that we would contact them as soon as you're up to it."

"Any other updates on Trudy's condition?"

"As of last night at eight o'clock, there was no change. I'll call Robson after breakfast and find out how she's coming along."

There was no more news to report, so we read the paper and finished the last bits of breakfast in amiable silence. Afterward, I stayed seated at the table while Derek washed the dishes, dried them, and put them away. I knew he had to leave in a little while to chaperone the odious Noland Garrity into the caves in order to view the artwork once again.

"I'm not completely incapacitated," I insisted, trying not to sound too whiny. "I could go with you."

He gave me a look over his shoulder, then shut off the water and returned to the table. "Darling, less than twenty-four hours ago you were coshed in the head and came away with a bloody bad gash and a concussion. One woman is dead and the other is in a coma. The only reason you escaped a hospital stay is because I swore I would wake you up every two hours to make sure you weren't seeing double and slurring your words. So, while the doctor has given you a clean bill of health, I think you should stay close to home today. Rest. Take a nap, read a book."

"Sounds so boring."

"You'd honestly rather spend the day with Noland Garrity?"

"Ugh. Maybe you're right. But I hate knowing you'll have to deal with him alone."

"So do I."

"Can't we make him go away?"

He laughed and folded the dish towel, hanging it on the small rack under the sink. "It won't be a pleasant day, but I'll survive him."

"I hope so. I'll miss you if you go to jail for throttling him."

He chuckled. "I won't throttle him, I promise."

I felt a sudden throbbing and rubbed my head. "I was thinking I might have lunch with China, but I'd better not push it yet." Saying it out loud reminded me of my last lunch in town. "And you didn't say whether anyone's heard from Elizabeth yet."

Derek scowled. "I don't know. I'll give Detective Parrish a call to see if she's heard anything."

"You don't think she could've . . ."

He gazed at me for a long moment. "I don't, no. But it's suspicious, her being gone like this."

I didn't know what to think. I liked Elizabeth and couldn't imagine her doing anything that would hurt Trudy. But then, what did we really know about her? Almost nothing, except what she'd told me. And who was to say she'd told me the truth? But recalling what she'd said about her beloved grandma Reenie, I couldn't believe she'd been lying. It made my stomach hurt to think about it.

"Before you leave," I said, changing the subject, "can we call and find out how Trudy's doing?"

"Funny you should say that, darling, because I was just going to call Robson to find out that very thing."

"I hope she's awake."

He sat down beside me at the kitchen table and made the call on his cell phone. When Robson answered, Derek pressed the Speaker button so I could listen in.

"I am at the hospital now," Robson said, "and it is very good news. Trudy is awake and seems to be doing well despite her ordeal."

"That's wonderful," I said.

Derek agreed. "Please give her our best."

"Yes, we're looking forward to seeing her soon," I said.

"Thank you both for your kind thoughts. She will be pleased that you called." Robson hesitated, then said, "May I ask you to hold on for a moment?"

"Of course," Derek said.

It was a full minute before he came back on the line. "I am sorry I kept you waiting. I wanted to step outside Trudy's room to give you the rest of the news."

I glanced at Derek. We could both hear the tension in his voice.

"What's wrong?" I asked. "Is she really okay?"

"Trudy is fine physically," he assured us. "There is a problem, though. She does not remember a thing."

*A*fter calling to reschedule his morning meeting with Garrity, Derek drove us to the hospital. Guru Bob's news had been a shock, and there was no way I was going to sit around waiting for updates. We both wanted to see Trudy, even if her memory was temporarily gone.

And as long as I was at the hospital, I was determined to have this headful of gauze and bandages removed. I was pretty sure a simple, small bandage would do the job. I didn't want to scare poor Trudy half to death by walking into her room looking like the Invisible Woman.

"Poor Guru Bob," I said to Derek as he drove down Shakespeare Lane toward Ridge Road. "He's the one who's always being called on to comfort the sick and troubled. So who comforts him when he's suffering?"

"Looks like it's you and me," Derek said.

I nodded. "I guess we'll do what we have to do."

Derek took hold of my hand as he drove, and we talked for another minute or two, until the gentle movement of the car made me drowsy and I closed my eyes. The good news about sneaking a little car nap was that it would help in my healing process. The bad news was that Derek was probably regretting taking me along while I was still a little wobbly on my feet. The sooner I was completely back to my normal self, the sooner I could start figuring out who the hell had killed Amelia. Because if Trudy couldn't remember anything that happened yesterday, we were still at ground zero.

I woke up as we pulled into the hospital parking lot. Derek agreed to go with me to the clinic to have my bandages removed. It only took a few minutes, and I was looking and feeling much better after the new dressing and small bandage were applied.

We took the elevator up to Trudy's floor, and I was happy to see an armed guard stationed outside her door. I was even more gratified to see her looking so well. Someone had come by and fixed her hair. She was sitting up in bed, and Guru Bob was seated in the chair beside her.

"Oh, how sweet you are to come by," she said, holding out her arms to greet us. When she saw my small bandage, she faltered. "What is this? Were you hurt?"

I gave Guru Bob a quick glance, and he shook his head. So he hadn't told her anything yet? I could hardly scold him. He looked so upset, it broke my heart.

"I had a little accident," I said lamely. Derek, meanwhile, had brought two more chairs into the room and set them down on the opposite side of the bed from Guru Bob.

"We could be having a party," she said.

I smiled. "Trudy, do you remember what happened? Why you're in the hospital?"

"I can't remember a thing. The doctor says my memory is temporarily missing because I hit my head." She laughed lightly. "But I can't even remember doing that."

Derek closed the door to the room, and I moved my chair closer to Trudy's side. "It's not good news. I'm sorry."

Guru Bob reached over and took her hand in his.

"Oh dear. You all look very serious." She tried to smile. "Am I dying of some rare disease?"

I leaned in and held on to her other hand. "I came to your house to see you yesterday because you said you had a surprise for me. Do you remember what that was?"

She gazed at me blankly. "I have no idea."

"When I arrived, I heard a loud noise, like a gunshot. I ran into your house, and you were lying near the fireplace."

I glanced at Derek, who continued the story. "Someone was in your home, Trudy, and they had a gun pointed at you. As they pulled the trigger, Amelia ran over and shoved you out of the way. The bullet went through your shoulder and hit her in the chest. I'm sorry, Trudy, but Amelia died yesterday."

I gripped her hand as she gasped. She glanced from Derek to Robson to me, gasped again, and then couldn't seem to catch her breath. "No. No. No. No."

"I'm so sorry," I said.

Her eyes filled with tears, and she shook her head. "It's not possible. It can't be true. Robson, tell me the truth."

"Oh, Trudy." Robson stood up, leaned over, and pressed his cheek to the top of her head. He couldn't lift her up and hold her because her shoulder was bandaged.

I kept my hand locked on hers and felt her squeezing it so tightly, I could barely feel my fingers. I didn't care.

Derek walked out into the hall to find a nurse. I knew we'd dealt a crushing blow to Trudy's spirits. She would probably need a tranquilizer, and I wondered if she'd be able to come home as early as they'd said.

But almost as upsetting was seeing how distraught Guru Bob was. I'd never seen him like this before. It was perfectly understandable, of course, but I'd always known him to be so strong. He seemed to have aged overnight.

I had a feeling the best thing for Guru Bob—and everyone else—would be for Trudy to regain her memory and fully recover from this awful experience. But who knew how soon that would happen?

"Tell me everything," Trudy said abruptly, letting go of my hand and grabbing the remote control to bring her hospital bed to a fully upright position. "I want to hear it all, no matter how horrible. I'm heartsick and my head can barely accept what you're saying, but if you tell me the whole story, I might be able to remember something."

"All right," I said, thrilled that she was willing to act, not just sit back and worry.

Robson sat down just as Derek walked back into the room with a nurse, but Trudy waved her away. "Thank you, Lynette, but I don't want any shots or sleeping pills right now." She trembled and sniffled twice before her eyes narrowed in on Derek. "I want you to find the person who did this, and you can only do that if I can recall what happened. And dozing off for the next three days won't help."

Guru Bob's concerns for his beloved cousin seemed to dissipate slowly as Trudy spoke. He scooted his chair closer and took hold of her hand again. It seemed to comfort him as much as it did her.

Derek leaned against the wall facing her. "Can you think back to the last thing you do remember?"

Trudy stared at him for a moment, then said, "Dinner. Wednesday night. Amelia served my favorite, chicken stew with dumplings." She frowned. "After that, nothing."

For some reason, that filled me with sadness. Wednesday was the night before Amelia was killed. So she remembered nothing about Thursday.

I continued telling her what had happened. "When I saw you lying on the floor, I ran over to help you. I vaguely registered that Amelia was sprawled on the chair, but I was more worried about you. I didn't even think . . ."

"That she might be in worse shape than I was?"

"Yes. I'm sorry. My concern was with you. I felt your pulse and knew you were alive, so I pulled out my phone to call nine-one-one."

Derek added, "And she was attacked from behind by the killer, who hit her over the head with a vase."

Trudy's eyes were wide as she realized I'd been injured, too. "Dear God. Brooklyn, I'm so sorry."

"None of this is your fault," I insisted. "And I'll be fine. I've got a hard head."

She gave me a weak smile. "So much damage. Why? What in the world happened?" She took another glance at each of us. "I'm the only one who knows. And I can't remember."

"But you will," Robson said, squeezing her hand for encouragement. "Your memory will return shortly, and you will be able to tell us who did this horrible deed."

She nodded. "I will. I promise." Her eyelids fluttered closed. "I'm so tired."

I thought about asking her if she knew where Elizabeth was, but Trudy had been through enough trauma today. I didn't want to compound it by suggesting that her new friend had disappeared.

Lynette, the nurse, must've been hovering at the door, because she walked into the room just then. "I'd like you to let her sleep. She's been devastated by the news. Sleep will help her get her strength back and, in turn, it'll help with her memory."

"Yes, we'd better go," Derek said, looking at me as though he thought I could use some sleep, too. Frankly, he was right. I was exhausted.

"I will stay for a few more minutes," Robson said. "I would rather she have someone here in case she wakes up."

I walked to the other side of the bed and gave him a hug. "She's going to be all right."

"Thank you, gracious," he said.

Derek and I walked out of the room, just as another security guard approached. I was surprised to see that it was George from Derek's office. He had been undercover security when I worked on a television show several months earlier.

I looked at Derek. "I forgot that Robson told me you hired your own team for Trudy."

"Gabriel's men are busy at the caves, so it made sense to recruit a few of my own people. George is in charge of the security detail for as long as Trudy's hospitalized. He's doing a great job."

"Of course he is." George had worked undercover with me at my television studio gig last month. I had complete confidence in his abilities and knew Trudy was in good hands. It didn't surprise me a bit that Derek had gone the extra mile on this. But it did make me love him even more.

Smiling at his boss's words, George greeted me with a hug. We talked for a moment, then turned to leave, just as a woman dashed up the hall toward us in a state of complete panic.

I did a double take. "Elizabeth?"

She skidded to a stop. "Brooklyn?" She whipped her head around, looking for something. "Where's Trudy? I have to see her."

I stood my ground, unwilling to let her pass. "Where have you been for the past thirty hours?"

She seemed taken aback. "I was . . . I was out of town for a few days. Trudy knew I was going away. I was supposed to return tomorrow but . . ."

"But you're here now."

She shook her head as though confused. "Yes, because I happened to check my voice mail and heard a cryptic message from a police detective that something had happened. I rushed back home to Trudy's and saw the crime scene tape and called the detective back. She refused to tell me where Trudy was, so I tried to contact you, but there was no answer. So I called your mother."

"My mother?" I was getting dizzy from the twists and turns of her story. Frankly, I hadn't checked my messages since the attack occurred, so I rifled through my purse for my phone. Sure enough, there was a missed call. "Okay, it looks like you tried to call me. But where were you? When did you leave? How did you get my mother's number?"

"From, um, your sister Savannah."

"Savannah?" That was weird, but possible, I supposed. She'd met Savannah when we all had dinner at her restaurant the other night. "And my mother told you what happened?"

"She just told me that Trudy was in the hospital, so I raced over here as fast as I could. Will she be all right? I want to see her. What happened?"

"She was shot," I said bluntly. "Why did you disappear?"

She shook her head a few times as though she hadn't heard me correctly. "Brooklyn, I didn't just *disappear*. I've been out of town since Saturday. What in the world happened while I was gone?"

"Somebody shot Trudy and killed Amelia," Derek said. "Can you confirm where you were on Monday?" He was being blunt, too.

"Monday?" Elizabeth swallowed nervously. "You mean yesterday?" Her gaze was diverted to something behind us. I turned and saw Robson standing at the door to Trudy's room, listening to every word she said.

Elizabeth blinked and looked back at Derek. "I—I was out of town. I told you."

"Can you be more specific?"

She scowled. "No."

"So that's all you have to say?" he asked.

"Yes. Are you accusing me of something?"

"Not yet. I'm simply gathering information. Can anyone corroborate your story?"

"You mean, do I have an alibi?"

"Yes."

She stared at the floor for a long moment, then glared up at Derek. "It's none of your business where I've been or who might've seen me. I don't have to tell you anything. You have no authority over me."

I almost sputtered. The man had *authority* written all over him. And as far as the town of Dharma went, Robson Benedict was the supreme authority, although the Sonoma County Sheriff's Department might've balked at that description.

"True," Derek said mildly. "You don't have to tell me a thing. But you will have to tell the police." He pulled out his cell phone and made the call.

*D*erek dropped me off at the house and drove off to keep his rescheduled appointment with Noland Garrity. After all the excitement at the hospital, I spent the rest of the day sleeping and recuperating. I barely managed to do much else but sip from a bowl of soup that night.

The following afternoon, Derek returned home from yet another meeting with Garrity. As he fixed a pot of tea, we returned to the topic of Elizabeth's brief disappearance and her reluctance to tell us anything.

"She was right, of course," Derek said as he pulled two teacups out of the cupboard. "We can't force her to talk to us. But we weren't exactly interrogating her. We just wished to know where she's been for the past few days."

"I'm glad you called the sheriff." I was still miffed that Elizabeth wasn't willing to tell us where she'd gone. I'd been so worried, but now I was just suspicious.

"I'm confident they'll obtain more information from her than I was able to get."

"I really hate to think that she killed Amelia. I mean, she did go to the trouble of showing up at the hospital yesterday. I suppose that's a mark in her favor. And she did call the local police to find out what happened at Trudy's. If she was the killer, she would've just kept running, wouldn't she?"

"Would she?" Derek's gaze narrowed. "Perhaps she believed that coming back, showing concern, taking all those steps, would make her look innocent. I don't buy that angle. Until she's willing to tell us where she's been, I have to assume the worst."

We were silent for a full minute while he filled a small plate with a half dozen of his favorite English biscuits. Normally at this time of day, we might've been sipping a glass of wine and munching on cheese and crackers. But with my head injury, Derek had automatically switched to tea and biscuits. Just one more reason to love him. As he poured tea, I thought about Elizabeth and her lack of an alibi. Why wouldn't the woman talk? What was she hiding? And why?

It was all too confusing and depressing to think about, so I changed the subject. "The good news is that Trudy is feeling better every day." I picked up my teacup and took a cautious sip, then frowned. "My head is a little fuzzy still. I don't suppose you'd like to get a pizza delivered and hang out at home tonight."

"I would love to. It's my favorite way to spend an evening."

"Mine, too." He led the way into the living room, and we sat together on the couch. After taking a bite of a biscuit, he remarked, "You didn't even ask me how my day went with Noland Garrity."

"Oh no." My shoulders drooped. "I must have been so out of it, I forgot completely. How did it go?"

"I survived," he said wryly. "But I've come to the realization that he has somehow obtained access to the caves from someone besides me."

That got me sitting up straight. "What? No way. You're the only one he's allowed to go in there with."

"Yes, and I thought I made that very clear. But he was quite eager to let me know that he didn't have to kowtow to me. He has other means of access."

"He's lying."

"I would've thought so, but there were items out of place since the last time I took him into the caves."

I froze. "Out of place? Or missing altogether?"

"There were three silver candlesticks missing from the first cave. Originally they were standing on top of the large ormolu dresser."

"I remember them."

We both sipped our tea. It was a strong, dark blend and I marveled at the difference between this and the insipid tea bags I'd grown up with.

"I finally found them in the back cave," he said. "Behind some of the rolled artwork."

"On the floor?"

"Yes."

"That's just weird," I said, resting my elbows on the table. "Did you ask Garrity if he moved them?"

"He insisted that he didn't."

"He must be lying," I repeated. "Who else would move stuff around? The only person I can think of would be Robson. Or maybe Gabriel. Did you ask either of them?"

"I phoned Gabriel. He said he never would've given the fellow access, first of all, and second, he would never move anything. I didn't have a chance to ask Robson when we saw him at the hospital today."

"It wasn't a good time to ask, anyway."

"No."

"Maybe it was one of Gabriel's men."

"Possibly." Derek was frowning now and so was I. I didn't like to think about people coming and going from those caves.

"Gabriel assured me he would talk to his entire security team. And he insisted that no one could breach the doors without him being aware of it. So who knows? I'll discuss it with Robson when the time is right, and we'll get to the bottom of it. In any case, Garrity will be gone within the week."

"Thank God," I groused. "Because I am really sick of Noland Garrity."

"I'll admit he does wear on a person." Derek reached for another biscuit. "He was in rare form yesterday."

"I'm sorry," I said, sympathizing, but quickly added, "Do tell me everything he did and said. All the dirty little details."

Derek smiled, but the emotion didn't reach his eyes. "He tried to convince me that someone in Dharma has stolen something from the cave."

My own eyes widened. "He's right, sort of. I took the Jules Verne book, remember? And Trudy took her bird sculpture."

"Both of those items were already gone when Garrity arrived, so he's not referring to them." Derek shifted on the couch, turning to face me more directly. "He's insisting that one of the paintings is missing. The Renoir 'facsimile,' as he puts it."

"The man refuses to suggest that it might be a genuine Renoir." I shook my head. "He's probably right, but I would love it if he were wrong."

"I'll admit he's not working under the most ideal circumstances, but I'm not willing to let him take anything out of the caves. I don't trust him. And Robson must agree; otherwise, he might've arranged for him to work in a more spacious, well-lighted studio somewhere."

"Do you think the painting is actually missing? It might've been moved to a different place. Like the candlesticks."

"I'll keep looking," Derek said, but he didn't look optimistic.

So we had thieves as well as a murderer in Dharma. Someone who had access to the caves? It didn't seem possible. How could they have gotten inside with no one noticing, let alone bring out a valuable painting?

"I hate to mention a sore subject," I said, "but what about one of the Frenchmen? You toured the cave with them last week, right? Could one of them have slipped the canvas under his shirt?"

"I was watching them closely. Then again, if we're willing to believe that one of the Frenchmen could get away with it, then so could Garrity. Although I always watch him closely as well."

"Good. I don't trust him, either." I gave in and reached for one of the sweet biscuits. "What if Garrity stole the painting," I theorized, "and now he's making a stink over it because he wants to appear above the fray while at the same time throwing suspicion elsewhere?"

As theories went, it wasn't a bad one. Especially given Noland Garrity's generally foul attitude.

"It's possible," Derek admitted casually, although I knew better than to think he was as relaxed as he sounded. "Perhaps the reason he calls the Renoir a facsimile is to draw less attention to it. If it truly is a Renoir, the fact that it's missing would be a massive scandal."

"I don't remember seeing a Renoir listed on any of the families' inventories, so chances are, it's not an original."

"Good point, darling."

"But it's still missing." An idea was bubbling inside my head, and I had to talk it out. "What if Garrity met Trudy somewhere in town and charmed her—I know it's hard to fathom, but humor me. He's not a bad-looking guy as long as he keeps his mouth shut. Anyway, he talks Trudy into asking Gabriel or Robson to let her into the cave to visit some of her own family's treasures. Garrity sneaks in after her. And then maybe later, she invites him to her house to show off some of her own pieces of art. And while they're talking, he tells her he needs to go back into the caves, but this time she refuses to help him. Maybe she's getting suspicious."

Derek jumped in. "So he pulls out a gun and shoots her, killing Amelia? Do you honestly believe he's capable of that?"

"I think he's pretty awful." But I thought it over and came to a sad conclusion. "But no, I guess not. Even though he's a bully, he doesn't seem to have a killer instinct. Cold-blooded maybe, and cowardly, but not a killer."

Derek rose and walked to the kitchen, returning with the teapot. He sat and poured more tea into each cup before continuing. "I don't see any evidence telling me that Garrity has ever met Trudy."

"Thanks for the tea." I took a bite of my biscuit. "We should ask Trudy about him, just to be sure, but you're probably right. If she'd asked Gabriel or Robson to let her back into the cave, I think they would've mentioned it. Especially after she was shot."

"True."

As I sipped my tea, something else occurred to me. "Wait. What if it wasn't Trudy? What if Amelia was the one who met him in town? Those two sourpusses would have plenty in common. He flirts with her to get closer to Trudy. She invites him over to the house for lunch and . . . I don't know. Something happens. She catches him going through Trudy's purse, trying to find the key. Or something. She screams bloody murder."

"So he pulled out a gun and killed her?"

I mulled it over. "Okay, what if he was aiming the gun at Amelia, but then Trudy ran into the room to intervene and Amelia pushed her away? What if his original target was actually Amelia?"

"But why, darling? What could Amelia have said or done that would cause him to react so violently? I know you dislike him. I do, as well. But I can't see a motive."

"I know, I know." I slumped back in the couch. "It's all ridiculously far-fetched."

"I'm not discounting it completely. Garrity could very well have stolen the Renoir. And since we have nothing concrete to go on so far, any thoughts or theories are welcome."

I pushed myself off the couch and found my purse. Pulling out a little notepad and pen, I began to jot down names.

"What have you got there?" he asked after swallowing another sip of tea.

I grinned. "A suspect list. So far we've got Elizabeth Trent and Noland Garrity. Any or all of the Frenchmen, but especially Henri. And I'd love to add Darlene and Shawn, but I have a feeling they're long gone. But I'm adding Josh Atherton because he asks too many questions and he's probably going to go out with Annie. So of course, we need to investigate him."

"Of course," he said, smiling.

"Darlene and Shawn are the perfect suspects," I said sentimentally. "Alias Smith and Jones. Even their name sounds criminal."

"And they're quite friendly," Derek remarked. "They could easily have struck up an acquaintance with Trudy and finagled an invitation into her home."

"Wow, that's true."

"But they're so easily recognized with all that bright red hair," he said. "They'd be taking a big chance showing their faces in Dharma again."

"It could be worth it to them."

Derek's mouth twisted into a frown. "And they did have all those lock-picking tools. Although, truth be told, they couldn't have broken into the caves with those tools. Gabriel would've been after them in a heartbeat."

"But somebody got into the caves, right? Maybe they snuck in while the door was open. Could one of the winery workers have gone in there and left the door open for a minute or two?"

"Anything's possible," Derek said. "But Robson announced that the caves were off-limits, so I can't imagine anyone in Dharma going against his edict. Although it's conceivable that an employee would have to go in there for some legitimate reason. Even if they were locked and secured."

Something occurred to me. "My brothers probably have the security codes to the doors."

"And it's quite possible that they've gone inside once or twice in the last week or so."

"And if some felonious critter has been watching the doors, he could sneak in behind them."

Derek smiled at my words, but he quickly sobered. "That might indeed be the way Garrity obtained entry."

"Sneaky bastard," I muttered, and stared at my list of names. "Does Gabriel's security system make a note each time the doors are opened and closed?"

"Yes, of course," he said, contemplating the possibilities. "And the closed-circuit cameras record everything. It all shows up on an elaborate printout."

"Can we get a look at it? I'd like to create a timeline for all these suspects and add the security information to it."

"Excellent idea, darling." He pulled out his cell phone. "I'll set up a meeting with Gabriel first thing tomorrow morning."

Chapter Fourteen

Bright and early Thursday morning I followed my doctor's advice and took the last of my bandages off. I was giddy with relief that I could finally take a real shower and wash my hair. By the time we left for our meeting with Gabriel at eight o'clock at his house, I felt as fluffed and fresh as a pretty flower.

Derek drove for a full mile up a winding road high in the hills above Dharma. When he came to a stop, I was mystified. I hadn't even known this place existed until that moment. I'd grown up in Dharma and was familiar with most of the town's nooks and crannies and hideaways, but I'd never realized there was a beautiful home tucked away at the tip-top crest of Dragon Valley Road.

As I gazed down one side of Gabriel's steep mountain, the view was of green terraced vineyards with grapevines that seemed to spread out forever. On the other side of the hill, I could see the ocean in the far distance as the marine layer was beginning to break up.

His home was a modified log cabin, similar to Austin and Robin's alpine home, only bigger. There was a pool in back with a good-sized patio deck, and along the side of the house were three large satellite dishes. These were the really big ones, the kind found at television studios and around airports.

What in the world? Maybe Gabriel really loved television, but this was ridiculous. Then I remembered how he talked about his drones and wondered if there was a connection between the drones and these dishes.

"Brooklyn," Derek said, "are you coming?"

"Yes, but did you see those dishes? They're huge."

"Gabriel does a lot of communicating by satellite."

"Oh." I didn't even know what that meant.

Gabriel met us at the door, looking impossibly sexy in a black T-shirt and stonewashed jeans. "Hey, babe," he said, giving me a hug. He smelled delicious and made me wonder how a simple citrus-and-spicy scent could be so dangerous.

Derek smiled indulgently, secure in the knowledge that I considered him even more dangerously handsome than our dashing friend. He shook Gabriel's hand. "Thanks for meeting us on short notice."

"No problem," Gabriel said, and led the way down a wide hallway and into a small conference room next door to his office. On the wall was a giant map of the world with lots of little pins stuck in certain spots. There was also a map of the oceans and the sky. I was afraid to ask what all those little pins signified.

A full coffee service along with an inviting basket of croissants and scones was laid out on the credenza under the window. The view out the bay window was of the pool and spa.

"Your home is beautiful," I said. "I didn't realize you'd moved to Dharma permanently."

"It's permanent for now," he said, grinning as he glanced out the window. "I like it here. And being at the top of the mountain has its advantages."

"I'll say. Your views are spectacular." I could think of other advantages that probably had something to do with those satellite dishes.

"Can I get you some coffee or tea?" he asked.

"I'd love some tea, but I can take care of it."

"Okay. Help yourself to the goodies, too."

"Thanks." I took a blueberry scone and a cup of tea. Even though the coffee smelled delicious, my system wasn't quite ready for it yet.

Derek poured coffee for himself, and we sat at the conference table.

Gabriel handed us a thick printout of the security system log and pointed out that he'd arranged it so that the top three pages listed the activity at the doors to the storage cave. The hours were listed in military time. As soon as I solved that little puzzle, I was able to read the information more comprehensively.

I pulled my desk calendar out of my satchel and opened it to the first week we'd moved to Dharma. I angled it on the table so that both men could see it. Pointing to Monday of that week, I said, "This was the day we excavated and discovered the first cave and the body of Jean Pierre Renaud. The police investigators were in and out numerous times, but you didn't have your security up and running yet. Later that day, I found the note in the book, and on Tuesday, Derek and I found the second cave. Wednesday we spoke to Trudy and showed her the cave. That night, we all met with Robson at my parents' house, and he asked you to beef up security for the caves."

"Right," Gabriel said, "and the following morning, Thursday, my team was installing new alarm systems on the cave doors." He used a pencil to point to the first line of data on his sheet. "This first log-in time corresponds to that moment. We were testing the systems all day, so you can see a series of notations. They aren't as important as the times on the next page."

"That's the same morning I started my inventory list."

Derek consulted his phone calendar. "And later that day, we had lunch with the Frenchmen."

"That feels like such a long time ago," I marveled, "but it's barely been three and a half weeks."

"A lot has happened since then," Derek said.

"I'll say."

We went through all of our calendars and tried to match up our visits to the cave with the corresponding times on Gabriel's security log.

"I've got seven entries logged that first weekend," Gabriel said.

"We were in and out of the caves those first few days," I recalled. "I was still doing the inventory and you and Derek were setting up light trees to help illuminate everything. And the police were there a couple more times, weren't they?"

"Yes," Derek said. "And Robson brought a few members of the commune board over to see what we were up to. Everyone was quite excited."

"I get that," Gabriel said.

"It took me three days to complete the inventory, working a few hours each day." I went through my calendar and told Gabriel which days I was in the caves. He checked off the corresponding log entries.

"If my notes are correct," Derek said, staring at his phone screen, "that following Tuesday, Robson called us over to request that we talk to the press. He had heard from the town mayor back in France, and he'd already hired the art appraiser. Word of the discovery had spread around the world."

"Yeah, I've got that on my calendar, too," Gabriel muttered.

"And Mom did a cleansing ritual the next day, Wednesday morning."

"Can't leave that out," Gabriel said, smiling. "And it's indicated right here on the chart."

"Now it gets tricky," I said. "Because Wednesday afternoon, Derek went to see the Frenchmen to set up a tour of the caves for them. And Trudy heard from Elizabeth for the first time. It doesn't have much to do with the caves, but I mention both incidents because all of them are suspects as far as I'm concerned."

"How did Elizabeth contact Trudy?" Gabriel asked.

"Elizabeth called her out of the blue," I said. "She's the grand-daughter of an old friend of Trudy's. I guess that part's true enough, although we should probably double-check. Elizabeth told Trudy that she'd seen something about the cave discovery in her local paper, and she asked Trudy if she wouldn't mind having a visitor for a week. Trudy was thrilled."

"Sounds reasonable so far," Gabriel said.

I glanced at Derek. "By the way, it was during that same visit with Trudy that she gave me the letter that I wanted translated. I contacted my online group that night."

"Busy day," Derek said.

"And for the next three or four days, we were preparing for the photo exhibit. Robin and I were in and out of the caves, taking pictures, while Mom was setting up volunteers and such."

"Can you pin down the number of times you and Robin were there?"

I thought about it. "Okay, twice on that Thursday, once on Friday for four hours, and once on Saturday, but just for about a half hour."

Gabriel checked off a number of items on his sheet. "Okay, got 'em. Except there's another entry on Saturday afternoon."

"That was the tour I gave the French families," Derek noted.

"When did Elizabeth arrive in town?" Gabriel asked.

"The following Wednesday." I frowned, remembering something else. "Now that I think about it, Trudy waited until Amelia was out of the room before she told us about Elizabeth's visit. I wonder if Amelia was suspicious of Elizabeth from the very start."

"Interesting," Gabriel murmured.

"On the other hand," I said with a shrug, "Amelia never liked having anyone around, so maybe Trudy just waited until she was out of earshot to save herself the aggravation of an argument."

"That's the more likely scenario," Derek admitted, having met Amelia himself.

"I guess so." I checked my notes. "But wait. Before Elizabeth arrived, the horrible Noland Garrity showed up. He came on Monday, two days before the exhibit opened."

"What day did you go to lunch with Elizabeth?" Derek asked.

"That was Thursday, the day after the exhibit opened."

Gabriel leaned forward in his chair. "Were you able to learn anything about her?"

"She told me she lives in some dinky town in Wisconsin. No, sorry. It's in Michigan. She didn't give me the name of the town, but it's somewhere on the Upper Peninsula. She was lamenting that there aren't any good Mexican restaurants in the area. She's a navy brat. Spent some time in Sicily. None of this is helpful, is it?"

Derek chuckled. "It's a start, love."

"You'd be surprised what we can find out from that little bit of intel," Gabriel said, winking at me.

I was smiling back at him when I suddenly realized something and jumped from my chair. "Oh my God," I cried, pacing the floor. "Oh my God, I completely forgot to tell you this part." I stopped and pressed my palms against my forehead. "How could I have forgotten?"

Derek stood and put his arms around me. "What part, love?" He clearly thought I needed comforting, and maybe I did.

"I'm so sorry. I think this might be significant, but I have no idea why." My head was starting to spin from the exertion. Derek helped me back into the chair as though I were an invalid.

"I feel so silly forgetting to tell you, but there's been a lot going on."

"That's putting it mildly," Derek said, taking another moment to rub my back.

"Sorry to be such a drama queen," I said, feeling even dumber for causing that little scene, "and it's probably not even important."

"Tell us and we'll help you figure out what it means," Gabriel said.

"Okay. After we had lunch, I took Elizabeth over to the town hall to show her the photograph exhibit. Her attention was immediately drawn to the alleged Renoir painting. She forgot all about me and just stood there staring at that photograph. So I wandered around for a while, ran into the odious Mr. Garrity and exchanged a few insults, and after he left, I saw Robin. She was there to show off her photos to Austin and Jackson."

"I'm with you so far," Gabriel said.

"So I stopped to talk to those guys, and then Robin and Austin walked away to check out the exhibit. Jackson stayed with me, and I invited him to dinner the next night at Savannah's restaurant. I wanted to introduce a bunch of people to Elizabeth because Trudy's hoping if she makes enough friends, maybe she'll move here."

"That's the dinner I had to turn down," Gabriel said. "Sorry about that."

"I know you were busy," I said, smiling. "We'll do it again sometime." I frowned. "If Elizabeth doesn't turn out to be a psychopathic killer."

Derek pointed to the calendar. "That dinner was Friday night, so your conversation with everyone at the exhibit would've been Thursday."

"Right," I said. "Same day as my lunch with Elizabeth. So there I am, talking to Jackson, and he agrees to go to dinner with us, and suddenly I hear this big gasping sound behind me. I turn and see Elizabeth, who looks like she's seen a ghost. She can't breathe. And now I'm worried, so I turn back to Jackson for help. And he's gone. Vanished."

"Where'd he go?" Gabriel asked.

"I have no idea. It was like he vanished in a cloud of smoke."

"What did Elizabeth say?"

I rolled my eyes. "She made up this story about how she thought she saw some woman she used to know. I told her we should go find the woman, but Elizabeth insisted that it wasn't that woman, after all. She got over it pretty quickly."

"Sounds bogus," Gabriel said.

"I thought so, too. And then Jackson didn't show up for dinner the next night."

"Yep, definitely bogus," Gabriel said.

"I totally agree."

"So you believe they knew each other," Derek said.

"Doesn't it sound that way to you?"

"Yes, it does," he said. "I think we should have a talk with Jackson after we finish up here."

"Can you get me a photograph of Elizabeth?" Gabriel asked.

"I'll take care of it," Derek murmured as he typed a note into his calendar.

I'd watched *NCIS* enough times to know that Derek could submit Elizabeth's photograph to a facial recognition program and find out who she really was within minutes. Hopefully she wasn't some sort of criminal mastermind, but you never knew.

"Let's get back to the caves," Gabriel said. "Since last Thursday, the day of your lunch with Elizabeth, and up until yesterday, I've got log entries once each day and twice on Saturday, Sunday, and Tuesday."

Derek checked his calendar and frowned. "I had time scheduled with Garrity every day but Saturday."

I sat back in my chair. "So Saturday there were two entries and neither of them were yours?"

"That's right. Along with one extra entry on Sunday and Tuesday." He thought for a moment. "No, Garrity and I only entered the caves once on those days."

"What times? Do you remember?"

Derek told him the times he met Garrity and Gabriel checked off the applicable entries. "So we've got a question mark for Saturday morning, Saturday afternoon, Sunday morning, and Tuesday morning."

"Were they all the same times in the morning?"

"Different times," Gabriel said.

"I tried to meet Garrity in the mornings," Derek said, "Usually around ten. But there were a few afternoons, as well."

"I think I've noted them all." Gabriel double-checked his log-in list. "So we've got four entries unaccounted for."

"That's disturbing," Derek said.

Gabriel shrugged. "It could be completely innocent. Maybe Robson stopped by to check on something."

"Or an employee had a valid excuse to go in there." Derek's eyes narrowed in concern. "Brooklyn and I were discussing the possibility that the appraiser or one of the reporters was able to cajole someone into letting them inside the cave. Even Trudy might've asked Robson if she could take a look. After she opened the door, someone could've snuck inside. This is all conjecture, but it's worth considering."

I had stopped listening and simply stared at my calendar page until my eyes went blurry. "Oh no. Oh my God. This time it really is all my fault."

"What is it, love?" Derek said, taking hold of my arm. "What's wrong?"

I jabbed my finger on the calendar note. "My chat room! I sent them all the first paragraph of the letter that Guru Bob's grandmother sent to her sister. It was in some medieval language, remember? And I described the watermark on the paper. I told them the letter came from a storage box in a friend's house. It wouldn't be hard to track it down. It must be connected."

"Not necessarily, darling," Derek said in his most soothing tone. Usually it worked to calm me down, but not this time.

"Something else is going on here," I said, growing more agitated. "Look at the timeline, Derek. My online communication about that letter might've set everything in motion. What if something in that ancient language triggered some kind of reaction in cyberspace? What if someone connected to my chat room killed Amelia?"

*A*n hour later, after an extended rant on my part combined with Derek's lightning-fast skill at pointing out the obvious flaws in my hypothesis, I managed to compose myself. But though I'd stopped sharing my ideas on this, my brain kept racing. Had I brought all of this trouble to Dharma? Was it my fault Amelia was dead?

Gabriel sat back and enjoyed the show until Derek and I were finished with our little discussion. Then he poured himself another cup of coffee and said, "Let's go back to some more realistic possibilities. Like, Elizabeth."

I sighed and let go of my careening thoughts. After all, I had to admit it would be better if Elizabeth was at the bottom of all this, rather than my longtime chat group filled with book geeks like me. They'd been my virtual friends for years.

"Fine," I said.

Gabriel pointed to my calendar. "So she first called Trudy on Wednesday, ten days after the artwork and furnishings in the caves were discovered. She said she'd read about the treasures in her local paper and that reminded her that Trudy lived in the area. So now she wants to come visit. Out of the blue. That right there raises a red flag, wouldn't you agree?"

"Absolutely," Derek said.

Gabriel nodded. "Seven days later, she arrives in Dharma. And five days after that, Trudy is in a coma and her companion is dead."

"That's fairly compelling," Derek said.

It was. I glanced from one man to the other. "So you don't believe I could've sent a paragraph written in some obscure, ancient French-Coptic-Aramaic language out to the inter-webs, and set in motion a hundred-year curse on the Benoit family?"

Gabriel grinned. "It's a cool theory, babe, but it's straight out of science fiction."

"Damn," I grumbled. "It was a very cool theory." But if Gabriel and Derek were right, then I wasn't to blame for Amelia's death, and that was even cooler.

Of course, I wasn't ready to let go of my little notion quite yet. But I let the conversation return to the suspects who were actually in town and involved in some way or another with the cave discoveries. I had zoned out for a few minutes, but I tuned back in just as Gabriel began to talk about his drones.

"We've already programmed one of them to activate whenever there's any kind of motion near the cave doors. It'll record everything it sees and hears. If you'd like something more invasive, we can add more motion-detection lights and cameras."

"That's an excellent idea," Derek said. "Because you know they'll be back. If they've gotten away with stealing one painting, they'll want to return for more. And if they've gotten away with it once, they're familiar with the positions of the cameras. They won't be expecting any additional ones. We could also beef up the locks."

Gabriel stared at his notes and shook his head. "I'm just afraid it might be an inside job."

"I refuse to believe that," I said, not caring if I sounded like a Pollyanna. "If someone from Dharma is allowing the thief access, it's got to be inadvertent. Nobody who knows Robson would do it deliberately. This means too much to him."

"I'd like to think you're right," Derek said.

"But here's the big question," I said, gnawing at my lip as I tried to figure it all out. "How is the theft of the painting connected to the murder at Trudy's house?"

"Maybe there's no connection," Gabriel said offhandedly. "Maybe it's all just a weird coincidence."

"You don't honestly believe that," Derek said.

"No," Gabriel said with a crooked grin. "Just throwing it out there for us to munch on."

As much as I hated being a magnet for dead bodies, experience had taught me that there was always a *reason*.

"Anything's possible," I said, "but it's crazy to think it's not all connected, don't you think?"

"Sure," Gabriel said lightly. "But if you seriously believe the theft and the murder are connected, then you have to ask yourself what the connection is."

"Something tells me you've already done that," I said. "So what do you think the connection is?"

His smile was resolute. "It's Robson Benedict."

*A*fter the intense morning at Gabriel's, my head was pounding, so I spent the afternoon resting on the couch. Derek had gone back to the caves to do a little investigating because we theorized that whoever stole the Renoir—*alleged* Renoir—might've left a clue somewhere. Chances were slim, but we both thought it was worth following up.

I had finally found a comfortable sleeping niche and was dozing off when someone knocked on the front door. I groaned out loud and waited a few seconds, thinking they might go away. But then I realized it was probably my mom, and she wasn't going to go anywhere.

I shuffled across the room and swung the door open without

first peeking to see who it was. That was something I had to stop doing, given that someone had tried to kill me in the last forty-eight hours. Luckily, I saw that gorgeous head full of dark curly hair and knew it was a friendly visitor.

"Hey, you," I said, grabbing Annie in a hug. "Come in. I'm so glad you came by."

"Since you've refused to visit me, I thought I'd better."

"I'm sorry," I said, leading the way into the living room and returning to my comfy corner of the couch. "I've been meaning to get into the store to see you. It's been a little crazy lately."

"Yeah, I've heard."

Annie's real name was Anandalla, and she was the daughter that my mentor Abraham Karastovsky never knew. Her mother never told him she was pregnant after she moved back to her home-town of Seattle, where Annie was raised. It wasn't until her mother was dying that Annie had learned the truth. Her father was alive and well and living in Dharma. She and Abraham met for the first time only days before he was murdered.

Annie was petite, adorable, and in her midtwenties, all quali-ties I'd held against her when we first met. She'd been a goth princess back then, all kohl-rimmed eyes, skull earrings, and black leather vests. These days, however, she was clean-scrubbed and tie-dyed, pure Dharma right down to her Birkenstocks.

Several months after she'd moved to town, she'd opened her kitchenware store and named the shop *Anandalla!* The exclamation point fitted Annie's personality and the Hindu-inspired name suited Dharma perfectly. The store was very popular with locals and visitors alike.

She sat down in the chair opposite me and took her time look-ing me over. Taking in my disheveled appearance, she said, "You know, you didn't have to go to all this trouble just to avoid me."

I chuckled. "Very funny."

"Seriously, though, I'm sorry. I heard about Amelia and

Trudy." She shook her head in sadness and disbelief. "Amelia was in the shop just three days ago. She used to come in at least once a week, and she could easily spend an entire afternoon in one aisle. I can't believe she's gone."

"It's sad, isn't it?" I was surprised to hear that Amelia had taken such an interest in kitchenware, but it made sense since the kitchen seemed to be her realm at Trudy's.

"She was a sweet lady," Annie said.

"Was she? I'm glad to hear it, because she didn't seem to like me at all."

Annie grinned. "Did I mention she had good taste?"

"Ha ha." I bit back a smile. "I forget how funny you are when I don't see you for a while."

"It's a gift." But then she frowned. "I know Amelia was an oddball, but she loved to cook and bake, so we got along well."

"I think you and Trudy might've been the closest thing she had to friends."

"That's entirely possible. She wasn't exactly the most outgoing woman in the world." Annie stood and asked for some water. I told her to help herself, pointing the way to the kitchen. She walked out of the living room and was back in her chair a minute later, gulping down a glass of water. "Ah, much better, thanks. So how are you feeling, really?"

I sighed. "The pain comes and goes, but mainly I'm going crazy here. I need to be doing something."

She got up, came over to the couch, and peered more closely at my head where the wound was still healing. "It doesn't look too bad, but I guess they nailed you good."

"Yeah. I'm lucky to be alive."

"I'd say so." She sat down, and I scooted back so I could sit up straighter.

"So, what's new with you, Annie?" I asked, anxious to change the subject away from head wound. "I haven't seen you in at least two months. How's business? Do you still love it here? Do you have a boyfriend?"

She thought for a moment. "Um, nothing much. Great. Yes. And none of your business."

I laughed. "None of my business? You know this is a small town, right? All I have to do is ask my mother. She'll tell me everything about your love life."

Annie rolled her eyes. "Unfortunately, that's not a joke. That woman knows everything about everyone in town."

"Yeah, we've all given up trying to keep secrets from her."

She smiled fondly. "Your mom is the best."

"She loves you, too."

She stared out the window at the beautiful blue sky and the line of pine and oak trees that covered the ridge. "I was so lucky to find this place."

"Lucky?" I said. "If memory serves, I was the one who introduced you to Dharma."

It was her turn to laugh. "You just keep believing that."

I gave her a smile. "It's really good to see you."

"You, too." She glanced at her watch. "But I'd better leave you to rest. I've got to go meet someone in a little while."

"Hot date?"

She shot me a suspicious glare. "Since you'll find out anyway, I might as well tell you that I'm meeting that reporter for coffee. Your sister set me up."

"Reporter?" I frowned before remembering my conversation with China. "You mean Josh Atherton?"

"Yeah. Oh, I guess you must've met him since he's here to research the caves. China wouldn't tell me anything about him. Well, only that he's nice and cute."

"He's perfectly pleasant and very cute," I agreed with a nod. I hesitated, then added, "Just please don't forget that he's a, you know, a reporter. Watch what you tell him."

"Don't worry," she said. "He won't get anything out of me."

"Good." I grinned. "Have fun."

"Always." She gave me a quick hug and took off, leaving me to contemplate Josh Atherton. Annie was a lot more confident in her ability to resist his interrogation techniques than I was. I could only wonder what sort of information he would try to wangle out of Annie.

*F*riday morning, I washed dishes while Derek finished up a phone call with our contractor, who assured him that the work was moving along and everything was on schedule. Our home would be ready and looking beautiful within a month. Derek let him know that he planned to be in the city next week and would stop by to inspect everything done so far.

After the phone call, we drove to the supermarket to stock up on groceries and incidentals for the week.

On the drive home, we got more news, this time from Gabriel, who announced that Trudy had come home. As Gabriel had predicted, Trudy had refused to leave her home for the sake of her own safety, so he was in the process of moving into her spare bedroom. Trudy had only weakly protested his presence, and now it was clear that she was happy to have him there, especially since Elizabeth would be visiting for only a few more days.

If she wasn't arrested for murder first.

We drove by the house to welcome Trudy home but stayed just a short while. I had to endure Elizabeth's hugs while she expressed the hope that she and I could get together for lunch soon. But how could she possibly think I would want to get together with her when I didn't even know if she was guilty of killing Amelia or not? She carried on as if nothing had happened, and I made some lame excuse about being too busy this week to go to lunch.

Derek sensed my unease, and we left as quickly as we could, leaving Gabriel to watch Elizabeth's every move and keep Trudy safe. If anyone could multitask under those circumstances, it was him.

*A*melia's memorial service took place the following day in the tiered theater side of the town hall, opposite the exhibit hall.

Robson had been hoping that Trudy's memory would return by then, but the poor woman was still at a loss as to what had happened to her companion and friend. But since the sheriff had released Amelia's body and the funeral home had gone ahead and performed the quiet burial—with just Trudy, Robson, Elizabeth, Gabriel, Derek, me, and my parents in attendance—Robson decided not to wait any longer to hold the larger memorial service.

It wasn't a religious ceremony but a simple and sweet memorial to a woman who was known by very few of us but who nevertheless had left an indelible mark on Dharma. There were several lovely short speeches, including a few words from Annie. A string quartet played in the background.

At the last minute, we had tried to track down any possible relatives of Amelia's. Trudy was unaware of any and expressed the belief that the woman was alone in the world. Amelia had been an only child, she said, and Trudy was fairly certain that both of her parents had been as well.

"I never saw her write a letter to anyone," Trudy had said. "She never called any family."

It was sad to think that the woman had no one who would care that she was alive or dead. But that wasn't really true. She had Trudy. And I was pretty sure that Trudy was the reason why most of the town had gathered together to give her friend a decent send-off.

"She died a hero, saving Trudy's life," Robson stated in his eulogy.

It was true. There was no better way to say it. But as I listened to his words, guilt rained down on my soul. I had been so ambivalent toward the woman. She was finicky and judgmental and always scowling at me, and I had no idea why. Was she jealous of Trudy's time or affection? Or was she just a sourpuss? I guessed it was both.

Glancing around the tiered assembly room, I spotted Trudy sitting in the first row and found Elizabeth in the seat next to her. A quick chill tickled my spine at that sight, but then I spied Gabriel seated directly behind the two women. He was clearly taking very seriously his job of guarding Trudy. Mom and Dad were sitting with my two brothers and Robin a few rows down and over from me and Derek. China and Savannah were seated together nearby.

Seeing my brother Jackson reminded me of his odd disappearance that day at the exhibit hall when I was about to introduce him to Elizabeth.

I leaned over and whispered to Derek, "We need to talk to Jackson."

He nodded. "As soon as this is over."

I smiled, glanced around, and found myself staring right at Detective Hannah Parrish from the Sonoma County Sheriff's Department. Her smile was a lot less friendly than the last time I'd seen her and I quickly looked away. Then I had to try and remember exactly when I'd seen her last. I recalled seeing her at the press conference, but I also had a vague recollection of seeing her at Trudy's house the day Amelia was killed.

Was she annoyed with me? Did I say something strange while under the influence of painkillers? I would have to make a point to talk to her after the service. I didn't need a local cop focusing her anger on me.

I continued to wonder why she was so annoyed. Though to be fair, I seemed to have that effect on police officers.

. . .

*M*s. Wainwright."
         I turned and looked directly into the eyes of Detective Parrish. Again.

"Hello, Detective. Can I offer you some crudité? Or something a little heartier?"

We were standing in the attached dining hall where an abundance of savory food and delectable desserts was always served after events.

"No, thanks." She looked around. "Everything looks great."

"We know how to throw a party, even when it's a sad occasion."

She seemed uncomfortable, but I didn't know if it was the surroundings or me, specifically. "I'd like to ask you a few questions about the day you were attacked."

"I remember seeing you there. It's a very foggy memory, I'm afraid."

"I can understand. I'm sorry you were hurt."

"Mine was the least of the injuries that day."

"Indeed. I was hoping to hear from you before now."

"Oh. I thought you got all my information from Derek. Derek Stone."

"I asked him to have you call me."

"He might've said something, but I was probably still out of it and didn't follow through. I apologize."

She seemed to relax a little as she reached for a carrot stick and took a bite. "No worries. Can you tell me what happened?"

I related everything exactly as I remembered it, and exactly as I'd told Derek before. She listened and nodded and crunched on her carrot stick.

"Mr. Stone said that you heard the floor creak?"

"That was my only warning. I thought it was Amelia, but it wasn't."

She nodded again. "I appreciate your help. I may call you again to ask more questions, if you don't mind." She pulled a business card from her jacket pocket. "And if you remember anything else, please feel free to call me."

"Thank you. I will. I'm sorry again that I got my wires crossed."

Detective Parrish smiled and walked away. I stared after her, wondering where she'd received her training. The cops in San Francisco never would've been so polite or nonjudgmental. I always felt as if I were being put through the wringer with the city cops, and right now, I almost missed the feeling. *Almost.*

I was crossing the hall to get a glass of juice, when I caught a glimpse of Annie bringing in another tray of desserts. I detoured over to help her.

"Hi," she said, setting the tray down on the table and spreading the individual tart plates across the table. "You're looking a lot better than you did the last time I saw you."

"Thanks," I said, laughing. "That was a whole two days ago."

"Hey, you were wearing pajamas."

"I clean up well." I helped her move plates around so she could fit all the tarts on the table. "These look so good."

"I've had two of the apricot tarts, so I can promise they're fabulous."

"How have you been?" I asked.

She glanced around the crowded room, gave me a look, and whispered, "You mean, 'How was your date?'"

I laughed. "Well, now that you mention it, yeah. How was it?"

"You're such a bozo," she said, shaking her head. "I didn't think I would like him because of you."

"What do you mean? I told you he was pleasant."

"You made him sound like a snoop. Like he might go prying into my underwear drawer or something."

"I never meant that."

She laughed. "I know you didn't. And I realize he's a reporter, but you're right—he's really pleasant and very attractive and seems pretty interested in me." She smiled shyly. "We're going out again tomorrow night."

"I'm glad," I said, and meant it. "I want you to be happy. And as I already said, I like him. It's just that . . ."

"I know, I know." She rolled her eyes. "He's a reporter."

I grinned. "Exactly."

"Don't worry," she said, picking up the empty tray. "I won't divulge any of your deep, dark secrets."

I smiled indulgently. "If only I had any."

*L*ater that afternoon, once the memorial service and reception were over, Derek and I tried to find Jackson, but he had disappeared again. We swung by the vineyard offices, but he hadn't checked in. We even made the long drive up to his house, but he wasn't home.

Giving up the search for now, we decided to stop by Trudy's to visit and commiserate. Robson had arrived a few minutes before us, and shortly after we got there, my mom and dad walked in. Mom was carrying her briefcase, so I had a feeling we'd be witnessing another purification ceremony at some point. I had no problem with that. It would be fun to see her work her magic on someone besides me. And any little ritual that would help Trudy cope with the loss of Amelia was okay with me.

I was happy to see Elizabeth doting on Trudy. I had to admit I liked the woman, although my suspicions prohibited me from getting close to her. I seriously hoped she had nothing to do with the attack, but we wouldn't know for sure until Derek's facial recognition people were able to figure out if she was anyone other than who she claimed to be.

Derek had managed to take a good picture of her during the memorial reception earlier and had instantly texted it to his assistant at his office in San Francisco. She would forward it to their London office, and he was certain we would hear back from them within a few hours.

Mom and Dad had brought some of the leftover desserts and several bottles of wine from the reception, so we had a little commemorative party in Amelia's honor. Mom worked her magic, conducting a wonderfully bizarre cleansing ceremony that made Trudy laugh and cry, declaring it the most life-altering thrill ride she'd ever experienced.

But none of it shook up Trudy's memory, and I wondered if she would ever recall the face of the person who'd tried to kill her. Or even if she should try. Because maybe, just maybe, her amnesia was all that was keeping her alive.

Chapter Fifteen

The first thing I saw on my phone the next morning was a message from Claude from my chat room. He included his translation of the first paragraph of Marie's letter and apologized for taking so long.

"If you send me the rest," he wrote, "I can probably get it done within a day or two. Last week you caught me in the middle of a three-day continuing education class. OMG! Boring!"

Claude went on to explain that the language was exactly as he'd thought, mainly a combination of schoolgirl medieval French and Chouadit, the long-extinct Jewish language he had mentioned in our first chat room talk.

I wrote down what he'd translated. The first few sentences were the usual chitchat and news sent to a friend concerning different family members, the weather, and her health.

As I looked at the original letter, I was reminded that it was written by Marie, Guru Bob's grandmother, to Camille, who was Marie's sister-in-law and Trudy's mother. I hadn't paid much attention to the date when I first saw the letter, but now I did. It read *4 April 1946*, and I realized its significance.

Jean Pierre Renaud's ticket for passage on the ocean liner was dated April 12, 1946. So this letter was written the week before.

I assumed that both women were living in Sonoma with their husbands. According to Trudy, they and their families had all moved here from France during the war. They probably didn't have telephones at the time, but they couldn't have lived far from each other. Why didn't Marie simply ride her bike over for a visit? Was there something in the letter that couldn't be said out loud?

The last sentence Claude translated was troubling: "Oh, dear sister, I have witnessed something so terrible that I'm almost afraid to tell you about it, but I must get it off my chest."

I wanted to know what Marie had seen. What was so terrible that she had felt the need for a confession of the soul?

I showed the translation to Derek and voiced my thoughts.

He sipped his coffee. "There must be something in this letter about Monsieur Renaud."

"Shall I send Claude the rest of the letter?"

"Absolutely," he said. My face must've betrayed my fears, because he put his cup down and wrapped his arms around me. "Are you afraid your friend Claude might be Amelia's killer?"

Derek really did know me much too well. Yes, my brain had actually considered that very idea before dismissing it.

"No, of course not," I said. "And when you say it out loud, it sounds even more ridiculous." I pressed my cheek against his chest. "But the timing is still disconcerting."

He leaned back and tilted my chin up to meet my gaze. "If it means anything, I am absolutely certain that your chat room friends are not responsible for Amelia's death."

"I know you're right," I said, pouting a little. "Claude lives in Indiana and can barely afford to take the bus, let alone fly out to California to go on a killing spree."

"There, you see?" He smiled, but then sobered up to add, "I hope it hasn't escaped your attention that if someone in the chat room did kill Amelia, you would be in even more danger now."

I thought about that for a few seconds. "But I've never seen any of them in person."

"But they would know you," he reasoned. "They would have to get rid of you because of the chat room connection. You would be a threat to them."

"I suppose that's true." I shook my head in defeat. "Luckily it's too ridiculous and convoluted to contemplate, which means you were right in the first place."

"I never tire of hearing that."

"Fine, I'll say it once more. You were right. It was a ridiculous theory. But it was a fun one."

"Oh, fun. Absolutely." I had a feeling he was trying not to laugh. "If you want my opinion, I say you should go ahead and send Claude the rest of the letter and find out its contents. If nothing else comes of it, it'll be an interesting bit of ephemera for Robson's library."

I smiled at his use of my bookbinding and conservation terms. "Good plan. I'm going to scan the letter and send it to Claude. Then I'll join you for breakfast."

"My heart awaits your presence."

"Such a funny man."

His handsome grin was so rakish, I might've sighed a little as I hurried off to take care of sending the letter to Claude.

*T*alking about Monsieur Renaud reminded me that I still hadn't dealt with the ownership issue of *Journey to the Center of the Earth*. So after breakfast, I took a quick drive over to Robson's home to show it to him. Since it was his grandfather Anton who'd written the pledge on the back flyleaf, I figured the book belonged to Guru Bob as much as to anyone. I wanted to ask him if he would like me to rebind it or simply refurbish it and leave it as close to the original as possible.

I had a feeling I knew what his choice would be, and I was right. He preferred to have it spruced up, but he wanted it to remain in the same basic condition as when his grandfather read it as a boy. I promised I would simply clean the gutters, tighten the text block, and replace the flattened bands on the spine. The endpapers were still beautiful, and the flyleaf with its remarkable pledge in his grandfather's blood would naturally stay as I'd found it.

An hour later, I was home, packing up my satchel in anticipation of spending the day in Abraham's workshop. I wanted to take Charlie with me, but since Derek was working from home today, I left her to play with him and Maggie.

As I strolled down the hill to the workshop, I marveled at how quickly I had grown to love the darling creature. And by that I meant Charlie, not Derek. Although he was darling as well, and I loved him more than I thought possible. They were both awesome and wonderful. My little family. And if I daydreamed about adding Maggie to the group, it was only because she was such a sweetie pie with so much love to give. The Quinlans were lucky to have her.

I walked into Abraham's workshop and sniffed the familiar scents, and felt at home once again. Now that I had Robson's approval to work on the *Journey*, I wanted to get it done right away. I pulled it out of my satchel and, setting it on the worktable with my tools, felt a wave of sadness because of what had happened to those two young boys who'd signed their blood pledge all those years ago.

At the same time, I was relieved that the book hadn't been the cause of the tragedy that took Jean Pierre's life. I'd worked on too many valuable, rare books for which people had willingly lied, cheated, stolen, or killed. This wasn't one of those.

I took a quick minute to check on my medical books. Volume one was still in the book press where I'd left it a few days ago. Its leather cover was completely dried and looked fantastic if I did say so myself. The spine was ready to be gilded, but I wasn't sure I'd have time to do it today.

Back at my worktable, I pulled out my brush to continue cleaning the pages. But first, I grabbed my magnifying glass to give the Jules Verne book another close-up look. Even though the book had been battered by the boys who'd read it over and over again, Robson didn't want a new cover. I would eventually apply some high-quality leather rub and leave it at that. But first I would remove the leather and replace the six raised bands on the spine that had gone flat. Once I had the leather cover pasted back on the boards, I would gild the titles again and fill in where the gilding on the spine and covers had faded. I could also spruce up the tattered crown and foot of the spine where it was splitting from that front hinge.

Beyond that, a thorough sweeping of all the pages would finish the job. Then it would be Robson's to do with what he wanted.

I took another look at the back flyleaf where the boys had written and dated their pledge in blood. I felt a twinge, wondering if they had bled for each other on more than one occasion. I was sad to think that their friendship had ended in that cave with Jean Pierre's death. Had Anton mourned him always? Was he the one who walled off the cave? Would we ever find out the truth?

I hoped Claude would be able to translate Marie's letter quickly, because the suspense was killing me. I had a feeling it might hold some answers to my questions.

I stared one last time at the faded rust-colored ink and shivered again. "Blood," I muttered. "Boys are gross."

And thinking about gross little boys reminded me that we hadn't tracked down Jackson yet. There was no time like the present, so I pulled out my cell phone and pushed his number.

"Hey, sis," Jackson said upon answering. "What's up?"

"I was wondering if you'd be around sometime tonight. Derek and I wanted to ask you a question or two."

I used Derek's name in case he was inclined to balk. It was a sisterly thing to do.

"What's this all about?" he asked, sounding ready to balk regardless.

I could've lied and told him it was something to do with the vineyards, but he wouldn't have believed me anyway, so I told him the truth. "We're wondering if you know anything about Elizabeth. That woman who's visiting Trudy?"

"Why would I know anything about her?"

So male, really. He didn't answer; he just asked another question. Which told me that my brother knew something he didn't want to talk about.

"Well, you were acting weird last week when I was about to introduce her to you. Remember how you disappeared? And then you canceled dinner? And now we have a situation. . . ."

"A situation?"

It was just as well that he stopped me, because I was blathering, digging myself into a hole. "Yeah. So will you be around tonight?"

Jackson didn't answer right away, and I thought maybe he'd hung up on me. He was an elusive guy, so I never knew quite how to deal with him. But he was my brother and I loved him, so I was prepared to pester the heck out of him until I got an answer.

"Hello?" I said. "Are you there?"

"Yeah, I'm here."

I breathed a sigh of relief, although I could hear the annoyance in his tone. I didn't care. I'd heard that tone in his voice all my life.

"Listen," he said finally, "how about if you guys come by the winery tonight around eight? We're having a barrel tasting this afternoon, and I'll just be finishing up then. We can have a glass of wine and talk."

"That would be perfect." Better than perfect, I thought, because there would be wine. "Thanks, Jackson."

"See you then."

He ended the call, and I immediately telephoned Derek to let him know what we were doing that night.

I spent the rest of the afternoon sweeping the gutters of each page of the *Journey* and then bringing new life back to the raised bands on its spine. I reattached the leather cover and rubbed it with leather cleaner until it was gleaming.

Before I was ready to quit for the day, I took a half hour to cut and pare down the leather for the next medical text cover. I also wrapped the text block in wax paper and then packed up my bags to go home.

When I arrived, I found Derek working in the office with Maggie asleep at his feet.

I gave Derek a smooch on the lips and asked, "Where's Charlie?"

"She's dozing in my lap," he said, wrapping his arm around my waist. "Otherwise I'd have you sitting there."

I laughed. "I'll have to wait my turn."

He glanced back at his computer screen. "I'm just waiting for one more e-mail before I quit for the day. Then we can grab a bite to eat and go meet your brother."

We decided on Chinese food and drove a mile outside of Dharma to the best Asian fusion restaurant in the world—or in Sonoma, at least.

At eight o'clock, Derek parked in the winery's lot, and we walked into its cavernous bowels, looking for Jackson. The place was empty and the lights were dimmed. It was obvious that the barrel tasting had been over for some time.

"Hello?" I called. "Jackson?"

"I'm over here," my brother shouted from the other side of the warehouse-sized barrel room.

The room was kept cool, and I suppressed a shiver as we

walked past a dozen massive, stainless steel vats that held thousands of gallons of wine. We found Jackson standing against the far wall at a wine-barrel table surrounded by three stools.

"Hey, Derek," he said, and the two shook hands.

I gave him a hug and took a seat at the table.

Jackson grabbed the bottle. "I'll pour you some of the reserve Meritage we were tasting earlier."

"Wonderful," Derek said, straddling the stool next to me.

As he poured, Jackson gave a short lecture on the Meritage concept. The word was applied when at least two grape varieties were blended together, as long as none of the varieties made up more than ninety percent of the final merging. So it was a true blend, and it usually included cabernet sauvignon and merlot grapes.

Meritage was actually the name of an association formed by local winemakers in the Napa Valley back in the day, after many of them voiced frustration with the U.S. labeling requirements and decided to form their own brand. They combined the words *merit* and *heritage* to create a name for both their new alliance and their new blending style.

"There's more to it," Jackson said, "but that's enough for tonight. Let's taste it."

I took my first sip, rolling the dark red liquid around my mouth and tongue. "It's yummy."

"That's a technical term," Jackson explained to Derek, who chuckled.

"It's yummy indeed," Derek said after his first taste. "It has a nice spiciness to it. Also a hint of blackberry and . . ." He paused. "Mocha?"

"Yes!" Jackson said. "I get that, too. That's probably from the barrel, but it may be left over from the fermentation process." He pondered the question as he took another taste and gazed at the legs streaking down the side of the glass.

"It's mellow, but spicy, too," I said, taking another small sip.

"Plummy. Herby. Nice tannins. And I'm getting a little toasted oak, definitely from the barrel."

"What do you think of that?" Jackson asked, always looking for opinions on barrel fermentation.

"You know me," I said. "I love an oaky red."

We continued the wine talk for another ten minutes. Jackson estimated how many days were left until the harvest, and Derek expressed his interest in taking part in the event.

"We'll welcome every able-bodied human we can find," Jackson assured him. "And you've already proven yourself to be an excellent field-worker."

"High praise," Derek said. "I appreciate it."

Finally, I met my brother's gaze and said, "So."

"So?" he said coolly in response.

There was no soft and easy way to introduce the subject, so I got right to the point. "Last week in the exhibit hall, you disappeared the moment I tried to introduce you to Elizabeth. So, do you know her? Why did you run away? What's the story? Do you think she's dangerous? She's living in a house where a murder took place. Do you think she did it? Is Trudy in danger?"

"Slow down, speedy," he said. "Nobody's in danger from . . . What did you say her name was?"

"Elizabeth."

He raised an eyebrow. "Right. I . . . know her. No, she's not dangerous." He frowned and added, "Well, at least not to Trudy."

"But you ran away that day. What was that about?"

"Is that important, love?" Derek asked softly.

I looked at him. "Well, maybe not in the larger scheme of things, but I want to know if my brother is hiding from the law or something."

Jackson snorted, and I turned back to him. "Well then, what's up with that? Why did you leave?"

"None of your business, squirt."

"I'm thirty-three years old," I said through gritted teeth. "Stop calling me that."

"All right, punkin'."

"And that." Another dreaded childhood nickname. "Just grow up and answer the question." Brothers, no matter how old and mature they grew to be, always retained a talent for obnoxious behavior.

"Okay, okay," he said with a stiff laugh. "Look, this is not something I'm prepared to discuss with anyone."

I could see Derek studying him more closely than usual, and I wondered what he was thinking.

"Fine," I said. "We don't have to talk about it anymore. But look, if there's a problem or if you're in some kind of trouble . . ."

"There's no trouble," he assured me.

"Okay," I said, stifling a smile. "But if she turns out to be your probation officer, all bets are off."

"Very funny," he said, not laughing. "Look, just accept the fact that Elizabeth didn't have anything to do with Trudy's attack and Amelia's murder, and let's change the subject."

Derek's gaze focused in on him. "Are you her alibi?"

"Damn it," Jackson swore, and clawed his fingers through his hair in frustration.

"Wait a minute," I said, the light dawning. "You're her alibi? She was with you those couple of days when she was gone from Trudy's?"

He sighed. "Yes. And that's all you have to know."

"But how do you know her?" I frowned. And all of a sudden the pieces fell together. "Wait. She didn't come here to see Trudy. She came to see you. But why? Where did you meet? I'm more confused than ever."

"So just let it go," Jackson insisted, but then couldn't help but add, "And she didn't come to see me. She was just as shocked to see me as I was to see her."

"Fascinating," I murmured.

"Overseas," Derek guessed. "Africa? The Middle East?" He thought for another few seconds. "Of course. Southeast Asia."

"I'm not saying anything else." Jackson glared at Derek. "You, of all people, should know that."

My eyes widened, and I stared from Derek to Jackson. "Oh no. Not you, too. What are you, CIA? Military intelligence?" I waved the question away. "Never mind. Don't tell me. You'll just have to kill me, right?"

Suddenly Jackson was grinning. "Yeah, I'll have to kill you, so stop asking questions."

"All right, all right," I muttered. "But what about Elizabeth, *if* that's really her name. What is she? Some supersecret spy you met while rapelling down some treacherous cliff in Burma?"

"Maybe, in your own warped mind." He was laughing at me now, but he still wasn't spilling the beans. And why did that not surprise me? Jackson had always been the stoic one in the family, quietly going about his business. He'd been great at keeping secrets, like the time he caught me behind the school gym, kissing Richie Kirk. Back then, I was shocked that he hadn't told my parents about it. There were other incidents as well.

So I guess I didn't care if he told me the whole story. For now. It was enough to know that much of Jackson's past was truly secret. I would honor that. And I was glad to know that Elizabeth—or whatever her name was—was innocent of harming Trudy or Amelia.

Which meant that I could take her off my suspect list. And we would have to look elsewhere for the killer.

The three of us walked out to the dark parking lot together, and Derek and I waved good-bye to Jackson.

"That was fun and educational, too," I said as we watched Jackson drive his truck out of the lot.

"The wine was very good, too," Derek said, smiling broadly as he unlocked the car and held my door open for me.

"Always." I turned to look at him. "Do you believe Jackson was telling the truth when he said he didn't know Elizabeth would be here?"

Derek's expression sobered. "I do. He has no reason to lie to us, other than evading other details of his past. But I don't hold that against him."

"I guess you're right." I shut my door and watched Derek circle the car and climb into the driver's seat.

"I should've known he was in intelligence," Derek muttered a moment later as he glanced in his rearview mirror.

"I'm surprised you didn't," I said lightly. "You people seem to have a built-in radar when it comes to detecting that aspect of one another."

"And I missed the signs with Elizabeth, too." His frown deepened.

"I don't blame you for that. She's a whole different story. She told me the reason I wasn't able to place her accent was because she was a navy brat and had traveled all over the world. Now I wonder if she just said stuff like that so I wouldn't realize that she's a German spy or something."

"I doubt that she's German," Derek said, chuckling.

"You've probably figured out what she really is."

"Mossad, I imagine," he murmured.

I stared at him. "You think she's Israeli?"

"Not positive, but it's an educated guess," Derek said, checking his rearview mirror again. "Mossad has a discreet relationship with Thailand's intelligence community."

"Okay. So what's the connection?"

He glanced at me. "The tattoo on Jackson's left arm is a Thai phrase."

I stared at him in disbelief. "What tattoo? My brother has a tattoo?"

Derek grinned. "You'd know about the tattoo if you had toiled in the fields like I do."

I laughed. "Oh great. So what's the word?"

He pronounced the phrase using a sharp, guttural tone, sounding completely unlike himself.

"Wow. What does that mean?"

"Tranquility."

I thought about it. "That suits him. But couldn't he have gotten it anywhere?"

"It's possible, but not likely. Thailand is made up of hundreds of communities, each with its own language and colloquialisms. The phrase tattooed on Jackson's arm is from an obscure area in northern Thailand. I doubt he could've gotten it anywhere else in the world."

"How do you know so much about Thailand? Did you work there, too?"

"Yes, briefly. I had to take immersion courses in languages and customs in order to complete the mission." He glanced in the rearview mirror once again.

I could tell he was distracted, so I relaxed and enjoyed the ride. Two seconds later, I gasped and turned to him. "Wait a minute. If she's Mossad, she could be looking for artwork stolen from the Jews. That's brilliant, Derek. It has nothing to do with Thailand, but it's brilliant."

"Thailand simply provides a possible connection between Jackson and Elizabeth."

"Right. There are so many different threads to this situation, I can't keep them all straight." I thought of the rest of Elizabeth's backstory. "Is she really the granddaughter of a friend of Trudy's?"

"We'll have to ask her." He pulled over to the side of the road.

"What're you doing? Is something wrong with the car?"

"No. I saw someone sneaking over the hill back there."

"It's so dark out, how could you see them?"

"They had a flashlight turned on for a moment. They were headed in the direction of the caves."

"Damn it! We've got to stop them." I shoved my door open and had one foot on the ground before Derek grabbed my arm.

"Brooklyn, wait," he ordered, yanking me back. "Close the door, please. The interior light might alert them."

"Oh crap." I scrambled back into the car and tried to shut the door quietly. "I'm sorry. That was stupid."

"Never mind," he said more calmly. "I believe we're far enough away that they didn't notice the light through the tinted windows. But I don't want you charging off without a plan."

I thought about the last time I had charged in without a plan. I had gotten bashed in the head. "Okay. Sorry." I took a few deep breaths to chill out. "With all the trauma we've been through, my first thought was to hunt them down and throttle them."

"Perhaps you'll get your chance." He glanced up at the sky through the windshield and then scanned the landscape in four directions. The moon was a sliver and the sky was cloudy, so there was almost no light shining down on the nearby vineyards and surrounding countryside.

"How did you see him?" I asked.

"I saw his silhouette—that is, I assume it's a man, but it could be a woman—when he or she skulked across the fire lane that runs parallel to the cabernet vineyard."

"That was lucky. It's the only spot around that isn't covered in vines or thicket."

"Yes, lucky indeed." He looked at me, frowning. "I don't suppose you'll wait in the car."

"Not a chance," I said, buttoning up my jacket. I was glad I'd

gone with a dark wardrobe tonight. "But I promise I won't get in
your way."

"Damn straight you won't." He reached across me, unlocked
the glove compartment, and pulled out his scary-looking gun.

"I suppose that's necessary," I said, basically to myself.

"Yes, it is."

"Fine." I pulled my cell phone from my purse. "But do you
mind if I call Gabriel so you have some real backup?"

Derek checked his rearview mirror. "He knows we're here."

"He does? How?"

"One of his drones is hovering above our car."

"You've got to be kidding."

He grinned, took another look out the windshield, and waved
up at whatever was above us. "I've got to get one of those."

"You guys scare me. You really do."

He reached for his door handle. "Ready to go?"

"Yes."

"Stay behind me." Derek opened the car door and was out in
three seconds. I tried to duplicate his moves, but I wasn't quite as
smooth or fast as he was. We snuck across the road and hiked up
the shallow hill above the lighted parking lot. Here there were
rows of graceful birch trees lining the ridge along the bottom of
the vineyard acreage.

I stopped behind one tree and looked up at the terraced hill
above us. It was really dark out here tonight. The storage cave was
fifty yards in front of us, so we continued following the line of
trees, staying in the safe shadows as long as we could.

Derek held up his hand, and I stopped immediately. He
pointed to something in the bushes at the end of the tree line. I
had to squint to try and see what he was looking at, but I couldn't
see a thing.

"Stay here," he whispered, barely loud enough for me to hear.

I nodded, and he took off toward whatever he was seeing. I

waited. I had no interest in getting in the way of his gun. After a few moments, I had a sudden attack of cowardice. Did I really want to see what he'd found? It was a lot easier to be brave while sitting inside the luxurious Bentley. But out here in the elements, with some bad guy skulking around? Not so much.

"Brooklyn," Derek said aloud, breaking the silence of the dark night. "Get Gabriel on the phone. Tell him to call the sheriff and get an ambulance over here."

I forgot my fears and went running over to his side. "What happened?"

He pointed to the ground behind the bushes. "It's Noland Garrity."

"I knew it!" I leaned over and looked down at Garrity's body, sprawled motionless on the dirt and hidden by the hedgerow. "You caught him."

"No, someone else did," he said grimly, "and left him for dead."

"Just to be clear," Gabriel said, "nobody entered the caves tonight."

"Good," I said, pacing the room, trying to shake off the nerves and fear I'd felt out there in the dark.

After the ambulance had whisked Noland Garrity away and the police had finished asking their questions, Gabriel, Derek, and I had returned to our house. The two men were seated at the dining table, munching on pretzels while I continued to pace around the room.

"Garrity must've been trying to sneak inside, right? Did you find a key in his pocket? Anything?"

"No key," Derek said. "More likely, he was planning to meet someone else who had the key."

"He definitely met someone," I muttered, "and they beat the

heck out of him. Two fractured ribs and a broken nose, plus bruises everywhere." I shivered. "I mean, I can't stand the guy, but I'm sorry he was so badly injured."

Derek sat back in his chair. "He'll be able to tell us who did it when he's awake and talking again."

"Maybe." But I frowned. It had been pitch-black out there on the hill, so I was doubtful that Garrity even saw who had attacked him. With Trudy's memory not yet recovered, we were still completely in the dark.

The ambulance had arrived in record time, followed by the local police. Within minutes, Garrity had been rushed to the hospital. The police had stayed around and cordoned off the area behind the bushes where we'd found Garrity unconscious. I figured we would see the sheriff's detectives sometime tomorrow.

"This is really disturbing," I said, continuing to pace. "Since we talked to Jackson and decided that Elizabeth is in the clear, I had Garrity pegged for the most likely suspect. Not so much for the murder of Amelia but most definitely for the theft of that Renoir."

"Yes," Derek said, nodding. "He was certainly the most likely candidate."

"So who is it we're not suspecting that we should be suspecting?" Gabriel and Derek looked at each other, then at me.

I sighed and pulled my notepad out of my purse. "I guess we'd better go back over the list."

*T*he next morning, I stopped at Trudy's to see how she was doing. Gabriel answered the door, grinning like the devil as he let me into the house.

Trudy sat on the couch and waved a small handheld computer tablet over her head. "Look at this, Brooklyn. I can open and lock my front door from my tablet."

"What if I decided to break in?"

She smiled broadly. "I have an app for that. It's a panic button."

I looked at Gabriel. "She has an app for that?"

Gabriel chuckled. He was having fun while looking hot at the same time. Go figure.

I was thrilled and grateful that Gabriel had set up this elaborate security system and had taught Trudy how to operate it directly from her tablet. So she could work the sophisticated, computerized system, but she still couldn't remember who had tried to shoot her.

I was also grateful that Elizabeth wasn't a suspect anymore, but now I felt guilty for putting her at the top of my list. I knew I'd get over it and maybe we'd laugh about it someday, but right now, I watched her surreptitiously as she cleaned the breakfast dishes off the dining room table. I knew she was beautiful, but I'd never noticed her almond-shaped eyes. I'd thought her exotic looks were from her Italian father, but now I realized it was entirely possible that she was Israeli. Of course, I'd seen Israelis with blond hair, so what did I know?

She glanced up and saw me watching her and smiled. I knew then that Jackson must've told her what he'd said to us the other night. She had to know I'd suspected her of killing Amelia, but she didn't look angry and I appreciated that. I guessed the next step was mine if I wanted to repair our fledgling friendship.

As I'd made a habit of doing, I gently quizzed Trudy again, asking if she remembered the surprise she wanted to show me.

"No, Brooklyn. I'm so sorry. I wish I could."

"You will," I said, keeping my tone upbeat and positive. "Do you mind if I keep asking you?"

"Not at all! I want to remember."

"You will," I repeated. "In the meantime, I hope I'll see everyone at the Pre-Harvest celebration on Saturday."

"I'm looking forward to it," Elizabeth said.

Trudy beamed. "Wouldn't miss it for the world."

I believed her, just as I believed she would get her memory back. I wanted *her* to believe it, too. I just wished it would happen *now.*

Somewhere inside her mind, she was holding some vital, dangerous information, and for that reason, even though Gabriel and Elizabeth were here with her every day, I was determined to visit as often as I could. Trudy needed all the protection she could get.

Chapter Sixteen

Two days later on Wednesday, we held the first official gathering of Robin and her girlfriends to help plan her wedding. With Robin's permission, I'd invited my new friend and neighbor, Alex Monroe. Derek and I had become good friends with her after she helped me fight off some really bad guys a few months back. Alex was a gorgeous, tall, high-powered businesswoman with the best wardrobe in the world. She was also an expert at Krav Maga and other defensive disciplines. I had introduced her to Robin and Austin a month ago at a dinner party Derek and I had thrown, and my two friends had hit it off nicely.

My sister London had driven down from Calistoga to join us, along with China, Savannah, Annie, and Barb, another old friend Robin and I had gone to school with. The eight of us spent an hour chatting and giggling foolishly about every little thing before settling down to plan Robin's wedding of the century. It helped to have a few true experts at the table, namely Alex, the cupcake and wardrobe queen; China, the textiles maven; Savannah, the gourmet goddess; and Annie, who knew everything about kitchenware. Much to Annie's delight, Robin would be registering at her store. The rest of us fell into the general know-it-all category and blithely added our homegrown expertise to the conversation as often as we could.

After lunch, I spent a half hour in the parking lot, chatting and catching up with Alex. She filled me in on how well the construction was moving along and assured me that our new loft was going to be fantastic. We made plans to meet for dinner and then Alex took off to check in to one of the spa hotels in town.

When I arrived home, I felt much more relaxed than I had in a while.

Part of my feeling of calm came from knowing that Elizabeth hadn't killed Amelia. But as I walked into the house, I suddenly wondered if she was the one who'd taken the Renoir. She'd been obsessed with the photograph of the painting at the town hall photo exhibit. Could the painting have belonged to a Jewish family before World War II began? Had Elizabeth been assigned by Mossad to look for it? Had she somehow gotten into the cave and taken it? Had Jackson given her the key?

"Impossible," I muttered. My brother would never allow that to happen.

Not only that, but I couldn't see Elizabeth sneaking in and stealing it. If she had found evidence that a piece of artwork in the cave was once owned by a Jewish family, it would be a simple matter of alerting the local authorities and starting an investigation. She was welcome to do so, as far as I was concerned.

But knowing the history of how this artwork had made it from a village in France to a wine cave in Sonoma, I didn't see how any of our treasures could be what she was looking for.

That evening, Derek and I took Alex to dinner at Arugula. She had already given me the highlights earlier, but now she elaborated, filling us in on all the news going on in our building. Our new space was beyond wonderful, she assured us. Derek and I planned to drive into town next weekend to see it for ourselves. And Vinnie and Suzie's little girl, Lily, was growing so fast, she reported.

It was during dessert that Gabriel stopped by the table. "Hello."

We greeted him enthusiastically and introduced him to Alex. I watched his face as she spoke to him and it reminded me that Gabriel was very good at hiding his reactions. But I did see one of his eyebrows lift appraisingly and that told me a lot. It was easy to see why he would find Alex attractive. She was simply beautiful. Tall and confident with a good sense of humor. What was there not to like? But unfortunately for Gabriel, Alex would never get involved with him because as a super-high-powered woman, she preferred the attentions of more passive men. She called them beta types, as opposed to alphas like Gabriel.

Of course, knowing Gabriel, I doubted that he'd give up after just one meeting. I couldn't wait to talk to Alex about him, but she was unusually quiet once we were in the car.

After dropping Alex off at the inn, we drove home. I did a quick check of my e-mail and found a message from Claude. He had translated the letter completely. I thanked him profusely, but he turned around and thanked me instead.

"You lead a much more interesting life than I do, Brooklyn," he wrote. "This was the biggest thrill I've had in months. Normally, the only excitement I ever experience is when I read it in the pages of a book."

I smiled at that, since much of my excitement came from books, too. Sometimes, though, it was a little *too much* excitement.

I printed out Claude's translation and found Derek at the kitchen table, scanning his phone for messages while waiting for me to finish. He glanced up. "Are you ready for some news?" he asked.

"I was about to ask you the same thing."

"You go first," he said.

"No, mine will take some time."

"All right then. I just heard back from the London office." He read from his phone screen. "'Elisheba Asimov, known as Elise, is a high-ranking Mossad agent in charge of tracking down artwork stolen from the Jews during the Second World War.'"

"Wow, just as you suspected. I was right. You are brilliant."

He smiled. "It was a good guess."

"And Elisheba," I said. "That's an interesting name."

"It's the Hebrew version of Elizabeth, according to Corinne."

"Corinne knows everything," I said, smiling at the picture of Derek's delightful assistant. She had followed Derek over from his London office last year, and she and her husband had fallen in love with San Francisco.

"Yes, she does," he agreed.

"So I guess the name Elizabeth wasn't far from her real name."

"No." He set his phone down on the table. "What is your news, love?"

"Claude sent me his translation."

"Excellent," he said, pulling out a chair. "Sit and read it to me."

"I already read you that first paragraph, remember? But I'll start it there so we can get the full picture." I began to read Marie's words from Claude's translation.

"Dear sister,

"Oh, Camille, I have witnessed something so terrible that I'm almost afraid to tell you about it, but I must get it off my chest.

"First I must say how wonderful it has been having Jean Pierre visit. Anton was so happy to have his best childhood friend here! He's been so carefree, like the boy I met and fell in love with so many years ago. But in the last two days, the two men have been like strangers to each other, avoiding each other and casting dark looks. Anton refused to tell me what was wrong.

"Then late last night, he rose silently, got dressed, and left the bedroom. I was nervous and decided to follow him. He walked

across the vineyards to the cave where they store the wine barrels. I hid outside the entry, afraid that if I went inside, he would see me. I heard someone walking in the brush and ducked down to escape detection. It was Jean Pierre! They were meeting in the cave. Oddly, he carried a suitcase and was dressed for traveling. At three o'clock in the morning!

"I ventured a few feet inside the cave and hid in an alcove near the entry. Anton and Jean Pierre were too wrapped up in an argument to notice me.

"Jean Pierre insisted that he had to give everything back. But Anton . . . Oh, Camille, you know how he can be. His mind is no longer right. Every day he grows more afraid that the Nazis will arrive in California and kill us and take our possessions. It isn't reasonable, of course, but somehow he believes his dark dreams more than he believes the newspapers and news reports. I'm terrified that the war has taken a grave toll on Anton that he will never recover from.

"But back to the argument. Jean Pierre kept shouting at Anton, telling him he couldn't keep those things; they didn't belong to him.

"And Anton was shouting back, telling Jean Pierre that he had shared the secret with his beloved childhood friend and no one else. He trusted Jean Pierre. And now he was threatening to betray him.

"At first, I didn't understand what they were talking about. Then Anton promised he would give the precious treasures back after the war was over. Jean Pierre shouted that the war was over and it was time to return everything. But Anton swore that the Nazis were poised to attack again at any moment.

"They continued to talk back and forth about the Nazis, the villagers' belongings, the artwork and cherished bits of silver that they had entrusted us with.

"Anton told me he had already sent everything back to the

village. But instead he hid it all away, thinking the Nazis would track him down and take it if he didn't. He lied to me, Camille. Did he think I would turn him over to the Nazis or something equally evil? Does he not trust his own wife? Is he so sick in his mind that he believes his own words? I was praying that with Jean Pierre's arrival, things would be straightened out and poor Anton would come to his senses. But instead they argued incessantly. Jean Pierre knew my husband better than anyone in the world, and instead of helping him, instead of understanding his sickness, he accused Anton of stealing and lying about it.

"'I have packed my bag,' Jean Pierre said, 'and I'm taking with me the one thing from your home that always meant the most to both of us.'

"'Not the book,' Anton shouted. 'Give it to me.'

"'No. You are breaking the blood bond we've had from the age of seven. You are no longer my blood brother.'

"'You are the one breaking it! But I will always be your blood brother, and you will be mine, no matter what you say.'

"'I wash my hands of you.'

"'No!' Anton screamed the word. 'You have to help me. I'm so afraid.'

"I could hear Anton sobbing, Camille. The sound stabbed at my heart. My poor broken husband.

"'I can't help you, Anton,' Jean Pierre said. 'You've lied to everyone. I've only come back to the cave to salvage what little I can and return it to our friends.'

"I crept closer until I could see Anton and Jean Pierre. They were in another alcove at the back of the larger cave. The ceiling hung down so low that I could see only Jean Pierre's hands as he began to gather up small items from the dressers and bookshelves. Jewelry, several pieces of gold, a precious kitten sculpted from marble.

"Anton fought with him over every piece. He shouted at him again, trying to persuade him to stay, to change his mind. They *could become partners. Jean Pierre would not bend. Anton was beside himself, and he lashed out. Jean Pierre shoved him, and Anton fell, hitting his head. I was afraid he was knocked unconscious, but he stumbled back onto his feet. And then—I hesitate to write this down, but I must—Anton pulled out a gun and shot Jean Pierre!"*

I swallowed hard, looked up at Derek, and saw the same grim resignation I felt carved into his features. After a moment, I began reading again.

"I ran from the cave, no longer caring if Anton saw me or not. He didn't, though. And over the next few days, he banned the workers from the storage cave. I watched him push a heavy wheelbarrow back and forth from one of the supply barns to the cave. It was filled with bricks and stones. A week later, Anton was called into town on business, and I ventured back into the cave. He had plastered over the entire alcove! The small inner cave where he'd hidden all of our friends' treasures was completely concealed behind a wall of brick and cement.

"And suddenly I wondered if Jean Pierre's body as well was hidden forever behind that wall. We will never know, because as you know, Camille, Jean Pierre's mother and father passed away during the war. He has no brothers or sisters, no family left to question where he disappeared to. No one will inquire why he has not returned home to France. I thought to myself, if only your Luc had been home during Jean Pierre's visit. Of all times for him and Jacques to go fishing! Now no one will mourn the poor man's departure. Except me. And perhaps Anton, in those moments when his mind is clear.

"Anton seems happier now that the cave is closed off. He goes about his days, working in the fields and pressing the grapes. But I can't look at him without thinking of poor Jean Pierre.

They were best friends, Camille. I know you must remember what great comrades they were when we were all in day school together. I yearn for those carefree times.

"*I don't know if I will mail you this letter, knowing my words will betray my husband. But if I do, please remember that he was a good man, Camille. Never forget that, I beg of you.*

"*I feel relieved to have written down my story, and I pray that my dear Anton will find peace someday. I am not sure I ever will.*

"*With much love,*
Marie."

Speechless, I looked up at Derek and shook my head. It was unbelievable.

He placed his hand over mine and squeezed. "I can tell by your expression that you're thinking of Robson."

"I feel awful. I'm going to have to give this to him and watch him read it."

"I'll go with you when you do."

"Please. I'm dreading it."

He stood up and went to the refrigerator to pour each of us a glass of ice water. He handed a glass to me and remained standing as he drank his. "You probably need this after all that reading."

"I'm parched," I admitted. "Thanks." After taking several long sips of water, I said, "I don't believe Marie ever mailed the letter. So no one else ever knew."

"I think you're right." Derek leaned back against the kitchen counter. "Now we have to ask ourselves if Anton was essentially a good man or if he had some underlying need to steal from his friends."

"I seriously doubt that. It sounds like the war and the fear of the Nazis drove him crazy."

"Probably so. But can we honestly believe that he kept all of those things hidden inside that cave, that he killed his best friend because of some sort of post-Nazi stress disorder? Did he truly slide down into madness, or was that Marie's excuse for his behavior?"

"She didn't sound as if she was making excuses for him. She sounded heartbroken. It was much worse to lose her husband than to lose a painting or a fancy dressing table."

I took a quick sip of water and added, "Frankly, Derek, the world still suffers from post-Nazi stress disorder. To this day. Look at Trudy. She remembers the tragedy at Oradour-sur-Glane as if it happened yesterday. Millions of people suffered and died, and we're still dealing with the aftermath."

He nodded. "It was a devastating time."

We sat in silence for a minute or two. My mind was reeling from Marie's letter. I couldn't imagine having to witness one's own husband killing his best friend. I sighed. "Did I tell you what Guru Bob said that day we met the Frenchmen?"

Derek thought for a moment. "I don't recall your telling me."

"He talked about his grandfather and wondered if Anton's purpose was altruistic or not. If he was a thief, why didn't he sell off the pieces or display them in his own home as if they were his? But he never did. That must mean something."

"It must," Derek agreed, "but who's to say what?"

"We'll never know." I frowned at Derek. "I hate that."

I stood up. He met me halfway and we hugged each other. "I'll call Robson in the morning," he said, "and arrange a time to meet. He should know as soon as possible, for his own sake."

"Yes, he should. I remember telling him that there was absolutely no way his grandfather could've killed that man in the cave, but Guru Bob wasn't so sure. He said he didn't have my confidence simply because he never met his grandfather. I mean, I never met the guy, either, but I couldn't imagine Guru Bob would be related to someone who would do something so . . . well. I guess he was right to withhold judgment. Even of his own flesh and blood."

We sat quietly with our thoughts for a minute; then Derek said, "The letter does answer a question I had about the cave itself. Why did Anton build a second chamber? What was the purpose?"

"It sounds like the small, inner chamber was already there," I said.

"Yes. He filled it to capacity with the rarest artwork and silver, plus a few pieces of furniture. The big furniture and other items remained in the larger storage-cave area."

"That makes sense, especially if he believed he'd be sending things back to France eventually."

"Yes, but he never did. He was completely mad by the time Jean Pierre showed up. Marie's letter says that in so many words. And once Jean Pierre was killed, Anton had to single-handedly wall up the area in front of the small chamber, creating a second cave with his friend inside.

"He did a darn good job with that wall," I said, trying to lighten the mood.

"Indeed," Derek said. "None of us, not even the excavation team, suspected there was anything behind it except a mountain of rock and packed dirt."

I rested my head on Derek's shoulder, and he rubbed my back. "Let's go to bed, love," he said. "Tomorrow's going to be another busy day."

Upon reading the translated letter, Guru Bob was overwhelmed. "I'm so sorry," I said.

"I appreciate that, gracious." He took hold of my hand. "You have been so good and kind throughout this ordeal. I wish there was some way to relieve the pain you are feeling at having to de-liver this unfortunate news to me."

"My pain?" Shaken, I glanced at Derek and then back at Guru Bob. "No, Robson, I'm not the one in pain. I'm worried about you and your pain."

He smiled. "You have such a beautiful heart. I know you were not prepared to discover the truth about my grandfather, while I have had years to prepare myself for this inevitability."

"You have?"

"Yes." He sat back in his chair, calmer than he had been a minute ago. "I have been struggling with how to deal with the news if it was bad, and now I know. As reparation for my grand-father's deed, I plan to build a museum of tolerance and justice in Dharma. It will be a serene space where people can come to cele-brate mankind's goodness while never forgetting that it coexists with evil. What do you think?"

I smiled and blinked away my tears. "I think it's a dandy idea."

"Dandy." He grinned. "I like that."

*D*erek and I split up after our meeting with Guru Bob. I drove into town to meet China for lunch and follow up on some official bridesmaids' duties while Derek drove over to Frenchman's Hill to discuss the delivery of the inventoried items. I tried not to worry about him having to confront Henri, but I knew he could take care of himself. And if worse came to worst, he did have that big, badass gun in his glove compartment.

Derek had insisted that Henri had been on his best behavior since our first meeting, so I figured the only weapon he would have to use was his innate charm.

I parked on the Lane near Annie's shop. Since I was early, I decided to stop in to say hello.

"Hey, you," she said as she gathered a red-and-white-checkered tablecloth into a decorative knot. She surrounded it with all sorts of pastas and jars of red sauce. On the table display were pasta makers and bright red bowls and utensils for stirring and mixing sauces. "Wish I could meet you guys for lunch, but I'm manning the store this afternoon."

"Don't worry, I'll take notes on everything."

"Okay. Just let me know what you need me to do."

"I will, thanks." My gaze settled on the jar of rich, thick red sauce filled with basil and mushrooms and onions. "Wow, this display is making me hungry for pasta. That hardly ever happens."

She laughed. "Only every other minute, right?"

"Right. I could pretty much eat it every day."

"Mm. Me, too."

I looked at the red bowls and decided on the spot to buy them for the Quinlans. They would look cheerful and bright in their glass-fronted kitchen cabinet. Then I picked up one of the cellophane-wrapped bags of pasta and the jar of red sauce. The perfect meal. Now if only I could boil water. But maybe Derek would handle that part.

"You just made a sale," I said, holding up the bowls, the bag of pasta, and the jar of sauce.

She laughed again. "Hurray."

"You're awfully chipper. How's it going?"

"It's going great. Life is good."

"That's so nice to hear. Oh, hey. How was your date?"

"It started out great, but then Josh had to cut it short. He got some message about a deadline."

"That's too bad. What time did you get home?"

"Around nine o'clock. Maybe nine thirty."

"Do you know what he was working on?"

Annie gave me a frown. "What is this, twenty questions?"

"Sorry, just wondering. No big deal."

But Derek had seen Noland Garrity sneaking up to the storage cave around that time, and then he'd been attacked. The timing was about right, if Josh Atherton left Annie and drove to the winery.

I was grasping at straws again. Josh Atherton specialized in antiquities, so he was researching the cave discoveries and maybe even the caves themselves. He seemed like a really smart guy. Would he honestly care enough to get caught stealing a Renoir? And what could possibly connect him to Trudy? I was only suspicious of him because I was protective of Annie, and that wasn't fair. So I brushed those thoughts away, paid for my pasta, and went to meet China for lunch.

On Saturday the winery held its big Pre-Harvest celebration of the fall season. We had made plans to take Trudy with us, but then Elizabeth wanted to go, too. And since Gabriel refused to let Trudy out of his sight, he was in, too. He drove the two ladies, and Derek and I met them all in the parking lot.

I waved at Annie, who had arrived with Josh. They did indeed make a cute couple, and I felt a twinge of guilt for discouraging her about him. When we walked into the tasting room, Robin and Austin were both at work at the bar along with Jackson and Dad. Mom joined us five minutes later, and it was officially a party.

We'd been tasting wine for fifteen minutes, laughing and chit-chatting about everything under the sun—but mostly about wine and the attack on Noland Garrity. Robin noted that some of the winery employees were a little nervous about it, but Derek and Gabriel assured her that the attack was an isolated incident and they had nothing to worry about.

It was interesting to watch Jackson with Elizabeth. There was definitely sexual tension ringing between them, although they barely made eye contact. I took a quick trip to the ladies' room, where Robin cornered me.

"What's going on between Jackson and Miss Universe?"

I laughed at her title for Elizabeth. It fit the statuesque woman, but she was so much more than a beauty queen. I couldn't say too much, but I managed to tweak her interest. "Apparently they knew each other in a past life, so there's some residual smoldering."

"Smoldering," she said, nodding slowly. "Good word. Darn, I've got to get back, but we need to do lunch."

"Absolutely. We've got a lot to catch up on."

"Yippee."

As we walked back into the tasting room, the heavy French doors swung open and a well-dressed couple walked in. I was taken aback as I recognized Monsieur Cloutier and his charming wife, Solange, from Frenchman's Hill. We'd had lunch at their home with Guru Bob that first day when we went there to tell them about the cave discovery.

Seconds behind them, Henri and his wife, Sophie, entered, followed by Felix, the old man who had the habit of smacking Henri to keep him in line.

"Bonjour," I said, greeting them all politely since they had been civil with Derek the other day when he went to talk to them.

"Bonjour," Solange said, and her husband nodded. The others greeted me in a friendly way, and I felt the beginnings of a rapprochement. The thought made me smile.

"Welcome," Austin said jovially, and set five wineglasses on the bar in front of the visitors. "Your tastings are on the house today, compliments of Robson Benedict."

"No, no, that is not necessary," Henri protested.

I walked over to Henri and gave him a big smile. "Please, we insist. You are our honored guests."

Felix smacked his arm. *"Imbécile.* When someone offers you free wine, you take it."

Everyone laughed, including Henri, and I figured this had to be their regular routine.

As I walked back to the bar, Annie stopped me. "Josh and I were just talking about you."

"Me? What's up?"

"I think we should all go out some night this week."

I glanced at Josh, who was biting back a grin. The action only made his dimples more prominent. "It wasn't my idea," he said.

I gave him the benefit of the doubt, especially since he seemed to make Annie happy. "Okay, I'll see what Derek's schedule looks like and I'll call you."

"Super," Annie said.

I started to walk away, when Josh pulled me aside. Pointing at Trudy, he said, "Is that the woman who was attacked last week?"

I frowned. "Yes."

"Please don't think I'm being crass, but do you think she would be willing to talk to me?"

"As a reporter?" My frown grew deeper.

"Well, yeah," he said, shoving his hands into his pockets. "I mean, that's my job. I won't push her, but she's been inside the caves, right? I'm trying to paint a complete picture of your discovery, and she would be a good one to talk to."

Paint a complete picture, I thought. It sounded like the same blathering nonsense I'd heard from Darlene and Shawn when we caught them by the storage cave that night. Were they all in cahoots? I tried not to think about it as I glanced at Trudy and then back at Josh. "She's not quite ready to talk yet."

"I understand," he said, backing off instantly. "And I didn't mean to bother you. I'd like us all to be friends."

Over his shoulder I saw Annie looking tentative. I hated to cause her worry, so I nodded and smiled. "No problem."

I returned to Derek and Trudy just as Robin was pouring us the first glass, a wonderful muscadet that Dharma was famous for. It was light-bodied and mineral-edged, with a hint of apples. But it wasn't sweet at all, just crisp and refreshing.

"Oh, this is a favorite of mine," Trudy said after her first sip. She looked so healthy and happy to be out among friends, I almost forgot she'd been viciously attacked only days ago and that Amelia's killer was still on the loose. The fact that Trudy was in her seventies was another fact I tended to forget, but in that moment I felt a new resolve to protect her.

"It's lovely, isn't it?" Elizabeth said, swirling her glass.

Out of the corner of my eye, I could see Jackson watching her, and I wondered idly if she might stay in town for a while.

Elizabeth took a step forward to avoid bumping into a new group of people coming into the room. A fellow behind her moved even closer, and Elizabeth's glass bobbled in her hand. I tried to grab it, but it fell and shattered on the concrete floor.

She pressed her hands over her mouth in embarrassment. "I'm so sorry."

"It's my fault," the fellow insisted, and stooped down to pick up the broken stem. On his way back up, his gaze scanned her entire body, ending at her gorgeous waterfall of black hair streaming down her back.

He looked dazed.

As a way to get Elizabeth's attention, it was doomed to fail. I caught a glimpse of Robin, who studiously ignored the fellow and pushed a new wineglass over to Elizabeth. "No worries, occupational hazard," she said with a wink, and poured her another few ounces of white wine.

Jackson walked around the bar and came over to sop up the spilled wine and pick up the pieces of glass. When he stood, his muscled chest created a wall between Elizabeth and the clod who had bumped into her. She didn't mind Jackson's closeness at all.

I took another taste of muscadet and was marveling at the speed at which the broken glass was cleared away, when Trudy began to sway next to me.

"Oh my," she said, pressing a hand to her head.

"Trudy, are you all right?" I asked.

Derek grabbed her arm and braced her.

"What's wrong?" Gabriel demanded, taking hold of her other arm. "Let's go outside."

"No. No, I'm fine." She blinked a few times, trying to regain her equilibrium, and then she stared at me. "Oh, Brooklyn. Oh my. I had a surprise for you."

"You remembered?" I whispered.

"Yes." She inhaled and let her breath out slowly, glancing around as she did so. "My goodness. It must've been the broken glass. He broke a glass that day."

"He did what?" Gabriel asked in a low voice.

"Who?" I demanded quietly. "Who broke the glass, Trudy?"

Derek closed ranks, shielding Trudy from the crowd. Gabriel remained close beside her, and Elizabeth's entire personality changed in a heartbeat. All of a sudden, she looked taller, stronger, like Wonder Woman with her hands clenched into fists, ready to do battle.

Jackson morphed into the powerful soldier he'd obviously been once upon a time. His shoulders rose and his muscles tightened. I seemed to be shrinking next to all of them, but I managed to maintain a cool, calm exterior. I also imagined that Derek would laugh at me for painting that picture of myself.

Trudy scanned the crowd for a few seconds. "Yes, there he is. He's the one. He came to my house to interview me. He stole my quail sculpture, and he killed Amelia."

"Who?" I asked again.

She pointed at Josh Atherton. "Him."

I watched Josh as he realized what was happening and his eyes turned cold.

"Annie, run!" I shouted, but it was too late.

Josh had pulled out a gun and grabbed Annie.

Someone screamed.

"I'll kill her," he said, his voice flat and deadly. "Don't think I won't."

Annie looked absolutely terrified and confused. Her fear radiated right into me. I made eye contact with her, and she kept her gaze on me. When I glanced up at Derek, she did, too.

Yes, keep watching Derek, I thought, hoping she could read my mind. *He'll get you out of this.*

"Don't do it, Josh," Derek said, his tone composed yet urgent. "I can speak to the sheriff. It's not too late to work out a deal."

I prayed that his cool, calm British accent would lull Josh into a false sense of security. Otherwise, someone was going to get hurt. I glanced around. Gabriel had disappeared.

"You're lying," Josh said angrily, clutching Annie's arm and waving the gun. "Just back off, let me out of here, and nobody gets hurt."

Who was lying now?

Behind Josh and Annie, the doors swung open, and Gabriel strolled into the room behind them. How had the man moved so quickly? He had to have snuck back into the fermentation room and raced around to the front of the building.

"Hey y'all, what's happening?" Gabriel said loudly. "Can I get a drink around here?"

Distracted by the newcomer, Josh whirled, dragging Annie with him.

Annie cried out, and the sound made me hurt inside. But now Josh had his back to us.

Before I could mutter, "Get him," Derek took three strides forward and snatched the gun from Josh's hand.

"Hey!" Josh shouted, and twisted to grab the gun away.

Derek popped him on the forehead with the butt of the weapon, and he wobbled. Elizabeth sprang forward and grabbed him in a light choke hold.

Annie was about to crumple and faint dead away, when Jackson jumped out and swooped her up in his arms.

The Frenchmen began to applaud and whistle.

I glanced at Trudy, who was shaking her head in amazement. "I am surrounded by heroes," she said.

I looked over at Robin and started to laugh.

"I love this family," she cried.

"Me, too," I said fondly as I watched everyone in action. All we needed now was for Mom to come in and shake burning sage over Josh's head. For once I wasn't the one being threatened or rescued at the last possible minute, and I really preferred it that way.

It was a phenomenal show. And other than the shattered glass that had brought Trudy's memory back to her, not a thing was broken or lost. Except Josh Atherton's freedom.

Once the cops carted Atherton off to jail and the paramedics gave Annie a clean bill of health along with a mild sedative, Guru Bob arrived, and we gathered chairs together in the fermentation room and listened to Trudy's story.

"I met him at the photo exhibit," Trudy said, clutching Guru Bob's hand tightly. "He was such a sweet young man, so interested in what I had to say. He had attended the press conference and was interested in writing some more in-depth articles. He told me he wanted to feature me. Said I was living history." She glanced around the room and sighed. "I think he meant I was old, but I was foolish enough to be flattered."

"You are beautiful inside and out," Robson said.

Trudy leaned over and squeezed his hand. "Thank you, dear. I didn't see any harm in agreeing to an interview. He came by the house the same day I called you, Brooklyn."

I simply nodded.

"Amelia didn't like him at all. In this case, her instincts were correct." She sniffled, then said, "In any event, I left him sitting in the living room and went to help Amelia with the tea and cookies. She was in a mood because he didn't want tea but preferred to have a glass of water. I can remember her muttering, calling him a heathen. She was so funny."

I had to marvel at Trudy's kind impression of her curmudgeonly friend.

"A minute later," she continued, "I returned to talk to him, and that was when I noticed that my quail sculpture was gone."

"Was he holding it?" I wondered aloud.

"No. He'd brought a briefcase with him, and he probably hid it in there. I didn't think anything of his carrying a briefcase. He's a professional journalist after all." She sighed. "Perhaps he thought that with the abundant objets d'art I have in my house, I wouldn't notice one missing, but my quail is my pride and joy."

"What did you say to him?" Elizabeth asked.

"I looked right at him and shook my finger. 'What have you done with my quail?' I said."

"Did he admit he'd taken it?" I asked. "What did he say?"

"He didn't say a word. He just pulled out a gun. I believe I gasped, and that was when Amelia walked into the room. She saw the gun and dropped the tray. Cookies went flying, and his water glass shattered on the wood floor just as she shoved me out of the way. The gun went off, and I hit my head. And that was it. My memory was gone."

I looked at Derek. "I never even thought about checking for missing items after that. If I'd noticed the quail was missing, we might've been able to track it down more quickly."

Trudy waved my comment away. "Don't blame yourself, Brooklyn. I didn't notice it was gone, either. I have so much stuff in that house, he must've thought I'd never notice." She shrugged helplessly. "I suppose he was right."

"But you did notice," I reminded her. "You noticed right away."

She considered that and smiled. "That's true." Her smile faded. "I wish I hadn't noticed. Amelia would still be alive if I'd kept my mouth shut."

We were all silent for a minute. It must've been hard for Trudy to relive the moments leading up to Amelia's death, but she was handling it like a trooper. In that moment, I felt sorry for Annie, too, who was curled up with a blanket on one of the benches in the room.

And that was when I recalled that she'd mentioned that Josh cut short her date the other night. That was the night Noland Garrity was attacked. Had he left Annie and gone off to meet Noland? Had the two been in cahoots together? Probably not in the beginning, but once they got to know each other, maybe they figured they could do each other a favor. And what about Darlene and Shawn? Had the four of them recognized a familiar streak of larceny in one another?

Annie was dozing, but I suspected she was listening off and on to Trudy's story. I glanced at my mom, who was sitting on the bench, stroking Annie's hair. I knew she considered Annie one of her own daughters, and I was happy that Annie had someone in her life like my mom.

I couldn't predict the future, exactly, but I could foresee a rollicking good cleansing ceremony in Annie's future.

Elizabeth cleared her throat. "While the police were cleaning things up a little while ago, I ran a quick survey of Josh Atherton's last four years of articles. He wrote feature stories from archaeological digs, museum events, and art gallery events from around the world. And with each article he wrote, there was a corresponding story in various local newspapers noting that a small item of significance was found missing sometime after the event concluded." She glanced down and read from her phone screen. " 'Items missing included a shard of pottery, a book, a ring, a length of cloth, a small bell.' "

"Tokens," Gabriel murmured.

Elizabeth looked up. "Yes, tokens. Souvenirs. Each newspaper story mentioned that the particular item was small and not an essential part of the event, but historically important nonetheless."

"Like my quail sculpture," Trudy said.

Elizabeth's jaw tightened. "Yes, like your sculpture."

"Why was he never caught?" I asked.

"The items were insignificant. They wouldn't have been missed right away."

Annie dragged herself up to a sitting position for the first time. "Knowing Josh, he probably arranged for someone else to look guiltier than himself."

Mom frowned. "Why would you say that?"

Annie looked straight at me. "He was already talking about how that appraiser you guys hired . . ."

"Noland Garrity," I said.

"Yeah," Annie said, nodding. "Josh told me that he saw Garrity sneaking into the storage cave. When I asked Josh why he didn't report the guy to the police, he said that as an investigative journalist, he often worked undercover with the police."

"What a crock," Jackson muttered.

"He told me the police had asked him to keep an eye on Garrity, get to know him, and see what made him tick. They suspected him of stealing the artwork he was hired to appraise."

"So Josh was setting you up to point the finger at Garrity," I surmised. "Much later, of course, after he and Garrity were gone and we finally discovered something missing."

"That's horrible," Mom said.

I sucked in a breath and stared at Derek. "The Renoir. Did he take that, too?"

"No," Elizabeth said.

At the same time, Jackson said, "It's safe."

"Yes, it is," Derek confirmed.

I gazed from one to the other, shaking my head, then looked back to Derek. "I think there's a story here."

"I found it hidden behind the false wall of the wardrobe," Derek said to me. "It was just the other day, when I went back to investigate further."

"You never told me," I said.

He took my hand and squeezed it. "We've had a lot going on," he said, then glanced at Jackson and Elizabeth. "I'd like to hear your take on it."

"When I saw the photograph of the painting at the town hall," Elizabeth said, "I was sure it was the Renoir we've been looking for. The Nazis stole it from a wealthy family living near Oradour-sur-Glane shortly after the massacre. I asked Jackson to get me into the caves to study it up close."

"And then you hid it?"

"No. I found it in the wardrobe, right where Derek found it. I have two theories. One is that Garrity planned to steal it, but he couldn't get it out of the cave without Derek catching him, so he hid it in the wardrobe until he could sneak back in and steal it for good."

"What's your other theory?"

"That someone in La Croix Saint-Just was a master forger. The painting in the cave was a remarkable likeness of the original, but it was fake. I wonder if one of your local Frenchmen tried to hide the painting so as to avoid bringing shame to his ancestor."

"Clever," I said. "So when the wardrobe was delivered to Frenchman's Hill, the painting would go with it."

"I believe your second theory is correct," Derek said. "And I know exactly who it was who tried to hide the evidence of forgery."

It had to be one of the people from Frenchman's Hill. I knew better than to ask Derek in front of the whole crowd, but I knew he'd tell me later. For now, I was happy to change the subject. "So Noland Garrity was only guilty of being a total jerk and not a crook."

"True, gracious," Robson said. "He is not a crook."

"But he is a jerk," I insisted, although I tried to say it lightly. "Why do you work with him?"

Robson smiled. "I appreciate Noland for his ability to force me to consciously work against negative emotions."

I shook my head. "I failed that test."

"It is not your test to fail, gracious. You are perfect just as you are."

I laughed at that one and noticed Mom and Dad snickering, too. I was pretty sure Derek was biting his tongue.

I looked at Elizabeth and said what I hadn't been able to say before this. "So you hunt down stolen treasures? Are you really the granddaughter of Trudy's old friend?"

"Of course not, dear," Trudy said. "Elizabeth is a highly trained secret agent specializing in stolen artwork. We made up that granddaughter story so that she'd be able to slip into town and do her work without anyone suspecting."

I felt my mouth gaping. "Trudy?" I blinked a few times, completely bowled over. "You knew all along?"

"It was my idea," she said, and couldn't keep from flashing a proud grin. "As soon as I saw all those treasures in the cave, I worried that there would be some hanky-panky. So I called an old friend of a friend, who recommended another friend, and Elizabeth called me back." She gazed fondly at Elizabeth. "I think we worked very well together."

Elizabeth's eyes glistened with unshed tears. "I think you are the bravest woman I know."

"I agree," Robson said.

When I was over the worst of my shock, I said, "Wow. Good job, you two."

Robson held up his wineglass. "A toast, to all the brave women we know."

"Hear, hear," Dad said, giving Mom's shoulder a light squeeze.

As I watched Trudy take a slow sip of wine, I was reminded of something else. "Trudy, you said you remembered what the surprise was."

She brightened. "Oh, Brooklyn! Yes, I wanted to give you my bookends."

I frowned at her. "Your kitten and quail?"

"No, no. I would never give up my darling kitten and quail. They were gifts from my father. No, the bookends I had for you are two lovely brass angels. Your mother always says you need a guardian angel to watch over you because you're always finding . . ." She blinked. "Oh dear."

She didn't have to say it. I was always finding dead bodies. Trudy was probably stammering because she realized I'd done just that when I'd run in and found Amelia lying dead in her living room.

"Well," Trudy said, a little flustered as she fluffed over that detail. "I decided that morning that I wanted you to have the angels because when I talked to Robson, he called you an angel. And it's true. You are."

"Oh."

Derek handed me a tissue before I asked for it. He knew me, knew that tears were already welling up in my eyes.

"And that day before the young man arrived," Trudy went on, "I was straightening up my mantel to make more room for my marble bookends. That was when I saw the angels and was reminded of you. So I wanted you to have them."

"That's so sweet." I gave her a big hug. "Thank you, Trudy."

"I wish I had them to give you right now."

"That's okay. I'll get them next time I'm at your house."

"Oh, wait!" She laughed. "I took a picture of them with my

phone that day. Just like the kids do." She fished her phone out of her purse, found the photo, and passed it to me.

My eyes widened as I stared at the photograph of one of the angels she planned to give me. One angel was bent over, comforting a child, and the other had a sword raised above his head. The avenging angel. I handed the phone to Derek, who studied the picture for a long moment.

He passed the phone back to me, and I could tell from the bemused look on his face that we were thinking precisely the same thing: Trudy's angels looked exactly like something sculpted by Rodin. We had both done a bit of research when we were wondering who might've sculpted Trudy's kitten and quail.

We stared at each other and began to laugh. So it was possible that Trudy really did have a pair of Rodin bookends. Or they could be wonderful forgeries. It didn't matter one bit.

"Thank you, Trudy," I said, handing back her phone. "They're beautiful. I will cherish them and the thought behind them always."

Robson leaned over and kissed Trudy's cheek. Then he turned to the small crowd and held up his wineglass. "I would like to propose another toast."

"Hear, hear," Dad repeated, and winked at me as he lifted his glass with enthusiasm.

"To the angels among us," Robson said, his affectionate gaze touching all of us in the room. "May they always guard our treasures, great and small."

Epilogue

Two months later, on a gloriously sunny day in Sonoma, at the top of a terraced hillside overlooking the beautiful green valley, my best friend Robin married my brother Austin, surrounded by several hundred family and friends.

The food was fantastic, the wine was delightful, and the dancing continued late into the night. I was thrilled to be able to call Robin my sister every chance I could, mostly because she was brought to tears every time I said it. But more important, because we had been sisters of the soul since we were in third grade. I loved her as much as, or maybe a little more than, my own sisters. She had lived in my house for months at a time, and my parents considered her the fourth daughter—or was she the fifth?—they always wanted.

I finally took a break from dancing to rest my feet. I rarely wore heels, preferring to wear Birkenstocks when I worked in my studio—shoes that Robin referred to as "Hobbit wear." Needless to say, my feet were feeling the stress.

The party had been going on for six hours now, and I was more than ready to leave. But as maid of honor, I felt it was my duty to stay until the bride and groom left. As soon as they were gone, though, I would be dashing out of there.

It wasn't just the dancing that had exhausted me. No, it was something much more insidious. It was my mother's girlfriends. They were on some kind of mission. Frankly, if I had a nickel for every time one of them had asked me when Derek and I were going to tie the knot, I'd have ended up with a great big pocketful of change.

Besides being a rude, clichéd question to ask, it was embarrassing for me. None of them seemed to care, though. A few of my mother's friends had even asked me the question right in front of Derek. He had smiled politely, uttered some charming bit of fluff about me being the love of his life, and then extricated himself as quickly as possible. I didn't have that luxury, since my mother would find out if I'd been impolite to her girlfriends. No, I had to stand there and smile and make excuses. It was weird. I should've come up with something funny to say, but those women caught me off guard every time.

I brushed those thoughts away and concentrated on all the wonderful parts of the day. Several of the Frenchman's Hill families had been invited to the wedding, and it had been so much fun to see them enjoying themselves. I hadn't seen them since Robson had rented a massive truck and a few of us had driven over to Frenchman's Hill to deliver the heirlooms and treasure back to their rightful owners. That was a day I would never forget. And now we were all celebrating together as friendly neighbors. It was a lovely thing to see.

I watched Elizabeth slow dancing with Jackson on the dance floor. Those two looked awfully lovey-dovey, even though they continued to insist they'd never known each other in a past life. I wondered again if she might ever consider moving here. I knew that Trudy would love it if she did, and I would, too. Elizabeth and I had become good friends again, but it was more than that. If she made Jackson happy, we would all love her forever.

"Darling, are you ready to go?" Derek whispered in my ear.

I turned and wrapped my arms around him. "Almost. Where are Robin and Austin?"

"They left a half hour ago."

"Oh. Darn." I looked up at him and laughed. "We could've been out of here a lot sooner."

"You were still dancing."

"And my feet will kill me tomorrow." I laid my head on his shoulder. "I'm glad Robin escaped without too much fanfare. She was afraid everyone would make a fuss."

"They snuck away soon after the cake was served. I overheard your mother suggesting to Robin that they get out 'while the getting was good,' as she put it."

"Smart woman."

"The party appears to be winding down," Derek said, "although the caterers and bartenders are still on duty."

"Robin asked them to stay until midnight. But if she's already gone, then as maid of honor, my work here is done. Let's go."

We walked arm in arm to the car, and just as Derek opened the passenger door for me, I noticed two people standing in the shadows nearby, under an oak tree.

"Who's that over there?" I asked quietly, trying to see in the dark.

"Some neighbors, perhaps."

"Wait. No, that dress looks familiar." I looked closer. "Are they arguing?"

"It's none of our business, love." He tugged at my arm.

I gazed up at him. "You know that's not true. We introduced them."

"Let's go." He gently shoved me into the car and jogged around to the driver's side.

"Why were Alex and Gabriel arguing?" I asked myself.

"None of our business," Derek reiterated as he pulled out into the narrow lane and headed down the hill.

"He can't possibly be interested in her."

"Why not?" he asked. "She's a lovely woman and very accomplished."

"But she's a dominant, remember? She likes submissive males."

Derek laughed. "How could I forget? I was rudely informed of that news many months ago."

"Oh, right." I felt myself blush as I recalled an old, slightly crazy conversation from months ago, about handcuffs and masking tape. "But that's just it. Gabriel is the second most alpha man I know. They'll never get along."

"That doesn't mean they can't be friends," Derek said reasonably.

"This is terrible."

"Darling, don't take it so hard."

"No, it's terrible because Alex is leaving for a business trip in New York," I whined. "I'll have to wait a whole week before I can get any news or gossip from her."

"One week without gossip," he said with a laugh. "That is a terrible shame." As he drove, he reached for my hand, slowly lifted it to his lips, and kissed my palm.

I smiled. "I knew you'd understand the problem. That's why I love you."

"And I love you, darling. Perhaps we simply ought to make our own news instead of waiting to hear from others."

"What do you mean?"

He pulled the car to the side of the road and stopped. I watched, mystified, as he reached over to the glove compartment, removed a small box, opened it, and held it in front of me. "Marry me, Brooklyn."

CHURCH COOPERATION

IN

THE UNITED STATES

The Nation-Wide Backgrounds and Ecumenical Significance

of

STATE AND LOCAL COUNCILS OF CHURCHES

in their

HISTORICAL PERSPECTIVE

By

Ross W. Sanderson

The Association of Council Secretaries

(Local, State, and National)

1960

3

CHURCH COOPERATION IN THE UNITED STATES

Copyright, 1960.

by the

ASSOCIATION OF COUNCIL SECRETARIES

Library of Congress Catalogue Card Number: 60-13189

Printed in The United States of America
BY FINLAY BROTHERS PRESS
Hartford, Connecticut

CONTENTS

FOREWORD

The conciliar movement has come of age—not just twenty-one years old, but a century of existence. In the last five years, a number of state and local councils of churches have observed their centennials. Thus, this cooperative work of the churches has become an accepted as well as a growing expression of the Church of Jesus Christ.

A fledgling organization usually isn't much concerned about the past. Its time and energy are taken up with the demands of the present and visions of the future. As it reaches maturity, though, increasingly it becomes conscious of its rootage.

The council of churches movement has now reached this stage, but very little has been written about it. Of all the areas of the work of the Church, this has been the least treated. Only in a few councils has a good job been done in collating and preserving historical records. Where it is happening it has taken some specific occasion, such as the celebration of a centennial, to cause a history to be written.

For fifteen years now the Association of Council Secretaries has been concerned about the publication of a history of state and local councils of churches. As the professional organization of all employed staff members of interdenominational organizations (city, county, state, national and international) cooperating with the National Council of the Churches of Christ in the United States of America, the A.C.S. three years ago took formal action to have a committee appointed with power to raise funds and publish a history.

The writing of a history isn't done by committee. In choosing an author, though, our group had a very happy opportunity. Ross W. Sanderson was the obvious choice. And he was available and willing. There are very few men now living who have had the breadth of experience in the conciliar movement as he. From 1920 to 1929 he served as Executive Secretary of the Wichita, Kansas, Council of Churches. For the next three years he was associated with H. Paul Douglass as Project Director of the Institute of Social and Religious Research. Then from 1932 to 1937 he served the Maryland-Delaware Council of Churches and Religious Education as Executive Secretary. From then to 1942 he occupied a similar position with the Buffalo Council of Churches. In the National Council of Churches he has served as interim

7

executive for United Church Canvass as well as in the Department of the Urban Church. From 1952 to 1954 he was a visiting professor at the Boston University School of Theology. He is the author of *Strategy of City Church Planning* and *The Church Serves the Changing City.* In addition, he has a long series of survey reports and other articles to his credit. Then, too, he has served his own denomination, the Congregational-Christian, in capacities as pastor and director of Field Research for its Board of Home Missions.

Another fortunate circumstance is that this book was ready for the annual conference of the Association of Council Secretaries at Lake Geneva, Wisconsin, June 19-25, 1960. The theme of this meeting was: *The Conciliar Movement: An Appraisal in the Light of Yesterday, Today and Tomorrow.* The book was a valuable resource.

If this book, *Church Cooperation in the United States,* aids churchmen not only to appreciate the vision and labor of our forerunners but also to equip them to serve the present day and hand on a goodly heritage to their successors, it will serve its purpose. It is our hope that this volume will be introductory only, and will be but the first of many to follow.

Hartford, Connecticut
May 3, 1960

The History Committee
Association of Council Secretaries

Harold B. Keir, Chairman

Presidents of A.C.S. during the years of the Committee's existence

1957-58 Virgil E. Lowder
1958-59 Forrest L. Knapp
1959-60 Harvey W. Hollis

Ellis H. Dana
R. H. Edwin Espy
F. Ernest Johnson
John B. Ketcham
G. Merrill Lenox
J. Quinter Miller
Bruce Roberts
Lauris B. Whitman

PREFACE

Fifteen years ago I was bequeathed a large file of archives accumulated by Roy B. Guild and John Milton Moore over a period of three decades. Dr. Guild had long wished to write a history of the state and local council movement, with major emphasis on the personalities whom he had known. It seemed a happy and relatively easy task to take over where he had left off, filling in details of a story already outlined. The idea of such a narrative won general approval. The chief necessity seemed to be merely to find time to get at the job.

Meanwhile there were other things to do. The materials were however repeatedly examined and carefully arranged, geographically and chronologically; and the writing process was more carefully assessed. Finally, there came freedom to get seriously to work. Once at it, the task loomed larger and larger, as some of those best informed were sure it would. The assembled data, a mixture of the priceless and the inconsequential, needed supplementing at many points, especially for the intervening years; the movement had snowballed, and the size of the task had greatly increased. The primary problem now was not to find data, but to evaluate and compress; not to find something to say, but how to say it briefly enough to suit the initial market.

Obviously one could not write a detailed history of more than two score state councils, or nearly three hundred local councils with paid staff, or nearly seven hundred volunteer local councils, or more than two thousand councils of church women. Even selected case studies seemed to provide no adequate answer. What was really needed was a crew of historical workers, and at least a decade for their investigations and writing. But such dreams require money and time, neither of which was available in the necessary abundance. So we have done what we could, hoping that this little volume will serve as a sort of *historical primer* to open up a vast quest for more adequate documentation of state and local church cooperation.

He who reads may well ask, fairly enough, "Why is *this* omitted, and *that* neglected?" If this all-too-brief story of state and local beginnings and national backgrounds serves to stimulate the writing and publication of a whole series of historical monographs, already well begun, it will have served one of its most important purposes. If it informs those who bear the burden and heat of our day as to some of the pioneering events of earlier years, it will have been well worth the long months that have gone into its making.

For the patient, loyal, and generous support of the Association of Council Secretaries, expressed through the work of its special committee, and for the helpful counsel of many a colleague, my most hearty thanks. Dr. Samuel McCrea Cavert, Prof. Robert T. Handy, and Prof. Winthrop S. Hudson, who read the entire first typescript, are particularly to be thanked for their constructive criticism and generous encouragement, as is Prof. Paul H. Vieth for his helpful comments on an early version of Chapter II.

Like Charles Clayton Morrison, I am "no longer a 'young man in a hurry;'"[1] but forty years of interdenominational experience, at the local, state, and national levels, do dig deep foundations for solid convictions. I too have "no illusion that Protestantism will become ecumenical overnight," but many of us are on our way toward ecumenicity. If we are not to share in the satisfactions accompanying arrival, we can at least, with Robert Louis Stevenson, "travel hopefully."

If the church historian of a century from now can read the history of church cooperation in America a little better, because this volume has put one foot in the door that leads to the conditioning past, we shall be grateful.

January 14, 1960

Ross W. Sanderson

SOME INTERDENOMINATION ABBREVIATIONS

The complexity of the church cooperation task has deposited the following, along with many other "alphabetical" agencies:

ACS Association of Council Secretaries (1940-)
AES Association of Executive Secretaries (1915-1940)
BFA Board of Field Administration (ICRE)
CDFA Central Department of Field Administration (NCC, 1950-1954)
CWHM Council of Women for Home Missions (1908-1940)
DCE Division of Christian Education (NCC)
DCLW Division of Christian Life and Work (NCC)
DFM Division of Foreign Missions (NCC)
DHM Division of Home Missions (NCC)
DUC Department of the Urban Church (DHM, NCC)
DUCW Department of United Church Women (NCC)
ECOA Employed Council Officers' Association (1934-1940)
EFSC Education Field Services Committee (DCE, NCC)
EOA Employed Officers' Association (ISSA)
FC Federal Council of the Churches of Christ (1908-1950)
FCB Federal Council *Bulletin*
FMC Foreign Missions Conference of North America (1911-1950)
FCFD FC Field Department (there were various predecessor commissions and committees)
GCPFO General Committee on Program and Field Operations (NCC)
HMC Home Missions Council (1908-1940)
    Home Missions Council of North America (1940-1950)
ICFC Inter-Council Field Committee (1934-1939)
ICFD Inter-Council Field Department (1939-1950)
ICRE International Council of Religious Education (1922-1950)
IJRE *International Journal of Religious Education* (1924-)
ISSA International Sunday School Association
NCC National Council of Churches
NCFCW National Council of Federated Church Women
NCCW National Council of Church Women
OCC Office for Councils of Churches (NCC, 1954-)
UCM United Church Men
UCW United Church Women

The American Scene

Ecumenical Opportunity

Cooperative churchmanship as we now know it did not begin until the present century was well under way. The characteristic pattern of our nineteenth century religious cooperation tended to be undenominational and unofficial. At the outset America did not face, as it now does, "the ecumenical necessity."[1] The very word "ecumenical" is a twentieth-century addition to our church vocabulary. Rather, we were gradually confronted with an ecumenical opportunity.

The historic phrase *"cuius regio, eius religio"* reflects a characteristic aspect of the life of many European nations. While the prince might choose his religion, his subjects were expected to submit to that choice, unless they preferred to emigrate. The multiple origin of the American people automatically produced a novel amount of *religious heterogeneity,* which the American scene proceeded to accentuate. As the residual legatee of Europe's demographic diversity, and of its language and nationality differences, America inevitably experienced unprecedented religious diversification. Wide differences of polity and doctrine were reflected in different types of Protestant life in the several colonies, but this phase of sectionalism was later sharply modified.

The rapidly moving frontier compounded this original diversity. "The early years of the nineteenth century (saw) the beginnings of an astonishing growth of the denominations that are now numerically the largest in the country."[2] By 1808 Baptists, Methodists, and Presbyterians had all begun work as far west as Indiana.[3] While the home mission journals "of the early nineteenth century called continually for greater consolidation of effort,"[4] the period from the Revolution to the Civil War was one of ecclesiastical division, in which "churches became competitive with one another and broke the ties which bound them to the community." This competition continued for decades, later to be softened somewhat by the beginnings of "comity," but remains a fact still to be reckoned with in church extension, especially in the areas most rewarding institutionally. Individually influential neighborhood churches often "made no united impact upon the new communities." "The competitive churching of the West . . . eventually placed several ministers in communities that could hardly support one . . . Ultimately many communities had too many churches for too few people. . . . Underchurching often resulted in a no less pagan community than over-churching with its attendant evils of discouragement, over-emphasis upon maintaining building and leadership, and the inevitable struggles for membership. . . . The minister, once an important figure in community life, lost this leadership because he did not belong to the whole community."[5]

According to H. Paul Douglass, as the frontier moved westward our "nation created a new religious type the essential mark of which was sectarianism." In his judgment, "The occasion of the multiplying sects was obviously the extreme individualism of the frontier and the unlimited opportunity it afforded for persons under emotional strain to follow their religious hunches. . . . Sociologically speaking, however, the cause of the multiplying of sects was primarily the fact that social changes were taking place at unequal rates."[6]

Nevertheless, it has been urged, "the neighborliness of the frontier softened the asperity of conflicting theologies, and the practical nature of life on the frontier caused people to look askance at the theoretical and speculative nature of theology and creeds."[7] Accordingly, as we grew accustomed to religious differences, we evolved our characteristic, novel, and historically necessary principle of the *separation of church and state*. This peculiarly American arrangement helped to accelerate the *secularization* process that Philip Schaff noted even in 1848: "The secular interests, sciences, arts, governments, and social life have become since the Reformation always more and more dissociated from the Church."[8]

On the other hand, during these years church people had acquired the habit, aided and abetted both by revivalism and by the gifts of rich philanthropists, of organizing independent agencies for the furthering of all sorts of good causes. Even the foreign-mission enterprise was in a number of instances separately organized, making its own corporate appeal to local churches. Only tardily did many societies come under denominational control. During the first half of the nineteenth century there were no less than eight large societies, with large membership, undenominational in their character but largely supported by church people, which one historian of the period says constituted a benevolent "empire."[9] Intended to influence the political, economic, and social order, they sought to further a variety of good causes and needed reforms (peace, temperance, the abolition of slavery, etc.); but they were independent agencies, not associated with the ecclesiastical

13

process. "As extrachurch agencies, the voluntary societies were explicitly designed to overcome the disadvantages of the denominational system, and to provide an opportunity for Christians to unite in matters of common concern."[10] Though providing a "new feeling of solidarity," and often called *inter*denominational, they were technically *un*denominational societies. In a sense, the social gospel was actively preached by the characteristic revivalist, but "social action" as a function of organized church life was to take on new significance a century later.

The decades succeeding the Civil War involved increased sectarianism and division. In spite of the impact of *industrialization and urbanization,* and their consequences for rural life, not until early in the present century did serious concern for the condition of the churches in rural America cause a definite swing toward rural church cooperation. Both rural and urban church cooperation had their beginnings soon after 1880.

A Common Book, Allied Service

The religionists of 1850 had far less to do with one another ecclesiastically than they have now. To be sure, the American Bible Society had been organized in 1816, after the still earlier organization of certain state societies, "for the circulation of the Holy Scriptures without note or comment"—a necessary restriction in those days.[11] Moreover, "a Lutheran leader, Samuel Schmucker, as early as 1838 (had) issued a fraternal appeal to the American churches urging an 'alliance' of the several Protestant bodies which would not disturb their denominational organization and would enable them to render united Service . . . He reissued the appeal in 1870."[12] Thus early was the idea of some sort of "federal" unity for practical cooperation enunciated in the midst of the more isolationist denominational loyalties so characteristic of America.

Outstanding *lay developments* in the field of religious cooperation included the Young Men's and the Young Women's Christian Associations, neither of which became assimilated to the ecclesiastical process. On the contrary, their freedom from formal church control had its distinct advantages, for flexibility of organization and program, specialized service to age and sex groups and to the community, and cooperation with other non-ecclesiastical agencies. In 1850 there was as yet no YMCA in our entire nation. (So much the more, therefore, does the organization of the Young People's Society of Christian Endeavor in 1881 seem a surprisingly early harbinger of all that is now taken for

14

granted by denominational youth fellowships and by their associated efforts in the United Christian Youth Movement.)

The sixth decade of the nineteenth century was a dynamic period. "Whereas in 1850 plank roads, canals, river boats, and scattered short rail-lines provided haphazard communication and transportation, by the end of the decade more than 30,000 miles of rails connected the major regions of the continent except the Pacific Coast. In 1861 a transcontinental telegraph line was completed . . . (Chicago) . . . trebled its population, to pass the 100,000 mark by 1860. . . ."[13] Pennsylvania's first commercial oil well was opened in 1859. From 1852 to 1860 there was rapid growth in antislavery sentiment.

For the YMCA (which took root in America in 1851) and the Sunday School Movement the consequences of the revival of 1857-8 were far reaching. It involved "a large measure of lay activity, a phenomenon which increasingly became a part of the American religious pattern."[14] "Revivalism brought the layman into his own as he had not been since the first century. . . . The nineteenth century in America was the age of the lay worker in religion quite as much as it was the day of the common man on the democratic stage." Moreover, "revivalism was essentially above denominationalism. The evangelists tended to ignore sectarian walls and play down denominational distinctions."[15]

This was all the more significant at a time when—as one who was then a young man was to remember the situation half a century later— "Sectarian" jealousies were fierce; ministers of the different churches were hardly on speaking terms; an exchange of pulpits was a thing never heard of."[16]

The decade of the Civil War presented the churches both opportunities for cooperation and many difficulties. The American Christian Commission would long prove helpful to the cause of church cooperation.[17] On the other hand, during the war "congregations dwindled, the Sunday schools were decimated, the whole work of the church seemed to come to a sudden pause."[18] How the Christian forces of the nation sought to serve the men in uniform, and civilians caught in wartime emergencies, would be a story worth linking up with the growth of church cooperation and its prompt expression in later conflicts.

Not until 1874 was the WCTU to be organized, the Anti-Saloon League not until 1893. The Student Volunteer Movement began in 1886; the World Student Christian Federation in 1895. These latter were non-denominational associations, made up of interested individuals.

15

Ministerial alliances, especially when officered by men who took their opportunity seriously, while primarily fraternal and professional, not representative of the churches as such, and therefore without ecclesiastical standing, were frequently more enduring, and less ephemeral in their local influence, than some of the national movements.[19]

Rhode Island's *"Westerly* Plan" began in 1870 when "seven pastors, from Seventh Day Baptist to Episcopalian . . . had their pictures taken together to prove that 'the Church of Christ in Westerly, R.I., is one,' "[20] "though meeting, for reasons, historical and practical, in seven congregations."[21] This plan, Dr. E. Tallmadge Root reported to the Federal Council in 1908, as chairman of its Committee on State Federations, "assumes that the pastors ex officio represent the churches, and may, without formal authorization, organize and act in their names. In some cases, such a ministerial body has even adopted the name 'Federated Churches.' The advantage of this plan is its simplicity and economy of time and organization. Pastors know what is needed, and it can be done with less discussion. The success and permanence of the plan, however, depends on the personality and mutual confidence of the ministers."

Similar developments, ministerially, were to take place in the more metropolitan centers. As early as 1885, "The *Baltimore* Ministerial Union . . . announced its purposes and limitations as: 'The cultivation of a more intimate acquaintance and the promotion of fraternal feeling among the various evangelical bodies, the discussion of questions affecting the general Christian life of our city, and the securing of united action in evangelical and moral enterprises. No matter affecting the distinguishing practices or tenets of any denomination or church represented in the Union shall at any time be brought forward for discussion or action unless by unanimous consent.' "[22]

This natural proclivity on the part of pastors to pioneer in church cooperation had then and still tends to exhibit a lack of faith in the cooperativeness of lay Christians, and a certain clerical exclusiveness from which the ecumenical movement seeks to escape. For example, "the *Chicago* Federation in its earliest phase included no laymen, its membership consisting of delegates from cooperating denominational ministerial associations. It was therefore a federation, neither of churches nor denominations, but simply of ministers."[23]

16

Though it is true, as is frequently held, that in many communities "ministerial association provided the original basis for councils of churches," it is equally true that in the nineteenth as in the twentieth century ministerial associations have often resisted the organization of councils of churches, for a variety of reasons, including a sincere feeling that ministers themselves could adequately handle all necessary and desirable church cooperation.

Genuine Church Federation Beginnings

Massachusetts meanwhile presented *"Methuen's* Method." A sketch of the history of The Christian League of Methuen from 1887 to 1897 includes its constitution as adopted in 1888. Here "the *churches* join the League by formal vote, and agree to certain lines of cooperation, as stated union meetings, a periodic canvass, etc. They may appoint pastor and delegates to constitute the voting body; or all the members of the churches may be entitled to vote at its annual meeting. The advantage of the plan is that it commits the churches themselves, and renders permanence less dependent on the personality of pastors."[24] This simple structure, called by Dr. Root "perhaps the oldest local federation in the country," seems to have survived continuously for more than seven decades. (Novel as all such beginnings were, they are now matched by many hundreds of local councils of churches, simply organized, and operating under volunteer leadership, many of them in places like Methuen, with a 1950 population of less than 25,000.)

The Ecclesiastical Imagination of a Social Prophet

As early as 1866 "Henry Clay Trumbull, then in charge of the New England Department of the American Sunday School Union . . . in his tours, especially through the rural towns of Connecticut, had been deeply impressed with the needs of interdenominational comity and the federation of Christian forces."[25]

Yet, says Mark Rich, no "general awakening to the distress of the rural church . . . registered itself in the literature or institutions of the day." From the standpoint of comity, rural churches, and state-wide church federation, Washington Gladden's writing in *The Century Magazine* in 1882-3 was widely influential. His "fictionalized serial, 'The Christian League of Connecticut,' . . . first conceived as a single article, . . . (then) extended to four," finally resulted in a little volume of 192 pages. "His dealing with the principle and means of unity in the community, with spiritual fellowship among the denominations and a cooperative program for community improvement evoked a spontaneous response."[26]

It is significant that the writing of these articles stemmed from a request of Mr. Roswell Smith, president of *The Century Magazine,* who had said to Dr. Gladden, then pastor of the North Congregational Church in Springfield, Mass., "I want you to write a kind of a story showing how the people in some New England town got together and united their forces in practical Christian work." This was still the century of lay initiative.[27] It is perhaps no accident, however, that a pastor who had written "O Master, Let Me Walk With Thee" in 1879 should so soon sketch ways in which leaders in many churches could walk together in the community with their One Lord.

Washington Gladden looked forward: "The measure of unity to which the churches have already attained is by no means to be despised; their relations are vastly better than they were forty years ago, when Presbyterians and Congregationalists had no more dealings with Methodists or Baptists than the Jews once had with the Samaritans; when keen contempt and bitter abuse were common currency among the sects. . . . The spiritual unity to which we have attained, though not worthless, is ridiculously inadequate to the present need of the Church; and the organic unity for which we are exhorted to labor, though it may not be impossible, is yet a long way off. Is there not somewhere between the emotional fellowship of the present and the organized ecclesiasticism of the future, a measure of cooperation that is desirable and attainable?"[28]

Gladden was convinced that in 1883 it could be said, "We have reached a period of reconstruction and synthesis."[29] His imaginative writing was to have far more influence in subsequent developments than some seem to have realized. The details of the organization of a local Christian League, then of County Leagues, and finally of a State League, need not concern us. The story is fanciful, high-handed, visionary, headed in the right direction, and contagious in its idealism. Much of it is now standard practice among all cooperative Protestants. Divine discontent was beginning to mount: "The improvement of the social relations of the churches is a great gain; it signifies more to have the people meet in this friendly way, and show each other neighborly courtesies, than to have them talk the cant of Christian union now and then in a prayer-meeting—but it is not enough."[30]

A host pastor, in entertaining the League, is said to have confronted it with possible new techniques of church extension, common enough now, but unprecedented then: "The town is growing rapidly; other religious organizations will be needed; strife may arise among the denominations for the occupancy of new fields. Is it not possible for a band of Christian men, representing all the churches, to exert an influence which shall lead to the amicable adjustment of all such questions?"

When one reads this little volume, even "the Westerly Way" seems less original. One of Dr. Gladden's characters, Captain Conover, a Baptist, is made to say, "The fact is that we haven't got but one church here in New Albion. There are several different meetin'-houses, and several different congregations, and they have various ways of workin' and worshipin', but there ain't but one church." Were Gladden and the Captain quoting Westerly, or were Westerly and Root quoting Gladden? Or were these words part of the folklore of the period?

In the light of the Gladden proposals, the Methuen story also needs an added word. Speaking informally at the first meeting of the Federal Council, Dr. Root said,[31] "Some years ago a young man had read Dr. Washington Gladden's book, *The Christian League of Connecticut.* . . . In his new pastorate he at once proposed the organization of a Christian League of Methuen."

The effect of Gladden's writing on what was to happen in *Maine* is even clearer. In villages that were losing population, many of Maine's churches were impoverished.[32] Mark Rich tells how "Methodist Rev. Charles S. Cummings, a fraternal delegate to the 1890 Congregational Conference of Maine, quoted from Washington Gladden's *The Christian League of Connecticut;* the idea of cooperation flamed. President William DeWitt Hyde of Bowdoin College . . . found the ideas so congenial to his previous thinking that he got a Committee on Conference appointed by his own denomination. Representatives of other denominations were invited to a meeting at Brunswick where 'with rare tact and judgment . . . he with his associates set in motion the machinery which in 1891 brought together in Waterville accredited representatives of the five leading denominations in Maine—Congregational, Christian, Baptist, Free Baptist, and Methodist; and then was created *the Interdenominational Commission of Maine, the first federation,* or interchurch organization, *within a state,* to be formed in the United States, if not in the world.' "[33]

According to Dr. Sanford,[34] some time in the 1880's an "American Congress of Churches . . . held two meetings . . . and then . . . came to a sudden end." Perhaps these were the days to dream and hope, with national action still in the future.

19

Revivalism Characteristic

Among emphases characteristic of nineteenth-century religion in America were *revivalism* and the Sunday School Movement. Chapter II is devoted to the latter, which was in some sense a competitor of revivalism, though a sturdy ally of evangelism. According to one historian of Home Missions in America, it was "in revivalism (that) Protestantism found the key that unlocked the century."[35] Another student of American church life went further: "For two hundred years a conventional revivalism was the chief external feature of American Protestantism."[36] Periodic in the eighteenth century, revivalism became dominant in the nineteenth.[37] Recurrent, discontinuous, often ecclesiastically independent, revivalism reflected widespread interest on the part of many churches and their leaders, but not all. In any case, "successive waves of revivalism made for a common pattern that cut across denominational lines."[38] The modified type of revivalism exemplified during the latter part of the century by the great lay evangelist Dwight L. Moody, whatever its limitations, "was superb for ending denominational warfare."[39]

Home Missions and Social Change

An "upsurge of denominational consciousness (appears to have been) characteristic of many Protestant churches in America during the middle of the nineteenth century. (Even) the church boards based upon a congregational order . . . began to feel their need for intensified fellowship and cooperation within their own denominational circles."[40] This affected foreign as well as home missions. (Such a development is readily understandable in the light of the current increase in world confessionalism at the very time that church cooperation has arrived at the planetary stage.)

In contrast both to revivalism and the Sunday School Movement, in their more massive aspects, "nineteenth century *home missions* was strongly denominational in character," exhibiting a "tendency to proliferate agencies." "Women's national denominational societies" contributed "a further complicating factor."[41] But, according to its latest chronicler, "this complex movement . . . succeeded brilliantly in its main effort. In a century that saw the population increase roughly fourteen times, the proportion of church members in the total population rose from less than ten to over thirty percent." There was "one church for every 1,740 inhabitants in 1800, and for every 895 in 1850."[42] In 1850, however, only sixteen percent of the people were affiliated with any form of organized religion, as compared with sixty-one percent in 1957.

"Profound social changes were concentrated in the great cities, with their rapid growth and their puzzling combinations of interdependence and depersonalization." In fact, "urbanization . . . brought to the church 'the greatest inner revolution it has ever known,' " as the dean of America's urban church studies put it.[44]

"Mushrooming cities were as much in need of evangelization as the Western frontiers in an early day;" yet "the missionary movement was slow in regrouping its forces and reorienting its thinking." This now became imperative, however, for all organized religion "was soon to see other new and stronger frontiers . . . emerging." Accordingly religion, like the nation, was forced to turn back on itself and consider new beginnings. "The impact of scientific and historical thinking," moreover, meant that "the denominations confronted simultaneously new social situations and new patterns of thought." In the midst of such sudden change "Home Missions was driven to find new strategies."

Once the spanning of the continent by the railroads had seemed a precarious dream, the laying of a transoceanic cable a hazardous adventure. Now wonders began to multiply. Radio was not yet, television was undreamed of, but by 1876 both the telegraph and the telephone were a reality. Who would have dared to predict that the descendants of pioneers would so soon cross the continent by air in fewer hours than the months it had taken their forebears by ox-cart?[45]

The Evangelical Alliance Breaks the Trail

The isolationism of language groups was being challenged, and there had been valiant efforts to bridge the social distance between the contrasting denominational heritages, with their differences of creed, cultus, and polity. Organized Protestant cooperation's "most immediate forerunner" in America was the Evangelical Alliance. Because of the rise of this movement, Dr. Schmucker, who had been arranging to send out a call for a Conference of American Churches, gave up the further prosecution of his "Plan for Protestant Union on Apostolic Principles," which had received the endorsement of five major denominational bodies. But his 1838 "Fraternal Appeal" had given him such recognition in different churches and countries that at the 1846 London meeting one Irish leader dubbed him "the father of the Alliance."[46]

21

Established in 1846 in London, the Alliance "was nationally organized in the United States in 1867. . . . Under its auspices local Alliances were organized in various states and cities, and interchurch cooperation, both in its evangelistic and social service aspects, was invited."[47] Though the Alliance "was an organization of individual Christians, without any organized attempt at reaching the churches as official bodies, as this was not then considered practical,"[48] it nevertheless "did, as a matter of fact, within a limited sphere, speak and act . . . for American Evangelical Christianity."[49] An 1846 credal statement, issued as a guide for determining Alliance membership, included "the utter depravity of human nature in consequence of the fall." Theologically rigid, according to our standards, "for the churches as they emerged from the Civil War it was a specially fitting instrument. Denominational consciousness ran high; a more militant organization for church unity could not have maintained the confidence of the denominations."[50] In 1873 the Alliance held a "remarkable and significant meeting" in New York, as the result of "the tireless labors of Rev. Philip Schaff, prophet and pioneer of Christian unity."[51]

Religion Rediscovers the Social Order

In contrast with earlier independent organizational attacks on social problems, of a sort that continue until now, especially under secular auspices, the social implications of the gospel, and particularly their consequences for churchmanship and the ecclesiastical process as such, began now to find new spokesmen.

In 1883 Canon Freemantle, in his Bampton Lectures, spoke on "The World as the Subject of Redemption." The publication of *Our Country* by Josiah Strong in 1885 (to be followed later by *The Challenge of the City*) was undoubtedly a major influence in awakening many church leaders to the social and urban significance of Christianity and of the consequent need for church cooperation.[52] From 1886 to 1898 Strong served as the full-time general secretary of the World Alliance, which in 1887 called a meeting in Washington of all "evangelical Christians in the United States." Three questions were there considered: "1. What are the present perils and opportunities of the Christian church and of the country? 2. Can any of them be met best by hearty cooperation of all evangelical Christians, which, without detriment to any denominational interests, will serve the welfare of the whole church? 3. What are the best means to secure such cooperation and to awaken the whole church to its responsibility?"[53] The Church, like other aspects of our culture, was now no longer able to think of persons as isolated human units, for "by the Eighteen-Nineties the individual was dwarfed by the organization of business, finance, and politics on a grand scale."[54] The rise of psychology and sociology was also soon to underscore the social nature of personality.

By the time of the 1892 Chicago meeting of the Alliance " 'social problems' . . . were taking a larger place than ever before." The churches are now unquestionably developing "a growing awareness . . . that they cannot deal effectively in isolation with many of the social factors of community life upon which the Gospel must be brought to bear."[55] Meanwhile by 1890-91 the Interdenominational Commission of Maine had come into being; and in 1888 a preliminary conference, including representatives of several denominational mission societies, had been held in *New York* to consider religious conditions in that city. The widespread local interest in practical church cooperation was reflected in the 1890 report of the field secretary of the Alliance that 1,888 meetings had been held in 52 cities in 18 states.[56]

Aspiration and Experiment

In 1892 an unsuccessful effort was made to secure a conference of representatives of home-mission societies of a number of denominations.[57] A "proposal of the Brotherhood of Andrew and Philip in 1891 resulted in the formulation of a constitution which provided for a 'Federal Council' of officially appointed representatives of brotherhoods. A first convention was held at the Marble Collegiate Church in New York in 1893."[58] That more did not come from such efforts may be due in part to the "hard times" that began in 1893. But that year was one of cultural progress as well as difficulty. By 1893, too, the Foreign Mission boards, the first of which had been organized in 1810, had begun to confer; and at a great conference at Carnegie Hall in 1900 they were to use the word "ecumenical." Later (in 1911) the Foreign Missions Conference of North America would be organized.

In America as in Europe it was the foreign missions movement, whether denominationally organized or interdenominationally cooperative, together with its powerful allies, which first caught the ecumenical vision, as contrasted with the merely cooperative ideal within any given area. These allies in time included various aspects of the Student Christian Movement, the Student Volunteer Movement, the great Christian Associations, the Laymen's Missionary Movement, and the tremendous interest of church women in the world mission of the Church. It is significant, also, that the "centennial celebration of the

23

Williams College 'Haystack Meeting' in 1906 at Williamstown" occurred two years before the organization of the Federal Council.[59]

Dr. Philip Schaff, of the Reformed Church in the U.S., "at a meeting of the Alliance in Chicago coincidentally with the World's Parliament of Religions in connection with the Columbian Exposition in 1893, in his address on 'The Reunion of Christendom,' . . . declared for a federal type of union, defined as follows: 'Federal . . . union is a voluntary association of different churches in their official capacity, each retaining its freedom and independence in the management of its internal affairs, but all recognizing one another as sisters with equal rights, and cooperating in general enterprises, such as the spread of the Gospel at home and abroad, the defense of the faith against infidelity, the elevation of the poor and neglected classes of society, works of philanthropy and charity, and moral reform.' "[60]

Having "opened up the way for the churches" to act in the field of social problems, the Alliance now began to relinquish its aggressiveness in this field. Meanwhile there had been a significant development in "institutional churches," which seemed to Elias Sanford to provide a new approach to interdenominational fellowship; "and under his inspiration *The Open and Institutional Church League* was organized in 1894."[61] Leaders in this enterprise were Dr. Charles L. Thompson, pastor of the Madison Ave. Presbyterian Church, and later the first president of the Home Missions Council, and Dr. Frank Mason North, of the New York City Church Extension and Missionary Society of the M.E. Church. Dr. Sanford was elected secretary in 1895. Gaylord S. White of the Union Settlement, first secretary of the League, was later elected vice president.

The cumbersome name of this body reflects the slow transition from the now almost forgotten practice of pew rentals and firmly assigned seats to a more cordial and democratic attitude toward the stranger and newcomer, and a less rigid sense of proprietorship on the part of members who had once been literally pew "owners." This new League championed "Christian unity as a spiritual reality and as a practical factor, bringing the denominations into federative relations through which they can work out the problems of Christian service in city, country, and abroad, without the present waste of forces." "Of this word 'institutional,' Dr. Josiah Strong once aptly said, 'It is a word we all dislike but all have to use.' "[62]

The general story of the rise of the "social gospel" is familiar, and has been ably told.[63] It began to provide a third approach to religion, in addition to revivalism [64] and the Sunday school, as the nineteenth century drew to a close; and was a major factor in conditioning the atmosphere in which church cooperation, local, state, national, and world-wide, now developed with such relative rapidity.

Metropolitan Experimentation

In New York an East Side Federation of Churches, organized in 1894, "gave the impulse that brought about the founding, the following year, of the City Federation."[65] Accordingly by 1895 the Federation of Churches and Christian Workers of New York City first blazed a trail in a metropolitan city that had already been pioneered in a more modest way in the smaller New England communities already cited. By 1898 Wisconsin was experimenting with its first Federation of Reforms; and in 1899 Vermont's Interdenominational Commission was under way.

While the one urban example that soon dominated national thinking, the New York City Federation, was in the end to prove as atypical as was the metropolis itself, it provided a concrete demonstration of one way of tackling the interdenominational urban problem, in its most advanced and complicated form. Beginnings elsewhere would have to be as different as the many cities now sensing the need of cooperative churchmanship. Meanwhile New York City afforded a base of operations, and its Federation, it was felt, "illustrated the spirit, methods, and purpose of local cooperative service which we believe a national organization would do much to foster and advance in other cities and communities." At the outset New York, under the exceptional leadership of Dr. Walter Laidlaw, had concentrated on acquiring "a comprehensive knowledge of facts" according to scientific methods. This quest had a profound influence on federal census procedures, and decades later was to become standard procedure for all well-engineered church cooperation. At first, however, it was so far ahead of average ecclesiastical comprehension as to seem somewhat eccentric; also sufficiently expert and detailed to be prophetic of later nation-wide urban studies. Of the New York City Federation Dean George S. Hodges of Cambridge said, "This and similiar movements are in the right direction. . . . Cooperation is not enough and does not satisfy our prayers, but it is at least a long step up the hard hill, and it is possible tomorrow."[66]

National Contagion

By 1898, when a religious newspaper reported that in a Missouri town with 600 inhabitants and three churches (Congregational, Methodist, and Baptist), two branches of another denomination were coming in to organize new churches, everybody was properly scandalized[67]; and the name of the town might just as well have been Legion, in almost any state. Yet leaders were endeavoring both to push forward and to keep their feet on the ground. To men like Sanford it seemed that "Organic unity is still a dream of the future. Federation is a present reality. The churches of the community are the Church of the community."[68]

An undated New York Federation publication, listing Dr. Sanford as for the time being a staff associate of Dr. Laidlaw, sought thus to indicate the need, purpose, and work of a national federation:

"Widespread interest in many parts of the country is crystallizing into purpose and effort to form local federations. The call is increasing for the aid of an organization that will give all the help possible to those who desire information regarding the work that others have done and are doing along federative lines. A national organization would best provide the facilities that would place at the disposal of every community and interested person the literature and guidance that would be helpful both in the founding and development of Local and State Federations.

"Already a considerable number of Local Federations are in existence and others in process of formation. These organizations join in an earnest request that a bond of union be supplied that will enable them to come into closer relation with each other for the interchange of thought and suggestion on matters of common interest. For this reason they advocate the formation of a National Federation.

"The Federation would be only advisory in its plans and purposes. It is reasonable, however, to expect that, without the slightest interference with denominational or local church autonomy or affairs, it would, as a national organization, exert a very strong and helpful influence in advancing the spirit of Christian comity and cooperation that is already a hopeful sign of the hour."

Was this wishful thinking? How widespread was the demand, how profound the urge? Did New York really have its fingers on the pulse of American Protestantism? How hearty would be the response? In any case, according to this claim, "the field" was asking for cooperation nationally, i.e., a national federation. Likewise it is now evident not only that local councils preceded the establishment of the national body, but also that the national body, once it was organized, would in turn stimulate "the establishment of more local councils and the growth of some of those councils already in existence."[69] In thus exercising hindsight, however, we are running ahead of the story. (Centuries from now church historians may still differ as to whether the initial instances of local and state church cooperation accelerated national and world interdenominational organization more or less than they were themselves strengthened by these larger forces. Doubtless it was a two-way stream.)

The competent contemporary historian may well regard this first chapter as a quite amateurish prelude to what follows; the scholarly reader will do well to substitute for it any more adequate frame of reference available to him. We twentieth century cooperative American Christians stand on the shoulders of many a previous epoch. The topmost of these is that long dynamic century between the American Revolution and the Spanish-American War. Accordingly the more ecclesiastical aspects of nineteenth century Protestantism in America, with particular reference to church cooperation, have been briefly presented. Ecumenical opportunity had by 1900 become ecumenical necessity, and an increasing number of church leaders were alive to this change. With the coming of the new century, change will accelerate.

Meanwhile Chapter II will concentrate on a most significant aspect of American church life, the Sunday school, and its consequences for Christian cooperation.

REFERENCE NOTES

Preface

1 *Christian Century,* Dec. 23, 1959

Chapter 1

1 Raymond A. Gray, "The Ecumenical Necessity," STM Thesis, Union Theological Seminary, New York, April 1958. Unpublished MS.

2 Sanford, E. B., ed., *Church Federation*—The Interchurch Conference on Federation, New York, November 15 to 21, 1905. p.v.

3 Mark Rich, *The Rural Church Movement,* Juniper Knoll Press, 1957, pp. 5, 9, 16. Used by permission.

4 Hutchison, *We Are Not Divided,* Round Table Press, 1941, p. 8. Used by permission.

5 Rich, *op. cit. pp.* 13, 16, 21.

6 H. Paul Douglass, *Christian Unity Movements in the U.S.,* Institute for Social and Religious Research, 1934, p. 30.

7 Hutchison, *op. cit.,* p. 8.

8 Quoted in Macfarland, *Christian Unity in the Making,* Federal Council of Churches, 1948, p. 13.

9 See particularly, Gilbert Barnes, *The Anti-Slavery Impulse, 1830-1844,* Appleton-Century, 1933; especially Chapter II on "The New York Philanthropists."

10 "As extrachurch agencies, the voluntary societies were explicitly designed to overcome the disadvantages of the denominational system and to provide an opportunity for Christians to unite in matters of common concern." Though providing a "new feeling of solidarity," and often called interdenominational, they were technically *un*denominational societies. Winthrop S. Hudson, *The Great Tradition of the American Churches,* Harper, 1953, p. 77. Prof. Hudson ably sets forth both the greatness and the weakness of organized Protestantism in American life; his volume will provide the reader with excellent collateral reading.

11 Macfarland, *op. cit.,* p. 18.

12 *Ibid.,* p. 19; also his *Christian Unity in Practice and Prophecy,* Macmillan, 1933, p. 36.
Likewise, Prof. John W. Nevin, of the faculty of the Mercersburg Theological Seminary (Reformed Church in the U.S.), a denominational representative on the American Board of Commissioners for Foreign Missions from 1840 to 1865, has been called by R. Pearce Beaver "the great father of the Mercersburg Movement (in the German Reformed Church)—the most important native American contribution to ecumenical thinking in the nineteenth century." (Quoted by Fred Field Goodsell, in *You Shall Be My Witnesses,* ABCFM, 1959, p. 136 note.)

13 C. Howard Hopkins, *History of the YMCA in America,* Association Press, 1951, p. 12. Used by permission.

14 Hutchison, *op. cit.,* p. 12.

15 Hopkins, *op. cit.,* pp. 7, 8.

16 Washington Gladden, *Recollections,* Houghton Mifflin, 1909, p. 34.

17 According to Winthrop S. Hudson, there is ground for believing that the whole grass-roots organizational development "was sparked by the sociological studies of the religious needs of the cities by the American Christian Commission during the late 1860's and the 1870's, for the need for united action was constantly stressed and numerous proposals were offered and implemented." Personal letter, December 15, 1959.

18 Gladden, *op. cit.,* p. 114.

19 Just when and where, in the nineteenth century, ministers were interdenominationally associated, and how effectively, would make an excellent topic for a doctoral dissertation. Did ministers pioneer church cooperation or thwart it? To what extent? Doubtless documentary evidence could be discovered supporting quite different impressions as to what actually happened before 1900 among the clergy of America. Mass revivals afforded opportunity for frequent and widespread cooperation.

20 E. Tallmadge Root, "New England's Quest: Community and Liberty," unpublished MS.

21 Bulletin No. 4, April, 1905, E. T. Root, New England Secretary of the National Federation of Church Workers and Field Secretary for the Rhode Island Federation of Churches.

22 H. Paul Douglass, *Protestant Cooperation in American Cities,* Institute for Social and Religious Research, 1930, p. 41.

23 *Ibid.,* p. 42.

24 Dr. E. T. Root's 1908 report, previously cited, in 1908 report of Federal Council, Revell, 1909.

25 Sanford, *Origin and History of the Federal Council,* Federal Council, 1916, p. 17.

26 Rich, *op. cit.,* pp. 38 and 215. Cf. also *Information Service,* Vol. XXXIII, No. 16, 1958.

27 Washington Gladden, *op. cit.,* p. 274.

28 Washington Gladden, *The Christian League of Connecticut,* Harper, 1883, pp. 10, 11.

29 *Ibid.,* Postscript, as published in *Century* magazine, September, 1833.

30 *Ibid.,* pp. 15, 16.

31 1908 Federal Council proceedings, p. 131.

32 Alfred Williams Anthony, reporting on "Work in the States," 1905, in *"Church Federation,"* pp. 313-322.

33 Rich, *op. cit.,* p. 41, citing a Robert W. Roundy 1950 pamphlet.

34 Sanford, *Origin and History of the Federal Council,* p. 113.

35 Handy, Robert T., *We Witness Together,* Friendship Press, 1956, p. 3.

36 Douglass, *Christian Unity Movements in the U.S.,* p. 34.

37 Rich, *op. cit.,* p. 17.

38 Hutchison, *op. cit.,* p. 8.

39 Weisberger, *They Gathered at the River,* Little, Brown, 1958, p. 171. *Cf.* also Hudson, *op. cit.,* Chapter III, pp. 137-156: "The End of An Era: The Last of the Great Revivalists" (Dwight L. Moody.)

40 Goodsell, *Ye Shall Be My Witnesses,* ABCFM, 1959, p. 41.

41 For this and the next two paragraphs, *cf.* Handy, *op. cit.,* pp. 6-9.

42 Weisberger, *op. cit.,* p. 151.

43 *American Year Book of the Churches,* 1959, p. 293.

44 H. Paul Douglass, in *Religion—The Protestant Faiths in America Now: An Inquiry into Civilization in the United States,* Harold E. Stearn, ed., Scribner's, 1958, p. 514; quoted by Handy, *op. cit.,* p. 8. *Cf.* also Handy, *op. cit.,* Chapter VI, pp. 110-136, "The City and The Churches" (during the nineteenth century).

45 A January, 1928, Omaha interchurch bulletin noted that "some men who came west in covered wagons have lived to see mail planes flying over their heads."

46 Sanford, *Origin and History of the Federal Council,* pp. 90-92. *Cf.* also H. Paul Douglass, "Christian Unity—1839 and 1939," in FC *Bulletin,* May 1939.

47 Douglass, *Protestant Cooperation in American Cities,* p. 41.

48 Macfarland, *Christian Unity in the Making,* p. 19.

49 Macfarland, *Progress of Church Federation,* Revell, 1921, p. 28.

[50] Hutchison, *op. cit.*, p. 20.

[51] FC 1913 Report, Resolution, p. 55; cf. also Macfarland, *Christian Unity in the Making*, pp. 19 ff.

[52] *Cf.* Winthrop S. Hudson: "The Evangelical Alliance was organized in some cities on a local basis, and in some of these cities the monthly house-to-house visitation proposed by Josiah Strong was carried out by these local Alliances" (personal letter, previously cited).

[53] Macfarland, *op. cit.*, p. 22.

[54] Walter Johnson in the *N.Y. Times Book Review,* November 9, 1958.

[55] Gray, *op. cit.*, p. 19.

[56] Macfarland, *ibid.*, p. 23.

[57] Handy, *op. cit.*, pp. 13, 14.

[58] Macfarland in *American Journal of Theology*, Vol. 21, No. 1, July, 1917, from Notes by Dr. Roy B. Guild, *Cf.* also *Progress of Church Federation,* p. 29.

[59] Goodsell, *op. cit.*, p. 116.

[60] Douglass, *Protestant Cooperation in American Cities,* p. 44; and Macfarland, *Christian Unity in the Making,* p. 19.

[61] Macfarland, *ibid.*, p. 24.

[62] Sanford, *Origin and History of the Federal Council,* pp. 31, 36-49, 49, 67.

[63] C. Howard Hopkins, *The Rise of the Social Gospel in American Protestantism,* Yale University Press, 1940.

[64] As Barnes, *op. cit.*, points out, pp. 7-162, there was a difference among revival leaders. For example, Charles G. Finney was a leader in the antislavery movement, and Oberlin College, of which he became president, pioneered both desegregation and coeducation.

[65] Sanford, *op. cit.*, p. 42.

[66] *Ibid.*, p. 83.

[67] *Ibid.*, p. 77.

[68] *Ibid.*, p. 80.

[69] Gray, *op. cit.*, p. 31.

The Sunday School Movement
In The United States

Prophetic Movement

It would be difficult to exaggerate the part the Sunday school movement has played in educating American Protestantism for more effectiveness in the Christian nurture aspect of their churchmanship, now recognized as central for persons of all ages. As contrasted with the missionary and student movement origins of European ecumenicity, the most conspicuous forerunner of later American church cooperation at the state and local levels was the Sunday school movement. This persistently lay enterprise, which for many decades was undenominational, by substantially supplementing Protestantism as denominationally organized had become a chief precursor of American ecumenicity.

Earliest Beginnings

Francis Asbury established a Sunday School in Hanover County, Virginia, in 1786.[1] Sunday schools were started in Philadelphia and Boston in 1791, in New York City in 1793, in Paterson in 1794, in Pawtucket in 1797, and in Pittsburgh in 1800.[2]

A marker at Greensboro, Vt., commemorates "the first Sunday School *Convention* in New England, June 25, 1817." There were Sunday School "Unions" in New York, Brooklyn, and Boston as early as 1816, in Philadelphia in 1817.[3] Numerous local, county, and city conventions were held about 1820. The American Sunday School Union was organized in 1824.

The Sunday school enterprise, which had quickly gained support from enthusiastic lay persons, was met with initial indifference, apathy, or even open hostility on the part of some clergy. Many church leaders viewed it with open concern, partly because it so often proceeded without getting permission from the ministers, and did not involve itself in the regular denominational procedures.

Soon the Methodist Sunday School Union and similar denominational bodies were also organized. Sunday schools, too, soon tended to "become parts of churches, and came under denominational care." By 1829 even the early publication work of the American Sunday School Union proved "no longer indispensable."[4]

31

State and Local Conventions and Organizations Before 1832[5]

Connecticut had a convention as early as 1825; but not until 1857 did it hold its first regular state convention. (In then electing H. Clay Trumbull as state secretary, with particular attention to Hartford institutes, Connecticut pioneered both a standard statistical process and the important leadership education aspect of the Sunday School Movement.) State "Unions" were organized in Connecticut (1825), in Maryland (1844 or 1846), Wisconsin (1846), and Massachusetts (1854) —but their history was not always to be continuous. For example, in 1889, thirty-five years later, Massachusetts had to be entirely reorganized. New York got an association permanently under way in 1856 or 1857, Connecticut in 1857, New Jersey in 1858; in 1859 Illinois, Minnesota, and Ohio were also permanently organized as convention-holding states that were to evolve Sunday school associations.

As early as 1846 *county* conventions were held in Pike and Scott Counties in Illinois, and by 1856 townships in that state were being organized "to ensure good county work." By 1865 Illinois had 102 counties organized, each with a secretary and a convention. New Jersey had also provided for a secretary in each county.

The permanent nation-wide movement was clearly an outgrowth of these state, county, and township developments, as well as a source of organizing inspiration for them.[6]

First National Conventions

Full visibility for the Sunday school movement was achieved at the exceptionally representative[7] First National Sunday School Convention, held in New York in 1832, at a time when "Chicago, the second city of the United States, was yet unborn."[8] No nation-wide overhead promotion followed. By and large, "the denominations had not yet discovered the Sunday school, except as a customer for printed goods."[4] Twenty-seven years elapsed before the next national convention, in 1859 at Philadelphia. The 1859 Convention came immediately after the 1857 revival period, and gathered up the momentum of state and local developments.[4] A committee appointed to plan for 1861 could not know that there would be a long interruption of all national meetings. Here, however, in Philadelphia in 1859 were the beginnings of The International Sunday School Association, as distinguished from a mere series of conventions.[4] It would be another forty years before corporate responsibility would be taken seriously enough to call for the election of a general secretary.

National progress in the Sunday school as in other movements was of course seriously interrupted by the Civil War; but state Sunday school bodies continued to take shape. In 1859 there was spirited discussion over the use of the words "in connection with the teachings of the Family and the Pulpit" in a resolution approving the Sunday school.[9] But, "the clause was retained, and the Sunday school brought yet closer to the other departments of the Christian Church." The 1869 Convention, postponed from 1861, held at Newark, N. J., was intended to be "a mass convention, open alike to all who come, but every state convention, by its executive committee, (was) invited to send a delegation, not to exceed twice the representation of the State in both houses of Congress;" and it was expected that these delegates would "probably hold a business session at some time during the Convention."[10]

By 1869 there were nineteen organized states:

*	—Maryland	1862	—Pennsylvania
1854 or 1855	—Massachusetts	1864 or 1865	—Indiana
1856 or 1857	—New York	1865	—Iowa
1857	—Connecticut	1865	—Kentucky
1858	—New Jersey	1865 or 1866	—Missouri
1859	—Illinois		(possibly 1859)
1859	—Minnesota	1866	—Kansas
1859	—Ohio	1867 or 1868	—Nebraska
1860	—Michigan	1868 or 1869	—Maine
1860	—Wisconsin	1869	—Vermont

* The Maryland Sunday School Union, organized in 1844 or 1846, seems to have cooperated with the national Sunday school forces from the outset, but not until 1904 did it become an auxiliary of the International Sunday School Association. (Other states also had Sunday school unions before their associations were organized.)

With the 1872 date set, and convention officers elected for the triennium 1869-1872, national Sunday school gatherings were now to be held every three years until 1914. The 1869 mood was significant for later ecumenical developments: "We rejoice in the spirit of Christian union that has been manifested by this Convention, demonstrating that whatever our denominational differences, we are one in Christ and in Christian work."[11]

At Newark, in 1869, "no tolerance was given to the idea that the Sunday school was in any sense an institution independent of the Christian Church." Whatever may have been true half a century earlier, or in the minds of some, the Sunday school was now well on its way to becoming part of that educational enterprise of the Church now known as the church school.

Permanent National Organization Effected, 1872

In 1872 a still more representative gathering convened at Indianapolis, in the heart of "the field." The significance of this midwestern location is better understood when it is remembered that "by the midpoint of the nineteenth century, the five states of the Northwest Territory alone—Ohio, Indiana, Illinois, Michigan, and Wisconsin—contained 4½ million souls, more than the entire population of the country in 1789."[12] Four decades had now passed since the first convention in 1832. The call for the 1872 Convention provided for credentials from the executive committees of the several state assocations;[13] actually, 254 delegates represented 22 states and one territory.

According to H. Clay Trumbull's interesting comparison, in his invaluable "Historical Introduction to the 1872 Convention Report,"[9] "The individual power and responsibility of members was greater in the First Convention (1832) than in the Fifth (1872). The *representative* character of the delegates was weightier in the Fifth Convention than in the First. The action of the First Convention was chiefly for a constituency which had summoned it. In looking at the record of these two conventions, one is likely to be most impressed with the sagacity and foresight of the *men* who planned so wisely at the New York Convention in 1832, and with the magnitude of the *cause* represented by the assembled workers in Indianapolis in 1872. And the contrast indicates the growth of the Sunday school system in America during the last forty years. Who shall say what is to be its growth in the next forty years?" The corporate process had begun, a full generation before the more ecclesiastical forces were to develop the Federal Council of Churches.

This 1872 convention named a first salaried officer, E. Payson Porter of Illinois, as *statistical secretary,* on the basis of his record; but it would be another fifteen years before a paid official field secretary was to be added in 1887. Nevertheless, "The era of sporadic convention impulses was over."[4] In 1872 the Uniform Lessons Committee, a chief by-product of the movement, began a half-century of helpful domination of the lesson-making process. Uniform lessons, which as late as 1940 constituted three-fifths of publishers' sales, have probably been of more value in the economy of the Kingdom than many are now able to realize.

34

By 1820, in spite of its earlier emphasis, first on secular subjects, then on the catechism, the Sunday school had become primarily a Bible school. (The denominations had some of the same problems in connection with the Bible Societies that they had in connection with the Sunday School Movement.) Extension was largely a "Union" responsibilty, and in the earlier years sometimes overdone. Evangelism was central, as is clear from the state reports. Temperance and missions evoked enthusiastic loyalties. Mass conventions stressed inspiration; but the counties began to substitute institutes for mass meetings. (As early as 1860 Illinois was pioneering institutes at the local level.) The need for leadership was the occasion for the beginnings of leadership education ("teacher training," at first).

By the time the first "International" (i.e., including Canada) Convention was convened in Baltimore in 1875, twenty-one state Sunday school associations were under way, all of which survive as functional portions of state councils of churches, or as (in the sole case of Pennsylvania) a closely cooperating agency.

The International Convention Period, 1875-1899[4]

According to its early theory, each convention left behind it a committee to see to it that the next was held at the end of the triennium. Though the International Sunday School Association was organized in 1881, for nearly two decades it continued as essentially a series of conventions rather than as a body with a continuous program. From the outset, however, its executive committee exercised real power, and developed significant leaders. In 1881 B. F. Jacobs was made its chairman; it included representatives of each state, territorial, and provincial organization. Each convention was regarded as a separate entity. Costs were modest, but increasing.

"The first paid secretaries (sustained by the fields they worked for) were Samuel W. Clark in New Jersey and W. B. Jacobs in Illinois, both starting in 1882. In Maryland and New York State and possibly elsewhere there were missionaries in the field, sustained by their states and not by the American Sunday School Union."[4]

At Louisville in 1884 much field work was reported. All bills had been paid, and there was a balance on hand. At Chicago in 1887 too there was rejoicing over the tremendous amount of volunteer field work, and a *field superintendent* was soon to be employed at a "$2,500 salary —a tenth of his previous income." The statistical secretary reported eight "banner states"—every county organized: *Connecticut,* Illinois,

35

Maryland, New Hampshire, *New Jersey,* New York, and Pennsylvania. (The three italicized were reported as completely organized by townships or districts, each county being a banner county.)

In 1890 at Pittsburgh, however, it was admitted that "Many of the states organized before had lapsed and needed complete rebuilding." By 1893 at St. Louis the field superintendent was able to report that only three states remained unorganized (Nevada, New Mexico, and Oklahoma Territory). But it had been difficult to maintain the state bodies in the late 1870's—while six new states were being reported between 1875 and 1878, five had lapsed. Likewise in the early 1880's there was a slight temporary loss, which seems to have been speedily recouped through staff increases. In 1893 eleven states were said to be "completely" organized: Connecticut, Delaware, Illinois, Iowa, Kansas, Kentucky, Maryland, Missouri, New Jersey, New York, and Ohio. The national objective was "an effective organization in every township of every county of every state and territory of this country and Canada," a goal worth remembering.

The proliferation of the work into subsidiary groups was now well under way. In 1884 a national Primary Union had been organized. In 1892 an International Field Workers' Association became the organizational beginning of what is now the Association of Council Secretaries; it gathered momentum in Boston in 1896.

The Period of the International Association, 1899-1920

The Atlanta 1899 Convention had marked effect on the whole *South.* Prof. H. M. Hamill was now made the field superintendent, and Marion Lawrence of Ohio was called to the new position of *general secretary.* Two Georgia ministers were employed for the colored work.[15] Only now had "the intangible movement of 1875" become, in fact as well as in name, the International Sunday School *Association,"*[4] as distinguished from a mere series of conventions. Yet the term "Convention" was long retained, not only for legal purposes, but even as the designation of the body represented by the staff, often becoming a confusing but necessary legal anachronism.

The Denver 1902 Convention was significant for its effect on the *West.* Lingering opposition was still occasionally reported. Even in 1902 Texas called one of "the greatest difficulties to be overcome the indifference of the ministry (and) their allegiance to the old-fashioned revival meeting." Meanwhile the whole question of Christian nurture, raised as early as 1847 by Horace Bushnell's provocative volume, was

36

taking on new urgency. By 1903 the Religious Education Association began its noteworthy career, not as an administrative agency but as a climate-changing body, which spread enthusiasm for education and criticism of stereotyped procedures.

At Toronto in 1905 Dr. H. H. Bell declared, "I am delighted to be here because of the Personality we represent."[16] Likewise Dr. Benjamin B. Tyler reminisced: "Twenty-four years ago, in this city, I attended an International Sunday School Convention. When we came to the registration booths the loved and lamented B. F. Jacobs was just in advance of me. When he was asked about his denominational connection nobody suspected that he was ashamed for a moment of his denominational label. He replied, 'Isn't it good enough in this place to be simply a Christian?' "[17]

At the 1905 Convention W. C. Pearce told how a county convention blackboard map, locating every Sunday school, had revealed a thickly inhabited territory ten miles wide and thirty miles long without a single Sunday school or church—a situation that, once seen, was quickly changed. This procedure appears to have been one of the forerunners of later comity and field research. But there seems to have been too little recognition of the desirability of thinning out the ranks in other too crowded fields.

Recent emphasis on mission and unity, and on Biblical theology, is forecast in remarks at this convention by Carey Bonner on William Carey, who dreamed, saw visions, and "learned something of God's plans:

1. God's love is not for a tribe but for the world.
2. Divine 'election' is to service.
3. The greatness of redemption consists not in what a church is saved *from,* but in what it is saved *to.*"[18]

An important innovation had been the creation of a Department or Committee of Education in 1903 by the Executive Committee of the International Association.[19] Since 1901 there had also been a Sunday School Editorial Association, denominationally constituted. By 1905 it "stands sponsor for a business that represents an investment of perhaps fifteen million dollars."[20] The vested interests of the denominations—not to mention undenominational private enterprise—were beginning to ·affect the corporate structures of the Christian education movement.

37

A significant resolution by the Central Committee, concerning "the relation of the International Sunday School work to the denominational," disavowed any intention on the part of the International to go into the publishing business, and pledged full cooperation rather than competition with the denominational publishing houses.[21]

In modest and irenic spirit, it was also asserted that "We must remember that the Sunday school is not the whole of the church, nor does it cover all the educational functions of the church."[22] Yet there was pride in progress. It was reported that "Over 2,000 counties are organized (and) fully 10,000 townships and districts. At an estimated average of ten people each, there are 120,000 people in our field who are giving solid blocks of time to this work without any remuneration whatsoever."[23]

But the national staff was also growing: by 1905 it included six executives, three stenographers, and special help.[24] Half a century ago the dream of the sort of ecumenical headquarters, which by 1959 had become a reality on New York's Morningside Heights, began to take shape. In 1905 it was felt that "the idea of an International Sunday School building (as suggested by the Executive Committee) is a good one, but we recommend that its disadvantages as well as its advantages be carefully considered and reported on at the next convention."[25] Actually, however, it was not until 1907 that the Association office was removed from the Lawrence home in Toledo to Chicago.

Increasing Corporate Strength

By virtue of the Association's incorporation by Congressional charter in 1907, when it was already twenty-six years old, "the members of (its) Executive Committee . . . became the members of the Association, responsible for its business and affairs," constitutionally.

At Louisville in 1908 expenses for the triennium had mounted to $106,733, as staff, office, travel, and administrative costs increased.

One begins to hear an increasingly defensive note. There were obvious fears of "legislation," and already, even at this undenominational stage, the problem of "authority" began to raise an issue that would later be termed the threat of "super-church" imposition. A conciliatory resolution, introduced in 1908, was adopted;[26] but a clear crisis was already at hand. The retiring president spoke vigorously of Christian loyalties transcending denominational commitments.[27] There was candid differences of opinion as to the relative merits of "uniform" and "graded" lessons.[28]

38

Quantitatively the movement was making progress. Three years before the Federal Council was organized, practically every state had a Sunday school association that was a going concern, and these were bound together in a strong national body. On the other hand, as of 1908-9, the Federal Council listed only sixteen state federations of churches, of which only Massachusetts had a paid secretary, a meager budget, and a continuous history under full-time professional direction. State association papers were now listed in the national report.[29] Likewise the enrollment figures for union Sunday schools—14,118 of them —seemed significant.[30] In fact these union schools were a matter of increasing concern to the denominations.

A total enrollment of approximately fifteen million for the Sunday schools of the nation, undenominationally reported for the most part, was probably less than the figures reported to the denominations.[31] In 1914 it was said that 2,387 out of 3,034 counties were "organized"; in 1918, out of 3,069, there were 2,476. An undated publication recording "Half a Century of Growth and Service" asserted: "There are 63 State and Provincial Associations, approximately 10,000 Districts or Township Associations. The large cities have active Associations."

Growing Denominational Initiative

Behind this impressive quantitative strength the necessity for drastic change was already becoming evident. To be sure, even Dr. J. M. Frost, secretary of the Sunday School Board of the Southern Baptist Convention, spoke generously on[32] denominational cooperation. Likewise, a United Brethren bishop gave eloquent testimony as to what we now call the ecumenical significance of the Sunday School Movement. Yet, in spite of far-flung organizational lines, and increased financial resources, all was not well.

This was a yeasty period of cooperative beginnings in America. The denominations were coming into new self-consciousness as the instigators and controllers of church cooperation. Within three years after the tardy incorporation of the International Sunday School Association in 1907, the whole interdenominational picture in America had perceptibly changed. In 1908 the organization of the Federal Council and of the Home Missions Councils emphasized the new determination of the denominations, as such, to work together. The Foreign Missions Conference, informally organized by denominational boards in 1893, was to be consolidated in 1911 into a more permanent and functionally significant body. Newly aware of their responsibility

39

in the field of education, the denominations were now strengthening their own agencies, while at the same time seeking to play a team game for the control of such hitherto maverick agencies as the Sunday school. The organization in 1910 of The Sunday School Council of Evangelical Denominations provided a fourth combination of denominational forces, functional and ecclesiastical. In a little more than a single critical decade, its crash program was to result in the significant merger of Sunday school "Council" and Sunday school "Association" forces at Kansas City in 1922, and the organization, on a new basis, of their combined strength in the International Council of Religious Education.

Between 1908 and 1914, particularly, says Dr. Arlo A. Brown, " 'a battle royal' was on" between the established International Sunday School Association representing the states and provinces, and the newly organized Sunday School Council, representing the denominations.[34] For interpretation of this determinative blitzkrieg we turn to a sympathetic and participant student of these changing patterns of power. Let E. Morris Fergusson tell the story as he prepared it in the sixth of "Ten Lessons" published in 1922 as a 25-page manual for association field workers.[35]

"And now the denominations began to call the Association to account; just as they had done in the twenties of the last century with the Bible and Tract Societies and later with the American Sunday School Union, and in the eighties with the United Society of Christian Endeavor. The International Sunday School Association had challenged their leadership, and the challenge was ably met. In 1908 the Board of Sunday Schools was created by the Methodist Episcopal Church, superseding the Methodist Sunday School Union. Its secretaries[36] . . . called in question the right of the Association and the states to promote methods and standards in Methodist Episcopal Sunday schools without their sanction, and particularly objected to state normal courses, the enrollment and care of local training classes, and the certification of organized classes in their schools. In a conference held in Chicago in 1909 the bounds of activity between state and denominational agencies were agreed on. The denomination was to have charge of work in the local school; community work and work in union schools and those not denominationally supervised being left to the Association.

"In July 1910 the denominational Sunday school secretaries, editors, publishers, editorial leaders, and extension superintendents came together and formed the Sunday School Council of Evangelical Denominations, replacing the Editorial Association formed in 1901. It became a nucleus for the expression and fostering of the sense of denominational responsibility for Sunday school leadership. Many of its members were strong friends of association work; but they joined with those who emphasized denominational rights in the new spirit of question and audit as to the character and limits of proper association and state activity. Constructively, the Council contributed much to the progress of method, succeeding in some respects to the leadership of the Committee on Education. In 1911 at San Francisco a further issue was raised over the conduct of the Executive Committee in the exercise of its powers under the new constitution, which accentuated the growing friction with the denominational leaders."

Staff increases, especially departmental, meant that "growing expenses, despite the large number of personal and special gifts, kept the financial question acute. Expenses reported at Chicago in 1914 totaled $148,449, with a deficit of $13,105 unprovided for. The Association found itself in need of an appeal to its field constituency through a general financial campaign; and here it was forced to reckon with its denominational critics.[37] Because they were denied an official vote on its executive councils, some of their representatives proceeded to block the plans for campaign organization. The situation was growing acute.

"Educational leadership began to be taken by Prof. Walter S. Athearn (still known to many leaders as their dean at Boston University's School of Religious Education and Social Work) with his report at Chicago in 1914, attacking the existing 'First Standard Teacher Training Course.' As the new chairman of the Committee on Education he continued to develop the educational policies of the Association, and at Buffalo (1918) presented these in broad and detailed form and secured the hearty acceptance by the Convention (now quadrennial). This practical change of the Association from a conservative to a progressive educational body removed one large basis of denominational criticism; while its steady magnifying of its call to lead the community educational forces, leaving the local school field to the denominational agencies, had sensibly reduced the friction of a few years before. It was now possible to consider plans for unification. The example set by the reorganization of the Lesson Committee in 1912 showed how this might be done.

"So it was in June, 1920, at Buffalo, after two years of hard work by an able joint committee, the International Executive Committee admitted to its roll denominational members in full balance of its members elected territorially; while the Sunday School Council, not to be outdone, admitted all the International and state and provincial employed workers to sit with the denominational workers in advisory counsel on plans, standards, and methods of local work. With the carrying down to the state organizations of the same principles of unified counsels guiding a unified field program, the era of the New Cooperation will have begun."

Thus it seemed to an experienced leader in 1922. His appraisal is amply supported by the minutes both of the "Council" and of the "Association."

Part of the problem was what seemed to many the competitive, over-organized state of the movement. As H. H. Meyer put it in his 1913 report to the "Council," there were "four major organizations interested and engaged in the Sunday school enterprise in its larger interdenominational aspects: The American Sunday School Union, The International Sunday School Association, The Religious Education Association, and The Sunday School Council of Evangelical Denominations."[38]

As Dr. Meyer saw it, "the seriousness of the Sunday school task with which every denomination is confronted, and responsibility for which rests upon the denominational leaders, will make it quite impossible for the denominations permanently to cooperate with each other in interdenominational work through the channels offered by an outside, independent organization, in the inner councils of which the responsible denominational Sunday school executives, as such, have no voice."[39] Again, "the denominations, as such, cannot conduct their cooperative educational and extension propaganda except through channels over which they have immediate control. There will always be a broad field of usefulness even to independent organizations, but ultimately, though perhaps gradually, every important department of work, on both the educational and administrative sides, must be taken over by some organization officially constituted by and for the cooperating denominations themselves."[40]

Though in 1914 no evidence of real cooperation on the part of the American Sunday School Union [41] was seen by the "Council," its Committee on Reference and Counsel reported real progress with the "Association," and suggested "the advisability of requesting the International Sunday School Association as soon as practicable to transfer to the denominations cooperating in the Sunday School Council the

42

whole matter of the making of lesson courses for the Sunday schools."[42] This suggestion was the result of a significant report made by the Association's Committee on Teacher Training at a conference in Philadelphia in April, 1914: "In the early days of the teacher-training movement, when the denominations had neither the resources nor the machinery available for this purpose, the work was taken up by the International Sunday School Association. From the beginning it was clearly recognized that ultimately the responsibility of training teachers must rest with the various denominations."[43]

Interdenominational vs. Undenominational

In 1917 the new "Council" secretary, George T. Webb, reporting on the significance of that body, called the Sunday School Council "the finest expression of interdenominationalism that can be found anywhere in the world. . . . Interdenominationalism today means nothing less than the denominations in their organic capacity working together for a common end, and does not favor that free and independent course where men, with however good intent, work together without regard to the plans and policies of our regularly constituted church work."[44] Seen from this safe distance, this problem is now in part clearly one of semantics and terminology; it took decades of experience to make clear—and then only to the initiated—the difference between "un-" and "inter-" denominational.

By 1922 the battle was all over but the shouting. The Kansas City Convention of that year (attendance 7,034) was "more than twice as large as any previous International Convention." Delegations from all but four states were there, ranging from ten to 3,245 persons. There could be no question as to the representativeness of such a gathering. The official Convention Report makes plain what was bound to happen.

The 1914 By-Laws had clearly read: "The Triennial Convention is the supreme authority in all matters pertaining to the policy of the Association."[45] Meanwhile, "The Sunday School Council (had) held its first meeting on the new basis at Indianapolis, January 18-21, 1921. . . . Previously representative of the denominational interests, (it) now was a body composed of the professional workers in the field, both territorial and denominational."[46] There was thus obvious duplication with the now similarly organized International Executive Committee, which had met June 3, 1920, at Buffalo. The two organizations, as newly constituted, had resulted from actions of the Buffalo 1918 Convention.

43

Their merger was now easily accomplished, and *The International Council of Religious Education,* as it soon came to be called, duly constituted. But the Preamble to its revised by-laws, as adopted in 1922, included these important words: "We recognize that in the field of religious education, the local communities and local institutions and organizations have rights of initiative and local self-government. . . . We recognize the rights of the cooperating local churches and organizations to be represented as such in the direction and control of the community movement, which has for its purposes the training of workers for the local churches or the religious instruction of the children of the churches."[47]

Lest it be forgotten by the younger or uninformed leaders of our generation, the International Council clearly intended to make both state councils of religious education and constituent denominations full *members* in the new body. This provided a dual basis, on an intended parity between the two historic sets of interests. Later the criteria for membership, of either type, would come up for more careful review, properly and inevitably.

Of course it was obvious to all that this was only the beginning of an important new story. Said Dean Athearn, speaking on "The Outlook for Christian Education," "The problems of organization whose solution we are beginning here today, must be reenacted in every village, hamlet, and countryside in the days that are just ahead."[48]

That this was not just a temporary, personal, erratic viewpoint was evidenced twenty-five years later by the 1947 General Administrative Report of the International Council: "We note with pleasure the rapid strengthening of the staffs and program services of state and local councils of churches and religious education. If we are to make our ecumenical ideals effective, our cooperation through world and continental units must be rooted in strong local and area avenues and programs. It is here we provide avenues for those types of cooperation and unified actions which the denominations desire and for which they have nationally provided personnel and program resources."[49]

Among the needs listed by this same statement were "a series of mass meetings and demonstrations which will arouse American citizens of good purpose to the actual and potential contribution which the Sunday schools and other agencies for Christian education are making to the public welfare."[50] Mass functions and legislative gatherings had now been differentiated. In the strengthening of the national educational mechanism something of value had been at least temporarily lost.

44

Convention enthusiasm seemed likely to become largely a thing of the past. Could it be regained?

The International Council of Religious Education (ICRE), 1922-1950

The International Council, once organized, existed as a separate agency for 28 years, before becoming a division of the National Council of Churches in 1950. (The Home Missions Council of North America, a 1940 merger of two earlier bodies, existed separately only ten years.) The year 1910, with its consolidation of denominational Sunday school forces, had apparently been definitely related to the ecclesiastical decisions made in 1908. The 1922 merger at Kansas City followed more or less inevitably, once the battle was joined; for the absorptive power of the ecclesiastical process had begun to assert itself.

This regularizing of the Sunday school movement as part of the denominational structures was of course success, not failure. The movement was, to be sure, to a considerable extent professionalized, and largely ecclesiasticized; but this was far more than a victory for the denominations—it was in reality the establishment of an emphasis long pioneered by lay amateurs, who believed that their common Christian witness was even more significant than their particular church loyalty.

Hugh S. Magill, a layman, formerly field secretary of the National Education Association, was elected the first general secretary of the ICRE, and served it ably for more than a dozen of its first, formative years. A capable administrator, he was "thoroughly familiar with the American public school system and with the new movements that were so profoundly affecting the philosophy, content, method, and organization of general education in the first quarter of the twentieth century. He brought to the Council a wide perspective for religious education in relation to the total education of American childhood and youth."[51]

Dr. Magill had brought with him a business manager from the N.E.A., and within a few years a greatly enlarged and increasing budget was in balance. "The first seven appointments made to the new staff had or were within a few months' reach of their Ph. D. degrees, mostly in the field of religious education. . . . The new curriculum of leadership training (was) built on the excellent work that had been done through the Committee on Education and the pioneering work of Walter S. Athearn and others preceding the merger." "The strong and controlling influence of denominational leadership in the committees at work" was of very great assistance.[52]

As one member of that brilliant young staff now sees the situation in retrospect, "More and more the logic became clear that the International Council was and of necessity had to be an interdenominational organization in which the official ecclesiastical representatives constituted the determining body, but with the addition of territorial representatives for their contribution to the development of an interdenominational program."[53] To many of the territorial representatives, however—who had agreed that the new organization should be set up to provide a "fifty-fifty" basis of representation from denominations and territories—it looked as if interdenominational experience was being submerged, and that those who had originally been full partners were being relegated to second-class citizenship. The "accreditation" process, as it developed, appeared to be more insistent in its effect on state councils than on member denominations.

Here now is a powerful agency, possessed of double strength—territorial and denominational; prepared to function sturdily in one phase of the life of the Church, from parish to national and world levels. Within three decades, taking its place alongside the missions councils (home and foreign), it will testify that the task of the Church and of the churches is one task. The result of the growing appreciation of this fact is shortly to be inclusive councils—local, state, and national. Most of these subsequent (post-1922) developments in religious education will be considered later, after we bring the discussion of ecclesiastical cooperation abreast of this Sunday school mile-post. Meanwhile this chapter may well emphasize three phases of the Sunday school history only hinted at previously.

----

1. Urbanization

Unfortunately the International Sunday School Association, based as it was on state bodies, maintained very little record of Sunday school work in the cities. But in February 1912 Fred A. Wells, chairman of the executive committee, had received from various sections of the nation a partial report[54] as to the extent of city-wide Sunday school organization in 39 cities of 100,000 or more in 1910. Twenty of these were organized; twelve were thought to be unorganized, but at least one of these was active in the county organization; information as to the others was inadequate. (Budget figures for church federations in fifteen of these cities are still available; almost all of them now have inclusive councils of churches.)

46

At the 1914 convention fourteen cities were represented by general secretaries of Sunday School Associations, exactly the same as the number of church federation secretaries in 1915. By 1918 there were 25 cities with Sunday School Association executives, in a dozen states; Ohio led, with seven. (By 1918 the number of city church federations with executives had increased to 31.)

2. Shifting Basis of Financial Support

Secondly, a massive piece of evidence as to the change in the relative proprietorship of the states and of the denominations can be quickly sketched in terms of dollars and cents. At the 1890 Convention receipts for the triennium were reported as $14,755.81; expenses, $14,602.78. Of $19,536 pledged for the next three years, $16,470 was promised by the constituent state associations. (This was before a general secretary was employed.) Unfortunately acutely "hard times" followed throughout the nation; and a serious shrinkage in actual as against expected income, with consequent indebtedness. Expenses for the triennium, 1890-1893, amounted to nearly $18,000.[55]

Between 1903 and 1918 field support more than doubled. By 1918 the International was receiving $15,000 a year from the field, with five of the 51 state associations each contributing from one to five thousand dollars. Measured in terms of geography and finance, the undenominational Sunday School Movement seems to have reached its peak of nation-wide support in 1918.

The inevitable decline in state and local financial support of the national work during the depression was never matched by corresponding recovery. At the lowest, in 1932, state support of the International Council, then ten years old—not including the gifts of city and county organizations—dropped to only $1,120.54. (That same year denominational support, while at a temporary low ebb, amounted to $24,011.18.)

During the last four years of its existence the International Council received only an average annual total of $3,539.68 from the State Councils of Religious Education, plus $2,575.02 from city and county organizations. In 1950 state contributions ranged from $25 to $635, and averaged $181.77 for each of 35 states contributing. Not only was the number of dollars reduced; as compared with 1918, the number of contributing councils in 1950 was down a full 30 percent.

After a momentary increase, total state, city, and county contributions to religious education shrank rapidly when the National

Council was organized in 1950. (Since 1954 all receipts from state and local councils have been credited to the Office for Councils of Churches.) Meanwhile annual denominational contributions for national interdenominational religious educational work rose sharply from a pre-depression total of approximately $27,000 to $30,000 in 1930, dropping back in the next years almost to $24,000, then climbing steadily to more than $90,000 in 1950. (In 1950 the work of the International Council became merged with the tremendously inclusive tasks of the National Council's Division of Christian Education, which now handles literally millions of dollars annually, including a variety of enterprises in the field of higher education.) What the state Sunday school associations had pioneered has prospered mightily under the support of the denominations.

A century ago the denominations may have looked askance at the Sunday school. By 1950 they had adopted it, and all that went with it, as a major phase of church life, and had come to consider religious education as a proper charge on all denominational budgets.

3. Professional Personnel

Not until 1892 did the question of organizing paid Sunday School Association workers into a professional group arise. An editorial in the Missouri *S. S. EVANGEL* for August of that year advocated a conference of field workers.[56] The plan was approved by the International Executive Committee, and preliminary organization effected at Chautauqua that same month.

In 1893 at St. Louis the program of the first Conference of Field Workers was carried out as planned.[57] In addition to the paid superintendents employed by the Sunday school associations of 19 states and four Canadian provinces, there were from two to seven assistants in each of eight of these associations. The total of paid workers at the state and provincial level was 54, only 37 of whom were full-time.[58]

Three years later at Boston, in 1896, an International Field Worker's Conference, "auxiliary to the International Sunday School Convention," was held.[59] "The membership shall consist of international, state, territorial, and provincial field workers and officers, paid and volunteer, and all other Sunday school workers endorsed by state, territorial, or provincial associations." Thus by more than four decades was the Association of Council Secretaries anticipated in one major program field. (The inclusiveness of the membership left ample room, of course, for later jurisdictional uncertainties.)

48

In 1899 the name "International Field Workers' Association" was changed to "The Field Workers' Department of the International Sunday School Convention."[60] The tenth annual conference of this Department, held in Denver in 1902, reported 57 full-time and 29 part-time paid workers.[61] In accordance with the basis of organization adopted in 1896,[62] the executive committee of the Department was "authorized to provide for such annual conferences as may be practicable in each year when the International Convention is not held, said conference to be arranged with a view to distributing most widely the benefits of this Department"; and "to spend not more than $100 in any one year for the travelling expenses in arranging for conferences." The International Executive Committee was respectfully asked for an appropriation of $300 a year to supplement the Department's revenue. One of its published papers, "Meeting Difficulties in a New Country," by Rev. John Orchard of North Dakota, reported that "workers of almost every denomination are with us heart and soul, each seeking by every possible means to reach the most people for the most good. Nevertheless, personal and denominational jealousy . . . are not . . . unheard of." A membership of 264, in 45 states, territories, and provinces was recorded; and 50 of these were registered attendants.

Three regional conferences were approved for 1903 (Seattle, Memphis, and Portland, Me.); and three for 1904 (Minneapolis, Indianapolis, and Philadelphia). Whether held or not, here was an obvious beginning of later "pow-wows" and other regional gatherings. By 1905, at Toronto, the "Field Workers' Association," in listing its officers, included ten district vice presidents.

By 1912—not a convention year—a conference of general secretaries was held in New Orleans, under the auspices of the Field Workers' Department. Twenty-eight were present, along with eighteen other state and county workers. They spent eight days together, including suggested periods of rest. One topic, which will recur in a later chapter, was "Making the Most of the Men and Religion Forward Movement."

In 1914, at Chicago, 153 full or part-time workers (not including office secretaries and stenographers) were reported to be present.[63] In 1916 this professional group appears to have become more formally organized as "The Employed Officers' Association."[64]

At Buffalo in 1918 the general secretary of the International recognized "the 'E.O.A.' (as) a family group, consisting only of those who are giving their time to the organized Sunday school work, under salary . . . Many a State and Provincial officer has been saved from making a mistake by hearing some other officer tell how he fell into it. No meetings connected with our work are so 'full of ginger' as are those of the E.O.A. It is a royal fellowship, and promises much for the welfare of the work. The sparks fly sometimes when the discussions get warm, but there is always the undercurrent of choice brotherliness. Our International Association can never measure the extent of its obligation to the E.O.A."[65] So much the more surprising is it that this professional fellowship, fourteen years a-borning, was so soon to be allowed to lapse.

From 1896 to 1918 the number of paid workers reported by the state associations had increased rapidly:

Year	Paid Workers	Part-time Workers included in the Totals
1896	54	17 (in 1893)
1899	62	?
1902	86	29
1905	136	53
1908	155	52
1911	174	41
1914	288	122
1918	336	179

Athearn appears to have been fully justified in declaring[66] that by 1917 there were 300 paid workers; and in the 1922 report[67] Marion Lawrence spoke of "approximately 300" persons "in the various State and Provincial offices, and cities and counties where they have paid workers devoting their full time, under salary, to organized Sunday school work." But in 1923 Brown claimed only 275 such workers in the United States and Canada.[68]

Meanwhile the number of denominational state and national religious education personnel had more than doubled in a decade, increasing from 241 in 1910 to 498 in 1920.[69] While the Association staff appeared to have reached its peak in 1918, the denominations were just beginning to become alert to their staff responsibilty by the time of the Kansas City merger. Denominational personnel now moved to the fore, to dominate the leadership of the new International Council. Impressive as was the development of the Sunday School Association field forces, they were quickly outnumbered by those denominationally employed, once the established Protestant bodies began to take the Sunday school as part of their normal field program responsibility.

Larger Cooperation Ahead

The story of this whole educational aspect of the American ecumenical heritage is now interrupted while the parallel church federation developments are rehearsed. There seems to have been a strange lapse of a dozen years (1922-1934) in the national organization of state and local Sunday school personnel, prefaced by an apparent absence of records of their separate professional association after 1918. In later chapters their resurgent self-consciousness as a group will prove to be a strong stimulus toward the integration of all paid interdenominational staff persons in the nation into a single body, and indirectly therefore toward the establishment of the National Council of Churches in 1950.

To the thorough student of the history of religious education in America this chapter too may appear to be only a dilettante sketch of matters worthy of a volume from the pens of some far more competent educator and some much abler historian. If so, let the reader be patient. As the story proceeds, this writer becomes not merely a compiler and interpreter of documents; as six twentieth-century decades unfold, they will prove to be those of his late adolescence, young manhood, pastoral experience, and denominational and ecumenical apprenticeship. He himself has been a participant in, as well as an observer of, many of the events presented in the rest of this volume.

REFERENCE NOTES

Chapter II

1 The *Columbia Viking Desk Encyclopedia,* p. 1,230, calls this school the first in the present United States. According to E. Morris Fergusson, *Historic Chapters in Christian Education,* Revell, 1935, in December 1790 Philadelphia organized "The First Day or Sunday School Society" (p. 14). Fergusson gives 1785 as the date for the first Virginia Sunday school.

2 *Henry Clay Trumbull, 1888 Yale Lectures,* quoted in the 1905 International Convention Report, p. 44.

3 Arlo Ayres Brown, *A History of Religious Education,* Abingdon, 1923, p. 50.

4 E. Morris Fergusson, "Ten Lessons for Association Workers," 1922 (mimeographed). *Cf.* also his *Historic Chapters in Christian Education,* Revell, 1935.

5 *1872 Convention Report,* p. 15.

6 Brown, *op. cit.,* p. 170. For the "Illinois Band" see *1905 Convention Report,* p. 31.

7 *1872 Convention Report,* p. 11; *1869 Convention Report,* p. 15.

8 *1905 Convention Report,* p. 153.
When the Boston and Albany Railroad was built in the 1830's, "The officials celebrated the amazing fact that the two cities were now only fifteen hours apart by holding a banquet in the United States Hotel in Boston. The bread served at this dinner was made from the wheat which had been growing in Albany only two days before, and it was shipped in a barrel which had been a living tree the previous day. The world was beginning to shrink." *(Boston Ways,* George F. Weston, Jr., Beacon Press, 1958, p. 20.)

9 Historical Introduction to the *1872 Convention Report,* by H. Clay Trumbull, pp. 9-23.

10 *1872 Convention Report,* p. 18.

11 *1869 Convention Report,* p. 153.

12 Weisberger, *op. cit.,* p. 10.

13 *1872 Convention Report,* pp. 21-23.

14 *Cf.* Erna Hardt, "Christian Education in New Jersey," 1951, N.Y.U. Ph. D. dissertation, School of Education. Unpublished MSS.

15 *1902 Convention Report,* p. xxx.

16 *1905 Convention Report,* p. 135.

17 *Ibid.,* p. 119.

18 *Ibid.,* p. 387.

19 Reported at length, *ibid.,* pp. 486 ff.

20 *Ibid.,* p. 561.

21 *Ibid.,* p. 502.

22 *Ibid.,* p. 164.

23 *Ibid.,* p. 421.

24 *Ibid.,* pp. 418 ff.

25 *Ibid.,* p. 403.

26 *1908 Convention Report,* pp. 16, 55.

27 *Ibid.,* p. 333.

28 *Ibid.,* pp. 512, 536.

29 *Ibid.,* pp. 118, 139.

30 *Ibid.,* pp. 141, 142.

31 *Ibid.,* pp. xiv ff., 160.

32 *Ibid.,* pp. 638 ff.

33 *Ibid.,* p. 642.

34 Brown, *op. cit.,* pp. 183 ff.

35 Pp. 13, 14.

[36] Drs. David G. Downey and Edgar Blake, in charge of the new Methodist Board of Sunday Schools, organized a month before the 1908 Louisville International Convention.

[37] *Fifth Annual Report,* SSCED, 1915, p. 41.

[38] *Third Annual Report,* SSCED, 1913, p. 29.

[39] *Ibid.,* p. 30.

[40] *Ibid.,* p. 31.

[41] As Prof. Hudson points out, there was early a "distinction between the activities associated with the ASSU (which is still in existence) and those associated with the Sunday School Conventions. The first was to establish and promote Sunday schools. . . . The Sunday school Conventions were quite different. They were gatherings of Sunday school workers, and the movement had a mass base. . . . City and state Sunday school conventions with the continuing organizations they fostered were the organizational nuclei for many of the later councils of Churches" (letter previously cited). This last point has often been overlooked by "church federation" leaders; sometimes it has even been unknown to them.

[42] *Fourth Annual Report,* SSCED, 1914.

[43] *Ibid.,* p. 99.

[44] *Seventh Annual Report,* SSCED, 1917, pp. 22 ff.

[45] *1922 Convention Report,* p. 62.

[46] *Ibid.,* p. 67.

[47] *Ibid.,* p. 68.

[48] *Ibid.,* p. 171.

[49] *1947 ICRE Year Book,* p. 37.

[50] *Ibid.,* p. 39.

[51] Bower and Hayward, *Protestantism Faces Its Educational Task Together,* Appleton, Wis., 1949, p. 18, (C. C. Nelson Pub. Co.) Used by permission.

[52] *Ibid.,* p. 263.

[53] Personal Letter of Dr. Paul H. Vieth, April 29, 1959.

[54] *1902 Convention Report,* p. 57.

[55] *1893 Convention Report,* pp. 144, 164.

[56] *Ibid., see Historical Note,* p. 66.

[57] *Ibid.,* pp. 19 ff.

[58] *Ibid.,* see list on p. 158.

[59] *1896 Convention Report,* p. 367.

[60] *1899 Convention Report,* p. 327.

[61] *1902 Convention Report* devotes 57 pp. (361-417) to this "fourth regular meeting."

[62] *1896 Convention Report,* p. 367.

[63] *1914 Convention Report,* p. 111.

[64] *Half a Century of Growth and Service,* p. 9.

[65] *1918 Convention Report,* p. 85.

[66] *Religious Education and American Democracy,* Pilgrim Press, 1917, p. 195.

[67] *1922 Convention Report,* p. 93.

[68] *Op. cit.,* p. 171.

[69] *Tenth Annual Report,* SSCED, 1920, pp. 17, 18.

Federative Progress, 1900-1908

While Chapter II brought the Sunday school story in America down to 1922 and to the organization of the International Council of Religious Education, Chapter I covered only nineteenth-century aspects of American federative beginnings. During the first decade of the new century the urge for cooperation in the entire life of the churches gained rapid and cumulative embodiment. This third chapter deals with twentieth century interdenominationalism before 1908.

National Leadership Emerges

A 1900 conference in New York looked toward a *National Federation of Churches and Christian Workers*. In 1901, in spite of "strong opposition on the part of a few" New Yorkers,[1] this national federation was organized at Philadelphia; but largely through representatives of local churches or a variety of state and local bodies, not delegates with national denominational credentials. Those attending represented Evangelical Alliance branches in Pennsylvania, Boston, and Philadelphia; the Connecticut Bible Society; the Maine Interdenominational Commission; and local federations in cities in Connecticut, New Jersey, New York, and Ohio. As yet organizational policies were still experimental, and membership requirements relatively generous and a bit vague. However, as Dr. Macfarland was to write in 1948, "during the period beginning with (the 1902 meeting of the National Federation) we have seen . . . the movement for federation being developed from the bottom up as well as from the top down."[2] Under the auspices of the National Federation of Churches (1900-1905), "local federations were actively promoted."[3]

Church Women Pioneer

The nineteenth century, according to Mrs. Fred S. Bennett, was not only the period when lay activity emerged; because of the new status of women—especially organized women—in church life as well as other aspects of our American culture, it was "destined to be known as the Women's Century."[4] In the early twentieth century three national phases of church women's work were organized.

(1) In 1901 the Central Committee on the United Study of Foreign Missions was organized by interested women.

(2) In 1903 the Women's Interdenominational Committee on Home Mission Study was organized. (These two bodies were later

united, and by 1938 had merged into the Missionary Education Movement, which had stemmed from the Young People's Missionary Movement, organized in 1902. By 1906 there was also a Laymen's Missionary Movement.) In 1906 representatives of five women's Home Mission Boards met in New York to consider the establishment of regional interdenominational home missions conferences for women, and in 1908 the Council of Women for Home Missions was organized.[5]

(3) A wide variety of local federations of church women sprang up during these years. For example, as early as 1907 the Woman's Auxiliary of the Federation of Churches of Providence, R.I., had a printed constitution.

States Organize Church Federations

Maine already had its Interdenominational Commission; New York State organized a Federation of Churches and Christian Workers, at Syracuse, November 13, 14, 1900; Massachusetts, Rhode Island, and Ohio followed in 1901; New Hampshire created its Commission in 1903. Some of these beginnings proved abortive, but the movement had begun to seed itself at the grass roots. Socially minded Christian leaders everywhere found themselves "wrestling with the practical tasks of the churches, in what was becoming a hostile or increasingly unaccommodating social order."[6] Wisconsin in 1902 changed its "Federation of Reforms" to a Federation of Churches.[7] In 1902 Michigan and Illinois were organized. "This seed sowing, however, both in Michigan and Illinois, did not root into permanent life, not from lack of interest but simply from lack of executive secretarial care. Voluntary service was inadequate to meet the requirements of plans that called for constant and wise adjustment of forces."[8]

In November 1904, the year in which *The Shame of the Cities,* by Lincoln Steffens, appeared, Dr. E. T. Root began to give part time to looking after the interests of the general work in New England. Maine's Interdenominational Commission had now acquired extended experience and was looking forward to making its work more effective than ever; and, said Dr. Sanford, "similar federation committees, appointed by fraternal action of denominational bodies in Michigan, South Dakota, and other states, are doing a work most important and far-reaching in its influence."

New Local Federations

In discussing the "Development of State and Local Federations Prior to 1900," Dr. Sanford[9] also cited federations in Oswego, N.Y., and Hartford, Conn. (1900), and reported that the Connecticut Bible

Society was pressing toward a Connecticut federation of churches. In his report for 1900[10] he added that Chicago had organized a Federation of Religious Workers; and that "local federations have been formed in Syracuse, Schenectady, Jersey City, Portland, and Auburn, Me." Later[11] he mentioned Rochester, Troy, Amsterdam, Albany, Utica; Detroit, Toledo; and Ohio, with unanimous adoption of its constitution by representatives of fourteen denominations on December 3, 1901.[12] He quoted Theodore Roosevelt as saying, "There are plenty of targets we need to hit without firing into each other."[13]

Confident Expectations

Dr. Sanford then regarded "the growth of cooperative effort and counsel (as) not only convincing but successful. The conviction deepens that with wise executive care and leadership success will follow federated efforts, both state and local. Without this service little can be accomplished."

These are obviously, though guarded, the words of a man of sanguine temperament, an optimist and a promoter. It was easy to dream, easy also to exaggerate the solidity, stability, and genuineness of progress already made. The denominational leaders were proceeding by faith. To most of them interdenominational achievement was an extra, all "velvet," so to speak. Failure would be disappointing but not fatal. Traditional church business would proceed pretty much as usual at the old stand. To the slowly expanding group of interdenominational specialists, however, now beginning to constitute the tiny nucleus of a new type of functional ministry, whether lay or clerical, bread-and-butter aspects of the problem were soon to become, at best, a matter of serious interest; at worst, life or death concerns.

Denominational Representativeness Established in 1905

It was now clear that the proposed 1905 conference should be made up "wholly of delegates from national church bodies," as contrasted with the relatively "nondescript" National Federation, however commanding its personnel.[14]

At a Washington, D.C., conference in February 1902, at Dr. Sanford's suggestion Dr. William Hayes Ward wrote a resolution that was unanimously adopted providing for the procedures leading up to 1905 and 1908.[15] A Committee on Correspondence was appointed, made up of eleven members, representing five denominations, to which were added Dr. Sanford and, as chairman, Dr. William H. Roberts.[16] Dr. Frank Mason North, in a significant article in *The Methodist Review* (Sept.-Oct. 1905) looked forward to the 1905 Interchurch Conference on Federation as "among those which rise to a universal significance."

In *Carnegie Hall,* from November 15 to 21, 1905, "the most officially representative gathering of the Protestant forces (in America) up to that time," as it was characterized by Dr. Charles L. Thompson in his welcoming address,[17] gave distinguished consideration to many issues. There were present 436 members officially appointed by 29 evangelical denominations, along with 93 alternates and 16 honorary members. About 70 of the participants were laymen, an exceptionally impressive group, but "not a woman's name appears on the roll."[18] "Two subjects were introduced which then seemed radical, if not indeed dangerous: Social Christianity Including Industry, and International Relationships." "But, alas, not a woman's voice was heard."[19]

In the call for this Interchurch Conference on Federation it had been "understood that its basis would not be one of credal statement or governmental form, but of cooperative work and effort; . . . also . . . that the organization shall have power only to advise the constituent bodies invited." Long consideration was given to "the relation of the national body to the state and local federations," many of which, in their first experimental stages, antedated the national beginnings. This issue, still unresolved five decades later, was and is complicated by the fact that "a few state and local federations have included" non-evangelical congregations.

The problem is of such persistent relevance that some details of what happened in 1905 may well be here recorded. Dr. Alfred Williams Anthony, of Maine, moved that the words in Article V of the Plan of Federation, "The question of representation of local councils shall be referred to the several constituent bodies, and to the first meeting of the Federal Council," be omitted.[20] Said he, "Seven distinct ideas have been enunciated on this platform during the progress of this Conference." He favored making "the unit of membership . . . the denomination or church bearing a distinctive name," allowing "these local organizations . . . to form their alliances as they will, but not with this body," the main concerns of which seemed to him to be "the union of the churches, the denominations, the great Christian bodies."

The motion to strike out was adopted, but Dr. William Hayes Ward won a reconsideration. Dr. Frank Mason North explained, "We shall try to secure some sort of representation in the Federal Council that shall come not directly with the appointment by authority of the legislative bodies of the Churches, but from the representative organizations which are at work in the field." How and to what extent this could be done, it was proposed to refer to the constituent bodies for study, and to the Council itself on its organization three years later.

The President of the Rhode Island Federation thought the national organization was being formed "on a narrow basis," and believed Rhode Island did not intend to join it. "We desire to retain our power to organize our local federations as we wish." One delegate thought cumbersomeness and divisiveness would result from any attempt to provide representation for hundreds of local organizations. A Southern Methodist spoke against "a double basis of representation." A motion was made to restrict the reference to the Federal Council alone.

Dr. Ward explained the division of opinion in the Executive Committee. The Business Committee stated, "We think we can safely trust the action which will be considered later, and we do not think there is time or opportunity here for a full discussion of the matter." Dr. Ward himself believed "that the men that are in the local councils will be the interested ones who will be active and useful. . . . These local councils are as much official as we are. They represent the local churches. Those local churches are just as official as the supreme bodies."

Dr. Roberts said the action proposed in the Plan of Federation was in the nature of a compromise, but called attention to the fact that in the 1903 letter calling the Conference the statement was made, "What we propose is a federation of denominations, to be created by the denominations themselves." He personally favored restricting the movement to the denominations. The corresponding secretary of the Baptist Home Mission Society, while eager for the presence of "experienced and able men, who know the most about the workings of the local council," and sure that the power of the Federal Council would depend on their interest "rather than upon men who are outside the local council," pointed out that the proposition before the Conference was simply to defer decision until 1908. He did not feel that they could then and there "deliberately and judiciously" favor single representation.

Both amendments were lost.

There was further discussion[21] of what was meant by "other Christian bodies," and the consequences of requiring their approval both by two-thirds of the members and by two-thirds of the bodies represented. A proposal to amend the plan to permit state federations to organize local councils on any basis they may deem fit, "if it shall not be questioned by the Federal Council," was voted down on the grounds that nobody wished to restrict "absolute liberty of action."

Earlier, with only one dissenting vote, the words "their Lord and Savior" had been amended to read "their *Divine* Lord and Savior." When the one dissenter now proposed to amend the plan to exclude "any doctrinal basis whatever, save that implied by the broadest Christian unity," it became immediately clear that the Conference was quite unapologetically and explicitly trinitarian in its thinking. The chairman of the Business Committee said unequivocally that the plan was "strictly on a trinitarian basis." Extremes of reaction included those of Methodist editor Dr. James M. Buckley: "I here and now declare that I cannot associate in any Conference . . . as is here called for with any person who does not heartily worship the Lord Jesus;" and the more irenic statement of Baptist home missions leader, Dr. L. C. Barnes, who subscribing heartily to all that had been said "covering the supremacy of the Lord Jesus Christ," went on also to remark, "I have no fear that a million Presbyterians and four or five million Baptists, and five or six million Methodists, and so on, and so on, should in the least be harmed if a few thousand Unitarians and Universalists would be willing to come into an organization with such a preamble as this." He "would like to have the door left open."

Dr. Roberts pointed out the danger, in adopting any amendment to a plan representative of the hard-won unity and "absolute harmony" already achieved, that the Conference might "introduce elements of discord." The amendment was lost.

Dr. Charles L. Thompson [22] remarked that "a hundred years ago opinions were often mistaken for conscience . . ." and that "theological wars" had continued "well into the middle of the century," when "indifference took the place of hostility. Churches no longer fought each other; they only passed by on the other side. Then gradually—and it is within the last generation. . . . Churches began to feel kindly toward each other . . . Churches began to say, 'We want to keep out of each other's way.' . . . It was peace secured by distance . . . Another step in the upward path is cooperation."

Pragmatic Orthodoxy

Dr. Samuel B. Capen of the ABCFM was one of those who stressed the possible economies and increased efficiency for the same expenditure in cooperative work.[23] Bishop John H. Vincent, too, was sure[24] that "while the Federation will not diminish in the faintest degree

59

our denominational enthusiasm and effort—but rather increase both—there must grow out of this fellowship a wise economy in our work—in some cases, possibly, the diverting of funds used in unprofitable rivalry, to a wise and promising aggressive effort." He went on to say also, "I should not be true to my profoundest conviction if I did not confess to a serious regret that any sincere worshipper of our Father in Heaven should be entirely excluded from this fellowship. It is to be hoped that in some way (not perfectly clear, I confess to my own mind), every philanthropist who through religious motive and by religious agencies seeks to promote social reform might be able to cooperate with us, whatever his doctrinal views concerning Jesus of Nazareth may be."

In his closing address Dr. Roberts made three suggestions:

"1. We are organized in antagonism to no body of persons claiming the Christian name. . . .

"2. We are ready to cooperate as an organization with good men of all creeds and races for the moral uplifting of mankind, both at home and abroad . . .

"3. (Our) chief work . . . is to bring salvation from sin to the lost race of men through Jesus Christ, our Divine Savior and Lord."

Aside from theology, which is rarely an issue in the newer councils, the matter of structural relationships remains a moot point, involving many difficulties not yet cleared up.

State and Local Developments, 1905-1908

Dr. Walter Laidlaw reported in 1905 on "Ten Years' Federative Work in New York City";[25] and Dr. Root on "Work in the Smaller Cities and Rural Districts."[26] Dr. Root quoted the secretary of the Massachusetts Civic League as saying that "while the churches might be the strongest factor for social betterment, in most towns, because of their divisions, they are themselves the cause of faction and discord."[27]

Rev. J. Winthrop Hegeman, field secretary of the New York State Federation, spoke on "Work in the States."[28] He said that at the organization of the New York State Federation five years earlier, nine denominations were represented, five of which sent official delegates. Unfortunately, "some local federations were soon in a state of suspended animation." He listed as causes of their failure:

1. Lack of a proper idea of the Kingdom.
2. A Church as existing for itself.

60

3. The people are for the church instead of the church for the community.

4. Ignorance of conditions requiring cooperation.

5. Ignorance of the nature, purpose, and method of cooperation.

6. Lack of training to do work outside of the parish-routine.

7. Lack of social mixers to break up the denominational caste, and of social centers favorable to spiritual growth.

8. Lack of use of the lay element; lack of a program and a secretary to carry out its details. "Some federations, having nothing to do, did it, and died."

9. Peculiar characters in the ministry conditioned by their seminaries and denominational individualism. The denominational jingo, the small man in a big church, the small man in a church afraid to lose some advantage to competing churches.

"In the outworking of our Federation it was found that a federation of denominations in the state was not desirable until enough local federations had tried out the possibilities of our method and had developed a strong enough spirit to persistently carry out our basic principles. The unit of our state work is the local federation—not the denomination as yet."

Josiah Strong said:[29] "I rejoice that this great gathering aims at the oneness of God's people—at what might be called *federation at the top:* i.e., closer relations through the action of ecclesiastical bodies. Let me also urge *federation at the bottom:* i.e., the active cooperation of local churches. The churches of the same community, being charged with Christianization, having the same great aims, holding essentially the same great doctrines, enjoying the same opportunities, contending against the same obstacles, have much more in common than the churches hundreds or thousands of miles away, with which the only distinctive bond is a denominational name, a nonessential doctrine, a common form of government or ritual."

Bishop Daniel A. Goodsell, Methodist, pointed out[30] that in "new communities . . . born of the strange drawing of men westward . . . beyond the Alleghanies . . . they met others, drawn by the same drawing, yet of different speech and different Christian doctrine. . . . All had been trained, in the Old World and in the New, in controversy. Controversy, especially when it hardens into exclusion and privilege under law, embitters, segregates. By so much as conscience was in such differences were the lines drawn between the churches. By so much as one church preceded another by age and number, by so much

61

was a newcomer an impertinent intruder, to be chilled by indifference, turned back by contempt, rejected by controversy, or isolated by ostracism. . . . 'Ours is the faith once delivered. Yours is the religious novelty. We do not need you, and will not receive you.' Such for a long time was the spirit of American religious life." The bishop was obviously rejoicing in the change now taking place.

Now "two related bodies continued to function at the headquarters in the old Bible House in Astor Place, New York—the original National Federation of Churches and Christian Workers and the Executive Committee of the Interchurch Conference on Federation." In October 1906 the latter body agreed that "the general work of promoting federations, state and local, remains with the original national Federation." "Just as Dr. Sanford was the personal embodiment of the federal idea in national terms, so E. Tallmadge Root personalized it in those of the community and state." Some have forgotten, many have never known, that "from 1903 to 1913, Mr. Root was field secretary of the Rhode Island Federation, and from 1904 to 1930 executive secretary of the Massachusetts Federation."[31]

Evidences of state and local church cooperation are included by Dr. Sanford in his annual report for 1906, made January 1, 1907, to the Executive Committee of the Interchurch Conference on Federation.

Dr. Root reported that 16 out of 27 denominations in Rhode Island, with 93 percent of the Protestant members of the state, were cooperating in the State Federation. The *Church Messenger* had been taken over as a Federation organ, and mailed to every pastor and church clerk. Three years of experience had thus defined the Federation task: "(1) To secure comity; (2) to secure local cooperation in cities, villages, and rural townships; (3) to voice the common Christian consciousness against evil and for social betterment." A *Handbook,* issued by this Federation in January 1907, and still extant, contains its constitution as adopted in 1901, together with brief statements as to its history, work, and financial policy. These sixteen closely printed pages (less than 4" x 6" in size), plus cover, are characteristic of the celebrated Yankee thrift Dr. Root so ably exemplified, and are a far cry from the more pretentious and costly "public relations" printing of today. But these same prim pages pulse with pioneering vision, giving clear evidence of the courage it took to make even abortive beginnings in a day of high but modest expectations. Two states shared the same field secretary. "The time has now come when clerical assistance and at least one permanent parish visitor are urgently needed. It is estimated that we require $2,000 a year, which is only one-fourth of one percent of the total income of the Protestant churches of the state. . . . At present it is necessary to supplement the contribution of the churches by appeals to individuals." Fifty years later most councils are still under the same necessity!

In *Massachusetts* the number of denominations federated had increased to twelve. A hundred of the smallest towns, with a population of 1,000 or less, had been studied.

In *Connecticut* nine denominations had adopted a constitution, but the full Council membership quotas awaited another round of denominational meetings.

In *Vermont,* out of 174 replies, 71 had acknowledged that their towns were overchurched. Federated churches seemed at least a partial solution.[32] Vermont had evidently been conditioned to cooperation and fact-finding as it fought its rearguard action while many of its most energetic citizens moved westward.[33] A "Report of the Moral and Religious Conditions of the Community" was given in an address by Professor Edward Hungerford before the Union of Evangelical Churches in Burlington, March 10, 1867.[34] The "Vermont Interdenominational Commission (was) organized April 6, 1889 . . . after the pattern of the Maine Committee, which by then had almost ten years of experience. Vermont became, it appears, the principal experimental field for the adjustment of local churches. The organization of state federations went forward apace; six were invited to send delegates to the New England Conference on Rural Progress March 8, 1907."[35]

In 1886, also, Henry Fairbanks had made a report to the Vermont Congregational Conference on "The Problem of Evangelizing Vermont," "based on an examination of the religious conditions in twenty-four towns."[36] Daniel Dorchester, in an article in the *Methodist Review* for November, 1884, presented "chiefly a statistical statement which gives census exhibits for the various Protestant church bodies and the relative status of the Roman Catholic Church."[37] While some communities were better off with two or more churches,[38] among 28 communities studied in Vermont, 15 were over-churched, six of them seriously so. It seemed to Vermont leaders that "federation was a successful method of meeting the problem of over-churching."

Dr. Sanford reported a recent meeting of the "efficient" *New York* State Council in Syracuse. "They have the assurance that several of the secretaries in charge of church extension interests in different denominations will heartily cooperate with them in their efforts. It is recognized on all sides that there is a lamentable waste of men and resources caused by the over-churching of some of the communities and the shifting of population in others."

New Jersey was still in the organization stage, but an executive committee of "influential ministers and laymen had been appointed."

The Evangelical Alliance of *Pennsylvania,* organized some years earlier as an auxiliary to the Alliance in the United States, had developed local alliances. Since the death of its executive, however, no action had been taken to fill his place. A meeting scheduled for early 1907 was to consider formal action to make the State Alliance a "Federation Council."

Dr. Sanford attended the November 1906 annual meeting of the Council of the *Ohio* Federation of Churches in Dayton, where the state executive board was well represented; and he was to spend a month in Ohio in the spring of 1907. The Federation was to seek to secure $500.

Dr. Sanford was also present at the Ninth Annual Convention of Churches and Workers of *Wisconsin,* and H. A. Miner, secretary of its Federation, reported at length concerning its work.[39]

Other reports concerned a group of *Home Mission States:*

In *South Dakota* the Federation Council of the Churches of Christ planned to create a commission "through which it is hoped that practical definite results will be secured in the matter of comity."

In *Montana* an interdenominational Federation Commission, under consideration for a year and a half, was soon to be organized.

In *Kansas* there had been "no success as yet."

Washington reported Congregational-Presbyterian comity, also "much rivalry to occupy new fields where there is any promise of growth, much friction, and considerable loss."

In *Oregon* "we have a committee to prepare a plan (under consideration by the denominations) . . .; we have not yet made much progress . . . but . . . are hopeful."

In *Wyoming* and *Colorado* denominational home missions secretaries were showing increasing care in investigating, to avoid interfering with rights already established. "There is no department of work where the churches are insisting more earnestly that the spirit of comity shall prevail than in the planting of new churches."

Various *cities* also reported. The president of the *Toledo* Federation told of their evangelistic programs and other cooperative activities.[40] The secretary of the Connecticut Bible Society recounted the experience in *Hartford* with tent meetings.[41] Rev. E. P. Ryland, a Methodist pastor in *Los Angeles,* spoke at length for that Federation.[42]

According to a statement from the Executive Committee of the Interchurch Conference on Federation, "in nearly all our cities the assembly rooms of the YMCA are freely granted as the meeting places of the ministerial unions and the local church federation."[43] Incidentally, the word "federation" appears to have had an ambivalent meaning in this period, and perhaps still has: it refers to the cooperative activities of strong churches that presumably should remain separate, and also to some sort of relationship by which weak churches can unite for purposes of greater usefulness. There continues to be ambiguity at this point, with a resulting prejudice against one meaning of the word because of the other.

By September 1907 it could be confidently proclaimed, "The Federal Council of 1908 is assured."

Dr. Sanford's second annual report as secretary of the Executive Committee of the Conference, made in 1908, covering the year 1907, is similarly valuable as an evidence of the progress of federation at that time. Dr. Root[44] had met with the *Portland, Maine,* Federation in February. It was reorganized, and in November voted unanimously, at a meeting at which every member church was represented, to raise $1,000, employ a lady as secretary, and introduce the cooperative parish plan. "This secretary is spending January, 1908, in Providence, New York, and Worcester, studying methods."

The *Vermont* Interdenominational Commission had empowered its Executive Committee to appoint a secretary to collect thorough statistics bearing on the problem of federation.

Connecticut completed its organization December 10, 1907. Its constitution was to be submitted for the consideration of the state constituent bodies before aggressive work was undertaken.

The *New York State* Federation was active against race track gambling.

"The *Wisconsin* Federation is undertaking, during the coming year, to make a thoroughly scientific study of religious conditions in every town and city in the state." (One wonders if the size of such a task was adequately grasped.)

Reports from other states (Pennsylvania, Ohio, Michigan, California, North and South Dakota) made it clear that

"(1) Church Federation offers a solution in meeting needs that are recognized on every hand;

"(2)   That in order to secure these benefits plans must be worked out that will support efficient and permanent secretarial and executive work. The statement made in the report for 1906 will bear repetition. The attempt to develop and carry forward any large work . . . local, state, or national, . . . when the details are left in the hands of volunteer agents, lay or clerical, will in most cases soon end in comparative failure. . . . As soon expect a church to thrive without pastoral oversight, or the smallest business to run itself without direction, as to expect federation to work out large results by putting the best plans on paper, endorsing them in a mass meeting, and then leaving them to be wrought out by a group of overworked pastors and busy laymen, who wonder how they will find time to do the duty that lies nearest to them as the servants of those who have a first claim on their time." Half a century later the absolute necessity of adequate, sustained financial support for professional leadership is clearer than ever; so also is the continuing value of volunteer service. In those earlier days budgets were modest. For example, the corresponding secretary of the *Trenton, N.J.,* Interchurch Federation reported that they had collected a thousand dollars. This was obviously regarded as a bit of an achievement, and no doubt was.

Federal Council of Churches (FC) Organized, 1908

Now, in spite of untoward events, came great ventures of faith. In 1908, one of the most important ecumenical benchmarks in all this history, "race riots and labor conflicts marked the scene in the United States," and international "tensions . . . were to eventuate in a world war."[45] The first Model T Ford had not yet been produced. The significance of what the Wright Brothers had accomplished at Kitty Hawk five years earlier was still little realized—who could have thought that ecumenical secretaries would soon be shuttling back and forth *over* the seven seas? Wireless communication was still in its infancy. Sound was soon to transform the silent movies, but technicolor was very much in the offing; and television lay far in the hypothetical future. The Theodore Roosevelt Country Life Commission was being organized; the *Christian Century* was being reconstituted for the assumption of its place of undenominational leadership in religious journalism.

Truly, 1908 was an *"annus mirabilis,"* as Handy terms it;[46] fortunate were those of us who entered into our ordained ministry as seminary graduates in a year of such opportunity. In March *The Home Missions Council* (HMC) was organized, in November *The Council of Women for Home Missions* (CWHM); and in December came the

66

long-awaited assembly of 352 members and alternates, representing 33 Protestant denominations, gathered to organize *The Federal Council of Churches* (FC). "Again women had been ignored, or, shall we say overlooked."[47] "Twenty-eight national church bodies . . . had approved the constitution. . . . State and local federations had made some progress," the nature of which has just been set forth and will shortly be detailed still further.[48] How modest were the resources of these founding fathers, even at the national level, during this extended period of preparation when a permanent national agency of church cooperation was still "in process of formation," is shown in the financial figures reported: "During the six years of preliminary preparation the average expense had been but $3,000 a year, and during the three years following the Interchurch Conference of 1905 the annual cost had been $6,000."[49] Yet the Federal Council, once organized, assumed "the $3,000 deficit of the National Federation of Churches and Christian Workers."

The sources of income for the fiscal year 1904-5 are significant. Forty-seven personal contributions, ranging from one dollar to five hundred, amounted to $3,151; from one to eleven churches or church bodies in each of three denominations (Baptist, Congregational, and Presbyterian), in seven states, paid amounts varying from five to one hundred dollars, to a total of $485; from three state interdenominational bodies (the Ohio and Wisconsin "Federations" and the Pennsylvania "Alliance") came, in sum, $65; and offerings seem to have added $460 —to provide, in all, an income of $4,161. The proportion of generous individual and local church gifts deserves note, as do the denominational and the geographical concentration, and the meagerness of the financing constituency. This seems like "Operation Shoestring," but fortunately obligations were as yet limited. Doubtless it is fair to add that no very vigorous push for widespread support had as yet been made. In any case, it was clearly not a very broad financial base on which patiently and courageously to erect so significant an ecclesiastical structure. Nobody could have been accused of starting a lucrative "racket" in such terms. The 1905 Conference had been expected to cost $18,000. Actual expense, not including the estimated cost of printing the *Book of Proceedings* ($2,500), amounted to only $12,912.99, as compared with receipts of $16,797.70. The balance of $3,884.71 appeared more than adequate for publication and other costs. Mr. Alfred Kimball, treasurer, regarded the expenditure of only $3,000 a year for the first six years as "a very small sum for the work accomplished."

Issues were faced, and some of them allowed to "rest for a time." "The further formation of so-called 'Union Churches' was discouraged in favor of federation," which was held to be an unsectarian principle "still consistently denominational."[50] The major work of the (proposed four regional) district offices was to be that of organizing state and local federations, but in the "rather grandiose plans" of the Committee on Organization and Development it turned out that "the cart was placed before the horse." Developing permanent, firmly rooted state and local federations of churches proved to be a far more serious undertaking, requiring much more thought, work, personnel, and financial resources, than was at first realized. Nevertheless, in 1908 beginnings of significant ecclesiastical cooperation were reported in sixteen states and a number of cities.

High Intention, Low Income

The report of the Committee on Organization and Development[51] was presented by its chairman, Bishop E. R. Hendrix. It called for the strengthening of state and local federations already in existence and the organization and development of federations in all the states, and through their agency, the multiplication of town and city federations. (This decentralized, from-the-top-down method of organizational promotion was for long largely theoretical, but still has much to commend it in the minds of experienced council leaders.) The committee's report also proposed to provide, as rapidly as funds would permit, for a district superintendency that would establish at least four offices in strategic centers of population representing different sections of the country. Immediately the question was raised, Is the Federal Council moving too fast? Is it going beyond its mandate? But on a reassuring word from the treasurer, who had prepared a careful memo, the committee's proposal was adopted.

The next question was one of maintenance.[52] How could the proposed expenses be met? The treasurer, Mr. Kimball, proposed a $30,000 annual budget, chiefly to be allocated to the denominations *pro rata*. On paper that looked good, and was unanimously favored. Unfortunately, as we shall discover, this did not assure that the money would be in the treasurer's hands as needed.

A Committee on Cooperation in Home Missions hailed the progress made by the Federal Council with gratitude, and its report was adopted, but not without discussion, which included reference to one town of 3,000 people, with fourteen churches, as a sample home missions problem.

Local and State Progress Assessed

In introducing Rev. E. P. Ryland, president of the Los Angeles Federation, and chairman of the Committee on *Local* Federations, Bishop Hendrix said, "Brethren, this is where your whole work reaches a special culminating point, in the matter of local federations."[53] The local federation was defined by Dr. Ryland as not a ministerial union, nor a self-constituted committee of individuals; there were about 150 churches in the Los Angeles Federation. Its Council (the pastors of cooperating churches, together with one layman for each 300 members) met once a month; its Executive Committee once a week. Its annual expenses totaled $1,800.

Dr. H. B. MacCauley, of Trenton, N.J., reported[54] that their federation, which had been organized at the initative of the ministerial union, included 37 Protestant churches with 11,000 communicants. Federations in Camden, Paterson, New Brunswick, Bound Brook, Somerset Co., and Hubbardton, N.J., were also reported.

It was voted[55] that "the time has come when the churches of every community should join their forces in federated effort," and that "the Federal Council . . . should plan for the support of work that will give aid in stimulating and helping the development and organization of local federation in every part of the country." To the actual implementation of these high resolves the succeeding chapters of this history are shortly devoted.

Said Dr. Root, chairman of the Committee on *State* Federations, "A state federation is a joint committee, officially representing the denominational bodies, to learn all the facts and ally all the factors, and thus to overcome our overlapping and overlooking. . . . All existing state federations make denominational representation the basis (of their membership); although some add representatives of interdenominational organizations or local cooperative councils." In practice, some interesting adjustments to denominational geography, which did not always conform to state lines, were required; and Dr. Root found that part of "the difficulty of the task arises from the inertia of our present ecclesiastical organizations." "The only serious embarrassment in the development of a state federation now arises from the side of finances. We believe that *the proper method of providing adequate income is by appropriation of its just quota by each denominational* body. This principle is slowly but surely establishing itself, in spite of admitted difficulties . . . The next best method . . . is to ask for appropriations from the funds of the stronger local churches. Both methods must at present, probably, be supplemented by personal contributions from individuals. . . . A modest amount of endowment would stimulate progress immediately." (How contemporary this sounds more than five decades later!)

Dr. Anthony, speaking of Dr. Root's report,[56] its four "declarations" and its four recommendations, pointed out that "we do not approve of so-called union churches, independent of denominational associations, although we recognize their utility in many places." "We wish to defend the existence of the denomination, but the denomination without taint of sectarianism, which forbids united action." He also underscored the implications of a federal compact," including the suggestion "that the functions of the federation be plainly stated and described as an advisory council without ecclesiastical authority, so that each state organization of a denomination may clearly understand . . . that . . . it is surrendering no powers or responsibilities inherently its own, . . ." and the clear agreement "that the federation be regarded as not a new organization . . . but the churches (themselves) federated."

Incidentally, he pointed out the economy of operations of the Maine Commission. It had made annual levies of ten dollars per denomination, or five, or none at all. If this seems a feeble and timid beginning, it is to be judged not in terms of present budgets but in the light of what was accomplished, and also of the fact that the chief actors in the Maine ecclesiastical drama had denominational expense accounts. As if to caution against too low financial sights, Dr. Root reported that Massachusetts, on the other hand, when asked to raise $1,000 a year, had promised to raise $3,000; and that Rhode Island had closed out a debt of $500. Even so, it was day of small beginnings.

Bishop A. B. Leonard asserted: "If we are to make this organization effective in localities the state federation is an absolute necessity. . . . Unless we have state federations this general Federation will amount to comparatively little."

The resolutions presented in the printed report of Dr. Root's committee were now carried by unanimous vote. Just how church cooperation in the states was to be organized and financed was by no means clear; but everybody was for it. Perhaps the Lord would provide.

Basic Denominational Loyalties

In bringing the report on "The Relation of the Federal Council to Interdenominational Organizations," Rev. Ame Vennema spoke of such bodies (The American Bible Society, The American Tract Society, The Evangelical Alliance for the U.S., The YMCA, The YWCA, The YPSCE, and the Laymen's Missionary Movement) as "the Church of Christ in America at work." The report regarded them "as an integral part of the church." Their "cooperative work along special lines of effort" had done so "much to prepare the way for that broader work contemplated by this body" that, Vennema felt, "this Council could not have been convened except for the fact that through these organizations the churches had been working together side by side for a long time." Subsequent events and more careful study of relationships would lead to a number of questions as to the technical accuracy of some of this language; but its courtesy and gratitude remain unchallenged.

What now seems a bit amusing was distinctly less so, when Dr. James L. Barton, in reporting for the Committee on Cooperation in Foreign Missions, quite informally remarked "that the lines that divide these various denominations . . . are bird tracks in the mud in a prehistoric age; fossilized controversies for which we can make no explanation that will satisfy." This was going entirely too fast and too far. Said Bishop E. E. Hoss, M. E. Church South, "I do not believe that denominational lines are simply bird tracks in geological mud." Accordingly he objected to the proposed "elimination, as far as possible, of denominational distinctions" in the foreign field. An interesting debate ensued, for as yet there had been little or no "rethinking" on foreign missions. Bishop Earl Cranston pointed out that "as long as missions abroad are to be supported by denominational treasuries," there was involved in any such action "risk of creating friction between the workers in the field and the administrative boards at home." "We are here as a federation . . . One of our fundamental propositions, without the full recognition of which this Council could not have been organized, is the recognition of our denominational autonomy. . . . We are on dangerous ground when we attack the very foundation on which we have met."

Dr. Roberts urged the deletion of the offensive words. Dr. Robert Mackenzie spoke of "the marks of our fathers flying from the mighty storm of persecution." Dr. Barton defended the report; but it was adopted as amended: "We favor the closest possible federation of all Christian churches in foreign mission lands."

This is not a study of the Federal Council as such, but only of its importance for the organization and maintenance of state and local cooperation. In 1908 there was as yet no world-wide structure of a

71

comparable sort; and the determinative 1910 Edinburgh Conference was still two years off. It was "Life and Work" that was shaping up its machinery in the United States; "Faith and Order" had relatively few devotees, doubtless fewer than it deserved. Ecumenicity, as we now know it, was just acquiring visibility in the dreams of a comparatively small number of church leaders. Yet the organization of the Federal Council was to make the situation vastly easier for every local and state federation of churches.

Deeper Meanings

Though they were a long way from any adequate assumption of their responsibility, in terms of money and volunteer service, the denominations had now firmly established *the principle of representativeness*. Hereafter federations were to represent churches rather than the cooperation of individual Christians, however influential. Yet the words of the Federal Council's famous "preamble," long in the thinking of the leaders, have persisted as a symbol of the deep interest of multitudes of people in some broader concept of the Church than that provided either by the single local congregation or by the machinery of any denomination, even the greatest. The churches could not constitute The Church, but "in the providence of God, the time has come when it seems fitting more fully to manifest the essential oneness of the Christian churches of America, in Jesus Christ their Divine Lord and Savior, and to promote the spirit of fellowship, service, and cooperation among them." Such language, proposed in 1905, and adopted in 1908, furnishes a milestone from which there can be no turning back. On the contrary, more than four decades later, the vaster implications of such a declaration would reach a greatly expanded fruition in a degree of ecclesiastical integration of a federative sort in the National Council of the Churches of Christ in the USA, quite exceptional in church history.

On the other hand, at the time, the denominational partners to this compact had small notion of the logical consequences and implicit demands their action at the national level would require of them in terms of American community life. Had they adequately sensed the world-wide implications of their proposal, all would have admitted that ecumenicity (a concept only beginning to appear on the ecclesiastical horizon) could not become real until it was everywhere local, but the accomplishment of the task to which they had set their hands would test their resolution and resources for many years to come. At the outset, local and state federations would mushroom, many of them

72

with very little depth of root. The criteria of permanence would have to be forged out on the anvil of experiences, or painfully learned in the school of cut-and-try.

"Soon after the turn of the century," Dr. Charles L. Thompson had "invited a few of the secretaries of the various home mission boards to a dinner, that they might get better acquainted and discuss common interests." (Down the years those words, "get better acquainted," were to prove the secret of cooperation at every level.) Out of this modest beginning was to grow the *Home Missions Council,* later to become the division of Home Missions of the National Council of Churches. Dr. Thompson, called by Handy a "Presbyterian architect of Cooperative Protestantism,"[57] was becoming convinced that in all phases of their work "cooperation must take the place of rivalry among denominations."[58] In his 1924 *Autobiography* Thompson wrote, "We had remained too long in denominational valleys. The denominations must yield to the larger view of what is best for the Kingdom of God."[59]

With the organization of the Home Missions Council there would be appropriate differentiation between state councils of home missions and state federations of churches, as a prelude to a long process of organizational consolidation soon to be described. As Dr. Thompson later remembered the situation, "The denominations were not only trying to keep out of each other's way. They were . . . joining hands in a common crusade."[60] Shortly it would be painfully discovered that much boasted organizational growth was far less significant than it seemed; and workers in many a present state and local organization will read some of these early dates with an amused realization of how discontinuous was much of the development of early local church cooperation, and how long it took to perfect an ecumenical motor that, once started, would continue to run, especially if it had to "idle" over a period of considerable time under unfavorable atmospheric conditions, economically and ecclesiastically.

Appearances during this first decade of the new century were sometimes deceiving. Twenty years later, in the late 1920's, Dr. H. Paul Douglass wrote:[61] "Partly as indigenous movements, but partly because of the national agencies preceding the Federal Council, long lists of (places) now began to be reported . . . where the evangelists and organizers of the new movement supposed that they had effected permanent local organizations. . . . But of all the federations named, those of Massachusetts and New York City are the only ones that have had a continuous life under paid leadership from the time of their foundation."

But church cooperation now had explicit denominational sanctions; to experiment locally was far less lonely business. There was now a "pattern in the mount," and those who sought to order the life of the churches in accordance with it were less queer, more honored as pioneers of an approved sort, as builders of a new ecclesiastical ethic. To be cooperative at the state and local level had now become a recognized and approved *modus vivendi,* difficult but commendable. Nationally, Protestantism had set its face in the direction of a unified strategy.

REFERENCE NOTES

Chapter III

1 Sanford, *Origin and History of the Federal Council,* p. 116.

2 Macfarland, *Christian Unity in the Making,* p. 27.

3 Douglass, *Protestant Cooperation in American Cities,* p. 42.

4 For the development of federated women's work in American Protestantism see "All That is Past Is Prologue" (compiled and edited by Mrs. Fred S. Bennett, Miss Florence G. Tyler, and Mrs. E. H. Goedeke, United Council of Church Women, 1944, 24 pp.), which traces "The Emergence of Inter-denominational Organizations among Protestant Church Women"; and "Forward Together," An Historical Sketch of Interdenominational Women's Work and the United Council of Church Women, by Mabel Head, 1950, 28 pp.

5 Handy, *op. cit.,* p. 26 (similar developments among women interested in foreign missions will be set forth in Chapter IV).

6 Gray, *op. cit.,* p. 27.

7 Sanford, *op. cit.,* p. 181.

8 *Ibid.,* pp. 185, 186.

9 Sanford, *op. cit.,* Chapter V, pp. 103 ff. (Development of State and Local Federations Prior to 1900).

10 *Ibid.,* pp. 138, 139.

11 *Ibid.,* pp. 156, 157, 165.

12 Thus in 1901 there already seemed to be "a vast grassroots organizational development." Unfortunately it frequently had much less depth of earth than was essential to permanence.

13 *Ibid.,* p. 173.

14 Macfarland, *op. cit.,* p. 28.

15 Sanford, *op. cit.,* p. 174.

16 *Ibid.,* p. 175.

17 Handy, *op. cit.,* p. 23.

18 Macfarland, *op. cit.,* p. 15.

19 *Ibid.,* p. 30.

20 Sanford, *Church Federation,* pp. 87 ff.

21 *Ibid.,* p. 95.

22 *Cf.* Dr. Thompson's address of welcome, *ibid.,* pp. 133 ff.

23 *Ibid.,* pp. 605-608.

24 *Ibid.,* p. 613.

25 *Ibid.,* pp. 299-307.

26 *Ibid.,* pp. 307-322.

27 *Ibid.,* p. 311.

28 *Ibid.,* pp. 322-332.

29 *Ibid.,* p. 421. (According to Frank Mason North, *Methodist Review,* Sept.-Oct., 1903, Josiah Strong had used this contrast as early as his 1903 Chicago address before the Evangelical Alliance.)

30 *Ibid.,* p. 422.

31 Macfarland, *op. cit.,* p. 35.

32 *First Annual Report of the Executive Board of the National Federation of Churches and Christian Workers,* 1906, p. 53. See also pp. 57-66, report by Wells.

33 Gray, *op. cit.,* pp. 29, 30.

34 Rich, *op. cit.,* p. 42.

35 *Cf.* 1906 *Report* just cited, pp. 56, 57.

[36] Rich, *op. cit.*, p. 43; *cf.* Wm. DeWitt Hyde, 1892 article on "Impending Paganism in New England," based on statistics gathered by the Maine Bible Society in fifteen communities.

[37] *Cf.* the Morse 1928 *Every Community Study of New Hampshire,* and the Sanderson 1948 follow-up.

[38] Rich, *op. cit.*, p. 44.

[39] *1906 Report,* pp. 75-79.

[40] *Ibid.,* pp. 34, 35.

[41] *Ibid.,* p. 69.

[42] *Ibid.,* pp. 66-68.

[43] Writing of the YMCA in 1905 (Sept.-Oct. *Methodist Review*), Frank Mason North said, "This mighty organization, with its sister association founded only a few years later, has been a mighty leveler of denominational prejudices." The extent to which the YMCA has "carried on much of the cooperative work among the churches" has been repeatedly assessed. In many cases the executive leadership and outstanding board members have "fathered the local council of churches." On the other hand, both experience and experiment have tended to differentiate the roles of the Association and of church cooperation as such. The writer, who was for two years a YMCA general secretary as well as Council of Churches executive, has had exceptional opportunity both to appreciate the contribution of the Christian Associations and to discover their distinctive, nonecclesiastical functions. Numerous YMCA secretaries have for longer or shorter periods served as executives of councils of churches. Sometimes this has tended to postpone the development of an adequate council; in other cases council progress has been greatly accelerated. Present participation by active and retired leaders of both the YMCA and the YWCA in council work, as staff members and as volunteers, is considerable, and deserves deep gratitude.

[44] *1907 Report,* pp. 10, 11.

[45] Macfarland, *op. cit.*, p. 38.

[46] Handy, *op. cit.*, p. 18.

[47] Macfarland, *op. cit.*, p. 38.

[48] *Ibid.,* p. 39.

[49] *Ibid.,* p. 39. (*Cf.* FC *1908 Report,* pub. in 1909, p. 19; also *Church Federation,* 1905, pp. 201, 641, 642.)

[50] *Ibid.,* p. 40.

[51] FC *1908 Report,* pp. 47 ff. and 206.

[52] *Ibid.,* pp. 54 ff.; also pp. 214, 215.

[53] *Ibid.,* pp. 110 ff.; pp. 274 ff.

[54] *Ibid.,* p. 132.

[55] *Ibid.,* p. 277.

[56] FC *1908 Report,* pp. 187-205.

[57] *Journal of the Presbyterian Historical Society,* Dec., 1955, pp. 207-228.

[58] Quoted by Handy, *op. cit.*, p. 22.

[59] *Ibid.,* p. 23.

[60] Charles L. Thompson, *Autobiography,* Revell, 1924, cited by Handy, *op. cit.*, p. 25.

[61] Douglass, *op. cit.*, (pub. in 1930), pp. 47, 48.

Shakedown Voyage, 1908-1915

Cumulative National Cooperation

While it is not easy to say just when the Protestant Reformation began, by the time Luther had posted his theses it is clear that the Reformation was well under way. Similarly, by 1908 cooperative Christianity, according to the twentieth-century pattern, was beginning clearly to emerge. By 1908 there were in America a whole cluster of national bodies representing various aspects of what was later to be known as the ecumenical movement: the International Sunday School Association, the Foreign Missions Conference (in its earlier and simpler form), the Home Missions Councils, and the Federal Council of Churches—to name only those most central to the integrating churchmanship of the period. As yet their common concerns and ultimate merger were obscured by a sense of discrete organizational autonomy, soon to be modified, but only slowly to be outmoded. Ecclesiastically, the Federal Council was doubtless the most significant of these bodies. Each of the others featured some functional specialization within the total work of the church; the Federal Council united the denominations as such in a federal approach to their entire task.

The year 1908 is the more significant because of the determinative occasions which it *antedated*. Not until 1910 was the Edinburgh Conference to be held, which was greatly to accelerate world-wide interests both in "Life and Work" and in "Faith and Order." Not until nearly three decades later were those two streams to begin to merge into the World Council of Churches, long to be "in process of formation." Not until 1911 was the Foreign Missions Conference to acquire more continuous administrative significance through limited but expanded processes of reference and counsel. Not until 1922 was the Sunday School Movement to involve the denominational controls recognized in the organization of the International Council of Religious Education.

But, as Dr. Samuel McCrea Cavert points out, two additional facts must not be overlooked: "(a) 'Life and Work' really did get a tremendous impetus from the Federal Council, whereas the American program in 'Life and Work' was not much indebted to European experience; (b) (even) 'Faith and Order' as a movement was American-born, originating in the Episcopal Convention in 1910. It is true that Edinburgh (1910) stirred up Bishop Brent as an individual, but the Edinburgh Conference itself completely avoided all issues of 'Faith and Order.' "[1]

Social Trends and Church Cooperation

Behind the organization of the Federal Council, and increasingly characteristic of the motivation of the other national bodies, the social emphasis was now sharply modifying earlier evangelistic and educational procedures. In 1906 Peabody had published *Jesus Christ and the Social Question*. In 1907 Rauschenbusch's *Christianity and the Social Crisis* appeared. Then, "thinking he had said all he had to say on the social question, he went to Europe to devote himself to historical studies. On his return to America, he discovered that the social awakening of the nation had set in like an equinoctial gale.' "[2] In the midst of this new popular and ecclesiastical interest in human relations, as well as in the welfare and nurture of the individual soul, the Federal Council hoisted its banner, in the hope that many would gather round it. Many did.

"Urban" and "rural," two differentiating foci of life in the United States, now emerging, both constituted an increasing challenge to the policy-makers in all forms of organized religion. Revivalism did much to conserve agrarian values, and to exploit for good the commitments made by formerly rural people now city dwellers; but evangelism as such never faced up with population trends, except as they provided the new location of its mass audience, for it felt itself called to consider what seemed to it far more basic concerns. According to Rich, "Early efforts to restore the rural church did not arrive out of traditional departments of evangelism or missions. The 'social gospelers' were most concerned." Similarly the consequences of urbanization for church extension were even more slowly recognized by new forms of denominational and interdenominational organization.

Industrialization and urbanization, by contributing to rural decay, first called attention to the plight of the rural churches, facing constant loss of population, rather than to the equally serious problems of the rapidly expanding cities, in many sections of which local church growth was at first almost automatic. Only later—much later—was it understood that cities too could lose population, especially at their heart, as well as suffer changes in the ethnic, national, linguistic, and religious characteristics of their neighborhoods. These changes would prove fatal to churches that had unconsciously become little more than chaplaincies to "our kind of people"—the religious sanctification

78

of, or sanctions attached to, various forms of secular gregariousness growing out of the social heritage of their several constituencies. In the end the new significance of the urban potential, the need for denominational city strategy, and the necessity and significance of city federations of churches as the urban means of cooperation in religious work, would become evident. For the moment, the sense of need was focussed on the plight of rural America.

To the credit of the Presbyterians, it was actually twenty-five days before Theodore Roosevelt in 1908 issued his famous letter appointing the Commission on Country Life, which reported in 1909, that Warren H. Wilson began assisting country churches throughout the denomination. When, on November 1, 1910, the Presbyterian Department of the Church and Country Life became effective, other denominations began to follow suit. In 1911 the first County Farm Bureau was organized, followed in 1914 by the now taken-for-granted Extension Service. In 1915 Liberty Hyde Bailey put new spiritual sanctions under the rural life movement by his noble little volume, *The Holy Earth*.[3] Yet population continued to stream cityward, and one by one the denominations, and finally the interdenominationalists, found themselves forced to deal with urbanization as a determinative factor in church life. This meant new organizational portfolios and the ultimate employment of specialized field personnel. Before this cycle was completed, urbanization, mechanization, and mass communication had so wiped out the distinction between urban and rural that the whole nation, in all its aspects—educational, economic, political, and religious—found itself much more of a piece than it had been for a long time; but it was to be predominantly an urban piece rather than a rural one.

Nation-wide Cooperative Response

It was good to have the national church bodies federally related, but all informed leaders recognized that this nation had now become too great to permit the handling of all its problems, ecclesiastical or other, at the national level. State organizations were essential; so were local federations of churches. What were to be the consequences for state and local work of the increasing cooperation of church bodies nationally? Undoubtedly during the first years of the century the promise of greater federal unity produced an atmosphere of cooperativeness in local communities throughout the nation. The succession of significant national gatherings, culminating in the organization of the Federal Council in 1908, clearly accelerated the more local urge toward state and community federations of churches. Yet in fifteen years this thrust would have spent itself, and new beginnings and a more realistic strategy were to become necessary.

This first period of sanguine beginnings was followed by a reaction in favor of standardized practices of proven worth, on the basis of established criteria of organizational durability. This evolution, paralleled by that of many other forms of human association (e.g., the development of the social welfare and character building agencies, and various commercial, educational, and civic clubs or associations), resulted inevitably in a screening process, informal, unauthoritative, but increasingly experienced on a nation-wide basis. The significant and enduring were separated from the well-intended but transient and relatively ephemeral impulsiveness of those who had small notion of how much of an investment would be required before ever the interdenominational hope could match the actuality of denominational fact. Seen in retrospect, the free-enterprise, *laissez faire* spirit of American Protestantism, with its reaction from ecclesiastical authoritarianism in politics and religion, put a premium on spontaneity in the local federations, and only slowly systemized the national movement into some sort of recognized pattern of standardized procedures.

Initial Federal Council Field Promotion

Among the recommended resolutions, adopted in 1908, *nemine contradicente,* were these:[4]

1. "The time has come when the churches of every community should join their forces in federated effort."

3. "This Federal Council . . . should plan for the support of work that will give aid in stimulating and helping the development and organization of local federations in every part of our country."

Such sentiments won instant concurrence, but the wherewithal to make them effective was less easily secured.

One of the professed objectives of the Federal Council was "to assist in the organization of local branches . . . to promote its aims in their communities"; but implicit in these words were ambiguities that gradually made them a dead letter. Inadequately considered theory proved unworkable in practice. What was meant by "branch"? What were the Federal Council's community "aims"? Had it the resources to promote these aims? What about the aims of the local churches in the many communities and states already organized in some fashion? How were these aims to be related to those of the Federal Council?

80

In the school of trial and error, at least certain negative answers to such questions were to be learned rather quickly, in terms of the Federal Council's own structure, personnel, and finances. As we proceed with the story, all this will become abundantly clear. Perhaps our best first approach to the state and local facts during this period will be to take a preliminary look at a series of organizational inventories during the years 1908 to 1915.

In December 1908 a "Table of State Federations," including "the definite lines of work in which several of them are engaged," marked the supposedly permanent progress of no less than sixteen state organizations. In 1909 *North Dakota* also organized its Interdenominational Commission, and *Indiana* made federative beginnings.

In his 1910 report Dr. Sanford, aided by the district secretaries (whose offices soon had to be discontinued for lack of funds), reported concerning the situation in two dozen states. In sum, thanks to the district secretaries, "more progress has been made this year in organizing state federations than in five previous years." New local organizations included three counties in New Jersey; Harrisburg, Pa.; and Baltimore, Md. Reorganization in Chicago was planned, "so that (instead of) being simply a federation of denominational ministerial bodies, it will become a body representing the denominations officially." In 1912 the Federal Council listed twenty-one state bodies. By 1913 twenty-six different states had experimented with some form of interdenominational organization. This looked like a rather far-flung frontier of interdenominational experimentation. How about the local situations?

In 1912, in addition to these state bodies, the Federal Council listed 35 county and district federations in six states; 49 partial or tentative federations in 23 states and the District of Columbia; 27 federations now "in process of formation" in 13 states; and no less than 99 local federations in 27 states and in Honolulu—a total of 210 local federations, in addition to the many county and city Sunday school associations. In 1913 more than a score of these federations reported a paid staff; but in 1915 the number of part-or full-time executives appeared to be only a dozen, in a total of 218 federations allegedly existent.

Of 103 local federations existing in 1913, and reporting dates of their formal organization, only a dozen had been organized before 1908 (approximately one every other year, 1887 to 1907); eighteen

81

in 1908, 1909, or 1910 (two, seven, and nine, respectively); eighteen in 1911; thirty-three in 1912; twenty-two in 1913 or (in two cases) early 1914. Thus a marked organizational thrust in the years 1911 to 1913 resulted supposedly in at least 71 local federations.

Mushroom Growth, not Durable

Twenty-five denominations were represented in these local organizations, in addition to the thirty in the Federal Council.[5] Detailed inspection of a tabulation of the earliest organization dates of the twenty-six *state* bodies reportedly in existence before 1915, chronologically arranged, rather than by their appearance in the 1912 or 1913 lists, and another of organization dates for the forty-one *local* federations reputedly in existence before 1915, would probably occasion considerable surprise or skepticism. In a number of instances there has been no continuity with present organizations; and there may not now be any organization with paid leadership in the state or city listed. All the recorded dates, however, are based on seemingly reliable documentation, either published reports or private records. The line between normal ups and downs, through reorganization, and entire disintegration followed by organization *de novo,* is not easy to draw. Many abortive ecumenical beginnings had to be made before the seeds of cooperative churchmanship were finally to take permanent root. In only a few cases did the earliest beginnings survive in uninterrupted organizational history.

Of the federations, state and local, reported in 1913, twenty-seven stated that they had annual budgets ranging from $300 to $20,000; but only seven of these as much as $5,000. Even taking into consideration the change in dollar values, it is plain that these were the days of small interdenominational expenditures. A surprising aspect of this record is the number of local bodies or federations with sizable budgets before 1915 that have since dropped out of the picture—at least temporarily—as organizations with paid personnel. This discontinuity is one of the most baffling phases of the story, often perhaps to be accounted for by the inadequacy of the basis of organization. Wherever it could be reconstructed, this earlier local or state federation history, its failures and successes, and the reasons for them, would be instructive.

The 1913 local federation reports supply much evidence of both weakness and strength, and interesting details as to structure, program, and personnel, as well as finances. There are a number of references to proposed constitutions supplied by the Federal Council as a guide for local use. Several revisions are extant, and reveal the administrative thinking at various stages during this period. The data, filled in on 141 of the printed questionnaires sent out by the Federal Council, and supplemented by occasional letters, are an interesting mixture of sunlight and shadow.

Repeated credit is given the Men and Religion Forward Movement (1911-1912), soon to be discussed. Occasional printed letterheads, of local as well as of state federations, provide a seeming tangibility for the movement at this time; but they were sometimes only a facade, backed by no very active corporate reality. Additional significant personnel, already beginning to be well-known, loom out of these early reports, both of volunteer and paid officers, around whom—along with many others, including some mentioned earlier—the cooperative story was slowly being woven.

A Disappointing Facade

Sometimes the facts were not up to appearances. For example, not all the many organized cities in Massachusetts were blessed with vigorous federations. Lawrence was "not doing much." At Pittsfield "Our Federation started off too ambitiously, with a paid secretary and a budget which proved burdensome to the churches. We are now reorganized on a more modest financial basis, but expect to accomplish more." What work had been done at Salem? "Little or none." Springfield's "organization is as yet incomplete and there had been no work done." Chelsea's federation was "not doing its full work yet, but we hope soon to have everything under way." One small federation asked two cents a member from each of its six churches.

New Jersey reported a baker's dozen of small local federations, but three of these were "not active," and a fourth "organization exists in name only." The reporter for a fifth declared, more positively, that it "must be reorganized and revitalized." Cincinnati, Ohio, submitted its constitution and by-laws with the remark, "We are just starting." A Pennsylvania local federation complained of "indifference—undue emphasis by pastors and their churches on their own purely local tasks." Said Newport, R. I., "So far we have done little constructive work." Testimonies of this sort will help to show why the closing paragraphs of this chapter will re-emphasize the sharp shrinkage, already indicated, in the national audit of the number of effective state and local federations in 1915.

83

The Time Not Yet Ripe?

The Federal Council convened only once in four years, but between these plenary sessions an Executive Committee met annually, and between its sessions an Administrative Committee could be assembled. The first quadrennium of the Federal Council, from 1908 to 1912, was "a period largely of experimentation," during which "much effort was given to the development of state and local federations, the nation being divided into districts in charge of district secretaries. This method, however, did not avail. The cities and towns were not prepared for federation. Many, therefore, of the federations organized were short-lived. It became apparent that the Council would need first to develop the spirit of federation before it could proceed to successful local organization." So at least it seemed to Dr. Macfarland in 1920.[6] Or, as Shailer Mathews, president for the quadrennium, put it, "Human nature is so constituted that it is always easy to arouse enthusiasm for an idea not yet in operation. . . . Administration is always the test of ideals."[7] Statements like these need now to be put over against a sufficient background of national ecclesiastical thinking and action to show the setting of state and local federation work during this period.

First Philosophizing

At the 1908 meeting of the Federal Council, E. P. Ryland, chairman of the Committee on Local Organizations, had thought[8] that in cities of 100,000 or more "federation is most needed . . . and has its greatest opportunity." As if Los Angeles could be organized like Methuen, he went on to say, "All the members in all the churches in a local Federation should be members of the Federation. The idea is to bring the rank and file of our people to realize the essential oneness of the Christian church in America." One approves this last statement, and also his judgment that "Neither a ministerial union nor a 'self-constituted body of earnest individuals' is a church federation. Either of these may form a good basis on which to perfect a federation, however." Within the larger membership, he said, there should be a "federation council," "to be composed of men": "all the pastors and at least one layman from each congregation," chosen to act as a "governing body"; and a federation center already seemed important.

In 1909 progress in local and state situations was reported in some detail by Dr. Sanford and the district secretaries. That same year an address made earlier by J. H. Garrison, of the Christian Publishing Company, St. Louis, editor of *The Christian Evangelist,* to a national gathering of his own Brotherhood, was widely circulated. Speaking on church federation, after mentioning various worldwide denominational aggregations, and the Interdenominational Commission in Maine, he said, " 'The National Federation of Churches and Christian Workers' (the precursor of the Federal Council) is different . . . in that it is 'federation at the bottom' (quoting Josiah Strong) instead of at the top; in other words, it is the federation not of denominations but of individual churches. The local churches of a given community enter into an agreement to cooperate on a certain basis for the accomplishment of certain ends in which they agree.

"The plan of making the local congregation the unit of action, rather than a denomination, makes it possible for us to co-operate with such a movement, harmonizing as it does thoroughly with our idea of the local autonomy of the churches. It is entirely within the province of any local church to enter into co-operation with other churches of the community for the furtherance of any common purpose, without asking the consent of any convention or society or organization of any kind. We can safely assume that each local church may be depended upon to act within the limit of loyalty to its faith and its mission. It is also at the option of any local federation to act independently, or ally itself with a state or national organization." (Obviously this is the viewpoint of one particular church polity.)

Among certain 1910 "definitions," the following was referred back to the Federal Council's Business Committee with power:

"An Interchurch Federation is a voluntary association of two or more churches contiguously situated in any state, county, city, or other locality and *connected with the denominations which are in the Federal Council,* and organized under a code of by-laws adopted by them as a *branch* of the Federal Council, for the purpose of working together in behalf of the social, moral, and spiritual betterment of their communities" (emphasis added).[9]

Said Dr. Macfarland a generation later:[10] "This provision, if carried out, would simply raise all over again the discussions at the 1905 meeting. That is just what happened not long after. Another provision[11] also went into the same dubious grounds in assuming that state and local federations were to be composed of representatives confined to the constituent bodies of the Federal Council: The various state and local federations being already represented in the Federal Council, not directly but through delegates chosen by the highest national assemblies of the denominations federated, shall be expected, subject to the law of Christian liberty, to follow the rules as laid

85

down in the Standard By-Laws approved by the Federal Council and to be guided by its deliverances; and similarly the local federations within a state shall be expected to promote the unity of the federation movement within the state, subject to the higher law of denominational unity and fellowship as expressed in the organization of the Federal Council." (Can anyone long connected with state and local expressions of the ecumenical spirit read such words without smiling both at the assumptions implicit in them, and the differences between the witness of logic and the witness of experience, as local, state, and national, not to say world-wide councils have sought to work out some sort of pragmatic relationships down the years?)

Pioneering the Co-operative Frontier

Repeated citations have been made from the writings of Dr. Charles S. Macfarland. Not until May 1, 1911 (the year Kettering invented the self-starter for the automobile), did he actually begin service with the Federal Council, first as Social Service Commission secretary, soon as acting executive for the entire program, and then permanent senior secretary. In his reminiscences 25 years later he admitted that "Had I realized what a task the administration of the Federal Council was to be, I do not feel sure that I should have had the courage to undertake it."[12] (Doubtless many a state and local secretary, and pastor as well, could echo these words. For example, Walter Laidlaw after twenty years as New York executive confessed that during the first nine months of his term he had pawned his watch seven times!)

This pioneering phase of the story needs to be remembered by executives and volunteer officers of state and local councils, not only because "misery loves company," but because it goes far to explain what many of us have been guilty of forgetting, that the same forces which meant rugged pioneering at the state and local level, were at work at the national level. It was simply not possible at the outset for the national bodies to assist the states and local units with money or personnel in any such manner or to any such extent as would have been welcomed, and might have proven to be a good investment. Moreover—particularly at the national level—the movement had to run a continuous barrage of economic, theological, political, and other criticism, with increasing threats of boycott, and even efforts to control by gifts with strings attached. In some ways these earliest days were financially the toughest, for the sheer survival of the move-ment was at stake; in other ways, the worst was yet to come.

86

The 1911 record showed progress, with local organizations processes repeated over and over again. A printed *Bulletin of Results* was now being circulated; Number Two was dated November, 1911. These were also years when *organized church women were making marked progress*. In 1911 a series of jubilee meetings in the larger cities across the country celebrated 50 years of denominational women's work for foreign missions. These meetings prepared the way for the Federation of Women's Boards of Foreign Missions, first projected in 1912, and formally organized in 1915 after three experimental years. At the outset, 19 boards were involved; when integrated with the FMC in 1933, there were 33 member boards. The Federation's object was "to promote unity, Christian fellowship, and cooperation among women's boards; to encourage and disseminate the best methods of work, and to plead unitedly for the outpouring of the Spirit of God on the Church of Christ." (It was succeeded by the Committee on Women's Work of the FMC, active from 1933 to 1941.)

By 1913 the Council of Women for Home Missions, whose membership grew eventually from nine to twenty-four Boards, was involved in larger cooperation with the Home Missions Council, and in 1918 established offices adjacent to it, at 156 Fifth Avenue, New York. (In 1940 the two merged into one body.)

Cooperative Experience a Convincing Teacher

By the end of 1911 Dr. Macfarland had reached a number of conclusions:[13] It was "not financially possible to maintain the district offices." "The state and local federations could not be forced to make their constituencies identical with the constituency of the (Federal) Council. They must be left to determine their own constitutions and programs. The 'model constitution' now being circulated could not be imposed upon them."

"Instead of being a Council based on the state and local units we should bring the several agencies of the *denominations* into cooperation, and in such areas as (social service, international peace, race relations, and evangelism) the Council's leadership would be welcomed."

"Individuals and groups could be found who were especially interested in these objectives."

This was obviously opportunistic rationalizing of the necessary. As it then seemed, and also long after, "The state and local federations were frail organizations, without chart or compass." F. B. Meyer, after a long conference in England, had agreed that "the weakness of the

87

British Free Church Council was that it was based on local councils."
This weakness must be avoided in America, for the American experiment was of world-wide significance.

"Above all, it was clear that the Federal Council could not develop strong federations by simply presenting to them a general cooperative ideal and handing them the model constitution which the Federal Council had approved."[14]

By 1912 it was clear to Dr. Macfarland that "Neither the denominational treasuries nor the denominations themselves were as yet ready to be geared up to interdenominational cooperation. That there should be an experiment by the process of trial and error was inevitable."[15] (Has not every state and city executive found this to be true?)

In other words, the prime importance of official denominational representation, especially at the national level, was confirmed in experience. The functional approach was able to enlist the interest of individuals and groups, and their financial support, over and above what the denominations were prepared to underwrite. Autonomy and spontaneity had to be recognized as values at the state and local levels; and nationally regimented state and local structures proved impossible, while national counsel was eagerly sought, organizationally, and in terms of program specialization. All along the line, new habits of cooperation had to be learned, new resources for cooperative endeavor discovered.

Federal Council's Second Quadrennium, 1912-1916

At Chicago in 1912 the Federal Council's Second Quadrennial assembled 217 official representatives of 27 denominations, plus other interested persons, to a total of 400. In this connection there were two significant conferences: of the representatives of state and local federations; and of the new Commission on Interdenominational Movements that had been appointed by a Conservation Congress of the Men and Religion Forward Movement.[15]

"Taken as a whole . . . the second meeting of the Federal Council equalled in helpfulness the 1905 and 1908 meetings, largely perhaps because of its contrasts with the discouraging years which intervened between 1908 and 1912. . . . The general feeling . . . was that while the Council must find its way gradually through trial and error and experience, it was gaining a momentum that would be cumulative.

To have survived the difficulties from 1908 to 1912 was enough assurance for the future. The 'state of mind' was already becoming contagious."[17]

Under cumulative demand, articulated in three noteworthy addresses on the work of state and local federations, "The Council of 1912 appointed *a commission on state and local federations,* its chairman being one of the pioneers of interdenominational movements, Professor Alfred Williams Anthony of Maine, to give the whole question adequate consideration and to proceed in the development of the spirit and practice of the local federation according to its discretion."

The 1912 list, previously cited, was the work of this first commission, which had also "widely distributed additional literature."

To offset the loss of district staff, Dr. Macfarland himself in 1912 conferred with the executive committees of the Massachusetts and Rhode Island Federations, and attended the annual meeting of the *West Virginia* Federation; and he visited twenty cities, some of them several times. Accordingly it was out of some first-hand contacts that he reported,[18] "Some of the states and communities are organized with great efficiency; others do little more than exist in name. This is largely dependent upon whether or not some strong . . . pastor or group of pastors takes the whole situation seriously. One of the most hopeful signs is the effective organization of some of the city federations with executive secretaries. . . . It would not seem wise to attempt any organic relationship with local federations, which would disturb the (Federal) Council's present sound and effective basis (denominational representation). At the same time the Federal Council is the initiator and the creator of these local federations, and it must assume some responsibility for them." That the "Commission on State and Local Federations" had been duly authorized was evidence that the Council did "assume some responsibility" for local cooperation.

New Masculine Initiative

"Meanwhile the *Men and Religion Forward Movement* had swept the country and had made many fields white unto harvest. Therefore it was the part of statesmanship to look to the Director and Executive Secretary of that movement for leadership, resulting in a (second) commission, first called the Commission on Federated Movements, with Fred B. Smith as Chairman, Rev. Roy B. Guild as Executive Secretary, and James A. Whitmore as Field Secretary, these three men having had the larger part of the direction of the Men and Religion

Movement."[19] What was there about the Men and Religion Forward Movement that had enabled the leaders of the federation movement to get their sights so much higher? Just what was this 1911-1912 lay campaign? To answer this question we must again cut back a year or more.

As Dr. Macfarland remembered the situation,[20] preparations for the 1912 Quadrennial of the Federal Council had found only "three fields of interdenominational cooperation . . . clearly open": social service, peace and arbitration, and state and local federation. As we have seen, the first attack on state and local federation had been only partly successful.

"The effort to sectionalize the country in the interest of state and local federations had proved premature and impracticable, and, in view of the financial situation, it was necessary to discontinue the sectional offices . . . I felt that the best thing to do was to get in touch with the life of the Men and Religion Movement. So far as I know, the only person to realize the importance of such a course was Dr. Guild. Through his intervention, I participated in the campaigns in Williamsport, Hazleton, Mahanoy City, and Wilkesbarre, Pennsylvania; Greensboro, North Carolina; Poughkeepsie, New York; and other places, serving as the director of the social service end of the program, and in some instances acting as the dean of the corps of so-called 'experts.' I have always been profoundly grateful to Dr. Guild, because this experience gave me new insight into many of the problems with which the new Council was to deal. Later on, to my great joy, and to the furtherance of progress, both Mr. Smith and Dr. Guild became associated with the Council. . . . Forward movements of this kind are of great value when they realize their significance, but more so when their promoters do not take themselves too seriously, to the detriment of permanent, slower-going, but more constructively organized bodies."[21]

The Men and Religion Movement was one of those "crusades" characteristic of a period that was drawing to a close, mentioned by Weisberger in his study of revivalism.[22] "Highly organized, carefully publicized, efficiently managed,"[23] as Handy termed it, it matched clerical timidity and conservatism with lay vigor and imagination, ecclesiastical inertia with pragmatic initiative, and theological hurdles with dynamic fact-finding processes. Freedom from established organizational restraints plus confident and persuasive personnel, armed with data and vision, made it possible for this movement to sweep

90

the nation in the brief period from Sept. 15, 1911, to May 15, 1912, with a campaign that was impetuosity itself as compared with the more ponderous processes by which the partners in the Federal Council had so far been able to implement their professed intent.

That Dr. Macfarland's contemporary judgment as to the providential character of this Movement was not a passing enthusiasm is attested by his statement many years later: "The Men and Religion Forward Movement was a vital factor in the preservation of the Federal Council."[24] Doubtless one of the best contributions the Movement made was the unique Smith-Guild combination, which provided "oomph" and lilt during the next years. They were a sort of Gilbert and Sullivan team, not without tensions and differences; together they tremendously advanced the cause of state and local federation. Smith viewed the wide horizon with imaginative dreams, and Guild tilled many a particular field[25] with devotion and skill until a permanent leader could take over.

Federal Council Restructures Its Field Approach

The Men and Religion Forward Movement had paved the way for the organization of a new committee of direction for the extension of state and local federation activity. Dr. Anthony, in a personal letter written in 1913 as chairman of the Commission on State and Local Federations, asked for criticism and advice as to a number of possible Commission undertakings, including:

"III. A Federation of Federations, or Conference of Workers in State and Local Federations. It may be desirable to hold conferences, nation-wide, annually; or conferences within denominations at denominational gatherings or apart from such gatherings. . . . I see the possible value of such conferences. I fear also the multiplication of organizations and the increase of cumbersome machinery. Whatever is done in this direction should be simple . . .

"IV. The relation of federations to the Federal Council. Plainly there should be a conference of federations in connection with the next quadrennial meeting of the Federal Council. Should representation be sought on the program of the Federal Council? Should other relations be sought? I think the question has been settled, that federations, not being of the same class as denominations, nationally organized are not eligible to direct representation in the Federal Council." (This relatively hesitant policy was nevertheless preparing the ground for more vigorous procedures in the near future.)

By 1913 "state and local federations . . . had increased to thirteen state and 130 city and county federations,"[26] of which "about 95 local (federations were) actively prosecuting their work," while eight additional state bodies were also listed but could not be called active.[27] Likewise Dr. Macfarland remembered as significant that "the Commission on State and Local Federations proposed a conference of federations"[28]—a proposal whose implications have never been adequately explored.

"The Commission on State and Local Federations, of which Alfred Williams Anthony was chairman, again cleared an atmosphere which was still hazy. Several federations had objected to any effort on the part of the Federal Council to exercise authority over their composition. The Commission advised against any further effort to standardize federations: 'The federation ideal, expressing a principle, does not require a set form or fixed phrases. The principle of cooperation and concert of plan and purpose may find expression in as varied forms as there are places and people. A standard form or organization may suggest an ideal; but carries with it no inherent virtue, and requires subservient imitation. In our recognition of federations and with our propagation of the federative ideals we should allow every legitimate variety.' This settled the issue, but it may be added that later on the federations largely reversed their attitude and voluntarily sought closer relations with the Council."[29]

A dual provision for state and local extension now begins to be evident. Reporting to the Executive Committee of the Federal Council, December 3, 1913, the secretary said, "In response to a request from Mr. Fred B. Smith, representing certain interdenominational organizations and movements, the Administrative Committee has been authorized to appoint a Commission on Interdenominational Movements."[30] Meanwhile, the secretary reported, Dr. Anthony's Commission on State and Local Federations, "composed largely of executive officers of state and local federations, has entered seriously upon an attempt to formulate principles for the work of the local federations; to define such cooperative relationship as they may have to the Federal Council; and to provide ways by which they may through this Commission be of mutual help."

Tentative Conclusions

"This work is still in its elemental, formative, and experimental stage. In some cities and towns it has approximated or reached success. In places where it has been taken seriously and where strong pastors and laymen have gotten behind it to a sufficient extent, it has clearly shown its promise, demonstrated its possibilities, and proved its effectiveness.

92

"Relatively few, however, of either pastors or laymen comprehend the significance of this federated movement. In many places it is considered simply as an occasional coming together for good fellowship.

"The federations that have proved successful are in the main those that have been formed around some very definite concrete and pressing problems. . . . The laymen seem to appreciate and understand the movement, when it is brought to their attention, better than the pastors as a whole. It seems to appeal more strongly to their sense of efficiency.

"Local federation work . . . is of necessity very opportunistic . . .

"When one or two cities succeed in (determining the functions of the local federation) . . . it may be fairly predicted that the federation movement all over the country will move up not only with rapidity, but also with greater efficiency than it has had up to this time."[31]

Read half a century later, these paragraphs seem singularly up-to-date in some of their insights.

Finances and Relationships

Economic conditions throughout the nation continued to affect church program and promotion policies, inevitably. "All (Federal Council) Commissions are to secure their own support. . . . The budgets of the several Commissions . . . are subject to the supervision and control of the Executive Committee."[32] This was unavoidable, but underscored the inadequacy (in 1913, at least) of denominationally contributed funds to push interdenominational organization, whatever the level; if national funds were inadequate even for national work, so much the more were they likely to be insufficient to promote state and local co-operation. In other words, there was as yet no field budget, since the district offices and secretariats had been abolished. Even the volunteer commissions had no resources save those that they themselves were able to secure.

On December 4, 1913, a Special Committee on Principles and Functions of the Federal Council reported concerning "Relation to Local Federative Agencies":

"It is held by many . . . that the Federal Council should be the initiator, creator, inspirer, and so far as possible the directing agency of (state and local federations).

93

"There is, however, no organic relation between the Federal Council and state and local federations, and it can assume no responsibility for the constituency of such federations or the form which they may take, or indeed any responsibility, except as they may carry out the principles and policy of the (Federal) Council."[33]

The 1913 report of the Commission on State and Local Federations[34] seems to have been, at least in part, the statement of its chairman, Dr. Anthony. The Commission had not been able to meet until the time of the Federal Council's Executive Committee's sessions in Baltimore, in December. The Executive Committee, on hearing this report, "voted to adopt the same."[35] Just what was implied in this action is not clear—perhaps was not then clear. In line with information listed earlier in this chapter, Dr. Anthony reported, "We have data ready for publication concerning 20 state federations, 80 city, and 15 county (or a total of 115) besides a mass of information covering many other organizations." Dr. Anthony had obviously applied some criteria in sorting out the data; and evidently more blanks came in after his report had been completed. Many blanks provided "no data." (The original signed replies are still on file.)

This report asked, can local federations be regarded as outstations of the Federal Council (according to the original theory of "branches")? The answer was that state and local federations, which are "organically independent, . . . have with the Federal Council only the relations which spring from similarity and sympathy." Together they maintain "a cooperating fellowship."

"No uniform name need be employed for the designation of a federation." One judgment, then confidently expressed, may cause a smile now: "It certainly would appear advisable in the future to avoid the use of the name council for a state or local federation, inasmuch as that is the technical designation of the national organization." (In the years to come, the same considerations were to argue precisely in the opposite direction.)

"The membership of State and Local Federations should be kept entirely to local determination. . . . The delimitations or the extension of the membership of the state and local federations need not concern the Federal Council, since the Federal Council has neither called these Federations into existence nor is responsible for their specific agreements and functions." (Here surely is delightful ambivalence. Has the Council decided to lop off its "branches" as non-income-producing? Has it abandoned its own children? Plainly, one cannot make any figure

94

of speech, applied to such a situation, walk on all fours; but the time was to come when the National Council would approach this whole issue from a much more rigidly logical organizational viewpoint.)

"Not a few state and local federations, once promising and exuberant in the zeal of their beginning, have ceased activity and are dormant, if not indeed defunct. Not infrequently the failure of a federation is due to the fact that it has not represented its own constituency, or been true to its own environment."

The Commission favored "a bulletin service and the creation of a new literature in form of circulars, pamphlets, and possibly books, describing federation state and local, what it has accomplished, and what it may become." (Those of us who have struggled to actualize such sentiments know how much easier it is to express them than it is to implement them, in the light of the demands for adequate editorial work, and mounting costs for the simplest printing.) The Commission also favored local and regional conferences, as convenience might permit, and a Conference of Federations in connection with the next Federal Council meeting. There was to be immediate progress along all these lines, in spite of previous hindrances.

Tabulation of denominational participation in the federation movement at this time makes clear that one evidence of the success of the world and national councils is the gradual reduction in the number of denominations.

Dr. Macfarland, who was now unanimously elected as general secretary, said again in his 1914 report:[36] "The federations which are being formed at the present vary, as has always been the case, in their effectiveness. In states where the movement is taken seriously by the pastors, it is correspondingly effective. . . . We need one or more Field Secretaries for this work, and I would recommend that this matter be considered in connection with the proposal of a Commission on Interdenominational Movements."

New Beginnings in 1915

World War I had begun during the summer of 1914, but the sinking of the *Lusitania* did not occur until May 7, 1915, and America did not enter the war until April 6, 1917, only nineteen months before Armistice Day. Yet this entire epoch, including the early years covered in Chapter V, was affected by the expectation of war, its prosecution, and its aftermath.

95

A *Directory of State and Local Federations in the United States* was compiled by Dr. Anthony and edited by Edward M. McConaughey; Dr. Anthony also made certain "Suggestions for State and Local Federations." Reporting for his Commission,[37] he called "the Massachusetts Federation the most efficient of all Federations. (It) authorizes this year a budget of $4,000, and has voted to become incorporated, in order that it may receive bequests." In view of the inadequacy of correspondence, Dr. Anthony seconded the general secretary's recommendation that a national field agent be named. This report was received and approved.[38] The Administrative Committee was now "authorized at its discretion, to employ a Field Secretary in the interest of state and local federations and interdenominational movements and organizations, when conditions shall warrant such action and when the special resources necessary for the maintenance of such a Secretary shall be provided."[39]

After significant studies in Vermont and in New York State, C. O. Gill was now engaged in the famous Ohio Survey, under the Committee on the Church and Country Life.[40] The Commission on State and Local Federation, as listed,[41] contained fifteen members; and a new Commission on Federated Movements, first listed as "in process of formation," was duly appointed as an *ad interim* body by the Executive Committee of the Federal Council, which at its 1914 Richmond meeting had approved the recommendations of the general secretary that the Administrative Committee be empowered to provide such a commission. At the end of 1915 the general secretary made a careful summary of all these happenings, pointing out the well-considered nature of a step that had been three years in the making.

We may now well interrupt the story, leaving to Chapter V the employment of Dr. Guild, and the 1915 reports made by the two commissions. The Commission on Federated Movements, now to be considered, soon made the surprising report that it had received (sources not given) contributions amounting to $13,676.00 in 1915, as against expenses of $11,462.14, thus showing a December balance of $2,213.86.

This sort of financial wizardry marked a new day. *A fresh start had been made.* In time the temporary spurt would spend itself, but for the moment the interest in state and local federations moved in high gear, sponsored by a whole galaxy of nation-wide forces and new dynamic personnel. Timid minimums were now out the window; the signal was full speed ahead. There was no let or hindrance in the national denominational controls in the path of any commission that could pull itself up by its own financial bootstraps. This was the genius of Federal Council economics: specialized mickles of functional interest could easily be synthesized into a considerable and impressive interdenominational muckle. If the state and local bases could grow strong, so much the better for the interdenominational senate at the top of the cooperative edifice.

With the accession of new structure, funds, and personnel, nationally there is first to be a quick deflation of the alleged strength of the federative movement among the states and cities. New criteria of evaluation, new definitions of effectiveness, will promptly debunk much of what has been hitherto asserted as law and gospel, and the whole movement will be ruthlessly pruned, looking forward to a heavier crop in the next harvest.

Forgetting the insecurities of the past, a new beginning is about to be made, equally fallible but more enduring.

REFERENCE NOTES

Chapter IV

1 Personal letter, December 21, 1959.
2 Rich, *op. cit.*, pp. 216, 222. *Cf.* also Hudson, *op. cit.*, Chapter X, "A Lonely Prophet" (Walter Rauschenbusch), pp. 226-242.
3 *Ibid.*, pp. 25, 50, 53, 57, and 87.
4 FC *1908 Report*, p. 110.
5 FC *1913 Report*, p. 100.
6 Macfarland, *The Progress of Church Federation*, p. 36 (pub. in 1921).
7 *Ibid.*, pp. 38, 39.
8 FC *1908 Report*, pp. 274 ff.
9 *Cf.* FC *1910 Report*, p. 13.
10 Macfarland, *Christian Unity in the Making*, p. 56.
11 FC *1910 Report*, p. 14.
12 Macfarland, *Across the Years*, Macmillan, 1936, pp. 86-91.
13 Macfarland, *Christian Unity in the Making*, pp. 66, 67.
14 *Ibid.*, p. 68.
15 *Ibid.*, p. 65.
16 *Ibid.*, p. 70.
17 *Ibid.*, pp. 72, 79.
18 FC *1912 Report*, p. 64.
19 Macfarland, *Progress of Church Federation*, p. 126.
20 Macfarland, *Christian Unity in the Making*, p. 64.
21 Macfarland, *Across the Years*, pp. 93, 94; *cf.* also *Christian Unity in Practice and Prophecy*, pp. 68 ff.
22 Weisberger, *op. cit., pp.* 129, 130.
23 Handy, *op. cit.*, p. 39.
24 Macfarland, *Christian Unity in the Making*, p. 64.
25 To concrete this statement would take a book in itself. Twice Dr. Guild spent long periods in Boston, and repeatedly months on the West Coast. When this writer went to Wichita in 1920, Dr. Guild had laid careful foundations, including responsible financial underwritings, which permitted a new and inexperienced secretary to give major attention to the cooperative task itself rather than its financing. Many other executives, who began work during Dr. Guild's term of office, would likewise rise up and call him blessed.
26 *Ibid.*, p. 85.
27 FC *1913 Report*, pp. 35, 36.
28 Macfarland, *Christian Unity in the Making*, p. 86.
29 *Ibid.*, p. 88.
30 FC *1913 Report*, p. 35.
31 *Ibid.*, pp. 35, 36. (*Cf.* also Douglass, *Protestant Cooperation in American Cities*, p. 225).
32 *Ibid.*, p. 59.
33 *Ibid.*, pp. 66-69; for adoption see p. 56.
34 *Ibid.*, pp. 96-102.
35 *Ibid.*, p. 60.
36 FC *1914 Report*, p. 55; *cf.* also p. 168.
37 *Ibid.*, pp. 162-168; *cf.* also p. 55.
38 *Ibid.*, p. 104.
39 *Ibid.*, pp. 101, 106.
40 *Ibid.*, pp. 51-53.
41 *Ibid.*, p. 222.

First Period of Expansion, 1915-1924

Just what was to be the Federal Council's interest in state and local cooperation? Was it essential that state and local church federations should also be constituted ecclesiastically, by appropriate representation from member units? Or could they continue to be agencies or societies affiliating individual Christians? And was the Federal Council interested primarily in church cooperation for its own sake, or was its main objective favorable social change, including community betterment and the affiliation of all local agencies for its achievement? If its interest covered both these matters, which was to have the priority? Did some leaders regard church cooperation as a more urgent necessity, rather than the purposes to be accomplished by it? If so, what was to be the outcome?

This chapter provides an answer somewhat different from what some might have anticipated, and from what some have thought to be the case. Whether the answer was correct or incorrect is not here the question. Our next query is merely, What actually happened when the Federal Council faced up to the problem of state and local church cooperation?

A Vigorous New Thrust

For state and local cooperation 1915 marked as definitely new a beginning as 1908 did for national interdenominational federation. Each of these dates, coming at the close of a long succession of preparatory events and forces, was distinct in the sequence of American ecumenical developments.

From 1915 to 1924 the Federal Council staff included Dr. Roy B. Guild, a man peculiarly adapted to field promotion, deeply devoted to the cause of church cooperation, and backed by the volunteer services of Fred B. Smith, with whom he had been so closely associated in the Men and Religion Forward Movement. By 1915 also the local and state executives were beginning their annual assembling, a habit carried on almost uninterruptedly until now.

On January 7, 1915, the Federal Council's Administrative Committee made Fred B. Smith chairman of a Special Committee on

Federated Movements "to shape up the whole proposition." Its report was accepted on March 11, and Dr. Guild's employment authorized.[1] A "First Suggestion" memorandum from this distinguished committee outlined the appointment of a new, large Commission on Federated Movements, in recognition of two services the Federal Council could render:

1. Organizing, inspiring, and standardizing local and state federations. "No community with two or more churches" should lack a federation. While "remarkable work" has been done in "several cities," the "whole country needs such a plan continuously promoted."

2. Bringing the various kindred Christian organizations into closer fraternal, cooperative relations with each other and with the Federal Council.

Atlantic City Conference, 1915

A Conference on Interchurch Activities, for "the prayerful consideration of another advance in 'Working Together' among the Christian forces of America," proposed by the Special Committee on Federated Movements April 27, was duly convened on June 3 and 4, 1915, at the St. James Protestant Episcopal Church, Atlantic City, N.J. The more than one hundred persons attending represented (a) sixteen nation-wide denominational, interdenominational, and undenominational bodies, all of which were dealing with the problems of local federation; and (b) state and local federations of churches, whose leaders had seemingly not met since the Federal Council's 1912 Quadrennial. Though there were only sixteen local organizations with paid personnel, and two of these had only part-time executives, eleven men representing seven cities and three states actually made reports of their work. Marion Lawrence spoke in favor of the proposed annual conference of the participating bodies.

The findings of this Conference favored the proposed Commission and its appointment by the Federal Council itself, after consultation with the agencies to be officially represented, to avoid any seeming pressure for premature organizational commitments. A fully representative conference, to be held within twelve months, was suggested, "to study state and local policies; to strengthen existing federations; to encourage the organization of new federations in selected places, laying emphasis not on the number of such new organizations but on thoroughness and comprehensiveness of effort in relation to existing needs; and to study the policies and programs of local federations with

100

special reference to (those) of the agencies represented in this Conference."[2] Thus the cooperative program adopted "would take into account all the agencies involved in a voluntary and unofficial way."

The president of the Federal Council appointed Fred B. Smith as chairman of the strong new Commission. At its first meeting, September 21, 1915, with 32 members present, Dr. Guild was elected secretary, and Mr. James A. Whitmore Field Secretary, "to assist in the formation of the Commission." A Committee of Direction of not to exceed nine members was to be appointed by the Commission's chairman; and at its call the annual meeting of the Commission would be held. To Raymond Robins these developments meant "the age of cooperation is really here."[3]

State and Local Executives Convened

On December 8, in making his first report to the Executive Committee of the Federal Council,[4] Dr. Guild cited a new leaflet, "Christian Conquests through Interchurch Activities," one of a long series to be issued. The Commission report, as amended, was approved by the Executive Committee,[5] an action, with the approval of a 1916 budget of $15,400, that was reported to the Commission the next day, December 9. The Commission "enters upon its work with great enthusiasm," largely because of *the First Conference of Church Federation Executives,* held at Columbus, O., December 7 to 9, 1915. Eleven men represented as many cities and at least two states; five national staff and committee members also attended. In five prolonged sessions these sixteen guests of the Commission discussed budget, comity, Bible study, boys' work, missions, survey, delinquency, recreation, etc. Actual budgets ranged from $800 in Dayton to $12,000 in New York City; salaries from one (part-time) of only $120 per year to $3,500.

The functions of a city federation were held to include: aid to specialized agencies; the making of surveys, religious and social; direction and endorsement of rescue missions; organizing missionary propaganda; relating boys' work to the churches; arousing and molding public opinion for welfare work; stimulating public officials. (The precise language was "to force action on the part of public authorities"!) In general, the federation was to be a clearing house rather than an operating agency. The experienced recording secretary, E. T. Root, condensed the conference report into a careful one-page summary. (Five pages of full minutes are also still extant.) This "first" conference is clearly another important bench mark in the history of American ecumenicity. Here are some of the early roots of the Association of Council Secretaries.

A year later Dr. H. K. Carroll, writing of these pioneers, said, "Each . . . was working without precedents, yet when these men came together for the first time, there was remarkable agreement between them as to principles, scope of work, and methods."[6] In his June 1916 report, and repeatedly later, Dr. Guild hailed this new body as "establishing a new religious order in the United States," a statement in which Dr. Macfarland concurred.[7] Fred B. Smith's prediction, "There will yet be such a gathering of a thousand men," carried on the organization letterhead, though still far from fulfilled, now seems quite possible of attainment. The need for training this new profession was recognized from the outset, and steps were taken to bring it to the attention of the theological seminaries.

Permanent organization was effected; "The Church Federation Secretaries' Council" proved to be a short-lived designation for an enduring body. Dues of one dollar per year per federation were voted. Morton C. Pearson of Indianapolis was elected chairman, and Root of Massachusetts for what became a three-year term as secretary. The order of business for a meeting in connection with the 1916 Federal Council Quadrennial was left to the officers in consultation with Dr. Guild.

In January 1916 the Commission's Committee of Direction proposed a second Atlantic City Conference of 250 delegates from cooperating agencies, to be held in June. Cooperation with the Home Missions Council in some state-wide campaigns was also authorized.[8]

In February Dr. Frank Mason North wrote to Fred B. Smith: "So far as the Commission is charged with the development of local federations, there is before it a field of opportunity that seems to me limited only by the number of communities in the United States. This phase of the program appeals to me with great force. Some of us who shared in the effort that resulted in the organization of the Federal Council had at the beginning and still have the conviction that federation in the local community, though a less splendid achievement, is particularly more immediate in its power of reducing friction and releasing forces for the promotion of the Kingdom." What this statement by the president of the Federal Council does not say is perhaps as important as what it does. For the time being the Federal Council was to give its attention to the extension of federative effort rather than to the integration of nation-wide forces. The latter would come later.

Realistic Inventory

After surveying nearly a hundred federations, Dr. Guild found that many of them were inactive. Failure in most instances was due to dependence on voluntary service. Often the leading officer was a clergyman who moved away. "It is very evident that in cities with a population of over 100,000 not much can be accomplished without . . . an employed executive." "To insure permanence of work, it is necessary to have the burden of support fall on the shoulders of laymen." "Most of the federations have been formed to deal with some evil condition existing in the community. . . . It is a waste of time to form federations merely because that is the proper thing to do."

Dr. Guild asserted that seven federations had grown out of the Men and Religion Forward Movement, while another was reputedly the result of the Laymen's Missionary Movement, as was the United Stewardship Council. He also ventured the opinion that "the closer the central organization is to the official ecclesiastical organizations of the community, the greater is the assurance of permanency. Federation budgets now ran as high as $18,000. "As in all religious work, the financial problem is the source of much difficulty. . . . Fifteen federations secure funds through church contributions."

On December 5 and 6, 1916, at St. Louis, the Conference on Organizations, first suggested for Atlantic City, was tardily held, with 89 persons present at five sessions.[9] It was guided by a characteristic page of "Principles"[10] concerning the cooperative relations of Christian organizations, drawn up by Dr. John R. Mott, and considered to be of sufficient importance to be published separately, as well as included in the five-page report from a distinguished committee of ten on "Suggestions."

New Momentum

Thus in two years the Commission had to a considerable extent accomplished its second purpose, to bring various Christian organizations into closer fraternal, cooperative relations with each other and to the Federal Council; and the Federal Council had won an acknowledged place of leadership, especially in integrating the Christian forces of the local community. Accordingly, Dr. North's judgment, as to the relative importance of the first or promotional function of the Commission, was seemingly sustained. (The quite unexpectedly successful fulfillment of the Commission's second function, through the organization of the exceptionally inclusive National Council of Churches, was now less than a generation away. In only 34 years there would be a massing of ecclesiastical agencies that to a few had begun to seem logically desirable, even in 1916, though then almost hopelessly remote.)

103

On December 5, 1916, the Council of Church Federation Secretaries had also met, with four national and eleven state and local men present. Differences of local names now seemed justified, in spite of the feeling that a "common name (was) highly desirable." While similar variety of organization was felt to be permissible, all agreed that ideally a local cooperative agency should include both pastor and layman from each church, an executive committee, and an employed executive secretary. Comity, it was declared, could best be handled by a committee composed of denominational representatives who "have the say" as to the location of new churches. (The problems of "old" churches, especially at the heart of the cities, had seemingly not yet registered.)

Badges, with the privilege of the floor, granted by the Federal Council for its quadrennial sessions, December 6-11, 1916, were gratefully accepted. The growing though meager strength of this Association is evidenced by its increase in membership from twelve in 1915 to twenty-four in 1919; at no time during this period was its cash balance at the end of the fiscal year as much as $18.50! One answer to a question as to what makes a church a member of a federation was, "Do not insist on delegates or dues. Keep on sending literature and get all the cooperation possible. The Federation, if it is doing things, will draw them in." Was this obviously opportunistic, free-sample, interim ethic realistic and unavoidable at the time?

A resolution,[11] offered by Dr. Root, sought the inclusion of executive secretaries either as corresponding members of the Federal Council or as denominational representatives, in "due proportion of such men with a practical experience in the details of church federation." Thus early was this issue raised, for continuance until now. In response to the query as to how federation could be extended to smaller cities, Indiana reported that it had a desk in the Indianapolis office, and Massachusetts that its promotional materials specialized on extension. Toledo, O., North Dakota, and Gary, Ind., plans for teaching the Bible in the public schools were presented.

The printed report of the Commission for the 1916 Quadrennial of the Federal Council[12] included much detailed documentation of how it had been organized and how it had begun its work, together with a discussion of such topics as standardization of program, executive leadership, and basis of organization. Signed by Fred B. Smith as chairman, it also included Dr. Guild's June report and that of the Field Secretary. In the six months before this December meeting, Guild

104

and Whitmore, who "had visited practically all the larger cities west of the Mississippi, had found many communities clearly ready to revive old federations or to create new ones." Earlier in the year they had visited from one to six cities in each of eighteen states and the District of Columbia.

Consolidated Emphasis on State Federations

A Committee of Fifteen now recommended "that the Commission on Federated Movements and the Commission on State and Local Federations be united under the name Commission on Federated Movements."[13] The Business Committee, however, on December 7, 1916,[14] substituted "Commission on Interchurch Federations (State and Local)," and its recommendation was adopted rather than the language proposed by the Committee of Fifteen. Commission members were not to be chosen with reference to agency representation.

On its Business Committee's recommendation,[15] the Council also directed "its newly appointed Commission on Interchurch Federations (state and local) to give special attention to the development of *state* federations, in order, in the most efficient and economical manner, to cover the whole field of interchurch work, rural as well as urban, the combination of churches as well as cooperation by the churches." Thus was begun a long campaign, of far-reaching importance, that was to continue for decades, to reach local situations from state centers, and to cover areas lacking metropolitan cities. This thrust for stronger state councils was seen to be the more necessary in the light of Dr. Anthony's analysis of cooperation in home missions, which "found great weaknesses, especially at the state level."[16] (The matter of the "combination of churches" was to involve differences of opinion as to method.[17])

In his 1916 statement Dr. Carroll cited the Federal Council's 1913 disavowal of responsibility for local and state federations, "except as far as they may carry out (its own) principles and policy,"[18] but in the Federal Council Year Book covering 1916 he noted the purposes, plan, organization, and history of the new consolidated Commission.[19] Thus duplication, transition, and consolidation had led to "more aggressive" field outreach.

Pittsburgh, 1917

On January 25, 1917, the Committee of Direction nominated 24 new members of the Commission, in addition to the 54 earlier members. Plans for a Pittsburgh Congress [20] on Purpose and Methods of Interchurch Cooperation were far enough along by this time to permit the naming of eight chairmen for subcommissions. On February 23, with only four declinations among Commission nominees reported, four other names were added. The Pittsburgh dates were set for October 1 to 4, and appointments made to the subcommissions. By April 16 (ten days after the United States had declared war), much was being written on "The War and the Churches." In spite of the war, it was voted to proceed with the Pittsburgh Congress, a statement of the need of which was now widely circulated. The subcommissions were in session from 9 a.m. to 5 p.m.

By June 22 wartime committees seemed essential, as did also a proposed field secretary. While more than half of the Congress fund had been raised, another $3,000 was needed. Said Dr. Guild's semi-annual report, in words like those used earlier, and to be used repeatedly from now on: "We do not encourage the formation of a federation in a large city unless there is the prospect of establishing a central office and employing a capable secretary. The task is too great for volunteer service alone." Again an impressive list of cities had been visited by the secretary or the chairman.

The historic Pittsburgh Congress, with its effective promotional material, program format, and careful body of discussion material, was held, according to plan, during the first four days of October, 1917. It resulted in a useful volume, *Purpose and Methods of Interchurch Cooperation,* a manual of interchurch work; and was attended by 506 delegates, representing 31 denominations, three dozen states, and 134 towns and cities.

In this connection a brief informal business session of "The Council of Church Federation Executive Secretaries" was held. The organization's letterhead was now carrying the slogan: "For a Trained Ministry—Representing All the Churches in Service to the Whole Community"; it listed twenty members, including executives from Atlanta, Buffalo, Chicago, Cincinnati, Cleveland, Duluth, Erie, Gary, Indianapolis, Kansas City, Los Angeles (and California), Louisville (2), Lowell, New York City, Pittsburgh, Portland Me., San Francisco, and Toledo; and Massachusetts. The help of local and state secretaries in field visitation was acknowledged.

On October 4, at the Wm. Penn Hotel, the Commission also met. On October 17 an editorial committee was appointed, for the important task of issuing the proposed *Manual.* An additional (ninth) commission report had been added on "War-Time Local Interchurch

106

Work," printed separately. On October 11 *The Continent* printed an extended editorial on the Congress.

Dr. Guild felt that "The success of the Congress has increased greatly the responsibilities of this Commission. There are now more than twenty employed executive secretaries. A new religious order has been established." "Plans should be made for visits to theological seminaries, that certain schools may begin the preparation of men for this work as they do for the missionary field."[21] His recommendation "that plans now be initiated for holding next year a summer school for executive secretaries, those who are contemplating entering on this work, also ministers and laymen who as officers and workers in federations are now giving volunteer service," was favorably referred to the appropriate committee; and in December 1917 was approved by the Executive Committee of the Federal Council. On the request of the Federal Council's Executive Committee, the president of the Federal Council was asked to add the president of the Council of Executive Secretaries and Morton C. Pearson of Indianapolis to the Commission, thus relating the local and state executives to the Federal Council.

The 1917 Commission[22] report began: "At the present time there are twenty-six employed executive secretaries, an increase of over 30 percent during the year. This new religious order is now well established and will increase steadily in number." The report appropriately included the purposes and recommendations of the Congress. These however were now available in the new *Manual,* orders for which had been received from all parts of the country.[23] Dr. Guild was doubtless right: "The Pittsburgh Congress marks a definite stage in the progress of Christian cooperation."[24]

En route to and from Hawaii in November and December, 1917, Fred B. Smith visited many cities, making 89 addresses. New federations were organized in Butte, Mont., and Seattle, Wash. Likewise Dr. Guild had been in Ohio, Illinois, Missouri, Kansas, and Pennsylvania. "The fruits of the Pittsburgh Congress are in evidence on every hand." •

Interruptions: World War I and the Interchurch World Movement

On January 1, 1918 *The Federal Council Bulletin* began to be a valuable news medium. On February 7 a budget of $16,600 for 1918 was adopted by the Committee of Direction. By June 18 the proposed Lake Geneva Summer School, in spite of previous approval by the Federal Council's Executive Committee, had to be postponed—so many men who had intended to enroll in it were now engaged in some kind of war service.

107

At a business session in connection with the Secretarial Conference on Principles and Methods of Interchurch Work, September 25, 1918, at the Sherman Hotel, Chicago, Fred L. Fagley of Cincinnati was elected president of the secretarial fellowship. This gathering was also a joint session of the Chicago Inter-Church War Work Commission, and the Federal Council's Commission on Interchurch Federations, in cooperation with the National Committee on the Churches and the Aims of the War.

At this Conference "twenty-six secretaries from all parts of the country were in continuous session for four days, interchanging and discussing experiences with a view to further understanding the aims and methods of interchurch work. The men who were doing the work conducted the discussions. Each man answered three questions: "What did you do?" "How did you do it?" "What do you plan to do this season?" With these secretaries were officers of federations, men who had been sent from cities to find out how to form a federation at home, and prospective secretaries. The Council of Church Federation Secretaries is a new but already well-established order of Christian workers. There are now over 30 employed secretaries of state and local federations."[25]

By October 23, 1918, the *Manual* was in its third thousand. Dr. Guild had visited 32 cities in six months. In his detailed report he said, "It is no longer a question of whether or not the churches of a city will be federated—it is only a question of when." Yet, he felt sure, "undue haste" was to be avoided.

An important background factor in these days was the Interchurch World Movement, which, on December 11, 1918, exactly a month after the Armistice was signed, began its brief, ill-starred history of approximately nineteen months. The wartime psychology lingered, and the task of demobilization and of bringing the troops back from Europe took many months. On December 30, 1918, it was reported that Rochester, N.Y., was organized; that Columbus, O., had reorganized on December 16 and was seeking an executive; and that Chicago was reorganizing. It was hoped that ten new federations with employed secretaries could soon be announced. A committee was named to arrange the regional conferences suggested by the Federal Council's Executive Committee. Fred B. Smith now reported that these conferences had been merged into the Interchurch World Movement.[26]

According to the General Secretary's 1918 report,[27] "The Commission on Interchurch Federations has made wonderful progress in

108

the development of substantial and effective local federations of church-es." The Commission's report, signed by Fred B. Smith, substantiated this statement.

Relationship Problems

Early 1919 appears to have been a slack time, but twenty-five secretaries were guests of the Church Peace Union at Pittsburgh, September 15 to 18, 1919, at the Hotel Chatham, where there was a continuing "desire that there might be a closer relation between the federations and the Federal Council." At the annual meeting of the Association of Executive Secretaries on the 16th the Pittsburgh executive, Charles R. Zahniser, of "Case Work Evangelism" fame, was elected president. Thirty-four persons were present. An executive committee was created, to include the officers and three others to be named by the president. Dr. Guild then stated that more than forty cities had full-time executives. Dates of the organization of fifteen of these were recorded in the minutes.

No less than thirteen program items were discussed at this conference, and 25 pages of minutes recorded. These included: comity, women and federation, young people, international justice and good will and the League of Nations, federation and industry, publicity, evangelism, religious education, the Interchurch World Movement, civic reform, administrative problems, and the Sabbath. E. R. Wright of Cleveland reported that in their Federation they now had enlisted two laymen for every minister; and Guild advised that "Those should be on the comity committee who do the spending, the raising, and the giving of the money."

On November 25, 1919, the Committee of Direction learned that the year marked "the largest developments" ever; field contacts had included six months of the secretary's time on the Pacific Coast. By then, five states had employed executives (California, Connecticut, Indiana, Massachusetts, and Pennsylvania), and "Ohio will soon have one." Twenty-five cities were listed, six of them with additional part-time personnel, and two with office secretaries. Four strong federations were looking for executives. Relations with the Interchurch World Movement, which had provided $504.57 for the work of the Commission, were discussed. The Commission welcomed nominations to its membership from the federations. Another "Pittsburgh" in 1920 was approved, with the Committee of Direction to be supplemented by the Executive Committee of the Council of Secretaries.

On December 30, 1919, the General Committee for the Church and Community Conference met at the Union League Club, with ten persons present. Fred B. Smith presented elaborate "Suggestions." With Mr. Smith as chairman, and Dr. Guild as secretary, nine persons from the Commission and the five members of the Executive Committee of the Council of Federation Secretaries were named to the Committee on Arrangements. Wright had invited the conference to Cleveland; a Cleveland cooperating committee of 58 members had been named. The general Committee of Arrangements finally numbered 42, and the Program Committee had nine members. An eight-page memo presented: "I, Purposes; II, Program; III, Delegates." An incidental question was, "Should there be a report of the Allied Christian Organizations at Cleveland?" The stage was being set for a second significant national gathering, with adequate organizational preparation.[28]

Cleveland, 1920, A New High

At a February 12 meeting, with three dozen persons present, at the Pennsylvania Hotel, followed by dinner at Delmonico's, the agenda for the Cleveland Conference began to take shape. It was suggested that Negroes and representatives of foreign groups be added to the personnel; and also some representative women. On May 24, 1920, in connection with an open meeting of the Cleveland Church Federation, and again on June 2, sessions of the Council of Secretaries were held. Dr. Laidlaw spoke on his work in the Census Bureau. Rev. E. R. Wright, the host, was elected president; and Orlo J. Price, executive of the Rochester, N.Y., Federation, began a three year term as secretary, to be followed for eight years by his colleague, Mrs. C. T. Simonds.

On May 26 Dr. Guild reported the reorganization of the Committee of Direction to include representatives nominated by state and local federations: "This relates the work of the Commission to the Local Federations and indirectly relates the Federations with the Federal Council," even more intimately than through membership in the Commission.

Boston was reported to have $9,000 in the bank, and expected very shortly to name an efficient secretary. *Washington, D.C.,* had organized a strong federation and had employed a capable executive. The writer had begun as executive of the new *Wichita* organization, like many others at first called a federation, later a council. Finance campaigns had been helped in *Dayton* and *Toledo*. Progress in *Philadelphia* had been delayed by the Interchurch World Movement situation. *Six states* now had church federations—still a tiny development, in sharp contrast with the nation-wide Sunday school movement; while two county and 36 city federations had secretaries on full or part time. Employed personnel now numbered 52. Splendid cooperation between the Interchurch World Movement and the Commission was reported.

Mr. Smith said that funds had been provided to meet the expense of the Cleveland Convention, but did not indicate the source. "The secretary stated that as the result of the past five years the Federation Movement had assumed such proportions that it was no longer possible for one man to carry on the work." On May 31, 1920, Dr. Guild declared that "The organization of *state* federations is one of our next tasks. To make haste slowly is the policy of this interchurch work." (This was in deliberate contrast to the policy of the Interchurch World Movement, which was just about to fold up.)[29]

The Cleveland Convention marked the end of an epoch. Some of us were drawn into the work on the crest of a wave. In 1930 Dr. H. Paul Douglass was to write, "Nearly one-third of the existing federations take their origins from the three years 1918-1920."[30] These included Boston, Detroit, Washington, and Wichita—to mention only a few. World War I had been more than an interruption: one of its cumulative by-products had been the discovery of unusual resources for community development. Dr. Douglass felt that it had "stimulated the organization of new federations in many cities," though their formal beginnings did not occur until the war was won.[31] To him the years 1920-1924 evidenced not as much continuous advance as a slightly delayed post-war period of "slowing up." In 1920 the tide was at the flood. With the collapse of the Interchurch World Movement, could it do anything but temporarily recede?

No such misgivings were evident, however, when the Commission met on June 2, 1920. Dr. Guild had again been five months on the Coast. He now reported *forty cities* organized. He had helped cities raise over $200,000. Confidently it was said, "There are fewer than a score of large cities without a federation or council of churches. It is . . . expected that within two years practically all these will have formed a suitable organization; . . . the Commission must now plan its work on a larger scale." The immediately succeeding years were unfortunately not to sustain these optimistic hopes.

As compared with the trifling financial resources of the AES, the huge resources of the Commission at this time looked almost inexhaustibly large. Incidentally, it was announced that Raymond Robins

111

and Fred B. Smith were soon to make a world tour for the World Alliance and Church Peace Union. Few of us who attended the Cleveland Convention June 1-3, 1920, had any realization that, just as some of us set our hands to the task, the peak was for the moment passing. Like the Pittsburgh Congress, this Church and Community Convention also had commanding printed matter, including impressive reports, available for all delegates in proof sheets, and subsequently embodied in the volume *Community Programs for Cooperating Churches. The Continent* was again impressed, as well it might be.[32]

The Commission was now one on *councils* rather than federations of churches, the transition from "federation" to "council" as the more normative word having been accomplished. Its 1920 report included 42 local, two county, and six state councils. One of these last (Pennsylvania) was for the time being served by a pastor (Wm. L. Mudge) on a part-time basis.[33]

By November 23 the Committee of Seven on Post-Cleveland Plan and Program was confident and expectant. Structural changes within the Federal Council, making its outreach a department rather than a commission, were suggested; and it was held that "the Commission's staff and organization, strong as they are, are not commensurate with the work to be done." Staff increase was therefore recommended; one or two additional secretaries ("men of ability and judgment") seemed imperative as soon as support could be secured. It was optimistically believed that first in larger cities, then in the states, councils "will be easily established on permanent and practical foundations," while more attention should also be given to smaller cities unable to employ executives. Because of a request for a statement covering the basis of federation organization as related to Christian forces, it was now explicitly reiterated that "the Commission . . . is seeking to develop the Cooperation of Christian forces in the various cities."

"Local Federations of Churches, through the Commission on Interchurch Federations, have multiplied and developed during the Quadrennium, so that whereas four years ago there were only twelve cities with substantial federations and employed executive secretaries, today there are more than forty with substantial federations, with executive secretaries."[34]

At the 1920 Boston Quadrennial Dr. Joseph Vance, president of the *Detroit* Council, addressed the Federal Council on "The Church and Its Service to the Community." E. L. Shuey, layman, *Dayton* president, and Rev. L. W. McCreary, *Baltimore* Federation executive, also spoke briefly.[35] In March the Commission on Councils of Churches adopted a 1921 budget of $26,000.[36]

The Pace Begins to Slacken

After another relatively slack period in early 1921, the AES annual meeting was held June 10, at the Spinning Wheel Restaurant in New York City, in connection with what had amounted to a "school of methods" at Union Theological Seminary, June 6 to 10, where rooms were free to the three dozen secretaries attending. Thirty-one attended the business session at which Rev. A. H. Armstrong of St. Louis was elected president; forty members paid dues in 1921. Two federations also paid ten dollars each; and nine, fifteen dollars—a total of $155 in organizational dues.[37]

On June 10 the Commission also met, at the Marble Collegiate Church. In presenting his report Dr. Guild said, "There is every reason to believe that by the end of 1921 practically every large city in the country will be organized." But again events were a bit slower in action than expected. The *state* field was said to be especially ripe. Women representatives of local churches were increasing. Sixteen men and women were named as the Committee of Direction for 1921-1922, and were empowered to fill any vacancy in their Committee.

On August 23, at Chautauqua, as part of Federal Council Week, Dr. Guild spoke on "Church Federation Problems" and "Community Conquest by Cooperating Churches"; Orlo J. Price of Rochester on "The Picture of Local Cooperation"; and Bishop McDowell on "The Ministry of Cooperation."[38]

On December 16 the Executive Committee of the Federal Council, on recommendation of its Business Committee,[39] in adopting the Report of the Commission on Councils of Churches, declared, "It is gratifying to note the steady advance of the cooperative principle in the larger cities, and the significant achievement of the churches when acting in accord and in union, especially in the field of evangelism. We heartily approve of the extension of the practice of cooperation into the states which as yet have but few effective federations."[40]

Smith and Guild, in the Commission's report on "Local Councils of Churches in 1921," said,[41] "Each council has no official connection with any other council," but there is "a most fraternal relationship." It was then not so difficult to organize the larger cities that had two to ten (or more) years of continuous success. "Fewer than a dozen large cities do not have a council and an office"! The "Men's Federa-

113

tion," as the women literally often termed it, now included an increasing number of representative women delegates and committee members. In 1921 the FC Commission on Councils and Federations of Churches and the AES made a survey to see what place women had in councils and federations, and what societies of women were doing. Two states and twenty-four cities responded. It was agreed that local churches should be represented in federations or councils by laymen and lay women, as well as by their pastors; and that the lay woman should be chosen by the combined vote of the women's missionary organizations of the local church. Autonomous departments of women members, it was also agreed, should be related to the women's boards, home and foreign. In "unorganized" places, women were to be encouraged to organize their own councils, and "hold themselves ready to affiliate when a federation or council comes into existence."

The state situation was necessarily slow, since denominational action requires from twelve to eighteen months. The work done by the Commission was largely the result of that done by city and state secretaries—more than fifty men, and a few women, were then employed. Significantly, a list of *volunteer* councils was then being prepared. The financial situation was difficult, and there was also the pressure on the local churches of denominational Forward Movements.[42]

At the 1922 annual meeting of the Association of Federation Secretaries, held May 31 at the Haskell Museum at the University of Chicago, as part of what again amounted to a "school of methods," May 29 to June 2, Rev. C. McLeod Smith of Toledo was elected president. Individual dues were increased to two dollars. Findings concerned evangelism, publicity, the international situation, religious education, state federations, civic betterment, moving pictures, race relations (apparently a new item), survey and comity, and women's work (also new).

The Price of Progress

On June 16, 1922, the Commission's Committee of Direction met for the first time in nearly a year, because of the almost continuous absence from the city of both its chairman and its secretary. Fred B. Smith had now returned from an eight-months' trip around the world in the interest of evangelism, church co-operation, and world peace. Chief unorganized cities included: Syracuse, Providence, Richmond, Va., Birmingham, Ala., New Orleans, Dallas, San Antonio, and Memphis. After reporting on developments in a number of other cities, "The secretary is of the opinion that he cannot out of justice to the

114

work nationally, devote so much time to single cities." "We are steadily reaching the point where the most important step must be taken, viz., developing the *state* councils of churches." "We are still confronted by the problem of finding . . . men. Between now and November about five will be required. One advantage we have today is the recognition of the fact that the man who makes good as a secretary can be sure of permanent employment. Men are less afraid to step out of established positions into a secretaryship." "With the passing of each year the program of work becomes both more intensive and extensive. The effort is being made to divert to other agencies the task that can be performed by them, and having the churches occupied in work that is peculiar to the church and will be done only as the churches co-operate." Elim A. E. Palmquist of Philadelphia, and Morris E. Alling of Connecticut, were elected to fill vacancies in the Commission, as representatives of the AES.

On December 7 increasing budgets and steady progress in specific cities were noted; and the organization of state councils, e.g., in such key states as New York and Illinois. The report to the Executive Committee of the Federal Council said that in comity there is "no short cut." Now about sixty men and women are employed by state and local councils. A budget of $28,800, including $3,000 for special agents and conferences, was approved.

A request was made by the Committee of Direction to the Church Peace Union for an appropriation to assist in the employment of a secretary to work in smaller places. It was recognized that "the Association of Employed Secretaries of Councils of Churches is the true dynamic of this movement."

In his 1922 report Dr. Guild featured developments in Minneapolis and in Ohio. Though Fred B. Smith was back, and addressed the Executive Committee of the Federal Council on "The Call of the Present Hour for Fuller Cooperation among the Churches,"[43] one suspects that the spell of his dynamic leadership had somehow been broken. In writing about "The Increasing Cooperation of the Churches" in their comments in "Community Cooperation,"[44] the general secretaries said, "To deal in any adequate way with the problem of cooperation in the community obviously requires an increase in resources both of men and money. Next to the need for strengthening the Council's work in evangelism, there is no more compelling necessity than at least one added secretary for the Commission on Councils of Churches." So wrote Drs. Macfarland and Cavert. In November, 1917, the latter had become assistant secretary of the General War-Time Commission, thus beginning "a long and distinguished career with the Federal Council." After 1918 service as army chaplain he became secretary of the important special Committee on the War and the Religious Outlook. In April 1920, at the request of Dr. Macfarland, with whom he was associated for nearly thirty years, Dr. Cavert was elected associate secretary of the Federal Council, "having revealed just the qualities, in both nature and scope, which adapted him to the Administration."[45]

A Long Pull Ahead

The Commission's report[46] on "The Churches Organizing for Community Cooperation" stressed the organization of new councils, the strategic place of the state council, and the full findings of the Conference of Allied Christian Agencies, held in Washington, D.C., October 17 and 18, submitted by a committee of which Dr. John M. Moore was chairman. In a Federal Council Executive Committee session Dr. Guild introduced the general subject of community cooperation;[47] Rev. F. E. Taylor spoke on city situations; and Rev. B. F. Lamb on state situations. Six official representatives of local councils were presented and addressed the Executive Committee briefly. In all, thirteen state and local councils were represented,[48] an indication both of the hospitality of the Federal Council and of the concern of the local leaders.[49] Here was sympathetic consideration, and large mutual interest; but somehow the situation began to bog down; the former momentum slackened; progress is leveling off. The best proof of this is the year-by-year count of effective local organizations:

Year	Number of City Federations	Year	Number of City Federations
1915	14	1920	47
1916	18	1921	48
1917	24	1924	48
1918	31	1929	43
1919	41	1931	49

What had been a crusade had become a chore; romance had changed to hard work. Gilbert and Sullivan are both as necessary as their successors in later decades, if there is to be light opera. Had the team of Smith and Guild drifted apart? The holding of national assemblies to rouse cooperative interest seemed to have reached the point of diminishing returns. The war was over; grandiose schemes and pan-

116

aceas proposed to put the church world to rights, and civilization along with it, had collapsed. After proposing a League of Nations, our nation refused to ratify it. Denominations had a new self-consciousness. Inter-denominationalism must seemingly plod along for a term of years, content to hold the ground it had gained. The stock market would pyramid, but in the decade then begun benevolence would not keep pace with prices.

In January, 1923, Harry N. Holmes was called to be an associate of Dr. Guild's, with particular reference to local agency relationships, in the light of the Washington Conference. On March 28 he cabled his acceptance. This action was in line with the vote of the Federal Council's Executive Committee recommending "to all national, re-gional, and state officials of the denominations that they give their fuller cooperation in the development of local councils of churches throughout the country"; and approving "the appointment of an addi-tional secretary for the Commission on Councils of Churches as soon as funds can be secured."[50] Here was formal backing, with a clear Commission responsibility for securing the resources needed, and a staff increase in sight.

From May 28 to June 1, 1923, the Association of Executive Secretaries met at the Southern Hotel, Columbus, and elected Rev. L. W. McCreary of Baltimore as president. Sixty-six persons were listed and photographed, including 39 executives, Dr. Guild, and 40 secretaries from Ohio counties present at the May 31 annual meeting. Dr. Hugh S. Magill, General Secretary of the I.C.R.E., was present for a full day, considering mergers then pending. As Dr. Guild at the end of the year looked back on this gathering, he noted "a remarkable sense of unity (among) these entirely autonomous organizations be-cause of this Association."

High Resolves

On December 12 to 14, 1923, the Executive Committee of the Federal Council voted: "That the method of church cooperation in local communities developed successfully by the Commission on Coun-cils of Churches be pressed in cities that do not yet have organized cooperation, and that special attention be given to plans for securing effective cooperation under volunteer leadership in all communities where it is not practicable to employ executive secretaries."[51]

The 1923 Federal Council reports featured a section on "Co-operative Christianity in Action," and a review of the year by the

117

general secretaries,[52] as well as a section entitled "Building from the Bottom Up."[53] A preliminary organization had been effected in Wyoming in 1923.[54]

The Executive Committee again heard a presentation on "How Can the Movement for Community Cooperation among the Churches Be Strenghened and Extended?" Rockwell Harmon Potter of Hartford spoke for city situations, B. F. Lamb of Ohio for state situations. Eight others, at least half of them federation secretaries, also spoke. A total of eighteen state and local executives were present. The Commission's annual report[55] mentioned developments in Wilmington, Del., Illinois and Springfield; Buffalo and New York State; Omaha; and Scranton, Pa. According to the Federal Council's Board of Finance, there was now significant competition for the ecumenical dollar.[56]

The Federal Council was now entering the fourth year of its fourth quadrennial. On May 2, 1924, Dr. Cavert raised the question with Dr. Guild as to whether the Federal Council was "expecting too much" of local councils; did it send them too much mail? Its purpose was to keep local councils informed, and maintain contacts with them in matters of varying importance, including finances. Would it help if all outgoing circulation cleared over Dr. Cavert's desk? In any case, "The cooperation of the Executive secretaries throughout the entire country has done more to make the Federal Council a reality than any other single thing. We deeply appreciate this cooperation, and will gratefully welcome any suggestions that will make this relationship stronger and more mutually helpful."[57]

On May 20 the question of regional conferences in the South was raised, and another nation-wide conference, in the 1915-1917-1920 tradition, was referred to the AES for discussion in June. The possibility of a women's conference was also mentioned. In these minutes one brief, cryptic paragraph read: "Mr. Smith reported on the probable readjustment of the work of the Commission as to the scope of the program, the organization and personnel of the Commission, and the name." One senses possible changes in the offing.

On June 3 to 5 the AES met in Harris Hall, Northwestern University, Evanston, with 34 present, five of whom represented the Federal Council, to the great satisfaction of the state and local executives. A Conference on Women's Work was approved for the fall, in Pittsburgh. Provisional authorization of representatives of the AES as members of the Federal Council's Executive Committee was taken, subject to the action of the quadrennial meeting. Regional conferences

118

were discussed. Helen Yergin of St. Louis provided a five-page memo on the cooperation of churches, religious education, race relations, office management, evangelism, missionary education, women's work, radio, coordination, non-Protestants, and denominational competition. Dr. Charles R. Zahniser of Pittsburgh gave answers, and there was general discussion. Rev. E. T. Root, after twenty years of interdenominational service, was elected President.

The 1924 Atlanta Quadrennial Report ("United in Service, 1920-1924") shows forty-eight cities with paid executives, as compared with fewer than a dozen ten years earlier, but no more than there were in 1921. The organization of the ICRE had simplified religious education relationships at least nationally. "More and more the churches are recognizing that the Council is literally a council of churches." The Commission's 1924 report was made over three names: Smith, Guild, and Holmes.[58] During 1924 Colorado organized a Home Missions Council, and North Dakota an Interchurch Superintendents' Council.[59]

Organized Church Women, The World, and The Community

One aspect of local federated women's work had been the widespread adoption of the Day of Prayer for Missions—Home and Foreign. For its promotion both the *Federation* of Women's Boards of Foreign Missions and the *Council* of Women for Home Missions joined in 1920. That same year marked the beginnings of what has now become a nation-wide program of migrant work, first suggested as an allocation to women's sponsorship in certain Interchurch World Movement surveys. In 1923 the first offerings for national and world projects were received at national women's headquarters. By 1924 there were approximately 1,200 local councils or federations of church women, probably mostly World Day of Prayer groups.

On December 11 and 12, 1924, at Pittsburgh, in response to the call of the FC and the AES, representatives of the Federation of Women's Boards considered the matter of unified approach in local communities. "No woman appeared on that program, but some did take part in discussion." There is considerable evidence that the clerical mind, chiefly masculine, was in danger of making the same misappraisal of women's work that it had earlier made in the reaction of many ministers to the Sunday School Movement and to the development of youth work. Women as an organized force, instead of being recognized as an asset, were too often regarded as an inescapable "problem." It was now "becoming increasingly evident that the two mission groups, organized for particular services, were not prepared

119

without certain internal adjustments to assume full responsibility for the inclusive programs foreshadowed in local organizations." Thus in every church of every communion, in every community, and throughout the states and nation, the integration of the program and machinery of the churches was undergoing constructive change.

The End of a Decade

On December 17, 1924, after a year of serious health impairment, Dr. Guild had written to Chairman Smith announcing his return to the pastorate December 31, thus terminating nearly a decade of service. The fourth quadrennial report[60] omits his name as senior secretary of the Commission. Times had changed. Said the retiring veteran, "It has been my hope to go forward with the more tedious but important work of forming state councils of churches. I fear, however, that this can better be carried on under new leadership." Attached to this letter is the 1915 memo of "Suggestions" about the work he had then been called to undertake. The aims there set forth had been largely accomplished.

On December 31 S. Parkes Cadman, president of the Federal Council, wrote to twenty-one persons requested to serve as the Committee of Direction of the Commission on Councils of Churches, nominated by Fred B. Smith, who had again been asked to serve as the Commission chairman: "It is believed that . . . the way will be clear by which the Commission will be called on to undertake larger responsibility, as the result of the striking program up to the present time."

Nearly a two-year interval followed, however, without executive leadership other than that of Harry Holmes.[61] Seemingly Dr. Guild had secured money, though not always enough, for the regular Commission task, including his own salary, thanks to the loyal support of friends able to give it; and Fred B. Smith had been able to get the money for the more spectacular gatherings. The two men, with their complementary gifts, made a good team. Dr. Macfarland wrote years later of Fred B. Smith as an "exponent of the ideal" of church and community organization, and of Dr. Guild as "the organizing genius" of the federation movement.[62]

Details of Commission finances need not concern us, but the overall picture may be of interest. First, the comparative size of the Federal Council operations is indicated by the increase in its budget from less than $35,000 in 1913 to nearly $150,000 in 1916, with the $300,000 mark in sight in 1924. Church cooperation was beginning to strike its stride. Did those in the local and state federations, who eagerly sought help from the Federal Council, and a share in the making of its policies, have any adequate comprehension of what hard work it had been to transform the meager resources of the Federal Council into these relatively ample figures?

Only during the past two years of the Federal Council's second quadrennium did the Commission on Federated Movements begin to get under way. Its financial status from year to year, as reported in its minutes and by the Federal Council treasurer, was substantially this: For its first seven years all had gone well with the Commission, financially; at the end of 1922 it was still in the black. So far, so good. Expenditures in 1923 had increased to $21,749.97, with no corresponding increase in income; at the end of that year—in spite of a contribution of $4,000 from the Church Peace Union—the Commission had a deficit of $2,377.98.[63] There were now two men on the staff; could the craft carry so much sail?

The expenses of the Commission in 1924 increased to $23,939.84, producing, in spite of a second contribution of $4,000 from the Church Peace Union, a $7,277.62 "debit balance," due the general treasury of the Federal Council. This was only one—but the largest—of four Federal Council deficits, fortunately offset by two balances, but leaving a net deficit of $8,789.48, over against a reserve fund of $10,000.[64] There would seem to be an obvious connection between the departure of Dr. Guild and this financial situation.

Two budgets were proposed for 1925. Concerning the $17,000 for local and state organization,[65] as part of a regular Federal Council budget of $272,100, it was stipulated that "This addition to the budget will need to be raised by special effort on the part of friends of the extension of local federations." To a second provisional addition to the budget amounting to $19,400 was added the proviso, "In view of the reorganization of measures for the development of local and state organizations, the following addition to the budget is authorized, contingent on the organization of this work and the securing of funds from special sources. The name and program of the Commission (were still) under consideration."

Such proposals were clearly ambivalent. Was it the intent to revive the dual purpose of the original Commission on Federated Movements? Was Fred B. Smith dissatisfied with merely ecclesiastical forms of cooperation? In the light of so serious a deficit, was this the time to expand? What was the cause of the deficit? Was there a difference

121

of opinion as to objectives? Could the former momentum be retained? Seemingly Dr. Guild felt stalemated, perhaps through sheer lack of financial resources. Whatever the reason, physical or otherwise, he resolved to withdraw from the scene at least for a while.

Health considerations[66] were accepted as a valid occasion for his seeking less strenuous employment, but they were not mentioned in his letter of resignation.

Throughout this entire determinative period there were two forces clearly at work: the down-from-the-top, out-from-the-center promotion by the Federal Council's Commission, slow as compared with the Interchurch World Movement, but sure; and the up-from-the-bottom, outward from city to city and state to state teamwork, chiefly professional, of the state and local federations or councils of churches. In retrospect it is plain, too, that a number of impersonal factors had contributed to the "slowing up" process noticeable between 1920 and 1924. Not the least of these was the economic cycle through which the nation was passing. In addition to minor "recessions," long before the stock-market crash in 1929, local churches and denominations began to anticipate or experience the effects of lessening benevolences, even at a time when there seemed to be plenty of money. And it was during this period that the long-standing organization of Sunday school workers, state and local, begun in 1892, and organized as the Employed Officers' Association in 1916, seems somehow to have been allowed to lapse.

Moreover, the meteoric coming and going of the Interchurch World Movement, with its first brilliant promise, its brief span, and its sudden demise, had doubtless induced a weariness comparable to that of the post-war reaction: December 1918 to June 1920 was more than an interruption—it served also to burn over the ground and induce a certain skepticism concerning all "ambitious" projects. This in turn made necessary a down-to-earth reality in the organizing and conduct of councils of churches at every level, not without its permanent values.

The year 1915 had marked a new beginning; 1924 saw the completion of this period of vigorous expansion. Fortunately, within five years Dr. Guild, his health recovered, was to return to his old task, and see the movement reach forward to a time when under new circumstances it would again expand with greater vigor than ever. Meanwhile Chapter VI will cover another period of appraisal, when the movement sought to catch its breath for a new start.

REFERENCE NOTES

Chapter V

1 *Cf.* FC *1915 Report,* pp. 53, 54.
2 Abbreviated from the findings of the June 1915 Atlantic City meeting.
3 Macfarland, *Progress of Church Cooperation,* p. 128.
4 FC *1918 Report,* pp. 46-48.
5 *Ibid.,* p. 81.
6 *Cf. The Churches of Christ in Council,* 1917, Vol. I of *Library of Christian Cooperation,* MEM, pp. 184, 185.
7 Macfarland, *Progress of Church Federation,* p. 49.
8 As it turned out, a whole group of Home Mission Councils expanded into or became part of inclusive councils of churches, under the strong encouragement of the HMC. (*Cf.* the earlier discussion of home mission states, in Chapter III.)
9 Macfarland, *ibid.,* p. 129.
10 Cited in *ibid.,* p. 130.
11 *The Churches of Christ in Council,* pp. 45, 46.
12 *Christian Cooperation and World Redemption,* pp. 245-274; *cf.* also Macfarland, *Progress of Church Federation,* p. 128; and Dr. Guild's semi-annual report.
13 *The Churches of Christ in Council,* p. 74.
14 *Ibid.,* p. 23.
15 *Ibid.,* p. 45.
16 Handy, *op. cit.,* p. 62; (also HMC *1916 Report.*)
17 *Cf.* also *International Journal* editorial, November, 1930: "Why Not the Consolidated Sunday School?"
18 *Ibid.,* p. 95.
19 FC *1917 Year Book,* pp. 36, 38.
20 "In April, 1912, at the close of the Men and Religion conventions, a group of Christian men agreed that in five years there ought to be a representative gathering to summarize the progress of cooperative Christian effort and to issue the manual which is here submitted." (From Fred B. Smith's introduction to the 1917 *Manual of Interchurch Work.*)
21 *Cf.* this writer in FC *Bulletin,* March, 1950—33 years later.
22 The Commission's 72 members were listed in the *1917 Year Book,* pp. 276, 277; again in 1918, pp. 208, 209; and in 1919, pp. 210, 211. The Smith-Guild report for 1917 appears on pp. 146-152 of the FC *1917 Report;* Dr. Anthony's on pp. 139-145 (*cf.* pp. 42, 43 for the list of Dr. Anthony's commission).
23 FC *1917 Report,* pp. 22, 64.
24 Footnote, p. 51 of the (Pittsburgh) *Manual.*
25 Minutes of the Committee of Direction, October 23, 1918.
26 *Cf.* Macfarland, *Christian Unity in the Making,* pp. 142, 148; also the FC *1917-1918 report,* pp. 14, 15, 90, 91, 155, 156.
27 FC *1918 Report,* pp. 6, 85-91.
28 FC *1919 Report,* pp. 8, 86-92.
29 Handy, *op. cit.,* pp. 80-82.
30 Douglass, *Protestant Cooperation in American Cities,* pp. 43, 50.
31 On the other hand, "No war has ever helped the cause of vital religion. Religion always slumps as a result. At no time in the history of organized religion in America has it been at such low ebb as after our great wars." Sweet, *The Story of Religion in America,* Harper, 1930 (revised edition, 1939), p. 564.

32 See *Continent,* June 24, 1940, editorial.

33 *The Churches Allied for Common Tasks,* 1916-1920, p. 225; the Commission's report, "The Churches United in Service to the Community," appears on pp. 217-224. The entire Commission is listed on pp. 221 ff., the names of the Committee of Direction on p. 411.

34 *The Churches Allied for Common Tasks,* pp. 9-18: "An Interpretation," by Dr. Samuel McCrea Cavert; *ibid.,* p. 12 (contrast p. 70).

35 *FC Bulletin,* January, 1921, p. 18.

36 *Ibid.,* March, 1921, p. 30.

37 *Ibid.,* June-July, 1921, a two-page lead-article, "Building from the Bottom Up," by Orlo J. Price, reported this meeting. (The October-November issue included a page of AES findings.)

38 *Ibid.,* August-September, 1921, p. 104.

39 FC *1921 Report,* p. 185.

40 *Cf. ibid.,* p. 17: "A United Approach to Common Problems."

41 *Ibid.,* pp. 49-53.

42 *Cf.* Handy, *op. cit.,* p. 77.

43 FC *1922 Report,* p. 183.

44 *Ibid.,* p. 15.

45 Macfarland, *Christian Unity in the Making,* pp. 136, 175, 183.

46 *Ibid.,* pp. 27-33.

47 *Ibid.,* p. 184.

48 *Ibid.,* p. 193.

49 Only the officers of the Commission are now listed, *ibid,* p. 222. The western office begins to assume importance for field relationships, *ibid,* pp. 113 ff.

50 Letter, Dr. Macfarland to Dr. Guild, January 13, 1923; see also FC 1922 Minutes.

51 *United in Service* (1920-1924), p. 301.

52 FC *1923 Report,* pp. 14 ff.; 33-37.

53 *Ibid.,* pp. 30 ff.

54 *FC Bulletin,* March, 1928.

55 *Ibid.,* pp. 38-43; "The Development of Local Councils of Churches."

56 *Ibid.,* p. 209.

57 *Cf.* letter, this writer, to Dr. Cavert, October 7, 1932.

58 *United in Service,* pp. 101-104. Similarly, all three men are listed on p. 233 of the FC *1923 Report.*

59 *FC Bulletin,* March, 1928.

60 *United in Service,* p. 373. (Dr. Guild had accepted a call to the Trinitarian Congregational Church of New Bedford, Mass.)

61 Though Dr. Macfarland (*Christian Unity in the Making,* p. 267) says that Holmes succeeded Guild, it was hardly more than an interim arrangement.

62 *Ibid.,* p. 133.

63 FC *1923 Report,* p. 221; also p. 233. (The relation of corporate to personal and ecclesiastical contributions merits and has received study.)

64 FC *1924 Report,* pp. 333, 338.

65 *Ibid.,* pp. 328, 330.

66 Macfarland, *op. cit.,* pp. 102, 261, states that Dr. Guild's "health broke in 1925" and that he "had resigned because of a breakdown."

Appraisal and Testing, 1925-1931

Midway in the baffling twenties 1925 was significant for all of Christendom by reason of the *Stockholm* Conference on "Life and Work," but in America it marked an unquestionable slump in the promotion of state and local cooperation. On the other hand, these years were to show that state and local church cooperation involved a variety of existing national agencies. If Chapter II of this volume seems extraneous to the interest of some readers, and if the assumed centrality of ecclesiastical mechanisms is offensive to others, this is all of a piece with the frustration by which some of us, working enthusiastically at the grass-roots, were confused. But, out of complexity coherence and unification were already beginning to appear, first on the far horizon, soon in the foreseeable future.

Defining the Federal Council's Field Task

The Federal Council now voted to approve "the principle of a division between the task, on the one hand, of organizing, assisting, and maintaining relations with local councils of churches, and on the other hand, of promoting on the field the ideal and aims of the federated movement as a whole"[1]; and to secure a secretary to carry out the former task.

The 1925 *FC Report on Field Organization,* in the "Review of the Year," "proposed that the work of helping to organize and sustain local and state councils of churches will in the future be a direct responsibility of the Federal Council itself, under the immediate supervision of the Administrative Committee."

Here was explicit recognition of two facts: (1) Whatever the responsibility of the Federal Council might be for the wider integration of all federative efforts in the community, it had an unavoidable responsibility for state and local councils; and (2) in the light of the accumulated deficit, which presumably had to be absorbed, it might be wise to make this concern less peripheral, and subsume it under the general work of the Council so that fiscal as well as program policies could be more closely supervised. The depression was nearly four years away, but the field work of the Federal Council had already temporarily crashed.

In 1925 the Church Peace Union contributed $2,000 for the Federal Council's field work, and other designated receipts amounted to $600; costs were $4,747.30. A 1926 estimated budget of $14,000 for state and local field work was suggested, as compared with much larger dual proposals a year earlier.[3]

State and Local Thinking

While the April 16, 1925, meeting of the Executive Committee of the AES at the Town Hall Club, New York, seemed strange without Dr. Guild, by this time the Association had acquired its own momentum. State and local leaders were becoming articulate as to the nation-wide cooperative task. Representation on various Federal Council groups was discussed, and "suggestions were made for training secretaries." It was felt that "if the Federal Council was now in a position to employ two field men, one should be a specialist in state organization."

"By unanimous verdict one of the most profitable sessions ever"[4] was held by the Association of Executive Secretaries June 16 to 18, 1925. Its annual meeting in connection with a conference and retreat on evangelism at East Northfield, Mass., was made possible by the Church Peace Union. Thirty-four were present. Ralph C. McAfee, then executive at Kansas City, Mo., was elected president. Twenty-seven federations had contributed toward total receipts of $273.36 for the fiscal year, which closed with a balance of $60.06. Replies to a questionnaire, sent out by E. T. Root and this writer, came from forty city and five state councils.

Suggestions offered for improving local conditions sound strangely contemporary:

Special training for secretaries and assistants.

Development of the spirit of fellowship.

More adequate financing.

More intimate relations between local and national work.

Regional conferences.

Larger and more active lay participation.

Continuous kindly effort, showing and cultivating the spirit of cooperation.

Taking more time for reading and study.

TIME and KEEPING AT IT.

While findings on evangelism were central, consideration was also given to comity, international justice and good will, religious education

126

(especially in its merger aspects), women's work, and finance. Proportionate dues ($5, $10, or $20) were suggested from federations with budgets of varying size, together with the recommendation that dues be paid "from the local budget and not by the executive secretary"! "Past, Present and Future" were discussed. "Of the eleven secretaries who attended the first conference, three are still in the service and attendance at this meeting."[5] "Further Steps That Should Be Taken" concurred with the Federal Council field proposals.

Joint Search for New Leadership

In December 1925 the AES Executive Committee appointed a committee to confer with the Federal Council concerning Dr. Guild's successor. Meanwhile, in November, a special Committee of Five, named by the Administrative Committee to consider the Federal Council's responsibility for the development of local councils, had nominated B. F. Lamb, of the Ohio Federation of Churches, to help both the Federal and the Home Mission Councils in field organization. The Committee was to continue its consideration of state council promotion. Nominated November 30, on December 10 Dr. Lamb indicated that he could not accept the nomination on the terms on which it had been proposed.

June 3 to 5, 1926, in connection with the FC Commission on Social Service meeting at the National Conference of Social Work, the AES met at the Hotel Winton, Cleveland, with an attendance of 57. Dr. Elim A. E. Palmquist of Philadelphia was elected president. A 1927 Women's Work Conference was proposed. The committee to confer about Dr. Guild's successor was continued. Income for the year had risen to $434.40, and there was a balance of $42.46 in the treasury.

In January 1926 Dr. Anthony had raised with the FC Administrative Committee four basic questions as to local, state, and national council relationships.[6] There was also discussion of closer coordination among the various interdenominational bodies (particularly the FC, HMC, and ICRE) for the sake of simplifying the problem of cooperation in the local community and closer relations with the local councils. (This was nearly a quarter of a century before the organization of the National Council of Churches.) In February, in deference to "the secretaries who will have responsibility in this field," the Administrative Committee felt that thorough-going discussion of all such issues should be postponed until "after the new secretary for work in connection with state and local councils of churches is secured."[7]

Nevertheless in July the Administrative Committee gave important consideration to relations with the ICRE.[8] A historic letter, approved by the AES on June 5, was presented in behalf of that body by Orlo J. Price of *Rochester, N.Y.;* W. L. Darby, of the *Washington, D.C.* Federation, also spoke. Both men reported that the AES favored expanding its annual meeting into a conference of the secretaries of the Federal Council and all State and Local Councils. In receiving the communication from the AES the Administrative Committee expressed warm sympathy with its general intent, and recognized "the great importance of giving special attention to the development of church cooperation in state and local communities." The AES secretaries had in turn developed a considerable ecclesiastical sense, with increasingly clear realization of the dependence of the federations on the churches and the denominations.

John Milton Moore, a Federal Council Secretary, 1926-1931

At this July 9, 1926, meeting, on nomination of the Policy Committee, the Administrative Committee now proceeded to elect Dr. John Milton Moore, who had been for four years (1921-1924) chairman of the Administrative Committee, as a general secretary, to give special attention to developing state and local cooperation. "Successsively president of the Brooklyn and Greater New York Federations of Churches," as well, "Dr. Moore brought to the staff a rare combination of wisdom, genial fellowship, and loyalty. Under his administration interest in state and local federation was revived and to some extent reorganized," wrote Dr. Macfarland.[9]

On November 1, while still serving part-time as pastor of the Marcy Ave. Baptist Church, Brooklyn, an important congregation soon to be caught in the throes of swift population change, Dr. Moore sent out a cordial letter, as one of the general secretaries of the Federal Council. All rejoiced with him "now that we have an office again in the Federal Council which you may use as a clearing house." It was twenty-two months since Dr. Guild's departure, and this long interval had been keenly felt by state and local federations and councils. Doubtless it was symptomatic of deeper forces, now rearranging themselves in new patterns of field outreach.

Incidentally Dr. Moore reported: "We are moving to get the New York State Council (of Churches) into action, and with prospects of success; there has recently been organized a State Council in New Jersey." (In 1908 the New York State Council had been reported as first organized in 1900, and New Jersey was then "in process.") Significant, also, as a first inkling of a determinative report now in the offing, he added, "There is likely to be conducted by the Institute of Social and Religious Research a study of Protestant cooperation which will mean a careful scientific survey of perhaps twenty-five or more federations. I am hoping that this project will go through, for it seems to be what we greatly need."

By November it had been decided that the whole program of the Federal Council's Executive Committee in Minneapolis the following month should be centered on problems of state and local cooperation.[10] under the general theme: "How to Make Church Cooperation Real and Vital in the Community."[11] The careful findings of these December 1926 meetings do not seem to have blazed any new trails, in spite of a series of two to four groups of questions raised on each of a dozen discussion themes.

Designations for state and local work in 1926 provided the Federal Council with $7,335.00. Expenses were low enough to result in an unexpended credit balance of $3,862.34 as contrasted with the crippling deficit of two years earlier.[13] A 1927 budget of $15,000 for state and local cooperation was accepted.[14]

Journalistic Straws in the 1926 Wind

The Federal Council Bulletin for January-February 1926 included a significant article by Orlo J. Price of Rochester, voicing the growing desire "to hold back the tides of denominationalism." (Later strategy was to exploit denominational loyalties in behalf of interdenominational cooperation.) The July 1926 Christian Union Quarterly was largely devoted to the Federal Council. Its editor Dr. Peter Ainslie asked, "Shall We Federate the Federations?" (So far, a negative answer to this question has always been made, at least in practice.) During these and the ensuing years both the FC Bulletin and the ICRE Journal provided many interesting details of organizational development and personnel changes, and of the difficulties involved in the merging of councils of religious education and federations of churches.

Lessened Momentum

The year 1927 wrote "Faith and Order" and Lausanne into the memory of all ecumenical Christians. In February Dr. Moore sent out a brief questionnaire, replies to which enabled him to make interesting statistical comparisons for the years 1917, 1922, and 1927. By March he was convinced that "We need to do some solid thinking about our whole enterprise. . . . It may be . . . that we have fairly exhausted

129

the initial momentum of our federation movement; . . . no new organizations are being formed, and we are having some difficulty in keeping alive the existing ones."[15] (This is a little like watching a doughnut maker, and remarking, "What large holes there are in all these doughnuts!" From 1895 to 1915 there had been heavy losses, but a dozen permanent federations survived; from 1915 to 1925 there was substantial growth, after deducting all casualties.)

In 1926 state councils of religious education spent $651,185.82, and had 137 staff and 91 office employees. Said Robert Davids, ICRE director of organization and promotion, "The financial problem in our state and provincial councils (of religious education) is acute. They are struggling with debts amounting to over $200,000, or an average of one-third of their operating budgets. Only eleven are free of debt."[16] Too often the emphasis was necessarily on finance, rather than on education, even in the years before the depression.

The ICRE and Its "Auxiliary" Councils

As has been indicated, the ICRE started off in 1922 with both denominational and territorial member units. Though the question as to what requirements denominations might properly be expected to meet was inevitably considered, denominational educational forces were always considered full members in the enterprise. Imperceptibly perhaps as a result of long-standing denominational pressures dating back to 1910 or earlier the nature of state and provincial council participation began to change. In a very few years the territorial units began to be termed "auxiliaries" rather than members. This is not to blame anybody, but simply to record a fact.

The ICRE too had been slowly evolving its field policy. One phase of the problem that had faced the Federal Council faced the ICRE also in 1925. The new *Salt Lake City* Council of Religious Education had sent a request for supervision by the ICRE, which felt that "some plan should be outlined whereby City Councils of Religious Education in unorganized territory may have direct supervision from the ICRE."[17]

Standards of representativeness and competence were being worked out, and the dependence of the ICRE on the state councils was generously recognized;[18] but perhaps unconsciously the role of the state councils as agents of the ICRE was increasingly stressed. In January 1926[19] Dr. Magill was writing about the purpose "of the International Council and its auxiliary councils." The February *Journal* honored the

130

state councils by featuring the pictures of 48 state secretaries. In an April 1926 "Interpretation" of the ICRE,[20] while recognizing that "local councils of religious education represent the churches of the city, county, or community in all cooperative efforts," Dr. Magill again spoke of these local councils as "auxiliaries of the International and state councils, to carry into effect the cooperative interdenominational programs developed through the International Council." Thus the agreed reorganization of the state bodies on a more representative basis seemed to have shifted their status from the constitutive role to that of agent.

In June one of the old guard, E. W. Halpenny of *Michigan,* representing the Sunday School Association tradition, was given the opportunity to put in a constructive comment on "The Place of the State Council":[21] "For twenty-five years I gave the best that was in me to the cooperative Sunday school effort under the old regime (independent), and some may still contend therefor, doubtless with good arguments in favor. I am compelled to express delight at being now privileged to direct the activities of a state, 'reorganized' as carefully as possible, both in letter and spirit, auxiliary to the International Council. There are some who feel that the strength of the ICRE lies at the top where an ever-increasingly efficient correlation of forces is demonstrated. I would not in any sense underestimate that feature, but am convinced that the more important function is that of the state council, where the principles involved must be demonstrated."

In February 1927, after stressing the importance of having councils of religious education administered by persons with "special educational fitness and particular interest in religious education,"[22] Dr. Magill generously continued, "Councils of religious education should have autonomy of action, but there should be *the closest possible cooperation* between them and the federations of churches which function in the general field of denominational cooperation." He then went on: "Although as the constituent bodies that make up the International Council, state councils have equal powers with the cooperating denominations, they should function as auxiliaries of the International Council and not as autonomous or independent organizations. The purpose of state and city councils of religious education is to serve as the accredited agencies of the cooperating forces within the various areas, just as the International Council serves as the accredited agency of the cooperating forces for the entire continent." (Was there ever any corresponding discussion of voluntary self-limitation of autonomy on

131

the part of the denominations? Certainly the ICRE never spoke of its "auxiliary" denominations, nor was there ever any question as to the autonomy of the member denominations. Yet the State Sunday School Associations thought they were going into the new relationship on a basis of equality with the denominations, i.e., "50-50." In practice, "equal powers" soon became unequal.)

Perhaps sensing that the ICRE's service role needed emphasis, Dr. Robert M. Hopkins, in the October 1927 *Journal,* insisted, "The Council is not a super-organization, giving orders to its constituent bodies, but is rather their accredited agency through which they federate their forces for cooperative service. The program of the International Council is determined by the duly chosen representatives of these cooperating forces." (Fortunately the word "accredited" has also largely dropped out; it was more of an irritant than some suspected.)

"Cooperation and Beyond"

Meanwhile, on the other hand, in April 1927[23] Dr. Moore of the Federal Council staff had become convinced that some sort of ecclesiastical "federal union," more intimate than that provided by the Federation movement, was possible and desirable. To him "the Federal Council . . . and the fifty standard state and city councils (of churches) now in existence . . . would seem to have reached a stage of cooperative action corresponding to the period of the American Articles of Confederation." (The correctness of this analysis need not be questioned; but could anything be done about it?)

By May Dr. Moore was writing, "See you soon in St. Louis." The May *FC Bulletin* gave half a page to announcing the AES meeting and the topics to be discussed; and the June number featured "National, State, and Local Councils in Annual Conference," in generous recognition of the FC interest in state and local organizations. What had really happened, however, was that only the church federation professional staff people were again in helpful sessions together. On June 1, at Eden Theological Seminary, Webster Groves, 34 local and state members of the AES and no less than 14 representatives of the Federal Council had held a four-day annual meeting. Here Dr. Moore was affectionately greeted as the new leader, and secretaries were requested to send both to him and to Dr. F. Ernest Johnson, of *Information Service,* "every piece of well-conceived publicity material." Dr. Macfarland graciously invited attendance at all important Federal Council Commission meetings. In its findings the AES declared that "the next outstanding objective in the program of the Federal Council is the

132

further extension of the cooperative movement throughout the nation." This writer was elected AES president. Receipts had amounted to $475.95, and a balance of $32.96 remained.

By early August Dr. Moore reported that he had travelled 43,000 miles in ten months; he was seeing the field. In September he asked local and state executives:

"1.   Have you grave financial problems?

"2.   If not, tell us briefly what your financial plan is.

"3.   Do you think that the Federal Council should . . . furnish expert financial leadership to the councils at small cost?" At the end of 1927 Dr. Moore was sure that "we need a more thoroughgoing philosophy of the whole enterprise."

The 1927 *Report of the Federal Council* devoted only a single page [24] to state and local cooperation, mentioning that Dr. Moore's more than 50,000 miles of travel had made for "much closer contacts." In the reported findings of a comity conference[25] attention was given to city councils of churches as essentially church city planning commissions, and to[26] relations with the YMCA. At the end of the year, though designated income appears to have been only $3,862.34, there remained an unexpended balance of $256.62 for the extension of state and local cooperation;[27] and a budget of $12,500 was deemed sufficient for 1918.[28] Extension was now central, but it was not creating a very big splash!

Reduced Resources

Perhaps the causes for what was failing to happen lay deeper than the actors in the play realized. Handy[29] speaks about "the decay of Protestant vitality in the 1920's," and the general tone of the decade is well remembered. He is impressed that "interdenominational organizations . . . were less deeply rooted than the denominations."[30] He found "the Cooperative road running through rough country in the middle and later 1920's." (If some of us were unaware of this, we may have been blessed by the help of exceptional lay backers.) Moreover, Dr. W. R. King, who became executive of the Home Missions Council in the fall of 1927, said in January 1928, "Almost all major *denominations* are now in a period of financial stringency in the conduct of mission work. We are in the days of falling budgets. There has been more or less retrenchment all along the line, and new work has been for several years at a standstill." By 1928, a year and a half before the stock market crash, "twenty years after their founding, the home mission councils were facing a crisis."[31]

In January 1928 Dr. Moore circulated a Christian unity "Syllabus," which he feared might be loaded in favor of federal union. From May 1928 to June 1930 a printed four-page Council *News Letter* kept all its readers informed of changes in personnel and other significant news.

An important Conference on Church Comity was held in Cleveland, January 20 to 22, 1928, under the auspices of the Home Missions Council and the Council of Women for Home Missions.[32] This was also the year of the Jerusalem Conference,[33] which marked great progress as compared with the 1910 Edinburgh meeting, when Orientals had been almost entirely absent. At Jerusalem many nationals were present, dominating the delegations from China, India, Burma, and Japan. This was not without significance for cooperation at the grassroots, even in America.

Awakened Desires

The 1928 annual meeting of the AES, May 31 to June 2, at the Statler, Buffalo, attracted 27 state and local executives, nine of the Federal Council staff, and eleven others—a total of 47. Dr. Moore spoke on Federal Union. An evening communion service was memorable to all present. The Institute of Social and Religious Research was asked to study seminary instruction on interdenominational cooperation. The National Conference of Church Women had now been effected, with a budget of $10,000; this was one stage in the long development of the United Council of Church Women. B. F. Lamb, newly elected president of the AES, had a vigorous column in the September *News Letter*.[34]

The only surviving minutes of the Advisory Committee for several years during this period are those of the November 5, 1928, meeting. Fifteen persons were present. Dr. Moore reported as to the status of local councils as revealed by questionnaire replies. A letter from Fred B. Smith was read. There was discussion as to how a local federation should be related to the state federation and to the Federal Council. To the question, "Is the movement stalled?" the answer was *No*. When asked what was the matter with it, Root replied: "The fundamental difficulty in organizing a state council is money." Was more national field staff needed? In any case, insisted Dr. Moore, "We need to undergird the movement with a better theory."

The Federal Council annual reports for 1928[35] discussed "Two Fruitful Decades of Community Cooperation,"[36] listing 44 city councils of churches, most of them with full-time executives. Said Dr. Moore, "The experience of cooperation has awakened desire and expectation that mere Cooperation is not able to satisfy. Some larger unity calls, and its call will be heard." (These prophetic words could be countered not so much with denial as with questions as to tempo.)

A January 1929 *FC Bulletin* editorial on the Rochester quadrennial likewise remarked: "The cooperative movement meets with general approval. But it is quite apparent that Cooperation has awakened expectations which are not going to be permanently satisfied with cooperation only"—a good instance of the freedom of the Federal Council to publicize individual viewpoints, while at the same time unable itself to implement the desires of some for greater union.

Proposals for Radical Change

On November 12 and 13, 1928, in connection with a meeting of the World Alliance for International Friendship, ten representative local, state, and national secretaries had met at the Waldorf-Astoria for breakfast. They discussed the work of the AES and how to strengthen it, and relationships with the Federal Council. A committee of five *recommended that the Association be reorganized as one of councils* rather than secretaries, and that each employed executive be matched by a board member from his council. All the members of the AES were to be informed of these proposals, and the Federal Council was to be requested to consider their effect on its By-Laws. Final action was deferred until the next AES annual meeting.

At Rochester on December 5 to 8, 1928, in connection with the Federal Council quadrennial, 30 state and local secretaries, several members of the Federal Council staff, and a number of guests attended three special breakfast sessions and a dinner meeting of the AES. The reorganization proposals were approved, and a new Constitution and By-Laws (mimeographed under date of December 7) unanimously adopted. It was voted "to consider the new organization fully authorized when the majority of the federations and councils of churches with executive secretaries have approved the Constitution and named their delegates." Action by March 1 was to be sought from all state and local boards.

Voting membership on the Administrative Committee of the Federal Council for four representatives of the AES was speedily granted. The December 1928 and January 1929 *Council News Letter* featured the action that "extension of local federation be made a major feature

135

of the Council's policy for the coming quadrennium," and the seeming formation of "The Association of *Councils* of Churches, State and Local." Dr. Cadman in his retiring presidential message had stated that in his judgment the most important task before the Federal Council was that of organizing state and local councils. Representatives of state and local councils were welcomed on all Federal Council commissions as appointees. It looked like a new day. Extension was now central to national staff responsibility. A strong Committee on Function and Structure was to reassess the whole Federal Council process. But Dr. Charles R. Zahniser of the Pittsburgh Council of Churches pointed out that "promising outlook itself is not fulfillment."

Within three weeks, on December 27 and 28, at New York City, eleven members of the Federal Council Administrative Committee and six representatives of the AES took affirmative action on general principles, but avoided discussion and decision on many matters of detail. Somehow the revolutionary character of the Rochester proposals began to ooze out, and trickle down the drain. They seem soon to have been entirely forgotten. But an enlarged Advisory Committee on Church Extension was created by the Administrative Committee, replacing a rather informal, chiefly staff, group. This new committee met February 20, 1929, to organize.[37]

Extension expenses for 1928 had been[38] $12,184.48, and a balance of $1,481.08 remained toward the 1929 $12,500 budget.[39] During 1928, at the beginning of "seven lean years" for the Home Missions Council, Dr. King also "travelled widely, visiting every home missions council and cooperating in the organization of seven new ones."[40] This was fractional and functional organization, rather than inclusive; but it was a beginning. The cooperative toe was again, or for the first time, in many a door.

Between 1924 and 1929 there was a loss of only five federations, and in only one southern state were two local organizations dropped from the list (Richmond and Norfolk, Va.).[41]

Beginning with the 1929 *News Letter,* "volunteer" councils were first noted, then listed; increasing attention was also given to ministerial associations as incipient councils of churches. On February 20, 1929, with 19 present, the new Committee on Extension of Local and State Cooperation met and organized, with Dr. L. W. McCreary, former Baltimore Federation secretary, as chairman. The next day the Administrative Committee approved this committee's recommendation, and referred it back for further discussion: "that two additional members be added to the extension staff, a field man and an educational man, but that the educational position be provided for first." ("Educational" here referred to the training of students in theological schools for inter-church cooperation).[42]

Dr. Guild Returns

On March 21, 1929, a little more than four years after he had withdrawn, the Committee on Extension recommended that Dr. Guild be elected Associate General Secretary, to serve with Dr. Moore, and to be resident in Chicago. On the following day he was elected by the Administrative Committee; he began work on April 10, to continue until his retirement in 1937, and in fellowship with the movement until his death in 1945. Provision was also made for a special lecturer in theological schools, for an experimental period of a year.

Within months the depression was to hit. How largely morale and finances were intertwined is a matter of keen remembrance on the part of all surviving oldsters. On March 25 Dr. Moore wrote confidently, "At the quadrennial meeting at Rochester it was agreed that extension of state and local federation should be a major feature of the Council's work for the coming quadrennium. The calling of Dr. Guild indicates that this proposal is being taken seriously, and significant developments in this field may reasonably be expected." To this all those veterans who had worked with Dr. Guild responded with a fervent "Amen."

In early 1929 everybody was still talking big. The idea that a world-wide financial collapse was just over the hill had occurred only to the relatively few people of superior economic literacy and experience. In spite of the strengthening of his hands by the reemployment of Dr. Guild, and partly because of his disappointment over the failure of the Federal Union movement to make concrete progress, Dr. Moore, along with millions of others, was in for a rough experience. In March he sent out his annual questionnaire, as the basis of a later valuable historical summary.

In April the FC Committee on Extension stressed the desirability of relating local federations of women, with proper autonomy, with local councils of churches; and considered how, in practice, the work of the various Federal Council commissions might be more closely correlated in their field contacts. Dr. Zahniser was to be nominated as special lecturer in the seminaries.

Dr. Zahniser had resigned at Pittsburgh May 15, and was to be professor of Community and Interchurch Relationships at the Boston University School of Theology. (This was thirty-one years ago!) In a first summer term, June 17 to July 24, at the University of Chicago, Dr. Arthur E. Holt and Dr. Cavert each taught four hours a week; additional lectures over a four-week period reached a larger audience. A beginning of the training process, at the graduate level, had been made.[43]

By May 1929 there were 43 city and six state councils of churches, in addition to one in Puerto Rico. The 1929 Federal Council report included a far-reaching statement: "The Federal Council agrees in so far as practicable to look to the Educational Commission of the International Council for the service hitherto rendered by its Commission on Christian Education."[44]

From June 17 to 21, 1929, the AES held its annual meeting at the Hotel Bellevue, Boston. Including five guests, fifty-four persons were present. Simultaneous committee meetings were featured; also sightseeing and addresses. "Certain changes in the situation" were said to have occurred since the December meetings in Rochester. In spite of the fact that an "organization committee" had been voted, the "provisional" president of the proposed new Association of Councils continued to function as head of the old AES, and the proposed reorganization seems to have died a-borning. Considerable wood was being sawed, however, while it was still day, before the dark night of depression would reduce all cooperative work to a minimum. Organizationally we had marched up the hill and down again. The uninterrupted continuity of the professional association of council executives proceeded as if nothing had happened at Rochester. The exceptionally competent and complete minutes (51 mimeographed pages) contain a full list of the committees for the previous year, and fifteen other reports.

On September 27, with eleven present, and again on October 25, the Committee on Extension discussed relationships, including those with the Federated Church Women. The October 1929 FC Bulletin in an editorial on "The Genius of Church Federation" said, "The federal movement represents the attempt of the Protestant bodies to achieve practical unity among the churches while at the same time fully maintaining the freedom and the diversity for the sake of which the denominations came into being." The final paragraph said, "Roughly speaking, the Church had unity at the expense of liberty for a thousand years

138

before the Protestant Reformation; and for four hundred years after the Reformation there was liberty at the expense of unity." Federation is an "effort to conserve both sets of values."

The 1929 "Review of the Year"[45] featured extension; the report on state and local federations[46] was signed by McCreary, Moore, and Guild. McCreary's recommendations were voted by the FC Executive Committee.[47] Extension expenses for 1929[48] totaled $18,192.46, and there was an unexpended balance of $1,481.08;[49] $1,635 had been designated for the special lectures account.[50] The 1930 budget was set at $16,000.[51]

Church Women Push Forward Again

The forces already at work in 1924 were further in evidence at a second Conference on Women's Organized Interdenominational Work, at Cleveland in 1926, and a third at St. Louis in 1927. By this time Mrs. E. Tallmadge Root of Massachusetts had published a 24-page pamphlet on "Local Federation (of Church Women) the Next Step."[52]

After further discussion among the leaders of church women as to relations, both local and national, in New York City in December 1927, a nation-wide fourth conference of representatives of state and local Federated Church Women, at Buffalo in 1928, resulted in a National Commission of Church Women. This Commission existed only two years, but in 1929 at Boston a National Council of Federated Church Women was organized. (NCFCW or NCCW—"Federated" was dropped in 1928.) Announcement of this event to 1,300 local groups before ratification by the Federation of Women's Boards of Foreign Missions and the Council of Women for Home Missions, while unfortunately premature, was greeted with great enthusiasm. At the 1929 Boston meeting it was voted to ask for affiliation with the FC. No direct affiliation was ever granted, though the president of the NCCW was made a member of the FC Administrative Committee.

From 1936 to 1950 the Federal Council had its own helpful Women's Cooperating Commission, which in its closing years numbered nearly 100 members. Dr. Mary E. Wooley was the first chairman. In 1940 the vice chairman, Mrs. Henry Sloane Coffin, moved up to the chairmanship, which she held until 1947. Miss Anna E. Caldwell was the paid secretary until 1942.[53]

Tough Times, Tough Thinking

By 1930 Handy noted a "theological drift to the left." That was the year that William P. Montague wrote: "Fear and sorrow are no

139

longer the major themes of our serious culture; . . . a new confidence in man's power to make life happy and secure by purely secular devices" was reported.[54] (The silent movies had found their voices of synchronized music and spoken word; and technicolor was just around the corner.) Yet paradoxically these were years of grievous insecurity for millions. "The depression, which began in the early twenties for the farmer, hung heavy over the entire country. . . . Not until 1935 did it begin to lift."[55]

At the end of 1930 Dr. Root of Massachusetts retired; the December *FC Bulletin* honored him for his 26 years as the outstanding veteran of the movement. Said Dean Vaughn Dabney, of Andover-Newton, "In 1906 the annual income of the (Massachusetts) Federation was but $552." A January 1931 appreciation of Dr. Root by Dr. Anthony occupied most of a *Bulletin* page. Dr. Root (and his wife) will be remembered for their famous slogan: "Keep the facts before the people till the people change the facts," which they borrowed from a State Federation[56] of Women's Clubs.

A 1930 headline, "Universal Life and Work Movement Develops Permanent Organization," marked a major foundation of the coming World Council of Churches. *Protestant Cooperation in American Cities,* the long-awaited Institute study by H. Paul Douglass, was published in 1930. Now little known, this determinative and significant volume proved to be a cause as well as a result. To some it represented chiefly "the paralysis of analysis"; to others it was the take-off for the beginnings of profounder ecumenical thinking. More than one secretary was deeply grateful for the way in which the Institute's field staff discovered even more about a local federation and its significance than those intimately at work in it had realized. Dr. Douglass was reporting as objectively as possible on the basis of empirical data. Some of us were forced to reach a larger measure of agreement with his conclusions, when we too became better acquainted with the facts. Dr. Douglass tried not to read his own ideas into the situation as he found it; he rather sought merely to "tease out" of it generalizations that he was sure were implicit "in the data" themselves.[57]

This huge volume (xviii, 914 pp.) involved field work by three men over a period of thirty months, an average of six weeks to each of twenty federations, nineteen of which were urban. The Massachusetts State Federation was also studied intensively. (There were 43 city federations with paid leaders in 1929, half as many more having reverted to volunteer leadership or dropped out since 1920.) With an adequate budget provided by the Institute, this study was able to trace the typical life-cycle of the surviving federations, which had by then begun to find themselves, and to examine their structure and program in considerable detail. Primarily factual, the report also interpreted the larger meanings of the church federation movement in terms both stimulating and provocative. Fifteen chapters in the "general" report were supplemented by nine others of a more "technical" nature. These latter covered the committee system, paid staff, three major program items, women's cooperation, finances and facilities, promotion and publicity. Sociologically the volume measured the social distance between religious groups and the response of constituents to federation programs, as well as the frequency of program items. Here then is both a monument of value to subsequent surveyors, and a methodology for the use of students seeking to compare the greatly expanded church cooperation of a generation later with the carefully documented situation in 1929.

By 1930 the extension staff were making excellent reports to the Extension Committee. For example, at the February 28 meeting Dr. Guild and Dr. Moore reported to the eleven persons present their activities in state work in Illinois, Kansas, Michigan, Ohio, Oklahoma, and Wisconsin, and in numerous cities throughout the nation. Dr. Moore had shared in the pace-setting conference on "The Church in the Changing City," in Detroit, February 17 to 19.[58] By March Dr. Zahniser's reports, which had begun in December, had become a regular feature. A new directory of councils was[59] issued. An interesting analysis of state and local relationships showed conflicting emphases on mass meetings and on field organization.

"Forward on the State Front"

"The state council is today the most needed line of advance," the June 1930 *FC Bulletin* editorialized. For many years only four fully organized state councils of churches had existed—Massachusetts, Connecticut, California, and Ohio. "The budgets of city councils of churches now total more than $750,000 a year." The significance of the action taken at Rochester is held to be that "The state is the necessary line of approach of the cooperative movement to the thousands of small communities."

While one able local executive thought "the chief business of a state council is to organize local communities," he added, "frankly, I do not know one single state secretary who is giving this more than a minor fraction of his time and interest." It was as easy for state

141

councils to become absorbed in other work as it was for the Federal Council, and the costs of field work were considerable. Dr. Cavert wrote, "We seek to organize state councils of churches in order to attain in state areas the same objectives for which the Federal Council is working nationally."

June 16 to 19, 1930, at the Windermere Hotel, Chicago, AES attendance was down, as a result of illness as well as financial stringency, but more than forty persons were present. Two joint sessions were held with the NCFCW. Don D. Tullis, then of Cleveland, was elected president. Receipts had amounted to $1,173.54, leaving a balance of $829.90, in accordance with a policy initiated by B. F. Lamb to build up a reserve. Dues were now as high as $50 for the largest organizations.[60] The AES Executive Committee, with both Dr. Moore and Dr. Guild present, held a delightful meeting in Cleveland at the home of President Tullis, then local executive, on June 26. Committees on personnel, program, and promotion, as well as relations with the National Council of Federated Church Women, were named; and preliminary steps taken looking toward a well-organized study of the philosophy of the federated movement.

On December 2, 1930, Dr. Macfarland became secretary emeritus. Dr. Cavert soon proved abundantly able to succeed him. On September 26 the Committee on Extension, with sixteen members present, faced up to "present problems," including its financial inability to continue the *Council (Church Federation) News Letter,*[62] a matter of committee study for a full year. Dr. Guild's report was one of realistic courage and never-say-die spirit.

On September 23 the Executive Committee of the AES, assembled in New York to consider religious education relationships and a progress report from the Philosophy Committee, was asked "for a clear definition of what is involved in evangelism." The five members of this Executive Committee met the next day, October 24, with ten members of the Extension Committee. Seven pages of valuable discussion material, covering five major questions, concluded with the query, "What are we on the Extension Committee to extend?" (That such a question was asked carries its own evidence of uncertainty.) Before adjournment Dr. Moore defined his relation to the federated movement as over against the trend toward church union, and his own interest in "Federal Unity," in a manner that foreshadowed events to come. On December 1 and 2 at the Hamilton Hotel, Washington, sixteen members of the AES were present. Committees reported and personnel problems were discussed.

In his 1930[63] report on state and local federation, Dr. Moore cited the Douglass report as "a formidable volume of 500 pages," which, by reason of its penetrating suggestions, merited widespread and earnest attention. Expenses for 1930 amounted to $15,801.61;[64] the $17,500 budget for 1931 included the expenses of the midwest office.[65]

The FC *Bulletin* for April 1930 featured an article by W. R. King on "Home Missions Faces the Future" by means of the organization of state councils (of churches, or of home missions; or interdenominational comity commissions; or superintendents' councils), survey (state by state, county by county, community by community), and adjustment. This was leading up to the North American Home Missions Congress, December 1 to 5, 1930.[66]

At the January 26, 1931, meeting of the Committee on Extension, with fourteen present, it was noted that as many as thirty-six letters had gone out from the Federal Council in 1930 to state and local councils—an average of three a month; six had been sent by the Commission on International Justice and Good Will. Dr. Moore's resignation, January 23, was then announced;[67] the FC Personnel Committee recommended its acceptance as of May 1, and the Administrative Committee followed this recommendation. A new list of councils then available included "volunteer" organizations. In April the Advisory Committee approved Don Tullis, AES president, for its membership.

A special feature characteristic of these years was the promotion of *State Ministers' Conferences*. The March 1930 *Bulletin* also featured "Ohio Churchmen and Christian Unity" as evidenced by the more than 3,500 people at the fourfold conference of pastors (1,261), laymen, women, and young people. The January 1931 *Bulletin* gave a schedule of 1931 statewide conferences, and the March issue had more than two pages about these developments, under the heading, "Statewide Convocations of Ministers Cultivate Spirit of Unity," in Minnesota, Nebraska, Kansas, Illinois, New York, and Pennsylvania. And in November "State-wide Convocations of Pastors Planned" listed Illinois, Maryland, Delaware, Ohio, Nebraska, and Massachusetts. On June 19, 1931, in Chicago a conference on state convocations of ministers was held, with twenty persons present. Eight 1932 convocations were listed, with dates, and six others were being proposed.

The ICRE Studies Its Field Supervision Responsibilities

Relationships are a two-way street. Smaller units related to larger units may be required to meet certain requirements, as a condition of this relationship; by the same token, larger units have certain obligations and opportunities in connection with the smaller units related to them. In 1927 an ICRE Committee of Nine had made suggestions concerning accredited state councils. The 1928 *ICRE Year Book* (pp. 114, 115) included a "Basis for Accrediting State Councils of Religious Education as Auxiliaries of the ICRE." By July 1930 Dr. Magill was pointing out[68] that "state councils meeting certain conditions have been designated as accredited auxiliaries of the International Council." That this idea of accreditation also put certain obligations on the denominations, at the local level as well, was likewise pointed out by Fred H. Willkens of Rochester.[69] "The old-fashioned spirit of competition and rivalry is giving way to fruitful cooperation." "Local churches can do their best work only when they cooperate in the fullest extent in the common cause." "If the denominations do not look on the city director of religious education as their representative, then all our talk about . . . cooperative program is of no avail."

After preliminary consideration in September 1930, on November 14, 1930, the ICRE issued "A Guide to the Evaluation of State Councils of Religious Education" (8 pages).[70] In those days religious educators were chiefly concerned with methodology and organization— far less interested than now in theological considerations. Accordingly conditions were appraised for the most part in terms of certain "non-theological factors." Actual state situations were found to range "from the ideal to the unsatisfactory."

These developments were part of the forging of a new ICRE field policy. On September 12, 1930, Harry C. Munro, director of field work, in presenting "Proposed Objectives, Job Analysis, and Time Budget for 1930-1931," had made "the assumption that the ICRE staff will organize itself as a Board of Field Administration in dealing with all field policies, problems, and programs which bear primarily upon state or local councils; and the director of field work will be the executive secretary of that Board."

The proposed Board seems to have got promptly under way. In November it withdrew accreditation from two states where there had been decided changes since April. Elsewhere accreditation was continued until February 1932.

On February 4, 1931, in connection with the agenda for a February 14 Conference of State and ICRE Staff at the Stevens Hotel, it was felt that "more opportunity is needed by this council group for mutual acquaintance and fellowship, for the sharing of problems and experiences, and for thinking through together solutions, policies, and principles which underlie the work for which as a group we are responsible." "As a basis for the day's program 25 state secretaries were requested to submit problems or topics. Nearly 100 suggestions came from the 15 who responded." Item V in a proposed manual for state councils outline was: "What is involved in accrediting state councils as Auxiliaries of the ICRE?"

In some states a closer integration of field forces seemed possible.[71] A financial policy covering field services of the ICRE staff to state councils was considered. By February 26, 1931, field engagements of five ICRE staff members were studied with a view to more adequate clearance. Further consideration was given to information needed from state councils, to suggested scales, and to an expanded (7 page) draft of a proposed basis of accrediting.

In March, after considering a revised statement on the "Purpose of a Field Program," and "Principles Underlying Interdenominational Field Work in Religious Education," attention was given to "The Background for the Calling of a Conference on Closer Cooperation of Field Forces in Religious Education," and to a revised 32 page statement on "Relationships between Councils of Religious Education and Councils of Churches." The situation in two states (Illinois and Wisconsin) showed that the educational forces were by no means a monolithic structure, and that denominational leaders, if requested to cooperate on one important function, like religious education, were now seemingly eager to cooperate "across the board."

The staff "Board of Field Administration" had now evolved to a point where on April 30 and May 1, 1931, there could be held the first meeting of the ICRE Committee on Field Program, for the consideration of "A Guide to Field Supervision in Religious Education."

Rethinking Cooperation and Relationships

More than fifty persons were present at the AES annual meeting, June 20-22, 1931, at the Hotel Windermere, Chicago, to consider "Basic Principles in Church Cooperation and Their Expression in Federation Activities." The Philosophy Committee (Evans, chairman) was continued, and conference with the Federal Council's Committee on Function and Structure authorized. The Committee on Personnel reported on qualifications and needs of the secretariat, and a prolonged study was recommended. A committee on biography (Guild, Price, and Darby) had been at work gathering data, now on file at the Office for Councils of Churches. Social service gained new visibility about this time. Linn A. Tripp of the Indianapolis staff gave a 6-page report on "Social Service Problems" to which the local church federations were now beginning to give departmental status.[72] On the basis of a careful 5-page report (McAfee, chairman), the Association was in favor of thoroughly rethinking evangelism. 2,200 Women's Groups were reported.

Receipts for the year amounted to $1,521.83, and the balance on hand was slightly increased to $848.85. George L. Ford of Youngstown (later of Scranton, Pa.), was elected president. This writer presented a 6-page report on the relationships between councils of churches and councils of religious education, which affords interesting evidence of how events sometimes outrun the fondest expectations. Emerson O. Bradshaw of the Chicago Federation gave a careful 5-page report on "The Present Status of Week-Day Schools of Religion." AES findings included "the opinion of this body as to the essential need of geographical as well as denominational representation in the Federal Council," and astonishment at the "variety of technical problems we have been obliged to face." An AES resolution suggested the wisdom of another conference like the one held in Cleveland in 1920.

On July 9 the executive committee of the AES, meeting at the Hotel Commodore Perry, Toledo, decided to maintain as fully as possible the reserves established by the Lamb administration. In the fall, however, AES apportionments were reduced 50% for the year.

In October 1931 the FC Extension Committee elected to its membership George L. Ford, new AES president. On December 3 a textbook on *Principles and Methods of Church Federation Work,* suggested by the AES, was approved. Dr. Guild's removal to New York at the end of the year was authorized.

In spite of their irritation at what sometimes seemed excessive mail from the Federal Council, on December 2 and 3, in connection with a Philadelphia meeting of the Administrative Committee, fourteen members of the AES Executive Committee requested "the Federal Council to take steps to arrange for as many as possible of (its) major executives to make one visit each year to every state and local organization."

Extension Increasingly Central

The 1931 Federal Council Report on Extension of State and Local Cooperation,[73] signed by Dr. Guild, explained that while "the work of

146

organizing and maintaining councils and federations of churches is under the direction of the Administrative Committee of the Federal Council," it had in turn appointed the Advisory Committee on Extension of State and Local Cooperation. (This change from Commission to Advisory Committee may seem a distinction without a difference, but the intent was to integrate extension more closely into the Federal Council task.) This report cites the fifth objective of the Federal Council: "To assist in the organization of local branches . . . to promote its aims in their communities"; but it points out that state and local "councils are affiliated with, but not organically a part of, the Federal Council. The autonomy of each . . . is preserved." Thirty-four city councils of churches then employed executive secretaries; 16 others had part-time or office secretaries. There were six state councils with employed personnel. (This was honest and conservative reporting.) A printed list now contained the names of 49 councils, or more than the previous peak in 1922 and 1924, and six more than in 1929, the low point at which Dr. Guild returned. It was still slow going, and there would be only a small increase in numbers of local councils of churches for another decade, but the slump was over. The ground lost had been regained, precisely at the time when some were lamenting that the movement was stalled. The next push forward would be at the state level.

"On account of the present economic condition, effort has not been put forth to organize and finance new city and state councils during this year, save where volunteer leadership might assure the success of the work," as, for example, in Madison, Wis. Progress toward affiliation of state councils of religious education with federations and councils of churches, and the trend toward mergers, is noted and illustrated. Close alliance with the Home Missions Council occasions satisfaction,[74] and Dr. Zahniser's work is appreciatively featured. Committee expenses for the year were $8,522.67. A budget allocation of $16,200 had been made for extension and for the midwest office, which actually spent $9,936.12. Extension receipts seem to have amounted to only $1,784. Evidently the general treasury absorbed the[75] difference.

First Thoughts of National Merger

Late in 1931 Dr. Guild wrote,[76] "I had a long visit with Dr. Wm. R. King as he passed through Chicago last week. We talked still more over his scheme of forming a combination of the organizations engaged in interdenominational work, such as the Federal Council, the Home

Missions Council, the International Council of Religious Education, the Foreign Missions Conference, etc. In such a combination Dr. King feels that his great task would be to continue as he is, directing the home missionary part of the work. In view of the fact that such matters have been discussed ever since the Men and Religion Forward Movement, I am not very much in hopes of anything being done suddenly. Representatives of these organizations had a memorable conference at Silver Bay soon after the close of that movement. When it was over they were farther apart than ever before. In the meantime we must push the work for which we are responsible."

Further, a December, 1931 *FC Bulletin* article by W. R. King, "A Suggestion for Reorganization," asked, "Is it not time to begin thinking of some changes in form and structure and relationships of several other organizations" besides the Federal Council? He pointed out that the Federal Council federated only limited functions, and was little related to important denominational boards. There were other unrelated interdenominational organizations; why not relate the Federal Council, the Home and Foreign Missions Councils, the International Council of Religious Education, and the Church Boards of Education? "This may be impracticable," he admitted, "and visionary—but it is worth thinking about." (Is there any earlier statement along these lines? Within less than two decades the National Council was to put to shame the faint hearts of those days; and yet was to be itself the victim of the retention of function by the member denominations in a spirit of increasing insistence on denominational responsibility.)

There had now been more than two years of depression. In some ways the worst was yet to come; yet necessity might here too prove to be the mother of ecumenical invention. The frustrations of the period were soon to be marked by consolidations of forces, and renewed vigor. The 1931 annual report noted progress toward the affiliation of state councils of religious education and councils of churches, and the trend toward state mergers; already these had begun to take place in the cities. In 1932—not without opposition— would come the first state "merger." That event makes 1932 significant, and determines the chapter division of this history at this point. In spite of vague thinking and economic blocks a ferment was at work, uniting all cooperative minds and hearts; and the results in ecumenical organizations were to appear shortly in a great new push forward, whether the radius of organized church cooperation was short or long. The baffling twenties were passed. The decade now begun constituted the *merging* thirties.

REFERENCE NOTES

Chapter VI

1 Minutes of a March 17, 1925, meeting of the Joint Committee on the Future of the Commission on Councils of Churches, appointed by the Administrative Committee of the FC and the Commission. (On March 11, as luncheon guests of Fred B. Smith at the Waldorf, the Committee of Direction had discussed at length the revision and modification of the work of the Commission.)

2 FC *1925 Report,* p. 17. For the Commission Report, signed by Smith and Holmes, see pp. 64ff.

3 *Ibid.,* pp. 217, 200, 222.

4 *1925 Commission Report.* A full page in the July-August, 1925 *FC Bulletin* was devoted to this meeting. The March-April issue gave more than three pages to E. T. Root's prize-winning essay on "Church Federation a Necessity."

5 For personnel changes, see *FC 1925 Report,* p. 65.

6 *Cf. FC 1926 Report,* p. 109; also *FC Bulletin* January-February, 1926. On December 29, 1925, the Special Committee had agreed that a requested conference with secretaries of local councils be held on January 8, 1926.

7 *FC 1926 Report,* p. 113.

8 Recorded in full in the minutes of the Administrative Committee for July 9, 1926. *Cf. FC 1926 Report,* pp. 126, 127.

9 *Cf. FC 1926 Report,* p. 127; and Macfarland, *Christian Unity in the Making,* pp. 206, 226.

10 *Cf. FC Bulletin,* November-December, 1926.

11 *FC 1926 Report,* p. 144.

12 *Ibid.,* pp. 159 ff.

13 *Ibid.,* pp. 172, 173.

14 *Ibid.,* p. 174.

15 General Letter, March 24, 1927.

16 Art. on "Field Organization in Religious Education," in *International Journal,* March 1927, p. 33.

17 *International Journal,* February, 1925, p. 56.

18 *Ibid.,* September, 1925, pp. 10, 11.

19 *Ibid.,* January, 1926, p. 6.

20 *Ibid.,* April, 1926, pp. 9-11.

21 *Ibid.,* June, 1926, pp. 68, 69.

22 *Ibid.,* February, 1927, "Relationships in Interdenominational Cooperation."

23 *FC Bulletin,* April, 1927, "Cooperation and Beyond."

24 *FC 1927 Report,* pp. 8, 9.

25 *Ibid.,* p. 115.

26 *Ibid.,* p. 127 f.

27 *Ibid.,* p. 141.

28 *Ibid.,* p. 148.

29 Handy, *op. cit.,* p. 116.

30 *Ibid.,* p. 113.

31 *Ibid.,* p. 116.

32 See *FC Bulletin,* December, 1927; also January, 1928 (more than a full page of interpretation); and February, 1928 (2½ pp. of findings, including "education for cooperation.")

33 See *FC Bulletin,* May, 1928.

34 *Ibid.,* ½ p. announcement of this AES meeting; June issue, full-page report.

[35] *FC 1928 Report,* pp. 38 ff.

[36] This report also appeared as a 2-page article by Dr. Moore in the December, 1928, *FC Bulletin.*

[37] *Cf.* the March, 1929, *News Letter.*

[38] *FC 1928 Report,* p. 279.

[39] *Ibid.,* p. 287.

[40] Handy, *op. cit.* p. 119.

[41] *Ibid.,* p. 130: The years 1928 to 1934 were for the HMC also a period of "over-all decline . . . of stabilization and retrenchment as the home mission slowed."

[42] See memo by Cavert and McCreary, February 21, 1929.

[43] *FC Bulletin,* June and September, 1929.

[44] This statement appears as a first item in a memo dated May 15, received by the Administrative Committee on May 24. While referred for study, it appears to have been promptly implemented, in fashion parallel to similar arrangements with the Home Missions Council. (*FC 1929 Report,* pp. 134, 135.)

[45] FC *1929 Report,* pp. 14, 15.

[46] *Ibid.,* pp. 20-23.

[47] *Ibid.,* pp. 121 ff.

[48] *Ibid.,* p. 190.

[49] *Ibid.,* p. 195.

[50] *Ibid.,* p. 188.

[51] *Ibid.,* p. 197.

[52] Pilgrim Press, 1920.

[53] See *FC Reports,* 1937-1950, each of which includes this Commission's report and a listing of its officers.

[54] *Cf.* Handy, *op. cit.,* p. 131.

[55] Rich, *op. cit.,* p. 113.

[56] *FC Bulletin,* October, 1930.

[57] *Cf.* this writer's 16-page "Study Manual," based on the Douglass Report, published by the AES in 1930.

[58] *Cf.* the *FC Bulletin,* February, 1930; and April, 1930 ("The Churches Look at the City.")

[59] The *FC Bulletin,* March, 1930, in announcing "Michigan Institutes Council of Churches," noted: "No provision has been made as yet for funds to provide paid leadership." In the June 1931 issue: "Iowa Leaders Plan State Council of Churches."

[60] See the June 1930 *News Letter,* and the full page article in the September 1930 *FC Bulletin.*

[61] His address in this connection, *FC 1930 Report,* p. 142, is a mine of historical and biographical material; see also the January 1931 *FC Bulletin,* "Dr. Macfarland Completes Unique Service in Church Co-operation," by Dr. Cavert (2-pages).

[62] In those depression years it did not seem to occur to any of us in the state and local councils that we might offer to *pay* for as welcome a bulletin service.

[63] *FC 1930 Report,* pp. 18, 19.

[64] *Ibid.,* p. 163.

[65] *Ibid.,* p. 168.

[66] See the *FC Bulletin,* September, and November, 1930; and January, 1931, an editorial on "A New Level in Home Missions Planning," and a 2-page article, "Home Missions Congress Prepares for a New Epoch"; followed in April by 2 pages of the Congress "Message."

67 See the *FC Bulletin*, February, 1931.

68 *International Journal*, July, 1930—"Some Achievements of the Past Quadrennium."

69 *Ibid.*, "The Function of the City Council of Religious Education."

70 See the ICRE Board of Field Administration file in the Office for Councils of Churches.

71 *Cf.* ICRE action taken February 17, 18, 1931.

72 *Cf. FC Bulletin*, October, 1930, art. on Indianapolis, by Tripp.

73 *FC 1931 Report*, pp. 16-19.

74 *Ibid.*, pp. 70, 71.

75 *Ibid.*, p. 134.

76 In a personal letter to Dr. McCreary, October 5, 1931.

The Merging Thirties

When Money Was Scarce

The depression that began in late 1929 was at its worst in the early thirties. National bodies were as hard hit as local, perhaps even harder; church organizations were as much hampered as secular, perhaps even more so. In 1932 the AES interrupted its series of annual meetings for the only time in its history, omitting a session already scheduled for Detroit in June. "All our councils and federations are having financial difficulties which would greatly limit the attendance."[1] By March it was clear that the AES ought to concentrate on getting state and local executives to attend the Indianapolis FC Quadrennial in December. June 28 Dr. Guild wrote to the field, "If you are having difficulties in the financing of your work . . . we are all in a large and splendid company . . . (splendid because) the secretaries are courageously meeting the issues that are at hand." September 23, 1932, Dr. Guild reiterated to Dr. Cavert, "The whole federation movement is in a very serious condition." Extension cost the Federal Council only $9,851.36 in 1932,[2] and the Field Department budget for 1933 was fixed at $10,000—obviously a depression figure.[3]

In the autumn Dr. Guild said again, "The first nine months of this year have tested the councils of churches severely. (But) of the 50 councils with employed leadership, only two have temporarily given up that policy."[4] Yet 1932 saw the publication of three significant volumes: Zahniser's *Interchurch Community Programs*,[5] Hartshorne and Miller's *Community Organization in Religious Education*,[6] and *Rethinking Missions* (the Laymen's Foreign Missions Inquiry).[7]

From 1933, when in many ways the depression was deepest, to 1937 there was drought on the Great Plains;[8] the cities also in the middle thirties saw rough days. But in 1933 it was said that "only three (council of churches) secretaries have resigned with the knowledge that a full-time successor would not be employed." "Other secretaries have wondered how they would carry on, but while wondering, have carried on just the same."[9] This was the first year of "The New Deal."

152

At the AES in Chicago in 1933 Detroit reported its church and council finances at the bottom; and the same was true elsewhere. Debts had increased 30%; eleven cities reported debts from $1,000 to $17,500; Rochester, surprisingly, none. The 1933 budgets of 18 cities were 33% below the 1932 figures; one old federation had to cut 66%. Staffs were reduced by 30%; salaries, 40%. In one case back salaries were 49% of the budget.[10] The AES had only $185 in available funds—the rest of its considerable bank balance was "frozen." The previous year's receipts had been about half the former peak. A new level of askings was set at only a third of the previous high figure, the treasurer suggesting a minimum payment of $10, with $25 for the larger six councils.

And Merger Was Epidemic

From 1932 to 1940 there was rapid consolidation of councils of religious education and councils of churches into a single nation-wide network of state and local cooperation. This trend had been under way *locally* for years. In 1918 Myron C. Settle of Kansas City's Sunday School Association had also become secretary of its council of churches;[11] a plan adopted late in 1924 for the merging of the two councils became effective in 1925, with mingled regrets and satisfaction. In 1920, the Wichita executive served not only the Federation of Churches but also the County Sunday School Association; he could soon report, "There is not one Sunday school office and another weekday office and another Council office. We are to all intents and purposes one organization."[12] Likewise by 1922 the Wayne County Sunday School Association had become the Department of Religious Education in the Sunday schools for the Detroit Council of Churches, the two bodies having their offices together.[13]

On September 20, 1923, the Cleveland Federated Churches and the Cuyahoga County Sunday School Association united to form what soon became known as the Federated Churches of Greater Cleveland, of which the Sunday School Association now became the Department of Religious Education. This was accomplished before the arrival of J. Quinter Miller as the first religious education secretary, and appears to have been the earliest complete local merger, as distinguished from joint employment of the same staff. Naturally Dr. Miller, having seen it accomplished locally, later reasoned, Why not at the state level also? Chicago's Sunday School Association and Church Federation forces were merged in 1924; and that same year the quiescent Monroe County Sunday School Association became active again with a modest budget and joined with the Rochester Federation of Churches in employing a

153

director of religious education for the county. After several years of "closest affiliation," the two bodies effected a complete merger in October, 1927, when Rev. Fred H. Willkens began his service as religious education director. In 1925 the Council of Religious Education in Portland, Ore., became the Department of Religious Education in the Council of Churches, both organizations continuing as autonomous bodies, but with one budget, and one executive.[14] By 1926 the Federation of Churches in Youngstown and the Mahoning County Sunday School Association had established "an intimate form of cooperation . . . without destroying the identity of the Sunday School Association."[15] In 1926 an International Standard Training School for Church Workers in Omaha was sponsored by denominations cooperating both in the Omaha Council of Churches and in the Douglas County Council of Religious Education. Five years later the two councils were merged. On April 1, 1930, the Erie County Sunday School Association and the Buffalo Council of Churches were happily merged.[16]

In June 1931 an AES paper on "Religious Education and Protestant Cooperation" was able to say:[17]

"By and large, the *merger* of local councils of religious education with federations of churches is a fact accomplished. There are exceptions. They must be recognized. Exceptional situations may continue for a long time. Let us be very patient.

"On the state level, it is the merger that is exceptional. The state councils of religious education are better entrenched than the few state federations of churches. Mergers will come slowly. Within a decade (or two at most) the story will be different: Eventually the independent councils of religious education on the state level will be exceptional. By that time we shall begin to talk seriously about national unification."

(Perhaps the most interesting fact about that paper is its date. In less than two decades the National Council was to be a going concern; and as early as 1951, seemingly only Pennsylvania had a separate council of religious education.)

The Brooklyn, N.Y., merger was effected in 1932; Baltimore, Md., united its councils in 1937; Cincinnati followed in 1938. The necessary economies of the depression years perhaps helped to merge local councils of religious education and federations of churches, as, for example, in Duluth, where layman W. L. Smithies had now served two decades, the first five years as president of the federation, and fifteen as executive of the now merged organizations.[18]

154

"Connecticut Leads on a New Path"

In 1932 the first complete merger at the *state* level was happily accomplished. January 1, 1931, Rev. J. Quinter Miller had become secretary both of Connecticut's Council of Religious Education and of its Federation of Churches. "On June 1 the headquarters of the two organizations were united, . . . the office secretariat of both continuing to carry on their functions. Mr. Miller is now engaged in studying the work of both organizations, with a view to submitting plans for the complete co-ordination of their activities."[19] Connecticut's "epoch-making union" took place at the annual meetings in December 1932, "the first of its kind in the United States"—"the most advanced step taken in any state unifying the Protestant Cooperative forces"—"the realization of the ideal that there should be one organization to carry out the whole program of the whole Church for the whole state."[20] Something new had happened in Connecticut, and it appeared to be catching. Down the years it has become increasingly clear that this was the contagion of health.

Other States Follow

In the spring of 1933 Illinois was voting on its merger. Massachusetts had also been working on its consolidation problems, and in November 1933 its merger was consummated. New York State's merger also was now all but completed, with Dr. W. G. Landes, of the State Council of Religious Education, slated to be the new executive.[21] The endowment funds held by his organization added greatly to the solidity of the combination of two organizations that were both "going concerns." As in local situations, state mergers were consummated only after years of negotiation, sometimes patient, sometimes less adroit.

For clarity's sake, the state merger process may now be previewed to the end of the decade by listing the years in which inclusive state councils were created by merger or expansion, or *de novo:*

1932 Connecticut	1936 No. California
	So. California
1933 Massachusetts	Michigan
	North Carolina
1934 Illinois*	Oregon
Nebraska*	Vermont
	Wisconsin
1935 New York	
Washington-No. Idaho	

1937 Maryland-Delaware   1940 Ohio*
     Rhode Island (revival)

1938 Maine
     Missouri
     Montana
     West Virginia

* In several cases the process involved two or more stages, and dates a year or two later are sometimes cited.

These 20 councils involved churches in 22 or more states. By 1940 there were eight additional state councils of churches (some of them without a paid executive): Colorado, Kansas, Minnesota, New Hampshire, New Jersey, Oklahoma, Pennsylvania, and South Dakota, all of them parallel with councils of religious education.

Sample Merger Situations

"A pastors' convocation was held, under the auspices of the *Nebraska* Council of Christian Education, in Lincoln, January 19-21, 1931. More than 200 pastors from all parts of the state attended."[22] Said John C. White, CCE executive, two years later,[23] "What we are doing . . . is asking the denominations who now own and direct the Nebraska Council (of Christian Education) to make it a Council of Churches and Christian Education." At the Third Annual Convocation it was voted to do just this. This expansion of the CCE was thus a patient result of three years of ministerial state-wide interdenominational fraternization. In presenting a constitution it was said, "The enlarged Council does not contemplate an expanded staff." (When one agency absorbed another, or expanded to perform its functions, there was always the question as to whether the added tasks could be adequately done.) Secretary White concluded an article on "Expanding the Field of Cooperation in Nebraska" with the assertion: "The Council of Churches and Christian Education will be the creation of the Protestant bodies of the state."[24] The new inclusive council (NCC&RE) was organized January 15, 1934.[25]

In 1934 *Massachusetts* and *Boston* were integrating their councils, an arrangement that persisted for more than two decades. In 1937 three organizations in *Maryland-Delaware* and *Baltimore,* which had one staff and only meager financial resources, found it expedient to consolidate their forces. (*Per contra,* in 1958 it seemed clear that *Seattle* might better have its own council, separate from that of Washington-Northern Idaho, a 1935 merger.)[26]

156

Merger details, including tensions, infelicities, personalities, variations from state to state, etc., would be worthy of a doctoral dissertation; and are instructive in terms of what not to do, and how not to do what ought to be done, as well as in terms of successful unions finally achieved.

In 1940 the *ICRE Journal* traced the merger process in *Ohio* in successive issues: In February the state was "considering merger," "after several years of discussion and conference." In May the merger plan had been approved, with details to be worked out; in June it had been ratified, and the date for making it effective was to be set. In November the completion of the merger in September was reported. Ohio, with relatively strong councils, was late in merging; *Pennsylvania,* which has not yet effected a merger, and may never do so, had more than 3,200 paid registrations at its 1934 Sunday school convention.[28] In some instances, state as well as local, bankruptcy and lack of leadership, both in church federations and in councils of religious education, accelerated the merger process.

For example, in *Illinois,* after the debacle of 1929, not only the "new Council of Churches organized in the days of prosperity" but also "by 1930 the Council of Religious Education was suffering from undernourishment. One by one the staff was decreased and cheaper quarters had to be sought." Most of 102 counties had formerly been organized; only 75 were now. "With our new conditions of rapid transportation and improved roads the county unit does not seem to be always the best plan"—so it seemed to Dr. Walter R. Cremeans, a Springfield pastor.[29] But by 1940 the Illinois merged Council was having exhibits in its own church house.[30]

In 1933 the *Oklahoma* Council of Churches and the Council of Christian Education held a joint meeting (it would be 1942 before they could merge); and the New York Council of Religious Education and the Council of Churches had their first joint state convention.[31] They would merge in 1934.)

In 1935 *North Carolina* held its first convention in five years, with 500 registered and 700 attending. Thirteen denominations were looking forward to more effective cooperation. Harry C. Munro of the ICRE and H. Shelton Smith (since 1931 of the Duke University faculty) collaborated in the leadership.[32] After a 1934 conference of leaders, *Wisconsin* held an organization meeting to plan its inclusive council in January 1935.[33] (This too became effective in 1936.)

157

In July 1935 a convention of the *Kansas* Council of Religious Education was articulated with the sessions of the state Council of Churches. The latter (though organized in 1922) was just getting under way; the former had preregistered 4,000 delegates.[34] By the fall of 1935 *North Dakota* was out of debt, had a comfortable cash balance, and was ready to move forward; but it seemingly did not achieve an inclusive council, with paid executive, until 1949.[35] *Oregon* its Council of Churches organized in 1935, joined its forces in 1936. (Its Sunday School Association beginnings dated back to 1870, 1872, and 1885.)

On October 31, 1938, the *Maine* Council, which had voted in 1934 to seek a general secretary, became inclusive.[36]

Other Glimpses of the Field

In May 1932 the IJRE editorialized on the need for both denominational and interdenominational field workers, and how to relate them. Dr. Munro wrote on "Unifying the Field Forces," with comments on the situation in seven states; and C. A. Hauser reported "Some Experiments in Cooperation in Pennsylvania." A leap year analysis of the situation in many states added to the significance of this issue of the *Journal*.

During these years there was repeated emphasis on evangelism and on the local community. J. Quinter Miller wrote on "The City Organization and Program of Cooperative Religious Education" after four years of experience as director of religious education with the Federated Churches of Greater Cleveland.[37] Visitation evangelism, an early phase of Sunday school work, now re-emerges as "Reaching the Unreached."[38] An article by Minor Miller on "Religious Education in the Community" proved of sufficient importance to warrant reprinting after three years.[39] One by Charles E. Shike of Illinois, "A State Council in Action,"[40] contained maps showing population change by counties, index of levels of living, and percentage of the population in church membership. P. R. Hayward's three annual meeting addresses on "Changes in the Population of America—What They Mean for Christian Education" were publicized.[41] Frank M. McKibben wrote on "Next Steps in Community Coordination."[42] Successive issues of the *Journal* during this period afford interesting evidence of rapid shifts in professional leadership.[43]

By April 1940 the Intercouncil Field Department found that councils of churches were being proposed in *Montana* (had 1938 beginnings proved abortive, or were they only in the field of home missions?) and *Wyoming* (but without permanent success until 1958);

that closer correlation in *Indiana* was being discussed (its merger to become effective in 1944), and that correlation had been accomplished in *Minnesota* (but with no merger until 1947). *Iowa* agencies were getting acquainted (and would merge in 1945). Since 1938 the *Missouri* CRE was "continuing to become" a Council of Churches. Expansion was also being considered by the CRE in *Virginia, New Jersey,* and *Oklahoma;* (and effected in 1945, 1947, and 1942 respectively). The *Maine* situation was now in doubt, by reason of a resignation. In *Washington, D.C.,* W. L. Darby had resigned after eighteen years, and coordination seemed worth considering. Dr. Miller had met with representatives of both *Kansas* agencies as to their relationships, but it would be several years before a merger could be effected. The *Colorado* situation was complicated; it would be another decade before a merger could be accomplished. In *Kentucky* the CRE and the HMC had conferred, but there was no executive; merger would be accomplished in 1948.

Greater Inter-Council Field Cooperation

In all this integrating process, three levels were involved: city or county, state, and nation. There were many problems, and real causes for hesitation, each of them matched by the impatience of those who did not understand all that was involved. At the national level negotiations proceeded steadily, if sometimes jerkily. Developments in the field had accelerated events at the "summit."

As early as July 1926 the Federal Council had appointed a committee on relations with the ICRE. A two year inter-council agreement (subject to ratification) made in 1929 recommended no particular form of relationship between organizations in states and local communities.[23] All the national interdenominational agencies now moved toward larger field cooperation with one another.

The religious educators had a concrete, established functional program, and a considerable field structure and personnel. As one able student of the movement put it, the problem involved in merger tensions "is not merely a question of misunderstanding. It is more one of *our own people* (i.e., the church federation group) having narrow, distorted ideas of function. I am convinced that more federations have died because they never found worthwhile jobs, than for any other reason. I am concerned because so commonly the churches are turning over to the Councils only the fringes, only the nick-nacks of their work. Things they consider vital they carefully held back. In comity we are getting into vital things, but where else?"[24]

Federal Council Establishes a Field Department (FCFD)

In the fall of 1932 the Federal Council expanded its Extension Committee into a representative Field Department, including persons denominationally chosen to the Executive Committee of the FC, others nominated by the AES, and representatives of the Home Missions Councils and other interdenominational agencies willing to cooperate in working out the most effective cooperative programs in state and local areas.

At the end of 1932 the FC had to confess, "The past quadrennium has been a very difficult one in which to carry out the proposal that extension of state and local cooperation be made a major task. . . . Special attention has been given to the extension of *state* cooperation . . . Most of the cities in which councils might be organized and adequately financed were already organized."[46] The state council was increasingly regarded as the key to the growth of local work.

"Primary attention" to organizing state and local federation was again voted in 1932, and the Field Department personnel was listed as the first of eight departments. It was further voted, "In order to make certain that the experience and the point of view of the local church and community shall be taken into full consideration in the development of all Cooperative programs, the membership of all the Federal Council's departments shall include representatives of city and state councils of churches."[47]

This sincere, generous, permissive action proved less worldshaking than it seemed; and the proof of the pudding, as always, was in the subsequent eating. Here too were both the seeds of progress in national-local relationships, and the beginnings of distinctions between corporate controls and program cooperation; yet it seemed to some that the chief structural problem was dodged. The effect in 1950 will become apparent.

The International Council Faces the Field

The year 1932 was also marked by the emergence of a new emphasis on field work on the part of the ICRE. The new national set-up, which had for a decade so largely absorbed the energies of denominational educational leaders, was by this time taken for granted. Renewed attention could now be given both to the state auxiliaries and to community aspects of religious education. In 1930 Harry C. Munro had been made Director of Adult Work and Field Administration.[48]

In February 1932 the Committee on Field Program made a significant report to the Educational Commission on "The Purpose and Principles of Field Supervision."

Dr. Hugh S. Magill of the ICRE had at first been critical of local mergers, and in 1929 he was still sharply opposed to state consolidations; but he now said, "I agree . . . that the Connecticut Council of Churches and Religious Education is the type of organization best suited to present-day needs and present overlapping and duplication."[49]

On February 13, 1933, the National and International Executives of the ICRE, in spite of grave misgivings on the part of several persons, agreed to experiment, in one or two states, as proposed by the HMC, and adopted a resolution indicating conditions under which they would favor state organizational unification. Mr. Russell Colgate and Dr. Harold McAfee Robinson, acting general secretary, were now convinced that the general merger principle required action.

On March 23, 1933, the new Field Department of the Federal Council, at its gratifyingly large first meeting, on hearing of the February action of the ICRE, found itself in hearty accord with its spirit and purpose, and on its recommendation the Executive Committee of the Federal Council the next day approved it with enthusiasm. Dr. King of course promised the equally hearty cooperation of the HMC.[50]

The new AES President was Irvin E. Deer, executive secretary at Kansas City, Mo., who had been elected in December. He assured the Federal Council that "the (state and local) secretaries will be very happy to be used at any time by the Field Department in its extension work or to send representatives of their councils to places where help is needed." Progress on a new manual of organization and program methods, in process since June, 1932, was indicated.

At the June 1933 Chicago meeting of the AES only 23 secretaries were able to assemble; eight others sent regrets. "Good and Bad" aspects of fourteen local council situations were reported, and various aspects of church cooperation reviewed. The findings were important: "In our judgment a primary function of the Field Department should be the articulation of the various departments of the (Federal) Council, especially where these represent denominational emphases, with the programs of local and state councils established and to be established." Study of field services available, on a cooperative basis, was urged; and close cooperation between the Field Department and the AES Executive Committee. Very great satisfaction

161

was expressed for the presence of Dr. Harry C. Munro of the International Council. "We urge cities and states to move with such deliberation that whenever mergers are desirable there shall be the largest possible conservation of historic values and traditional loyalties." Dr. Deer was continued as president.

At the September 21, 1933, meeting of the Field Department of the Federal Council the manuscript and editorial process of the forthcoming little booklet "Community Programs for Cooperating Churches" were presented. Dr. Ralph C. McAfee of Detroit made a careful report of AES actions, remarking that "this movement is far behind where most of us thought it was going to be."

The next day (September 22, 1933), the Executive Committee of the Federal Council, having heard with appreciation the proposal of the AES for a Study of the Federal Council's field service, and of other interdenominational agency service in relation to the programs of state and local councils of churches, as presented by Dr. McAfee, requested the Federal Council's Field Department to undertake such a study, and also "to make recommendations after study and inquiry, as to ways in which the national and regional leaders and agencies of the denominations can use their influence more effectively in behalf of cooperative programs in states and local communities."[51] Foreign Mission leaders were also now turning to the local and state councils with new interest, especially for statewide conferences; and the local councils were expressing appreciation for the stimulation of local church interest by denominational leaders.

In 1933 the ICRE took the important action that "in order to be a constituent member a state or provincial council (of religious education) shall be duly accredited as an auxiliary of the International Council, having its educational policies and field programs determined by an educational committee representing the cooperating denominations within its area."[52] (28 accredited councils, 7 not, had employed secretaries).

At the end of 1933, there were still only eight state councils of churches with employed secretaries. "The one hope of developing continuous cooperation in cities of less than one hundred thousand population, and in counties and smaller communities, is to have in the state an executive secretary who can organize and help maintain these councils which must depend largely on volunteer leadership. Such a secretary can make effective the cooperation of state denominational officials. He can organize and aid city and county councils as well as direct the cooperative church work."[53]

162

On November 16, 1933, an informal meeting of the executives of certain national interdenominational organizations was held at the Hotel Pennsylvania, New York City, on invitation of Mr. Russell Colgate, president of the International Convention of the ICRE, who was made chairman, with Dr. Cavert as secretary. There was "general approval of the suggestion that there be some more adequate means of conference through which the national interdenominational organizations may consider ways and means of developing a more closely coordinated program for the total task of Christianity." This cautious rather than radical language was to have far-reaching results for all of American Protestantism.

At Dr. Cavert's proposal it was[54] soon arranged to make the ICRE offices the Chicago headquarters of the FC after January 1, 1934. It was now[55] recognized not only that "in several states substantial progress in the unification of the Protestant forces is already under way through the union of councils of churches, councils of religious education, and home missions councils," but also that "foreign missions and the Christian colleges ought to be included;" "that the real unit for all our work is the local church, and that we need to guard against disintegrating its support because of competing appeals."

The 1933 *FC Report* included "Twenty-Five Years of Church Federation." Dr. Cavert was now the only general secretary. Associate general secretary Guild was executive of the Field Department, with a 1934 budget of only $9,000.[56] Receipts designated for extension in 1933 had amounted to only $130.34; Field Department expense was $9,273.95.

In 1934 church leaders, beginning to recover a bit from the depression spirit, started to talk about various types of "Advance." In January the Home Missions Councils adopted plans for "The New Co-operative Home Mission Advance." "It had been hoped to have major conferences in each state, followed by a series of smaller conferences; but for a number of reasons—chiefly the inability of the boards to supply needed funds or to loan the necessary staff—this whole side of the new advance never developed."[57]

The Christian Youth Council of North America, which had met in Birmingham in 1926, and Toronto in 1930, now gathered again in 1934 at Conference Point. Its slogan, "Christian Youth Building a New World," reflected the recovery of optimism.[58] Later in the year United Church Adult Conferences were scheduled.[59]

Organization of the Employed Council Officers' Association (ECOA)

The ICRE Committee on Field Program now began a period of vigorous functioning under the chairmanship of Dr. M. N. English; and what makes 1934 most significant for this narrative is the stirring among directors of state councils of religious education. Beginning with 1892, the Field Workers' Department of the International Association had proved of great significance; and out of the 1912 meeting of general secretaries, held under its auspices in New Orleans, had grown the Employed Officers' Association, formally "organized at Conference Point in the summer of 1916." "This organization continued until 1922, when it was disbanded because the continuance of it was considered 'contrary to the spirit of the merger' formed in 1922 uniting the Sunday School Council of Evangelical Denominations and the International Sunday School Association into the International Council of Religious Education."

A fellowship that had flourished for thirty years (1892-1922) had been strangely allowed to evaporate; and many of the old-timers felt that something important was now missing, something more than the Fellowship of Christian Workers promoted late in 1933.[60] Accordingly, in July 1934, a year when the AES was not to meet until December, "a group of seven men (representing the former Sunday School Association heritage) met on the Tipi-Wakan porch at Conference Point Camp (on Lake Geneva, Wis.). Out of this informal discussion the Employed Council Officers' Association (ECOA) came into existence. In effect this professional fellowship continued the traditions of the old E.O.A."[61]

At the first full ECOA session, July 17 to 21, 1934, fifteen state and seven ICRE staff persons were present; and six visitors. Its convener, Harry C. Munro, executive secretary of the Committee on Field Programs of the ICRE, was made permanent ECOA executive. Hayden L. Stright of Minnesota was elected president; Otto Mayer of the ICRE staff secretary. A full-time field director for the ICRE was favored, and increased services to the state councils of religious education in financing their programs. It was suggested that state financial reports, already given to the ICRE Committee on Constituent Membership, might also be circulated confidentially among all other reporting councils.

It was recognized that religious education faced intradenominational tensions between specialized workers and ecclesiastical administrators as well as interdenominational problems of the same sort;

164

and the cooperation and understanding shown by some ecclesiasts was recognized with grateful appreciation. Merger situations proved of very great interest. The secretary was asked to find out what was happening in merged cities. An assessment of 25¢ per member for the year 1934-5 yielded $12.75 from 51 persons.

The state religious education council secretaries, somewhat lost in the shuffle, had been hungry for closer fellowship and responsible cooperative status. They had been caught between denominational processes, in which their advisors shared fully and intimately, and the emerging ecclesiastical cooperation, which was often educationally amateurish, inexpert, unappreciative or even scornful of technical religious education. On the other hand, the dominance of state religious education secretaries in the ECOA now seems conspicuous, in contrast with the primarily urban leadership in the AES.

Since 1915 the AES had been able to maintain a small but increasing and uninterrupted fellowship; but the AES and the old EOA had never had any dealings with one another. In the 1930's the ecclesiastical climate was changing; the ecumenical spirit was beginning to thaw former icy walls of program partition, and iron curtains of functional separation were beginning to wear thin. Yet when it became probable that state religious education executives would be meeting at Lake Geneva in July, and Dr. Guild asked the AES men whether they would like to join in some of these sessions, he found that the time was not quite ripe. National leadership was now two steps ahead of state and local.

But, now that Connecticut had had a full year's experience with an inclusive council, and other states had experimented with various forms of cooperation between church federations and councils of religious education, and the field staff leaders of three national councils were achieving a new unity, the contagion of unified action began to spread. On January 12, 1934, seven national interdenominational executives conferred informally.

On February 17, 1934, on recommendation of its Executives' Advisory Section, the International Council took significant action toward closer integration of interdenominational agencies in the states. Over the next two years, however, a word of caution was repeatedly urged, lest by the neglect of strongly organized county units, or the provision of inadequate state budgets for religious education, councils of religious education find themselves "submerged" rather than parts of effective state mergers.[62]

165

In March President Deer of the AES and Dr. Guild announced the proposed publication of a free quarterly AES news bulletin, subject to the approval of the Federal Council Finance Committee, and asked for news and orders. Meanwhile the Department of Field Administration of the ICRE had begun a mimeographed quarterly, *The Field Counselor,* with emphasis on itineraries of field personnel.

Secretaries Munro, King, and Guild, who had met together on successive days and agreed on quarterly meetings, were now formally appointed as an Intercouncil Staff Committee on Cooperation in the Field, and each of the three men was to be a cooperating member of the field planning and program building body of the other two councils. Seven Councils (FC, ICRE, HMC, CWHM, Ch. Bds. of Ed., MEM, FMC) now agreed not only to exchange information as to field itineraries but to make a united field approach.

On April 26, 1934, at the Parkside Hotel, New York (luncheon 70¢, with free use of tenth floor solarium!), Dr. Cavert told the Federal Council's Field Department, "The proposed plan for closer cooperation of field forces and programs of the interdenominational organizations represent one of the most significant advances made in recent years in the whole cooperative movement." The Federal Council had now agreed to finance the *News Bulletin* up to $200 for one year. (*Church Federation Field* survived until the autumn of 1935). A 1935 Department budget of $9,300 was approved, toward which it raised $1,730.

In January 1935 48 city councils or federations of churches, with headquarters and one or more employed officers, with budgets ranging from $1,500 to $50,000, were reported, with many more depending on volunteer leadership. There were now eight state councils of churches with employed personnel and seven with volunteer.

At the end of 1934 the FC was told, "The most important factor in developing cooperation is the forces out in the field, constituting the AES. No group of Christian workers has been more severely tested by the depression. In spite of decreased income they have carried on and kept with them most of their assistants. The total indebtedness incurred by these councils is now less than at any time in the last three years, and larger budgets are being raised than last year. Only two cities closed their offices during the depression. The work of the city and state executives is the heart of the Field Department. The integration of the services of the city and state councils and of the Federal Council must be given more consideration than ever before. One of the serious losses resulting from the depression has been the necessary reduction in the amount of travel."[63]

"By far the larger part of the country is still unorganized."[64] The need for more field staff was reiterated; but lack of funds again prevented its employment. Church cooperation was now old enough to make the "Necrology" report increasingly significant.

In January 1935 Walter R. Mee, Chicago Federation executive, now president of the AES, was made a member of the ICRE Committee on Field Program, so that consideration could be given to a joint meeting of ECOA and AES at Lake Geneva that summer. (One of the standard jokes of this period had to do with the proper salutation of the AES president. One year we were writing, "Dear Deer"; and the next, "Dear Mee"!) January 9 Dr. Guild wrote, "The atmosphere has changed wonderfully as relates to the merging of the meetings of the ECOA and the AES." On February 2 Dr. Munro reported that 23 of the 26 ECOA replies were unqualifiedly in favor of joint sessions; two others were favorable "under conditions which will undoubtedly be met"; and only one raised any questions.

Inter-Council Field Committee (ICFC), 1935-1939

On January 6, 1935, at the Robert Morris Hotel, Philadelphia, the Joint Committee of the FC Field Department, the Joint Administrative Committee of the two HMC's, and the ICRE Committee on Field Program, called to consider relationships and issues involved in mergers of state councils," elected Dr. W. R. King as chairman and Harry C. Munro as secretary. This was only a little over three years from the time when Dr. King had made his first proposals for unification. This Joint Committee now recommended "that the FC, the HMC's, and the ICRE consider the possibility of a joint field staff and field department; and that a joint committee on integration of field activities, program, and staff be regularly appointed to assist the executives responsible for such integration and to study the possibility and wisdom of such a joint field department."[65] No standard form was recommended for every situation, but assurance was sought "that religious education will have adequate financial support, leadership, promotion, and supervision." (In the light of the history set forth in Chapter II, and the organizational patterns already achieved, was this not a proper insistence?)

The unification that had become routine at the local level, and more and more widespread at the state level, was now well on its way at the national level, specially for those staff persons in charge of field outreach and relationships.

In February 1935 on the suggestion of a representative meeting of its Committee on Field Program, after consideration by its Educational Commission and its Committee on Reference and Counsel, the ICRE approved appointments for the proposed Inter-Council Field Committee (ICFC), whose function would be to clear, integrate, and allocate responsibilities for those field activities in which two or more of the national interdenominational agencies were involved. Though the January 6 joint action on "Principles for Guidance in State Council Mergers" was approved, the question was raised as to whether "relations broader than those involved in field activity do not call for more adequate provision than now exists for their clearance." *The Field Counselor* and *Church Federation Field* were each to be sent to the other's list. The difficulties in relating program items of interest to religious education personnel only, or to church federation men only, or to both secretarial groups, in planning for Lake Geneva, were faced.

On May 1, Dr. King wrote, "I regard the work of field organization as fundamental and basic. Without an inclusive council of churches in each state and city we cannot hope to do a constructive work. The time is ripe for this organizational work."[66] On May 8 participation in the proposed Joint Committee was recommended by the FC's Field Department, to its Executive Committee, with nominations. Careful study of pensions was urged, with AES cooperation requested.

On June 29 and 30, at Conference Point, a joint staff session,[67] after reviewing the various actions already taken, favored working cooperation, as a step toward a more formal merger. Dr. King and Dr. Munro were to formulate a policy statement. On July 1 three Federal Council secretaries, four ICRE, a Home Missions staff representative, and the executive secretary of the NCFCW met as the Inter-Council Field Committee (ICFC) and elected Dr. King chairman. Though there was a question as to whether the relationships of state and local to national bodies were a function of this committee or of the field departments of each national body,[68] it soon "became perfectly obvious that closer relationships and more frequent conferences among these staffs are indispensable to proper correlation of the several agencies."[69] Separate and joint sessions of the state and local secretaries followed, with certain national personnel also present.

Simultaneous Sessions of ECOA and AES, 1935-1940

At Conference Point, June 29, July 2, 3, and 5, 1935, the ECOA ended its first year with 35 cents on hand! Dues, which had been paid by 51 persons, were now raised to 50¢. Walter E. Myers of Pennsylvania was elected chairman of ECOA. Cooperation with the State and Regional Executives' Section was voted in February. The ECOA now took over, for its last years, the conduct of the Conference Point Council Officers' Training School (C.O.T.S.).

The AES also met, July 1 to 6, with 31 present. There were *parallel and joint assemblies,* with a number of persons belonging to both bodies. At the AES there were 23 city and state and eight FC secretaries present, and Dr. Harold McAfee Robinson, representing the ICRE; also four guests and fifteen wives or children. Joint sessions of the AES and ECOA for 1936 looking toward more vital relationships were voted, with representatives of the HMC, FC, and NCFCW to be invited. The study of pensions was continued. At the conclusion of these sessions it was suggested that "at next year's meeting we have less program from national leaders, and more time to discuss our own problems."[70] Later the same local secretary said, "I earnestly hope the Program Committee will not hand over all the time to the Federal Council secretaries." "We want the FC secretaries with us, but they felt they could not afford to come unless they could promote their work." The officers were continued until the biennial meeting of the Federal Council in December. A June balance of $145.78 was reported.

Seventy-seven persons were present at these simultaneous sessions, which "suited the convenience of more than a third of the total number who are secretaries of merged councils."[71]

After a 21-week trip by car of 13,500 miles, Dr. Guild said to the FC Field Department December 11, 1935, "Protestant cooperation has reached the highest point nationally it has attained." "In nearly every city unification has taken place. The states are swinging into line." At the close of 1935 Dr. Guild pointed out that many executives were members of both the ECOA and the AES. "These (he said) are the men and women who are actually doing the cooperative work and are most vitally concerned. They created the conditions that necessitated national readjustments. The unification of cooperative work on city and state levels has preceded unification on national levels, even such limited unification as is manifested in the work of the Joint Committee on Problems of Relationships."

He also reported that though city and state councils had been "seriously handicapped by lack of funds, in some cases this has resulted in arousing volunteer service that has given renewed vitality to councils. Today there are as many cities having employed executives

169

and established headquarters as there were at the beginning of the depression, one having failed and one new having been formed. Some cities are reporting improved financial conditions."

Dr. Roy G. Ross (now general secretary of the National Council of Churches) was elected general secretary of the ICRE at its 1936 annual meeting.[72] In March 1936 responses from ten states where mergers were well along or completed, and four where unification had been discussed, revealed perceptible differences in ICRE, FC, and HMC perspectives.

A meeting of the ICFC planned for November 1935 had to be cancelled, but by early 1936 the time was ripe for cooperative action. On April 13 and 14, at the Parkside Hotel, New York, the ICFC voted that "we recognize the ultimate desirability of a complete union of the Field Departments of the FC, the ICRE, and the HMC's."[73] The general secretaries were asked to draft a general plan of procedure.

Similarly on April 15 at the FC Field Department the actions of the ICFC were approved or properly referred. (On June 5 the FC Executive Committee took the required actions.) Dr. Cavert now presented a "Procedure Suggested for Moving Toward a Joint Field Department."

Toward an approved 1936 budget of $9,300 the FC Field Department was supposed to raise $2,000. Need was felt for a finance man, and for regional offices. Expenses for three months had exceeded the budget by $55.

On June 25, at a meeting of national executives at the ICRE office, the field policies and staff duties of each agency were considered. There was consultation as to field staff appointments. It was suggested that in the field each might act for all. On the 26th the Joint Staff, meeting at Conference Point, felt that there might well be two meetings of the total staffs each year, perhaps in June and December, with one meeting of the ICFC in December.

The AES met at Conference Point June 29 to July 3, 1936. (Rates: $9.00 for six days; or $2.50 a day, two in a room, $3.00 single —including meals!) There were joint sessions with the ECOA, which held its meetings June 29, 30, and July 2. At the AES Dr. Cavert spoke of the federal and local councils. Church federations and community agencies were discussed. Dr. Miller of Connecticut made a significant analysis of the philosophy of state council work. There were 27 persons in the ECOA travel pool. Dr. Ross made a "General

Statement on the Relations of the ICRE and State Councils," and presided at a joint session where relations of national and state councils were considered.

Dr. W. C. Bower led a joint seminar July 1-3. Joint dates for 1937 were approved. Harry C. Munro was made chairman of a joint program committee. In 1937 all save business and some evening sessions were to be made joint.

At the September 23, 24, 1935, meeting of the ICFC it was voted to make the Committee more inclusive. "The need of a more systematic means of selecting, training, and placing secretaries in state and city council positions was discussed." A subcommittee was appointed. Should there be a *Field Bulletin?* Why? What for? A committee was appointed.

On November 19 the FC Field Department gave appropriate recognition to the service rendered by Fred B. Smith, who had died September 3, 1936; also to that of Dr. Roy B. Guild, who was again to drop out of the picture at the end of the year. Said Dr. Cavert of Dr. Guild,[74] "To him the churches are indebted more than to any other person for the remarkable development of interchurch cooperation in state and local areas during the last quarter of a century." In his own biennial report Dr. Guild predicted, "The next great and permanent advance in united Protestantism will come through state-wide mobilization of Protestant forces."

The evidence of slowly accelerating, solid growth in the church federation movement, chiefly in the states, is clear: The 1931 March FC mimeographed directory listed 49 city, 7 state, and Puerto Rican councils. In 1934 there were 50 city and 10 state councils of churches; in November 1936 there were 17 state councils, each with an office and one or more employed secretaries. Chairman H. Paul Douglass led a discussion, "What Next for the Field Department?"

Organizationally, at the national level, the field committees of the cooperating agencies were now growing closer and closer together, through involvement in the same state and local situations. Their perspectives were still different, but their concerns were increasingly mutual.

A joint staff conference was held at the Parkside Hotel December 14 to 17, 1936. On the 15th and 16th the ICFC voted that in 1937 the AES be requested to give "adequate consideration of criteria or goals essential for evaluating and guiding in the organization, relationships, procedures, and program of a state council." Experimentation in states without any interdenominational agency was considered. Intensive cultivation of selected merger situations was suggested. Expanding functions of existing organizations (a CRE into an inclusive CC) was a possibility. No action was taken as to a bulletin.

Now that the great depression was becoming only an unhappy memory, and World War II (rather than peaceful prosperity) was still around the corner of the years to come, the Oxford (Life and Work) and Edinburgh (Faith and Order) Conferences marked 1937 as a year of major ecumenical importance. At home a new set of leaders was displacing the old.

The ECOA mustered an attendance of 33 at the YMCA Hotel, Chicago, on Feb. 9, chiefly to discuss the 1937 C.O.T.S. In connection with the April 9 and 10 conference on the projected 1937-8 United Christian Advance (Deshler-Wallick, Columbus) there was a called meeting of the ICFC, which included the United Stewardship Council (USC). Events were moving rapidly toward the greater coordination and unification of seven interdenominational bodies, and eventually still others would be involved. The "ultimate objective" was recognized as "the fullest possible measure of unity among all Christian forces." "As a preliminary step" it was proposed to "integrate so far as possible all field activities and programs of denominational and interdenominational organizations." The ICFC and the Inter-Council Staff were now going concerns.

Dr. Merle N. English (Methodist), speaking for the ICRE's Committee on Field Program, was "glad the ICRE is becoming 'field conscious.' " Dr. Munro said: "Our difficulties (*re* state councils) are due to our failure to make administratively effective on a wide scale any adequate philosophy of the total task of Christian education." Dr. Walter D. Howell (Presbyterian, USA) spoke on "Making State Councils More Truly Interdenominational" and "Denominational Assistance to State Councils." All sorts of experiments were reported. Financing was crucial. Plans for future field service were suggested.

On May 13 the FCFD appointed a committee to give thorough study to the best basis of representation in city and state councils. The USC indicated its desire to belong to the ICFC. The choice of a new FC field executive was to be made in consultation with the HMC and ICRE. The ICFC was requested to formulate procedures by which the new field executives might plan and administer a common field program for the councils to which they are responsible. The question was raised, "Are state mergers too rapid?" Another, "Could the ICRE and FC Field Committees be identical?" Also, "Should the FC re-open the question of territorial as well as denominational membership?" Dr. King was reported to be in the hospital for a complete rest. In June the ICRE Bureau of Research issued a document on "Community Cooperation in Religious Education—Brief Case Descriptions."

July 2 to 7, 1937, at Conference Point, the AES assembled 34 persons, including guests. Pensions were again discussed. A year book was suggested. Duplications in denominational and interdenominational mailings caused some concern. The treasury showed a June 30 balance of $332.56. The 20th Christian Education Convention was announced for Columbus, June 28 to July 3, 1938. A joint field man for the FC and the ICRE was favored. The difference between the two national bodies in the matter of geographical representation was pointed out. Dr. Munro was made chairman of a joint committee—seven from AES, and seven from ECOA; and two from each group were placed on the 1938 program committee. W. L. Darby, of Washington, D.C., was elected president of AES; and Emory M. Nelson of Scranton began a term of several years as secretary.

The ECOA also met on July 4, 8, and 9 at the same place, with 38 persons participating in the $119.10 travel pool. Receipts for the year had amounted to $57.83; there was a balance of $29.03. E. T. Albertson of Indiana was elected chairman. A joint panel discussion considered the "Relation of City, State, and National Councils and Federations." It was agreed that secretaries of merged state councils should be put on the ECOA mailing list—no mention was made of merged city councils. Quotas (from 5 to 1,500) were allotted to 37 states for the 1938 ICRE Convention. It was recognized that "Just as state mergers are calling for a joint field service, a joint field service may lead to a demand for a merger of national interdenominational agencies."

On October 13, 1937, Roy G. Ross reported on "Future Plans for Field Service." Dr. Forrest L. Knapp was now transferred to part-time work in general field administration, and John B. Ketcham was called as his associate director.

The joint staff met on December 1, and the ICFC on December 2. Dr. King had now retired, having been succeeded December 1, 1937, by Dr. Mark A. Dawber. It was voted to appoint a subcommittee to study and report at the next meeting on the possibilities of developing a Joint Field Department for two or more of the councils. Dr.

Hermann N. Morse was elected ICFC chairman. (Dr. Morse, long the executive of the Board of National Missions of the Presbyterian Church, USA, brought to this post, and later as secretary of the Planning Committee for the National Council, a breadth of knowledge and depth of wisdom, along with an abundance of good humor, that made all his utterances and writings a tremendous contribution to church cooperation at every level.) At this ICFC meeting there was discussion of the United Christian Advance and of the Christian Adult Movement.

December 16 to 20, 1937, a special conference called by the ECOA convened 27 state and city council executives and ICRE leaders (39 regrets). The ECOA also met in Chicago on February 8, 1938, with 40 present. Dr. Ross said, in summarizing the discussion: "The relationship of the state and national work interdenominationally ought to be comparable in close-knit fellowship and in service to that which exists in the national denominational staff and the state denominational staff. . . . The time must come when all the state and city secretaries will meet with the International Council staff and face the interdenominational task together. In no other way can we succeed."

By February the suggestion[75] was made that the secretaries might well meet in or near Columbus, in connection with the ICRE Convention, rather than at Lake Geneva, with at least one period for each group (AES and ECOA), and some joint emphasis on theology! By March 5 this suggestion crystallized into a call for joint sessions at Otterbein College, Westerville, Ohio, for 3½ days, at a cost of $5.00 for room and board.

Early in 1938[76] it was announced that Dr. J. Quinter Miller would head the FC field program, to begin, part-time, on September 1. He actually got started on September 15, also continuing in Connecticut for a time. Because of his interest in religious education, his appointment was particularly happy. The ICFC met April 21, 1938; the next day, with 17 present, F. L. Knapp was made executive secretary. No action was taken as to a suggested bulletin. Revised proposals for the preliminary organization of an Inter-Council Field Department (ICFD) were adopted.

At Otterbein on July 5 the ECOA elected W. T. Clemens of New York State as its president. A June 30 balance amounted to $102.01. A joint meeting at Lake Geneva in 1939 was approved, with invitations to national staff people—denominational and interdenominational; and the NCFCW was to hold its annual conference on adjoining dates. A repetition of the February meeting in Chicago was not favored.

The AES met simultaneously, electing J. Henry Carpenter of Brooklyn as president; Dr. Guild was present. Dr. H. Paul Douglass spoke on the "new ecumenical note." Increased Sunday school attendance was reported. Pensions were again up for discussion. Should the new organization include lay persons? What about relationships to the FC? Was a new manual of cooperation needed? The need of a new financial policy for the AES was pointed out. Joint sessions at Lake Geneva in 1939 were approved. Probably a merger of the two groups could have been voted at this 1938 session—but not unanimously. Two years more were needed to make the action a wholehearted one.

On December 6 to 8, at the Buffalo Statler, six field secretaries of the FC, HMC, CCW, and ICRE, met; on the 9th the ICFC met. Action of the agencies on proposals for preliminary organization was reported. There was tentative definition of functions, relationships, staff functions and responsibility, and frequency of meetings; also as to the relation of the proposed department to other phases of the work of the cooperating agencies.

"Experiences in Cooperation" came out in a mimeographed edition on June 30, 1939; to be issued again, in printed revised form, functionally arranged, in 1941.

On February 9 and 10 in Chicago the ICRE Committee on Field Program met, and was continued; but it transferred all possible functions to the ICFD. The March *FC Bulletin* notes that the ICRE had approved the ICFD.

Thirty AES and 31 ECOA members met at Conference Point as part of a "National Conference of the Employed Staffs of Interdenominational Agencies, July 2 to 7," attended by a total of 74 persons, including guests. The ECOA showed a balance of $104.91; $84.13 was due on bills outstanding. Frank Jennings of Massachusetts was elected president. The AES, which showed a balance of $466.73, elected Harlan M. Frost of Toledo as president, and Evah Lane of Kansas City as secretary. Plans for the possible merger of the two professional organizations were now implemented, to become effective in 1940. Much of the discussion had to do with program emphases; and it was discovered that the interests of the two organizations overlapped so much that joint consideration of many issues was desirable and more or less inevitable.

Inter-Council Field Department (ICFD), 1939-1950

On October 5, 1939, was held the first session of the ICFD, succeeding the less formal ICFC. Attendance indicated interest; eight councils, entitled to from three to a dozen representatives, or a total of 47 persons, were actually represented by 41 people; each council had at least one person present, and regrets were received from ten absentees. The work of the ICFC from July 1, 1935, was reviewed. By February 1937 nineteen major projects had been considered. A definite plan for the ICFD was proposed in April 1938 for a suggested experimental period of two years.[77] "The state, city, and local councils of churches now have an affiliated relationship through which more democratic sharing in policy and program-making is possible. With them we maintain the type of harmonious cooperation resulting between two or more completely free and autonomous agencies that mutually recognize and serve a common purpose and program." Six possible functions of the ICFD were[78] voted, and it was decided that the emphasis for the next two years be "Making Ecumenicity Local."

Association of Council Secretaries (ACS), 1940

The grass-roots personnel had also been getting together. The year 1940 was noteworthy for the merger of the ECOA and the AES into the Association of Council Secretaries, which held its first meeting as an integrated professional group in July. Though this "historic occasion" was more than ten years before the national unification was to take place, it had already been preceded, as we have observed, by seven years of inter-agency conference and by six years of staff unification with reference to national field outreach. The pressure of their common interest in the field task was bringing together the national interdenominational agencies. A 1938 overture from the General Assembly of the Presbyterian Church, USA (not previously mentioned) had greatly accelerated the impulses toward closer national relationships, and was to result in formal processes beginning in 1941.

Meanwhile the state and local base was being securely built. In 1931 there had been 49 city councils; by 1939 there were 52. In 1940 there were 58 cities listed as served by city or state councils; and 22 state councils with paid executives, serving 23 states. The state situation had advanced much more rapidly—partly through necessity, largely through the concentrated, cooperative effort of the national agencies of interdenominational cooperation. The inevitable result of the development of inclusive state councils was to be a rapid increase in city and county councils of churches. Many county councils of religious education expanded their horizons and became inclusive councils of churches. Not all of these survived, as the fluctuations in national totals make evident.

176

In Chicago, February 5 to 10, the Executive Committee of the ICRE was " 'not as yet convinced of the desirability or practicability of the proposal for union in a single corporate body.' It expressed its approval, however, of cooperation with the FC and other agencies in all matters of common interest, and appointed a committee to study relationships, with the proviso that this did not involve any committal to actual union."[79] Differences in tempo were involved, but the trend continued to be unmistakable. The inherent tension between cooperation and union was as clear among interdenominational bodies as among denominational.

On February 7 and 8, 1940, the ICRE Committee on Field Program (CFP) heard from Dr. J. Quinter Miller a verbal report of the first meeting of the ICFD in October 1939 and its staff council; of its functions and procedures. Mr. Ketcham reviewed the functions already transferred to the ICFD and the remaining tasks of the CFP. A study of the whole field situation inevitably involved the question of the overlapping of denominational and interdenominational field activities. The ICRE CFP met again April 12 and 13 in Chicago.

The ICFD held its second meeting at the Stevens Hotel, Chicago, April 15 and 16, 1940.[80] A revised statement of its functions and procedures was given careful consideration, and referred to the member agencies. A study of national interdenominational pamphlet literature, its production and distribution, was authorized. Numerous field reports were made. Coordination of professional field service was again discussed, and calendar clearance procedures. The preparation of volunteer field leadership was given attention. Sample constitutions, for councils without paid leadership, were discussed.

On April 17 the Inter-Council Field Staff (five present) considered how to get clearance for "tools," etc. It was agreed that each council would make such use as it could of materials issued by the others.

On May 24 the Joint Committee of the AES and the ECOA met to consider a proposed ACS Constitution and the reasons for a merged professional association. On June 3, as part of the FC appraisal, Ralph C. McAfee, now returned to the pastorate, sent out a letter of inquiry. One four-page reply, dated June 6, from this writer, ventured the opinion that "Protestants do not and cannot understand the maze of interdenominational overhead. We must move as rapidly as possible toward a single federal structure in America." It was little realized that even with "a single structure" the "maze" would still be present, inevitably and desirably.

In connection with the National Conference of the Employed Staffs of Interdenominational Agencies, July 8 to 13, 1940, at Conference Point, 53 persons were in attendance at the first session of the Association of Council Secretaries (the ACS, merging the AES and ECOA). Eight of these represented state bodies; nine other states had city council personnel present; twenty cities were represented by 24 secretaries; four national councils had a total of 17 persons in attendance. O. M. Walton of Cleveland and Evah Lane of Kansas City, Mo., were elected president and secretary. The ECOA had a July 10 balance of $124.86; the AES, August 1, $238.01.

Dean Weigle (seminar on "The Christian Community") and Miss Ruth Seabury ("Building the World Christian Community") were conference leaders. Various matters were referred to the ICFD, including the circulation of four significant papers. "The development of the Association of Council Secretaries is closely associated with the Conference Point Camp at Lake Geneva."[81] That which had started out with complex and competitive origins was now seen to be a unity of distinguishable but closely inter-related interests. Party lines, as expressed in the former professional organizations, had almost vanished; and the merger was now speedily effected, with little or no opposition.

At its September 27 and 28 meeting in New York, the ICFD continued Dr. Morse as chairman, and named Rev. John B. Ketcham as secretary.

Merger, First Stage, Accomplished

From 1932 to 1950 there was marked consolidation and steady, slowly accelerating growth in the council movement, until the organization of the National Council of Churches in 1950. The year 1940 had been significant in that the unification of state and local leadership, and much of the national, in a single professional organization, had been achieved. Along with this perhaps as one cause of it—in any case as an accompaniment of it, in part the occasion and in part the effect of it—had come the consolidation of a variety of national field approaches. The merging 1930's, with their strengthening of the state councils, were now giving way to the expectant 1940's with their even more vigorous and unified field promotion.

This new thrust was again accelerated by events outside the ordinary life of parishes, local communities, or even states and commonwealths. On September 1, 1939, Hitler, long regarded as a nuisance, attacked Poland; in 1940 his forces invaded Denmark, Norway, the Low Countries, and France. The second World War was no longer "phony." The world was breaking up, but church forces were getting together.

178

REFERENCE NOTES

Chapter VII

1 Letter of AES President, George L. Ford, March 28, 1932.
2 FC *1932 Report,* p. 265.
3 *Ibid.,* p. 270.
4 (Probably) in his report to the Advisory Committee, October 28, 1932.
5 Thos. Nelson & Sons.
6 Yale University Press.
7 Harper, xv, 349 pp.
8 Rich, *op. cit.,* p. 13.
9 See 1932 *FC Report,* pp. 92 ff.
10 See "Highlights" of the AES 1933 Meeting, including brief summary of this writer's study of church federation finances that year.
11 *FC Bulletin,* October, 1918.
12 *Ibid.,* December, 1921; January, 1922; May-June, 1926.
13 *Ibid.,* December, 1922; January, 1923. (*Cf.* also AES 1923 finding, reaffirmed in 1924.)
14 *Ibid.,* January, 1927.
15 *Ibid.,* March-April, 1926.
16 *Ibid.,* April, 1930.
17 Paper No. 6 (6 pp.) at the 1933 AES, by this writer.
18 *FC Bulletin,* May, 1932.
19 *Ibid.,* September, 1931.
20 *Ibid.,* January, 1933 editorial.
21 Guild memo, November 15, 1933.
22 *IJRE,* March, 1931.
23 Letter to Dr. Guild, March 4, 1933.
24 *IJRE,* December, 1933.
25 FCB, February, 1934.
26 *Cf.* this writer's "Toward Still More Effective Councils of Churches" (in Seattle and Washington), 1958, pp. 14-17. Will new conditions argue in favor of a separate organization for Baltimore?
27 See Appendix II for additional state council developments.
28 *IJRE,* December, 1934.
29 *IJRE,* September, 1935.
30 *IJRE,* February, 1940.
31 *IJRE,* May & September, 1933.
32 *IJRE,* March, 1935.
33 *Ibid.*
34 *IJRE,* July, 1935.
35 *IJRE,* September, 1935.
36 FCB, December, 1938.
37 *IJRE,* December, 1927.
38 *IJRE,* September, 1932.
39 *IJRE,* October, 1931; September, 1934.
40 *IJRE,* January, 1936.
41 *IJRE,* May, 1940.
42 *IJRE,* October, 1940.

43 A few instances of personnel changes will illustrate:
September, 1931: Paul H. Vieth goes from the ICRE to Yale; New Jersey is fruitfully experimenting with a "cooperating Staff" made up of denominational religious education workers whose services are made available interdenominationally. (But the New Jersey merger was not effected until 1945.)
October, 1931: Myron C. Settle goes to Kansas.

December, 1934: Robert W. Searle succeeds W. B. Millar in the Greater New York Federation.
February, 1935: Wilbur T. Clemens succeeds W. G. Landes in New York State.
April, 1935: E. E. Halpenny resigns in Michigan, Ione Catton becomes acting secretary.
May, 1935: J. W. McDonald, former Presbytery executive, begins service in Kansas City, Mo.
November, 1935: Frank Jennings goes to Massachusetts.
January, 1936: A. T. Arnold of Ohio "has spent more years in interdenominational work than any person now living and more than any one who has ever lived" 43 in Illinois, West Virginia, and Ohio.
November, 1938: I. George Nace (later of DHM, NCC) had now gone from the pastorate, after service in Japan, to Portland and Oregon.

44 *FC Bulletin,* September, 1929, pp. 20, 21. See also Minutes of Extension Committee, March 21, 1929 and February 28, 1930; and of AES Executive Committee, October 23, 1930.

45 Personal letter, Dr. Zahniser to Dr. Guild.

46 *Cf.* the *FC Quadrennial Report,* 1928-1932, pp. 92-101.

47 FC *1932 Report,* pp. 7, 36.

48 See *International Journal,* October, 1930.

49 Personal letter to Dr. Guild, January 1, 1933.

50 The *FC Bulletin,* March, 1933, carried a half-page article, "Toward Fuller Co-operation in State Areas," with Dr. Magill's full approval.

51 FC *1933 Report,* p. 113.

52 *International Journal,* April, 1933.

53 Dr. Guild's 1933 Report.

54 December 12, 1933. *Cf.* Dr. Guild's December 30, 1933 general letter.

55 Informal Conference, December 21, 1933. Adjournment to March, 1934.

56 *FC 1933 Report,* pp. 34-36.

57 Handy, *op. cit.,* p. 151.

58 See *IJRE,* April, 1934; cf. also, *IJRE,* November, 1940: "Another Milestone—Recent Developments of the UCYM," by Ivan M. Gould; also *IJRE,* December, 1959, pp. 6 ff.: "The Five Stages of the UCYM," a history of its first 25 years, with pictures of executive staff members—"I. The Idealistic Period," "II. The Period of Reappraisal," "III. The Theological Period," "IV. The Ecclesiastical Period," "V. The Period of Dialogue." Obviously this too is a phase of this history that deserves a whole chapter, or even a separate volume. Any adequate treatment of youth work would also give extended attention to the noteworthy achievement under the leadership of John L. Alexander, in relation to subsequent significant contributions of the Danforth Foundation.

59 See late 1934 issues of the *Journal.*

60 The April 1935 *Journal* said, "The Fellowship of Christian Workers has been made entirely local in its administration."

61 *Cf.* Chapter II. See Hayden L. Stright's historical statement in the 1954 AES Minutes.

62 Dr. Munro in particular faithfully sounded this warning note.

63 "Biennial Report" of the FC Field Department.

[64] FC Field Department memo, January, 1935.

[65] See Minutes and Findings of this meeting, Finding No. 9, p. 3.

[66] Personal letter.

[67] *Cf. International Journal*, July, 1935; also *ibid.*, September, 1935, p. 22—"Council Staffs in Joint Conference."

[68] Minutes of ICFC, July 1, 1935.

[69] P. 5 of 8-page. "Working Document," ICFC, April 13, 14, 1936.

[70] AES 1935 Minutes, p. 8—Executive Committee Session.

[71] *International Journal,* September, 1935.

[72] *Ibid.,* April, 1936.

[73] P. 4, item 5a, of the Minutes of the ICFC meeting.

[74] *FC 1936 Report,* p. 70.

[75] Forrest L. Knapp to ECOA members.

[76] *FC Bulletin,* April, 1938.

[77] J. Quinter Miller to the FC.

[78] Dr. Knapp to Dr. Miller.

[79] *FC Bulletin,* March, 1938. The April 1940 *Journal* reported the attendance of 947 members of professional and advisory sections, nearly 200 religious education students, and 152 other visitors.

[80] *Cf.* the *International Journal,* June 1940, "National Inter-Church Council Relationships," a statement by the ICRE General Secretary, recording the February 10 action. See 27 pp. of Minutes.

[81] *Cf.* Note (61) above.

CHAPTER VIII

The Expectant Forties

Planet Shrinks, Councils Consolidate

With consolidation of church cooperation forces now "just around the corner," the whole movement pushed forward vigorously during the 1940's. This chapter will sketch first the enlargement of the professional fellowship of local, state, and national executives; and will then turn to national and world developments, interspersed with instances of the state and local cooperative enterprise.

The "New Order" Enlarges Its Fellowship

A week after Hitler invaded Russia, the ACS met, June 20 to July 5, 1941, at Conference Point, in its first annual meeting as a unified body. Those attending included 36 city, 19 national, and 11 state secretaries; these with wives, special leaders, and others, made a total of 84 persons. Various ICRE papers were presented, and also documents on "Missions in Local Councils," "Field Program and Research," and other topics. It was felt that "a definite foundation of conviction (should be) brought to the committee on arrangements and also to the conference on relations of interdenominational agencies, expressing the mind of state and city executives with respect to plans for any new all-inclusive interdenominational agency, and that we should be represented on the committee and at the conference meeting at Atlantic City in December." It was accordingly voted to "refer to the executive committee for study, consultation, and report, the question of how the city, county, and state secretaries can be given more responsibility for national program building and time schedules." John W. Harms was elected president and this writer vice-president in charge of the 1942 program.

Dr. J. Quinter Miller, reporting for the ICFD, pointed out the staff lists now printed in the *Year Book of American Churches*. The origins of what was later to be the Committee for Cooperative Field Research emerge in a suggestion that the ICFD might make available survey and research field service.

Program personnel in 1941 included Dr. E. Stanley Jones (three addresses), Dr. Toyohika Kagawa (two addresses), and Dr. Chester S. Miao of China. In the light of the world situation the friendly relation between these two Christians from the Far East was especially significant. Dr. F. Ernest Johnson presented "Current Theological Trends"—a new emphasis for ecclesiastical technicians. Other significant items crowded a particularly opulent program.

A previous balance of $355.12 was now reduced to $252.59 (including $69 already paid in 1941-2); expenditures for the year ($607.31) had exceeded income ($435.78) by $171.53. Dues had been paid by 56 local, 29 state, and 32 national persons, and by two associate members; contributions had been received from 26 local, 13 state, and 4 national councils. Thus, 119 persons and 43 organizations had helped financially.

From June 28 to July 3, 1942, at Conference Point, the second annual session of the ACS[1] again attracted more than 80 persons. A balance of $218.90 was reported. Under the leadership of Dr. W. C. Bower, the chief seminar considered "Tensions in American Life Today," "The Reconciling Ministry or Function of the Church," and "Tension and Condition of Creative Thinking and Growing Values." In response to 165 queries sent out by O. M. Walton, 37 replies furnished significant "Facts and Figures." J. Quinter Miller presented the "Plan Book" for discussion as an initial step in showing how American cooperative Christianity was "Moving Forward Together." Inevitably a major concern was "The Ministry of the Church in Wartime."[2] Soon the emphasis would be shifting to returning service men, demobilization, and post-war activities; but meanwhile the war years had to be lived through, in increasing realization of the availability of terrifying new powers of destruction. Hugh C. Burr was elected president, Harry W. Becker of Missouri vice president and program chairman.[3]

The ACS, augmented by church workers in camp and defense communities, in the United Christian Adult Movement, and in Indian schools, met June 28 to July 3, 1943, at Conference Point. A total of 102 local, state, and national executives were present. J. Burt Bouwman of Michigan was elected president, with John W. Meloy of Wichita and E. C. Farnham of Los Angeles as vice presidents in charge of program and membership. On July 2 "The Stake of States and Cities in the New (National) Organization" was considered. As Dr. Harms put it, "the ACS desired representation in the policy-making processes of the organization. The basic philosophy developed in the discussion," he asserted, "is that the whole matter rests on the assumption that territorial councils are as valid ecclesiastical bodies as the national denominational bodies." This would appear to be an assertion or assumption most congenial to the typical ACS member, but not yet fully established in the mind of many denominational leaders without experience in interdenominational cooperation at the state and local levels. On the other hand, it is obvious that the measure of participation in the policy-forming process by members of the ACS, and probably by the Association as a whole, had been considerable. On June 30, 1943, a first draft of a report of a significant committee was presented to the ACS under the title "Toward a More Ecumenical Church." In a greatly revised form, this committee issued an article in the Autumn 1944[4] number of *Christendom* on "The Philosophy of Church Cooperation" by this writer.

June 19 to 22, 1944, the ACS, again augmented by workers in Camp and Defense Communities, met at Conference Point, with 89 city, state, and national executives present. E. C. Farnham was advanced to the presidency; and Willis R. Ford of Baltimore elected Program Chairman, a new position in its own right. A panel of a dozen, with eleven alternates, was elected to represent the ACS at the Federal Council. Dr. Hermann N. Morse lectured on "The Church's Task, How to Face It Cooperatively." Evening joint sessions were devoted to anticipating "The Church's Ministry to Post-War Needs." A "Primer for New Secretaries" began a series of helpful annual documents, intended to inform and inspire new workers. Paid ACS membership was now approximately 150, and there was a cash balance of about $1,100.

Because of war-time transportation restrictions, the 1945 ACS annual meeting was cancelled, and its officers continued. But 44 were present at a midwest regional conference at Conference Point June 19 to 22, when Dr. Harms read a close-packed paper on "The Relations of the Denominations to One Another through Councils of Churches"; and 62 staff persons gathered in the western area December 10 and 11.

The ACS[5] and workers among Indians met July 12 to 22, 1946, at Conference Point, and considered "Corporate Functions of the Church in the Community." Attendance totaled 225 in the evenings.[6] No roll seems to have been kept, and no finance report appears to be available; but the treasurer had a balance of $1,606.64, probably subject to reduction by accounts payable. Officers elected included J. Henry Carpenter, of Brooklyn, as president; and Hughbert Landram, then of San Francisco, as program chairman.

The June 16-21, 1947, ACS meeting was combined with a Conference on "The Church and Urban Life." Harry C. Munro made a report on "An Integrated Protestant Strategy," involving both denominational and council approaches. Certain "Suggested Normative Principles," first reported at the April 1947 ICFD meeting, were further reviewed. Receipts for the ACS year, exclusive of the $857.91 balance after the previous annual meeting, amounted to $1,423.98; this provided a balance on hand of $1,611.19, reduced to $465.79 when all accounts were paid. Expenses for 1946-7 seem to have exceeded receipts by $392.12. Willis R. Ford of Baltimore was elected president, Oliver B. Gordon of Philadelphia program chairman.

The ACS met as usual at Conference Point June 21 to 26, 1948, to discuss "Man's Disorder and God's Design in the Community"— in the effort to make ecumenicity local. Dr. H. Paul Douglass (ably reported by Lemuel Peterson, now of Seattle) spoke on "The Philosophy of the Community." "The Theology of the Community," and "The Sociology of the Community." Vesper talks by Dr. Ansley Moore of Pittsburgh were specially helpful. Seminar groups were organized.

City and county experiences in the field of social education and action in Los Angeles, Philadelphia, Cleveland, Indianapolis, Louisville, Scranton, New York, Columbus, and Cincinnati were cited. Cincinnati ventured the opinion that "the Protestant vice is revolutionitis, which accomplishes nothing." Similar reports were made on other functions.

One session was devoted to state and regional work, with particular consideration given to state councils and the denominations, and to state councils and local councils.

Dr. Earl F. Adams spoke on the representation of state and city councils in the NCC. Though J. Henry Carpenter (Brooklyn) insisted that "We need local men in the planning of national projects," Alton M. Motter (St. Paul) was sure that his denomination (Lutheran) would oppose such representation in the framework of the Federal Council. Dr. Miller explained the importance of action that was "constitutionally responsible." A panel of 18, representing eight denominations (Baptist, Congregational, Christian, Disciples, Evangelical and Reformed, Methodist, Presbyterian USA, Presbyterian US, and United Presbyterian), were elected as FC representatives. It was voted that the ACS take steps immediately to study relationships to the new NCC with reference to program, structure, and finances, through a committee to be appointed by the new executive committee, consisting of three city and three state executives, this committee to seek suitable representation of local, city, and state councils on the national planning committee. An effort was to be made to get denominational participation in the 1949 ACS sessions. A 1948 preconference orientation session

185

had involved 21 secretaries and staff persons, more than the total attendance at the early AES gatherings. (The ICRE had also held a special conference on co-operative education, preceding the ACS.)[7] An attendance of 168 persons was recorded, with 30 regrets. Balances for a three-year period show a healthy state of ACS finances:

July 15, 1946	$857.91
July 24, 1947	465.79
July 26, 1948	671.97

Henry Reed Bowen of New Jersey was elected president, and Harvey W. Hollis of Albany, N.Y., program chairman.

In June 1949 the ICRE again had a special conference on co-operative education, and the June 20-25 1949 meetings of the ACS were also preceded by a conference of field researchers. Dr. W. E. Garrison was headliner at the ACS, presenting six lectures on the "Implications of the Amsterdam Covenant." Three men (Burr, Jennings, and Bowen) were named to the Planning Committee, and Burr was made chairman of the ACS panel on the NCC. As Burr put it, "Double representation (was) not yet fully understood (and) indirect representation (was) not entirely familiar or as yet entirely acceptable." The United Church Women were urged to join the NCC.

Organizations paying ACS dues numbered 96; individuals, 194. A June 21 balance of $2,434.61 was reduced to $1,349.65 by June 30. A budget of $2,000 was referred to the Executive Committee. The final attendance total was 218, of whom 36 were visitors. Scores of absentees had paid dues. Dr. Gertrude L. Apel of Seattle was elected president; Dr. G. Merrill Lenox of Detroit program chairman.

June 19 to 24, 1950, the ACS was led by Dr. Glenn W. Moore in the consideration of "Upbuilding the Body of Christ through Co-operation," while Dr. Roswell P. Barnes presented "Church and State —the Real Issues." Receipts from 101 organizations had amounted to $1,663.35 (38 organizations did not pay); from 214 individuals, $534.00. Including the previous balance, total receipts had amounted to $3,576.16, expenses to $2,083.21; there was thus a July 1 balance of $1,492.95. A total attendance of 225 was recorded, with a detailed roll and mail addresses; 78 of these were guests or visitors. Among professionals, city and local leaders numbered 99; national, 50; state, 15. There were 23 regrets and cancellations, while 59 not present paid dues. A 1950-51 budget of $2,100 was approved. A 27-page primer was provided for new council secretaries. Ten regular and ten alternate representatives to the NCC were nominated; also seven persons, with alternates, to the Central Department of Field Administration, and five to the Central Department of Research and Survey. The 1951 Boston University summer course was commended. A resolution regarding principles of relationships for city, state, and national interdenominational agencies was referred to the Central Department of Field Administration for action. Lists of directors of Christian education and of social welfare were to be checked, with a view to widening the invitation to ACS sessions. A Social Welfare Group passed significant resolutions. Hugh C. Burr of Rochester was elected president; and Forrest C. Weir of Atlanta program chairman. Both were included among those named to the Central Department of Field Administration. In the September 1950 *Bulletin* Dr. Miller had a page and a half about this ACS meeting, entitled "Fellowship of Kindred Minds."

Consolidation Accelerates

Like World War I, World War II only tardily involved America. Hitler had lit a match to the world in 1939, and the conflagration was not to be put out until 1945; but for two years we seemed not to be involved as active combatants. But at the end of 1941 the Inter-Council Field Staff noted that "the shadows of war darken the horizon of 1942."

Just as a "chief positive result of the war was the formation of the United Nations,"[8] so the cooperative unifications of the denominations, at least as difficult a matter, already begun, was to be accelerated by international happenings. Depression and war—both world-wide—were making it crystal clear that a parochial or sectarian type of organized religion was outmoded on our shrinking planet. The necessities of cultural change were fuel for the fires of ecumenical zeal. Therefore, when an Inter-Council Committee on Closer Relationships met on April 18, 1941, the world situation re-enforced the overtures already made, denominationally and interdenominationally. To prophetic minds and spiritual insight the meaning of the world drama was clear, but now a whole series of ecclesiastical chores must be patiently accomplished.

At Atlantic City on December 8, 1941, the day after Pearl Harbor, a conference of delegations from eight national interdenominational agencies[9] "came to the clear conviction that closer cooperation is essential to the ecumenical movement in America." On the 9th, 10th, and 11th, under the chairmanship of Dean Luther A. Weigle of Yale, with Dr. Hermann N. Morse, as secretary, the Atlantic City Conference on Closer Relationships of General Interdenominational Agencies moved toward a more inclusive cooperative organization. "The Conference began its sessions on Tuesday, December 9, at a moment when the nations, through the declaration of war, had been welded into a visible unity by a great national emergency."[10] The ACS was here represented by seven state and local men; and Rochester's "Hugh Burr made an eloquent plea for a recognition of the necessity for the unification of interdenominational service nationally in order to meet more adequately the needs emerging in the local community."

The Committee on Further Procedures, with the same officers, now took up, to carry through to its completion in less than a decade, the ecclesiastical portion of the task that the Federal Council's Commission on Federated Movements had dimly glimpsed a quarter of a century earlier, and that the Federal Council had shelved until it could establish stronger beach-heads in the community life of the nation. This new committee convened on April 12, 1943; on July 1 it issued a printed report (revised April 25, 1944). By early 1944 the religious and secular press were able to report actions favorable to the merger of the national interdenominational bodies. Throughout the decade the consolidation of the interdenominational agencies in the nation was to proceed steadily, with a long record of tactical detail to implement an increasingly determined ecumenical strategy. As one of many aspects of this process, the ACS executive committee, as well as the entire ACS, would give increasing attention to the question of relationships, particularly of state and local councils to the emerging National Council.

Conciliar Experiments in Cooperative Churchmanship

For times like these the Council movement felt itself to be providential. February 10, 1941, at a fellowship dinner in Chicago, attended by 69 members of the ACS, as specific purposes for 1941 "it was proposed (1) to cement finally into one fellowship the professional religious education and the general interdenominational field workers of America; and (2) to achieve a sense of direction for the future and to make progress in clarifying the purpose and function of the new association." A revised statement for the 1941 ACS meeting included a definition of "The central purpose (of the ACS) to be progressively realized: to achieve a functional unity in the development and projection of a comprehensive strategy for Protestant or non-Roman Catholic Christianity in America. To this end, the annual meeting of the ACS should at once be the occasion when a two-way clearance is made between national agencies and the secretaries regarding program and promotional plans for the ensuing year; and ultimately, it should be the occasion for the expression of as much unity among city, state, national, and international agencies as may progressively develop."[11] "The Intercouncil Field Department should be asked to assume definite

188

responsibility in cooperation with the program committee for the ACS's summer conference; and the staff of the ICFD should be asked to provide executive leadership."[12] "The program shall have the proper balance between two types of consideration: (1) the more or less fundamental long-range problems, and (2) the more immediately practical and operative problems."[13]

Clearly the ACS felt itself to be important in the evolving ecumenical process, was seeking to arrive at self-conscious participation in it, but was aware of its limitations as a professional group without its own administrative status or executive leadership. Beggars could not always be choosers. Hence the constant interplay that was to develop between the ICFD staff, the ICFD itself, and the ACS. Increasingly the votes and the financial support were to be denominational, at every level. How the servants of the interdenominational agencies at the state and local levels were to be related to the national organization, already in process of formation, was to remain a question even until now. Meanwhile the separate national agencies still needed to make their several plans for field work, and maintain their own structures for consultative purposes.

During this decade the ICRE Committee on Field Program continued to function, usually meeting twice each year, with attendance ranging from five to twenty-two persons varying according to the location of the sessions and averaging a dozen members. Nearly 30 people showed an interest in this committee's work. Careful minutes were kept, and annual reports made to the Education Commission. Many working documents were considered, covering such interests as the viewpoints, policies, procedures, and organizational structures of the cooperating denominations, the tasks of the field executives in religious education, the particular field objectives and functions of the ICRE, how to organize county councils of religious education, the united field approach on the part of the associated national agencies (in preview, practice, and retrospect), and their growing unity as exemplified in the ICFD.

On February 13, 1941, at the meeting of the ICRE Committee on Field Program, 22 persons considered and rejected a regional staff plan for the ICRE alone, favored regional experimentation in the upper Mississippi Valley, talked about the more adequate denominational financing of state councils, and authorized cooperation with the ICFD for an additional year. In March "Christian Education in Unified Councils" was approved for experimental use, and a study of city councils approved for report to the ACS.

189

On the other hand, the Federal Council seems not to have held separate sessions of its Department of Field Administration, but to have deliberately concentrated on making the ICFD an increasingly effective instrument for unifying the field approach of all the merging national agencies. The Federal Council seems to have regarded its field service as "largely coterminous with the ICFD," and even its 1940 report had pointed out that "most of the field services of the (Federal) Council (had) been conducted in partnership with the seven national interdenominational organizations which (had) authorized the formation of the ICFD" in 1939.

The resources of the Federal Council's Department of Field Administration, and its responsibilities, greatly increased during this decade. Its budget, which was only $10,000 in 1940, had become $17,500 by 1948, in its general fund alone. Receipts from individuals, organizations, and denominations for the general fund ranged from less than $2,000 in 1940 to a high of nearly $8,000. They totaled nearly $51,000 in eleven years, but covered only 30.5 percent of the Department's regular budget. If there is to be fiddling in the field, somebody must pay the fiddler.

The cumulative thinking of the ICRE is shown by two editorials in the *Journal*. In April 1942 it was reported that "The Council wholeheartedly endorsed the proposed plan looking to closer relationships with seven other interchurch agencies. . . . If these plans are finally completed, there will be one general interdenominational body representing the united work of the Protestant churches in America." A year later it was said that 1942 "will be known as the year when the ICRE committed itself officially to the general direction being worked out for bringing together into one agency the eight separate national interchurch agencies in the country . . . after several years of most earnest consideration."

Church Women Build Their Divisional Unit in the Coming NCC

The saga of the Protestant woman in America now moved to a long-awaited climax. On December 11-13, 1941, at an Atlantic City constituting convention, "after three days of frank and amazingly friendly discussions there emerged a plan and outline of program for the United Council of Church Women which was to further the work of the National Council of Church Women and to continue the established relationships with the FMC and HMC, and to be a channel for the power of 10,000,000 Protestant Women working together on a local, state, and national level to do those things that no single denominational group of women can do alone." "It seeks to establish a local council of church women in every community. It sponsors the World Day of Prayer on the first Friday of Lent, May Fellowship Day on the first Friday in May, and World Community Day on the first Friday in November. It seeks to inspire Christian women in all communities to study the non-Christian forces of these communities and to oppose them by all means in their power; it seeks to cooperate with the national and foreign mission agencies in further programs of world evangelization." Its purpose, according to its constitution, is "to unite women in their allegiance to their Lord and Saviour, Jesus Christ, through a program looking to their integration in the total life and work of the church and to the building of the world community."

This brief chapter can only hint at the rich development of cooperating work among church women, under this new national setup, during the balance of this cumulative decade.[14] In 1942 Mrs. Ruth Mougey Worrell began her six years as UCCW executive secretary. "Her vision, enthusiasm, great devotion, and hard work are largely responsible for (its) rapid growth." In 1943 state council presidents were made members of the UCCW Board. In 1945 the UCCW asked 25 councils to study segregation in their own areas. In 1946 it pledged support of the "Study of Life and Work of Women in the Churches," undertaken by the World Council of Churches, and aid in the dissemination of the results of the study. The 1946 UCCW National Assembly, with the theme, "Until We All Attain unto the Unity of Faith," according to one masculine observer in attendance throughout, marked "the definite emergence of maximum inclusiveness of women's work in the Church—Ladies' Aid, Missionary Society, Temperance Society, Bible classes, Study Groups, Peace Committee, Race Relations, Social Action, Christian Family Life, etc., all welded into one inclusive program as wide as the planet."

In 1948, Mrs. William Murdoch MacLeod became UCCW executive secretary. In 1949 state councils were asked to add a committee to promote world missions; and the forming of an Inter-Faith Committee was recommended to local councils. "After much prayer and careful evaluation," by a vote of 75 to 3 the UCCW Board decided "that the UCCW join with the other national interdenominational organizations in constituting the NCCCUSA," in which it became, in 1950, the General Department of United Church Women. This lay woman's movement has worked through state councils to expand a fellowship carrying a unified program among church women, based on the combined strength of women in each local church. Its meetings have always been without discrimination of race or color. In 1941 there were recog-

191

nized state and local councils of church women in 17 states; [15] by 1950 church women were organized interdenominationally in all 48 states, Hawaii, and the District of Columbia.

"Inter-Council" Paves the Way for the National Council

The ICFD met semiannually throughout the decade, except in 1943, 1945, and 1946, when only one session was held. Scores of people were vitally interested in the work of this interagency group. The ICFD staff held additional sessions, from one to five times a year.

While the Committee on Further Procedures, gradually transformed into a Planning Committee for the NCC, was building the structure of the new inclusive nation-wide interdenominational agency, the ICFD was a prolonged clinic in program planning, clearance, and appraisal. It built up an invaluable fund of experience in the complexities and relationships involved in doing the field job that the National Council was to inherit from its multiple parentage. What happened under the auspices of the ICFD during the decade before 1950 was to prove most determinative not only nationally, but specially to the state and local interdenominational agencies. The one place where local and state council work could be seen even more continuously than at the ACS was the ICFD. In October 1941 the Vieth Appraisal Committee Report on the ICFD assured the continuance of this fruitful experiment, which was regarded as a step in the right direction, but only a step: "Even though efforts for possible closer relations were being made by a committee of representatives of member organizations, this Department represents a necessary intermediate step, and the best preparation for closer relationships when effected."

By 1942 a first inter-agency *Plan Book* was being discussed. So were such topics as "Wartime Necessities" and "Brotherhood and Christian Unity." At the spring ICFD session Dr. Morse gave searching answers to the question, "What are the implications in the Atlantic City Study Conference for the work of the Department?" He regarded the current cooperative approach in the field as entirely too feeble. At the October ICFD meeting it was reported that the ACS had thoroughly considered the proposed (1943-4) *Plan Book,* which was duly issued early in 1943, thanks to the careful work of Miss Sue Weddell of the FMC and Gilbert LeSourd of the MEM.

By early 1943 the staff found that the quantity of program events made it "somewhat difficult to encompass in one (consolidated) report . . . all that is happening." But what Dr. Miller and Mr. Ketcham took turns in summarizing—especially by way of state and local situations—

192

provides valuable data on the development of specific councils, as well as of the total field.[16] At first the eclectic process of endeavoring to use the materials tardily reported by the constituent national agencies, and put together at the last minute for ICFD scrutiny, resulted in considerable duplication. Gradually the unity of the task resulted in earlier and more unified and orderly reporting, and less repetitive, according to editorial processes forged out on the anvil of cooperative experience.

Japanese resettlement was now a major consideration. A "Unified Field Approach" was considered necessary in the interest of "Community Building in Wartime." Attention was accordingly given to interdenominational field services, especially those of a wartime nature; industrial defense centers; and wartime communities. The ICFD as a whole seems not to have met between March 1943 and December 1944.

During these months and years the origin and referral of various proposals and procedures, from the ICFD to the separate national agencies, to the ACS, and back again to the ICFD and its staff, seem cumbersome and complicated. But all this was educative and unifying; and it provided a foretaste of the complexity of "channels" that were bound to develop in any federal movement in a nation as large as ours. Cooperative churchmanship was necessarily much more like the national government, or some huge business corporation, than many of us were at first willing to admit; and more so than many may still be able to perceive. When the ecclesiastical process has once become institutionalized, it is hard to avoid "institutionalism." Perhaps the Church should not try to do so, but only seek to determine the nature of its institutional acts and attitudes.

In October 1943 the ICFD discussed a proposed study of the financing of state and local councils, but referred any action on this matter to the ACS executive committee. Here would seem to be important beginnings of a demand for services now represented so ably in the important financial studies made in recent years by W. P. Buckwalter, Jr.

By the autumn of 1944 expanding programs and budgets were the order of the day in state and local councils. Manuscripts for the first four Church Cooperation pamphlets were up for approval. In December 1944 the ICFD held its first meeting in 21 months. State-wide program planning conferences, using the new *Plan Book,* had been held in Iowa, Maine, Michigan, New Hampshire, New York, West Virginia, and Wisconsin. The process of literature production was formalized, the Church Cooperation Series reviewed. "The Philosophy of Church Cooperation" was further discussed by E. C. Farnham, H. N. Morse, and Harry C. Munro, secretary of the ACS Committee on Philosophy. A long list of local and state council staff changes was submitted at most of these ICFD meetings. The service of Dr. Worth M. Tippy as interim secretary at Springfield, Mass., after similarly acceptable earlier service in Washington, D.C., suggested the question, "Should the ICFD have a staff man available as a pinch hitter in local situations?" In connection with "A Look Ahead," cooperative field research, which had seemed a possibility toward the end of 1941, was now looming as a major opportunity. Of course there was continuous discussion of "Relations—City, State, and National."

At the April 1945 ICFD meeting Dr. Miller presented an up-to-date map of the councils throughout the nation. A new *Directory* was also available. Hugh C. Burr's challenging paper on "Next Steps in Field Organization and Strategy," with contemplated staff enlargement, was referred to the staff. Philosophy was again discussed, but no action taken. At the October 1945 ICFD meeting, after discussion at the ACS, the first steps were taken toward the writing of this history.

A special meeting of the ICFD staff, March 8, 1946, was held, chiefly to consider the proposed southeastern office at Atlanta. Miss Weddell was now to work on the second *Plan Book*. How to continue the *ACS News Letter,* eight issues of which had appeared during the three previous years, was referred to the executive committee. The amount of new personnel and the difficulty in assembling the membership led to the question, "Is the ICFD bogging down?" On the other hand, staff attention was given to five pages of "What's New in the ICFD?" and this material was to be further considered by the ACS.

There appears to have been no meeting of the ICFD between April 1945 and October 1946; but three staff meetings were now reported. By way of suggestion, the ICFD now "Resolved that the ACS petition the eight national interdenominational agencies to take affirmative action at the earliest possible moment concerning the merger to form the National Council of Churches as being highly important to the success of ecumenical relationships on the local level." When "Personnel Service" was carefully reported, those most responsible for it regretted to have to call current procedure inadequate. The number of staff changes was becoming very great. In 1943 new staff appointments had numbered 33; in 1944 they had increased to 62; and in 1945 to 71.

Dr. Wynn C. Fairfield presented a significant paper on "World Christian Fellowship Related to State and Local Councils of Churches." "Foreign" was becoming irrelevant to the local domestic field. Again, at the April 1947 ICFD meeting Dr. Fairfield presented an "Advance Program in Foreign Missions." A number of simultaneous committee sessions considered various phases of the Department's work. The southeastern office was now a reality, and a southwestern office at Dallas was proposed. The Committee for Co-operative Field Research was also a going concern. At the previous meeting Dr. Mark A. Dawber (HMC) indicated that for some time there had been deep concern for a better understanding of the relationships among national, state, and local councils. At this April 1947 session a special committee found itself in substantial agreement with the summary report, "A Study of Principles, Policies, and Procedures Governing the Relationships of Local (City and County), State, and National Interdenominational Councils."

By October 1947 the ACS had requested help from the ICFD in its procedures. Favorable action as to "An Integrated Protestant Strategy for America" was proposed, but referred to a committee of five. Personnel service and a possible statistical summary were considered. In recognition of the latter need a committee was appointed to study possibilities. Field aspects of national agency work and relationships (including those of the YMCA to councils of churches) were discussed. It was recommended that community churches be given a consultative status in state councils.

In April 1948, in reporting to the ICFD replies from 13 communions to six questions concerning joint planning, Dr. Earl F. Adams stated that the situation as regards a Protestant strategy for America was, if anything, more baffling than four years earlier. But progress was noted, and joint planning continued. An important Supreme Court decision as to "released time" was considered. It was felt that the national agencies should everywhere work through the councils in the field. A study of YMCA relationships was based on 75 reports. A Committee on State-National Relationships and Representation was to report to the Committee on Further Procedure. Tentative suggestions for coordinated program, 1948-1952, were considered.

The October 1948 ICFD meeting, while gratified at the 2,200 registrations at the Columbus Assembly of the Foreign Missions Conference, was told by its Committee on a More Integrated Protestant Strategy that it had been able to make little progress. This confusion, however, served only to underscore the need for the National Council of Churches. A conference on a more integrated strategy was authorized. There was now significant cooperation with Church World Service to Displaced Persons.

By April 1949 a committee to study and report on the need of a statistical survey of council financing was authorized; but later in the year the staff decided that it did not then have the resources or facilities to carry on this project.

In holding certain "Little Assemblies" throughout the nation, the FMC had found that there were marked advantages in working through denominational channels in the promotional process at the community level, but that council channels could not be neglected. This was a phase of field activity that had to be learned over and over again. Each new national program emphasis was inclined to ignore the state and local interdenominational structures already existing, and proceed too exclusively through the more familiar denominational channels. On the other hand, some felt that the earlier post-Madras meetings had inadequately utilized denominational resources, while others failed to realize the significance of the partnership of the councils in those gatherings. It was voted to convene a group of denominational leaders to explore further the whole matter of denominational emphases, in relation to a more integrated strategy.

A small committee was authorized to cooperate with the Planning Committee of the National Council in the drafting of by-laws or an operating procedure that would replace the document "Functions and Procedures" of the ICFD.

In October 1949, the proposed by-laws of the new National Council Central Department of Field Administration were considered. Some concern was expressed as to a seeming loss of 33 local and state councils, and the reversion of others from a paid-staff to a volunteer-service basis. A small committee, of which Wilbur C. Parry was later made chairman, was authorized to study procedures for an all-inclusive strategy of developing councils with respect to national sociological groupings. The staff now began to feel that there was need for a more comprehensive pamphlet on the program of a council of churches, and a committee was authorized. The task proved considerable, and required more time than may have been at first realized.

By April 1950 the NCC field budget was up for consideration. A wise paper by Wilbur C. Parry on "Developing Councils of Churches" was referred to a committee for study and revision, possible consideration at ACS, and report back to the ICFD. It was clear that "The value of the work of the present ICFD and much of the work of the new NCCCUSA is dependent on the development of strong councils of churches on both the state and local levels. Councils of churches basically incorporate two elements that, at least in the present church structure, are not found elsewhere. 1. The focus of their concern is the advancement of the Christian experience throughout the entire life of the community. 2. They offer a means by which both clergy and laity (men, women, and young people) come together to face effectively the task of reaching every person with the Christian message. If state and local councils of churches are essential to a complete program of Christian service to the entire life of the community, it is important that the national interchurch agencies perfect a strategy for their further development. They are too important to be allowed to spring up because of the momentary enthusiasm of one or two persons, and possibly die either because of the moving away of those individuals or the failure of those same well-meaning persons to secure the cooperation of others, who would have helped to guarantee broader service and continued existence" on the part of the particular council.

The need for certain specialized national service was suggested: financing, organization and relationships, and counseling with national leaders of the communions.

The ICFD now began to categorize cities and their councils according to population size. The Boston University Summer School on Ecumenical Administration won the joint sponsorship of the ICFD.

At its last session, in October 1950, nominations of state and city council representatives to the NCC were approved for proper presentation, after consultation with the ACS.

Church Cooperation Expands Rapidly

Just how many state and local councils were involved in the field contacts and outreach of the national agencies?

In 1941 there were a total of 247 local and state organizations:
    62 state (CC, CRE, HMC, or SSA).
    98 city and county councils or associations with paid leadership.
    87 city and county, on a volunteer basis.[17]

Beginning about 1942, the directory of state and local councils became more inclusive than before, as a result of more accurate reporting and the assistance of state council offices. A number of councils of religious education devoted chiefly to week-day instruction, and a few larger parishes were now included. The later figures are therefore not strictly comparable with some of the earlier listings. A temporary falling off in the reported number of councils with paid staff, during 1948 and 1949, with signs of recovery in 1950, was a cause for some concern; it suggests that some volunteer organizations may have undertaken to employ staff prematurely. Yet the growth in numbers of councils of churches of all sorts during the decade was remarkable:

Year	Councils of Chs. and of R.E.			Ministerial	Councils (c)
	Pd.Staff	Volunteer	Total	Associations	of Ch. Women
1942	108	162	270	1,400	
1944	127	243 (a)	370	2,176 (b)	1,441
1946	196	439	370		
1947	257	420	677	2,100	1,513
1948	227	485	712	1,775	
1949	214	624	838		
1950	222	699	921	1,827	1,764

(a)   239 in Federal Council annual report.
(b)   Only 1,600 in January; the larger figure seems inflated.
(c)   Includes state and district councils: 51 in 1946; 51 in 1950.

Bower and Hayward reported only seven fully merged state councils in 1938, five expanded councils of religious education, three states with parallel organizations but common staff, and six with only councils of religious education.[18] The number of inclusive state councils in 1941 was 22,[19] while ten additional states had both councils of churches and councils of religious education; two states had only councils of religious education, and five only Sunday school associations. In 1950, there were forty states with inclusive councils, while only Pennsylvania reported two statewide organizations. This increase in state councils was due both to the multiple thrust of various national agencies and to their cooperation in the field. The HMC had done yeoman's work in earlier years. The UCCW was blanketing the nation. Two men in particular pioneered together. Rev. John B. Ketcham (affectionately called "Jack"), elected to ICRE Field Administration in 1937, was first associated with Dr. Knapp; Dr. Miller ("Quinter") joined the FC staff in 1938. At the end of their first decade both could rejoice that the number of state councils of all types had increased by more than half.

In 1942 there were reportedly 270 men and women employed in local and state councils. State and local budgets had increased from

198

a reported total of $1,800,000 in 1941 to $6,100,000 in 1946. From any angle, this was a decade of phenomenal increase in state and local cooperation. Between 1942 and 1950 the number of volunteer state and local councils increased by 331 percent. Among the 699 volunteer local organizations reported in 1950, there were 55 Sunday School Associations, 79 Councils of Religious Education, and 565 Councils of Churches. The total number of state and local organizations increased by 241 percent. Councils with paid staff increased relatively slowly, by only 96 percent; but this appears to have been solid growth, maintained after a tendency to overexpand had spent itself. There had been only 44 inclusive local councils with paid staff in 1941, with both councils of churches and councils of religious education in five additional cities. In addition to 46 local councils of religious education, six Sunday School Associations, and half a dozen larger parishes reported in 1950, there were (counting the four Divisions of the Protestant Council of New York City separately) 121 inclusive local councils with paid staff.

It was this growth at the grassroots that had enabled the ACS to grow correspondingly. The expansion in its resources can easily be indicated:

Persons Paying ACS Dues		Organizations Contributing	Income excluding previous balances	Expended	Balance
1941	119	43	$ 435.78	$ 607.31	$ 252.59
1950	214	101	2,207.35	2,083.21	1,492.95

Accordingly, with five times the income that it had at the beginning of the decade, and nearly six times the balance—because of a great increase in dues paying members and more than double the number of organizational gifts—the ACS found no difficulty in expanding its budget to $2,100 for 1951. Similarly, attendance at the ACS had reached a new high in 1944, when 89 were present; but the figures for the last three years of the decade show how great had been the growth in number and interest:

Year	ACS Attendance
1948	168
1949	218
1950	225

In a single decade attendance had more than quadrupled.

199

We have noted that the ICFD staff found it very difficult to summarize the field situation semiannually. At the ACS meetings the combined national staffs also soon discovered how hard it was to tell "What's New Nationally" in one evening. Fortunately, in state and local council house organs one finds "Ecumenicity Made Local," to quote a *FC Bulletin* editorial. Morover, for years the *Journal* and the *Bulletin* featured "What's Happening" and "News of State and Local Cooperation." An article by Charles P. Taft found the "Growth of State Councils an Encouraging Sign."[20] Typical details, as listed in the *Bulletin* and in the *Journal,* include items like these:

1940. The *Kansas* Council of Religious Education and Council of Churches first appointed a joint committee, then voted to combine under one secretary, Sept. 1, 1940; and effected a merger in 1942.

1941. Colorado began studying a plan of merger, but did not unite its forces until 1950. There was close cooperation among three bodies (Church Federation, Council of Religious Education, and United Church Women) in *Minnesota. North Dakota* projected an integrated program; in 1945 it merged its Superintendents' Council with its Council of Religious Education, but did not have a fully united council until 1949. *Oklahoma's* Council of Religious Education voted to expand, and become an inclusive council in 1942. *South Dakota* leaders organized an inclusive council to be operative "when five denominations and twelve counties approved"; merger plans were completed early in 1943.

1942. Arizona had a new inclusive council. *Denver's* Council of Religious Education, Ministerial Association, and Council of Churches merged, with Harold M. Gilmore as first executive.

1943. Indiana began its inclusive organization, partly as an outgrowth of its annual Pastors' Conferences. The *South Carolina* Fellowship of Churches was organized. *West Virginia* also began its inclusive council. *New York City* organized its interborough Protestant Council, for a time including the Welfare Council, but without the Queens Federation. *New Jersey* considered a merger, moved forward in 1944 and 1945, but seems not to have fully effected it until 1947.

1944. Iowa began its reorganization; the *Montana* Council was revived. The *Virginia* Church Council then included the Council of Religious Education. *New York State* completely liquidated its $22,000 debt.

1945. New Hampshire's Council of Religious Education was expanded, and merged with the Council of Churches. Charles P. McGregor had served the former 21 years; Whitney S. K. Yeaple succeeded him January 1, 1946.

1946. Pennsylvania which had continued to maintain two councils, now experimented with one executive and an interrelated staff and a common headquarters building.

1947. Minnesota's Federation of Churches had ceased to function in 1944, and its Council of Religious Education became inclusive.

1948. "Oregon Council Takes New Life." "Progress in Maine." *Kentucky* organized.

1949. Florida and *Utah* organized.

Local inclusive councils were established in Fort Wayne, Ind. (1941); Portland, Me., Albany, N.Y., and Memphis, Tenn. (1942); Pittsburgh (1944, one stage); Philadelphia (1945); Honolulu, T.H., and Miami, Fla. (1946), and Dallas, Tex. (1949)—to pick only a few samples.[21] An Association of Christian Churches antedated by a decade the Council of Churches of Greater Houston, which was organized in 1950 with representatives from 52 churches of 12 denominations. Washington, D.C., was also studying reorganization.

The St. Louis Church Federation, for which a portion of the YMCA building was set aside by a generous donor, is now (1960) considering a *building* of its own. Illinois dedicated its headquarters in 1941, Buffalo was given its property in 1942. In 1960 there are 30 or more council buildings, some of which include one or more denominational offices, and some have living quarters for their staff leadership. Councils are increasingly making provision for the housing of their executive personnel.

Progress in *Social Service* is marked by such additional staff appointments as those of John L. Mixon in Los Angeles, 1942, after pioneering in Washington, D.C.; Virgil E. Lowder in Chicago, 1943; Dale Dargitz in Buffalo 1946, and Denver 1949. Here is a whole story in itself. Truly, the churches "Need More Trained Leaders in Social Work."[22]

Other examples of program progress, and a steady stream of staff changes, weaving a constantly changing personnel pattern, are recorded from month to month in the columns of the *Bulletin* and *Journal*. Two-thirds of the issues of these magazines yielded significant notes for the compilation of this history—sometimes as many as ten items in a

201

single issue.[23] While interested in the unique and relatively spectacular, these publications gave large stress to local situations in general. The emphasis on "A Common Strategy in the Local Community," stressed by Dr. Cavert's 1946 FC biennial report,[24] continued throughout 1947 in *Bulletin* articles, and the *Journal* gave equal or greater attention to this theme.

World Council Consummated

Toward the end of this decade, at Amsterdam in 1948, after an astoundingly useful prenatal career of world helpfulness, the World Council of Churches, in process of formation for more than a decade (London, 1937; Utrecht, 1938), had become a fully organized reality. Its very existence—though less inclusive than the all-out "closer cooperation" involved in American "closer relationships"—helped to create an atmosphere favorable to interchurch cooperation at every level, everywhere.[25]

The whole religious press was now to make increasingly frequent and generous reference to the ecumenical movement. The baffling 1920's and the merging 1930's had now fully given way to the ecclesiastically expectant 1940's. An October 1948 *Bulletin* editorial traced the encouraging story from the organization of the FC at Philadelphia in 1908, to Amsterdam 1948, when the WCC, first organized as a provisional body ten years earlier, had then been fully established. Said Bishop Oxnam, "I doubt we could have had the WCC without these forty years of FC history."[26]

Great Expectations Fulfilled

A foreword to the final report of the Federal Council rejoiced that "the inauguration of the NC will be the consummation of a decade of effort to bring a more effective unity among the American churches." (Not until late 1949 did the UCCW ratify the proposed NCC; and only in early 1950 did the FMC decide to do so.) Looking back 50 years to 1900 and the organization of the National Federation of Churches, or to 1910 and the Edinburgh Convention, or to the 1937 beginnings of Life and Work and of Faith and Order, a lot of water had run under the bridge. Some of the same forces that had finally brought about the organization of the World Council of Churches had led up to the functionally even more inclusive National Council, which was duly constituted at a convention beginning November 29, 1950, at Cleveland, Ohio. Of course "a whole network of non-

202

American forces were at work in relation to the World Council, while only American forces were involved in the National."[27]

The details of the establishment of this unique and powerful ecumenical body need not here concern us; they are too well-known, too recent, and too obvious in their significance, to require rehearsal in this connection. One wonders if the tremendous growth of local and state councils prior to 1950 was an effect or a cause of the national integration of American interdenominational cooperation? Only at one point was the NCC to be less articulately ecumenical, less broadly representative than the WCC: it included at the outset no formal recognition of "Faith and Order." On the other hand, the WCC was still paralleled by a World Council of Christian Education and by the International Missionary Council. In practical terms, the NCCCUSA represented an attainment in cooperative organization as inclusive as any yet achieved on the planet.

For, like it or not, the horizon of American life, and of its churches, had now become the whole inhabited earth. As C. Howard Hopkins put it,[28] "The decade of the Second World War and its undeclared continuation not only ushered in the atomic age but compressed within its short span the most momentous events of modern history. . . . Disruption of normal life was felt throughout the length and breadth of America. The turmoil following World War II, prolonged by the cold war, was marked by economic readjustment, moral laxity, political corruption, spy-hunting, religious uncertainty, and the rise of militarism." Over against all this, however, loomed "new heights of prosperity." Therefore, while it might naturally be said that the tremendously expectant 1940's would lead into fearsome 1950's, as a matter of actual fact the year 1950 was the beginning of a great new ecumenical impetus, and marked the start of still greater state and local cooperation in American Protestantism.

REFERENCE NOTES

Chapter VII

1 *FC Bulletin,* September, 1942.

2 *Cf.* September, 1942, *FC Bulletin,* "Councils Active in War Service"; also October, 1942, H. Paul Douglass. "The War Emergency and Co-operative Unity"; also, *ibid.,* "The Churches and Defense Communities" and "Wartime Trends."

3 Albert B. Denton of Youngstown, and O. M. Walton, then of Cleveland, were named to the ICRE and FC, respectively.

4 Vol. IX, No. 4.

5 *International Journal,* September, 1946, "ACS Has Inspiring Meeting."

6 *Ibid.*

7 *International Journal,* September, 1948 (nearly a full page); there were present 100 state and local executives from 27 states, D.C. and T.H., to consider a Protestant strategy in Christian education.

8 *The Columbia Viking Desk Encyclopedia,* p. 1379.

9 The ACS had four special representatives present, in addition to one city executive on the FC delegation.

10 *FC Bulletin,* January 1942.

11 Expansion of Paragraph 6 of "General Purposes for the Years Ahead," supplement to ACS 1941 Minutes, "for discussion only."

12 *Ibid.,* item 10, under "Policy as to Specific Aspects of the Annual Program."

13 *Ibid.,* item 11.

14 For year-by-year details, 1942-1949, see Dr. Head's "Forward Together," cited in Chapter III. See also the *International Journal,* February, 1942, *re* the December 1941 organization af the UCCW; also November 1950, "Women's Work in the New NCC" by Mrs. W. Murdoch MacLeod: "Nine short years ago . . ."

15 Councils of Women in 23 states had been listed by the ICFD in March 1941.

16 Later Don F. Pielstick of the HMC and George D. Kelsey, Dr. Miller's Associate in the FC, took their turn at presenting the staff report.

17 *FC 1941 Report,* p. 13.

18 *Op. cit.,* pp. 193, 196.

19 ICFD Minutes, March 24, 25, 1941.

20 *FC Bulletin,* December, 1947.

21 *Cf.* also *FC Bulletin,* January, 1948: 2 columns on the newly organized council in Mifflinsburg, Pa., a town of 2,000; and September 1948, a page on the Queens Federation.

22 *FC Bulletin,* May 1948, editorial.

23 Additional memoranda, not cited in this volume, have been preserved in summary in the Research Notes, filed with the Office for Councils of Churches.

24 *FC 1946 Report,* p. 14.

25 *FC Bulletin,* January, 1948, call to the First Assembly of the World Council of Churches, to be held in Amsterdam in August.

26 *Ibid.,* January, 1949.

27 S. M. Cavert, letter cited. On the other hand, Cate (see Ch. X, note 10) says, "The Federal Council of Churches . . . set the pattern for national, state, and local organizations, plus giving the general pattern for the World Council of Churches."

28 *"The History of the YMCA in North America,"* Assn. Press. 1951, p. 709.

Since 1950, Solid Growth

The Increasingly Ecumenical Atmosphere

With the organization of the National Council of Churches in 1950, many of the goals that had been sought specifically for more than a decade, and implicitly for half a century, had been reached. Interdenominational cooperation was now taken for granted, and the ecclesiastical climate was more favorable than ever before for the organization and maintenance of local and state councils of churches. As one careful writer[1] observes, "Whereas fifty years ago the churches in most communities tended to act unilaterally in all matters, now they usually take it for granted that there are certain functions they will perform in common." The decade now closing has therefore been a time of solid growth for cooperative churchmanship.

AN EXPANDING ENTERPRISE

More State and Local Councils, Especially with Paid Staff

The extent and nature of this growth will be shown if we can answer a few seemingly simple questions: How many councils, state and local, are there? What professional staff do they employ? Where are they located? How much income do they have? What are its chief sources? How are they associated? Just what do these councils do? This chapter seeks to suggest as accurate answers as possible to questions like these, and to show something of the trends since the organization of the National Council of Churches.

Number of State and Local Cooperative Church Organizations

Year	State	Local with paid executives	Volunteer Local Councils	Total Local Pd. & Vol.	Total State & Local
1951a	39	172	687b	849	898b
1959c	50	278	614	892	942

a—Nov. 1, 1951 Summary, *Mimeographed Directory of American Protestant Churches.*

b—Omitting certain larger parishes and exclusively WDRE organizations. With these, the total was 926.

c—OCC figures as of January 1, 1960.

Nine of the state councils (in eight states) are volunteer bodies, without paid executives: Alaska, Delaware, Nevada, New Mexico, South Carolina (Fellowship), southern Nevada, southwestern Idaho, Utah, and Wyoming.

California has two councils, northern and southern areas.
Pennsylvania has both a Council of Churches and a Council of Religious Education.

Thus there are councils with paid staff in 38 of the 50 states; and also in Puerto Rico. In several instances councils have served areas across state lines. The National Capital Area (Washington, D.C.) Council has state status in DCE, NCC. Arkansas now has a part-time executive, and Georgia has moved to a full-time basis. Delaware, long linked with Maryland, now has a volunteer council of its own.

Northern Idaho has been linked with Washington; southwestern Idaho now has its own volunteer council. Nevada, formerly served only by the California councils, now has two volunteer organizations of its own.

The number of volunteer councils was smaller in 1959 than in 1951, having temporarily increased meanwhile to 697 in 1955. On the other hand, with the exception of 1953, the number of local councils with paid executives increased 61.6 per cent in eight years. The percentage of local councils with paid staff increased from 20.0 in 1951 to 31.5 in 1959. Since 1952 the total number of state and local councils (not including separate women's organizations) has always exceeded 900; it reached a high of 960 in 1955.

At least thirty local councils—three or more in each of six states —moved from the 1951 volunteer list to the 1959 paid-staff list. A number of other states shifted one or two volunteer local councils to paid status during the same period. The trend is clear—the solid core of professionally staffed councils grows steadily larger.

A partial listing of state and local staff members in the 1959 *Year Book of American Churches* (including only "departmental heads" in the larger councils, and supervisors rather than all teachers in some week-day religious education systems) totaled 745:

Councils	Professional Staff Members		
	Ministerial	Lay	
State	91	63	
Local	257	334	
	348	397	745

206

Probably the total of *executive* staff in 1959 was well over 900 persons, plus another five or six hundred secretaries and other office workers.

Only three mainland states in the deep south (Alabama, Louisiana, and Mississippi) now lack some sort of state-wide interchurch organization. In at least one of these "conversations are in progress" looking toward possible organization, in another there are already hopeful beginnings. *Councils of church women serve all the states.*

Outside the south the number of cities with a population of 100,000 or more without a council of churches is being steadily reduced to almost zero. The smaller cities and the redevelopment of county or area councils in more sparsely settled sections of the nation appear to provide the largest opportunity for extension.

Organizational Names

From year to year, forty or more titles appear in the roster of state and local bodies.[2] More than two dozen names have been tried and discontinued, and as many new ones added. But in recent years the ten most used titles account for 93 percent or more of the total number of organizations. Councils with various inclusive names now constitute three out of four of the total, and Councils of Churches seven out of ten. Councils of Christian or Religious Education tend first to take on the functions of Councils of Churches, and then to adopt the more inclusive name as well as program. The number of Sabbath or Sunday School Associations reported to the Office for Councils of Churches varies from year to year, as attitudes toward the National Council and response to its inquiries change.

Great Expansion of Co-Operation among Church Women (DUCW)

The progress of the United Church Women during the decade is easily measured. Whereas in 1951 "more than 1,800 local councils"[3] of church women were known to national headquarters, in 1958 this number had increased in spite of much more rigorous standards of enrollment, to 2,135;[4] and 25,325 local churches are involved. State councils of church women include representatives of from five (Alabama) to twenty-nine (D.C.) denominations. In all but five states, where there is a council of churches, the women function as a department of the larger body; and there are councils of church women in four additional states, where there is no state council of churches.[5] By 1957 it was possible to list 41 state annual meetings,[6] with dates

207

and places; the last three years 49 have been listed.[7] At the Seventh Assembly of United Church Women in November 1955 46 states were represented;[8] at a 1953 Board of Managers (DUCW) meeting[9] presidents of 46 state councils of church women were in session together; and in a 1957 meeting 47 presidents gathered.[10]

The financial increase is even more striking. When the UCCW was organized its budget for the first year was $12,000 ("what faith it took on the part of the finance committee to adopt this!"),[11] and actual expenditures in 1942 amounted to only $9,600.[12] By 1954 expenditures were $354,000;[13] the 1955 budget (exclusive of the World Day of Prayer) was $423,800. In 1958 the Department handled nearly $800,000.

In 1952 it was reported that the last four national assemblies had adopted $50,000 a year as "the financial share for state and local councils, to support (UCW) national work."[14] Steady progress was made over the years, from $39,352.92 in 1952 until 1958, when this high goal was actually passed. [15] These figures are of course over and above an Ecumenical Register Fund of more than $300,000,[16] offerings received on the three great UCW days ($450,000 in 1953),[17] and other extras.

When the UCCW voted in 1949 to become a Department in the NCC, it recognized "the need for one co-operative agency in each state and local area." At the same time there were "organized councils of church women in state and local areas that came into being before there were councils of churches. Indeed, the councils of church women are frequently the only interdenominational co-operative agency in an area." In April 1954 important action was taken providing "Suggested Criteria for Organizational Participation of Church Women in State and Local Councils of Churches." These included objective study of possible patterns and mutual agreement in each situation, and provided for "autonomy in the operation (and financing) of distinctly United Church Women programs and projects," including a UCW annual meeting, to be held separately, in order to make possible larger participation on the part of church women in the annual meeting of the Council of Churches.[18]

EMPLOYED PROFESSIONAL PERSONNEL

In State Councils

In 1951 state councils in 34 states (two in Pennsylvania) and a Sunday School Association in Hawaii, reported a total of 128 employed executives, many of whom were undoubtedly part-time, and at least five of whom had double portfolios.

In 1959 professional staff positions,[19] full- or part-time, reported by 41 state councils, numbered 166. The number of councils had increased 13.9 percent, their professional staff 29.7 percent, and the average staff 11.1 percent. In recent years the median state council has had a professional staff of six persons.

General executive, managerial, and finance leadership available per council have increased slightly, as have miscellaneous program positions. Range of program and competence of administration have gained. On the other hand, the number of state inter-denominational workers assigned to the field of religious education, especially in traditional age group specialization, has decreased. This decline is in part offset by denominational and local council increases in religious education personnel, and in part by the fact that many of the council senior executives, especially in the smaller organizations, are primarily concerned with the educational task of the churches, and are trained religious educators.

In Local Councils

In 1951 Virginia reported 39 local or county organizations engaged in week-day religious education.[20] Eleven of these had a staff executive, who in most instances was also a teacher. Some of these staff executives had from one to four teachers on their staff. The other 28 organizations employed from one to six teachers, making a total of 73 persons, or an average of nearly two per council. In a smaller proportion of councils in other states also the organization is essentially a teaching enterprise, without some of the staff problems common to the more inclusive councils.

Omitting this significant and pioneering Virginia development, the number of other local organizations (city and county) increased from 131 in 29 states, with 395 professional staff positions[19] in 1951, to 215 in 34 states, with 551 professional tasks in 1959. Of senior executives, with seven different titles, more than seven out of ten are executive secretaries, and nearly two out of ten executive directors. Almost half of the employed personnel is engaged in some sort of administration. (The line between managerial and promotional tasks and purely clerical work seems not always to be clearly observed; but it is plain that there is an increase in administrative and business specialists.) The next largest group is the religious educators. In 41

209

councils from one to five chaplains, to a total of 75, are now employed. Social services, which are decidedly on the increase, engage more than 50 other persons. Radio and television directors number at least ten; nine staff persons serve local or state councils of church women; nine are research and planning specialists. The diversity of program undertaken by state and local councils is even greater than that of their employed personnel; a number of persons are employed at two or more unrelated tasks.

In 1951 more than one in three local councils reported a staff of three or more professional workers; a smaller proportion did so in 1959. On the other hand, in 1951 fewer than half of these councils reported only one executive; in 1959 nearly three out of five did so. Many newer councils report smaller staffs at the outset. While the average staff per council has declined, the base has been broadening, and the strong are growing stronger.

Geographical Distribution of Local Councils and Their Personnel

Most of the metropolitan centers are clustered in a small number of states. A considerable portion of the local councils with paid staff have been organized in these more urbanized areas. Of 84 new local councils with paid staff listed since 1951, nearly four-fifths are located in eleven states. In 1951 eleven states employed nearly two-thirds of the total local personnel; in 1959 this proportion had increased to three-fourths. The increase from 278 to 417 in local personnel in these eleven states was above average.

The total number of employed professional positions reported by local councils also definitely suggests the relative urbanization of the states in which they are located. In 1951 seven states reported 78 local councils with six or more professional staff members. In 1959 eleven states, including the 1951 seven, reported 162 councils with six or more professional employees. Local staff professionals in nine of these states now number a score or more: New York, 75; California, 67; Pennsylvania, 50; Ohio, 47; Illinois, 44; Massachusetts, 34; Indiana, 24; Michigan 23; Connecticut, 20.[21]

Increased Income

Like the National Council, local and state councils now have more dollars available, and from increasingly representative sources. The dollar volume of reported state and local business more than doubled in six years.[22]

Gross Annual Income, State and Local Councils

| Year | Councils with Paid Staff | | Volunteer Councils | Totals |
	State	Local		
1952	$1,316,726	$3,936,232	$848,870	$6,101,828
1953	2,097,233	4,288,297	775,762	7,161,292
1954	2,508,886	4,517,117	831,531	7,857,534
1955	3,011,463	5,748,780	719,457	9,479,700
1956	3,401,441	6,561,674	785,382	10,748,497
1957	3,527,173	7,360,711	747,395	11,631,279
1958	3,869,172	8,357,216	812,479	13,038,867

The impressive annual financial total of National Council operations is now approximated by the total amount received and spent by state and local councils.

More rapid increase in state as compared with local council income is due chiefly to the development of state benevolences, which now amount to almost as much as current expenses. Local benevolent programs have involved smaller sums. Of the total received in 1958 by all state and local councils, one dollar in five was given for benevolent projects.

In 1958 councils with volunteer leadership reported smaller receipts than in 1952, but the average per council ($1,328) was larger. (When volunteer councils are able to secure an income of four or five thousand dollars, they tend to shift at least to the part-time category. If several such changes occur in one year, the effect on the totals can be considerable.)

Increased Representativeness

During the last six years main sources of income have shown a decided trend toward member unit support. Half of state council income in 1957 came from denominations, local churches, local church organizations, and city and local councils, as compared with three-tenths in 1952. Local councils with paid staff received 23.3 percent from such sources in 1952, and 41.4 percent in 1957. Meanwhile the proportion of receipts from individuals showed a reverse trend: from 24.4 percent in 1952 to 13.6 percent in 1958 for state councils, and from 27.8 to 17.6 for local.

The larger the city, the more likely is the Council of Churches to receive designated funds for health and welfare work from such sources as Community Chests, to which are always added general

211

Council funds—in some cases approaching one-half of the cost of such programs. In 1957 councils in 14 cities of more than a million population received nearly a fourth of their current expense income from Chests and municipal funds, as compared with only a little more than a fifth for 15 councils with over $100,000 income, and less than one dollar in nine for all local councils with paid leadership. By the same token, in 1957 the most metropolitan cities received the smallest fraction of their income from local church budgets—22.9 percent as compared with the 33.6 percent average for 200 councils with paid staff.

Program Expands, Education Still Central

Only a thorough analysis of the annual reports, the structures and the finances of state and local councils could adequately appraise their relative program emphases. There is abundant evidence, in personnel, activities, and budgets, that the range of tasks undertaken has greatly expanded. The range of program interests reported by state and local councils, as summarized in the last three ACS annual reports of "Significant Developments," is impressive; and some trends seem clear.

Education—including age and sex group activities, week-day released time, and campus ministries—continues to be central; but—perhaps because it is established and taken for granted—it occupies, at least temporarily, a proportionately smaller place in the summaries. Administrative concerns are sharply to the fore, including finance and stewardship, increased support, public relations, planning and strategy, better quarters, and larger staff. Ecumenical studies are on the increase. Social action and social welfare have zoomed into a new place of attention. Pastoral services and counselling, institutional ministries, including various types of chaplaincies, along with service to migrants and minority groups, missionary interest and evangelism, assume important proportions. New program emphases like radio and television and the fine arts are increasingly regarded as imperative.

Starting from Sunday School Association beginnings, Maryland, New York, Connecticut, New Jersey, Illinois, Minnesota, Ohio, and Michigan, in that order, have all passed their 100th *anniversaries*. Buffalo celebrated its local centennial in 1957 by a dinner, attended by 783, honoring its church school teachers. Other cities had already passed their century marks. As the movement matures, golden anniversaries also grow more numerous and more significant.

212

Sample Happenings Journalistically Noteworthy

While the *International JOURNAL* published many special issues during this decade,[23] it also—especially from 1951 to 1956—featured much state and local council news, including personnel changes.[24] Attendance at the Directors of Religious Education section of the DCE meetings in 1948 was 165; in 1953 it had climbed to 451.[25] At the 1953 DCE Fellowship Dinner "Mr. Ketcham traced upon a large map the journeys back and forth across the nation of several of the persons present, showing how intertwined are the lives of people from many different denominations."[26] In 1954 "A rough guess would suggest that somewhere between five and eight million hours per week are given by the 2,699,327 teachers and officers in Protestant church schools."[27] In 1956 attention was called to the First Ecumenical Institute in the southern region, held in North Carolina.[28]

Four out of five of the 60 issues of the National Council *Outlook* issued during the six-year period 1952-7 contained items of "Church Council News," rarely less than two columns, a full page more often than not, and often two full pages. Here were chronicled smaller items of spot news, and personnel changes were frequently noted. In addition there were numerous feature articles on particular cities or states.

Approaching meetings of the ACS were repeatedly noted, and in the early fall generously reported. E.g., in September, 1952 the Van Dusen lectures rated the headline: "Wanted: First-rate Christian Leaders"; and in September 1954 appeared a picture of the newly elected ACS Executive Committee.

Of special importance—because of his position as the new chairman of the Central Department of Field Administration—was a February 1953 full-page article by Glenn W. Moore on "Achieving Spiritual Unity in Your Community." At Denver he had said to the NCC biennial, "Speaking from the standpoint of a denominational officer, . . . I do not believe a program of a council of churches should be overlapping, competitive, or unrelated to the program of the denominations. I believe that enthusiasts for councils of churches who support overlapping programs do a disservice to the cause of Christian unity. And I also believe a similar disservice results when denominational leadership fails to see that both our denominational programs and the programs of councils of churches are essential to the greater cause which each endeavors to serve." Likewise, in October 1953 Virgil E. Lowder of Houston had a two-page article on the council

213

movement in the U.S. under the title, "The Job the Churches Can Do *Only* Together."[29]

THE ACS GROWS

In Attendance

There is increasing co-operation of councils of churches, local, state, and national, and of their employed personnel, through the ACS. Though in 1951 total ACS attendance was 364, including 113 visitors (guests, husbands, wives, children), the sharp increase that year was not maintained; in fact, later attendance has not quite equalled the 1951 total. Of 363 present in 1959, council executives numbered 238, as compared with 251 in 1951.

A careful three-year breakdown (1953-5) showed that of those in attendance nearly three persons in four were professionals. The number of city executives present was twice that of national staff, which in turn was twice that of state personnel. That is, of every seven votes four were local, two were national, and only one was state.

In Membership

The following tabulation is instructive:[30]

	Number Paying Dues or Making Contributions to the ACS Treasury	
Year Ending	Individuals	Organizations
1951	253	109
1952	284	105
1953	293	105
1954	286	102
1955	270	94
1956	338	110
1957	309	114
1958	328	118
1959	354	115

The reasons for the fluctuation in organizational interest and support, whether administrative, economic, varying attractiveness of annual meeting programs, or other, have received attention from the officers of the ACS, and deserve continuing study in the light of the number of persons and organizations eligible for membership.

214

In Income

The total annual financial transactions of the ACS, omitting certain in-and-out items like publication funds, as compared with budgets authorized, are likewise worthy of comparison.

ACS Year Ending	Budget	Net Received	Net Expended	Balance
1951	$2,200.00	$2,460.88	$2,582.13	$1,341.40
1952	2,800.00	2,837.98	2,501.10	1,681.28
1953	3,700.00	3,614.57	2,898.60	2,399.25
1954	4,200.00	3,656.02	2,761.26	3,294.01
1955	4,525.00	3,831.79	3,361.69	3,764.11
1956	4,925.00	4,378.96	4,768.69	3,374.38
1957	6,685.00	4,631.55	6,163.69	1,842.24
1958	6,185.00	6,402.93	6,159.04	2,086.13
1959	6,495.00	7,286.82	4,981.04	4,511.51
1960	6,660.00			

Thus the volume of dollar business nearly tripled in less than a decade; and the balance in hand ebbed and flowed according to the financial controls exercised from year to year.

In Representativeness

The proportion of organizational contributions and of personal dues in the receipts of the ACS reflects both increases in the amounts requested, and an increasing emphasis on organizational representativeness.

Dollars Paid into ACS Treasury by

	Organizations	Individuals	Net Totals	Percent Organizational
1951	$1,828	$ 633	$2,461	74.3
1952	2,102	736	2,838	74.1
1953	2,730	885	3,615	75.5
1954	2,799	858	3,657	76.5
1955	2,796	810	3,606	77.5
1956	3,186	1,014	4,200	75.9
1957	3,407	927	4,334	72.9
1958	4,343	1,615	5,958	78.4
1959	5,331	1,790	7,121	74.9
9 yr. totals	$28,522	$9,268	$37,790	75.5

215

In 1958 it was agreed that . . . "membership in ACS as a professional organization is essential whether or not a member attends the conference that particular year." Closely related to the number of individuals paying dues is the question of the function of the ACS. It is—as it has sometimes tended to be—in line with some tendencies in the organizations that preceded it, a conclave of senior executives only, or does it provide a helpful meeting place for program specialists, and junior personnel, as others have steadily maintained? The answer to this question involves many matters of schedule, structure, finance, and specialized professional groupings of others than council personnel. The 1959 program was designed not for general executives only but for all staff personnel.

In Breadth of Program and Organizational Procedures

The records of the ACS begin to acquire a significant place in the history of church co-operation in America. Here, better than anywhere else, one catches the true flavor of grass-roots ecumenicity.

A list of the ACS presidents and program chairmen for the decade will serve to indicate something of the range of its official leadership. Scores of additional persons have been officers, and members of the executive, standing, and special committees, to which with increasing care many matters have been delegated, as the organization has expanded in size and range of interest.

Elected for the Year Ending	*President*	*Program Chairman*
1951	Hugh C. Burr	Forrest C. Weir
1952	Harold C. Kilpatrick	Jennie M. Doidge
1953	Hayden L. Stright	O. Walter Wagner
1954	William D. Powell	Ira C. Sassaman
1955	O. Walter Wagner	Dan M. Potter
1956	Forrest C. Weir	Virgil E. Lowder
1957	Harlan M. Frost	Grover L. Hartman
1958	Virgil E. Lowder	Frederick E. Reissig
1959	Forrest L. Knapp	B. Bruce Whittemore
1960	Harvey W. Hollis	Harold B. Keir
1961		Robert L. Kincheloe

ACS minutes have been prepared with an enlarging sense of their importance, though with varying attention to statistical details of enduring historical value as evidence of trends. The work both of the secretary and of the treasurer has loomed larger and larger, with the growth of ACS membership and its increased volume of business.

A program feature of central importance at ACS meetings during the decade has been the general seminar. Here an outstanding leader has lectured formally in a series of presentations on some serious and pertinent theme, and opportunity has been provided for the entire Association to join in a discussion period. The mere catalog of these seminar topics and their leaders shows how seriously the ACS has considered its task.

ACS General Seminars

Year	Topic	Lecturer
1951 June 18-23	"This Nation Under God"	Dean Liston Pope, Yale Divinity School
1952 June 16-21	"The Theological Roots of Ecumenicity in American Protestantism"	Pres. Henry Pitney Van Dusen, Union Theological Seminary
1953 June 21-27	"Social and Cultural Factors Affecting Ecumenicity"	Dean Walter G. Muelder, Boston University School of Theology
1954 June 20-26	"Looking Toward Evanston"	Dr. F. Ernest Johnson, of the NCC
1955 June 19-25	"Christian Unity—Its Relevance to the Community"	Dr. J. Quinter Miller, of the NCC
1956 June 17-23	"Christian Faith and the Cultural Situation"	Dr. George D. Kelsey, Drew Theological Seminary, formerly of the NCC
1957 June 16-22	"The Church and the American World"	Prof. H. Reinhold Niebuhr, Yale Divinity School
1958 June 15-21	"Seeking the Ecumenical Church"	Dr. Nils Ehrenstrom, Boston University School of Theology, formerly of the WCC
1959 June 21-27	"Our Witnessing Task"	Dr. Norman Goodall, London Office, IMC and WCC

Among these nine lecturers have been representatives of the faculties of four seminaries, two each from two of them; two representatives

217

of the World Council, and three of the National Council. Local and state council leaders have diligently sought not to be provincial.

In 1951 Dean Pope confronted the American secretariat with "Our International Responsibility"; in 1952 Dr. Van Dusen stressed the role of theology in ecumenicity; in 1933 Dean Muelder faced "The Problem of (so-called) Nontheological Factors" and "Institutional Resistance to Council Policy." Dr. Miller's 1955 lectures have become a part of the literature of the movement, in the volume *Christian Unity, Its Relevance to the Community*.[31]

The 1951 Tenth Anniversary Session of the ACS began the custom of special sessions for the orientation of newer secretaries, with brief but carefully prepared memoranda on "The Field of Interchurch Cooperation," "The Work of the Executive Secretary," "Departmental Program Administration," "The Secretary's Relationships," and "Resources for Continuous Growth as a Council Leader." Thus newly elected state and local workers were introduced to the thinking of five ACS leaders, as a basis for discussion and conference. Some such introduction to the profession has now become standard procedure at ACS meetings, and the syllabi used are an important part of the documenting of the growth of the council movement.

In 1951 Bishop Henry Knox Sherrill, president of the NCC, spoke on "Foundation Principles for the Council Movement." In a different field a special finance seminar (three sessions) was addressed by George E. Lundy, of Marts and Lundy. "The Philosophy of Interchurch Cooperation" came up for renewed discussion, with specific reference to undergirding the constitutional provision for relationships between the NCC and state and local councils. Difficulties experienced by state and local councils were aired in a panel discussion.

At this meeting Dr. Franklin Clark Fry also ably voiced certain denominational concerns. His president's report to the 1950 Convention of the United Lutheran Church in America on "Relationships with Other Evangelical Christians," including an emphasis on the "evangelical" and "representative" principles, was distributed. On the other hand, the executive of one of the strongest metropolitan councils of churches presented a five-page memo on "Relationships of City and State Councils and Federations to the NCC." Another panel considered "Lay Men and Lay Women in the Cooperative Movement." Threefold attention was given to "The Making of the Executive Secretary," through his habits of study, personal devotion, and relaxation.

Dr. Van Dusen's 1952 lectures contained several statements worth quoting verbatim, because they may well be regarded as deliber-

218

ately controversial. In speaking of the relation of local and state councils to the NCC, he said: "The NCC at present provides no logical or adequate relationship with the bodies to which it is, in fact, more intimately related than any others. The solution of some of the other important problems is to a large extent dependent on the right solution of this problem." "What is demanded is nothing less than an absolutely fundamental re-examination of the role of the church council within its community and among its churches, i.e., within the organization of society and within the Body of Christ."

And in his review of the changes in the American scene, he declared: "The cultural and sociological factors responsible for the origin of denominations have largely become obsolete." Persons like those who attend the ACS are not likely to forget such recorded statements on the part of an eminent and responsible theologian, in good standing in his own communion, but less involved than some in denominational mechanisms.

In 1953 four significant workshops sought to analyze the council task. One on "Metropolitan Areas" considered finance, radio and TV, public relations, and strategy. Dr. Kenneth G. Neigh, then Presbyterian synodical executive in Michigan, presented an important 5-page paper on "Protestant Strategy in Metropolitan Centers." The workshop on larger cities considered a vital program of religious education, keeping the churches in the black, being realistic about the Council's social-action program, and spiritual ministries to people on the fringe. One on smaller cities asked: "What are good public relations and finance? Do we have a mission? How to fill the gaps in Christian education?" It also discussed the community conscience at work. State council leaders talked about building the state council program on the program of the denominations; planning, promoting, and financing the state pastors' conference; teamwork between state councils and the NCC; and public relations, publicity, and finances. As might well be expected, the parallelism among these groups showed common interest in education, in denominational cooperation, in community action, public relations, and finance. G. Merrill Lenox of Detroit gave a well-documented three-page answer to the question, "Is the Validity of the Conciliar Movement on State and Local Levels Challenged by Present Trends?"

The ecumenical atmosphere in America in 1954 was of course tremendously vitalized by the Evanston sessions of the WCC. "Designs and Freedom in the Ecumenical Movement" and "Christ the Hope of the World" were very much in American thinking. Hence the special significance of Dr. Johnson's lectures.

On June 21, 1954, the executive committee of the ACS agreed in principle that the nominating group for representation in the various units of the NCC by state, city, and other local levels should be the Executive Committee of the National Council's Central Department of Field Administration or its successor, rather than the ACS, since it was felt that the ACS as a professional fellowship should have no organic connection with any council. Final action was deferred however, pending changes then in process in the NCC.

In 1955 the ACS shifted its attention from world unity to "Grass-Roots Ecumenicity." Under the leadership of Dr. J. Quinter Miller, the relevance of Christian unity to the community, for program, structure, staff, finance, and relationships, was carefully considered. His lectures on this theme, published in 1957, embody principles and procedures that have widely influenced all state and local councils of churches, and have helped denominational leaders without practical experience at the state and local levels better to understand the opportunities of all our communions in connection with community relationships.

By putting an item of $500 in its budget for the use of certain special committees, the ACS now began statesmanlike long-range, year-round consideration of several difficult problems. Three executives were asked to prepare a strong case for the adoption of an amendment to the Constitution of the NCC at its 1957 Assembly dealing with the representation of the cooperative work of the churches in states and cities, to be used as the basis of discussion in a 1956 ACS session. A committee on the "Present and Future Role and Function of the ACS" was authorized, as was also 1956 consideration of the "Place and Function of State and Local Councils of Churches in the Total Life of the Church." "Criteria for Self-Evaluation and Measurement by Councils of Churches" now came up for careful consideration. The establishment of the Office for Councils of Churches in 1955 was of course of major importance to the ACS, which has been greatly indebted to it for all sorts of services rendered.

The year 1955 was also noteworthy for the publication of the long-awaited *Growing Together,* a manual or operating handbook for councils of churches,[32] which began to meet a very great need for a solid volume on council work, after an interval of many years during which only pamphlet material had been available. The peril was that

220

the rapidly expanding movement would outgrow its inadequate guidance material.

In 1956 the ACS was greeted with 26 mimeographed pages of "Most Significant Developments in State and Local Councils of Churches," one of a long series of important historic memoranda. The special study committees and the Executive Committee had taken their work seriously. Reports were again made on "Representation in the NCC," "The Role and Function of the ACS," and "The Role of Local and State Councils in the Ecumenical Movement." The three special committees were continued, with the understanding that later more time would be allowed for discussion of their further findings. ACS questionnaires indicated:

(1) Growing satisfaction of seeing our work as councils in an ecumenical context;

(2) a uniform expression of favor for democratic participation;

(3) a realization of an increasing spiritual depth in our program.

A statement made at ACS sixteen years earlier, in 1940, concerning ACS work for 1941 and later, now seemed again valuable; and a summary of "Historic Episodes" by John B. Ketcham[33] whetted the appetite for additional historic documentation of the ecumenical movement in its more local aspects.

The year 1957 was significant by reason of the Oberlin Conference on "The Nature of the Unity We Seek," to which the ACS was invited to nominate ten persons as consultants. The ACS noted with satisfaction that the Oberlin section on "Cooperation in State and Local Councils recommended 'an ongoing study of the ecclesiological significance of local, state, and national councils of churches.'" At the June meeting of the ACS, the report of its committee on "The Role of State and Local Councils of Churches in the Ecumenical Movement" was adopted and ordered printed as a document of enduring value. The question of state and local representation on the NCC proved to be a complicated one. In October 1956 the Executive Committee of ACS had acknowledged, "We are not all agreed on what we want." Hence the importance of the reactions to the pertinent Committee report, which was approved at the 1957 meeting of ACS. The report on "The Role and Function of the ACS" was given careful consideration, and the Committee continued.

The exceptionally valuable mimeographed minutes of the 1957 ACS by Daniel R. Ehalt (Oak Park council executive), secretary, including committee reports and revised by-laws, were again supplemented

221

by "Outstanding Developments in Councils of Churches During the Year 1956-7." Special attention had been given to strengthening membership in the ACS, and vice president Ellis H. Dana of Wisconsin had devised and circulated a folder, "Why You Should Belong to ACS."

The year 1958 marked the tenth anniversary of the World Council and the golden anniversary of the Federal Council. On receipt of its report, the commitee on "Role and Function of the ACS" was discharged. Progress reports on professional standards, personnel practices, and representation in the NCC resulted in the continuance of these committees. (There appeared to be an honest difference of opinion as to whether a council secretary needs to be an ordained minister.) The general theme, "The New Dimension in Our Council Movement—Our Involvement with Faith and Order," harked back to the Oberlin Conference.

By 1959 the various ACS study committees had become so important an aspect of the organization's program that a Committee on Studies (Virgil E. Lowder, Grover L. Hartman, and Harold Kilpatrick) had been named, to consider the whole study task. On receiving this committee's thoroughgoing report, the ACS named a new committee of seven members, with Dr. Forrest L. Knapp as chairman, continuing the three men who had served in 1958-9, and adding Dr. William B. Cate, Dr. J. Quinter Miller, Dr. Stanley Stuber, and (as consultant) Rev. William A. Norgren of the NCC staff, Faith and Order Department. This committee is currently budgeted for $300.00, and ACS study committees have spent an average of more than that during four previous fiscal years.

In Influence

Some unavoidable repetition in reporting National Council aspects of the "Field" situation will underscore the increasing influence of the ACS. The necessity and desirability for all national interdenominational agencies and programs to keep in close touch with the ACS grows clearer to all concerned. This contact is made the more sure because so many of the National Council staff are themselves ACS members.

THE NATIONAL COUNCIL AND "THE FIELD"

The extent of the present representation of state and local councils in the various units of the National Council is impressive.[34] It is an open secret, however, that even the Division of Christian Education finds it not easy to maintain the intended balance of representation between councils of churches and denominations. Other units, where the habit of territorial representation has been less well established, may have even greater difficulty. Though the opportunity for participation by state and local council representatives has been widely accepted, the accompaning responsibility for sharing in policy-making has not been everywhere accepted. The degree to which elected state and local personnel have actually participated in National Council meetings, and by correspondence, is not clear; nor are the channels by which they can communicate to and from the state and local bodies.

The problem here is more than administrative, though limitations of state and local staff time and travel funds, and similar practical considerations, are an important factor; and so is the inadequacy of intercouncil machinery. In practice, do not denominational representatives in the National Council possess superior status? Has the National Council ever regarded state and city councils as loci of basic structure, comparable to the denominations? Should it? This is an ecclesiological problem, a matter of church politics in the high sense (the science of the possible); it is even a theological problem, quite as much as an organizational and institutional matter.

The General Assembly

From the outset, the NCC has been sure that its "membership" should be limited to delegates chosen by its member communions. But it has always been equally clear that it would be advantageous to all concerned if state and local councils could also name additional "representatives," to be individually authenticated as members of the particular cooperating communion to which each belongs. In this way the voice of community experience is added to the testimony of the denominations, which are the prime units of the corporation.

By 1954 the National Council Assembly, meeting in Boston November 28 to December 3, was seating one representative from each state council and a panel of ten representing the city councils, but the 1954 *Work Book,* in reporting field developments, found "a consistent and sound pattern of relationships between the NCC and state and local councils of churches . . . a complex problem." "Thus far we cannot report much progress in solving organizational patterns for comprehensive councils of churches for recommendation to local constituencies. Such patterns are needed in order to expedite effective functional relations among national, state, and local agencies. State and local constituencies want guidance on the basis of policies and plans that are acceptable to all units of the Council; they do not want patterns dictated by national staff people. But suggestions must take into account the types of structure that have been already adopted by

223

the denominations for the NCC. It is our conviction that substantial progress has been made."

At the General Assembly in St. Louis in December 1957 a proposal to amend the Constitution of the National Council printed in the *Work Book* as recommended by the General Board (after a disappointingly close vote, at the close of a discussion that seems to have strayed from the main issue under consideration) was withdrawn. Instead, a "thorough study by a special committee" of the General Board was authorized, and the General Board was "instructed to bring the 1960 triennial meeting of the General Assembly . . . such amendment or amendments to the Constitution as it may deem necessary to insure adequate representation of the co-operative work of the churches in the various states, cities, and counties, while preserving the nature of the National Council . . . as a council of *churches.*" So the matter stands as this history goes to press.

The Division of Christian Education (DCE)

Nowhere had the relation between national, state, and local co-operation been more real than in the field of religious education. Nowhere was the National Council under greater obligation to consult the thinking of the state councils. This it has faithfully done.

In the 1954 DCE *Year Book* "the growing trend toward fuller denominational participation in city, state, and national councils" was noted with satisfaction. There was increasing consultation with city and state councils, utilization of ongoing council programs, city and state sponsorship of nationally devised programs, and active participation in them. The February sectional meetings have provided a natural opportunity for learning field reactions, during advisory stages of new programs, and for sharing reports of cooperative activities. Field strategy was worked out in consultation with the ACS, and reactions and evaluations were cordially invited.

While the ACS has been the professional fellowship of staff personnel, local, state, and national, the National Council has continued to have administrative and counselling units devoted to field program and administration. One of these, appropriately, has been the Division of Christian Education's *Educational Field Services Committee.* This committee has cleared field concerns and projects and has calendarized events in the interest of effective utilization of personnel and enlistment of field response. By steady referral of all field proposals both to the denominations and to the state and local councils involved, the way has been prepared for increasing mutuality and participation.

224

As listed in 1955, this committee contained eight national denominational field staff persons, six denominational voluntary field staff persons, six state council executives, and six city council execctives, out of a total of 53 members, including ten staff members *ex officio,* without vote.

State and Local Representation in DCE

The first available listing of representatives of state councils in DCE as a whole appears in the 1952 divisional *Year Book.* Of the 33 state councils (including the District of Columbia and fractions of three additional states, with two councils in California) entitled to divisional representation, 26 (or fewer than the member associations in the International Sunday School Association thirty years earlier) had named a total of 167 representatives. In the 1958 *Year Book* representatives from 31 of 37 member councils numbered 209. State delegations have ranged from one person, usually the state council executive, to as high as twenty-two in the Pennsylvania Council of Christian Education. One suspects that there has been a certain loss in lay representation, and a number of the states have been tardy in their appointments. Certainly, however, DCE has given ample recognition, both in principle and in fact, to the rights of state councils of religious education agreed upon at the time of the Kansas City merger and the organization of the International Council.

Divisional year books have regularly provided a generous column for an ACS report. In 1956 Forrest C. Weir reported on the ACS attitude toward the approaching Oberlin Conference on "The Nature of the Unity We Seek," "Over and over we heard the conviction expressed: 'The time has arrived when ecumenical program at the community level must include participation in faith and order studies, though it cannot neglect its service activities developed over the years.' " Likewise in 1957 Harlan M. Frost reported, "The memorial service each year at ACS reminds one of how far it has come as the names of the stalwarts of yesteryear are read. But each summer the incoming group of new secretaries, educated and prepared as the earlier generation could not be, and full of purpose and dedication, give one the sense that this council movement is vigorous and still 'on the make.' " And all the 1958 report on the ACS noted that "the ACS yearly conference in personal enrichment, in professional growth, in helpful exchange of ideas, in evaluation of our own techniques, in finding solutions to crucial problems, in Christian fellowship, is often the most rewarding week of the year to a busy council executive."

Central Department of Field Administration (CDFA)

The National Council as a whole has given attention to state and local council relationships successively in two different ways, CDFA and GCPFO (General Committee on Program and Field Administration), to use the jargon or gobbledygook of American ecumaniacs. Until 1954 there was a Central Department of Field Administration. As finally constituted, this Department involved 112 persons, from 13 groups, in addition to the national field staff of seven. Attendance at seven sessions during four years averaged 43 members, in addition to staff and guests. With regrets recorded from a dozen to sixteen persons, a considerable degree of interest appears to have been maintained. Organized with Hugh Chamberlin Burr of Rochester as chairman, this Department took over the work of the former ICFD, adopted its own by-laws, and operated under an initial budget in excess of $60,000. It, rather than the ACS, now became the normal channel for the nomination of representatives of the cooperative work of the churches in cities to the National Council. Various subcommittees, including one on field organization, went to work.

Along with the representative principle, the evangelical principle and the principle of autonomy were both approved as basic. W. P. Buckwalter, Jr., was added to the staff, as Director of Financial Counseling, to work with city, county, and state councils of churches, effective April 1, 1952. Planning and adjustment were shifted to the Division of Home Missions. Dr. Glenn W. Moore, made chairman of the Department at the end of 1952, had presented a significant paper on "Criteria for Self-Evaluation and Measurement by a State and City Council of Churches." In 1953 important recommendations were made to the General Board by the Committee of the NCC on Policy and Strategy, looking toward strengthening cooperation in state and local councils of churches. Only after long discussion were basic structural changes in the national setup approved.

In November 1953 Willis R. Ford, then of Maryland-Delaware, reported progress on the long-awaited *Field Guidance Manual*. Mr. Buckwalter was then able to report that state and local council income exceeded six million dollars. The Department membership repeatedly broke up into eight or nine parallel seminars for the discussion of various aspects of the field task. In March 1954, in a discussion of field structure and relationships, it was voted that in the appointment of the proposed NCC Committee on Program and Field Operations due recognition should be given to having an adequate proportion of

226

the members represent state and local councils of churches, and that representation, lay as well as professional, should be available for consideration of program as well as administration. It was emphasized that stress should be put on "interrelationships" rather than on lines of "demarcation" between national interests on the one hand, and state and local on the other. A tentative statement on field outreach policy was referred to the new Committee on Program and Field Operations for further study.

General Committee on Program and Field Operations (GCPFO)

Authorized by the General Board March 17, 1954, after sixteen months of study by the Committee on Study and Adjustment, the General Program and Field Operations Committee met for the first time on November 27, 1954, with Dr. Glenn W. Moore as chairman. Its genesis was outlined. Functions were assigned, and in March 1955 sub-committees established. The committee membership was to "include general denominational leaders, general program executives of denominations, state and local council leaders, and representatives of the major program units of the Council, with the executives of major program units of the Council as consultants without votes." Temporary subcommittees were free to include additional personnel. The General Committee was "not operational." A temporary committee took over the issuing of the *Field Guidance Manual,* and was dismissed a year later, with the publication of *Growing Together* in 1955.

In March 1955 a permanent Advisory Committee of 21 for the Office for Councils of Churches was authorized, of whom at least seven were to be from the General Committee, as well as state and local officers and executives, pastors, and lay men and women experienced in the cooperative work of the churches in state and local communities.

As at present constituted, the GCPFO consists of 54 members, in addition to sixteen staff persons of several sorts. The membership includes six city and three state executives. Attendance at nine regular meetings held over a four-year period in six different places (repeatedly in connection with other NCC meetings, five of the nine in New York or Chicago) averaged 45 persons, including staff; and ranged from 37 to 52. Meetings varied from a single session to parts of three days. Early in 1959 attention was given to the importance of adequate information and clearance in any long-range planning for field operations.

The task of GCPFO includes the study of methods of work, procedures for interunit clearance, coordination of policy in program areas, and an advisory relationship to the Bureau of Research and Survey, the Office for Councils of Churches, and the Southern Office. Staff responsibility rests with two assistant general secretaries, one for program and one for field operations, who report to the associate general secretary.

Office for Councils of Churches (OCC)

For the purpose of this history the Office for Councils of Churches is perhaps the most significant phase of this new national field structure. Organized with fifteen members, its Advisory Committee has increased to 21 members from 9 denominations; these are supplemented by 10 consultants and three staff persons. Of the 21 members, nine are denominational persons not employed as council staff, while a dozen are state and local council persons authenticated by their respective denominations. Recorded total attendance has ranged from nine to sixteen. Annual sessions have been the rule. Each has been held in a different city, chiefly in the midwest.

Raymond R. Peters, recently executive at Dayton, Ohio, was the first chairman. At the first session of the Advisory Committee, held in July 1955, it was explained that the NCC was seeking to bring field administration into the central concern of the General Board. As part of the new structure, the functions of the Office for Councils of Churches were outlined, a baker's dozen of them. The OCC staff at the outset included one part-time person for Chicago relationships, and arrangement that was discontinued when DCE moved to New York in 1956. Specific staff responsibility rested with John B. Ketcham and W. P. Buckwalter, Jr.; but Dr. J. Quinter Miller remained responsible for the general supervision of this office and the southern office, and for assistance in field interpretation, evaluation of programs, and personnel counselling. It was agreed that reports of the Advisory Committee for the Office for Councils of Churches to GCPFO should be made by the OCC chairman.

At the outset Mr. Ketcham gave approximately a third of his time to the New York office, a third to the Chicago office, and a third to work in the field. The consolidation of the office in New York early in 1956 was of great help in unifying his task. Dr. Miller also continued to serve on the DCE Committee on Field Services, and on the Staff Field Operations Committee, which was retained. Gratitude has been expressed that the various units of the NCC are increasingly consulting the staff of the OCC as they develop policies and programs of concern to councils of churches.

As compared with an actual expenditure of $44,163.87, the OCC budgets for 1955 and 1956 were $53,710 and $56,483 respectively. There was anticipated income of $13,160 toward the latter figure, thus reducing the net amount needed to $43,323. Beginning in 1955, all undesignated income from councils of churches has gone to support field operations, including both the OCC and the Southern Office. How to increase this income has been a problem.

There was a feeling that, especially as regards councils with volunteer personnel, the movement had reached a plateau. Service rendered to these councils from state and national bodies was deemed inadequate. Decrease in numbers of volunteer councils was held to be due in part to sociological factors (e.g., the declining political significance of many counties), and the disappearance in some states of county councils as units of cooperation. On the other hand, 28 councils had moved from volunteer to paid status. The Advisory Committee felt it necessary to consider the advisability of adding another staff member by 1960 to work with state council executives in developing greater help for volunteer councils. The OCC was now issuing a *News Letter*. It employed two office secretaries to serve its two executives; a third typist position was projected, and later established. It was reported in 1956 that when city councils reach a $70,000 budget, or state councils $80,000, they need at least a part-time staff member to handle income, or the executive secretary will have little time to spend on program activities. Job analysis for staff members has also come up for increased attention.

In 1953 DCE received from 29 state councils a total of $4,614.05, in sums ranging from $25 (N.C.) to $505.05 (N.J.). OCC income from two sources for its first five years of operation was reported as follows:

	From Councils	From Local Churches and Individuals
1954	$12,547	$1,661
1955	14,592	2,046
1956	16,002	2,457
1957	16,593	?
1958	16,820	2,979
1959	16,329	2,475

OCC expenditures for 1958 amounted to $52,362. Obviously, "the field," while increasing its support, is paying only a fraction of the cost of serving it. The implications deserve more consideration than many have given them.

In March 1957 John B. Ketcham presented a November 1956 paper on "Cooperative Protestantism—A Strategy for Serving Metropolitan Areas." He took up developing patterns, relationship of larger city councils to growing metropolitan areas, geographical problems, differing philosophies and problems involved in these philosophies, and relationship to state councils of churches. The reaction of an inadequately attended, too brief session was voiced by one member of the group: "We are impressed with the fact that this is on the agenda, but depressed by the fact that there is not time to discuss fully its implications." One regrets to say that this seems too typical of the work of the Advisory Committee so far—too few present, and not enough time.

In 1958 G. Merrill Lenox of Detroit and Michigan became chairman. There was a careful check-up on how well and and to what extent assigned functions had been performed. There was extended discussion of a breakfast talk by Dr. Truman B. Douglass at St. Louis in December, 1957, on "Relations of Denominations to Councils."[35] Its widespread consideration was favored.

One cannot avoid the feeling that "not operational" applies to the GCPFO, the Advisory Committee for the OCC, and to the ACS —all three. This seems to mean that field work becomes operational only at the staff level. If this be true, the further question arises, Is the present national provision for facing up to state and local problems and increasing opportunities adequate? Is the available staff sufficient in number, in variety of skills, and in budgetary resources? To state it more positively, large matters are afoot; and the machinery for patient, long-range planning is available, but under-staffed and under-financed.

How Interpret What Has Happened

So much for the facts up to now, in swift summary, and in comparison with the tremendous volume of documentation in relatively brief detail. But such a mass of events needs interpretation. How shall one appraise the tendencies at work over so many decades? A concluding chapter endeavors as concisely as possible first to discover some of the possible meanings of all that has been so far recorded, and then to offer a few hints for possible future action.

REFERENCE NOTES

Chapter IX

1 Gray, *op. cit.,* p. 157.
2 See *Staff Titles in Local Councils,* App. V., pp. 114, 115, and in *State Councils,* App. VI, pp. 116, 117, in Miller, *Christian Unity—Its Relevance to the Community.*
3 *The Church Woman,* December, 1952.
4 *Ibid.,* June-July 1959.
5 *Ibid.*
6 *Ibid.,* January 1957.
7 *Ibid.,* January 1958 and 1959.
8 *Ibid.,* February 1956.
9 *Ibid.,* March 1953.
10 *Ibid.,* June-July 1957.
11 *Ibid.,* December 1959, Ruth Moguey Worrell, pp. 13-15.
12 *Ibid.,* March 1955.
13 *Ibid.,* November 1954.
14 *Ibid.,* May 1952, Edith L. Groner.
15 *Ibid.,* as reported in the March number of each succeeding year, state and local contributions to DUCW amounted to

1953	$42,870
1954	45,062
1955	45,685
1956	47,000
1957	49,694
1958	50,346

16 *Ibid.,* August-September 1952 ff.
17 *Ibid.,* February 1953.
18 *Ibid.,* August-September 1954, p. 39 (also mimeographed 8/2/54.)
19 As distinguished from the number of persons noted earlier.
20 *Cf. International Journal,* December, 1953, Elizabeth Longwell: "The Virginia State Council Services Local Communities." (More than 52,000 pupils are enrolled, 96% of the pupils in the grades where the program is offered. Nearly a third of these pupils have little or no connection with the church. Nearly 400 communities are served.)
21 Tabulation of the geographical distribution of subscribers to *The Church Woman* as of March 10, 1953 (back cover of April, 1953 issue), and December 1, 1958 (map, pp. 20, 21, August-September, 1959), visualizes the widespread and increasing interest in co-operative women's work throughout the nation. Excluding 246 foreign subscriptions, there were 19,932 subscribers to this journal in 1953, ranging from 36 in Nevada and in Utah to 1,369 in New York State; in 1958 the domestic total had increased to 27,655, ranging from 8 in Alaska to 1,903 in Ohio. Started as a quarterly bulletin of the NCFW in 1935, and in 1938 becoming the joint publication of the three groups merged in the 1941 UCCW, *The Church Woman* celebrated its 25th anniversary in 1959.
22 The figures used are compiled from Numbers 1 to 10 of the invaluable *Financial Counciling,* issued by the Office for Councils of Churches, and prepared by W. P. Buckwalter, Jr.
23 E.g., on age groups, alcohol, camping, drama, missions, peace, race relations, worship, etc.

24 Each personnel change was likely to be part of a chain of three or more moves. E.g., when Harold C. Kilpatrick became the first executive of the new Texas Council in 1953, J. T. Morrow moved from St. Paul to San Antonio, to fill that vacancy, and W. Bruce Hadley from Omaha to St. Paul, and Walter E. Daniels from the Cleveland staff to Omaha. What happens in pastoral appointments or calls to local churches is paralleled in council staff changes.

25 *International Journal,* January 1953.

26 *Ibid.,* April 1953.

27 *Ibid.,* November 1954, editorial.

28 *Ibid.,* June 1956.

29 The tendency in *The Outlook* over these recent years seems to have been toward longer feature stories. The February 1957 issue devoted 4 pages to state and local council work, and others only slightly less. Typical of this decade was the growth of the Council of Churches of Buffalo and Erie County, N.Y., under the fifteen-year leadership of Rev. Harlan M. Frost, recently retired.

30 These and other later similar data appearing in this chapter are compiled from the records of the ACS as provided in the mimeographed annual minutes.

31 Shenandoah Publishing House, 1957.

32 NCC, 1955.

33 ACS 1956 Minutes, pp. 59-64.

34 For an excellent factual statement, *cf.* the unpublished discussion paper presented by R. H. Edwin Espy at the NCC Consultation on Long-Range Planning, in November 1959; also Mr. Ketcham's careful 8-page mimeographed analysis of state and local NCC representation, February 1959.

35 Published in *The Christian Century,* January 8, 1958.

Meanings and Expectations

Accelerated Expectations

The pre-ecumenical era ended very recently. In the 1930's workers at the state and local level, however expectant, were often thwarted by a feeling of frustration, because of the complexity of the cooperative enterprise, its many national agencies, and the seemingly elephantine ponderosity of its movements. This confusion has slowly given way to orderliness, though complexity remains, by the very nature of the multiplicity of church interests in relation to such a complicated culture.

Forty years ago some of us had the joy of pioneering in local councils that were "inclusive"; nearly thirty years ago Connecticut effected a merger at the state level. Then followed, in quick succession, national staff and Inter-Council field cooperation. Finally, state and local executives, many of whom had clamored for larger unity "at the top," were themselves willing to pool their strength in the ACS. By 1940, in the midst of a changing world climate, it was only a question of time until the NCC would be a reality.

If Norman Cousins is right when he says that man "has to convert historical experience into a design for a sane world,"[1] church cooperation will rejoice in the progress it has made, but will be very sure that it has "not yet attained" much that the future will make necessary, if organized religion is to be a less chaotic aspect of our national life.

How Far Have We Come?

By and large, councils of churches seem to thrive in direct proportion to the density of the population. In 1956 the percentage of places (cities, towns, counties, and states) having councils ranged thus:

233

Size of Area (Population)	Number of Places	With Councils with Paid Staff		Volunteer	
		No.	% of places	No.	% of places
1,000,000 up	51	42	82.4	2	3.9
500,000-999,999	54	27	50.0	3	5.6
250,000-499,999	74	26	35.1	9	12.2
100,000-249,999	218	56	25.7	28	12.8
50,000- 99,999	383	49	12.8	65	17.0
25,000- 49,999	899	37	4.1	134	14.9
10,000- 24,999	1959	32	1.6	206	10.5
5,000- 9,999	1692	7	.4	81	4.8
Under 5,000	16371	18	.1	119	.7
	21701	294		647	

Or, as to organized and unorganized territory, these OCC figures may be summarized:

Population	Total Pd. and Vol. Councils	Percent of Places	Number of Places without Councils[2]
1,000,000 up	44	86.3	7
500,000-999,999	30	55.6	24
250,000-499,999	35	47.4	39
100,000-249,999	84	38.5	134
50,000- 99,999	114	29.8	269
25,000- 49,999	171	19.0	728
10,000- 24,999	238	12.1	1721
5,000- 9,999	88	5.2	1604
Under 5,000	137	.8	16234
	941		20760

We have come a long way, but in terms of the total potential we seem only to have begun to occupy the land. One conclusion is plain: Churches associated interdenominationally in state and local councils of churches have as clear a right and *as manifest* a *duty* to express their cooperative attitudes and convictions as they have when associated in their respective denominations.[3]

God can be in the experience of local churches of various sorts associated together in their communities, quite as much as in the history of their denominational fellowships. The communion of saints is geographical and contemporary, as well as continuous and historical. God

234

is still acting, His creation is not yet finished, He still reveals His nature and His will. Ecumenical discovery can be most vital when it is local.

WHY HAVE WE TRAVELLED THUS FAR TOGETHER?

Church cooperation in America has had a dual purpose. (1) It has been a means to get many necessary jobs done, of a sort that no individual church could do alone. (2) It has also been an effort to embody a sense of unity dimly felt, in recognition of the fact that the Church, and therefore the churches, as Visser 't Hooft said at Oberlin, are not merely human enterprises, "which (men) have a right to fashion according to their own will and insight."

Social Determinism

Secular pressures have included urbanization, international strife, depression, and other unsettling forces.

One aspect of urbanization has been the increase of Roman Catholic population in city neighborhoods, formerly Protestant, along with Jewish immigration that has bulked large in some cities. A Protestant minority, however diverse within itself, has tended to seek some solidarity. In some metropolitan areas this has been an acute need, and in some whole states it has undoubtedly been a contributory factor in increasing church cooperation.[4]

Emphasis on the need for community solidarity during World Wars I and II had two consequences. (1) Especially during World War I, the easy association of churches with non-ecclesiastical bodies in all sorts of community effort tended to blur the requirements of membership in a strictly inter*church* organization. Later the slogan "Let the Church Be the Church" made the churches emphasize their own unique role. (2) The 1917 Pittsburgh Congress, described in Chapter V, proved once more that God can make the wrath of men to praise Him, in terms of Christian Cooperation in wartime. That what ought to happen through sweetness and light is sometimes accelerated by military necessity is ground both for gratitude and sadness. In 1945, fifteen years ago, the uneasy ending of six years of terrible strife was an occasion of solemn joy, and of deep heart-searching. Said Bishop Eivind Berggraf, when the World Council forces were able to meet for the first time after the war, in the Cathedral of Geneva, in closing his sermon, "During the war, Christ has said to us: My Christians, you are one."[5] How now were the workaday churches to make more visible their unity in Christ?

Between the two World Wars other factors were at work. The period made a mood of moral let-down more or less inevitable, with consequences for all cooperative effort. In 1924, when Dr. Guild had been handicapped by so great a deficit, Dr. King's predecessor, Dr. Charles E. Vermilya, had confessed, "The most elusive and uncertain of all forces are those which are classed as 'interdenominational.' Inter-denominational ideals and organizations are still to a large extent in the realm of the abstract. They represent aspirations and phophecies that have not taken hold of the loyalties and practices of any large group in religious circles." (It may be more than a coincidence that 1924 was the year George Gershwin wrote *Rhapsody in Blue*.)

A couple of years later the able Rochester secretary, Orlo J. Price, told the Federal Council,[6] "The reason we are making such slow progress in church cooperation is because denominational officials are not holding up the practice of cooperation as one of the great tests of a successful pastor in the several denominations. When the Methodist district superintendent begins to ask not simply how many new members of Methodist churches the pastor has secured, but also how much he has cooperated in community programs with other pastors, then we shall really get ahead. When the Baptist state superintendent inquires of Baptist pastors not merely how much money they have raised for Baptist projects, but also to what extent they have shared in inter-denominational undertakings with other churches in the same town, then the cooperation of which we talk will become a reality. The responsibility cannot be delegated to the FC; if the denominations really meant what they said when they created the FC, it is the solemn duty of all denominational officials themselves to help educate their constituencies in the spirit and practice of cooperation."

Added to the moral confusion of the 1920's came the Depression. On May 15, 1930, the executive of a church council in a great metropolitan industrial center asked, "Is the cooperative movement going anywhere? Have we reached the top?" A couple of years later he knew that we had not yet reached the bottom! But far fewer church enterprises than banks went bankrupt; and the councils—almost all of them—somehow weathered the storm. By January 1936 Dr. Guild was saying, "There is full agreement to the fact that to close the city headquarters for cooperative Christian work would be more foolish than closing the Chamber of Commerce would be for business institutions."

The non-economic factor of the lesser loyalties, which so puzzled Dr. Price, still puzzles local and state council executives a generation later. "Speaking on the occasion of his retirement as executive secretary of the Rhode Island Council of Churches, Earl H. Tomlin warned that the ecumenical movement has slowed down and a resurgence of denominationalism has appeared where there was once a hope for Christian unity, . . . that 'vested interest' on the part of denominational leaders, a lack of real desire to minimize denominational barriers, and an emphasis on 'brand names' instead of world Christianity are largely responsible for the resurgence of denominationalism."[7] So Dr. Goodsell writes of "the virus of resurgent denominationalism."[8]

Meanwhile, among the "younger churches," new voices are heard. Says Bola Ige, former secretary of the Nigerian Student Christian Movement, "We (African Christians) cannot afford the luxury of denominationalism, which Americans seem to enjoy."[9] On the other hand, one of our most thoughtful and well-trained younger executives insists, "At the present moment in history a complete merger of all denominations into one church does not seem a necessity or a probability. What is important is that the church becomes one undivided body in fellowship."[10] If undenominationalism is in danger of being denominationalism *minus,* interdenominationalism faces an increasing opportunity for being denominationalism *plus.* In any case, the question keeps recurring, "Has church cooperation promised more than it has delivered?" What is the nature of the unity we have been seeking?

The Aspirations of Christian Leaders

A century ago last year Charles Darwin's *Origin of Species* appeared. In that same year, 1859, other books published included *A Tale of Two Cities* by Dickens, *Essay on Liberty* by John Stuart Mill, *Idylls of the King* by Tennyson, and volumes by Thackeray, Eliot, Ruskin, and other eminent writers.[11] The social origins of ecclesiastical species were as yet little realized, but there were stirrings toward a greater unity among the people of the faith.

> In 1866 Whittier wrote,
> "We faintly hear, we dimly see,
> In differing phrase we pray;
> But, dim or clear, we own in thee
> The Light, the Truth, the Way."

The 1869 Sunday School Convention went on record:[12] "We rejoice in the spirit of Christian union that has been manifested by this Convention, demonstrating that whatever our denominational differences, we are one in Christ and in Christian work." (Technically, what they were talking about was not "union" but spiritual *unity.*) Similarly in 1873 Dr. Charles Hodge said, "If all churches, whether

237

local or denominational, believed that they are one body in Christ Jesus, then instead of conflict we should have concord; . . . instead of rivalry and opposition we should have cordial cooperation."[13]

During the early years of our century Dr. Frank Mason North was moved by the common consideration of "a great central theme— the plea which faith and service make in this day and in this land for a united church, a church one in spirit and adjusted in its several branches for federation in organization and cooperation in action."[14] A little later[15] Edgar P. Hill affirmed: "Past, we trust, are the days when any branch of the evangelical church would insist that a community is not being evangelized unless *its* agents are doing the work." (One wishes that his hope had been more fully realized.)

But the new Home Missions Councils, organized in 1908, were "not widely known, largely because they were responsible not to denominations as such but to their mission boards," and "had relatively low visibility."[16] Moreover, as Dr. King pointed out,[17] "each member society had (only) one vote" in the HMC, which was "not intended to be a mission agent." It existed rather for "conference, fellowship, and cooperation"; and not for operational purposes, against which there has been steady denominational resistance until now.

In 1919 the FC general secretary said, "The denominational consciousness in the constituent bodies of the FC was never as strong as at the present moment, and it is rapidly deepening. We thus have these two seemingly contradictory phenomena—intensified denominationalism and increasing unity."[18] To be sure, Dr. Macfarland also cited a 1920 statement of Dr. Cavert's: "The Council rests on the principle that the pathway to the larger unity that we seek lies through the field of action";[19] but, as far as denominational boards were concerned, this action was likely to be simultaneous and cooperative, rather than operationally representative. At every level it was necessary and seemed desirable to keep the emphasis on cooperation, not some other more distant goal.[20]

Like the Federal Council, the National Council seems by its very existence to strengthen the separateness of its partners; but the chairman's address before NCC's DFM, in Pittsburgh December 7-10, 1958, sounded a new note: "Most of our cooperation has not been planned with the whole strategy of the mission of God in mind. . . . We have been reluctant to delegate to the cooperative bodies we have created . . . any creativity that places them in position to challenge the sovereignty of denominational control. . . . We should seek to encourage the DFM to seek a creative relationship with its cooperating boards which places it in a position of leadership rather than a group that merely executes the responsibilities allocated to it by the boards."[21] (How often in the DHM also have staff members been reminded that its function was to foster "co-operation" but not to "operate.")

The DFM leader continued, "We may be able to contribute more to the advance of the Kingdom of God through the emerging ecumenical movement than we will alone within a strictly denominational structure. . . . The continuing identity of our denomination is not of major importance, . . . the really important thing is whether the Church of Jesus Christ is free to develop along the lines that may not be familiar to us now and yet be within the purpose and intent of God. . . . The ecumenical era . . . is a new kind of thinking in which the nonessential lines of separateness within the field of religion become unimportant. The ecumenical era can become a new thrust in the mission of God."[22]

Word from the Field Increasingly Invited

Says the current folder, "The NCC, What It Is—What It Does," "About 900 local and state councils of churches, and more than 2,000 ministerial associations, work with the Council at the community level. State and local councils of churches are also represented officially in the Council."

In Chapter IX the impressive nature of this state and local representation in the NCC was noted, but its extent was only hinted at. Actually there is now such representation in no less than 55 NCC units: the General Assembly, the General Board and nine of its committees, the four Division Assemblies, the Commission on Christian Education and fourteen of its committees, three DCE, seven DCLW, two DFM, and four DHM committees, as well as on DUCM, DUCW, the Department of Evangelism, the National Christian Teaching Mission, the Department of Church World Service, the Broadcasting and Film Commission, the Bureau of Research and Survey and its committee on HM research, and the Washington Office Committee. Mr. Ketcham's computation shows 517 individual positions where state or local councils of churches have been represented, by a total of 415 different persons, from 43 states and Puerto Rico, and 27 city councils. Both quantitatively and qualitatively this would seem to be significant and generous representation. It provides an index both of NCC hospitality and of state and local interest. If there is a problem here, it lies in part, at least, in the realm of subnational structure and of intercouncil communication, where from the outset state and local councils have been entirely autonomous. If NCC is Barkus, it would seem that "Barkus is

239

willin',", far more than some impatient critics have thought. A major question is: "How can state and local councils organize their forces (not merely their professional personnel) and exchange the results of their wide-flung experience? Have they themselves been unwitting victims of a new sort of clericalism?"

More is now required than the testimony of brilliant individuals, however representative. Four hundred fifteen men and women, properly related to their constituents, could be a mighty force; and their combined testimony would undoubtedly be cordially welcomed at the national and world levels. What they need is not so much a vote, but a chance to witness, and to carry back word to the organizations they represent. They would appear to be entirely free to seek the mind of the field and to report to it. But how?

Desires of the Rank and File

A generation ago Dr. H. Paul Douglass found that the great loyalty of federation constituents, both lay and ministerial, was a symbol of unity achieved and in process. Even though "churchmen generally (thought) of federation as a working convenience rather than as an organic expression of the unity of the participating churches,"[23] the movement had already acquired "enormous symbolic meaning."[24]

There are no comparable data for recent years, but a new survey would probably confirm the earlier findings. Consider the popular response to Dr. E. Stanley Jones' presentation of "Federal Union," however over-simplified that proposal may seem to the experienced ecclesiastical administrator. Consider the widespread interest in the Oberlin Conference, and the growing attention paid by the ACS and local groups, as well as state councils of churches to questions of faith and order. President Eisenhower has whimsically ventured the guess that if government leaders do not get out of their way, some of these days the peoples of the earth, including our own, are likely to wage peace. Perhaps the same might prove true of church leaders and church unity. In spite of all lesser loyalties, do not the great rank and file of lay people feel that the Church is something vaster than their own particular communion, whatever it is, and however dear?

Ecclesiastical Action and Popular Thinking

In 1930 Dr. Douglass was convinced that "The Federation has to worm its way into nooks and crannies not yet pre-empted nor later discovered by the denominations. At no point has it been free to run and be glorified."[25] He felt forced to raise the question as to whether the denominations were afraid of federation as "the symbol of a unity

240

that in principle they cannot deny."[26] He found the "situation . . . safer denominationally speaking, because . . . headed up in a national system strictly subject to denominational action." This, to his mind, meant that "the cooperative movement as a whole (was) definitely fixed in the clamps of current denominationalism." He thought, however, that "the denominations (were) following a probably sound instinct in feeling that if they cooperate a little, Protestant public opinion will be slower in forcing them to a degree of unity for which they are not ready."[27] The national system of church cooperation would now seem to be more subject than ever to denominational action. On the other hand, much water has run under the bridge in thirty years, and it is now entirely safe to raise the question, "How permanent are the denominations themselves?"[28] On the other hand, have we sharpened the either-or aspect of this problem over-much? Should we have regarded denominationalism as an asset rather than as a difficulty?

As for the foreseeable future, denominations are of course to be taken for granted. Instead of being regarded as opponents of cooperation, it would seem more realistic to consider them as the basis of cooperative effort among Protestant and Orthodox churches. But as long ago as 1931 some of us were sure that "the federation movement favors those forces that make the church a servant of the community, rather than the community the servant of the church; which utilizes educational methods rather than mere propaganda."[29] Was this also too sharp an alternative to draw? We were sure, in any case, that the churches should build themselves into the life of the community, rather than build themselves up at the expense of the community.[30]

In 1931 it seemed necessary to confess, "It is a long row that must be hoed between the present competitive denominationalism and the cooperative Protestantism of tomorrow." Much of that long row has now been hoed—but by no means all of it. Then it seemed that "the church federation movement is an effort by the conciliar processes of democracy to provide that sort of fellowship that will make worship the foundation of social unity rather than the occasion of ecclesiastical strife."[31] In those days John T. McNeill was saying, in his *Unitive Protestantism*,[32] that "opportunity is for the courageous." How courageous have we been? Have we embraced our ecumenical opportunity with sufficient vigor and imagination? Or have we, with all our progress, been content with a smaller measure of advance than larger commitment would have made possible?

To attempt to answer the question, What is "the nature of the unity we seek?" might require another volume as large as this, if one

241

were merely to document the testimony of state and local councils. Suffice it here to say that, as never before, councils and groups within them are squarely facing up to that unavoidable question. In earlier years we could dodge it; but now it recurs with cumulative insistence.[33]

From Action to Thought

Thirty years ago H. Paul Douglass saw that there was already "a system of nation-wide Protestant federation . . . in the making."[34] To his mind, "no other movement rivals the federations in their direct and practical attack on the evils of the divided Church."[35] (Note that he did not say "of a divided world," but "of a divided Church.") That system, then only in the making, has now been tremendously extended, outward and upward, so that it is literally a world-wide venture. As William Temple, Archbishop of Canterbury, so well said, the ecumenical movement has been "the great new fact of our time."

Is the Council movement simply more ecclesiastical machinery? Is it merely an interdenominational administrative addition to the increasingly heavy denominational "overhead"? Is it one more aspect of the "bigness" that has developed in government, education, business, and labor? Is it dynamic and creative, or does it tend to "freeze" the ecclesiastical *status quo?* In what sense is it more Christian than separatism or autonomy, whether parochially exercised or sectarian in its world-wide practice? If we propose to "test our lives," and our culture, by His, how do our cooperative church relationships stand up under analysis? In what sense is "interdenominational" synonymous with "ecumenical"?[36]

Yet, even though ecumenicity has to face a renascence of denominationalism, ecumenicity can also easily be sabotaged by increasing parochialism. As John C. Bennett says,[37] "The community of Christ . . . never allows us to be merely Americans or people of the political West." By the same token, Jonesville and Middletown have their proper claim on religious loyalties, but a community church that does not look beyond the borders of a community too narrowly defined is in no position to censure denominations with world-wide horizons. The communion of ecumenical saints has to function in space as well as in time; else is it not ecumenical.

Over against sectarian narrowness there could easily grow up an ecclesiastical chauvinism. State and commonwealth provide opulent social differences, but Christ seeks to be Lord of them all. Regionalism can also show jingo traits, and parochialism can afflict Megalopolis and Manhattan as readily as it can Sauk Center. Nevertheless, as Leslie

Newbigin says,[38] in East Asia "one discovered . . . a thoroughly positive regionalism." To a lesser extent there are varieties of social and spiritual scene in America itself. Seattle and San Francisco, Indianapolis and Houston, Boston and Atlanta, are richly varied. The problem is: how to conserve the values of the indigenous and the charm of the local idiom without substituting them for the universals with their wider claim. If every denomination, and every church, and every Christian, in every geographical relationship (be its radius short or long), truly belongs to the Church Universal, then ecumenicity has begun to arrive. "The ecumenical community increases to the extent that communication expands among the churches."[39]

According to Gray,[40] "Leaders of councils discovered early that many churches are willing to 'do' but are not willing to 'talk.' " Because "the councils have been slow to develop an adequate doctrine of the Church . . . they are discovering that they have made their communities conscious of the churches but not of the Church."[41] (They could develop only pragmatically. Going denominations could talk on a world scale; talk at the local level would have meant no council.)[42]

"Heretofore," says Gray, "councils of churches have principally been regarded as instruments for cooperative activities among the churches. But there is emerging a concern for their *theological* implications, and a call for the serious study of faith and order in relation to them." He concludes: "While it is understandable that councils up to this point have not been very much concerned with theological meanings, and have thus been extremely slow to develop an adequate doctrine of the Church, this stage of their development is probably past. In order to fulfill their role in the second half of the century, they must correct what has been the lack by which theologians have been most deeply disturbed. It becomes for them the ecumenical necessity."[43]

Thus the ecumenical necessity is now in the field of thought rather than practice exclusively. For, as Goodsell says,[44] "Action in any sphere, undirected by sober thinking, is usually either futile or fateful." And Cate maintains that[45] "Unity in association must be solidified and given duration by a body of common doctrine." (He adds as a hypothesis, "Disunity is a result both of doctrinal and non-doctrinal barriers that block communication between church groups.") And it is interesting to see a state council secretary featuring on the front page of a recent monthly bulletin topics like these: "Technology and Service," "Sociology and Politics," "Theology and the Church."[46] Here again is an

243

increasingly thoughtful note as over against too exclusive emphasis on "activism" in years gone. Action is not less, but increasing thought gives it better grounding.

WHAT NEXT?*

The decades covered by this volume have stimulated many adjectives. Goodsell writes[47] of the *"drear* nineteen-thirties and the *warrocked* nineteen-forties."* (As far as America was concerned, World War I had been a briefer and less severe international earthquake.) According to Hal Boyle, writing at the end of last year,[48] "the *frantic* 1950's draw to a close. . . . At the start of the decade there were few things you could buy with a penny. And at the end of the decade there were few things you could with a nickle." Brooks Atkinson[49] found 1959 a "shabby season" in the theater, in which "small plays about small people suit (the) temper of a moody civilization." Now after the *"tremendous* fifties," come the *"amazing* sixties." [50] In magazine after magazine they have been called the *"soaring* sixties." But thoughtful analysts also talk about "the gathering haze of the *crucial* 60's."[51] The president of Columbia University thinks posterity may refer to the *"fumbling* fifties" in the United States, and points out that the new decade could turn out to be the *"slumping* sixties."[52]

The active council secretary would very much "rather make history than record it." To have point, this story should suggest some practical next steps. Three seem obvious:

I. *More Study,* † especially of the state and local councis as a whole.[56] Such studies might well cover at least seven areas:

    (1)   The extent and geography of the movement.[57]

    (2)   The structure and relationships of state and local councils.[58]

    (3)   The scope and range of their program activities. A first and very difficult question would be, How factorize the facts for statistical analysis and summary? At least nine foci of inquiry immediately suggest themselves: (i) religious education;[59] (ii) planning and strategy;[60] (iii) the UCW[61] and UCM[62] in relation to state and local councils; (iv) missions, home and foreign, as a state and local council task;[63] (v) evangelism;[64] (vi) public relations and communication;[65] (vii) social welfare;[66] (viii) human relations, international, inter-racial, interfaith, etc.;[67] (ix) faith and order.[68] Such a list could be easily extended.[69]

    (4)   Personalities and personnel.[70]

(5)   Budgets and finances; properties.[71]

(6)   Particular states and cities.[72]

(7)   Contemporary constituent attitudes.[73]

(8)   The varying religious needs of differing communities.[74]

II. *More Conference*

At St. Louis in 1957, when visitors were given a chance to react to NCC reports, they showed a much keener interest in discussing the working of state and local councils. Perhaps it should be frankly recognized that the NCC Assembly should consist of properly qualified delegates, and that the more popular interest should be directed not toward helping the NCC do its work but toward making the state and local aspect of church cooperation more effective and more widespread.

It is now forty years since the last nation-wide conference for the consideration of methods of church cooperation. Has the time come when another carefully planned congress could be held, comparable to those in Pittsburgh in 1917 and Cleveland in 1920? The Oberlin 1957 experience confirms the hope that such a gathering might prove popular and useful. If GCPFO, OCC, and ACS were to collaborate, it would be no very great task to enlist at least 1,000 persons in preliminary studies, to assure a body of material for consideration and discussion at such a congress. Discussion questions might include "The Significance of State and Local Councils from the Standpoint of the World and National Councils;"[75] and "Should there be some sort of a Council of Councils in addition to the ACS?"[76] These are only two of the many major questions that need far more serious study than has yet been given them. What is more important than finding answers is more careful thought on all the issues involved, not only by the paid executives of the council movement, but by experienced volunteer officers and division, department, commission, and committee chairmen and members as well.

(III) *More Vigorous Extension*

In Chapter II a national objective of the International Sunday School Association in 1893 was cited as "an effective organization in every township." Ought our objective in 1960 to be any less comprehensive? Whatever the sociological changes and their organizational consequences for geography and structure, ought we not now, more than ever, seek to blanket the entire nation with a network of church cooperation?

It must be confessed that "the cooperative movement in all its forms (local, state, national, and international) has to confront the

245

fact that very large sectors of Protestantism still hold aloof." While "the climate is . . . changing, we create too rosy a picture unless we take account," humbly, of our only fractional success, even within Protestant ranks.[77] Fortunately a number of local councils have found themselves able to win the cooperation of many local churches not allied with the national and world councils through their denominations, to the benefit of all concerned; and Divisional cooperation in the National Council is wider than the member bodies of the Council as a whole.

Moreover, impressive as is the number of state and local councils, even more so is the number of places where church cooperation is not yet adequately organized. As long ago as 1931 many of us had become convinced that "extension instead of being a detail on the fringe of things (had) become the central problem of the Federal Council."[78] Is it not now at least *a* central problem of the National Council?

Rural America is overchurched;—in many instances fewer churches would serve the community better. How can the denominations face this clear obligation with statesmanship, tact, patience, and courage? Is there a better instrument than the state councils of churches for building a sounder strategy for the more adequate churching of America under the counsel of the denominations cooperating in the National Council? Nowhere is the fragmented condition of the Church more in evidence than in the tragic inadequacy of little competitive churches, infrequent in their services, manned in many instances by non-resident pastors. Here is obvious opportunity for ecumenical statesmanship.

Even if all the churches ought to continue to exist, they would do far more effective work cooperatively than in isolation. Ministerial acquaintance is not enough. The rank and file of the membership need to acquire not only denominational loyalty, but some sense of The Great Church. The number of places of more than 5,000 inhabitants without councils of churches gives us a vast potential for the extension of church cooperation. With proper teamwork, at every level, by all the partners to the ecumenical enterprise, the number of councils of churches with volunteer leadership could easily be doubled. The number of councils with paid leadership would then more or less automatically increase, given proper field service.

How can the resources be found to add to the OCC staff the long-needed person to help state councils organize volunteer local councils? Doubling the number of volunteer councils would create many familiar problems of counsel, guidance, and the preservation of weak organizations through the vicissitudes of personnel change, especially among pastors, but difficulties should not be permitted to obscure opportunity and responsibility. Do the denominations and the councils really want to extend local and state cooperation? If they do, it can be done.

One person could easily spend all his time helping state councils cultivate ministerial associations and other local organizations, with a view to their slow expansion into more inclusive councils of churches. Even the slower spontaneous developments in the communities of less than metropolitan size will sooner or later force the employment of more coordinating staff. With greater opportunity than ever, the field staff now available is no larger than it was decades ago. Has not the time come for another advance?

There is doubtless room for honest difference of opinion as to whether emphasis should now be put on extending church cooperation by organizing new councils, or whether councils already existent should first rethink their reasons for existence, their programs and objectives, and the theology of interdenominational action, with its consequences for the meaning of the Church. Are not both courses to be followed?

The time is surely over-ripe for a more profound analysis of what church cooperation is all about. On the other hand, is it a time for coasting, in terms of the extension of the agencies of cooperation? As Seifert puts it,[79] "short steps ahead become long steps backward when the ground is rushing forward beneath our feet." Relatively, ought we not to do better than hold our own? Are state councils encouraging the growth of local councils? Are state councils giving adequate representative status to established local councils?

Can we recover the promotional and extension enthusiasms of half a century ago? If we do not, we could let the wonderful Interchurch Center, where people from near and far gather together joyously around cafeteria tables, in a sort of every-day ecumenical interchurch luncheon, become merely a monument to denominationalism, as certain European temples of international aspiration have served to enshrine a type of nationalism now outmoded in the minds of all penetrating analysts of the world crisis. In a world that could blow up at any minute, it is lesser loyalties, however rich our several heritages, that must prove their case. To put too much emphasis on the plural in churches is to fall into a sort of ecclesiastical polytheism quite inadequate to a time like ours. Is not a pantheon of autonomous denominations a rather impotent sort of anarchy in a jet-atomic age? In America too, as well as in lands where Christian communities

247

clamor for union, is not something more needed than "the outworn regalia of American denominationalism?"[80]

On the other hand, any attempted action outside the interdenominationally authorized channels, or action in any sense un- or anti-denominational, would seem as improper as it is unnecessary, undesirable, and ineffective; but the conclusion is unavoidable that truly denominational representatives now face the opportunity and the duty to transcend the limits of denominationalism while conserving the richness of every denominational heritage.

We Feel Our Way

To what do we look forward? Some think a group of national experts should tell us; the more experienced are more modest. We do not know what lies ahead. The number of major denominations may be sharply reduced during the next century. The possibility of new groupings, at first of an independent sort, with some of them soon more and more assimilated to the general type of American denominationalism, is equally clear. In any case, the need for church cooperation at every level will increase rather than decrease.

We cannot yet spell out the exact "Nature of the Unity We Seek." Is it not high time, however, that we confer more earnestly, and more open-mindedly, about so basic an issue? Not to know all the answers is no sign of weakness or ignorance. The general secretary of the WCC is sure that "while active collaboration . . . is an important part of the common calling of the churches, it is by no means the whole of that calling. Cooperation in service and witness has its own specific value, but it must not become a substitute for the realization of that fuller *Koinonia* and unity which is meant in John 17 and Ephesians 4."[81]

On this there would doubtless be agreement; but on the implementation of the implicit ideal there is room for wide disagreement. Therefore the WCC Central Committee at its August 1959 session, in considering the future of faith and order,[82] was clear that "The basic issues are not in the first place issues of organization, but issues of ecclesiology. We have come to a period in the development of the ecumenical movement when once again (as in Toronto in 1950) we have to define more clearly what exactly is the function of the World Council with regard to church unity." If this be true of the WCC, with the Lausanne tradition as part of its heritage, how much more is it true of state and local councils in the United States, where the tradition has been so overwhelmingly one of Life and Work. This would seem to be a time for study, hard thinking, prayerful quest, enriching fellow-

248

ship, rather than precipitate conclusions. We have been a long time separating; the reuniting process will not be easy or sudden, even though desirable and inevitable. Fortunately it is our Father's good pleasure to *give* us the Kingdom. We need not try in our own little wisdom to fashion the Larger Church that is to be; the Head of the Church will build it.

Our Times and Our Churches are in His Hands

Now that the World Council has been organized, the interest of all Cooperative Christianity supports the association of the denominations in National Councils of Churches. Now that the NCCCUSA has been organized, there is certainly nationwide interest in the strengthening of state councils of churches. Now that most of the states are organized, it ought surely to be a major concern of state councils of churches that local councils should be organized on an appropriate basis in every place where the Kingdom and the community would be served by such interchurch organizations.

The earliest roots of cooperation were at the local and state level. The national and world organizations have greatly improved the ecclesiastical climate, but the urge for cooperation began at the grass-roots. Says one of our most experienced, consecrated, and well-loved national leaders, "I believe the grass-roots movement helped in shaping or really interacted with other factors to make possible or force cooperation at the national level, or I would not have given 30 years to the work."

Somewhere along the road we have discovered that though "churches can cooperate without being changed, they cannot participate in the total mission of the Church without their life being transformed."[83] If sometimes this long story may seem like only another power struggle, between churches organized denominationally and churches organized territorially, it will be well to remember that in Christ there are neither denominations nor geography. As Visser 't Hooft reminded us in his Oberlin sermon,[84] *God in Christ still takes the initiative.* As long as all our churches serve Him, the exact nature of their relationships to one another can be left not merely to human compromise, but also to divine guidance. Our cooperative strategy can limit our ecclesiastical anarchy, but called pilgrims should be friendly. Given basic friendliness, under the banner of our One Lord, all the problems of cooperative relationships, at the local, state, national, and world levels, would seem to be on their way to solution. For "He will complete what He has begun."[85]

249

* *A Suggested Procedure.* This entire section ("What Next?") was roughed out before the writer had any adequate knowledge of a whole series of events that took place in the NCC in late 1959. These included such varied happenings as:

The Consultation on Long-Range Planning, called and sponsored by GCPFO, held at Atlantic City November 4-6, 1959; the Consultation on Personnel Needs in Church Planning and Research, Indianapolis, November 10-20, 1959; the special meeting of GCPFO and the Advisory Committee for OCC at Detroit December 3, 1959; and the Joint Assembly of DFM and DHM, held at Atlantic City December 7-11, 1959.

The records of these meetings show that the problems raised in this volume are very much in the thinking of all NCC leaders, whether denominationally or interdenominationally employed or related. Even the sovereignty, durability, and adequacy of the denominations as such is certainly to the fore, as never before.[53] Moreover, Section I of what follows ("More Study") was written before the 1959 ACS minutes, including the excellent report of the Committee on Studies,[54] and the action of the ACS setting up an enlarged committee and study program, were available. So much the more significant are this writer's conclusions as to the need and opportunity for study, reached after nearly two years' intensive perusal of the historical data afforded by the church cooperation movement. They strongly support, in principle, the widely publicized Wickizer proposal.[55]

In effect, this whole volume is a report to the ACS Committee on History. In authorizing its publication, the ACS has only received it for study, by its own members and other interested persons. *Perhaps the History Committee would like to refer to the ACS, and through it to the ACS Executive Committee, the careful consideration of the proposals for study and action that follow.*

† *Other Suggested Referrals:*

What immediately follows might properly be referred eventually to the Committee on Studies, for such action as they may see fit to take, in the light of the DHM proposals for 1960-1963 and of the faith and order ecclesiological study. Similarly, any suggested administrative procedures might ultimately be referred to the Advisory Committee of OCC, and if deemed worthy, by that body to GCPFO, in the hope that ACS and the Faith and Order Department of the NCC would also be involved in any long-range planning along the lines suggested. The purpose of this final section of the history is not to blueprint details but to indicate a possible sense of direction, with the hope that the obvious expectancy of the Committee on Studies may prove wholly justified.

Supporting this hope are such statements as those made by Dean Jerald C. Brauer of the Federated Theological Faculty of the University of Chicago, in connection with the installation of Lemuel Petersen at Seattle. While Dean Brauer insisted that *informal* representation "is a luxury (councils of churches) can no longer afford," he was equally sure that councils "can perform even greater service" and that "local (and presumably state) councils are entering the most crucial period in their history. They have vast new opportunities." (See FC *Outlook,* February, 1959, p. 8). This entire historical sketch seems to its writer to support this thesis. Wherefore the plea for accelerated momentum, along with profounder thinking.

Two dangers seem equally real. *We can be too impatient,* without justification. State and local council leaders will do well to join with NCC leaders in genuine *long*-range thinking. The problems of schedule mechanics, etc., involved, do not permit any quick, easy solution. On the other hand, *we can be too content with things as they are.* Personnel steeped in the denominational process will not understand the problems of state and local councils unless these are brought to their attention respectfully, loyally, but courageously and clearly. What is here sought is action as well as discussion, extension as well as enrichment.

REFERENCE NOTES

Chapter X

1 *Saturday Review*, April 23, 1959, from a talk at the dedication of the Colgate University Library. (The importance and the limitations of what happens at the United Nations Building may well serve as a restraining hand on extravagant claims of interdenominational progress, as well as a beacon toward ventures of co-operative effort yet to be undertaken.)

2 These figures are not exact: New York City has a number of councils; and some places are effectively served by councils in larger areas. However, the extent of the "unorganized" field is clear.

3 Ralph Canfield McAfee, long-time executive secretary (Portland, Ore., Kansas City, Mo., and Detroit, Mich., councils) and urban church pastor, amending language submitted to him by this writer; in a personal letter, February 24, 1959.

4 Two interfaith tendencies have been at work simultaneously. One, in the direction of greater mutual appreciation, has expressed itself in The National Conference of Christians and Jews, which soon swung away from its early FC moorings. The other has issued in movements like Protestants and Other Americans United.

5 *Ecumenical Review*, April, 1959, *World Council Diary*, p. 324.

6 At Minneapolis, 1926; *FC Bulletin*, January 1927.

7 W. W. Richardson, R. I., correspondent, *The Christian Century*, Nov. 4, 1959, p. 1292.

8 *Op. cit.*, p. 251.

9 Also co-secretary of the 18th Ecumenical Student Conference of the National Student Christian Federation, held in Athens, Ohio, December 27, 1959, to January 2, 1960; in an article in *The United Church Herald*, January 21, 1960.

10 Introd. to Wm. B. Cate: "Theoretical and Practical Aspects of Ecumenical Communication," Ph.D. dissertation, Boston University, 1953. Introd., vi, 305 pp., and abstract.

11 *United Church Herald*, November 12, 1959, p. 3.

12 *1869 Convention Report*, p. 153.

13 Cited by Frank Mason North, in *The Methodist Review*, September-October, 1905.

14 *Ibid.*

15 Handy, *op. cit.*, p. 28, citing "Cooperation in Home Missions" (undated).

16 *Ibid.*, pp. 27, 28.

17 *Ibid.*, p. 25.

18 Macfarland, *Christian Unity in the Making*, p. 182.

19 *Ibid.*, p. 185.

20 At times this was even at the expense of the prophetic, as "the price you pay for co-operation." (J. M. Artman, in *FC Bulletin*, October, 1931, editorial.) From the standpoint of the objective sociologist, functional cooperation was a legitimate end in itself. In his influential book *The Community* (Association Press, 1921), Dr. Artman had said, "Unfortunately, (church) federations have been largely nominal not functional" (p. 165).

21 *Cf.* the hope expressed by one nationally influential churchman in 1951 that this history might help state and local councils to be something more than "errand boys of the denomination."

22 "From Missions to Mission" by Virgil A. Sly in his address before the DFM, NCC, December 7-10, 1958, in Pittsburgh. Printed in full in *The Christian Evangelist-Front Rank*, October 25, 1959, pp. 1352 ff.; cf. also *Information Service*, February 28, 1959. At the same DFM Assembly John Coventry

Smith, associate general secretary of the Commission on Ecumenical Mission and Relations of the United Presbyterian Church in the USA, said, "If the Baptists and Methodists are strong in Burma, there is no reason why a Presbyterian should be unhappy until he also established a Presbyterian work in that country. The work of the whole church belongs to all of us" (*Information Service*, February 28, 1959). (Isn't the same true of Jonesville, USA?) *Cf.* also the address by Truman B. Douglass, a year earlier, already cited.

23 *Protestant Cooperation in American Cities*, p. 88.

24 *Ibid.*, p. 278.

25 *Ibid.*, p. 255.

26 *Ibid.*, p. 258.

27 *Ibid.*, p. 275.

28 *Cf.* Lewis S. Mudge, art. on "World Confessionalism and Ecumenical Strategy" (*Ecumenical Review*, July, 1959, Vol. XI, No. 4, p. 383). "Denominationalism is something essentially pre-ecumenical." (The problem would seem to be: How make the resurgence of denominational loyalties an asset rather than a liability?)

29 "The Status of Church Cooperation," by this writer, *Religious Education*, September, 1931, pp. 530 ff.

30 *Cf.* Lindeman, *The Community*, p. 24: "When an institution comes to think more of its own advancement than of the advancement of the community, it is out of harmony with true progress."

31 Art. cited in note 29.

32 Abingdon, 1930.

33 For an exceptionally well-informed and competent review of all that is here involved, *cf.* "The Ecumenical Movement—Retrospect and Prospect," by Dr. Samuel McCrea Cavert, *The Ecumenical Review*, April, 1958, pp. 311 ff.

34 *Protestant Cooperation in American Cities*, p. 213.

35 *Ibid.*, p. 280.

36 This writer has tried to edit out of the first portion of this book all use of "ecumenical" where "cooperative" or "interdenominational" was meant. The word "ecumenical" does creep in, especially in quoted statements, where it is sometime either an anachronism or inaccurate. There is now an increasingly careless use of the word, which should be guarded against, lest it lose its significant meaning.

37 *Christian Century*, December 13, 1959, p. 1502.

38 In a December, 1959, International Missionary Council general letter.

39 Cate, *op. cit.*

40 *Op. cit.*, p. 171.

41 *Ibid.*, p. 173.

42 Minear, *The Nature of the Unity We Seek*, p. 209; cited by Gray, *op. cit.*, p. 174.

43 The response to this need begins to appear. E.g., when Lemuel Peterson was installed as executive secretary of the Greater Seattle Council of Churches on February 1, 1959, he presented a distinguished paper on "Seeking Christian Unity in Greater Seattle" (10 pp., mimeographed), in which he drew on much recent Faith and Order literature. *Cf.* also "As the Secretary Sees It," Harlan M. Frost, in the *Newsletter* of the Council of Churches of Buffalo and Erie County, N.Y., January, 1959; "Why do and should churches work together? . . . We work together because we cannot do otherwise. The love of Christ constraineth us."

44 *Op.cit.*, App. III, *Toward a Theology of Missions*, p. 275.

45 *Op. cit.*

46 Vernon M. MacNeill in *Illinois Church Councilor*, December, 1959.

47 *Op. cit.*, p. 62.

48 AP to *Boston Traveller,* December 29, 1959.

49 *NY Times,* January 3, 1960.

50 *Cumberland Presbyterian,* January 19, 1960.

51 Martin E. Marty, *Christian Century,* January 6, 1960.

52 *NY Times,* January 8, 1960.

53 Elsa Kruuse, Office of Information, NCC.

54 Dr. Cate's paper (27 pp.) on "The Institutionalism of the Church as it Affects Ecumenical Communication in the Local Community," a contribution to a large WCC Faith and Order study, while only in tentative draft, provided a particularly thoughtful analysis deserving wide consideration. It is an excellent example of the respect a local council (Portland, Ore.) secretary can command, on the basis of real scholarship reenforced by practical administrative experience.

55 Willard M. Wickizer, vice president of the NCC for home missions, called for a six-year "comprehensive study of American life," with a "Convocation on the Mission of the Church in America" in 1963, which might be attended by thousands of Protestants.

56 National Council records will be carefully kept. Individual state and local council archives from now on are likely to be faithfully maintained. It is high time, however, that we begin to regularize the gathering of facts that will make possible "new generalizations" of a far more thoroughgoing sort than anybody is now equipped to assemble.

57 Could we have a year book giving details comparable to those provided in denominational summaries, with the integers not the local churches or groups of churches (synods, conferences, dioceses, conventions, and the like) but state and local councils of churches?

58 This field needs a fresh, new, objective approach. Empirical study of basic constitutional similarities and differences, and of administrative practices, other than matters of specific program activities and finance, might throw great light on the meaning of the movement, and its needs and opportunities.

59 Contemporary organizational structures, functions, personnel, etc. E.g., attention to age and sex groups.

60 Is the NCC able to strengthen this original aim of many state and local councils of churches? If so, how? By the action of denominational extension boards, or by the plenary action of the communions themselves, or both? Probably such an inquiry would require at least one, perhaps a whole series of specialized conferences.

61 62 Up-to-date appraisals are needed.

63 What contact do state and local councils have with DHM, DFM, IMC, and other national and international agencies? If the "Mission" of the Church involves united action, can state and local councils omit "missions" from their program? How can they most effectively supplement denominational activity in missionary work?

64 What are the actual and desirable roles of state and local councils in evangelism? Perhaps the NCC Department of Evangelism would be interested to share in such an inquiry.

65 Including house organs, the media of mass communication, etc. Here again various NCC units may be interested.

66 Nature and extent of specialized personnel, activity, and budgets. Certainly the NCC would be interested here.

67 This inquiry should be cleared with the proposed post-Oberlin ecclesiological study. How much attention are state and local councils actually giving to the study of the meaning of the Church? With what results?

68 Summaries of experiences in this field, and suggestions as to council responsibility, would seem appropriate. As one NCC leader puts it, theology is often used as an alibi for separateness maintained on quite other grounds. So Dr. C. C. Morrison (*Christian Century,* December 23, 1959) writes of "the

comfortable illusion that the cause of our continuing dividedness is doctrinal." J. Robert Nelson *(ibid.)* deplores the fact that our "brotherhood in Christ remains a fractured fraternity because of ecclesiastical schism"; but Dr. Goodsell *(op. cit.,* p. 276) believes that "the old era of theological isolation is drawing to a close." Field studies, with precise instruments of measurements, could estatblish the facts, empirically observed.

[69] Program study might also include such matter as: Departmentalization in larger councils, as the result of the proliferation of functions; special problems of smaller councils, where the leadership, whether paid or volunteer, must be of the "generalist" sort, but needs the counselling services of more specialized personnel (the role of the "amateur" and of the "expert"); additional or revised program guides, or a new manual of program possibilities.

[70] Suggested sub-topics: Effective leaders in the past—as many write-ups as possible, on the basis of suggested criteria, plus unique individual contributions; elements of present effectiveness in leadership; choosing and training leaders; professional standards; placement problems and practices; adequate pensions.

[71] Suggested sub-topics: Facts, and their meaning; suggested procedures and principles; additional field service; office headquarters, rented and owned; (this subject alone ought to produce at least one, perhaps several useful volumes).

[72] Such a study would involve establishing criteria of choice, method of treatment, enlistments of analysts, including graduate students, in seminaries and in university social sciences.

[73] Social distance tests, such as those used in *Protestant Cooperation in American Cities,* might well be used; also questionnaries as to program interest, and the significance attached to the council movement by constituents. New data could be compared with those gathered just prior to 1930.

[74] This is partly a matter of method, but even more of attitude, involving an empirical approach to cooperative function.

[75] Without anticipating what careful group study might discover, two assertions may be ventured. (i) More important than how many of what sort, and how chosen, is the question of *why* representatives of state and local councils in the NCC should be chosen. (ii) This whole problem could prove to be one of communication rather than of votes, largely, if not wholly. State and local councils are not now interested in acquiring status as "accredited auxiliaries" of the NCC. What they seek is a more adequate method of sharing their experiences and insights, both with the NCC and with each other.

[76] *Cf.* Harold E. Fey: "Councils of Churches should be encouraged instead of discouraged to form a national organization of Councils of Churches" (in "Ecumenical Christianity in Urban America," pp. 42-49 of the *American Baptist Urban Convocation Report,* Indianapolis, 1957, p. 48.)

[77] Letter from Dr. Cavert, previously cited.

[78] Personal letter, this writer to Dr. Guild, January 3, 1931.

[79] Harvey Seifert, "A Christian Reappraisal of Realism in Foreign Policy," in *Religion In Life,* Winter, 1959-60, pp. 75 ff. Capable of significant translation into the field of interdenominational policy.

[80] *Op. cit.,* p. 248.

[81] *Ecumenical Review,* October, 1959, p. 73.

[82] *Ibid.,* p. 102.

[83] *Ibid.,* p. 125.

[84] September 8, 1957 (Minear, *op. cit.,* pp. 121 ff.)

[85] *Ecumenical Review, ibid.,* p. 126.

A BRIEF BIBLIOGRAPHY

Materials most frequently used include the following:

General

H. Paul Douglass, *Christian Unity Movements in the U.S.*
Protestant Cooperation in American Cities.

Washington Gladden, *The Christian League of Connecticut.*
Recollections.

Fred Field Goodsell, *Ye Shall Be My Witnesses.*

Robert T. Handy, *We Witness Together.*

John A. Hutchison, *We Are Not Divided.*

Charles S. Macfarland, *Across the Years.*
Christian Unity in the Making.
Christian Unity in Practice and Prophecy.
Progress of Church Federation.

Paul S. Minear, *The Nature of the Unity We Seek.*

Mark Rich, *The Rural Church Movement.*

E. B. Sanford, ed. *Church Federation.*
Origin and History of the Federal Council.

Bernard A. Weisberger, *They Gathered at the River.*

Chapter II

Athearn, *Religious Education and American Democracy.*

Bower and Hayward, *Protestantism Faces Its Educational Task Together.*

Arlo Ayres Brown, *A History of Religious Education.*

E. Morris Fergusson, *Then Lessons for Association Workers.*
Historic Chapters in Christian Education.

Edwin Wilbur Rice, *The Sunday School Movement and the American Sunday School Union* (1780-1917).

International Sunday School Association Convention Reports.

Minutes of the Sunday School Council of Evangelical Denominations.

Chapters III to VIII make frequent use of *published* Federal Council annual reports and quadrennial summaries, containing minutes of its executive and administrative committees, and of its commissions; and its *Year Books* (various titles and editors).

Chapters V to VII make large use of *materials on file* at the Office for Councils of Churches, including:

Minutes of the Commission on Inter-Church Federations (State and Local), and of its Committee of Direction;

Minutes of the Association of Executive Secretaries;

Folders of supplementary data, including correspondence, chronologically arranged;

Other folders of material filed by states and communities.

Chapter VI cites the *Council News Letter;*

The FC Committee on Extension of State and Local Cooperation minutes; the ICRE Board of Field Administration minutes.

Chapter VII utilizes the minutes of the
　　Federal Council Field Department;
　　ICRE Committee on Field Program;
　　Inter-Council Field Committee;
　　Inter-Council Field Department;
　　Employed Council Officers' Association
　　and *Church Federation Field.*

Chapter VII consults the minutes of the Association of Council Secretaries, and the files of *Christendom* and *The Church Woman.*

Chapter IX uses the minutes of the
　　DCE Educational Services Commission, NCC;
　　Central Department of Field Administration;
　　General Committee on Program and Field Operations
　　and Office for Councils of Churches records;
　　NCC *Work Books;*
　　DCE *Year Books;*
　　NCC Outlook, and *Interchurch News;*
　　OCC News Letter;
　　ACS *Alerte*

Chapter X cites numerous other periodicals.

(For dates of publication, publishers, etc. and many additional sources, see Reference Notes).

ACADEMIC TREATISES

There is a slow but considerable accumulation of graduate dissertations on specific aspects of the ecumenical movement, including local and state cooperation. These include:

The Cooperation of Churches in Baltimore (1919-1949),
  by John W. Harms, M. A., University of Chicago, 1953.

A History of the Buffalo Federation of Churches, (1913-1930),
  by Dorothy E. Eells, M. A., University of Buffalo.

Christian Education in New Jersey,
  by Erna Hardt, Ph. D., Drew University, 1951.

Protestant Cooperation in Alleghany County, Pennsylvania, from 1889 to 1943,
  by Frank A. Sharp, Ph. D., University of Pittsburgh, 1948.
  (Cf. also *In Glorious Tradition* prepared for the tenth anniversary of the Council of Churches, September 25, 1953, based largely on the above, *Pittsburgh Council of Churches, A Historical Interpretation,* by Charles Reed Zahniser, 1944, and the *Golden Jubilee Year Book of the Alleghany County Sabbath School Association,* 1939).

A History and Comparative Study of Four City Councils of Churches,
  by Kenneth A. Garner, B.D., Union Theological Seminary New York, 1951
  (Hartford, Conn.; Washington, D.C.; Albany, N.Y.; Springfield, Mass.).

Factors of Success and Failure in Federated Churches,
  by Ralph L. Williamson, Ph. D., Drew University, 1951.

Theoretical and Practical Aspects of Ecumenical Communication,
  by William B. Cate, Ph. D., Boston University, 1953.

The Ecumenical Necessity,
  by Raymond A. Gray, S.T.M., Union Theological Seminary, New York, 1958.

If other seminary libraries have materials of this sort, a note to the Office for Councils of Churches, 475 Riverside Drive, New York 27, N.Y., would be a courtesy.

The Bergen County (N.J.) Council of Christian Education records have been sent to the library of the Union Theological Seminary in Richmond, Va., which is becoming a depository for these historical records.

A History of the Ohio Council of Churches (1919-1954) has been written by Fenton Fish.

APPENDIX I

Two Outstanding Local Councils

These two councils have been chosen because of the recent retirement of their distinguished executives, because they illustrate what has happened in the last two decades, because of available historical summaries, and to illustrate the merger process. The list could easily be multiplied by at least ten, to include a score or more of significant local demonstrations of church cooperation of long standing.

1. *Buffalo and Erie County, N.Y.*—Harlan M. Frost

Eric F. Goldman, writing in the January 1960 *Harper's,* called the 1950's a "stuffy decade." In terms of Buffalo church cooperation the facts were quite otherwise. During these years the growth of the Council of Churches, under the long leadership (1944-1959) of Dr. Frost, was conspicuous.

In June 1951 *The Christian Century,* in an article on "Christian Church Cooperation in Buffalo—A Study of a Successful Council of Churches," said, "To know Dr. Frost is to understand the position of trusted leadership the council holds in the life of the churches and the city. His notable traits of humility, sincerity, and democratic spirit are at the heart of great Christian leadership. He graduated from the University of Minnesota with Phi Beta Kappa honors in 1915. After completing his theological training at Colgate-Rochester Divinity School, he served pastorates in Minnesota, New York, and Ohio. At the end of a ten-year pastorate in Toledo, he was elected executive secretary of the Toledo Council of Churches in 1934. (Some of us still remember his exceptional counsel on "Undergirding Spiritually" at the 1936 joint sessions of the AES and ECOA.) In 1914 he was called to head the Federal Council's commission on camp and defense communities. When he came to Buffalo the budget of the Council was $17,000. Now it is four times as large." The 1959 budget was $110,354, with cash on hand January 31, 1958, in double the amount of the total budget when Dr. Frost went to Buffalo.

That this growth resulted from the labors of many others is part of the administrative leadership of this well-loved, representative executive, as well as evidence of the progress of the entire movement during the decade, in program, in personnel, and in support.

The Erie County Sabbath School Association was organized December 3, 1857. In 1886 its name was changed to the Erie County Sunday School Association.

The Interchurch Council of Women was organized in 1911.

Taking over a $600 debt from the local Men and Religion Movement, the Buffalo Federation of Churches was organized April 15, 1913. Its Committee on Religious Education paralleled the County Sunday School Association.

As early as 1916 thought and effort were expended to bring the Association and the Federation together. On April 1, 1930, the Sunday School Association became the Department of Religious Education of the Federation of Churches.

In 1941, when it was given its fine new home, the Federation sought incorporation as the Council of Churches.

Any adequate history of church cooperation in the city and county would wish to go into details concerning its earlier secretaries: Edward C. Fellowes (1913-1916), C. McLeod Smith (1916-1921), Lewis G. Rogers (acting 1921-1923), Don D. Tullis (1923-1930), John A. Vollenweider (1931-1934), Ross W. Sanderson (1937-1942). (It will be noted that there were repeated "interim" periods, between full-time executives.) After the International Sunday School Convention in Buffalo in 1918, R. George Lord was moved from part-time to full-time as County Sunday School Association executive (1918-1924), and his successor, Benton S. Swartz, is gratefully remembered. If only a few lay persons were to be listed, the names of Edwards D. Emerson, George T. Ballachey, and Ralph E. Smith would surely be included; so would Mrs. Albert F. Laub, donor of the Council property, and Mrs. Fred H. White, long secretary of the Council of Church Women. A long list of local clergy would include Bishop Cameron J. Davis, and many others.

The Federation's initial budget (1913-1914) was $3,200. In 1919-1920 a $20,000 budget was reduced to $16,640. In 1921 salary arrearages had reached $1,000, bringing about an interim arrangement. In 1923-1924, according to Dr. Tullis, "More than once this year the salaries of the staff have been a thousand dollars in arrears . . . rent as much as three months back." In the 1924-1925 budget of $21,000, a debt item of $6,600 was included. By 1929-1930 the budget was up to $24,000, and the debt reduced to $2,500. The first merged budget (1930-1931) was $35,000; but by October 1933 there were liabilities amounting to $8,452.41. The close of the Sunday School Association's separate existence was marked by sharp shrinkage in payments on pledges, excessive cost of solicitation and collection, and expenses incurred on the basis of expected rather than actual income. The Federation's financial situation, though difficult, was somewhat better, and its income larger. Part of the problem of councils like this has been the relation of city to county, in terms of service, support, and structure. The sociology of this and many other metropolitan counties has changed rapidly in recent decades, involving the sudden transformation of rural churches and neighborhoods to suburban.

Since his retirement in June 1959 Dr. Frost has been working part-time to help develop a stronger program for the councils in Niagara Falls and Lockport. He has been succeeded at Buffalo by Paul Anderson Collyer, former missionary to China and the Philippines, under the American Baptist Foreign Missionary Society, more recently in charge of Latin American and European distributions for the American Bible Society.

2. *Pittsburgh Consolidates*—Employs O. M. Walton

Similarly, if one local council and one executive were to be chosen to exemplify the perplexities, achievements, and expectations of the 1940's, it would be hard to find a better example than that afforded by Pittsburgh and its O. M. Walton.

The Pittsburgh Sunday School Union was organized in 1817, the Alleghany County Sabbath School Union in 1889. The Protestant Ministerial Union dates from 1900. After an Evangelistic Committee (1912-1916), and a Christian Social Service Union (from 1913), and a City Missions Council (from 1914) had been organized, the first Pittsburgh Council of Churches dated from 1916. With it a Week-Day Religious Education organization (from 1940) and the County

Sabbath School Association were merged in 1913, after two years of functional cooperation, to form (what has been called since 1955) The Council of Churches of the Pittsburgh Area. A Council of Church Women was organized in 1946. In 1956 the Area Council acquired its own Headquarters Building. In October 1959 the Council celebrated the 200th anniversary of the founding of Pittsburgh by a Bicentennial Rally of the church forces of the area.

In a succession of Pittsburgh leaders, including Dr. Charles Reed Zahniser and Dr. J. Kirkwood Craig, the name of O. M. Walton, executive director from 1945 until his retirement in 1957, stands out as the embodiment of the solid accomplishments of cooperative churchmanship in the American city. Graduating from Oberlin College in 1916, Mr. Walton later spent five years (1920-1924) in the Central and Lakewood branches of the Cleveland YMCA. In 1929, after five years as educational minister of the Lakewood Methodist Church, "O. M." (now with an M. A. from Northwestern) became religious education director of the Federated Churches of Cleveland, and was ordained in 1930. When depression conditions forced staff reductions on that organization, Mr. Walton served for four years (1932-1936) as the able church editor of *The Cleveland Plain Dealer,* an experience that later served him in good stead. Returning to the Federation in 1936, after seven months of service as acting executive during the illness of his chief, in early 1937 he succeeded Dr. Don D. Tullis in the executive secretaryship. Eight years later Pittsburgh called him.

A competent church administrator, with several types of specialized ability, Mr. Walton has also been a civic leader of outstanding stature. In his ministerial service in the local church when the cooperative movement was young and relatively small, as educational worker and senior executive during the difficult 1930's, and as executive director in a metropolitan council for more than a decade during the years when American Protestantism was achieving new cooperative unity, he won friends and influenced people by sterling worth and sturdy achievements. Since his retirement "O. M." followed Frank Jennings (retired Massachusetts executive) as interim secretary for the Ohio Council of Churches. He also compiled the *Story of Religion in the Pittsburgh Area* (72 pp. Committee on Religion of the Pittsburgh Bicentennial Association). His "interests and activities have extended across the lines of faith and denominations. In May 1958 he was awarded a certificate of recognition for leadership in the fields of human relations and religious brotherhood by the Pittsburgh Chapter of the National Conference of Christians and Jews."

The reason for this award is reflected in the final paragraph of Mr. Walton's "Summation" of the story of organized religions in Pittsburgh: "The test for the future will lie, not so much in the richness and variety of the houses of worship we build, nor in the zealousness with which we keep them separate and inviolable, but in how we share the treasures they represent and how we demonstrate the qualities of religious living through amity, good will, and the creation of a more righteous community." Here church cooperation becomes interfaith community-mindedness.

Pittsburgh and Walton symbolize quiet expectancy and hopes still being fulfilled, under the leadership of his colleague and successor, Robert L. Kincheloe.

APPENDIX II

Some Sample State Stories

1. *Massachusetts*

Organized Sunday school work in the Bay State goes back to 1854 or 1855. In 1869 it was reported that the commonwealth would soon hold its fifteenth annual convention. In 1875 a regular Saturday meeting was held in Boston to study the uniform lesson, which by 1872 "was carrying everything before it." Another meeting was held in Cambridge. Four or five hundred persons attended each week, "rubbing out our sectarian lines for the hour."

Partly because of the relative unimportance of the county in New England, only two Massachusetts counties were organized in 1875. By 1878 it was reported that a high percentage of all church additions were from the Sunday school.

Four thousand people were present at an 1889 meeting in Boston, and 60 conventions were reported. The movement had sought to provide a district meeting within reach of every school. A full-time worker was employed. By 1893 "the workers in Massachusetts are proving the proposition, take care of the township and county organization, and the state organization will take care of itself." The work was reorganized in 1889, with 53 districts; and by 1889 the organization was reported "thorough." In 1902 most of these districts had maintained their organization, and all but three had done good work. In 1900 complete reports came from 29. All but six held conventions at least annually, some of them more often. Contributions in 1904 amounted to nearly $10,000.

Among state federations of churches that have survived uninterruptedly, Massachusetts, the earliest, was organized March 31, 1902. Massachusetts Church Federation history divides itself into four main periods; only the first of these will be noted here in any detail.

(1) *The E. T. Root Era,* to 1930.

Dr. Root's unpublished manuscript and other materials (many of them printed) amply document this period. Dr. Root was primarily interested in people: "Comity and cooperation are means; and the end is not even 'successful' federations, denominations, or churches, but the perfecting of individuals and their communities." He testified that in spite of "the complexity and novel difficulties of interdenominational cooperation, involving constant salesmanship to individuals and congregations," and "much travel," "my health improved." He early "learned, in interviews and addresses, to appeal to the premises of each denomination." It was the official commitment of the churches themselves, not the cooperation of individuals, which gave significance "to a federation of churches, local, state, or national. This—not achievements however brilliant, not leaders, voluntary or salaried, however able, not the size of the budget—is its *esse;* these other things, however desirable, contribute to its *bene esse.*" A federation's "best work is to better (the churches') work. It is not their rival but their joint agency, maintaining and strengthening them, until, two by two, and ultimately all, they merge into one ecclesiastical organization." He recognized ecclesiasticism as a reality.

"During its first five years, work in Massachusetts would have collapsed but for the base of operations in Rhode Island," where Dr. Root lived in a rented summer cottage, two miles from the railroad. In 1909 the Congregationalists of Massachusetts agreed to give 50¢ per church, or $300, to the Federation. In 1913 this amount was raised to $1 per year per church as an asking from each denomination. In 1906 the amount raised was $552; in 1907, $343; 1908, $214; 1909, $1,149. At the end of 1912 the Federation owed the secretary $715. In 1914 the "quota" was raised to $2 per church, and $2,836 was received. The 1915 budget of $4,000 was not reached.

As a matter perhaps not unrelated was the fact that Barnstable County had one church for every 295 inhabitants. "Lowell, with a Protestant population no larger than 60 years ago, is attempting to maintain three times as many churches." In 1920 the secretary's salary was increased to $2,400. Half of his time was contributed to the rural survey of the state by the Interchurch World Movement, as it had been in previous years to the Committee on the Moral Aims of the War. The total raised in 1920 was $4,930; in 1922, it was $5,608, with all bills paid; in 1924, $8,374.

In 1925 Kenneth MacArthur was added to the staff, and $14,742 was spent. In 1926 the amount raised was $15,066. In 1928 religious education became a department, but the formal merger of the Sunday school forces and the Church Federation did not take place until 1933. By 1930 Dr. Root had seen the income grow from $200 to $21,000. Congregational Superintendent F. E. Emrich had quoted John R. Commons: "The two faults of American Protestantism are its *overlapping and its overlooking.*" Dr. Root rang the changes on these words, adding "and its overorganizing." He reported 1,199 Protestants in an urban "parish" distributed among 46 churches in 14 denominations—the church that had the most could claim only one-fifth of the total. "If there were found a village of 1,000 inhabitants with 46 churches, would it not be a scandal? Yet such is the overlapping in cities."

"The Federation is not a society, but the churches themselves consulting and cooperating. But . . . givers were accustomed to societies," and gave more to entertain a single convention than to the annual budget of a state federation. "The Federation had rivals and even enemies. I suspect that strong supporters of the Sunday School Association regard me as a deserter; and feared that the Federation with its broader program, if it gained a foothold, would absorb religious education, as it has done." "The Federation was judged by standards set for philanthropic organizations; in fact it was a council of the denominations to change the conditions created by their self-centered institutionalism." In 1929 it seemed "easier to secure from individuals contributions for special lines of work than for overhead expenses." So wrote E. Tallmadge Root, in 1940 and the years following.

This earliest (Root) period has been featured partly because it is so easily forgotten, partly because it exhibited such penetrating insight into continuing problems and opportunities. Later periods include:

(2) *The Period of the Merger;*

(3) *The Frank Jennings Administration* (1935-1952);

(4) *The Forrest Knapp Administration.*

Much published and private material is available on Massachusetts church cooperation since 1902, including files of *Facts and Figures, Bay State Church Life,* and *The Christian Outlook,* as well as Minutes. Here, with abundant historical library resources, is a rich field for some church history major to explore in a doctoral dissertation.

2. *Missouri*

As Massachusetts is enriched and complicated by the dominance of Boston, and Maryland by that of Baltimore, so Missouri is both the beneficiary and the victim of having two metropolitan cities within its borders: St. Louis and Kansas City.

When seemingly in 1865 "a small group of men in St. Louis gathered together to help each other find better methods and plans for the Sunday school, that was the beginning of the Missouri Sunday School Association" (historical memo by H. W. Becker). "The first statewide convention was held in October 1866." According to a 1915 Golden Jubilee Convention report, as early as 1869, with 80 out of 114 counties organized, "the Finance Committee reported a debt of $1,000," but it recommended the employment of a "state missionary," if funds could be found. In 1872 the office of State Agent was created by the Convention; but "not until 1886-7 does it appear that any salaries were paid." In 1878 the chairman of the state convention advised the organization of the townships first, believing that county organizations amounted to little without township cooperation. In 1891 the first state superintendent was employed, and three field agents served under him. A most aggressive decade began in 1888. In 1893 "all the 114 counties were reported organized." Of $12,438.41 expended, $8,290.68 came from St. Louis. There was a staff of ten persons, mostly full-time. When the Seventh International Convention met in St. Louis in 1893, the Missouri Sunday School Association, incorporated that year, "claimed to lead the entire field."

In the 1890's the hard times produced a "slump"; in 1898 receipts had dropped to $3,432.29, liabilities were $4,453.83, and there was no field force. In 1896 it was reported, "We believe in the international system of Bible study as the very best means man can employ to discharge the high duty to which he is called by the spirit breathed in the earnest prayer of our loving Lord recorded in the Gospel of St. John, 17th chapter 21st verse." In 1902 there were "struggles, trials, and victories. Every county was visited, many of them several times." Then came a come-back. Among many prominent names, only those of Lansing F. Smith, aggressive chairman of the executive committee for a number of years, and William H. Danforth, president from 1920 to 1925, can here be mentioned.

In 1922 the Sunday School Association became the Sunday School Council of Religious Education, and in 1937 the Missouri Church and Sunday School Council, taking on some of the functions that ordinarily belong to a Council of Churches. As early as 1929 there had been a demand from the field for the organization of a state federation of churches (*cf.* an article in the Missouri *Sunday School News* for May 1931 by Paul Barton, a Methodist pastor and County S. S. Council secretary.)

February 25, 1936, at a Ministers' Continuation Committee meeting in Sedalia, Mr. Harry W. Becker (executive of the Council of Religious Education) gave a brief historical account of the several attempts that had been made to organize a state council of churches, together with more recent efforts toward expanding the work of the Missouri Sunday School Council. The committee was unanimous in feeling that there should not be a Council of Churches for

Missouri, independent of the Missouri Sunday School Council. "We must preserve the assets we have." Dr. Munro pointed out the mistake made by a number of other states, namely that they built an overhead organization, a merged council, representing both the Federal Council and the ICRE, without much regard for the local county councils that had been functioning. He said there were in Missouri 65 county councils, some of which were weak, but some of which had a strong organization. It was the consensus that Missouri should move slowly toward a more inclusive organization. Dr. J. W. McDonald of Kansas City was helpful at this meeting. In 1940, which marked the Diamond Jubilee of Sunday school work in the state, the Council of Churches was organized. No attempt is made here to sketch the work of this council during the last two decades. Bishop Ivan Lee Holt proved to be one of its most helpful leaders. Missouri too provides a story for a competent student to write.

Missouri's last three executives have been Harry W. Becker 1919-1951; Morris H. Pullin 1952-1953; A. Greig Ritchie 1953-

3. *Other States*

The *California* situation has been complicated by the size of the state, the presence of two great metropolitan centers (San Francisco and Los Angeles) as well as other considerable cities, the early need felt for area organization within the state, the opportunity for service to Nevada and other adjoining territory, the tremendous immigration and consequent population increase, the secularized aspect of Pacific coast regionalism, etc. California seminaries and universities would perform a service if this complex history could be documented before priceless archives are lost.

Nearly a century has elapsed since the first state Sunday School Convention in California. In 1872 it was said that "there had been four" conventions. As early as 1899 the Sunday school forces were divided into northern and southern. Said the latter, "We date from 1880," but the first general secretary was not called until 1902, after organization in 1901 and a "first convention" in 1892, as reported in 1905. In 1899 the Northern California Association issued over 1,000 copies of its paper—"a powerful ally." It too employed its first general secretary in 1902.

From the church federation standpoint California was in the picture early, but not continuously. A series of reorganizations needs careful tracing, as do the relationships between the two chief cities and the Southern and Northern California Councils of Churches.

Similarly, the story in many midwestern states deserves better documentation. E.g., in *Wisconsin,* the 1872 International Convention was told, "Ever since 1846 a state Sunday school organization has been in existence, and with the exception of an interval of four years, it has held an annual convention ever since." How undenominational Sunday school forces and the repeatedly reorganized forces of church cooperation were finally integrated in a state with its own peculiar ecclesiastical complexion, is a story deserving scholarly understanding and sympathetic narration.

Connecticut has been featured in the text as leading the state councils in the acceptance of the merger principle. That full story is worth careful documentation, at greater length than has as yet been attempted. All the older state councils are similarly worthy of careful historical study. An entire volume could be filled with an account of their origins, development, opportunities, and problems. What seems more likely to happen is that state after state will publish its own history, assisted in some cases by the work of graduate students. When a sufficient accumulation of such material is available, providing factual detail and adequate insights, matched by increasing numbers of city council historical studies, it will become possible to make competent generalizations on the basis of empirical data systematically presented. Here is a field for church history departments to pioneer. The documentation of the multiple origins of church cooperation should complement the story of ecumenical beginnings at the national and world levels.

INDEX

NOTE—q.—quoted

267

268

269